ENDANGERED SPECIES

Scott and Rand were jockeying for a clear line of fire. It was hopeless, with Annie standing frozen right in front of the thing, hypnotized like a mouse before a rattlesnake. They were both armed with MARS-Gallant Type-H90s—the latest word in hip howitzers, but all that firepower was of little use with Annie in the crosshairs.

The *Eogyrinus* had gotten close, Rand knew, because it was an experienced shore hunter, just like the paleontology books said. Scott hollered at Annie to get out of the way. She threw herself flat on the ground just as the creature reared up to lunge for her. Then the neon-blue blasterbolts flew, making a mewing sound.

As the H90s spat, the torrid air got even hotter. The thing heaved up as the dazzling hyphens of energy hit it. Pieces exploded from it as the furious heat of the shots turned the moisture in its cells into superheated steam, blowing it apart. . . .

By Jack McKinney
Published by Ballantine Books:

THE ROBOTECH™ SERIES
GENESIS #1
BATTLE CRY #2
HOMECOMING #3
BATTLEHYMN #4
FORCE OF ARMS #5
DOOMSDAY #6
SOUTHERN CROSS #7
METAL FIRE #8
THE FINAL NIGHTMARE #9
INVID INVASION #10
METAMORPHOSIS #11
SYMPHONY OF LIGHT #12

THE SENTINELS™ SERIES
THE DEVIL'S HAND #1
DARK POWERS #2
DEATH DANCE #3
WORLD KILLERS #4
RUBICON #5

ROBOTECH: THE END OF THE CIRCLE #18
ROBOTECH: THE ZENTRAEDI REBELLION #19
ROBOTECH: THE MASTERS' GAMBIT #20

KADUNA MEMORIES

THE BLACK HOLE TRAVEL AGENCY:
Book One: *Event Horizon*
Book Two: *Artifact of the System*
Book Three: *Free Radicals*
Book Four: *Hostile Takeover*

ROBOTECH:
THE NEW GENERATION
THE INVID INVASION

INVID INVASION
METAMORPHOSIS
SYMPHONY OF LIGHT

Jack McKinney

BALLANTINE BOOKS · NEW YORK

Robotech: The New Generation: The Invid Invasion is a work of fiction. Names, places, and incidents either are products of the author's imagination or are used fictitiously.

2007 Del Rey Books Mass Market Edition

Copyright © 2007 by Harmony Gold USA, Inc.

ROBOTECH® and associated characters, names, and indicia are the property of Harmony Gold USA, Inc.

Published in the United States by Del Rey Books, an imprint of The Random House Publishing Group, a division of Random House, Inc., New York.

DEL REY is a registered trademark and the Del Rey colophon is a trademark of Random House, Inc.

Originally published as three separate volumes as follows: *Invid Invasion* copyright © 1987 by Harmony Gold USA, Inc., and Tatsunoko Production Co., Ltd. *Metamorphosis* copyright © 1987 by Harmony Gold USA, Inc., and Tatsunoko Production Co., Ltd. *Symphony of Light* copyright © 1987 by Harmony Gold USA, Inc., and Tatsunoko Production Co., Ltd.

ISBN 978-0-345-49901-1

Printed in the United States of America

www.robotech.com
www.delreybooks.com

OPM   9   8   7   6   5   4   3   2   1

INVID INVASION

METAMORPHOSIS

SYMPHONY OF LIGHT

APPENDIX

Published by Ballantine Books

ROBOTECH
NOVEL TIMELINE

Novelizations based upon the animated science fiction series produced by Harmony Gold.

Novels featuring all-new storylines not seen on television.

1999

THE MACROSS SAGA: BATTLECRY
GENESIS
BATTLE CRY
HOMECOMING

2009

THE MACROSS SAGA: DOOMSDAY
BATTLEHYMN
FORCE OF ARMS
DOOMSDAY

2014

THE ZENTRAEDI REBELLION

2022

THE SENTINELS
THE DEVIL'S HAND
DARK POWERS
DEATH DANCE
WORLD KILLERS
RUBICON

THE ROBOTECH MASTERS
SOUTHERN CROSS
METAL FIRE
THE FINAL NIGHTMARE

2030

BEFORE THE INVID STORM

THE NEW GENERATION
INVID INVASION
METAMORPHOSIS
SYMPHONY OF LIGHT

2042

2044

THE END OF THE CIRCLE*

* superseded by
THE SHADOW CHRONICLES

INVID
INVASION

For K.A. and the Kahlua Kid,
who have heard little else
this past year

SOMEWHERE A QUEEN WAS WEEPING...HER children scattered; her regent a prisoner of the blood lust, at war with nature and enslaved to vengeance.

But dare we presume to read her thoughts even now, to walk a path not taken—one denied to us by gates and towers our senses cannot perceive and perhaps never will?

Still, it must have seemed like the answer to a prayer: A planet newly rich in the flower that was life itself, a profusion of such incredible nutrient wealth that her Sensor Nebulae had found it clear across the galaxy. A blue and white world as distant from her Optera as she was from the peaceful form her consciousness once inhabited.

And yet Optera was lost to her, to half her children. Left in the care of one who had betrayed his kind, who had become what he fought so desperately to destroy. As she herself had. . . .

All but trapped now in the guise that *he* had worn, the one who lured the secrets of the Flower from her. And whose giant warriors had returned to possess the planet and dispossess its inhabitants. *But oh, how she had loved him!* Enough to summon from her very depths the ability to emulate him. And later to summon a hatred keen enough to birth a warring nature, an army of soldiers to rival his—to rival *Zor's* own!

But he, too, was lost to her, killed by the very soldiers her hatred had fashioned.

Oh, to be rid of these dark memories! her ancient heart must have screamed. *To be rescued from these sorry realms!* Garuda, Spheris, Tirol. *And this Haydon IV with its sterile flowers long awaiting the caress of the Pollinators—this confused world even my Inorganics cannot subdue.*

But she was aware that all these things would soon be behind her. She would gather the cosmic stuff of her race and make the jump to that world the Sensor Nebulae had located. *And woe to the life-form that inhabited that world!* For nothing would prevent her from finding a home for her children, a home for the completion of their grand evolutionary design!

News of the Invid exodus from Haydon IV spread through the Fourth Quadrant—to Spheris and Gàruda and Praxis, worlds already abandoned by the insect-like horde, worlds singled out by fate to feel the backlash of Zor's attempt at recompense, nature's cruel joke.

The Tirolian scientist had attempted to foliate them with the same Flowers he had been ordered to steal from Optera, an action that had sentenced that warm world's sentient life-form to a desperate quest to relocate their nutrient grail. But Zor's experiments had failed, because the Flower of Life proved to be a discriminating plant—choosy about where it would and would not put down roots—and a malignantly loyal one as well.

Deriving as much from the Invid as the Invid derived from it, the Flower called out from Zor's seeded worlds to its former guardian/hosts. Warlike and driven—instincts born of the Robotech Masters' transgression—the Invid answered those calls. Their army of mecha and Inorganics arrived in swarms to overwhelm and rule; and instead of the Protoculture paradises the founder of Robotechnology had envisioned, were planets dominated by the beings his discoveries had all but doomed.

And now suddenly they were gone, off on a new quest that would take them clear across the galactic core.

To Earth . . .

Word of their departure reached Rick Hunter aboard the Sentinel's ships. He was in the command seat on the fortress bridge when the communiqué was received. Thin and pale, a war-weary veteran of countless battles, Rick was almost thirty-five years old by Earth reckoning, but the vagaries of hyperspace travel put him closer to fifty or two hundred and seventy, depending on how one figured it.

The giant planet Fantoma, once home to the Zentraedi, filled the forward viewports. In the foreground Rick could just discern the small inhabited moon called Tirol, an angry dot against Fantoma's barren face. *How could such an insignificant world have unleashed so much evil on an unsuspecting galaxy?* Rick wondered.

He glanced over at Lisa, who was humming to herself while she tapped a flurry of commands into her console. *His wife.* They had stayed together through thick and thin these past eleven years, although they had had their share of disagreements, especially when Rick had opted to join the Sentinels—Baldon, Teal, Crysta, and the others—and pursue the Invid.

Who would have thought it would come to this? he asked himself. A mission whose purpose had been peace at war with itself. Edwards and his grand designs of empire...how like the Invid regent he was, how like the Masters, too! But he was history now, and that fleet he had raised to conquer Earth would be used to battle the Invid when the Expeditionary Force reached the planet.

Providing the fleet reached Earth, of course. There were still major problems with the spacefold system Lang and the Tirolian Cabell had designed. Some missing ingredient...Major Carpenter had never been heard from, nor Wolff; and now the Mars and Jupiter Group attack wings were preparing to fold, with almost two thousand Veritechs between them.

Rick exhaled slowly and deliberately, loud enough for Lisa to hear him and turn a thin smile his way. Somehow it was fitting that Earth should end up on the Invid's list, Rick decided. But what could have happened there to draw them in such unprecedented numbers? Rick shuddered at the thought.

Perhaps Earth was where the final battle was meant to be fought.

Ravaged by the Robotech Masters and their gargantuan agents, the Zentraedi, it was a miracle that Earth had managed to survive at all. Looking on the planet from deep space, it would have appeared unchanged: its beautiful oceans and swirling masses of cloud, its silver satellite, bright as any beacon in the quadrant. But a closer look revealed the scars and disfigurations those invasions had wrought. The northern hemisphere was all but a barren waste, forested by the rusting remains of Dolza's ill-fated four-million-ship armada. Great cities of gleaming concrete, steel, and glass towers lay ruined and abandoned. Wide highways and graceful bridges were cratered and collapsed. Airports, schools, hospitals, sports complexes, industrial and residential zones ... reduced to rubble, unmarked graveyards all.

A fifteen-year period of peace—that tranquil prologue to the Masters' arrival—saw the resurrection of some of those things the twentieth century had all but taken for granted. Cities had rebuilt themselves, new ones had grown up. But humankind was now a different species from that which had originally raised those towering sculptures of stone. Post-Cataclysmites, they were a feudal, warring breed, as distrustful of one another as they were of those stars their hopeful ancestors had once wished upon. Perhaps, as some have claimed, Earth actually called in its second period of catastrophe, as if bent on adhering to some self-fulfilling prophecy of doom. The Masters, too, for that matter: The two races met and engaged in an unspoken agreement for mutual annihilation—a paving of the way for what would follow.

Those who still wish to blame Protoculture trace the genesis of this back to Zor, Aquarian-age Prometheus, whose gift to the galaxy was a Pandora's box he willingly opened. Displaced and repressed, the Flower of Life had rebelled. And there were no chains, molecular or otherwise, capable of containing its power. That Zor, resurrected by the Elders of his race for their dark purposes, should have been the one to free the Flower from its Matrix is now seen as part of Protoculture's equation. Equally so, that that liberation should call forth the Invid to complete the circle.

They came without warning: a swarm of monsters and mecha folded across space and time by their leader/queen, the Regis, through an effort of pure psychic will. They did not choose to announce themselves the way their former enemies had, nor did they delay their invasion to puzzle out humankind's strengths and weaknesses, quirks and foibles. There was no need to determine whether Earth did or did not have what they sought; their Sensor Nebulae had already alerted them to the presence of the Flower. It had found compatible soil and climate on the blue and white world. All that was required were the Pollinators, a missing element in the Robotech Masters' equations.

In any case, the Invid had already had dealings with Earthlings, having battled them on a dozen planets, including Tirol itself. But as resilient as the Humans might have been on Haydon IV, Spheris, and the rest, they were a pathetic lot on their homeworld.

In less than a week the Invid conquered the planet, destroying the orbiting factory satellite—an ironic end for the Zentraedi aboard—laying to waste city after city, and dismissing with very little effort the vestiges of the Army of the Southern Cross. Depleted of the Protoculture charges necessary to fuel their Robo-technological war machines, those warriors who had fought so valiantly against the Masters were forced to fall back on a small supply of nuclear weapons and conventional ordnance that was no match for the Invid's plasma and laser-array superiority.

Even if Protoculture had been available to the

Southern Cross for their Hovertanks and Alpha Veritechs, there would have been gross problems to overcome: the two years since the mutual annihilation of the Robotech Masters and Anatole Leonard's command had seen civilization's unchecked slide into lawlessness and barbarism. Cities became city-states and warred with one another; men and women rose quickly to positions of power only to fall even more swiftly in the face of greater military might. Greed and butchery ruled, and what little remained of the northern hemisphere's dignity collapsed.

Though certain cities remained strong—Mannatan, for example (formerly New York City)—the centers of power shifted southward, into Brazilas especially (the former Zentraedi Control Zone), where growth had been sure and steady since the SDF-1's return to devastated Earth and the founding of New Macross and its sister city, Monument.

Unlike the Zentraedi or the Tirol Masters, the Invid were not inclined to destroy the planet or exterminate humankind. Quite the contrary: Not only had the Flower found favorable conditions for growth, the Invid had as well. The Regis had learned enough in her campaign against the Tirolians and the so-called Sentinels to recognize the continuing need for technology. Gone was the blissful tranquillity of Optera, but the experiment had to be carried forth to its conclusion nonetheless, and Earth was well suited for the purpose.

After disarming and occupying the planet, the Regis believed she was more than halfway toward her goal. By utilizing a percentage of Humans to cultivate and harvest the Flowers, she was free to carry out her experiments uninterrupted. The central hive, which came to be called Reflex Point, was to be the site of the Great Work, but secondary hives were soon in place across the planet to maintain control of the Human sectors of her empire. The Regis was willing to let humankind survive until such time as the work neared completion. Then, she would rid herself of them.

There was, however, one thing she had not taken into account: the very warriors she had fought tooth and claw on those worlds once seeded by Zor. Enslave a world she might, but take it for her own?

Never!

CHAPTER
ONE

The armada of Robotech ships T.R. Edwards had amassed for his planned invasion and conquest of Earth would be put to that very use years later when Admiral Hunter sent them against the Invid. Adding irony to irony, it should be mentioned that the warships had serious design flaws which went unnoticed during their use on Tirol. Assuming this would have been the case even if Edwards had managed to persevere, the invasion would have failed. Destiny failed to deliver Edwards the crown he felt justified to wear and likewise failed to deliver Hunter the quick victory he felt justified to claim.

Selig Kahler, *The Tirolian Campaign*

A FLEET OF ROBOTECH WARSHIPS MOVED INTO ATtack formation above the Moon, a mixed school of gleaming predators, radiant where the distant sun touched their armored hulls and alloy fins. Each carried in its belly a score or more of Veritech fighters, sleek, transformable mecha developed and perfected over the course of the past thirty years. And inside each of these was a pilot ready to die for a world unseen. War was at the top of the agenda, but in a narrow hold aboard one of the command vessels a young man was thinking about love.

He was a pleasant-looking, clean-shaven youth going on twenty, with his father's long legs and the wide eyes of his mother. He wore his blue-black hair combed straight back from his high forehead—save for that undisciplined strand that always seemed to fall forward—making his ears appear more prominent than they actually were. He wore the Expeditionary Force uniform—simple gray tight-fitting pants tucked into high boots and a short-sleeved ornately collared top worn over a crimson-colored synthcloth bodysuit. The Mars Group patch adorned the young man's shirt.

His name was Scott Bernard—Lieutenant Scott Bernard—and this was a homecoming of sorts. That fact, coupled with the anxieties he felt concerning the imminent battle, had put him in an impassioned frame of mind. The fortunate recipient of this not-so-sudden desire was a pretty, dark-eyed teenager named Marlene, a good six inches shorter than Scott, with milk-chocolate-brown hair and shapely legs enhanced by the uniform's short skirt.

Scott had Marlene's small face cupped in his hands while he looked lovingly into her eyes. As his hands slid to her narrow shoulders, he pulled her to him, his mouth full against hers, stifling the protest her more cautious nature wished to give voice to and urging her to respond. Which she did, with a moan of pleasure, her hands flat against his chest.

"Marry me, Marlene," he said after she had broken off their embrace. He heard himself say it and almost applauded, simply for finally getting the nerve up to ask her; Marlene's response was a separate issue.

Her surprised gasp probably said the same: that *she* too couldn't believe he was finally getting around to it. She turned away from him, nervous hands at her chin in an attitude of prayer.

"Well, will you?" Scott pressed.

"It's a bit sudden," she said coyly. But Scott didn't pick up on her tone and reacted as though he had been slapped.

"You'll have to speak to my father first," Marlene continued in the same tone, her back to him still. "My mother, too." When she turned around, Scott was staring at her slack-jawed.

"But they're back on *Tirol!*" he stammered. "They might not be here for—" Then he caught her smile and understood at once. He had literally known her for her entire life, and he still couldn't tell when she was putting him on.

Marlene was smiling up at him now, eyes beaming. But the sudden shrill of sirens collapsed her happiness.

"Defold operation complete," a voice said over the PA. "All wing commanders report to the bridge for final briefing and combat assignments."

Scott's lips were a thin line when he looked at her.

"Answer me, Marlene. I might not get another chance to ask you."

The command ship bridge was a tight, no-nonsense affair, with two duty stations squeezed between the wraparound viewports and four more back to back behind these. There was none of the spaciousness and calm that had characterized the SDF-1 bridge; here everyone had a seat, and everyone put duty first. It took something like the first sight of Earth to elicit any casual conversation, and even then the comments would have surprised some.

"I'm so excited," a woman tech was saying. "I can hardly wait to see what Earth looks like after all these years."

Commander Gardner, seated at the forward station of starboard pair, heard this and laughed bitterly to himself. He had served under Gloval during the First Robotech War and had been with Hunter since. His thick hair and mustache had gone to silver these past few years, but he still retained a youthful energy and the unwavering loyalty of his young crew.

The woman tech who had spoken was all of seventeen years old, born in deep space like most of her shipmates. Gardner wished for a moment he could have showed her the Earth of forty years ago, teeming with life, wild and wonderful and blissfully unaware of the coming tide. . . .

"What does it matter?" the tech's male console mate answered her. "One planet's the same as another to me. Robotech ships are all I've known—all I want to know."

"Don't you have any interest in setting foot on your homeworld? Our parents were born here. And *their* parents, right on back to the first ancestors."

Gardner could almost hear the copilot's shrug of indifference clear across the bridge.

"Just another Invid colony, color it what you will. So this place is blue and Spheris was brown. It doesn't do anything for me."

"Spoken like a true romantic."

The copilot snorted. "You get romantic thinking about the Invid grubbing around the old homestead looking for Protoculture?"

Commander Gardner was hanging on the answer when the door to the bridge hissed open suddenly and Lieutenant Bernard entered.

"Alpha Group is just about ready for launch," Bernard reported.

Gardner muttered, "Good," and rose from the contoured seat, signaling one of the techs to turn on the ship's PA system.

"Most of you know what I'm about to say," he began. "But for those who don't know what this mission is all about, it's simply this: Several months ago we became aware that the Invid Sensor Nebulae had located some new and apparently enormous supply of the Flowers of

Life. The source of the transmissions turned out to be the Earth itself.

"The Regis moved quickly to secure the Flowers, with the same murderous intent she demonstrated on Spheris and Haydon IV and a dozen other worlds I don't have to remind you about. Nor should I have to remind you about what we're going to face on Earth. It seems probable that the Invid decimated Wolff's forces, but we number more than four times the units under his command."

Scott noticed that the bridge techs, eyes locked on Gardner and grim faces set, were giving silent support to the commander's words. Marlene entered the bridge in the midst of the briefing, whispering her apologies and seating herself at her duty station.

"Admiral Hunter has entrusted us to spearhead a vast military operation to invade and reclaim our home-world," said Gardner. "And I know that I can count on every one of you to stand firm behind the admiral's conviction that we can lay the foundations for his second wave." He inclined his head. "May God have mercy on our souls."

A brief silence was broken by the navigator's update:

"Earth orbit in three minutes, Commander. Placing visual display on the monitor, sir."

Everyone turned to face the forward screen. Orbital schematics de-rezzed and were replaced by a full view of the Earth. They had all seen photos and video images galore, but the sight inspired awe nevertheless.

"It's beautiful," someone said. And compared to Fantoma or Tirol, it most certainly was: snow-white pole, blue oceans, and variegated land masses, the whole of it patterned by swirling clouds.

A computer-generated grid assembled itself over the image as the command ship continued to close. At her station, Marlene said, "So that's what Earth looks like . . . I'd almost forgotten."

The commander called for scanning to be initiated, and in a moment the grid was highlighting an area located in one of the northern continents. Data readouts scrolled across an adjacent display screen.

"Full magnification and color enhancement," Gardner barked.

Marlene leaned in to study her screen. The forward monitor was displaying an angry red image, not softened in the least by Earth's inviting cloud cover. She knew what this was but asked the computer to compare the present readings with those logged in its memory banks. She sensed that Scott was peering over the top of her high-backed chair.

"That's it, sir," she said all at once, her screen strobing encouragement. "The central hive. Designation... Reflex Point," Marlene read from the data scroll. "Picking up energy flux readings and multiple radar contacts... waiting for signature."

Gardner glanced over at her briefly, then turned his attention forward once again. "I want visuals as soon as possible," he instructed one of the techs.

"Shock Trooper transport," Marlene said at the same time.

Gardner's nostrils flared. "Prepare to repel."

Techs were already bending over the consoles tapping in commands, the bridge a veritable light show of flashing screens.

"Two minutes to contact," the navigator informed Gardner.

"All sections standing by..."

"Auto-astrogator is off... Ship's shields raised..."

Marlene flipped a series of switches. "Net is open...."

"All right," Gardner said decisively. "Issue the go signal to all Veritechs."

"One minute and counting, sir..."

The commander turned to Scott.

"It's up to your squads now, Lieutenant. We've got to get through their lines and set these ships down." Scott saluted, and Gardner returned it. "Good luck," he added.

"You can count on us."

Marlene had turned from her station, waiting for him to walk past. As he leaned down to kiss her, she smiled and surprised him by placing a heart-shaped holo-locket into his hand.

"Take this with you," she said while he was regarding the thing. "It's my way of saying 'good luck.'"

Scott thanked her and leaned in to collect that kiss after all. Resurfaced, he found Gardner and the techs smiling at him; he gave another crisp salute and rushed from the bridge.

"'Good-bye, sweetheart,'" one of the techs stationed behind Marlene mimicked not a moment after Scott left. "'And here's a token of my undying love.'"

Marlene poked her head around the side of the chair. Marf and one who liked to be called Red were laughing. "Knock it off," she told them. She was used to the razzing—personal time was hard to come by aboard ship, and Scott's open displays of affection only added fuel to the fire—but in no mood for it right now.

"What's the matter, Marlene?" Red said over his shoulder. "Don't you know that absence makes the heart grow fonder?"

She swiveled about in the cushioned seat and hid her face in her hands. "I don't know how it could," she managed, suddenly on the verge of tears.

"Don't let them get to you, Marlene," one of her supporters at the forward stations called out while Red laughed.

Come back, Scott, she prayed. *I'd give my life to keep you safe.*

* * *

Gardner's command ship was actually one of the fleet's many transport vessels—delicate-looking ships that resembled swans in flight, with long, tapering necks and thin swept-back wings under each of which was affixed a boxcarlike Veritech carrier.

Scott, his body sheathed in lime-green armor, was strapping himself into one of the Veritechs now. Fifteen years had seen only minor changes in armor and craft. Lang's Robotech design team had maintained the "thinking caps" and sensor-studded mitts and boots that were so characteristic of the first-generation VT pilots. Armor itself had become somewhat bulky due to the fact that these third-generation warriors were involved in ground-assault missions as often as they were in space strikes; but there was none of the gladiatorial styling favored by Lang's counterparts in the Army of the Southern Cross.

"The main engine and boosters are in top shape, sir," a launch tech perched on the rim of the Veritech bin told Scott before he lowered the canopy. "Good luck and good hunting."

Scott flashed him a thumbs-up as the canopy sealed itself. "Thanks, pal," he said over the externals. "I'll be seein' you Earthside."

Flashes of green and red light from the cockpit displays played across the tinted faceshield of Scott's helmet as he activated and engaged one after another of the Veritech's complex systems. "This is Commander Bernard of the Twenty-first Armored Tactical Assault Squadron, Mars Division," he announced over the com net. "Condition is green, and we are go for launch."

"The flight bay is open," control radioed back to him. "You are cleared for launch, Commander."

Scott gave a start as bay doors throughout the carrier retracted. The cloud-studded deep-blue oceans of Earth filled his entire field of vision. The sight elicited a sense

of vertigo he had never experienced before; it was difficult for him to comprehend a planet with so much water,
a liquid world that offered so little surface.... But Scott
was quick to catch himself.

"Mars Division attack wing," he said over the net,
"let's do it!"

The Veritech lurched somewhat as the bin conveyers
began to move the fighters toward the forward bay. Scott
saw that the grappler pylons that would convey the
mecha from belt to vacuum had already attached themselves. He readied himself at the controls, urging his
body to relax, his mind to meld with the VT systems. In
a moment he felt the grapplers release, the fighter drifting weightlessly, before he engaged the thrusters that
bore it away from the transport carrier.

"All right, look alive," Scott said as his wingmen
came alongside to signal their readiness. "Once we join
up with the main formation, I want eyes open and hands
on the trigger." Earthspace was filled with mecha now,
some two thousand Veritechs in a slow descent over a
silent world. Scott heard Commander Gardner's voice
over the com net.

"All wing commanders maintain loose battle formation.... prepare to break off for individual combat
at the first sign of enemy hostility. It shouldn't be long
in coming...."

It is unlikely that many of the men and women who
made up the Mars Division (so named by Dr. Lang to
convey a sense of attachment to Earth and its brethren
worlds) recognized the uniqueness of their position:
Their invasion represented humankind's first *deliberate*
offensive against an XT force. Up to that point Earth
had always been on the defensive, counterstriking first
the Zentraedi, then those giants' Tirolian Masters, and
lastly (and unsuccessfully) the Invid themselves. In this
sense the day was a red-letter event, if not the turn-

ing point Hunter and numerous others had all hoped it would be. . . .

Scott was one of the first to see the enemy ship; it was below him at nine o'clock, surfacing through Earth's atmosphere at an alarming rate. An Invid troop carrier, one of the so-called Mollusk Carriers.

"Here they are," Scott said to his wingmen, gesturing with his hand at the same time. The clamshell-shaped fortress was yawning now, revealing an arena array of Invid Shock Trooper mecha. "Fall in on my signal."

When Scott looked again a split second later, an Invid column launched itself and was locked in on an ascent to engage, the ships' crablike hulls and pincer arms a gleaming golden-brown in Sol's intense light. "Yeah, I think we're gonna see signs of hostility," Scott muttered to himself as his squadron dropped in to meet the enemy at the edge of space.

At Scott's command the pilots of the Twenty-first thumbed off flocks of heat-seeker missiles, which streaked into the ascending column. Short-lived explosions of violent light blossomed against Earth's blue and white backdrop. The VTs continued their silent descents, loosing second and third salvos of red-tipped demons against that horde which had overwhelmed their world. And countless Invid mecha flamed out and fried, but not enough to matter. For every one taken out there were three that survived, and those which broke through the line of fire began to strike back. Scott knew there were creatures inside each of those ships—huge bipedal mockeries of the Human form, with massive arms and heads that resembled elongated snouts.

Unlike the enemy forces of the First and Second Robotech Wars, the Invid relied on numbers rather than firepower. True, the Zentraedi had a seemingly endless supply of Battlepods and an armada of ships four million strong, but by and large the war was fought in conventional terms. Up against the Masters this was even more the case, with the number of mecha on both sides substantially reduced. With the Invid, however, humankind encountered a horde mentality to rival any that nature had produced. And true to form, whether army ants or swarms of killer bees, the Invid carried a sting.

As Scott and the others knew from their previous encounters, initial fusillades were what counted most. Once separated from its column, the individual Invid ship was blindingly maneuverable and often unstoppable. In close it favored two approaches: ripping open mecha with its alloy pincer claws and embracing a ship and literally shocking it to death with charges delivered by the ships' Protoculture systems. Scott saw both variations of this occurring while he did his best to keep his own fighter out of reach.

Veritech and crabship were going at it across the field, Mars Division troops and Invid mecha in deadly pursuits and dogfights, crisscrossing in the upper reaches of the stratosphere amidst tracer rounds, missile tracks, and laser-array fire from the command ships. Scott saw one of his team taken out by a claw swipe that opened the Veritech tail to nose, precious atmosphere sucked from the fractured canopy, the pilot flailing for life inside. In another part of nearby space, several Veritechs floated derelict after loveless Invid embraces.

Scott realized the hopelessness of their situation and ordered his squadron to reconfigure to Battloid mode.

Mechamorphosis, or mode selection, was still controlled by a three-position cockpit lever, along with the pilot's mecha will, which interfaced with the fighter's Protoculture-governed systems. But where all parts of the first-generation Veritechs participated in reconfiguration, the augmentation packs and energy generators of the Armored Alphas (essential for the space and ground missions that typified the Expeditionary Force) remained intact during the process. The forward portion of the craft telescoped to accomplish this, arms unfolding from behind the canopy while radome and cockpit rotated up through a 180-degree arc, now allowing the underbelly laser turret to become the Battloid's head, and the underbelly rifle/cannon to become the weapon that was grasped in the mecha's right hand.

Thus transformed, Scott's squadron fell in to reengage the Invid, blue thrusters bright in Earth's dark side.

Meanwhile, a second wave of Veritechs was launched from the transports to respond to another column of Invid approaching swiftly from Delta sector.

Scott's displays flashed coordinates and signatures of the second Mollusk Carrier even before he had visual contact. He ordered his team to form up on his lead and throw themselves against the column. Once again heat-seekers found their marks and took out scores of Invid ships; and once again orange hell-flowers blossomed. But reinforced, the Invid launched a frenzied counter-strike. Shock vessels broke through the front lines and went for the transports themselves in suicide runs and massed charges. Particle beams, disgorged from bow guns, swept like insecticide through their ranks, annihilating ship after ship.

Scott's team regrouped and gave chase to any that survived, blasts from the VTs' chain-guns blowing pincers to debris and holing carapaces. Still, Scott could hear the death screams of the unlucky ones piercing the tac net's cacophony of commands and reactions. VTs and Invid ships drifted from the arena, locked in bizarre postures, obscene embraces. Here, an Invid pincer was apparently caught in the canopy of the ship it had ensnared; there, another held a VT to itself, exchanging lightning flashes of death.

Scott, sweat beading up across his forehead, was in pursuit of two Invid ships that were closing in on Commander Gardner's transport; he had heard Marlene's terror-stricken call for help only a moment before and had one of the enemy ships bracketed in the chain-gun's sights now. He fired once, shooting a hole through its groin, and smiled devilishly as it disintegrated in a brief burst of crimson light. The second Invid, its pincers raised for action, was moving toward the bridge viewports. But fire from Scott's cannon decommissioned it before it attained striking distance.

"Saw two, swatted same," Scott told Marlene over the com net, a confident tone returned to his voice. The Invid were falling back on all sides.

"Good job, Commander," Gardner congratulated him before Marlene had a chance to speak. "Signal your team to begin their atmospheric approach. Our thermal energy shields are already seriously drained."

"Roger," said Scott, at the same time waving the chain-gun to signal his wingmen. "We'll escort you through."

Scott saw the transport's thrusters fire a three-second burst, realigning the ship for its slow descent. He sat back and punched up orbital entry calculations on the data screen, fed these over to the autopilot, and returned his attention to wide-range radar. Suddenly Marlene was on the net again, alerting him to a unit of bandits moving against him at four o'clock. He glanced over his shoulder and glimpsed them even as their signatures were registering on the mecha's radar screen.

"I see them," he answered her calmly.

Scott permitted the half dozen Invid to close in, enabling his onboard targeting computer to get a fix on all of them. It was a calculated risk but one that paid off a moment later when the Battloid's deltoid compartments opened and each launched a missile that homed in on its target. Scott boostered himself away from the silent fireworks and rechecked the screen: There was no sign of enemy activity.

"We're all clear, Commander," he reported, easing up the thinking cap's faceshield.

Gardner's face now flashed into view on the cockpit's small commo screen. "Scott! We must try to slip through and hit Reflex Point before the Regis's drones have a chance to regroup. Understood?"

"Roger Commander," Scott returned. At a signal from the HUD, he dropped the faceshield, the inside surface of which was displaying approach vectors and numerical data. He opened the tac net. "Our entrance azimuth is one-two-one-one . . . Reconfiguring for orbital deviation."

Scott armed the Veritech's shield after it had shifted mode and brought the fighter alongside Gardner's descending transport. The hull temperature of his own ship was reaching critical levels, and he reasoned that the same thing had to be occurring on the larger ship. A glance told him he was correct and more. The underside of the command vessel was radiating an intense glow that suggested an improper angle of approach. Scott waited for the vessel to correct itself, and when it didn't, he went on the net.

"Recommend you recalculate entry horizon, Commander. The ship appears to be entering too quickly."

"It can't be helped, Scott. We've got to put down. Our shields will never see us through another attack."

"Sir, you'll never live to see another attack if you don't readjust your course heading," Scott said more firmly. "That ship wasn't built for this kind of gravitational pull. You're going to tear her apart!"

Scott tried to suppress a mounting feeling of panic. He heard Marlene tell Gardner that the reserve thermal energy shields were now completely exhausted. Gardner ordered her to engage the retros.

Scott craned his neck to see if the retros were having any effect, his guts like a knot pressing against his diaphragm. He saw something break free from the tail section of the transport, glow, and burn out. He was trying to maintain proximity with the ship, but as a result his own displays were suddenly flashing warnings as well. *I'd better slow down myself if I don't want to be decorating a big part of the landscape.*

Scott pulled the mode selector to G position and stepped out of his fear temporarily to think the Veritech through to Guardian mode. As the legs of the mecha dropped, reverse-articulating, he engaged the foot thrusters, substantially cutting his speed. At the same time, Gardner's transport was roaring past him in an uncontrolled plunge.

"Commander, pull out!" he cried into the net. *Marlene!*

Caught between self-sacrifice and desperation, Scott could do little more than bear witness to the agonizingly slow deterioration of the command ship—the end of all he held dear in the world. The transport was a glowing ember now, slagging off fragments of itself into the void. The intense heat would have already boiled the blood of those inside. . . .

Marlene!

His mind tried to save him from the horror by denying the events, cocooning him in much the same way the Veritech did. But averting his gaze only worsened matters: Everywhere he looked ships-of-the-fleet were breaking apart, flaming out as they plunged into Earth's betraying blue softness, wings and stabilizers folded by heat, delicate necks snapped, molten alloy falling like silver tears in the night.

The Veritechs were faring better, but columns of Invid were now on the ascent to deal out their own form of injustice.

They fell upon the helpless transports and command ships first, helping nature's cruel reversal along with deliberately placed rends and breaches, spreading further ruin throughout the fleet. Scott saw acts of bravery and futility: a Battloid already crippled and falling backward into the atmosphere pouring cannon fire against the enemy; two superheated Veritechs attempting to defend a transport against dozens of Invid claw fighters; another VT, boosters blazing, in a kamikaze run toward the head of the column.

Scott instructed his ship to jettison the rear augmentation pack and increased his speed, atmosphere be damned. There was still an outside chance that some of Gardner's crew had made it into the evacuation pods. If only the Invid could be kept away from the hapless transport.

"Please, pull out!" Scott was screaming through gritted teeth. "Please, please . . ."

Then, all at once, the transport's triple-thrusters died out, and an instant later the ship was engulfed in a soundless fireball that blew it to pieces.

Marlene! Scott railed at the heavens, his fists striking blows against the canopy and console as the Veritech commenced a swift unguided fall.

CHAPTER
TWO

I don't think I'll ever forget the first time I laid eyes on Scott Bernard—beneath all that Robotech armor, I mean. He had the Look of the Lost in his eyes, and a stammer in his voice that was pure tremolo. The latter proved to be a case of offworld accent—some Tirolian holdover—but that Look...I just couldn't meet his eyes; I sat there tinkering with the Cyclone, trying to figure out whether I should run for the hills or off the guy then and there. Later on—much later on—he told me about that first night in the woods. I've got to laugh, even now: Ask Scott Bernard the one about the tree falling in the wilderness—and prepare to have your head bitten off!

Rand, *Notes on the Run*

TIROL, ONCE THE HOMEWORLD OF THE ROBOTECH Masters, then an Invid colony when the Masters had uprooted the remnants of their dying race and journeyed to Earth in search of Protoculture, was a reconfigured planet, much of its surface given over to humankind's needs, its small seas and weather patterns tamed. Not like this Earth, Scott thought, with its solitary yellow sun and distant silver satellite. He yearned for Tirol. It had been his home as much as the SDF-3 had been; he missed the binary stars of Fantoma's system, the protective presence of the motherworld itself. *How remote one felt from the heavens on this displaced world.*

Scott recalled Admiral Hunter's rousing send-off speech, his talk of the "cool green hills of home"—his home, Earth. Scott laughed bitterly to himself, the planet's native splendor lost on him.

The Alpha had found a soft spot to cushion its fall in some sort of highland forest. Oak and fir trees, Scott guessed. The VT was history, but cockpit harnesses and collision air bags had kept him in one piece. However, the crash had been violent enough to plow up a large hunk of the landscape. He had lost his helmet and sustained a forehead bruise; then came a follow-up thigh wound of his own making when he had rather carelessly climbed from the wreck.

He was sitting in the grass now, his back against the fighter's fuselage, his head and left leg bandaged with gauze from the ship's first-aid kit. He had gotten rid of his cumbersome armor just before nightfall but kept his blaster within reach.

The forest was dark and full of sounds he could not identify, although he was certain these were all *natural* calls and chirps and whistles—from what he had seen thus far, Earth was primitive and uncontrolled.

And there were just too many places for an enemy to hide.

"Give me a scorched Martian desert any day," Scott muttered.

He heard a rustling sound in the brush nearby and reached out for the blaster—a discette-shaped weapon developed on Tirol that was a scaled-down version of the one carried by the Masters' Bioroids during the Second Robotech War.

"Is there somebody out there?" he asked of the dark.

When the movement suddenly increased, he fired off a charge; it impacted with a blinding orange flash against a tree, flushing two small long-eared creatures from the undergrowth. Scott mistook them for Optera cha-chas at first—the Flower of Life Pollinators—then realized that they were rabbits.

What's happening to me? he asked himself, shaken by the cold fear that coursed through him. *Marlene and everything I loved destroyed, and now I'm losing my nerve.* He set the blaster aside and put his gloved hands to his face. It was possible he had sustained a concussion during the crash. A delayed onset of shock . . .

Lifting his head, he found that Earth had another surprise in store for him: The sky was dumping droplets of water on him—it was *raining*! Scott got up and walked to a clearing in the woods. He had heard about this phenomenon from old-timers but hadn't expected to encounter it. Scott could see that rain might not be a bad thing under certain conditions, but right now it was only adding to his discomfort. Besides, there was something else in the air that had come in with the rain: periods of a short-lived, rolling, explosive roar.

Clouds backlit by flashes of electrical charge were moving swiftly, obscuring the Moon and plunging the world into an impenetrable dark. Soon the angry bolts responsible for that stroboscopic light were overhead, launched like fiery spears toward the land itself, ear-splitting claps of thunder in their wake.

Scott found himself overwhelmed by a novel form of terror, so unlike the fear he was accustomed to that he stood screaming into the face of it, his feet seemingly rooted to the ground. This had nothing to do with enemy laser fire or plasma annihilation discs; it had nothing to do with combat or close calls. This was a larger terror, a deeper one, springing from an archaic part of himself he had never met face to face.

Unnerved, he ran for the safety of the Veritech cockpit as lightning struck and ignited one of the trees, toppling it with a second bolt that split the forest giant along its length. He lowered the canopy and hunkered down in the VT seat, hugging himself for warmth and security. Eyes tightly shut, ears filled with crackling noise, he shouted to himself: *What am I doing on this horrible planet?*

As if answering him, his mind reran images of the command ship's fiery demise, that slow and silent fatality.

"Marlene," he said through tears.

His hand had found the holo-locket she had given him on the bridge. But his forefinger was frozen on the activation button, his mind fearful of confronting the ghosts the device was meant to summon up. Still, he knew that he had to force himself to see and hear her again... before he could let the past die.

The metallic green heart opened at his touch, unfolding like a triptych; from its blood-red holo-bead center wafted a phantom image of Marlene.

> *"Scott, my darling, I know it isn't much, but I thought you'd get a kick out of this trinket. I'm looking forward to living the rest of my life with you. I can't wait till this conflict is all behind us. Till we meet again, my love..."*

The voice that had been Marlene's trailed off, and the shimmering message returned to its place of captivity. Scott closed the heart and clutched it tightly in his fist, wishing desperately that he could so easily de-rezz the images held fast in his own heart. Outside, the storm continued unabated, echoing the dark night of his soul. Lighting fractured the alien sky, and rainwater ran in a steady stream across the protective curve of the VT's canopy.

In the morning Earth's skies seemed as blue as the seas Scott had seen from space; the air smelled sweet, washed clean of last night's violence. But this was little consolation. Fear and sorrow had lulled him into a fitful sleep, and the stark images of Marlene's death were with him when he awoke.

At a clear stream near the crash site, he filled his canteens with water. Taking in morning's soft light, the spectacle of the forest itself, the profusion of bird life, he suspected that Earth could be a tolerable place, after all, but doubted that he would ever feel at home here. He promised himself that he would turn his thoughts to the mission and only the mission from this point on. Insanity was the ónly alternative.

He returned to the Veritech and stowed the canteens with the survival gear he had already retrieved from the mecha. He had enough emergency rations to last him the better part of an Earth week; if he didn't come across a settlement or city by then, he would be forced to forage for food. And given what little information he had about edible plants and such, the thought was hardly an appetizing one.

He turned his attention now to the one item that was likely to rescue him from edible plants or privation: the Cyclone vehicle stored away in the fighter's small cargo compartment. A well-concealed sensor panel in the fuselage gave him access to this, and in a moment he was lifting the self-contained Cyclone free of the cargo hold. In its present collapsed state the would-be two-wheeled transport was no larger than a foot locker, but reconfigured it was equivalent to a 1,000-cc twentieth-century motorcycle. Which in fact it was, after a fashion.

Originally one of Robotechnology's first creations, it had undergone some radical modifications under Lang's SDF-3 teams. The Expeditionary Force had come to rely upon the vehicle as much as it had on the Veritech fighters, even though its design was still a basic one: a hybrid piston and Protoculture-powered transformable motorcycle that was a far cry from the Hovercycles developed on Earth during the same time period. Unlike that Southern Cross marvel, the Cyclone required the full interaction of its pilot, whose "thinking cap" and

specially designed armor were essential to the functioning of the vehicle's Protoculture-based mechamorphic
systems. In addition, it was light enough to carry, and
wondrously fuel-efficient.

Scott carried the Cyclone several feet from the fighter
and set about reconfiguring it, which entailed little more
than flipping the appropriate switches. That much accomplished, he transferred his survival gear to the
cycle's rear deck and began to struggle into the mecha's
modular battle armor—not unlike the shoulder pads, hip
harnesses, and leg and forearm protectors worn by turn-
of-the-century athletes, except for the fact that the armor
had been fashioned from lightweight alloys.

Scott was wearing Marlene's holo-heart around his
neck now and gave a last look at it before snapping the
armor's pectorals in place. *It's time, my love,* he said to
the heart.

Again he told himself to concentrate on the mission.
He recalled Commander Gardner's words: *If only one of
you survive the invasion, you must locate the Invid Reflex Point and destroy it along with their queen, the
Regis.* Scott had no idea how many people from Mars
Division had survived atmospheric entry, but it was unlikely that any of them had touched down near his crash
site. He had been so caught up in the destruction of the
command ship that he had failed to lock the proper coordinates into the VT's autopilot. As a consequence, the
mecha had surely delivered him far from any of the
dozen preassigned rendezvous points and who knew
how far from the Reflex Point itself. The stars told Scott
that he had come down somewhere in the southern hemisphere, which put thousands of miles between him and
the Regis if he was lucky, oceans between them if not. In
any case, north was the direction of choice.

Scott donned his helmet and mounted the Cyclone. A
thumb switch brought the mecha to life; he found his

confidence somewhat restored by the throaty, synchro-
nous firing of the cycle's systems.

*Now let's get on with evening the score with the
Regis and her Invid horde*, Scott said to himself as he
set off.

The worst thing about being a lone survivor were the
memories that survived with you, Scott decided. If only
one could erase them, switch them off somehow. But
Scott knew that he couldn't; the people one loved were
more frightening ghosts than anything imagination could
conjure up. And they couldn't be outrun. . . .

Less than an hour from his crash site, Scott was surprised to find himself on what appeared to be a trail or an
ancient roadway lined with trees. But an even greater
shock awaited him over the rise: a veritable desert at the
foot of the wooded foothills that witnessed his crash,
stretching out toward distant barren mountains. Scott
slid the Cyclone to a halt and stared homesick at the
sight.

*Who said there were no Fantoma landscapes on
Earth?*

Scott had never heard Wolff, Edwards, or any of the
old-timers brag about this. It was almost as vast as
Spheris!

Now reassured as well as renewed, Scott twisted the
Cyclone's throttle and streaked down into the wastes.

Elsewhere in the wastes rode a survivor of a different
campaign; but his cycle was of a different sort, (twenty
years old if it was a day, and running desperately short of
fuel pellets).

A clear-eyed, short, sinewy teenager with a shaggy
mop of red hair and an unwashed look about him—both
by necessity and by design—he called himself Rand, his
inherited names long abandoned. He was born about the
time the SDF-3 had been launched from Little Luna, and

he had seen the rise and fall of Chairman Moran's government, the invasion of the Robotech Masters, and humankind's subsequent regression to barbarism, a turn of events that had culminated with the arrival of the Invid and their easily won conquest.

Just now Rand was doing what he did best: keeping himself alive. His old bike was closing in on the object he had seen plummet from the night sky two days ago, something too slow and controlled to have been a meteor, too massive for an Alpha. He had made up his mind to track its fall, abandoning his earlier plans to try for Laako City in the hopes of beating other Spotters, Foragers, and assorted rogues to the find.

Rand relaxed his wrist and let the bike come to a slow stop a good kilometer from the impact point. He threw back the hood of his shirt and slid his goggles up onto his forehead. The ship was even larger than he had guessed, like some great bird with enormous hexagonally shaped cargo pods strapped to the undersides of its wings. It was still glowing in places but obviously had been cooled by the rains that had drenched the irradiated wastes during the night. Rand cautiously resumed his forward motion, completing a circle around the thing at the same safe distance. There were no tracks or footprints in the still-moist sands, which meant that no one had left or entered the wreck during the past twelve hours or so.

He cycled through a second, tighter circle and headed in, convinced that he was first to arrive on the scene. Approaching the ship now, he could discern numbers and letters stenciled on the fuselage—M__R__ DIV____I____—but could make no sense of the whole —where it had come from or why.

The wreck had the stench of recent death written all over it. He wasn't in the least looking forward to walking into cargo bays wallpapered with Human remains, but he was just going to have to shut his eyes to that part of it.

There had to be something he could use, weapons or foodstuffs.

He began to circle the ship on foot now, searching for some way to get inside. The nose was throwing off so much heat there was no getting near it, but the rear hatch of one of the cargo carriers had sprung open on impact, and the place seemed cool enough to enter.

Rand threw himself atop the twisted wreck of the hatch and started in. The interior was dark and uninviting, and it smelled like hell. He knew he wasn't going to get very far, but not fifty feet into the thing—after whacking his head on a low threshold and falling flat on his face in the dark—he found more than enough to satisfy him: a bin of ten Robotech cycles.

He lifted one up and out of its rack and bent down to look it over. It was Robotech, all right, probably one of the Cyclone type the military had used before the development of the Hovercrafts. Rand had heard about them but never thought he would live to see one—let alone *ride* one!

Straddling the mecha now, he depressed the ignition switch, fingers of his left hand crossed for luck. The Cyclone fired, purring like a kitten, after a goose or two of the throttle.

"Awwriight!" Rand shouted.

He flicked on the headlight, screeched the Cyclone through a 360, and tore back toward the doorway, launching himself into the desert air from the sprung hatchway. He hit the sand and twisted the cycle to a halt, exhilarated from his short flight.

Then he noticed something else in flight: a three-unit Invid scouting party coming fast over a ridge of low hills to the west. Rand cursed himself for not figuring them into the picture; they, too, must have been aware of the transport's crash. And as always, their timing was impeccable. Even so, Rand was thankful that they were only Scouts and not Shock Troopers. In fact there was a good chance that the Cyclone would be able to outrun them—at least as far as the forest.

The three Scouts put down next to the downed ship, positioning themselves to prevent Rand's escape, the cloven foot of one them flattening the old cycle that had seen him through so much.

"I sure hope your insurance is paid up, pal!" Rand yelled at the Scout.

They were twenty-foot-tall bipedal creatures with articulated armored legs and massive pincer arms; there was no actual head, but raised egg-shaped protrusions atop their inverted triangular torsos were suggestive of eyes, while what looked to be a red-rimmed lipless mouth concealed a single sensor lens. Rand had seen brown ones and purple ones—these three were of the latter category—and more than anything they reminded him of two-legged land crabs. The Scouts were just that and were weaponless, except if one counted their innate repulsiveness. However, they could inflict serious damage with their claws, and just now one of the Scouts wanted to demonstrate that fact to Rand.

Rand shot the Cyclone forward at the Scout's first swipe, its claw striking the sand with a loud crunching sound. "Okay, but I'm going to be submitting a bill for damages!" he called over his shoulder as a second creature gave pursuit.

Rand's previous questions concerning the Cyclone's capabilities were soon to be answered. The three Invid were gaining on him, and ready or not he was going to have to put the cycle through its paces. He took a deep breath and kicked in the turbochargers. Instantaneously the Cyclone took off like a shot, living up to its namesake while Rand struggled to retain control. The Scouts meanwhile gave up their ground-shaking run and took to the air, thrusters carrying them overhead, pincer arms poised for the embrace that killed.

Their prey, however, had managed to overcome his initial ineptitude and was now leaning the Cyclone through a series of self-imposed twists and turns along the featureless sands, a tactic that more than once brought the Scouts close to midair collisions with one another.

"Just lemme know if you're gettin' tired!" Rand shouted above the roar of the mecha. He laughed over his shoulder and threw the Scouts a maniacal grin; but when he turned again to face front, he found trouble ahead. Something was approaching him fast, kicking up one heck of a dust storm. Two of the Invid were moving into flanking position, and it suddenly occurred to Rand that he would soon be surrounded.

Scott Bernard felt two emotions vying for his attention when he saw the Cyclone rider and the Invid Scouts: elation that he had found one of his Mars Division comrades and rage at the sight of the enemy. He couldn't figure out why the rider wasn't reconfiguring but knew that the situation called for immediate action. Lowering the helmet visor, he engaged the mecha's turbos. For a moment the Cyclone was up on its rear wheel, then it went fully airborne. At the same time, Scott's mind instinctively found the vibe that allowed it to inferface with the cycle's Protoculture systems.

Helped along by the imaging Scott's mind fed the Cyclone via the helmet "thinking cap," the mecha began to reconfigure. The windscreen and helmet assembly flattened out; the front wheel disengaged itself from the axle and swung back and off to one side. The rear wheel, along with most of the thruster pack, rode up, while other components, including the wheel-mounted missile tubes, attached themselves to Scott's hip, leg, and forearm armor. In the final stage of mechamorphosis, he resembled some kind of airborne armored backpacker whose gear just happened to include two solid rubber tires and a jet pack.

Scott let the thruster carry him in close to the Invid Scouts before bringing his forearm weapons into play—twin launch tubes that carried small but deadly Scorpion missiles. Right arm outstretched now, palm downward, he raised the tubes' targeting mechanism, centered one of the Scouts in the reticle, and loosed both missiles. They streaked toward their quarry with a deadly sibilance (Scott's armor protecting him from their backlash), narrowly missed Rand, and caught the Invid ship square in the belly, scattering pieces of it across the sands.

The unarmored Cyclone rider went down into a long slide while Scott took to the ground to dispatch his remaining pursuers. Once in their midst, he dodged two claw swipes before launching himself over the top of his would-be assailant. Another missed swipe and a second leap landed him atop one of the pair; he leapt up again and came down for the kill, firing off a single Scorpion from the left forearm launch tubes. While the Invid was engulfed by the ensuing explosion, Scott put down to deal with the last of them.

The thing tried to crush him with its foot, but Scott rolled away from it in time. Likewise, he dodged a right claw and jumped up onto the Invid's head. The Scout brought its left up now, almost in a gesture of puzzlement, but Scott was already gone. He toyed with the Invid for a minute more, allowing it another shot at him before polishing it off with the remaining Scorpion, which the Scout took right through its red optic scanner.

The Cyclone rider was still on the ground beneath his overturned mecha when Scott approached. "They're not really as tough as they look, are they?" he said to the bewildered red-haired civilian.

"*Hombre*, you're really something else in a battle," the man returned, his bushy eyebrows arched.

Scott raised the faceshield of his helmet. "The Cyclone does the work," he said humbly.

"Yeah, it's quite a rig," said Rand. He got up, dusted himself off, and righted the cycle, marveling at it once again. "You are a Forager?" he asked Scott warily. "Some kinda one-man army?"

"You might say that," Scott began. "Now listen—"

"It's the first time I ever actually rode one of these things!" Rand interrupted.

"I need some information—"

"I'll bet I could modify this to go twice the speed!" Rand was on his knees now, fidgeting with this and that. "Look at this control setup! I can't wait to try to reconfigure it!"

"Just where the hell are we, outlaw?" Scott managed at last. But when even that failed to elicit a response, he reached over the Cyclone and grabbed Rand by the shirtfront. "I'm talking to you, pal. Where'd those Scouts come from? Is there an Invid hive around here?"

Rand began to struggle against the mecha's hold, and Scott let him go. He was a scrappy kid but might make a decent partner.

Rand backed off, arms akimbo. "What do I look like, some kind of travel agent? I don't make a habit of asking them where they hail from—you just look up and there they are. I hate those things!"

"Take it easy," Scott told him harshly. He explained about the ill-fated invasion force and their abortive attempts at securing a groundside front.

"I didn't think you were from around here," Rand said, somewhat relieved. "Admiral Hunter, huh?" It was as if Scott had mentioned George Washington.

"Ancient history, I suppose."

Rand shrugged. "I've never heard of Reflex Point either. 'Course, I don't mix much when I don't have to. As far as I know, the Invid HQ is north of here—*way* north." Fascinated, he watched as Scott, now on his knees, collapsed and stepped out of the two-wheeled backpack, returning the mecha to Cyclone configuration. "You really going to try and find Reflex?"

"That's what I'm here for," said Scott, doffing the helmet. As he pulled it over his head, the chin strap caught the holo-locket's chain and took it along. The heart fell and opened, replaying its brief message to Scott and his stunned companion.

> "*. . . I'm looking forward to living the rest of my life with you. I can't wait till this conflict is all behind us. Till we meet again, my love . . .*"

Wordlessly, Scott stooped to retrieve the heart.

"Hey, that's great!" said Rand. "Is that your girl?"

"Uh . . . my girl," Scott stammered. He straightened up, clutching the heart against his pectoral armor, and turned his back to Rand.

> *Dolza's annihilation bolts had devastated the South American coastal cities and turned much of the vast interior forest into wasteland. Ironically enough, however, repopulation of the area was largely the result of the hundreds of Zentraedi warships that crashed there after the firing of the Grand Cannon. Indeed, even after Khyron's efforts to stage a full-scale rebellion had failed, the region was still largely under Zentraedi domination (the T'sentrati Control Zone, as it was known to the indigenous peoples), up until the Malcontent uprisings of 2013–15 and the subsequent events headed up by Captain Maxmillian Sterling of the Robotech Defense Force. But contrary to popular belief, Brazilas did not become the lawless frontier Scott Bernard traversed until much later, specifically, the two-year period between the fall of Chairman Moran's Council and the Invid invasion. In fact the region had seen extensive changes during the Second Robotech War and surely would have risen to the fore had it not been for the disastrous end to that fifteen-year epoch.*

> "Southlands," *History of the Third Robotech War,*
> Vol. XXII

COUNTLESS PEOPLE FOUND THEMSELVES HOMEless after the Invid's preemptive strike against Earth; the waste was awash with wanderers, thieves, and madmen. And, of course, children: lost, uprooted, orphaned. They fared worse than the other groups, usually falling prey to illness, starvation, and marauding gangs. Occasionally, one would stumble upon groups of them in devastated cities or natural shelters—caves, patches of forest, oases—forty or fifty strong, banded together like some feral family; and God help the one who tried to disturb their new order!... But this was the exception rather than the rule. The great majority of them had to make their own way and fend for themselves, attach themselves—more often, *enslave* themselves—to whomever or whatever could provide them with some semblance of protection, the chance for a better tomorrow.

Laako City, largest settlement in the southern wastes, saw its fair share of these nameless drifters, and Ken was usually the one who welcomed them with open arms. He was a tall, gangly streetwise eighteen-year-old with a reputation for dirty tricks, mean-spirited by nature but a charmer when he needed to be. His long hair was a pewter color, save for the crimson forelock that was his trademark.

His most recent conquest was a young girl named Annie, who claimed to be fifteen. But Ken had grown bored with her; besides, he had his eye fixed on a pretty little dark-haired urchin who had just arrived in Laako, and the time had come to kiss Annie off.

The trouble was that Annie didn't want to go.

"Don't leave me like this!" she was pleading with him just now, alligator tears coursing down moon-face cheeks.

"Hey," he told her soothingly, disengaging himself from her hold on his arm. "You knew from the start you'd have to leave someday."

This was and was not true: Laako did maintain a policy of limiting the time outsiders were allowed to spend in the city, but well-connected Ken could easily have steered his way around the regs. If he had been so inclined.

The two of them were standing at the causeway entrance to the city in the lake, the tall albeit ruined towers of the Laako's twin islands visible in the background. Sundry trucks and tractors on their way to the causeway checkpoint were motoring by, kicking up dust and decibels alike.

"*Please*, Ken!" Annie tried, emphatically this time, launching herself at him, hoping to pinion his arms with her small hands. It was push and pull for a moment—Ken saying, "Annie!... Cut it out!... Stop it!" to Annie's "I can't!... I won't!... I can't!—" but ultimately he put a violent end to it, bringing his arms up with such force that Annie was thrown to the ground.

Which was easy enough for him to do. She was a good foot shorter than Ken, with a large mouth, long, straight, carrot-colored hair, and what some might have termed a cherublike cuteness about her. Her single outfit consisted of an olive-drab double-breasted military jumpsuit she had picked up along the trail, set off by a pink frameless rucksack and a maroon visored cap emblazoned with the letters *E.T.*, a piece of twentieth-century nostalgia that dated back to a popular science-fantasy film. It was difficult to tell—as it was with many of the lost—whether Annie was searching for a friend, a father, or a lover. And it was doubtful that she could have answered the question either.

"I *told* you to cut it out," Ken started to say, but the sight of her kneeling in the dirt crying her eyes out managed to touch what meager tenderness he still possessed. "Don't you see I have no choice?" he continued apologetically, walking over to her and placing his hand on her heaving shoulder. "This whole thing is just as hard for me as it is for you, Annie. Please try and understand."

She kept her face buried in her hands, sobbing while he spoke.

"Nobody who comes from the outside can stay for more than a little while, remember? And if I left here, I wouldn't be allowed to return ..."

Suddenly the tears were gone and she was looking up at him with a devious grin on her face. "Then run away with me, Ken! We'll start our *own* family, our own *town!*" She was up on her feet now, tugging on his arm, but Ken didn't budge.

"Quit giving me a hard time," he told her harshly, angry at himself for being taken in by her saltwater act. "I'm not going anywhere—*you* are!"

Annie's face contorted through sorrow to rage. She cursed him, using everything her vocabulary had to offer. But in return he proffered a knowing smile that undermined her anger. "You're heartless," she seethed, collapsing to the ground once more. "Heartless."

Rand had led Scott to the site of the downed transport; the Mars Division commander held little hope that anyone had survived the crash but thought there might be an Armored Alpha Veritech still aboard. He was thankful for the Cyclone, but with perhaps thousands of miles separating him from the Invid Reflex Point, the journey would be a long one indeed.

Fearing a visit from Invid reinforcements—Shock Troopers this time—the two riders didn't remain long at the wreck. There were neither survivors nor Veritechs, but Scott was at least able to procure additional Scorpions for the battle armor launchers, several canisters of Protoculture fuel, and a sensor-studded helmet for Rand. Thus far the redheaded rebel had demonstrated no inclination to form even a temporary partnership, but Scott hoped that the helmet and battle armor would entice him somewhat. Scott would have been the first to admit his sense of helplessness; he was a stranger to this world and its ways. And if the unthinkable had occurred—if he alone had survived the atmospheric plunge—he was going to need all the help he could get.

Rand wasn't sure what to make of the offworlder. He was a good man to have on one's side in a fight and no doubt a capable enough officer in his own element, but he was a fish out of water on Earth, and a relic besides

—a throwback to a time when humankind functioned hopefully and collectively. In any case, Rand was a lone rider, and he meant to keep it that way. You joined up with someone, and suddenly there were compromises that had to be made, plans and decisions a single Forager wasn't caught up in.

Rand lived for the open road, and he was grateful that the offworlder hadn't lingered too long at the crash site, glad to have it behind him now. The two had ridden as far as the hills together, then Rand had waved Scott off and lit out on his own, the Cyclone throbbing beneath him. He was enchanted with the mecha, but there were a few other priorities that needed tending to: food, for starters. The tasteless stuff Scott had liberated from the wreck might be all right for spacemen, but it wasn't likely to catch on among down-to-earth Foragers.

Once again he had decided to pass on Laako City; it would be easy enough to get something to eat there, but the results probably wouldn't justify the paranoid garbage he would have to put up with. Rand had never visited Laako, but what he had heard from other Foragers was enough to give him second thoughts about the place.

Even so, he was headed in the general direction of the island city, putting the Cyclone through the paces on the twisting mountain road that connected the wastes with the grasslands and lakes of the central plateaus. The only such road, it was usually heavily trafficked and dangerous in spots—little more than a narrow ledge with deep ruts and steep drop-offs. But most of that was still ahead of him, and he was cruising along, oblivious to the fact that Scott was not far behind. Then Rand heard the roar of the second Cyclone and looked over his right shoulder, surprised to find the offworlder scrambling along the embankment above the roadway. Scott gave a nod and piloted the cycle through a clean jump that brought him alongside Rand.

"What's the problem?" Rand shouted, raising his goggles. "You got nowhere to go, or what?" He saw Scott smile beneath the helmet's wraparound chin guard.

"I want to head up toward that city you mentioned," Scott called back, maintaining his speed. "We might be able to get some information."

"What's this *we* stuff, spaceman?" Rand barked. "I go my own way."

Scott smiled again. "Come on, I'll show you how to convert to Battle Armor mode. Or maybe you're too frightened of the Invid, huh?"

"Hey, pal, *you* go ahead and wage your one-man war. This Cyclone's fine as is," Rand snapped. "See you around," he added, giving a twist to the throttle and pulling out ahead of Scott.

In a moment Scott came up alongside again.

"Make up your mind—you headed to the city or not?"

Scott made a gesture of nonchalance. "I'm just headed where I'm headed, that's all."

"Well, get off my tail!" Rand shouted, lowering his goggles. He popped the front wheel and accelerated out front.

Scott did the same, and the two of them toyed with each other for several minutes, alternating the lead. By now they had entered the shoulderless downhill portion of the highway, and Rand was nursing some misgivings about playing chicken with a dude who was decked out in armor. Nevertheless, he stuck by the offworlder, racing him into a wide turn where the roadway disappeared around the shoulder of the mountain. Neither of them saw the convoy of trucks headed for the pass until it was almost too late. The driver of the lead vehicle—an open-cabbed eight-wheeler—leaned on his horn and locked up the brakes, throwing the transport into zigzags. The Cyclones, meanwhile, were also locked up, sliding sideways down the narrow road. Rand, on the inside, saw a collapsed portion of an earthen wall and went for it, ramping his bike up to the high ground. Scott, however, kept to the road, dangerously close to the drop-off now, and brought the Cyclone to a halt a meter from the truck's front grille.

The driver, a long-haired rube wearing a tall brimmed hat, waved his fist in the air. "Ya rogue—somebody coulda got killed!"

"Sorry about that," Scott told him offhandedly. "Look, we need some information—"

"Wait a minute!" the driver cut Scott off, eyeing him up and down. "You're a soldier! What are you doing out here?"

Scott revealed just enough to satisfy the driver's curiosity. "I'm looking for others who may have bailed out. Have you come across anyone?" Scott saw the man give a start, then avert his gaze.

"Nope. No one . . . But lemme give you a free piece of advice," the driver answered him, throwing the truck into forward gear. "You're gonna wish you never came back!"

Scott legged the Cyclone off to one side, calling out for an explanation as the truck roared off. The other drivers in the convoy regarded Scott warily from the cabs of their trucks as they lumbered by, but no one said a word until a young boy in the back of the final one yelled out: "Hey, mister, don't tell anyone who you are or you'll be in deep trouble!"

Scott thought he would hear more, but the truck's headbanded elder put a hand over the boy's mouth. "Don't talk to that man," he threatened the kid.

Rand watched the convoy disappear around the bend and saw Scott's gesture of puzzlement. "You coming or not?" the offworlder asked him suddenly. Rand thought about it for a moment while Scott took off down the road. All his instincts told him to follow the trucks, but ultimately he coasted down the incline and set out to catch up with Scott; after all, *somebody* had to keep the guy from sticking his nose where it didn't belong.

In the trees at the edge of the roadway, the red optic scanner of an Invid Scout rotated slightly to track the rider's swift departure....

"Ken, *please* come with me!" Annie was shouting. "I'll be good for you, I promise! I love you! You promised you'd stay with me!"

He was dragging her down the road now, his hands underneath her arms. They were a good half mile from the causeway checkpoints already, and Annie was still causing a scene. Finally he dropped her on her butt.

"Whaddaya want from me—you want me to leave my family and friends?"

She looked up at him and said, "Yes."

Ken bent down eye to eye with her. "Look, I know it seems bad right now, but you'll find somebody to take care of you."

"Don't worry about me!" she yelled in his face as she got up. "I can find my own way around. Men are a dime a dozen for someone like me." Then suddenly she was all over him again: "*Please*, Ken!"

Ken shook her off, sending her down to the ground on her knees. Fed up, he began to walk back to the checkpoint. Ten steps away, however, he turned at the sound of approaching vehicles. Scott and Rand were just coming around a bend in the tree-lined road. They halted their Cyclones where Annie sat crying. Ken took one look at the cycles and saw a sweet deal in the making. He went over to them with a gleam in his eye.

Closest to Annie, Rand was asking, "What's the matter, kid, are you hurt?"

She looked up, surprised, and told him in no uncertain terms that *she wasn't a kid*. "So, beat it!"

Ken ambled up and gestured appreciatively at Scott's mecha. "Nice wheels, rogue." Ken smiled. "Where'd you forage 'em?"

"I'm Commander Bernard of Mars Division," Scott said when he had raised the helmet faceshield. "I'm looking for other survivors of my unit."

Ken glanced over at Rand and stepped back. "You're for real, then—soldiers, I mean."

"Have you seen any of the others?"

"Come with me," Ken said after a moment, already setting off for the causeway.

Scott was suddenly full of hope. "They're here?"

"And you can come, too, Annie," Ken added without turning around.

Annie's eyes opened wide. "I take back what I said." She hurried to catch up with him and attached herself to his arm lovingly.

Rand and Scott exchanged looks and brought the Cyclones back to life. "What's the chance of landing some belly timber?" Rand wanted to know. "We've got trade goods."

"Follow me," Ken told him.

Annie beamed. "You've made me so happy, Ken." She went up on tiptoe to kiss him on the mouth.

Ken whisked them through the checkpoint and escorted them along the causeway that led to the main island. It was a picturesque spot for a city, Rand had to admit: a crystal-blue lake surrounded by forested hills. But there was ample evidence of the war's hold over the place—the scorched and rusted hulks of Zentraedi battlecruisers, downed Adventurers, Falcons, and Bioroids.

He noticed that there was a second island, accessible only from the main one, and that it, too, was host to a densely packed cluster of tall, mostly ruined buildings, rubble, and debris heaped up in the streets. Up close the city was somewhat less than inspiring, literally a shell of its former self, but so far they hadn't been searched, hassled, or otherwise bad-vibed, and Rand was beginning to wonder where all those rumors had come from.

"These are Robotech soldiers!" Ken announced to the sullen-faced people huddled inside the buildings, postapocalypse cave dwellers in high-rise cliffs of slagged steel and fractured concrete. "They were with the forces who have returned to Earth to rid us of the Invid." No one moved, no one returned a word. There was only the slight howling of the wind and the steady throb of the Cyclones' engines. "They're looking for lost members of the assault group. I'm going to take them over to the other island."

Ken turned a wan smile to Scott and Rand. "As you can see, folks around here aren't used to strangers," he said by way of apology. "They're always a bit suspicious at first, but don't worry about it. They'll soon get used to you."

Scott, Rand, and Annie followed Ken's lead to the causeway linking the main island with its twin.

"There it is." Ken pointed. "If any of your comrades have come through here, they'll have been taken over to the other island."

"Thanks a lot for your help, Ken," Scott said.

Ken disengaged his hand from Annie's two-fisted lock on it. "Why don't you show them over the causeway while I go talk to the Elders about your staying here?"

Annie called out to him as he was walking away.

"Yes?" he said impatiently, not bothering to turn around.

"Bye-bye, sweet thing!"

"And don't forget that food!" Rand thought to add.

Annie made an elaborate gesture, then laughed. "Now, if you gentlemen will just follow me . . ."

Rand chuckled and patted the rear seat of the Cyclone. "Hop on," he told her. "It'll be fun."

CHAPTER
FOUR

The Invid Regis ruled her empire from Reflex Point (lo-cated in what was once the United States of America, spe-cifically the Indiana-Ohio frontier); but there was scarcely a region without one or two large hives (except the poles and vast uninhabited tracts in Asia and Africa). In this way her Scouts were always about, with Enforcers (a.k.a. Shock Troopers) not far behind. Brazilas was no different from other northern regions in that it was effectively an occupied zone. Like Vichy France of the Second World War, each town had its sympathizers and resistance fighters; but the former far outnumbered the latter, and it was not uncom-mon to encounter gruesome and ghastly acts of betrayal and butchery undertaken in the name of self-survival.

Bloom Nesterfig, *Social Organization of the Invid*

AS RAND HIMSELF WOULD LATER WRITE:

"There was something about Ken's telling Annie to lead us across the causeway that hit me like a cold wind, but for some reason I just turned my back to it. Scott's innocent enthusiasm had something to do with this. Psyched about seeing some of his friends, he was off in a flash, the Cyclone's rear end chirping a quick good-bye to me and the kid. So I told her to climb on and followed Scott's carefree course, Annie laughing and hanging on for dear life while I goosed the mecha into a long gold-card wheelie.

"The bridge was a simple affair, a flat span no more than fifteen feet wide and a quarter mile long, its plastar surface every bit as holed and bellied as the rest of Laako's streets. The causeway seemed to bisect the is-land's stand of colorless truncated towers, which rose before us like some ruined vision of the future, an emerald without its shine. Beyond it, a ridge of green hills and a soft-looking autumn sky.

"Scott was a block or two ahead of me when we hit the island, and talk about your low-rent downtown... the place looked as though it had seen some intense fighting with conventional weapons as well as the usual Robo upgrades. Scott had slowed his cycle to a crawl and was using the mecha's externals to broadcast our arrival.

"'This is Commander Bernard of the Twenty-first Armored Tactical Assault Squadron,' his voice rang out. 'I'm looking for any Mars Division survivors. If you can hear my voice, please respond...Is anybody there? I just want to talk!'

"Annie and I looked around but didn't see anyone moving. I would have been happy to see some more of those sunken-eyed citizens we had seen on the other side, but suddenly even those shadowy cliff dwellers were in short supply. Up ahead, Scott was stopped near a pile of trashed mecha, a perverse war memorial complete with Veritechs, Battlepods, Hovertanks, and Bioroids, arms, legs, and cannon muzzles fused together in a kind of death-affirming sculpture. I came up behind him and toed the Cyclone into neutral. We were on a small rise above the causeway, Scott off to my left, staring at the junk heap with a kind of morbid fascination.

"Then we saw the Cyclones.

"And the bodies.

"You couldn't ride the wastes in those days and be a stranger to death, and like everyone I had seen my fair share of Human remains, but there were fresh kills in the heap, and it was obvious what had happened.

"'This isn't any junk pile!' I heard Scott say. 'It's a goddamn graveyard!'

"Annie gave a start and hugged herself to my back. 'What's it mean?' she cried, panic already in her voice.

"Scott glanced over at us, his face all twisted up. 'It means I smell a rat and it's got your boyfriend's face!'

"All at once we heard a deep whirring noise accompanied by sounds of mechanical disengagement. I looked back toward the causeway in time to see it give a shudder, then begin a slow retraction toward the main island. But I was more puzzled than alarmed. I'd already seen Scott leap that mecha of his twice the distance to the island, so our being able to get off this one alive only meant that I was going to be learning the secrets of Cyclone reconfiguration in spite of myself. Moreover, I couldn't figure why Ken needed to resort to such elaborate plans to rid Laako of intruders.

"I think Scott must have been way ahead of me on this one, because he didn't seem at all surprised when two Invid suddenly surfaced in the lake. Annie's pounding me on the back, shouting, 'We gotta get outta here!' and Scott is just sitting silently on the Cyclone taking in the situation like he's got all the time in the world. I'll always remember the look on his face at that moment—and I would have reason to recall it often during the following months. I thought to myself: *The eye of the storm.*

"Two more Invid were now heading our way from up the street, looming over us, pincers gleaming like knives caught in the light, the ground shaking from their footfalls. These weren't Scouts but Shock Troopers, the larger, meaner version whose shoulder-mounted organic-looking cannons gave them a wide-eyed amphibious look. The lake creatures had submerged, only to reappear behind us, rising up through the plastar streets and putting a radical end to thoughts of escape. In a moment the four were joined by a fifth, who had also taken the subterranean route.

"I felt compelled to point out that we were surrounded, and Scott said, 'Take off!' Which I was all for. I spun the cycle around my left foot and was gone, Scott not two lengths behind me, his Cyclone launched from the street by an overhead pincer slam that nearly flattened him. Later, Annie apologized for the fingernail prints she left in my upper arms, but at that moment I was feeling no pain.

"I had what I thought was the presence of mind to head for the narrower streets, but the Troopers were determined to have us for lunch; their leader, airborne now, simply used its shoulders to power a wider upper-story path between the buildings.

"'How'd they find us!' Annie was yelling into my left ear.

"'Your boyfriend, Ken,' I told her. 'He delivered us right into their claws.' But she didn't want to hear it. Who—*Ken*?

"'He'd never do anything like that—*never!*'

"It wasn't really a good time for an argument, though. The Troopers were sticking to us like magnets, firing off bursts of plasma fire. The fact that I had seen what those annihilation discs could do to a Human body was probably responsible for the chancy moves I made on the Cyclone. But the memory of those liquid remains paid off, because I got us through the first stretch unscathed. Then, after we had taken them around one block, down an alleyway, and through half a dozen more right angles, Scott told me to get the kid out of there; he was going Battle Armor to lure them away. Scott was nothing if not noble. But I couldn't resist getting another look at that reconfiguration act, and caught some flack for it.

"'What're you *looking* at?' Scott berated me over the externals. 'Get moving!'

"Annie seconded this with a couple of cleanly placed kidney shots. So Scott and I parted company at a T intersection, and the next thing I heard was a massive exchange of cannonfire and a series of crippling explosions. But the Invid had done their part in sticking to Scott's tail, and Annie and I were in the clear for the moment.

"I pulled the bike over and told her to hop off. There was no way I was going to let Scott take all the heat; I just had to get my Cyclone to reconfigure, battle armor or not. Trouble was, the damn thing wouldn't respond. I thumbed the switch above the starter button, but nothing happened, so I started flipping switches left and right, cursing the thing for being so obstinate. Annie, the little darling, stood by me, hands behind her head, taunting me and telling me in no uncertain terms to hurry the hell up. Of course, I have since learned that that is precisely what you *don't* do with a piece of mecha, but what did this basically backwoods loner know about mecha then? I just kept jiggling this, pounding that, turning the other, and all of a sudden I found myself flat on my back in the seat, the Cyclone grotesquely reconfigured, with both wheels behind it now, its nose kissing the street.

"Annie was kind enough not to laugh in my face; she turned aside first. And I did something brilliant—like leap off the cycle and try to place kick it into the lake—which only resulted in an injury to my foot to match the one already sustained by my pride.

"But now Annie was shouting and pointing up at something. Scott, in full battle armor, had taken to the buttressed top of a building a few blocks away. One minute he was standing there like some sort of rooftop Robostatue, and the next he was playing dodge-the-plasma-Frisbees. I saw him drop into that annihilation disc storm and execute one of those Bernard bounces that carried him out of sight, just short of the explosions that turned the building into a chimney, flames roaring up from its blasted roof, black parabolas of slagged stuff in the sky.

"Meanwhile, I had worked through my frustration and managed to get the mecha back into Cycle mode. Annie still wanted to know why the thing wouldn't change. I started to explain about the armor and 'thinking cap,' and the next thing I knew she was running off toward the causeway.

"'I'm gonna go and find Ken and get him to tell me once and for all why he went and sold us out to the Invid!' she yelled after I tried to get her to stop. ''F you don't like it—*tough!*'

"I had to admit that I was thinking along those very same lines, but Annie's timing left a lot to be desired. And since I didn't relish the thought of finding that pink backpack of hers dangling from a bloody pincer, I threw the Cyclone into gear and went after her. I reached out, and she swatted my hand away, telling me to get lost. Angry now, I decided I would just scoop her up in my left arm and put an end to the foolishness, but I misjudged both my course and her weight. No sooner did my arm go around her waist than I was pulled from the mecha. Worse still, we were right alongside an open freight elevator; and down we went, eight feet or more, would-be opponents wrapped in each other's arms.

"I blacked out for a moment; perhaps we both did. But Annie came around first and laid into me as though I had just tried to maul her. I came to with her shouting: 'Get off of me, you monster! You dirty Forager sleaze! You're all alike!' She heaved me off her and scrambled up out of the shaft with a nimbleness and speed that surprised me. By the time I poked my head out, she was nowhere in sight. But I heard her rummaging around in a nearby pile of mecha scrap, still cursing men in general, me in particular. When I saw her come up with an old-fashioned automatic rifle, I started having second thoughts about showing myself. Fortunately, she was only interested in emptying the thing's clip against the already devastated facade of a building across the street. Then she tossed the depleted thing aside and dove back down into the scrap heap. Meanwhile, I was wondering what had become of Scott and whether the Invid would home in on Annie's gunfire. When I looked over at her again, she was wrestling an antitank weapon up onto her shoulder.

"'Watch where you point that thing!' I started to warn her. 'It might be—'

"And it was.

"The small missile nearly put a center part in my hair, then changed trajectory and detonated against the side of the building.

"A little to the right and she would have connected with the Invid who was just stepping around that same corner.

"I ran for the overturned Cyclone, hopped on, and darted over to pick up Annie, who now had control of the weapon. She located another missile and launched it against the approaching Shock Trooper. I backed her up with Scorpions from the front-end launch tubes of the Cyclone, but neither of us managed to connect with a soft spot in the thing's shell, and it kept up its menacing advance. Annie screamed and made a run for it, not a second before the creature's right claw came down at her; the tip of its bladelike pincer swept the pack from her back and ripped open the jumpsuit neck to waist but left her otherwise untouched. But the nearness of the blow paralyzed her; I saw her reach back, finger the tear, and collapse to her knees.

"Meanwhile, I had problems of my own: The Invid had turned its attention to me and fired off several discs, one of which blew the Cyclone out from under me and threw me a good fifteen feet from the blast. My back was to its advance now, but one look at Annie's shocked face told me everything I needed to know.

"'Heeelp!' she was screaming. *'Anyone!'*

"But there was something else in my line of sight as well: a glint across the lake, sunshine on gleaming metal. And even as my head was going down to the street in a gesture of surrender and ultimate indifference—some part of my warped mind wondering what that giant cloven foot or pincer was going to feel like—I knew Annie's call had been heard.

"A figure in red Cyclone battle armor launched itself across the lake and came down at the end of the street, hopping in for a rescue, dodging one, two, then three explosive blasts from the Invid Shock Trooper. I saw the soldier return fire from the rifle/cannon portion of the armor's right arm and heard the Invid take a direct hit and come apart.

"The soldier put down behind me as I rolled over, Annie *ooh*ing and *ahh*ing nearby, just in time to see Scott appear at the other end of the street with three Invid on his tail. He dropped one for the crowd and took off out of sight, the other two closing on him. I got up, hand shielding my eyes, and tried to follow the fight. Overhead now, Scott blasted a second Invid, then swooped in low and ass-backward to finish off the last. I saw him sight in on the Trooper, then loose the shot. It tore into one of the Invid's hemispheric cranial protrusions, loosing fire and smoke from the hole.

"Scott was thrown backward by the missile's kick and landed on his butt not ten feet in front of us—Annie, me, and the mysterious red Cycloner. The Invid came in on residuals, mimicking Scott's undignified approach with one of its own, and immediately fell face forward to the street, a sickly green fluid spewing from its wound, its outstretched pincer trapping and nearly mincing poor Annie. Scott had explained that the fluid was a kind of nutrient derived from the Flowers of Life, but I had yet to see exactly what it was that the stuff was keeping alive! Scott, his faceshield raised, turned to thank the red who had come to our aid. But it was obvious he had seen something I hadn't, because he stopped in midsentence, as though questioning what he was seeing.

"And Red bounded off without a word.

"At the same time, Annie was crying for help, and Scott went over to her, lifting the pincer enough to allow the pale and shaken kid to crawl free. What a picture she made, kneeling there in the dirt, tears cascading down her face, her torn jumpsuit hanging off her shoulders.

"'I'm so sorry,' she wailed. 'This is all my fault.'

"Scott didn't say anything; he simply walked over to the fallen Invid and regarded it—analytically, I thought, as though he had seen those things bleed before.

"I was sitting on the engine cover of my overturned Cyclone feeling twenty years older and wondering what had happened to solo riding.

"'We did what we could,' I told Scott. 'But it just wasn't enough.'

"Annie said, 'Now what are we going to do, Rand?'

"And Scott and I exchanged looks, remembering Ken and the other island . . ."

"We found Annie's knapsack, and I did what I could to sew up the tear in her jumpsuit. The causeway had been reextended to complete the span between the islands; Scott figured that Ken and the others had heard the explosions and realized they were going to have to deal with us one way or another. This was pretty much the case. Ken said, 'I'm glad you made it,' when he saw us cycle in. But Annie wasn't buying it; she leaped off the rear seat, even before I had brought the Cyclone to a halt, and whacked Ken across the face forcefully enough to spin him around. He gave us a brief over-the-shoulder look and decided he had better take it or he would have us coming down on him as well.

"He asked Annie to forgive him, and frankly, I was surprised by the sincerity he managed to dredge up. 'I only did it to save the others,' he explained. 'If we stood up to the Invid, all the people in Laako would suffer for it. The way things are, we get by all right.'

"Fire in his eyes, Scott dismounted, took off his helmet, and walked over to Ken. 'So you feed potential troublemakers to the Invid to save your own skins,' he growled.

"I'm not sure what would have happened next if a crowd of Laako's citizenry hadn't appeared.

"'You got that right, soldier!' their leader told Scott.

"They were only a dozen strong, men, women, and children, and they were unarmed; but there was an attitude of defiance about them that rattled us. The rest of the audience was glaring down at us from their cells in those shells of buildings.

"'You've got to leave here!' the man continued. 'I'm sorry, but we don't want any soldiers in this town. So get out—*now*!'

"I had to hand it to the guy: He wasn't especially large or well built, and his glasses and workman's blues gave him a kind of paternal look; but here he was standing up to an offworlder in Cyclone battle armor. I thought Scott would take the poor man apart; instead, I heard him laugh.

"'Well, was it something we said?' Scott asked.

"'There is nothing funny about the situation, young man,' the man responded angrily. 'I am in deadly earnest. Nobody here even wanted your Robotech Expeditionary Mission to begin with, and if it wasn't for you soldiers, this planet would still be living in peace! Now, get out! Save your rescues for somewhere else!'

"I winced at hearing this, knowing the man had gone

too far. Scott stepped into the guy's face, shouting back: 'Why you. . . . Don't you realize that without any kind of resistance, you've got no hope?!'

"'We know,' Ken chimed in from behind Scott. 'But we still want you to leave.'

"'Terrific,' Scott snarled. 'You're going to sit back and relax and let the Invid rule over you and the entire planet—'

"'Fighting the Invid will aggravate the whole situation!' the crowd leader interrupted. 'All we want is a peaceful life. What difference does it make who's at the top—some corrupt Council or the Invid? There's no such thing as freedom!'

"The man must have caught a whiff of his own words, because all of a sudden he was soft-spoken and rational. 'Look, anybody who hasn't seen it our way has already left. So will you please go?'

"I had heard the same speech so often that I hardly paid any attention to it, but you just didn't go throwing the reality of the situation into the face of a guy who had come halfway across the galaxy to fight your battles for you. Before I could open my mouth, Scott had grabbed the guy by the shirtfront and was ready to split his head open.

"I told Scott to leave him alone. After all, in their own way they were right: They had peaceful lives, even without the so-called freedoms that were so important thirty years ago. Besides, nothing Scott or I could say or do was going to change the way they felt.

"'Look around you,' I told Scott.

"He did, and the truth of it seemed to sink in some. He shoved the man aside and spat in the street. 'I don't believe what I'm witnessing here,' he rebuked the crowd. 'You people make me sick! You think I'm the only one fighting the Invid? Well, there are plenty of others. People who aren't ready to roll over and play dead, understand?'

"The crowd looked at him pityingly. He donned his helmet, mounted the Cyclone, and took off without a word to any of us.

"I felt that I had to back Scott up and made some kind of silly speech about selling out strangers, but it all fell on deaf ears. Except Annie's.

"'That goes for me, too,' she told the crowd. 'I wouldn't want to live in this rotten town anyway.' With that, she threw herself onto the cycle's rear seat and told me to 'let 'er rip.'

"Annie hugged herself to me for all it was worth, and I could almost feel her tears through my shirt. But when I asked if she was okay, she said she would make it all right. I was certain she had known worse moments in her life. . . .

"When we caught up with Scott, I asked about his plans.

"'Somehow or other I've got to find Reflex Point,' he yelled without bothering to look over at me.

"He had mentioned this when we first met and once or twice since but had never explained its meaning. 'You keep talking about this place as if it's the most important thing in the world.'

"'It is,' Scott threw back sternly, and accelerated out front.

"There was something about his attitude that put me off, or maybe I was just hoping for an argument that would split us up and return me to my solo riding. I said, 'You know what your problem is? You don't know how to communicate with people! Now that you've had a taste of the old homeworld, don't you think you'd be a lot happier back in space with your girlfriend?'

"His silence told me I'd gotten to him.

"'Lay off,' he snapped back, accelerating again. 'Marlene's dead.'

"It literally stopped me cold in my tracks.

"'He never told you?' Annie said as we watched Scott disappear over a rise up ahead.

"'Not one word about it,' I mumbled. It explained a lot about Scott's behavior, his obsession with waging this one-man war of his. . . .

"'I know how he feels,' Annie was saying. 'Being the woman so many men dream of, and yet so unlucky in love, has made me very sensitive to this sort of thing.'

"I didn't know whether she was trying to make me laugh or what, but her comment succeeded in lightening my spirits. Then she slammed me on the back: 'Hey, come on! We're gonna lose Scott if we don't get a move on!'

"I asked her if she was sure about leaving Ken behind, and she made a face.

"'Uh-huh. I have a feeling my next lover's going to be my last. Now, let's get moving, Rand!'

"She pounded her tiny fists against my back again, and we were gone."

CHAPTER
FIVE

> *Mom was, as they used to say at the turn of the century,
> one tough broad. She was the most respected member of the
> Blue Angels, and even after her falling out with Romy and
> her flight from Cavern City, her name was adopted by only
> those riders who shot for the narrows, and scrawled on
> many a wall.*
>
> Maria Bartley-Rand, *Flower of Life: Journey Beyond
> Protoculture*

IT WASN'T MUCH OF A TOWN—STRICTLY MAIN-STREET
frontier, run-down and dirty—and it wasn't much of a
bar, but at least the place offered cold beer (even if it was
locally brewed and bitter-tasting), shade, and a singer
backed by a decent pickup band.

> After all of the battles are over
> After all of the fighting is done
> Will you be the one
> To find yourself alone with your heart
> Looking for the answer?

Rook Bartley lifted her glass and toasted the singer.
The song was soft and downbeat, just what she needed

to ease herself into the blues, trip through memories she couldn't do anything about.

Rook took a look around the place over the rim of her mug. It was dimly lit and poorly ventilated but surprisingly clean and tidy for a joint in the wastes. There was the usual assortment of types, Foragers mostly, keeping to themselves in the corners, nursing drinks and private thoughts. A couple or two wrapped around each other on the cleared space that passed for a dance floor. And several bad boys on the upper tier, boots up on the table, midnight shades. Rook judged they were locals from the way they were scanning the room for action, your basic rough trade feeling safe on the barren piece of turf they had secured for themselves. Rook returned to her drink, unimpressed.

She was a petite and shapely eighteen-year-old with a mane of strawberry-blond hair and a face that more than one man had fallen in love with. She was wearing a red and white short-sleeved bodysuit that hugged her in all the right places. It was set off by forearm sheaths, a blue utility belt, and boots, an outfit styled to match the mecha she rode, a red Cyclone she had liberated from an armory just after her split from the Blue Angels, the assault by the Snakes. . . .

When it feels like tomorrow will never come
When it seems like the night will not end
Can you pretend
That you're really not alone?
You're out here on your own
(Lonely soldier boy)
You're out here on your own
(Lonely soldier boy)

Rook settled back in her chair to study the group's lead singer, a rocker well known in the wastes who called herself Yellow Dancer. The song had taken an unanticipated leap to four-four, guitar and keyboards wailing, and Yellow was off to one side of the low stage, clapping in time and allowing the band their moment in the spots. She was tall and rather broad-shouldered, Rook thought, but attractive in a way that appealed to men and women both. Her hair was long but shagged, tinted slightly lavender and held by a green leather band that chevroned in the center of her forehead. Yellow's stage clothes were not at all elaborate—pumps, tight-fitting slacks, and a strapless top trimmed in purple—but were well suited to her tall frame and flattering to her figure.

Yellow stepped back to the mike to acknowledge the applause. She was modest and smiling until one of the bad boys decided to change the tempo somewhat.

"Hey, baby face!" he called out, getting up from the table and approaching the stage. "Me and my friends don't like your music. It stinks, y' hear?"

Rook had expected as much. It was the one with the pointed chin and wraparound sunglasses, the apparent gang leader. He was wearing tight jeans tucked into suede shin boots and a short-sleeve shirt left unbuttoned.

"It's garbage, it ain't music," he insulted the singer.

Rook wondered how Yellow would handle it; the pickup band were locals, as was most of the room. No one was exactly rising to her defense, but neither was she showing signs of concern.

"Well, why don't you just give these people a sample of what *you* consider music?" she taunted back.

Some of the crowd found the comeback amusing, which only managed to put Yellow's critic on the spot. Rather than risk making a fool of himself, he decided to teach her a quick lesson and stepped forward swinging a lightning right.

"I'll give 'em a sample," he said at the same time.

But Yellow was even faster; still maintaining her place, she ducked to the left, leaving vacuum in her wake. The rogue's arm sailed clean through nothingness, wrapping itself around the mike stand, and threw him completely off balance. The crowd howled, and Yellow smiled. But in that instant, her assailant recollected himself, turned, and caught her across the face with an open-hand left.

Yellow's head snapped back, but not for long. She countered with a right, open-hand also but hooked a bit to bring her nails into play. The man took the blow full force to his temple and cheek; his glasses were knocked askew, and blood had been drawn.

"Now we're even," she said to the leader, whose back was still turned to her. But she now had the rest of the gang to answer to as well; they had left their tables and were approaching her threateningly. "How about calling it quits, fellahs?" she told them. "Tag-team wrestling isn't scheduled until Saturday night, and we wouldn't want to mess up the program, would we?"

Rook had to laugh; either she knew what she was doing or she was one of those who got her kicks face-down. Rook had reason to believe it was the former, however. Yellow was set like an upsprung trap, her legs slightly bent, her fists clawed. At the same time, she was keeping an eye on the one she had already wounded and was more than ready for him when he pounced.

"You little witch!" the man snarled. "I'll kill you!"

He moved in and swung a roundhouse left with little of the lightning that had characterized his first swing and none of the ambivalence of the second. But once again, Yellow was left untouched, and the momentum carried the man off the stage, practically into the arms of his henchmen.

"I've enjoyed our little dancing lesson," Yellow joked, backing away somewhat. "But if it's all the same to you, this place is paying me to *sing*." Her eyes darted right and left, plotting an escape if needed. "Of course, we can pick up where we left off after the show—you could sure use some work on your fox-trot, you know—and if you're all nice boys, I'll teach you to rumba. . . ."

The gang was closing in on her, and Rook was beginning to rethink her earlier evaluation of Yellow Dancer. Whatever happened now, she had some of it coming. Meanwhile the club owner had appeared on the stage to intercede. But Rook had to laugh again, grog making it up into her nose: Not only was the dude pushing seventy, but he began his little speech by referring to Yellow's opponents as *gentlemen!*

"If you can't control yourselves," he continued, his white mustache twitching, "I'm going to have to ask you all to leave!"

You and what army, Rook said to herself, quoting the punch line of an old T'sentrati joke.

One of the toughs, a mean-looking little guy in a muscle shirt, had whipped out a throwing knife during the old man's attempted reprimand. He gave the knife a backhand toss now, sending it whizzing past the owner's head and straight into the plywood wall behind the stage.

"Mind your manners, Gramps!" the youth cautioned.

Rook sighed tiredly, swallowed the last two drops of her drink, and stood up from the table.

"Boy, you guys sure have guts," she told the gathered gang members. They turned slowly toward her as she knew they would, looks of disbelief on their faces. "Think you can handle her all by yourselves?"

This brought immediate catcalls and challenges from the rest of the room. Rook smiled for the audience's benefit and winked at the gang leader. She had been through scenes like this too often to count, and she knew the leader's type as well as she knew herself. She was confident she could take him, and that would eliminate the need to go one on one with the others. All she had to do was go after the leader's pride, and she had already made a good start in that direction. . . .

"Blondie, take my advice and stay out of this or you'll be next," he warned her.

Rook looked away nonchalantly. "Maybe if two of you held her down while the others ran for reinforcements . . . Then you might have a chance."

The catcalls increased in volume and originality. Even the leader cracked an appreciative smile. He steadied his shades and gave Rook the once-over. "A comedian." He sneered. "Too bad for you I've got such a poor sense of humor, 'cause I'm gonna make you sorry you ever walked in here."

The nasty little knife thrower produced a second shiv, but the leader motioned him back. "She's mine," he told his boys, and launched himself into a charge.

Rook had plenty of time to prepare and position herself; plus she had already sized up the guy's strengths and weaknesses. He was coming at her full force, yelling at the top of his lungs, his hands at shoulder height slightly out front. On the balls of her feet now, Rook dropped herself into a crouch and brought her right arm in front of her face, elbow pointed outward. When the leader was within range, she twisted back, then sprang up and took her shot, catching the man square in the larynx.

Instantly, he went down on his knees, hands clutching his throat. "You almost killed me," he managed to rasp.

"Well, come at me again and let's see if I can get it right this time," Rook answered him.

The room was full of applause and cheers by now; even some of the gang members were laughing.

Rook heard Yellow Dancer say, "I think the baboon's overmatched," just before the leader growled and shouted, "Stop laughing!"

Then the knife wielder started to move in . . .

Outside the bar, two Cyclones were added to the long row of cycles and various hybrid vehicles that lined the town's main street. Scott and Rand glanced at the cycles and at the bar and traded questioning looks.

"Shall we go in?" Rand asked.

Scott shrugged and removed his helmet. "What've we got to lose?"

"That's not what I wanted to hear," Rand started to say, but Annie was already off the Cyclone and heading for the door.

"Come on, Rand. I'm dry enough to spit cotton."

Rand exhaled forcibly and dismounted wondering just how he had let things get so out of hand. *Just one more town*, he had told himself. A place where he could feel all right about leaving Annie and saying a final farewell to Scott. Then it was going to be back to solo riding and the open road. But that had been three days and several towns ago, not one of which suited his needs. Nor did he have especially good feelings about this one. Two rows of ruined high-tech prefabs split by the northern highway and squeezed between the stone walls of an arid canyon, the place had a filthy, forlorn look to it. It seemed as though the town had surrendered long before the Invid's arrival.

"They could at least clean the place up," Rand said to Scott now. "Bunch of lazy slobs. . . ."

"You country boys do things differently, I suppose," Scott said in a patronizing way.

Rand scowled. "At least we have enough self-respect

to keep our homes from becoming pigsties. You wonder why I'd rather live off the land, Scott? Well, look around."

"Oh, quit arguing, you two," Annie said, stepping through the barroom's swinging doors. "This dump isn't so bad. What do you think they do for fun around here?"

Inside, the first thing that greeted their eyes was a knife fight.

An attractive young woman in a red bodysuit was squaring off against a mean-looking youth wielding what looked like a hunting knife. Onlookers were cheering and offering words of encouragement to both parties. On the room's stage, a tall, lean female and a white-haired old man yelled for the fight to stop.

Scott stopped short. "It's her!?"

"Who?" said Annie.

"She's the one who helped us out the other day—the girl on the Cyclone!"

Rand's eyes went wide. "The *girl* on the Cyclone? Now you tell me!... Well what are we waiting for? Let's go—"

"No, hold up a minute." Scott put his arm out to restrain Rand. "I'm sure she can handle herself all right."

"But they'll kill her," said Annie.

Scott shook his head. "No, I don't think so."

Rand decided that Scott might be right. The woman moved like a dancer, dodging the youth's every thrust and overhand, her blond hair twirling about her face. One of the other men in the crowd was urging the knifer on with threats of his own.

"Stop your prancin' around! Stick her, man! Stick her!"

But the woman wasn't about to let that happen. She backed away with calculated deliberation, turning and folding at just the right moments. Rand could see that the rogue was losing patience and getting sloppy with his cover; he also noted that this was not lost on the woman in red. She set herself, legs wide, and waited for him to come in. Sure enough, the youth tried an over-the-top reverse and left himself wide open; the woman spun out from under it and completed her turn with a roundhouse kick that nailed him across the face, throwing him against one of the tables. The knifer went down as the table collapsed under him, but a second man, a large, dark-skinned tough wearing an earflapped cap, caught the woman from behind in a full nelson. She tried to struggle free but found herself overpowered. At the same time a third member of the gang sauntered in and took the knife from his fallen comrade. He tapped the tip of the blade menacingly against the woman's cheek.

"You can say good-bye to that pretty face of yours, sister," Rand heard the man say.

Scott was already stepping in, as was the female singer, who had started to grab for the knife stuck in the wall behind the stage. But Rand moved quicker than both of them: He swept up a heavy half-empty goblet from a nearby table and hurled it, knocking the knife from the gang leader's hand. As the youth screamed and dropped, holding his struck hand, Rand yelled, "Duck!" and launched a second glass.

Rook saw this one headed her way and stretched herself thin in the larger man's hold, arms fully extended as she slithered down. The glass hit the man in the face, and his hold on her collapsed; he was holding his nose and moaning when Rook brought her boot down onto his instep and turned away out of reach.

"I'm gonna kill you for that!" the man yelled. But when he took his hands away from his face, he found himself staring at Scott's drawn blaster.

"Get moving—all of you!" Scott told them.

Weapons were a common enough sight in the waste, but a blaster was seldom seen. Taken by surprise, the gang members began to back toward the swinging doors. "You win this one, soldier," the leader threw over his shoulder. "But the war's not over yet."

In a moment the sounds of revving and departing cycles filled the bar.

Rook looked disdainfully at her rescuers; she recognized them as the three she had saved from an Invid setup in Laako three days before. The redheaded one named Rand was eyeing her appreciatively.

"Why'd you have to butt in?" Rook said harshly, and left the bar.

"Guess there's no pleasing some people," Rand threw after her.

"Swelled head!" said Annie, making a face and gesturing.

"Well, I'm grateful for your help," said a lilting voice.

Rand turned and nearly fell over: It was *Yellow Dancer*! He hadn't recognized her before and could hardly believe his eyes now. "It can't be," he stammered, unable to control his excitement. "I've seen you at least twenty times, but I never thought I'd get the chance...." He turned and made a desperate lunge for a napkin and shoved it toward Yellow. "I know it's silly, but...it's for my kid sister, you know?"

Yellow smiled knowingly. The bar owner took a pen from his jacket pocket and passed it to her. "To your kid sister," said Yellow, chuckling. "As always..."

Annie saw Scott's look of bewilderment and said, "It's Yellow Dancer. Haven't you ever heard of her?"

Scott smiled thinly and shook his head.

"Boy, you're really out of it, Scott."

Scott ignored the comment and turned to the owner. "That gang, who are they?"

The man shrugged. "The usual riffraff. Their kind seem to be just about everywhere nowadays."

"Yes, but what about the local authorities—have you thought of asking them to do something?"

Rand raised his eyes to the ceiling in a dramatic gesture and turned away embarrassed.

The manager stared at Scott a moment, then said, "Mister, those *are* the local authorities."

CHAPTER
SIX

Tirolian society—that is, the generation of Terrans that grew to manhood and womanhood under T.R. Edwards, Dr. Emil Lang, and to some extent (by proxy, as it were), Admiral Rick and Commander Lisa Hunter—took a decidedly different course than its counterpart on Earth (under Chairman Moran, Supreme Commander Leonard, et al.). Thanks to Edwards's chauvinism, bigotry, and undisguised misogyny, one would certainly have been hard pressed to encounter the likes of a Dana Sterling or a Marie Crystal among the Tirolian contingent... Scott Bernard had been raised in such a milieu, and there were things, as well as attitudes, on Earth that he had never dreamed possible.

Xandu Reem, *A Stranger at Home: A Biography of Scott Bernard*

RINGO AND HIS BOYS ROARED AWAY FROM THE BAR and regrouped at the edge of town. Their cycles, one outfitted with a sidecar, were well equipped with weapons, and it would have been simple to blast and torch the bar; but that wasn't really an option: Pops' had the coldest beer within three hundred miles. So they decided to turn their frustrations against any newcomers who might wander into town; a bit of the old ultraviolence, as it had once been called. Instead, however, they soon found an even more suitable target in the form of the ex-soldier named Lunk, who had been in town on and off for the past two months. More than once Ringo had attempted to goad the man into a fight with less than satisfying results. The attempts had increased in frequency once Ringo found out something about Lunk's recent military past, but still he was unable to push the man into a hand-to-hand confrontation.

But now, after his humiliating run-in with the strangers in the bar, Ringo was in no mood for subtlety or verbal provocation. No sooner had Lunk's battered six-wheel personnel carrier lumbered by the gang's edge-of-town position than Ringo ordered his men into pursuit. There was nothing like a little manhunting to pick you up when you were feeling down.

Lunk was twenty-five, a huge, barrel-chested man with almost brutish facial features: a wide, prominent chin, heavy-lidded, soulful eyes, and a broad, flat nose. He had let his hair grow long these past few months and kept it out of his face with a yellow elastic headband. His size alone would have given most men pause, but there was something soft and secretive about him that often allowed smaller aggressive types to feel they could have a free hand with him.

One look at Ringo's impromptu roadside gathering and Lunk knew that he was in for it; he told his companion, Kevin, to hang on and began to push the ancient APC along the town's main street for all it was worth.

He could see four cycles in the carrier's circular outboard rearview mirrors now; Ringo's men were opening up with handlebar and faring-mounted weapons, toying with him as he swerved the heavy vehicle left and right.

"How many of them are there?!" Kevin asked in a panic from the shotgun seat.

"Too many!" Lunk yelled back as machine-gun rounds fractured the mirrors.

Two rockets exploded in the street in front of the APC, and Lunk braked hard, losing control. The vehicle slid off the roadway and crashed into an enormous pile of debris that had been 'dozed away from a fallen storefront. The impact left Lunk and Kevin momentarily stunned, but they quickly shook themselves out of it and scampered out of the carrier's open top, taking careless and crazed giant strides down the back side of the heap.

Ringo and his boys threw their bikes into the pile with equal abandon, launching themselves over the top only to career down the rear face, laughing maniacally all the while. Lunk and Kevin had taken an alleyway that led to the main street, so Ringo ordered his gang to split up, sending the sidecar cyclist one way and instructing the others to form up on his lead.

Lunk wasn't aware of the trap until he saw the sidecar skid around a corner and head his way. Turning, he heard Ringo and the rest of the bikes behind him. He shoved Kevin toward the debris-strewn sidewalk, hoping they would be able to make it into one of the abandoned buildings, but at the same moment the sidecar driver gunned it and came down on them. One of Ringo's gang —a dark-skinned dude every inch as big as Lunk— leaned out from the sidecar seat and made a grab for Kevin. Lunk flattened himself against the street, but Kevin sidestepped too late. Ringo's man managed to get a handful of shirt and shoulder, and by the time Lunk looked up, Kevin was being dragged down the street by the cycle.

Lunk heard him scream for help but could do nothing; Ringo's men were accelerating toward him now, shouting and yahooing. Lunk spun around and ran toward Pops' bar. Halfway there, the sound of the cycles ringing in his ears, Lunk noticed that a group of men and women were gathered out front. And one of them was raising a weapon of some kind. . . .

He dropped himself into a tuck-and-roll seconds before the weapon fired. The round impacted against an unbraced section of heaped-up vehicles and mecha parts and loosed some of it into a slide. Lunk heard shouts and the squeal of brakes behind him. One of the bikes went down, sliding uncontrolled along the street with a rasping, scraping sound. Lunk reached Pops' just as Ringo's cycle pulled up, but the gang leader found himself confronting the man with the weapon.

"You again," Lunk heard Ringo seethe. "You're really pressing your luck, robby."

Hearing Ringo use the derisive slang term for a Robotech soldier, Lunk turned to study his rescuer. The man was straddling a Cyclone and wearing a uniform with patches Lunk couldn't identify. Nor was the weapon familiar.

"Put your hands where I can see them," the soldier told Ringo. "Now turn your cycles around and get out of here. The party's over."

Ringo adjusted his dark glasses and flashed one of his infamous grins. "Have it your way. . . ." He looked over at Lunk. "If you wanna see your friend alive, come on out to the ranch—if you have the guts, that is!"

The three cycles roared off, and the soldier asked about Lunk's friend. Lunk quickly scanned the crowd: mostly locals he had seen before, but there were three or four he didn't recognize. Two attractive women and some carrot-topped kid. Another Cyclone rider. They were staring at him expectantly.

"Stay out of it," Lunk said, starting to walk off.

Spider stepped out of the crowd; they had ridden together previously, Spider, Lunk, and Kevin. . . .

"Hey, Lunk, you're not going to just walk away?" Spider said to him questioningly. "We've gotta go get 'im, man. We can't leave him with Ringo!"

Lunk stopped, hung his head, then resumed his heavy steps.

"With a friend like you, a guy doesn't need enemies," the soldier called out to the delight of the crowd.

Lunk spun around, ashamed but angry; Spider and the others were still waiting.

"All right," the soldier was saying, strapping on some

sort of pectoral armor. "Where's this ranch? How far is it from here?"

"About five miles—" Pops started to say, but the soldier's younger companion interrupted.

"Hang on a minute, Scott," the redhead said. "You can't keep fighting everybody's battles for them. You think you're going to whip the whole planet back into shape single-handed, and I think you're nuts!"

"I wouldn't advise tangling with Ringo, stranger," Pops added. "Just take our thanks and ride on out of here."

But Scott didn't answer either of them. He put his helmet on, started the Cyclone, and wheelied off. A woman in similar armor riding a red mecha followed him. Lunk heard the soldier's companion mutter a curse and yell for Scott to slow down; then he angrily straddled his own Cyclone and joined the others.

"Lunk . . ." Spider said leadingly.

Lunk spun around, a determined look on his face now. "All right, let's go."

"Really?"

"I won't let those bums make a chump outta me, Spider. Kevin's our friend, and we can't leave him out there." Lunk turned to the crowd. "I need some wheels. I've got scrip enough to rent 'em."

"Take mine," said Pops, fishing keys out of his shirt pocket. "And don't worry about paying me, either."

Lunk caught the tossed chain, threw a thanks over his shoulder, and ran over to Pops' olive-drab tri-wheel. Spider straddled the rear seat. Lunk noticed that the tall woman singer he had seen once or twice in the bar was also headed toward her vehicle. Meanwhile, the little kid with the E.T. cap was beside him, introducing herself as Annie.

"Are you married by any chance?" she asked Lunk.

Lunk's face twisted up in shock. "What, are you kiddin'?"

Annie threw open her arms and said, "You lucky boy!" as Lunk rode off, a look of bewilderment on his face. "The man of my dreams," she added a moment later, climbing into Yellow Dancer's pink roll-barred jeep.

Scott's improvised posse of seven followed the road out of town to a turnoff that wound up into the hills. They stopped once so that Scott and Rook could suit Rand up in Cyclone armor and run him quickly through the basics of mechamorphosis.

The ranch sat at the crest of a gentle rise near a wide stream that made it one of the choicest spots in the district. It was enclosed by a rustic post-and-rail fence, and there were patches of grass and a few beautiful old trees that had weathered more storms, natural and otherwise, than anyone cared to guess. Scott and company rode in without ceremony and found Ringo's gang waiting for them in the shade of an immense oak. There were five of them: the knife-wielding punk, the hulk, and two others who had been with Ringo in the bar earlier that day. They were all astride their bikes—the hulk in his usual sidecar seat—grouped close together in a shallow arc, cycle weapons pointed outward. Kevin was behind them, lashed by thick rope to the tree trunk.

Scott ordered his group to a halt two hundred yards from the tree. Ringo's group wouldn't have stood a chance against the firepower of one Cyclone, let alone three, but it was obvious from the start that Ringo wanted to go one on one with Lunk. Kevin's precarious position guaranteed against any Cyclone fireworks, so in a certain sense (as was always the case when hostages were involved) Scott's position was the more vulnerable one.

Lunk was aware of what was going down and asked Spider to climb off the triple-wheeler. It was likely, given Ringo's flair for dramatics, that he would begin the festivities with a bike joust, and Lunk figured he could handle the thing better if he was alone.

"Okay, but be careful," Spider said, stepping away.

Lunk snorted. "I'm sick to death of being careful."

Rand and Rook were side by side a few yards away, with Scott slightly off to one side behind them. "I can't figure out why you came," Rand was saying to the red Cyclone rider through the helmet. "You've got no stake in this."

"I've got just as much reason to be here as you," Rook said harshly without looking over at him.

"Everybody stay loose," Scott warned. "Keep your fingers away from the triggers. I don't want anyone getting hurt unless it can't be helped."

"No great loss, if you ask me," Rook muttered.

Rand glanced over at her. "Reminds me of a movie I saw once. *Gunfight at the* . . .I can't remember the title. But what happens is that—"

"People die in real life, pal. Keep that in mind."

Before Rand could say anything, Ringo called out: "Hey, Lunky-boy—I can hear your knees knockin' together! Is it gonna be just you and me, or do you need the army behind you?" Ringo's gang hooted and howled. "I mean, you didn't have much use for the army a while ago, did ya? In fact, you got a history of runnin' away from fights, the way I hear it. Ain't that right?"

Lunk gritted his teeth. Sweat was beading up across his face, and indeed, his knees were knocking against the valve covers of the cycle's engine. "You don't know nothin' about it, ya little shit!" he managed to bite out.

Ringo laughed and slapped his knee. "Sorry if I blew your cover. I keep forgettin' you're too modest to brag about your military record!"

"What're you trying to prove?" Lunk yelled, muscles and veins standing out like cords in his beefy neck.

"Nothin'," Ringo returned. "Nothin' at all. 'Cept the Invid *hate* soldiers, and since we don't have much use for them ourselves, we decided to help them along this time."

Lunk began to rev his cycle, but Scott gestured to him to hold his ground. "Hand over your hostage!" Scott demanded of Ringo.

The gang leader turned to his men and laughed. "We might just make you part of today's quota, robby!"

"Yeah, we ain't picky!" the knifer threw in.

"And we're not afraid of your firepower, neither," the hulk yelled from the sidecar, raising a bazooka-type weapon into view.

"They're psyching themselves up," Rook cautioned the others. "Be ready!"

On Ringo's word the four cycles leapt forward in a charge, but all at once a round detonated in their midst, throwing some of them off their machines. Scott, Rand, and Rook exchanged looks, wondering who had fired. Then they heard Spider and Annie's simultaneous screams and looked up: Three Invid Shock Troopers had appeared over the canopy of the oak tree. Ringo and his boys were bolting for the shelter of the ranch house as continued flashes from the Troopers' shoulder cannons shook the ground and blew their cycles apart. Kevin was trying desperately to free himself from the tree trunk, and Annie was shouting, "Do something!"

Scott took the initiative and shot his Cyclone forward, engaging the thrusters and going to Battle Armor mode as the mecha left the ground. Two of the Invid went after him, while the third dropped in low toward Lunk and the others. Rand was working the system switches frantically, eager for the mecha to reconfigure.

"Come on! Come on!... What the heck's wrong with this thing!?" he said to Rook.

"Just calm down," she told him. "Remember what Scott told you—your thoughts have to help it along. Relax and stop bashing away at it." Rook lowered her head and threw the thumb switch. Rand watched amazed as the cycle restructured, wrapping itself around her and integrating with her armor. "Treat it gently—like it's alive," Rook added, standing now.

Scott meanwhile was off in another part of the grassy fields dancing between the annihilation discs sent his way by the Troopers who had put down on either side of him. Lunk saw him lift off after half a dozen agile leaps and bounces and return fire from the suit's forearm rocket launchers.

"I can't escape it!" Lunk yelled to no one in particular. "I thought I'd never be fighting again!"

Rook was engaging the third Invid, while Rand continued to struggle with reconfiguration. He was about to give up on it, when he felt the mecha's reciprocal vibe, and suddenly the damned thing was actually conforming itself to his armor. He stood up, showing a look of disbelief under the helmet's faceplate, and gently engaged the system's hoverthrusters, searching the skies for signs of Rook or Scott. At last he saw the red Cyclone rider. She was powering up through a backflip one minute and dropping like a stiff-legged bomb the next. But her Invid target leapt away in time, hooking itself overhead and dishing out a blast that nearly caught her. She avoided the explosion by launching straight up, but the Trooper was sticking close, discharging two more bolts, one of which nicked her armor and sent her into a spinning descent toward a stand of trees.

Scott was handling himself well against the other two Troopers but had yet to land a Scorpion on either of them. He was down on the ground now, getting off another shot before the Invid surrounded him, pincers swinging, discs cratering the soft earth. Rand joined him, and together they managed to chase the Troopers off momentarily.

Scott was congratulating Rand on his mechamorphosis when Lunk pulled up alongside on the triple-wheeler.

"You weren't ever a member of the space battalion, were you?" Lunk asked Scott.

"Yeah?..." said Scott. "So what?"

"Then you can fly a Veritech."

"Of course I can," Scott said excitedly. "Do you have one?"

Lunk nodded. "Follow me."

Rand watched them zoom off, Scott running alongside Lunk's cycle. He dodged an Invid that attempted to flatten him into the ground and brought his forearm up to fire. But the Trooper was already flying off to link up with the other two, all three headed in the same general direction as Lunk and Scott.

If I hang around with this guy long enough, I'm gonna get myself killed for sure, Rand said to himself.

Then Rook was suddenly beside him, upright in Battle Armor mode and hovering two feet off the ground. "What's the matter," she asked him, "your joints rusting up on you or something?"

"No, I was just trying to—"

"You really aren't much use in combat, are you?"

"Hey, wait a minute!" Rand shouted as she began to hover off in the same configuration. "It's not like I'm *supposed* to be here, you know. I mean, technically I'm a noncombatant, did you know that? Did I ever tell you about the time I fought off three Invid patrols at the same time...?"

From the cover of the ranch house, Ringo watched Spider set Kevin free from the ropes that held him to the tree. Knifer was kneeling by the window, peering over the stool; the hulk was cowering in a corner under a shelf.

"Stop your whinin', you lily-livered rogue!" Ringo shouted from the window.

Knifer looked up. "Hey, Ringo, I think I can hear *your* knees knockin'."

Ringo made an exasperated face and brought his fist down on Knifer's skull. "It's because I'm *mad*, bonehead. Mad, mad, mad!" He punctuated each word with a follow-up blow.

Elsewhere, Annie was asking Yellow Dancer why she was hanging around. They were in the singer's pink armored vehicle, parked some distance from the scene of the initial fighting. "What do you want from them?" Annie wanted to know. "I'm warning you, I can get very jealous."

Yellow turned to her from the driver's seat with an enigmatic smile. "Believe me," she assured Annie, "there's absolutely nothing for you to be jealous of."

"Well, then, it's okay," Annie said, perking up. "You can hang around as much as you want."

The Veritech hangar was a dilapidated circular building, holed in numerous places, with a hemispherical red roof sectioned off and reinforced by curved trusses. A mostly ruined solar windmill rose alongside the structure, which Scott guessed was a barn of some sort. Up ahead, he saw Lunk give a wave, jump the triple-wheeler from the top of a small grassy embankment, and accelerate through the fallow fields that led to the makeshift hangar. The Invid Shock Troopers were in hot pursuit overhead, their gleaming crablike bodies filling the sky.

"Hurry!" Scott could hear Lunk shout.

Scott had been expecting to find the rusting shell of a first-generation Veritech, but once inside the building his hopes took a leap forward. Carefully positioned in the spacious loft was what looked to be a well-maintained Alpha Fighter, sans augmentation pack and boosters, and certainly a leftover from the latter stages of the Second Robotech War.

"Climb in," said Lunk. "She's ready to fly."

"Who's been maintaining it?" Scott asked as he struggled out of the reconfigured Cyclone.

"Listen, I'm not as stupid as you might think," Lunk said, raising his voice above explosive volleys from the Invid. Discs were striking the fields nearby, loosening dirt and debris from the exposed rafters. "I was a certified bio-maintenance engineer. Trust me, this baby will fly like a dream."

Scott climbed into the barn loft and gave the Veritech's radome an affectionate pat. He threw himself up to the open canopy, got a good handhold, and slipped into the cockpit. He hadn't bothered to change out of the Cyclone armor, but now he exchanged his helmet for the Veritech's own "thinking cap" and began a run-through of the systems. It was so long since he had piloted a VT in atmosphere, he wondered if he could bring it off now.

"Everything seems in order!" he called down to Lunk as an explosion tore out a huge section of wall.

Lunk's hands went to his ears, and he threw himself to cover. Through the breach in the wall, Scott glimpsed the three Troopers land and begin their approach on the barn. *I'll never be able to power up fast enough to get out of here!* he thought.

But just then Rand and Rook arrived to check the aliens' advance. The red Cycloner launched herself like a projectile straight into one of the Trooper's optic sensors, while Rand fired two Scorpions against a second. It was all the time Scott needed to bring up the Protoculture levels of the Veritech, and a moment later, much to

Rand's consternation, the radome of the VT was punching through the barn's roof.

Scott threw the VT into a steep climb, luring the Troopers away from their swipe attacks against Rook and Rand. Rand watched the fighter accelerate through a sweeping arc and head back into the faces of its pursuers, destroying one with a missile too swift for his eyes to track. But that was only the beginning: Now the fighter was reconfiguring to Battloid mode and leading the two remaining Invid on a high-speed chase over the countryside.

Scott thought the ship upright—a techno-knight standing in thin air—while salvos of annihilation discs beamed past him. He reached out, throwing levers that opened the missile compartments built into the Battloid's forearm, shoulder, and lower-leg armor, and thought the systems through to launch. It was all coming back to him now—*it had to!* For a moment, the techno-knight was encompassed in energy balloons; then dozens of missiles tore from their launch racks like so many red-tipped arrows of death. The Troopers took the full storm and were all but disintegrated by the force of the blasts.

Down below, Kevin and Spider were running toward the barn, a few steps ahead of Annie, who had just leapt from Yellow's jeep and was calling out for Lunk. Rook and Rand had already reconfigured their Cyclones and were doffing the hot and cumbersome battle armor when Scott brought the VT down, cut the engines, and threw open the canopy.

Lunk stepped from the barn unharmed and caught Annie midair as she jumped up and threw her arms around his neck. "There you are!" she gushed. "I knew they wouldn't get you, I knew you'd come back to me!"

Lunk held her away, offering a miffed but understanding grin.

"I've decided you're the only one for me!"

"Well, thanks," said Lunk. "I wish I could say the same." He smiled tolerantly and gently lowered Annie to the ground. "You're a little young for me ... And besides, I've got other plans."

Annie stared up at him, despondent, and asked what those other plans might be.

Lunk threw his massive shoulders back. "Join the resistance," he said to all of them. "See if I can make up for past mistakes."

"I'd be glad to join forces with you, Lunk," said Scott. "If you mean what you say ..."

Kevin looked from one to the other. "He's not serious, robby. Are you, Lunk?"

Lunk nodded. "I'm sick of sneakin' around like a frightened little weasel. Face it, Kevin, I'm a *soldier*, after all. And it's time I started acting like one."

"Use your head, Lunk," Kevin countered. "This war's a lost cause. What can two, ten, or even two hundred do against the Invid?"

"We can try," said Lunk.

Annie made a disappointed sound and turned her back to Lunk, hands behind her head. "And I thought you were special ..."

Lunk bent down, perplexed, to ask: "But a minute ago I was the man of your dreams, remember?"

Annie's lips tightened, and she shook her head. "A long time ago I decided I'd never marry a soldier. They don't last long enough nowadays."

Kevin and Spider laughed.

"The kid's no dummy, that's for sure," Rand offered.

Yellow stepped down from the jeep and approached the VT. "I'd like to sign up for the team, Scott."

Rook sent a knowing elbow into Rand's ribs at the

same time Kevin sent one into Spider's. But Scott's answer disappointed all of them.

"Thanks," he said from the cockpit. "But we don't have enough troops yet to hire an entertainer."

"There's a lot more to me than meets the eye," said Yellow.

"As if that isn't enough," Rand commented under his breath but loudly enough for Rook to hear.

"All I see is an attractive woman in a rather slinky outfit," said Scott.

"Wrong on both counts," Yellow answered him, walking back to the jeep. "I've got something to show you."

A buzz of general puzzlement swept through the would-be team as Yellow sauntered off, especially when she turned her back to them and began to undo the rear buttons of her strapless top.

"Hey, w-wait a minute," Scott stammered in protest. "I appreciate your wanting to, er—*show* me, but don't think for a moment that's going to change my mind. . . ."

"Is she going to do what I think she's going to do?" said Annie, gulping.

"Sure looks that way," Rook said in an interested way.

Yellow meanwhile had removed her top and tossed it into the open jeep. She still had her back to them, long lavender hair falling all the way to the narrow band of her brassiere.

"H-hey, now hold on!" Rand said with a desperate tone.

Lunk laughed. "Well, she's right about one thing— she's not wearin' no slinky outfit anymore."

Yellow turned to throw them a wink over her shoulder, then reached back the way only a woman can and unfastened the bra, letting it slip from her breasts. She still had her back to them when she undid her trousers and let them fall. The pink jeep concealed whatever treasures these moments might have held for the red-faced team.

"*Now* what's she doing?" Lunk said as Dancer picked up a towel and began to scrub her face with it.

"I don't know," Scott responded sternly. "But I want an end to it right now, hear me, Yellow? You can stop this little game, because we're not taking you with us, and that's final!"

Then Yellow swung around to face them.

And something was wrong, very wrong, indeed.

"Oh, no!" Rook screamed, and began to laugh hysterically.

"Y-yellow Dancer?" Rand said tentatively.

Lunk, Kevin, and Spider drew in stunned but disappointed intakes of breath. Annie was simply confused; Scott, wordless. It was plain enough to see that Yellow Dancer was a man—a tall, rather hairless, lean and attractive man.

"You can start by calling me Lancer," he told his stunned audience, his voice deeper now. "I think the name suits me a little better. So, I hope there are no further objections to my tagging along with you."

"Well, I don't know..." Scott started to say. Woman or cross-dresser, what was the difference? he asked himself. But looking down at Rook now, he began to have second thoughts about all of this. Earth was a fascinating but bizarre place where women seemed to want to mix it up as much as the men. So maybe there was a place for her, er, *him*.

Rand meanwhile was beside himself. There were all those dreams of Yellow Dancer he had lived with for months—all those *fantasies*! "It can't *be*!" he was saying. "How could you do this to me—your biggest fan?!"

"I wasn't exactly thinking about you, Rand," Lancer said.

"Yeah," Rook chimed in. "Not like *he* was thinking about *you*!"

Everyone laughed, except Lancer. "So how about it, Captain? Do I make the team or not?"

Scott and Lunk exchanged looks and shrugs. "Yes," Scott said at last. "I guess you do."

SEVEN

Mom, who thrived on adversity, had met her perfect foil in Rand. Fortunately for me, they eventually worked it through.

Maria Bartley-Rand, *Flower of Life: Journey Beyond Protoculture*

A TEAM HAD BEEN FORMED: SCOTT, RAND, ROOK, Annie, Lunk, and Lancer (although Scott wondered if the singer shouldn't be counted twice). None of them promised to accompany Scott all the way to Reflex Point—if such a place actually existed; it was simply a loose agreement among six people headed in the same general direction, each with a separate purpose in mind. Scott wanted to see the Invid defeated; at the very least he hoped to link up with other downed fighters from the Mars Division and establish an organized resistance. Lunk was searching for a redemption of sorts; Annie, for a family. But the aims of the others were less clear-cut; their pasts remained unrevealed, their motives somewhat suspect. Nevertheless, Scott had himself a team.

All he needed now was an adequate plan.

The present one wasn't working well at all. Rather than risk calling attention to their latest acquisition—the Alpha Fighter Lunk had so reverently maintained after his rather hasty departure from the Army of the Southern Cross—Scott and Lancer had flown the mecha north under the cover of night and secluded it along the river that marked the border of the neighboring territory. Lancer was to remain with the Veritech while Scott rode back to town on his Cyclone to collect the others. In the meantime, Lunk and Annie would be in charge of gathering up what they could in the way of supplies and foodstuffs. Rand and Rook would secure a safe route out for the loaded APC.

Things went smoothly enough at first; Lunk had seen to his assignment, and Scott rendezvoused with the APC/Cyclone convoy on schedule. They had begun their trek north and entered the highlands when the Invid appeared. It hadn't paid to leave enemies the likes of Ringo behind. . . .

Scott held the lead up the rugged mountain road; Rand and Annie were a few lengths behind, then came Lunk in the APC and Rook on her red Cyclone. There were at least five Troopers in pursuit, with annihilation discs striking the cliff faces above and below the roadway.

Scott waved for the others to pour it on and accelerated along the arid slope.

Rook pulled alongside him and shouted above the deafening explosions. "They're gaining on us!" To maintain their low profile, they had opted against suiting up in helmets or battle armor.

"We haven't got a prayer unless we can reach the Alpha." Scott turned to Rand, who had come up on the inside, and told him to take the lead. He and Rook would stay behind to armor up and reconfigure for combat.

Rand signaled his assent, cautioned Annie to hold

tight, and moved out front. But no sooner had they reached the crest than two Invid rose into view. Rand engaged the brakes, pivoting the mecha through a clean 180, and headed back down the hill.

Scott hadn't even dismounted yet. "Why are you turning around?" he shouted.

"They've got us surrounded," Rand reported. "We'd better go cross-country." He indicated the steep grade above the roadway and lowered his goggles.

"No. No detours," Scott argued. "The Alpha's only a few miles down the road—we've got to break through!"

Rand snorted and shook his head. "*You* break through, Captain. I'm heading for the hills." He stomped the Cyclone into gear and took off, scrambling up the rutted incline, heedless of Scott's shouts to stop. But not a moment later, Invid Troopers were ascending into view at both ends of the road, and Scott saw the logic of Rand's choice. He gestured to Rook and Lunk and screeched off up the hill.

There was a barren stretch of plateau at the top of the slope, separated from twin fingers of pine forest by steep crevices too wide to jump. The Invid Troopers realized their advantage and began to loose disc storms of energy from their cannons. As always, there seemed to be an effort made to incapacitate rather than kill the humans, but it could just as easily have been poor marksmanship on their part. In any case, the plateau—great swirls of weathered rock and shale—was being torn up and superheated by the Troopers' fusillades. Lunk's APC, slower and far less maneuverable than the Cyclones, provided the best target, and the Invid were soon concentrating their bursts against it. Inside the cab, the big man was bouncing around like a featherweight, barely in control of the thing anymore. When a blinding disc streaked by inches from the carrier, he lost it completely; the APC crashed into a boulder and overturned, hurling

Lunk twenty feet to a hard landing facedown on the shale. At the last instant, however, he had grabbed two sacks of supplies and had managed to hold on to them during his brief airborne journey. The sacks cushioned his fall somewhat, but he blacked out momentarily nevertheless. Coming to, he heard Rook's voice behind him, warning him to keep his head down. He did as instructed and *felt* rather than saw the red Cyclone streak over him.

Scott and Rand had witnessed the collision and stopped their Cyclones to return fire against the Troopers, bringing rear weapons into play. Behind them, Lunk was attempting to gather together and rebag items spilled from the sacks.

"Lunk! Forget that stuff and come on!" Scott shouted.

"But we need these Protoculture energy cells for the mecha!" Lunk countered, ducking as a series of annihilation discs Frisbeed overhead. The Invid were close at hand now, upright and laying out salvo after salvo of white-hot fire. Explosions began to erupt all around him, orange blossoms in the shale, and he was forced to abandon the supplies. He made a beeline for Scott's idling Cyclone, straddling the rear seat not a moment too soon.

"My toothbrush!" Lunk moaned, looking back at the wrecked APC as Scott gunned the mecha into a wheelie.

"So your teeth will fall out," Scott said into the wind. "It's better than having your head blown off."

They were headed downhill a moment later, across a smooth flow of solid rock with an inviting forest of tall firs and eucalyptis at its base. As they neared the trees, Scott spied an unpaved road and made for it, signaling the others to follow his lead.

Two of the Invid attempted to track them but eventually gave up; it was widely believed (but certainly unproven) that the Invid had a kind of fearsome respect for forests in general. The Troopers circled overhead for a long while, then began to fan out trying to cover all possible points of egress. Meanwhile, Scott directed his band north in an effort to strike the river. By his reckoning, they were now somewhat west of Lancer and the Veritech, but reaching the river would put them in good position for a direct eastward swing.

The forest thinned as they worked their way north, giving way to a series of tall grass terraces that dropped in measured steps to the river gorge itself. The grass was deep enough to offer places of concealment for themselves as well as the Cyclones, so they continued their cautious advance. There was no sign of the enemy.

"Do you think we lost 'em?" Lunk asked, poking his head above the grass. He could see tall buttes and stone tors in the distance.

Rand answered him from nearby. "We must have—there's no way those things can follow a trail through the woods. Believe me, I know."

"How 'bout some food, then?"

Rook showed herself. "You really take the cake, Lunk."

"I wish I could—"

"First you nearly get us all killed, and now all you can think about is that selfish stomach of yours!"

"Drop it!" Scott said more harshly than was necessary. He switched on his Cyclone briefly to read the system indicator displays. "You were right about those Protoculture cells, Lunk," he admitted. "It's imperative that I get back to the Alpha. Someone's going to have to draw the Invid off in case I'm spotted. We can't let them find the ship."

Rand suddenly shushed him. "They're coming," he whispered.

The team dropped themselves into the grass, raising weapons as they did so. Minutes later, three Troopers could be seen patrolling the gorge, their scanners alert for movement on the cliffs above the river.

"Everybody hold your fire," said Scott.

"How did they find us?" Rand said to no one in particular.

Annie put her hands to her breast. "I betcha they heard the sound of my heart pounding."

Rand stared down at the Mars-galant Scott had given him earlier; it was a long-barreled version of the sidearm blaster the offworlder wore, shaped a bit like an elongated closed-topped Y. *Time to go on-line with this thing,* he said to himself. But no sooner did he flip the switch than the Troopers stopped their bipedal patrol and turned on them.

"Open fire!" Scott yelled as globes of fulgent energy formed at the muzzles of the Troopers' cannons.

Lunk, Rook, and Rand stood up, bringing their H–90's to bear against the invaders. Phased-laser fire seared into the Troopers' armored bodies, while annihilation discs ripped into the cliff's grassy terrace, touching off violent fires and clouds of dense smoke. Two more Invid appeared above the cliffs behind the team, adding their own volleys to the arena.

"We've gotta get back to the trees!" Rand shouted above the angry buzz of disc fire and concussive detonations.

"Lead them away from the Alpha!" said Scott.

"*You* worry about the Alpha. I'm gone!"

Abandoning their Cyclones, the team broke ranks and began to belly-crawl their way through the grass back toward the tree line. They scaled slope after slope, beating a circuitous retreat across each terrace. The closest call came when Rook miscalculated and nearly slipped into a narrow ravine; but Rand was there for her, hauling her up and supporting her while they ran. In the forest once more, they took to the trees and hid themselves high up in the branches. Invid Troopers were walking sweeping patrols along the perimeter; two were actually braving the cool and dark mystery to probe deep into the woods. Rand flicked his gallant on-line again as one of the latter group was passing beneath him. Curiously, the Invid stopped short, its would-be head rotating upward.

Rand took a sudden, sharp intake of breath—not out of fear but from realization. *Of course!* he told himself. *At the river they stopped when I activated the power cell on my blaster. And just now . . .*

It made sense, but it was time to try an experiment to validate his findings: He disarmed the power cell, and sure enough, the Invid lost interest and stomped off. "Yeah, that's gotta be it," Rand said softly. He was exhaling pent-up fear when something orange and menacing suddenly dropped on him from the branch above. His throat refused to utter the scream his guts demanded, but he gave a start nonetheless, raising the weapon like a club, only to realize that it was Annie, upside down and dangling from her knees, carrot-colored hair like an unfurled flag.

"Were you talking to yourself?" she demanded. "Were you? Huh?"

"Don't *ever* sneak up on me!" Rand seethed.

Scott, Rook, and Lunk were on the ground now, telling Rand that the coast was clear. Excitedly, Rand scrambled down out of the tree.

"I think I know why we've been having so much trouble getting these blasted walking lobsters off our trail," he announced. He gestured to the weapon's on-line switch. "We've been giving ourselves away every time we switch on our Cyclones or our blasters."

"How so?" said Lunk.

"They can detect the bio-energy given off by our Robotech mecha."

Lunk helped Annie down from the tree. "You could

be right," he said to Rand. "Back at the river Scott left the panel gauges of his Cyclone on. They could've homed in on that."

"Right!" Rand agreed.

"It makes sense," said Scott. It had never been an issue on Tirol, but then, there were a lot of things about Earth that separated it from Tirol. . . .

"Of course it makes sense," Rand was continuing. "They thrive on Protoculture, right? Well, it's like they can *smell* the stuff, the same way a shark is able to smell blood in the water."

"Charming thought," Rook said distastefully.

Annie laughed. "Mr. Wizard! You really thought that out by yourself, huh?"

Rand smiled with elaborate modesty.

"Sure doesn't happen very often, does it?" Rook scoffed.

Rand whirled on her. "Yeah? Besides your looks, what have you contributed lately?"

Rook's nostrils flared. "All right, that does it! Let's step aside and settle this once and for all!"

"You sure you don't just want to get me alone in the bushes?" Rand said, smiling and stroking his chin. "Admit it—"

"Stop it!" Scott broke in, silencing the two of them. "Arguing among ourselves isn't going to help matters any. We're supposed to be friends, in case you've forgotten."

"Oh, is that so?" Rook said, arms akimbo. "Well, I don't remember him ever becoming a friend of mine," she threw to Rand.

"Then what the hell are you doing here?" Rand barked. "I didn't ask you along! We don't need this kind of nonsense."

Rook and Rand faced off defensively.

"Cool off," Lunk told everyone. "There'll be plenty

of time to scream at each other later. But right now we gotta get back to the Alpha."

"Kiss and make up," Annie said to Rand as Lunk walked off. "Or at least shake hands."

"Fine with me." Rand shrugged and glared at Rook. "But maybe you should ask the lady with the chip on her shoulder!"

Gradually, in single file, they began to work their way back to the river. Rook and Rand opened a second front in their war when Rook insisted that something was following them and Rand called her paranoid. Scott came down on them again and ordered Lunk to walk between them as a buffer. And it was in this way that the three men managed to avoid the leeches . . .

Scott and Rand heard Annie's scream and turned around in time to see the descent of the mutant worm rain. They dropped from the forest canopy, instantly attaching themselves to the two girls.

Lunk made a sound of disgust and backed away. "There's millions of them!"

Annie was crying and stamping her feet. Rook's face was contorted, her body shaking all over. "Do something!" she screamed to Rand, but he only smiled. "You creep! Get these things off me!" She stood paralyzed, as if not knowing where to begin—on her arms, her neck, her face . . . Just then another leech dropped from the trees and landed on her forehead; Rook screamed and collapsed to the ground, wailing and kicking her feet in frustration.

"Hold still," Scott said, kneeling alongside her and pulling the leeches off Rook's arm. But Rand stopped him before he had detached more than two or three. He took Lunk's lit cigarette and touched the lighted end to one of the creatures.

"Make things hot for them and they'll pop out on their own," he explained as the leech dropped off, sizzling.

"Pull them off and you end up leaving the sucker intact." Methodically, he moved the cigarette from leech to leech.

"I tell you, I get a real kick seeing city girls in the country," Rand told Scott while he labored. "They look so darn cute when they start screaming." He smiled at Rook. "You should've seen yourself..."

She made a face, averting her gaze from Rand's handiwork. "Can you blame me? It's *disgusting*." She shuddered. "I hate to break this to you, Daniel Boone, but there's something called civilization out there. Maybe you've heard of it."

Rand snorted. "That's where you have crime and filth, right?"

"Better than slimy little blood-sucking tree leeches."

"Sourpuss," Rand said, standing up and moving over to Annie. "Any leech that gets a good taste of you is gonna swear off human beings forever."

Rook stood up, angry at first, then flashing an enigmatic, almost seductive smile. "We'll see..." she said, walking off into the bushes to check for leeches off limits to Rand's search.

They stuck to the forest this time rather than risk showing themselves in the open ground that bordered the river. Two hours along they stopped to rest below the small falls of a tributary that fed the gorge. Rand stripped a sapling of twigs and fashioned a fishing rod for himself. He waded out to a rock midstream and cast in his line. Scott and the others sat under the trees along the bank.

"Hey, Rand," Annie taunted him. "Do you really think you can catch anything with that funny-looking *stick* of yours?"

Rand frowned while everyone had a good laugh. "Just

you wait," he told them. "I'm an expert, and if there's a trout anywhere in this river, it's mine."

It was a pleasant spot, full of water sounds, animal life, and cool shade stirred by a gentle breeze. "Almost makes you forget where you are," Scott mused.

Rook nodded absently. "I know. I'm starting to feel like we're at a Boy Scout picnic."

Rand meanwhile was addressing his would-be catch, when something small and mean hit him on the head. He looked around and found Lunk crouched on the limb of an overhanging tree. "Hey, what's the idea?" Rand started to ask.

"Invid . . ." Lunk said softly, cupping his hands to his mouth.

Scott, Annie, and Rook took to the cover of the brush. Rand was looking around for a place to hide when he noticed the line stretched taut. He grabbed hold of the anchored pole, ignoring Scott's orders to abandon the fish. It had to be a five-pounder at least, and he wasn't about to let it go. Even so, he could sense the ground-shaking approach of the Trooper. He pulled hard and saw the rainbow break water; it was bigger than he had thought. The Invid's cloven footfalls were increasing; Rand gave a mighty tug and brought the fish up. But just then the line snapped. At the same time the Trooper appeared through the trees.

Deciding it might behoove him to be the one that got away, Rand dropped the pole and dived from the rock.

Lunk was still in the tree, standing now, his back flattened against the trunk, when the Trooper passed. A second Trooper lumbered into view an instant later. Peering from the bushes, his H–90 raised, Scott saw that the two were headed toward the falls. Rand was nowhere to be seen.

Unless one happened to be a fish.

Running short on breath when the first Invid hit the

water, Rand had propelled himself downstream, hugging the rocky bottom, only to run into another pair of armored legs. His lungs were on fire, threatening to implode, but surfacing wouldn't necessarily improve the situation any. He swallowed hard, sensing a darkness creeping into the edges of his vision. . . .

The two Troopers stopped in the middle of the river and swung their sensors through a 360-degree scan. Concerned for Rand's safety, Scott ran from cover when the Invid had crossed the stream and moved off into the woods on the opposite bank.

Lunk dived in, and found his companion unconscious on the river bottom, arms still locked around the boulder he had hugged to keep himself submerged. He brought him up and laid him facedown on the bank; then straddled him and carefully began to use his big hands to pump water from Rand's lungs.

"Is he going to be all right?" Annie asked.

Scott nodded. "He just passed out."

Rand's color started to return, and he coughed up a few mouthfuls of water. Softly, Rook called his name.

Rand straightened up with an energy that surprised all of them, knocking an unsuspecting Lunk backward into the river. He looked around dazedly and dropped back to his knees exhausted.

"Uh, the Invid are all gone," Annie said.

"Yeah, you can calm down, Superman," Rook added.

Rand smiled thinly.

"All right," Scott said, extending his hand to Lunk and helping him to the bank. "Now that they're gone, we can get back to Lancer. We can't be too far—"

Rook saw Scott's eyes go wide. She spun around and saw the reason for it: An enormous black bear, frightened and up on its hind legs, was breaking through the brush. Scott had his weapon raised but froze as a bizarre giant tiger-striped spider dropped from a tree onto the weapon's barrel. Scott winced and uttered a startled cry, reflexively loosing a bolt from the thing that whizzed past the bear's head. Rook lunged for Annie as the animal's huge claw came down, narrowly missing her. Lunk almost caught the backlash and rolled for cover.

Rand missed with two shots from his own weapon, and the bear's right paw connected with the blaster, sending him and the weapon flying in opposite directions. Rand looked up into bared teeth and sharp claws, the face of furry black death. He made his peace with the Creator and glimpsed a brilliant flash of white light... But when the smoke cleared, he found himself still alive and the bear gone—*vaporized*.

The only problem was that there was now an Invid ship overhead—and not one of the Troopers either, but one of the rust-brown Pincer units!

"Well, I never thought I'd be happy to see you guys!" Rand said as he got to his feet, the smell of roasted meat in the air. He joined the rest of the team in a jog for the woods.

The Invid rained fire down on them as they ran, steering them away from the safety of the trees and bringing one of the patrolling Troopers in on the action. The team soon found itself cornered, fenced in on open ground by high-energy beams and annihilation discs. But Scott heard a familiar sound cutting through the tumultuous roar of the Invid's death-rays.

It was Lancer, riding one of the abandoned Cyclones.

Lavender hair trailing in the wind, he leapt the mecha over a surprised Invid Trooper and landed it not more than fifteen feet from where the team stood huddled together.

"All I had to do was ride to the sound of the guns!"

Lancer yelled when the Cyclone had skidded to a halt. "What're you waiting for, Scott? Climb on!"

Scott offered a silent prayer to the gods who governed silver linings and threw himself onto the rear seat. Lancer popped the mecha into a long wheelie that shot them through the legs of the bewildered Trooper. But the Pincer ship chased them, loosing continuous disc fire from its treetop course.

Lancer kept the Cyclone in the woods for cover. Scott saw that they were nearing the river gorge now and raised himself on the rear pegs in an effort to spot the Alpha. Lancer took one hand from the controls and pointed. "At the foot of the cliff on the right!" he shouted over his shoulder.

Scott realized that the land dropped away sharply up ahead, but he couldn't discern just how high they were above the lower terrace. Lancer was cutting their forward speed as they approached the ledge. Scott leaned in to ask him how he planned to negotiate the jump. But all at once Lancer threw his arms straight up and was gone.

Instinctively, Scott grabbed hold of the handlebar controls and saved the mecha from overturning. He looked over his shoulder and saw Lancer squatting on the overhanging branch he had swung himself to, smiling and waving Scott off. Scott was impressed: It had been one heck of a gymnastic feat. But neither of them was in the clear yet. An Invid Trooper broke through the woods and began to open up with disc fire. Lancer executed a Tarzan leap from the tree and disappeared into the undergrowth. Scott lowered his head to the rush of the wind and goosed the cycle. But the cliff face was close now, closer than he had realized, and an instant later he was sailing into blue skies above the treetops. He lost the Cyclone and plummeted on his own, no one to catch him or take note of his alarmed cry. . . .

Elsewhere, Lancer had worked his way back toward the rest of the team. He literally ran into them not a mile from where he had put Scott in charge of the Cyclone. They had three Invid Troopers behind them, devastating the forests with sporadic sprays of fire. Lancer took the point and led them along the same path he and Scott had Cycloned not an hour before. Twilight was giving way to darkness now, and Invid cannon sounds and annihilation discs lent a hellish atmosphere to the scene.

Once again the Troopers succeeded in boxing them in, and once again Rook, Lunk, Annie, and Rand yelled good-byes to one another while explosions rained leaves and forest carpet all over the place. But Scott turned the tide: He had survived his plunge into the trees and made his way to the concealed Veritech. The Invid Pincer ship, as he explained later, was history.

Now the Alpha came tearing into the woods and took out the Trooper whose cannons were ranging in on the team. Then Scott launched the VT straight up into the starry skies, reconfiguring to Battloid at the top of his booster climb and bringing out the mecha's rifle/cannon to deal with his pursuers. Two more Troopers fell to the Alpha's storm, but a third managed to work its way in close enough to inflict a pincer swipe that brought Scott tumbling back to the woods.

The Trooper roared into a long sweeping turn and headed back in on the downed Battloid. Inside, Scott shook himself to clear his head and ran through a rapid assessment of his options as he brought the techno-knight to its feet. The mecha's external pickups brought the team's cries of warning into the cockpit, especially Annie's high-pitched: "Behind you, Scott! Behind you!"

Scott thought the Battloid through a quick about-face in time to see the approaching Trooper. He reached for the launch-tube cover levers. The Invid fired first, blazing discs spinning and twisting out of the cannon muzzles. But Scott's aim was surer: Red-tipped heat-seeking missles ripped from the Battloid's shoulder compartments and homed in on the Invid's dark form, detonating against pincers and torso alike, and giving brief life to a blinding fireball, a brilliant orange midnight sun.

CHAPTER
EIGHT

> *Most commentators overlook the fact that Lancer was a singer long before he was a freedom fighter, and a cross-dresser long before a Yellow Dancer. But he was first and foremost an actor—malleable, dramatic, and narcissistic. And while it's true that he can be linked to certain literary traditions wherein heroes carried out their crusades under the guise of fops and other fabulous fools, Lancer was no Scarlet Pimpernel or comic Zorro: He was a fox of an entirely different order.*
>
> Zeus Bellow, *The Road to Reflex Point*

PRIOR TO ZOR'S ARRIVAL ON OPTERA, IT WAS THE FLOWER of Life that held the central place in the Invid's naturalistic pantheon. But that was no longer the case. They were aggressive species now every bit as warlike as the Tirolian Masters who defoliated Optera. And they worshipped Protoculture, the bio-energetic by-product Zor had coaxed from the Flowers themselves. They continued to subsist on the Flowers their captive Human population planted and harvested, but it was Protoculture that fueled the army of mecha which kept that enterprise running smoothly and without incident. Indeed, it could be said that the Invid themselves had become more dependent on Zor's discovery than the Robotech Masters ever were.

Enormous amounts of Protoculture were required to oversee and maintain Earth's diverse population centers and to put down uprisings and revolts in the farms and factories. (Exedore would have been chagrinned to learn that the Invid had found their own way to manufacture Protoculture without having to resort to the matrix device that had figured so prominently in the First and Second Robotech Wars.) These reserves, fashioned by Human hands into individual energy canisters suitable for Invid and Terran mecha alike, were stored in scores of warehouses across the globe and guarded by Humans "sympathetic" to the Invid's purpose. The privileges enjoyed by these sympathizers varied; sometimes hostages were taken to assure allegiance, while on other occasions outlaws and petty powerbrokers were given charge. Towns and cities bartered with the Invid overlords for simple freedoms: the right to enjoy a semblance of normal life in exchange for snooping out resistance groups or seeing to it that Protoculture cells did not fall into the wrong hands. Often the Invid allowed those in charge before the invasion to keep their lofty positions, except that there was a new authority to answer to—the Regis and her legions of territorial supervisors who dealt directly with their underlings.

Lancer explained some of this to Scott while the team licked its wounds after their encounter with the Troopers. Even though the episode had consisted largely in their outrunning the Invid, it had nevertheless served to unite the members of the team and instill in each of them a confidence that hadn't been there two days before. They were now beginning to understand and accept each other's strengths and weaknesses, and they were learning to trust one another as well. Without any formal vote or voiced acknowledgment, Scott surfaced as the leader, which was only right given his training and resoluteness. Lunk was something of a sergeant to Scott's lieutenant Annie, everything from den mother to mascot. Rook still held herself separate, but could always be counted on for her instinctive combat sense. And Rand was their backwoods provider, fishing and hunting when he wasn't sitting under a tree scribbling notes to himself. That left only Lancer.

Scott still had misgivings about the man, but as he listened to Lancer's detailed account of the Invid infrastructure and occupation techniques, he began to see him in a new light. The female-singer ploy had yet to be explained, but it was obvious from Lancer's report that the adopted persona of Yellow Dancer had opened many doors to him. He would discuss his former ties with the resistance only in a vague way, but Scott understood that his contacts were as numerous as his information was exhaustive.

The team had retrieved the two other Cyclones from where they had left them in the grass and spent three days in the river gorge dining on pit roasted fish, recuperating, and planning the next move in their northward journey. They were careful about using the mecha now, convinced that Rand's theory was correct. Most of the time the Invid Scouts and Troopers were operating in a kind of background net of Protoculture emanations and couldn't home in on any one source. But when they were engaged in a particular search, their senses were more acute at screening out the random waves from the usually nearby active ones. In any case, it was a moot point at the moment; the Alpha was depleted of charge, and there was scarcely enough left in the Cyclones to power them, let alone reconfigure or fire them.

That's where Norristown entered the picture. Located somewhat east of their present route, it was one of the Southland's largest cities, transplanted like so many others from the devastated north during the reign of Chairman Moran and the formation of the Army of the Southern Cross. The city had prospered throughout and boasted one of the continent's few surviving sports arenas. But most important, it was the site of one of the Invid's Protoculture storage facilities, a heavily fortified castle (constructed years ago in the Hollywood style) that overlooked the city.

Lancer had a map of the place.

And a rather ingenious plan.

Less than a week later, Rook and Annie were on one of the roads leading into Norristown. They made an interesting picture—the blonde in her red and white body-suit leaning almost casually against the parked Cyclone and Annie in her military greens and ever-present cap perched on the seat like some diminutive ornament. Not five miles away was the city itself, a tight cluster of buildings surrounded by forest, with Drumstick Butte and the hulks of two Zentraedi ships casting their giant shadows from behind. The Protoculture storage facility could be discerned at the foot of the oddly shaped, top-heavy butte, linked to the city below a well-maintained switchbacked roadway.

Rook straightened up at the sound of an approaching vehicle and glanced over at Annie; the youngster nodded and hopped down from the Cyclone's seat to stand alongside her traffic-stopping teammate. Up the road a truck came into view, and Rook threw the driver a play-ful wink and raised her thumb in a hitchhiker's gesture. Innocently and with well-rehearsed bashfulness, Annie pressed her forefingers together and called for the driver to stop and lend a hand.

The driver halted the truck and climbed down from the cab, taking in a long eyeful of the two marooned girls and their red Cyclone. He bent down to inspect the mecha, complimenting them on the fine condition of the thing, but was sad to report that they were out of Proto-culture fuel. This was so common an occurrence that the driver scarcely gave it a second thought; anyone might stumble upon some wonderful specimen of aged Robo-technology only to come to think of it as a worthless piece of junk when the all but irreplaceable Protoculture energy cells were depleted. True, there was a black market, but it was one that few people had access to. Between the needs of the Invid, the resistance, and your everyday 'Culture hounds, Protoculture had become a priceless commodity.

"We were hoping you could fix it," Annie said to the truck driver. "We're on our way to the Yellow Dancer concert in Norristown."

The driver smiled up at her. "Not without Protoculture. There's nothing I can do."

"Hey, mister," Rook said suddenly, as if noticing the driver's Invid-occupation double-C hard-hat emblem for the first time. "You're from the storage facility, aren't you?"

"So?" the man answered, wary now.

"Couldn't you spare us some?" Annie asked, leaning over the Cyclone's seat.

The man snorted. "What're you, nuts, kid? If anyone found out I'd shared my rations, I'd be in deep trouble." He turned his head at the sound of a mechanical click and buzz and found himself staring into the laser muzzle of a strange-looking disc-shaped weapon.

Rook grinned and gestured with the blaster. "Know what? You're *already* in big trouble, buddy. . . ."

Five minutes later the driver had been dragged to the side of the road. His arms and legs were bound with rope, and his mouth was sealed by a piece of wide tape. He continued to struggle while Lunk secured the final knots.

"Relax, buddy," Rook told him. "We're just going to borrow your truck for a while." She hastened off to the spot in the woods where they had moved the vehicle.

Her teammates had the back doors opened. "Well, the first stage went pretty well," Scott was commenting as she walked up.

Rand was leaning against the trailer with his arms crossed. "I had no idea that soldiers also doubled as hijackers, Scott."

Rook looked at both of them impatiently. "Are you guys going to stand here and argue, or are we going to get a move on?"

Scott and Rand exchanged looks. "Let's do it," they said at the same moment.

A short while later the truck roared into town with Lunk at the wheel, the former driver's hard hat and permits now part of his disguise. Rook, Rand, Scott, and Annie were in the rear, but not yet in what would soon be their hiding place. Originally the plan had called for all of them to hide underneath the chassis while the truck was cleared through to the storage facility, but good fortune was on their side in the form of a loft compartment built into the truck's trailer. They could only speculate on what the compartment had been used for, but it was perfectly suited to their present needs. Lunk made one stop along the way to the facility gate—just brief enough to allow Annie to hop out and work her way into the crowds that were already gathering for Yellow Dancer's concert.

"Be sure to make lots of noise," Scott reminded her.

"Come on," she returned, as though insulted. "How do you suppose I got the reputation for being such a loudmouth?"

Scott grinned and began to pull the rear doors closed. He was surprised by the size of the crowds and recalled what Rand had told him earlier: *When people find out Yellow's coming to town, they go completely berserk.* When Annie had jumped out, Scott had glimpsed a poster of the singer pasted to the side of a building: Yellow Dancer in a spaghetti-strapped sundress, some sort of matching turban, low heels, and a pearl collar.

Lancer had left for Norristown three days before the rest of the team. The plan called for him to put a pickup band together and cut a deal with a local promoter, who would secure the sports arena and take care of publicity and logistics. The promoter, a man named Woods, was an old friend of Lancer's and a member of the resistance.

Scott thought back to Lancer's departure—Lancer in his alter-ego guise. Scott couldn't help feeling that Yellow Dancer wasn't just Lancer in female attire but an entirely different personality. Lancer's demeanor changed as well as his voice and carriage. Yellow was a real entity living alongside Lancer in the same body. Scott found it incomprehensible and just a bit unsettling, but it didn't detract from the trust he had in Lancer. Scott was wondering how the second part of Lancer's plan was succeeding when he heard Lunk's fist pounding against the cab of the truck—the signal for Scott, Rand, and Rook to take to the overhead compartment. That meant the truck was nearing the twin-towered security gate on the road below the storage facility.

Farther along the road that wound up toward the base of Drumstick Butte was the barracks of the security force that staffed and guarded the storage facility. The chief of station, Colonel Briggs, was a large, beefy man with salt-and-pepper hair and a thick mustache. He was in his office in the barracks, feet up on the desk, daydreaming over a color photo of Yellow Dancer that had appeared in the morning edition of the city's newspaper when one of his staff arrived with good news.

"We've been asked to supply security at Yellow Dancer's concert this afternoon," the staffer reported. He wore a blue-gray uniform with a red upturned collar, similar in cut and design to that worn by the colonel. A single red star adorned the front of his brimmed cap. The Invid had made a point of allowing local customs and garb to remain unchanged in Norristown and numerous other strongholds throughout the Southlands. "Shall I refuse the request, sir?" the staffer wanted to know.

Briggs didn't bother to lower the newspaper, which effectively concealed him from the staffer. He hummed to himself, finishing up his fanciful daydream scenario before replying. "Are you out of your mind?" he said at last. "If something should happen to Yellow Dancer, it's *our* reputation that will suffer. Send every available man down to the arena."

"But sir," the staffer pointed out haltingly, "we can't risk leaving the facility unguarded. . . ."

"Nonsense," the colonel said from behind his paper. "What time is the concert scheduled to end?"

"Around three-thirty, but—"

"And what time are the Intercessors arriving to pick up the shipment?"

"Four o'clock, but—"

"Then there's no problem." Briggs set the paper aside, got up from behind the desk, and walked over to the office window. "What can happen?" he said, gesturing to the facility half a mile away at the top of the switchbacked access road. "The facility's impregnable . . . And besides, I'd like to oversee Yellow Dancer's security *personally*." He swung around to his lieutenant. "See to it that she expects me."

Rumor had it that the storage facility was originally a castle imported stone by stone from Europe during the mid-1800s by a renegade nobleman from Transylvania. It saw more than one hundred years of alteration and modernization before being substantially renovated (in the Hollywood style) by a sports event promoter who fell heir to the place in 2015. Much of Norristown, including the arena, owed its existence to the same man.

The building, with its mansard roof and numerous spires, still retained a Provençal look, but this was overshadowed by the fantastical elements added on during the last twenty-five years, primarily the east wing's crenellated tower. Three-quarters of a mile down the road was the twin-towered main gate, where Lunk and the others were presently stopped.

"I'm here to run a check on the cooling systems," Lunk said to the helmeted guard who approached the driver's side window.

"Your permit," the guard said nastily.

Lunk handed the papers down for the man to read, while a second guard moved to the back of the truck to have a look inside. "It's clean, Fred!" Lunk heard the man call out a minute later. The guard perused the permit a while longer, then returned it. "You'd better be clean on the way out, too," he warned Lunk. Lunk saw sentries at the other tower frisking a white-coveralled driver.

"You got it," he told the guard.

The guard waved him through and opened the fence that spanned the roadway. Lunk threw the truck into gear and drove off, removing his hat and wiping away the sweat that had collected on his forehead. Two trucks filled with security personnel passed him going in the opposite direction, a sign that Lancer's request might have been granted. At the top of the switchbacks, Lunk backed the truck toward the shipping entrance. There were only three or four guards on patrol, and not one of them even glanced at Lunk while he climbed down from the cab and threw open the rear doors.

"We're in, gang," he said loudly enough for his friends to hear.

Rook, Rand, and Scott lowered themselves from the loft compartment and entered the facility. Scott unfolded Lancer's map and checked it against their location. "This one," he told Rook and Rand, indicating an air duct grate along one wall. Lunk helped them move several crates over to the wall. Scott climbed up first, rechecked the map, and peered through the grate. Satisfied, he nodded, and Rook and Rand joined him. The two men went to work on the bolts that held the grating to its frame, and in a moment they were able to lift the panel free. Scott and Rand crawled in. Lunk handed rope, a tool pouch, and an aluminum carry case up to Rook. She waved him good luck and followed Scott's lead into the horizontal duct.

Less than fifteen feet into the duct, Scott stopped and whispered: "The control room is on the third floor. It should take us about ten minutes to get there."

Rook could barely discern him in the darkness. Ten minutes was going to feel like an eternity.

Down below, the arena was rapidly filling to capacity and Annie was circulating in front of the stage doing what she did best: inciting the crowd.

"...At her last concert a whole bunch of people got up on stage, and everybody started partying and having a good ole time," she told everyone within earshot. "Some of us even got to go backstage with Yellow Dancer after the concert and party some more! But this one's going to be the best! I hear that she might not perform like this again, so we better make this the one to remember. Right?!"

"All right!" several people shouted. "Party time!"

Meanwhile, Yellow Dancer was entertaining guests in her backstage dressing room. She had changed to a sleeveless pink and burgundy pants outfit with a matching bowed headband, which held her hair up and off her neck.

"At the last concert, some of my fans came up on stage and really made a mess of things," she was explaining, facing the mirror while she applied eye liner. "I'd rather that didn't happen again."

"We won't allow that here," Briggs, the facility security chief, said from behind her. Yellow smiled at him in the mirror. "We'll do our job and guarantee you complete security. As long as nothing happens to bring the Invid down on us."

"Those horrible creatures," Yellow said, twisting up her face.

"Aah, they're not so bad once you get to know them," the chief started to say.

Lancer's friend, Woods, threw him a conspiratorial wink from a corner of the room. He was a handsome young man with a pencil-thin mustache whose taste ran to calfskin jackets and black leather ties. Just now he was holding the large bouquet of flowers Briggs had brought along for Yellow Dancer. "We know you'll do your best, Colonel," Woods said encouragingly.

Lancer saw the chief's puffy face turn red with embarrassment. "You're damn right we will."

"And I want to thank you *so* much for the flowers," Yellow gushed, turning away from the mirror now to flash Briggs a painted smile. "They're lovely."

Briggs leered at her. "Anything for you, Yellow, anything you want."

Scott, Rook, and Rand had reached the third floor of the facility. The duct opened out into a small area that served as the relay center for the facility's security systems. Scott and Rand moved in to try to make sense of the tangle of wires and switches that covered two full walls of the room. It took several minutes to locate the feeds from the security cameras, but the rest was child's play. Rook unsnapped the clasps on the carry case and began to hand over the devices Lunk assured them would scramble the a/v signals. Scott and Rand quickly attached these to the feeder cables and set off on the next leg of their cramped journey.

The map called for a brief return to the air duct system before they could enter the actual storage area. But once through this, they would be free to move about at will—assuming Lunk's devices did the trick. They dropped out of the duct into a maintenance corridor that encircled the supply room but had no access to it except for a single elbow conduit located clear around the back of the building. Rand volunteered to test the effectiveness of Lunk's scramblers by making faces at one of the surveillance cameras. When no sirens went off and no guards came running, the trio figured they were in the clear and decided to use one of the maintenance carts to convey them to the conduit—an open-topped electric affair with two seats and a single headlamp that brought them around back in a quarter the time it would have taken them to walk.

They stopped at the first elbow conduit and commenced a careful count. Rook looked over the map, while Scott took charge of noting their position relative to the first main.

"Under the main line, thirteenth from the right," Scott said, recalling the scrawled notation on the map. He gestured to an elbow up ahead. "That must be it."

The conduit was made of light-gauge metal; it was a good four feet in circumference and stood at least six feet high from floor to right-angle bend. It was held in place by a circular flange, but promised to be flexible enough once the bolts securing the flange to the floor were undone. Rand and Scott took box wrenches from the tool pouch and immediately set to work. At the same time, Rook took a coil of rope from the cart and began to tie it fast to one of the adjacent elbows.

When the last of the bolts had been loosened and removed, Rook and Scott shoved the conduit to one side and bent down to peer into the shaft below.

Rand squinted and smiled to himself as his eyes fixed upon the objects of their search: crate after crate of Protoculture canisters, each the size and shape of a squat thermos.

"There's a mountain of it down here," he reported.

Scott gave a tug on the rope Rook had tied to the conduit. "Feels strong enough," he commented while Rook tied the other end around her waist. "The security system down there is still operative. You touch anything—the wall, the ceiling, the floor—and you'll trigger it."

Rook sat down and let her legs dangle through the opening. Rand and Scott took hold of the rope and signaled their readiness. "All right," she told them. "Let's get this over with before I change my mind."

Yellow Dancer's concert was under way. She streaked onto the stage like a comet, with the band already laying down the intro to "Look Up!" and the audience of several thousand roaring their appreciation. It was a heavy-message number that had become something of an anthem in the Southlands, and Yellow loved singing it. She stood with her legs spread apart, one hand on her hip, holding the mike like an upturned glass, her body accenting the beat.

Another winter's day
Another gray reminder that what used to be
Has gone away.
It's really hard to say,
How long we'll have to live with our insanity;
We have to pay for all we use,
We never think before we light the fuse . . .
Look up, look up, look up!
The sky is fall-ing!
Look up,
There's something up you have to know.
Before you try to go outside,
To take in the view,
Look up, because the sky
Could fall on you . . .

Yellow looked to the stage wings, where the colonel was eagerly trying to stomp his foot to the music, an ear-to-ear grin on his face, his men vigilant throughout the arena.

Loaded down with canisters of Protoculture fished from the storage room, the electric cart sped away from the maintenance corridor and entered a stone service-way, damp, foul-smelling, and seemingly unused for centuries. Rook, still dizzy from her upside-down descent into the storage room, had the map spread open in her lap while Scott drove. In the dim ambient light, she tried to match juncture points in the serviceway with the vague scrawls indicated on the map. Finally she told Scott to stop the cart. He got out and began to inspect the stones at eye level along the right-hand wall of the corridor.

"Should be over here somewhere," Rook heard him say. She watched him lay his hand against one of the stones, and in a moment the wall was opening. Another corridor was revealed, perpendicular to the first and decidedly downhill.

"And this is supposed to lead to the concert hall?" Rook said uncertainly.

"Looks to me like it leads to the dungeon," Rand said behind her.

Back at the wheel, Scott edged the cart forward into the dark passageway. "Lancer said it was an escape route constructed by the man who originally had this place built."

"Well, let's hope so," Rook answered him as the stone wall reassembled itself behind them.

The ramp dropped at a steep angle that sorely tested the electric cart's brakes, but the important thing was that they were leaving the facility behind.

Rand was encouraged. According to his own calculations the passageway was indeed leading them in the direction of the arena. "Piece of cake," he said from his uncomfortable position atop the Protoculture canisters stacked in the bed of the cart. "We should have taken more while we had the chance."

"Don't be so smart," Scott said stiffly. "We're not out of here yet."

Rand leaned forward between the front seats. "What's there to worry about now? The concert's on, we've got the 'Culture, Lunk'll be waiting for us with open arms . . ."

"Mr. Confidence all of a sudden," Rook snorted from the shotgun seat. Scott was easing up on the brakes, and the cart was traveling along at a good clip now. Rook was holding her hair in place with one hand when the cart's headlamp revealed a solid wall blocking their exit.

"Hold on!" Scott yelled, pulling up on the hand brake.

The rear end of the cart bounced and swerved as the brakes locked, but Scott managed to remain in control and brought the vehicle to a halt with room to spare. The trio regarded the wall and began to wonder whether they might have missed a turnoff earlier on.

"I didn't see any side tunnels," said Scott. "And according to Lancer's map there's only supposed to be this one passageway."

"The map's been accurate up to now," Rook added, running her fingers through her tangled hair. "Where'd we go wrong?"

"Maybe we have to give the wall a push or something, like up top," Rand suggested.

Scott was just about to step out and have a look, when he heard a deep rumbling sound behind him. The trio turned to watch helplessly as a massive stone partition dropped from the tunnel's ceiling.

"Now what?" Scott said after a moment.

"They must be on to us somehow!" Rook said. But Scott disagreed. "Those a/v scramblers still have fifteen minutes of life left in them. I think we must have—"

Scott cut himself off as a new sound began to infiltrate their silent tomb. It began with a grating sound of stone moving against stone, then softened to a sibilance before gushing loud and clear.

"Water!" Rand yelled. "We're being flooded!"

NINE

It was just a case of overcompensation again: We went from having no plan to too much plan!

Rand, *Notes on the Run*

YELLOW DANCER PRANCED ACROSS THE STAGE, pointing and gesturing to the crowd, swinging the microphone over her head as though it were a lariat. She was in the midst of a hard driving number now, a flat-out rocker that had the audience dancing in the aisles and pressing forward toward the stage.

Annie was helping this along.

"Let's get this party under way!" she shouted from her cramped space near the front. "Let's get up on stage!"

Yellow spied Annie in the crowd and smiled while she sang. She threw herself into an impromptu spin, shaking her hips and urging the band to kick up the volume somewhat. She turned again and launched herself across the stage in a kind of Jagger strut, inching her way toward the edge with each pass and beckoning the fans to join her.

Woods and the colonel looked on from the wings.

"What an incredible performer," Briggs was saying. Woods noticed the glint in the colonel's eye as he watched Yellow twirl herself like some sort of singing acrobat. "She's amazing... And these kids look like they're ready to jump out of their socks."

The man is practically drooling. Woods laughed to himself. "They are beginning to get a bit out of hand," he told Briggs, a forced note of concern in his voice. He motioned to the front ranks of the audience, where the crowds were pushing hard against the security force's arm-link cordon. "Don't you think it would be wise to keep a van ready out back just in case we have to get Yellow Dancer out of here in a hurry?"

Woods saw Briggs blanch. He called out to one of the men guarding the stage entrance and told him bring a van to the rear door, while Woods suppressed a smile and turned to watch Yellow strut her stuff.

On the cold stone floor of a small, seldom-used room beneath the stage, Lunk sat cross-legged, blowing up balloons. Several hundred of these helium-filled colored globes had already been inflated and secreted in a compartment behind the bandshell itself, but the ones Lunk was busy preparing had to serve a special purpose. To each grouping of four balloons, Lunk added a carefully concealed propellant device in addition to a sensor that would allow the four-color group to home in on a prearranged beacon signal transmitted from the outskirts of Norristown, close to the spot where the team had left the Cyclones and the Veritech.

When Lunk had filled the last of the balloons, he crawled over and shut down the helium tanks, only then realizing how spaced out he was from inhaling the gas.

He glanced at the room's brick rear wall and moved over to it now, running his hands over the stones and searching for any signs of the doorway indicated on Lancer's map of the facility and linking passageway. But he could find no evidence of seams or fractures in the mortar. Perhaps it could be opened only from inside the tunnel, he thought, checking his watch. He would know soon enough, in any case. . . .

The cart turned out to be watertight. Not that this would have been some wondrous piece of news under normal circumstances, but given the tunnel trio's present condition it was one of those small miracles to be thankful for. It meant that they were able to remain seated while the water rose around them rather than have to exhaust themselves trying to remain afloat in water that was well over their heads. Of course, this, too, seemed a minor consolation.

A few four-pack canisters of Protoculture were bobbing about in the cold water, and Rand was sitting on the front bumper of the cart looking like the world was about to end.

Which was certainly an appropriate enough response, seeing how the water was still pouring into their tomb with no signs of letting up, and the cold ceiling was only four feet above them now. But Rook, who seldom had a good word to say about anything, was trying to cheer Rand up.

"C'mon, pal, try not to get so down in the dumps."

Rand stared at her in disbelief. "Down in the dumps?" he said, gesturing to the room, their situation. "What d'ya think, I should be happy about getting a chance to wash up before I die?"

"It's my fault," Scott told them. "I should have considered the possibility that some of the older defensive systems would still be operational."

Rook shook her head. "Don't blame yourself, Scott."

"Let 'im," Rand argued. "Why not? He got us into this, didn't he?"

"*We* got us into this," Rook said, raising her voice.

Scott told them both to shut up. "Besides, we might get a lucky break yet."

Rand and Rook waited for an explanation.

"If the a/v scramblers fade before the water gets much higher, we'll probably get to face a firing squad instead of drowning."

In the stage wings, the colonel looked out at Yellow's screaming audience and swung harshly to Woods. "If this mob gets any more unruly, the Invid are to going to send a few Troopers in here and we'll have all hell to pay!"

Woods had to agree. Yellow was supposed to have finished up already, but instead she was going into yet another encore. The crowds were whipped up into such a frenzy that the arena seemed unable to contain it.

Yellow Dancer sensed Woods's concern and turned to him briefly as she gyrated around the stage. *Where is Scott?* she asked herself as the band revved up. She took several giant steps toward the wings and tried to flash her accomplice a signal, touching her earring and shaking her head as if to indicate that she hadn't heard from Lunk yet.

Woods acknowledged his understanding with a shrug and a slight gesture toward the chief, who was pacing in the wings like a nervous animal.

Yellow brought the mike up and asked if everyone was all right, holding the mike out to them as they screamed replies. Again they strained at the security cordon, and several kids succeeded in making it onto the stage before being scooped up by guards and carried off. Something had to be done *quickly*!

* * *

Scott, Rook, and Rand had scarcely a foot of breathing space left, and the water level was still rising. Things had reached the desperate stage a few minutes before, and now the three of them were in the water pushing up against each and every ceiling stone, praying that one would give.

"That story about the hero escaping through a loose stone is just a fairy tale," Rand was saying, when his hands felt the stone budge. For a moment he was speechless, but finally he managed to gulp out the words: "It moved! The stone moved!"

"She's *already* gone a half hour overtime!" the chief shouted to Woods. "I want the concert wrapped up—and I mean *now*!"

"But look at the kids," Woods tried. "They're having the time of their lives. I mean, after all, when do they ever get a chance to let off a little—"

"Now!" the chief said firmly. "Or this will be the last chance they ever get. Do you understand me?"

Woods backed away and threw a signal to the control booth: They were to cut the power as soon as Yellow finished her song. . . .

Lunk, meanwhile, was pacing back and forth in the small area beneath the stage. Scott was way overdue. There were no contingency plans other than to get out of Norristown as quickly as possible. Annie and Lancer would be all right, but Lunk could be identified by the guards at the facility tower. But just as he was resigning himself to this, he heard sounds of movement behind him. He swung around in time to see his waterlogged friends step through the parted wall. Each of them was toting Protoculture canister packs.

"Well, it's about time," Lunk said to them, eyeing

their soaked clothing. "What happened to you guys—
you come by way of the river, or what?"

"We'll explain later," Scott said hurriedly, already
fastening the packs to the balloon clusters. "Signal
Lancer, and let's get this show on the road."

Yellow was aware that the control room and sound
personnel had been ordered to cut the power, so she
was milking the final song for all it was worth, extending the chorus and encouraging the audience to join in,
in the hopes that Scott would appear in time. But by
now she had done all she could; the band was finishing
up with an interminable one-chord wrap-up, and she
was just about to make the grand leap that would cut it
off. Then she heard a small but unmistakable flashing
tone emitted by her left earring. It was Lunk's signal:
Scott had made it!

"Thank you! Thank you, all of you!" Yellow yelled
into the microphone over deafening applause. Yellow
gestured to Annie and watched as she began to worm her
way toward the cordon, readying the pass that would
admit her backstage.

People in the crowd were pointing to something in the
air now, and Annie got a glimpse of a skyful of balloons
before she disappeared through the door to the stage
wings.

"I love you!" Yellow added as she left the stage.

The plan called for Scott, Rook, and Rand to infiltrate themselves among Yellow Dancer's retinue of si-
demen and bodyguards, all of whom had been
handpicked by Woods. At the same time, Lunk's role
was to see to it that the waiting police van was ren-
dered safe and secure.

This was easily accomplished, thanks to the fact
that the guard was napping when Lunk stole up to the
driver's side door. Lunk pummeled the man into a

more lasting sleep. Scott, Rook, and Rand took to the canvas-backed van, while Lunk dragged the guard off to one side and began to change into the man's police helmet, shirt, and trousers. Annie appeared a moment later, followed by Yellow, who was clutching two wardrobe suitcases under her arms. The colonel was inside the arena, waiting patiently at Yellow's dressing-room door for the singer to arrive. Woods's team, meanwhile, had spirited her out a rear entry and was now doing its best to keep things backstage suitably chaotic.

"So, you're alive after all," Yellow said breathlessly, running to the truck and passing her valises up to Scott.

"Never underestimate the best," Rand said, full of importance.

Yellow gave Rand the once-over and smiled bemusedly. "Why are you so wet?"

"Come on, get in," Rook broke in. "It'll be your bedtime story."

Yellow climbed up into the back of the truck, already pulling off the clothes that separated her from Lancer. Rand threw himself in and unfurled the rear canvas drape. Annie ran around to the passenger seat and settled herself, while a smiling Lunk did the same behind the wheel. He knew how ridiculous he looked in the smaller man's uniform and helmet and couldn't keep from laughing.

A moment later the truck was screeching away from the stage entrance, just short of a crowd of fans who had found their way back there. Woods stood pleased in the doorway, silently wishing Yellow and her friends a smooth getaway.

Back outside the dressing-room door, Colonel Briggs was glancing impatiently at his watch and complaining under his breath about how much time women required to change outfits. He contemplated walking in on Yellow, wondering if he would be able to catch her at a vulnerable moment. The thought was blossoming into a Technicolor fantasy when one of his guards ran up to him and saluted.

"There's been a break-in at the facility," the staffer reported in a rush. "Thirty-eight cases of Protoculture are missing."

The colonel's mouth fell open. "B-but . . . *how*?"

"They used some kind of scramblers to disrupt the surveillance cameras and apparently lowered themselves into the storage room from one of the overhead maintenance corridors."

Briggs grabbed the man by the lapels and pulled him close. "How could they get through the towers? Were all vehicles searched?"

"Yes, chief, everyone was searched," the man managed to get out. "They must have found another way out."

The colonel shook the man, took a few steps, then whirled on him again. "Search the city! Set up roadblocks! I want them found—*alive*!"

The staffer saluted. "We'll do what we can. But most of our units are still working crowd control outside."

"Forget the crowds!" Briggs barked. "Get every man on it."

The city's streets were soon filled with police vans —sirens hooting, tearing around corners in search of a team of sneak thieves. But by this time, Lunk was edging the van out of town, way ahead of the roadblocks the colonel's currently understaffed security force were attempting to set up at all possible points of egress.

The colonel's own van screeched to a halt in a cobblestone square, where it rendezvoused with three others that were returning from various checkpoints. Briggs leapt out and approached one of his lieutenants, demanding all pertinent information.

"And don't tell me they've disappeared," he warned the already shaking staffer.

"We have reason to believe that they made their getaway in a police van," the lieutenant updated. "So we're in the process of having our men check each van they come across to ascertain the identity of those inside."

"Good," the colonel said haltingly. Then: "You mean to tell me that your men are out there *searching each other*?!" He was about to say more, when he heard a small crash behind him, as if something had fallen from a rooftop. Turning, Briggs saw a cluster of red, yellow, and green balloons weighted down by something he couldn't make out until he had taken three steps toward it.

"Protoculture canisters!" he exclaimed, kneeling beside the helium balloons and their precious cargo. He looked up and saw scores more drifting high over the city on a northeast wind. "Gather up all those balloons," he ordered the lieutenant. "Shoot them down if you have to!...And bring me that *singer*," he hastened to add, thinking back to the concert and its colorful finale...

Briggs was hurrying back to his van when a vehicle from the facility pulled alongside him.

"Have you found them?" he asked eagerly.

"No," the driver answered. "But the Invid Intercessors have arrived at the facility...And they wanna speak to you...."

The getaway truck and the rigged balloon clusters arrived at the transmitter site at the same time, a clearing in the woods that fringed the northeastern outskirts of

Norristown. The team hopped out and began gathering up the canisters. Rook and Lancer were heading for the Cyclones when they heard Annie yell and saw her point to the sky.

"Invid!"

There were five Troopers, coming in fast from the southwest but still several miles off. Scott told everyone to grab whatever canister packs they could carry and run for the mecha. Lancer, already suited up in battle armor, headed directly for one of the Cyclones and inserted a fresh canister into the cylinderlike fuel cell below the mecha's engine. He straddled the cycle and activated the ignition, watching with delight as the power displays came to life, glowing with an unprecedented brightness. Nearby, Scott was in the cockpit of the Veritech, Lunk attending to the refueling.

Rook was preparing to power up her red Cyclone when she saw Lancer lift off and reconfigure to Battle Armor mode. Beside her, Rand was strapping on the last of his Cyclone armor.

"Rand, did you remember to put in a fresh canister?" she asked him, certain he had forgotten.

"Oh, right," he returned, and stooped to insert the fresh pack.

"Dimwit," Rook scolded him as she roared off, going to Battle Armor mode a moment later. Rand followed her up and through to reconfiguration, and the two of them streaked off to assist Lancer, who was going head to head with two Invid Troopers.

Lancer had coaxed the Troopers to the ground and was executing leaps to avoid pincer swipes. Frustrated now, one of the creatures was ready to bring its shoulder cannons into play.

Lancer stepped back when he saw the muzzles begin to glow; Rook and Rand had set down behind him, and the three of them felt the blast of the first charge.

"Let's not push our luck until the Alpha arrives," Lancer said over the Cyclone's tactical net.

The two Troopers took to the air, then swooped down for strafing runs. But Rand had tailed one of them and launched shoulder-tubed Scorpions before the Invid could fire. The Trooper took two missiles to the face and went down, leaking a thick green fluid.

Rook took out a second creature; Lancer dispatched a third that was giving Rand a hard time, bringing the odds more to everyone's liking by the time Scott got the Veritech up.

The two remaining Troopers kept to the ground, dishing out annihilation discs against the incoming Alpha, but Scott flew undaunted into the fire, loosing the VT's own brand of vengeful energy. With a last-minute leap, one of the Invid narrowly escaped the Alpha's angry red-tipped missiles, but the second stood its ground and suffered for it.

Scott continued his power dive against the fifth and final Invid now; it had put down again, emptying its up-turned cannons against him. Scott dropped through the annihilation discs like some sort of slalom flyer, getting off one shot before pulling out of his dive. But that one connected, impacting the Trooper's midsection and splitting it in half.

Scott banked hard at the top of his climb and fell away toward Norristown and the enormous buttes which overshadowed the city. Down below he could discern a long line of police vehicles speeding from the city toward the team's somewhat ravaged forest clearing.

Hearing Scott's warning over the tac net, Rand, Rook, and Lancer landed their mecha and reconfigured to Cyclone mode. Annie and Lunk were running around gathering up late-arrival balloonloads of Protoculture canisters. They took to the police van at Scott's amplified insistence and sped off following the Cyclones' lead, the setting sun huge and blood-red at their backs.

> *Rook's hometown [Trenchtown, formerly Cavern City] typified an offbeat trend in city planning that was popular between the [First and Second Robotech] Wars. This plan, called the Obscuro Movement, was formed as a reaction to threats of invasion, real and imaginary, by Zentraedi, Tirolian Masters, Invid, or any of a number of self-styled conquerors and terrestrial invaders. Cities were constructed in the most unlikely places—on the tops of mesas, the bottom of ravines, the heart of darkness—anywhere deemed unassailable by founders and would-be leaders.*

> "Southlands," *History of the Third Robotech War*, Vol. XXII

RAND'S JOURNAL PICKS UP THE STORY:

"We had a good enough jump on Norristown's police force to lose them without too much hassle. But just to make sure, Scott saw to it that our escape route was wiped out behind us with a few well-placed missiles from the Alpha. Chances are that most of the vans turned tail as soon as they caught sight of the Veritech anyway. We could only guess what the Invid decided to extract in the way of retribution; at the very least some heads were going to roll.

"We were all feeling great. The Cyclones practically had to be reigned in, thanks to the fresh infusion of 'Culture. Scott thought that the Invid-manufactured batch was more powerful than the 'Culture Earth mecha had been operating on during the last twenty years. The only thing that held us back was the police

van we had commandeered. But it seemed a wiser idea
to accept the thing's limitations rather than carry Lunk
and Annie on the Cyclones or in the fighter. It continued to puzzle us why the Invid didn't simply overwhelm us with Troopers; with three Cycs running at
high speed, it should have been easy enough to track
us down. But Scott explained that they had demonstrated the same sort of tactical shortcomings in previous encounters. I was always trying to press him to
elaborate, but he was reticent to talk about Tirol and
the other worlds he had seen.

"We traveled north for two days almost without
letup, using the scrip Woods had given Lancer to
barter supplies and bedrolls in some of the settlements
we passed through. The terrain was arid and rugged,
characterized by buttes and tors and mesas similar to
those around Norristown but softened by small sky-
blue lakes and patches of hardwood forest. We made
our first real camp alongside one of these cold water
lakes. We had come across a dozen wild cattle earlier
on and shot one for provisions, so we were eating well
and getting good rest in the sleeping bags. Scott ran us
through a kind of mutual-appreciation debriefing on the
Norristown raid. More and more we were beginning to
feel like an actual team and not just six individuals on
the run.

"I tried to insist that we make camp in the woods,
but everyone else was intent on enjoying the sunlight
at the edge of the lake. I put Annie in charge of gathering firewood, and she kept coming in with nearly petrified pieces of hardwood. (Not that we really even
needed the fire—I was doing most of the cooking over
a propane stove anyway—but a fire was their idea of
camping out, and I wasn't into spoiling anyone's fun.)
Lunk whittled when he wasn't going over the Cyclone
and VT systems. Scott cleaned and maintained the

ordnance. Lancer was finding it easier and easier to relax around us, and he would often fall quite naturally into a kind of midway mode that was part Lancer the freedom fighter and part Yellow Dancer. He had fashioned a shower for himself by punching a series of holes in one of our old cook pots. He would bring in water heated on the fire and pour this into the holed pot he had fastened to an overhead branch. Lunk got a big charge out of this and once tried to interrupt Lancer while he was showering. It was a pretty comical exchange that ended with Lancer calling Lunk "a mindless brute," and Lunk amazed that Lancer of all people should be modest.

"Rook was the only one keeping to herself. I would see her standing alone by the lake, absently skimming stones across the surface. It was obvious that she had something disturbing on her mind, but she didn't want to share it with the rest of us. Scott also sensed it. I have since learned what the brooding was all about, but back then all I could sense was Rook's uneasiness and an inexplicable feeling of helplessness. The only time the team discussed it was after she had turned on Annie, who was only trying to entice her to join us around the fire.

"'What d'ya think's wrong with her?' Lunk asked the rest of us.

"'Women's mood changes are unpredictable,' Lancer said knowledgeably in Yellow's voice. He had just stepped from the shower and was wearing a long yellow terry robe and had his hair up under a towel wrapped turban-style around his head.

"'Just leave her alone,' I suggested. 'She'll come out of it.' But Scott took issue with me.

"'No. This is different.'

"'Let it go,' I started to say, but Scott was already on his feet and off to seek her out. I felt compelled to tag along at a discreet distance, probably because I was afraid of Scott's scoring points where I couldn't.

"Rook was standing near the lake. She didn't even respond when Scott called her; I saw him give a small shrug and pull out that holo-locket he wore around his neck—the one Marlene gave him shortly before she went down with her ship. I wasn't sure just what he was thinking, but what bothered me most was the idea that Rook's moodiness was going to have a contagious effect on the team.

"In a moment, however, we all had bigger problems to deal with.

"I saw Scott and Rook turn at the same moment to stare at something off in the distance, so I stepped out from cover to see what was going on and heard the tell-tale approach of an Invid ship even before I saw the thing appear from behind one of the buttes. It was a large patrol ship, a rust-brown number boasting twice the fire-power of a Trooper. I ran back to the fire and started stomping it out, while Scott and the others headed for the woods. The Invids hadn't spotted us, and it wasn't likely that a simple campfire was going to bring it down, but for all we knew the patrol ships had now been ordered to incinerate anything that moved. Rook's Cyclone was my main concern; she had thoughtlessly left it by the lake in plain view.

"The patrol ship swept along the shore directly over our smoldering campfire and headed out toward the lake, but suddenly it swung about, its optic sensor scanning the woods. I voiced a silent prayer that the thing wouldn't spot us, and what seemed an eternity later, the Invid blasted up and away from our small piece of tranquillity.

"'Close one,' I said when the thing had disappeared. 'But it looks like we're safe for the moment.'

"'Uh uh,' Scott said worriedly, shaking his head.

'We've got to assume they found us.' He saw the cha-
grined looked on my face and hastened to add: 'It might
have gone for reinforcements—we'd be foolish to remain here any longer.'

"Lunk was taking stock of our surroundings. 'Bad
place to get caught if they mean business. I'm for splitting.'

"'Then let's move it,' Scott said.

"I knelt down by the remains of our fire and poked at
the coals. 'So much for dinner...'

"Lancer sauntered by me, dangling an outstretched
limp wrist from the robe's broad sleeve and feigning a
bored yawn. 'Well, it didn't look very appetizing anyway,' he minced.

"Movement was likely to make matters worse, but
there was high ground nearby that provided substantially more in the way of cover. We rode out most of
the afternoon looking over our shoulders and waiting
for Scott's warnings over the tac net, but no Invid appeared. It was beginning to look as though we hadn't
been seen after all, but no one was making an issue of
having abandoned our campsite. The air in the highlands was invigorating, and we found an expanse of
conifer forest to call home for the night. Even Lancer
had to admit that the steaks were tasty, and Rook, who
had been sullen and lone-riding all day, seemed to be
coming around some.

"I woke up sometime during the night and noticed
that Rook wasn't in her bag. I took a quick look around,
counting heads and quickly realizing that Scott had the
watch. (Actually, it turned out that he wasn't on watch at
all, but I imagined him absent, once again falling victim
to a kind of irrational jealousy.) I unzippered myself from
the bag, egged on by thoughts of Rook and Scott cozying
it up somewhere in the woods. *Just lean on my shoulder
and tell me all about it, Rook,* I could almost hear Scott

saying, when it was *my* shoulder she should have been leaning on!

"The moon was full and low in the west, casting long shadows across ground cushioned with pine needles. To a sound track of insect songs, I stole silently through the trees and spied Rook, alone, in a clearing dominated by a tall oak. Her Cyclone was parked nearby; obviously she had wheeled it away from the pack while the rest of us slept. She seemed to be staring transfixed at something carved into the trunk, but I was too far back to make out what it was.

"I heard her say, 'Why—why did it happen?' and the next thing I knew she was hopping onto the Cyclone and moving off. I ran after her and thought about calling her. The word or name *ROMY* was carved into the tree trunk. It didn't mean anything to me, but it had obviously touched off something in Rook. I went back for my Cyclone and pushed it a good hundred yards from the woods before starting it up and going after her.

"It wasn't hard to follow her trail, and there was enough ambient moonlight for me to tail her without bringing up the Cyclone's headlamp. Straight off, it was apparent that she knew where she was going: She cut through the woods in the direction of the main road, headed north for several miles, then turned east along a rutted track that coursed over a barren, seemingly endless stretch of land. She was perhaps a half a mile ahead of me when I saw her suddenly veer off sharply to the right for no apparent reason. Fortunately, I thought to cut my speed some, because just short of the spot where she had made her turn I realized that the land dropped steeply away. I braked and threw the Cyclone into a sharp turn that brought me close to the edge of a narrow chasm, scarcely the width of a city block. In the darkness below I could discern two rows of ruined buildings backed against the canyon's walls, almost as tall as the chasm was deep and facing each other across a single potholed street. Still a good distance ahead of me, Rook was disappearing into a kind of open-faced bunker that projected from the land as though it were a natural outcropping. Nearby were the tops of two massive circular shafts I guessed were exhaust ports for the city below.

"I twisted the Cyclone's throttle and accelerated into the unlit tunnel, not knowing what to expect."

"The city was dark and deserted-looking, claustrophobic due to the closeness of the canyon walls but threatening in a way that had nothing to do with the uniqueness of its location. Rook was still unaware of my presence. She had parked her Cyclone halfway along the street, dismounted, and was now peering into the permaplas window of a lighted and apparently occupied ground-floor apartment. I think I came close to abandoning my little game just then; the sight of Rook eavesdropping on someone called into question my own position. But I decided to hang in, rationalizing that I was simply keeping an eye out in case anyone came wandering in on Rook's scene. Again, I was too far away to make out exactly what was going on: I heard Rook say, 'Romy,' as a man in a yellow shirt passed by the window. That at least explained the tree trunk carving and Rook's knowledge of the area. She had been here before; perhaps was native to the place. A moment later I heard Rook's sharp intake of breath. She had turned away from the window as if in disbelief.

"'My sister Lilly?' she asked softly.

"Rook took a few backward steps, straddled the Cyclone, and roared off. I stomped my mecha into gear and followed. I had all intentions of catching up to her now and having a heart-to-heart, but suddenly there were three more vehicles in the street, tearing out in front of Rook from an alleyway that ended at the canyon wall. They were solid-hubbed Harley choppers with twin front headlights, dressed down for rough and ready street riding. The riders were of the same ilk—Mohawked, shaved-skulled, maniacal. They were chasing down two young women, taunting, gesturing, and otherwise cat-and-mousing them. I saw the Mohawked rider come alongside and douse them with beer from the bottle he was carrying. Then, when one of the women fell—a cute brunette in knee boots and a full skirt—the riders began to circle her, revving their bikes and promising a wide variety of injustices. The only helmeted rider had taken hold of the second woman and was grabbing what he could, heedless of the fury of her fists.

"Rook, meanwhile, had edged her bike up to the perimeter of the riders' circle; now, as they were making grabs for the downed girl, she switched on the Cyclone's headlight and brought it to bear on the group. Stunned, the riders brought hands up to shield their eyes.

"'You Snakes haven't changed a bit,' Rook growled. She turned the front wheel aside so the bikers could get a look at the hand blaster she had trained on them. 'Well, now don't tell me you've forgotten my face . . .'

"The Mohawked rider, who I now noticed had a blue heart tattooed on his left arm, squinted and scowled. 'Why, it's Rook!'

"The two women broke free of their pursuers and ran to stand by Rook's Cyclone, one of them crying hysterically.

"'I suppose you degenerates have overrun the whole place since I've been gone,' Rook continued.

"The outlaw riders looked at one another and said nothing. Finally, they laughed and took off, warning Rook that she had made a big mistake in coming back.

"'Skull's right,' I heard one of the women say to Rook. 'You better split. The wars aren't like before. The Red Snakes have five times as many members now.'

"'Five times?...Is Romy doing anything about it? Are the Blue Angels still around?'

"'Broken up,' the other woman said between sobs. 'They've fallen apart. Romy spends all his time with...'

"'Say it, Sue—I already know.'

"'Your sister,' Sue said, lowering her head. 'He can't fight them alone. No one can.'"

"The canyon widened some at its eastern end, where there was a surprisingly well kept park. Rook spent the rest of the night there—what little there was left of it—still unaware that I wasn't fifty feet away from her. In the morning a small van drove into the park; a nondescript-looking guy and a girl who couldn't have been more than fifteen stepped out, opened up the back, and, for an hour or so, sold and refilled canisters of propane gas for what appeared to be steady customers. Rook watched for some time without revealing herself, until the last customer had been served and the duo was getting ready to pack up and leave. Of course it occurred to me that these two might be Romy and Rook's sister, Lilly, but I had no way of being sure until Rook opened her mouth.

"On foot, she had moved her Cyclone to the top of a wide stone staircase that overlooked the couple's business area and signaled her presence by starting up the mecha. The man looked up at the sound and said, 'Who the heck...?' then, 'Rook!' full of excitement.

"But she returned a cold sneer. 'Romy, how the heck could you just let the Snakes take control of this place?' she demanded.

"'Welcome back,' Romy said, nonplussed.

"'Sue tells me there's five times as many of them as there used to be.'

"'I worried about you, Rook.'

"'Liar!' she shot back. 'I'll bet you were *real* worried about me when Atilla and his Snakes were stomping the hell out of me in a rumble you and the rest of the Angels never attended!'

"'Rook—'

"'How could you have done that to me, Romy?' Rook said, sobbing now. 'If you only knew what they did to me...there was no way I could stay here after that.'

"While all this was going on, I saw the girl walk out from behind the van, her hand to her mouth in a startled gesture. Now she spoke to Rook through sobs of her own.

"'You don't understand—it wasn't like that at all!' she began.

Rook's younger sister! I thought. She bore almost no resemblance to her blond sibling. Lilly was raven-haired and petite, dressed in a pleated white skirt and a simple burgundy-colored sweater.

"'Romy didn't run away—he tried to help you, but he was ambushed by the Red Snakes. They beat him up so bad, he couldn't walk for a month. It was the Snakes' plan all along to make it seem like Romy deserted you. They knew you would leave the Angels, and without you, the Angels were nothing. So when you left, everything fell apart.'

"Rook wore a confused look now.

"'That's enough,' Romy was telling Lilly.

"'Please don't blame him,' said Lilly. 'He searched all over for you.'

"Rook looked from one to the other, former lover to sister.

"'Why should I believe you?' she asked. '*Either* of you!'

"Lilly took a step closer. 'Besides, you can't expect Romy to take on the Snakes alone.' She motioned to the delivery van and to Romy, who was tight-lipped and, I think, embarrassed by the scene. 'We're trying to build a life for ourselves, Rook. Romy isn't going to do the stupid things he used to do. He's . . . he's grown up.'

"I thought Rook was going to take offense at the remark, but she didn't. In fact, I could see that she was no longer angry.

"'Sure the Snakes are an evil bunch,' Lilly continued. 'But if you don't give them a *reason* to fight, they mind their own turf. Romy's not holding back because he's a coward, but for the good of *everyone*.'

"Rook smiled. 'So you're holding back, are you, Romy?'

"I'm not sure just what was on Rook's mind—maybe the idea that Romy was also holding back the affection he still had for her. In any case, Lilly answered yes for him, and Rook said that she was beginning to understand. 'I guess it took a bookworm to make him see the light,' she directed at Lilly.

"Lilly was about to say something, when one of the girls Rook had rescued appeared at the top of the staircase. Sue, if I recall.

"'You've got to run for it, Rook!' she said, out of breath. 'The Red Snakes are all over Trenchtown looking for you!'

"I saw Rook grin. 'Great!' she said, engaging the Cyclone. She asked Romy if the Snakes still hung out at something she named 'Highways.' Romy nodded warily. 'Rook, you're not thinking of—'

" 'It's what I've been waiting for,' she told him. *'Revenge!'*

"She stomped the Cyclone into gear and raced off, leaving all of us wondering if we would ever see her again."

CHAPTER
ELEVEN

"No one can dispute the accomplishment. The very fact that they undertook the journey [to Reflex Point] is in and of itself a measure of their courage and commitment; the very fact that they journeyed so far through such hostile territory a testament to their skills. But someone needs to point out the troubles the journey stirred up for those along the way. Can anyone name one Southlands settlement that survived their [the Bernard team's] wake?"

Breetai Tul, as quoted in Zeus Bellow, *The Road to Reflex Point*

"**I** DECIDED TO SHOW MYSELF AFTER ROOK SPLIT. I brought the Cyclone to life and pulled out from my place of concealment in the bushes, surprising the hell out of Romy and Lilly. I popped a small wheelie for effect and screeched to a halt, allowing the tail end to slide around to where Romy stood with his mouth half-open.

"'Well, don't just stand there waiting for flies to land,' I said to him. 'Hop on and let's give her some backup support.'

"Romy flashed Lilly a look that communicated several dozen things at once and climbed on. I could tell that Lilly wanted to hold him back, but she knew better than to try. Romy had to get this out of his system for his sake as well as Rook's. I mean, *nobody* likes to be thought of as a Khyron, even if it was all a misunderstanding.

"Cavalierly, I nodded to Lilly and powered the Cyclone up the staircase, getting a rise out of the fact that Romy was white-knuckling the seat grips all the while. I have to admit that I liked impressing would-be motorcycle toughs like Romy; they were an all too frequently encountered breed in the wastes, and I was bored to tears by them.

"Once up top, I asked Romy about this 'Highways' place Rook had mentioned; he shouted directions into my ear, and I wristed the Cyc's throttle, letting it open up along the undamaged sections of roadway that led back to the narrow heart of the city.

"It must have been about this time that the three Invid paid a call on Scott and the others. I had been wondering what they had made of our disappearance from camp. Perhaps they figured we had run off together or just decided that individually we had had enough of Scott's search for Reflex Point. As it came out later, Annie was all for going out to look for us, but Scott felt differently. 'I prefer not to meddle in people's private affairs,' is how Annie told me he had put it. But I guessed correctly that they had opted to hang in for another day, thinking that we would find our way back to them. There was a good chance they would have literally passed right over Trenchtown on their way north, but strangely enough, Scott found his own way to the city in the canyon—with a little help from the Invid, that is.

"They came swooping down on the camp early in the morning, laying waste to that beautiful patch of forest. Whoever was in charge had elected to send in the big guns again: combat ships like the one we had seen after our run-in with the black bear. The team had no chance to hit back, only take cover and keep their heads down. The other thing I learned afterward was that neither the Alpha nor Lancer's Cyclone was activated or otherwise engaged before the attack, which suggested that the combat units had a means of zeroing in on Protoculture even when it wasn't being tapped for energy.

"Scott did manage to make it to the Alpha, though. He brought up the VT's power and launched before the Invid reduced the camp to a fiery ruin, but apparently that was only the first of his woes. The three aliens formed up on his tail and went after him with an unprecedented fury, layering the zone above the forest with unforgiving streams of annihilation discs. When Scott glimpsed Trenchtown's canyon, he saw his out; he led the Invid down into the seemingly deserted city, intent on battling them there.

"Closing on Highways, I heard what I then thought was thunder but later learned were the detonations of the eight heat-seekers Scott had dumped on one of the Invid ships.

"Highways turned out to be the headquarters of the Red Snakes. It was on the roof of a skeletal fifteen-story building, reached by a series of jerry-rigged ramps that connected it with an adjacent (and equally devastated) ten-story parking garage. Romy and I arrived a few moments after Rook, who was braving it out on her own against more than a dozen outlaw bikers. At the center of the group stood the Snakes' main man, a mean-looking hulk named Atilla. He must have stood six six and weighed in at two eighty, most of which was pure muscle. He had a pot, like most of these rogue leaders do, and affected a getup that was part street, part costume, including armless goggles no larger than bottlecaps he had had stitched to his eye sockets, black leather wristbands, shin guards and knee pads fashioned to resemble poised cobras, and a kind of pointed, twin-horned Vikinglike helmet and cowl combination. There was a large S emblazoned on the front of his sleeveless T-shirt, and he had a face not even a mother could love, with a nose that was wide and flattened from countless breaks.

"'I've gotta admit it, Rook,' he was saying as we pulled up. 'You got a lotta guts. It's just too bad you ain't got the brains that go along with it.'

"At that, Atilla gestured to his assembled pack, and they responded with the appropriate litany of hoots and hollers. The implication was clear enough: Rook was about to receive a stomping that would make the first seem like a love fest.

"'I didn't think you had it in you, Rook,' Atilla added.

"But if Rook was at all worried at that moment, she had me fooled. Somewhere along the way she had suited herself up in Cyclone battle armor. But even so, she looked vulnerable, straddling her bike, glaring right back at them, her blond hair mussed by the wind.

"'I'd say *you're* the one who's the coward. Snake Eyes,' she fired back. 'You're nothing without this army of slugs you call a tribe.'

"During this little exchange we were parked on the remains of a roof balcony, above and behind Rook. Romy was eager to go down to her, but I told him to hang back a moment more, at least until the rules were laid down.

"'You're Mr. Mean,' Rook was saying, 'only because you've got the odds on your side, and not one of these rogues has the balls to challenge your position. But I think you're hollow to the core, and I came back here to tell you that.'

"This was the same Rook I had fallen in love with that day in Pops's biker bar . . . And unless Atilla was a lot quicker than the scuz she had seen to there, he was soon to be one sorry rogue, and I knew it.

"To Rook's taunts, Atilla returned something befitting his intellect—something like: 'Oh yeah? Prove it!'—before she got down to the challenge.

"'Just you and me,' she told him. 'One on one, right here in front of all your boys. And I'll even make it easy for you. We won't even fight; we'll just have a chicken race.'

"'A race?' Atilla roared laughingly. 'I thought we were gonna have some fun.'

"Rook grinned and said, 'The beam,' pointing to something off to her left.

"This brought a real chorus of cheers from the spectators. I didn't understand what she was talking about until Romy showed me what the beam was. It was either the remains of a bridge that had once linked Highways with the building across the street or a collapsed structural member from one of the two buildings. In any case, it was no more than foot wide and now ran roof to roof more than one hundred and fifty feet above the city's main street. But that wasn't all: The beam was not entirely straight. Midway along was a bend and a slight dip—from who knew what—to test the mettle of any rider. Reaching the beam first was only part of the game; reaching the other roof was something else again. It was obvious from everyone's reactions that the beam was one of Trenchtown's rites of passage, an initiation that had certainly ended in more than one death.

"While I was taking all of this in, Romy was dismounting from the Cyclone. 'We can't let her go through with this,' he told me, showing an intense anger that almost led me to reevaluate my initial impression of him.

"Atilla, meanwhile, was doing his best to back away from the challenge without losing face. He pointed out to his assembled buddies that what he had envisioned was a genuine physical mix-up with Rook—winner taking all, so to speak—and they were buying it.

"'Let's pluck this chicken *now*!' he shouted, leering at Rook.

"I could understand his misgivings, but if I were him I would have been pointing out the fact that Rook's Cyclone was not only faster than his old Kamikaze but capable of reconfiguring and actually *flying* across to the opposite roof should Rook misjudge the beam itself. Well, perhaps he had never seen a Cyclone before, I thought.

"Romy and I were standing side by side on the roof balcony now. Below, Atilla and his Huns were beginning to take a fancy to the idea of jumping Rook's bones, so I decided it was time for us to show our colors, pulled out the hand H–90, and fired off a quick vertical burst for the boys that stopped them dead in their tracks.

"'Stay where you are!' I warned them, feeling a little like Atilla with the blaster backing up my threats. 'The two of them fight it out alone, just like the lady says.' Rook was more surprised by my sudden appearance than any of them. I figured that by backing her I was doing a little better than Romy, who was now urging her to give up the idea. His presence elicited as many comments from the Snakes as Rook's idea of riding the beam had. It seemed that the former leader of the Blue Angels was not very well thought of in the Snakes' side of town.

"'Don't worry, Romy, I won't blow it,' Rook was saying, not entirely successful at hiding her concern. 'Let's just say my riding skills have improved a lot.' She looked hard at Romy and thanked him for standing by her. 'Coming back here was a good thing,' she said, smiling. 'I think it cleared my head of a lot of bad memories. More than you'll ever know...'

"'Rook,' Romy started to say.

"'I'm counting on you to take care of Lilly,' Rook added, activating the Cyc.

"I walked down the stairs and casually aimed the blaster in Atilla's direction. 'You gonna run this race, or what?' I asked him, unsure about my next move should he refuse.

"The Snakes threw words of encouragement to their leader, and Atilla stepped forward to accept the challenge. Romy ceremoniously handed Rook her helmet, and some of the Snakes ran to the edge of the roof for a better view of the race.

"Things got under way without the preliminaries and fanfare that usually characterize such events; Rook and Atilla positioned their machines on either side of a flag bearer, maybe a hundred feet from the beam. The starter, a shaved-skull Snake in T-shirt and fatigues, jumped up and brought the flag down with a shout. The two machines patched out and headed for the beam. Again, I thought I heard distant thunder but made nothing of it.

"I had noticed Atilla give the red Cyc a dismissive once-over before the flag dropped and figured he would be in for a surprise. But I was the one surprised: The old Kami was a real sleeper and must have concealed a turbocharger somewhere within its works, because Atilla beat Rook off the line and stayed a half length ahead of her for the first fifty feet. In fact, I'm pretty sure Snake Eyes would have hit the beam neck and neck with Rook if fear hadn't revealed his own true colors.

"Just shy of the beam he glanced over at Rook, saw that she wasn't about to yield an inch, and bailed out, bouncing and sliding all the way, his cycle plummeting over the edge and exploding when it hit the street.

"Rook rode the beam like a pro. She told me later that at no time did she even consider using the mecha's capabilities to save herself from wiping out. I ran forward to the edge of the roof, along with everyone else who was applauding her feat, including more than a few Snakes. The loyal members of the gang were ministering to their bruised and road-rashed leader, who knew, I think, that many more challenges would soon be coming his way.

"Rook had raised the faceshield of the helmet and was waving back to us when I realized that that distant thunder was no longer either distant or thunder. And an instant later, we saw Scott streak overhead in the Alpha, pursued by two Invid combat ships. The Snakes began to freak and scatter for cover. I turned and heard one of them shout: 'They found out about the Protoculture I stole! They're gonna blow us apart!'

"I looked back at Rook in time to see her spin the Cyc through a 360, accelerate along the roof, and launch herself into Battle Armor mode. This was lost on most of the Snakes, but I noticed Atilla staring at the transformed Cyclone like he had just witnessed some kind of miracle.

"Rook put down on a roof a few blocks down the canyon, raised the mecha's cannon, and took out one of the ships. Scott, at the same time, had thrown the VT into a booster climb and was now falling back down upon the second, unleashing a rain of six missiles to deal with the thing. The Invid dropped itself to street level, dodging as best it could, but ultimately took one of the heat-seekers full force and spun out of control, impaling itself on a spiked piece of construction infrastructure. You would have thought Rook and Scott had planned it that way."

"After the action died down, I used the Cyc's tac net to notify Scott that his errant troops would be home soon; we made plans to rendezvous on the north road.

"I didn't have any doubts about Rook's bidding a swift good-bye to Trenchtown, even though some wrongs had now been redressed and some old worries laid to rest. But I knew also that there was still a scene that had to be played out with Romy, and I was anxious to see it.

"The four of us—me, Rook, Romy, and Lilly—got together for eats at his place. Small talk for the most part; Romy made no mention of Rook's staying on in

Trenchtown, and we made no mention of Reflex Point, Lancer, or the others.

"'Rook, it's been so good seeing you again,' Lilly said as we were preparing to shove off. 'I just can't tell you ...If it hadn't been for your courage, the Snakes would still be ruling this city...' She started getting weepy about then, and it made Rook angry.

"'What on Earth are you crying about?' Rook said, putting her hands on the smaller woman's shoulders. When Lilly exchanged looks with Romy, Rook caught on and lightened up. 'Hey, don't worry about me,' she told Lilly. 'There's a person in my life now who means a lot to me...'

"I was leaning against the building with my hands behind my head when she suddenly turned to me. 'Rand,' she said, leadingly and with a sweetness that didn't fit her. She came over and took hold of my arm, finding a pressure point in my wrist at the same time. 'Come on, give me a kiss like you always do.' Under her breath, she told me to pretend to be her honey or else. 'Kiss me on the cheek—and make it look good,' she added.

"Romy and Lilly were watching with a mixture of bemusement and anticipation, and Rook was standing there, offering me her left cheek like she was my aunt or something, so I did what I had to do to make it look good! I took hold of her upper arms and pulled her to me before she even had a chance to close her mouth. I didn't hold her long, and she kept her eyes wide for the duration, not returning the favor, but it was long enough to bring a scarlet blush to her cheeks.

"'Rook is my baby and always will be,' I told Romy over Rook's shoulder, putting some bass in my voice to keep from laughing. 'Come on, honey. Let's get back to the ranch,' I said as I mounted my Cyc.

"Rook climbed on her mecha without looking at me. Lilly started to say something, but Rook just said good-bye and motored off. I did the same, leaving Romy and Lilly in the street, his arm draped over her narrow shoulders.

"When I came alongside Rook, she flashed me the anger she didn't want to show in front of her sister, and I decided to have some fun with it. 'You kiss pretty well for such a tough gal,' I ribbed her.

"'That was supposed to be the *cheek*, dirtbag.'

"'Jeez, I'm sorry...I must have misunderstood or something...'

"'Pea brain! Degenerate!'

"I laughed, then tried to switch tracks. 'What about your folks, Rook?' I asked her. 'Are they still living in this hole?' I was sincere about it; Rook's past was my way into her present.

"But she just shook her head and made for the conduit, not bothering to look behind."

CHAPTER

TWELVE

> *The book Lunk had promised to deliver was called In-*
> *herit the Stars, a piece of speculative fiction written by the*
> *noted twentieth-century British author and inventor James P.*
> *Hogan and first published in 1977. It was the first in a series*
> *of novels that dealt with humankind's contact with an alien*
> *race indigenous to Ganymede (the Ganymeans), who in*
> *many ways were the antithesis of the Opteran Invid.*

> Footnote in Xandu Reem, *A Stranger at Home: A*
> *Biography of Scott Bernard*

WHEN THEY WERE REUNITED AND ON THE ROAD
north once again, it was business as usual. Four hundred
miles north of Trenchtown the team was attacked by five
Invid Troopers, which they disposed of almost without
breaking stride. Scott took out the first two from the
Alpha and left the rest of the work to the three Cyclones,
piloted by Rook, Rand, and Lancer, who had by now
become a finely honed unit. There had been no signs of
Pincer ships for several days, and though the Troopers
were bothersome, they posed no real threat provided
that each one glimpsed was accounted for on the battlefield.

The desert terrain helped them to easily spot the
Troopers. They had left the highlands behind. Gone were
the forests and misshapen buttes of those plateaus, as
well as the cool air and sparkling rivers they had come to

take for granted. But this was not true desert, waterless and unforgiving, but rather a broad expanse of arid lowland, with solitary flat-topped mesas to break the monotony of the horizon and enough spring-fed lakes to support a wide assortment of settlements.

Lunk, demanding equal-time benefits after Rook's "dalliance in the Trench"—Rand's words—was calling the shots on the latest detour along the way. The group was headed toward a town called Roca Negra, sixty miles west of the north road and said to be a community that had managed to retain an old-world charm.

The team had an overview of the place now from the tableland a few miles east. Roca Negra looked neat and compact, enlivened by groupings of cottonwood and eucalyptus trees, and lent a certain drama by the mesa and rounded peaks that all but overshadowed it. Scott made a pass over the town in the Alpha, the VT's deltalike shadow paralleling the course of the main road, and reported his sightings. There was a large circular fountain and plaza central to the town, with an assortment of rustic-style buildings grouped around it and the few streets that radiated out from the hub like the spokes of a wheel. Scott could make out tile roofs and cobblestone streets, a church steeple, and a number of people, some of whom were staring up at the Veritech, while others ran off to inform the rest of the townsfolk.

Lunk smiled at the thought of the place and urged the van along with added throttle. Annie was next to him in the shotgun seat. It was the same police van they had commandeered in Norristown, but Lunk had removed the canvas top and given the thing an olive-drab once-over in memory of the beloved APC he had had blown out from under him in the highlands. Lancer, Rook, and Rand flanked the truck on their Cyclones.

"I sure hope we'll be able to get some food in this town," Annie said after Scott's message. "I'm starved!"

Lunk flashed her a bright-eyed smile and told her not to worry, then turned to Rand, who had come alongside on the driver's side of the van.

"What's so special 'bout this place?" Rand shouted into the wind. "You been here before?"

Lunk shook his head, maintaining the smile.

"Then why are we stopping here?" Annie demanded, joining in.

Lunk reached back and pulled a worn paperback book from the rear pocket of his fatigues, holding it out the window for Rand's inspection.

"To make good a promise I made to a friend a year ago," Lunk said to both of them. "To deliver this book."

Rand gazed at the thing but couldn't make out much, except that it was aged, yellowed, dog-eared, and smudged. Someone had thought to wrap the book in protective plastic, but too late to preserve the cover illustration.

"What sort of book is it?" Rand asked.

Lunk pulled the book in and regarded it. "I really don't know—I haven't read it. But it was important enough to my buddy for him to ask me to bring it to his father if I ever got the chance."

"Well, why didn't your buddy deliver it himself, if it's so important?"

"I wish he could. . . ."

Rand saw Lunk's smile fade and asked him about it.

"It was during the Invid invasion," Lunk began. "My friend was on recon patrol, and I was detailed to rendezvous with him for the extraction. When I found him, he was trying to get away from a couple of Shock Troopers, and I could see he was wounded. They blasted him again while I . . . sat and watched. How he could get up and run after that I'll never know, but he did, and started for the APC. I thought there might still be a chance, but the Invid caught up with him before I could move in, and he didn't have a prayer."

Annie could see that Lunk was torturing himself with the memory but kept still and allowed him to finish. Was this what he had run from? Annie wondered, recalling comments uttered months ago when they had first met.

"He called out to me," Lunk was saying. "Calling me to come get him, but there was *nothing I could do*. The Invid had spotted the APC and started after me, and I had no choice but to make a run for it.

"I don't even remember how I got away from them . . . But I can still hear my buddy's voice coming over the net, as loud and clear today as I heard it then, calling me to help him. I can't forget . . ."

Lunk's face was beaded with sweat, and Annie fought down an urge to hold him. But he was through it now and sort of shaking himself back to the present, looking hard at the book again.

"This had some special meaning for him, I suppose. The one thing he wanted most was for his old man to have it. I promised on the day he went out . . ."

"Oh, Lunk," Annie broke in, touching his arm lightly. "You've been carrying more than that book around, haven't you? I feel so bad. . . ."

Rand looked in through the driver's side and noticed Annie crying. "Lunk," he said all of a sudden. "We've got a book to deliver. So let's get on it!"

Lunk saw Rand wrist the Cyclone's throttle to wheelie the mecha into lead position. He smiled to himself, thankful for the company of his friends, and pressed his foot down on the van's accelerator pedal.

* * *

Roca Negra had a secret of its own, a dirty little secret compared to the one Lunk wore like a scarlet letter.
But no one on the team was aware of this just yet; the
only thing immediately obvious was that the town
seemed deserted despite Scott's recent claims to the
contrary.

"Where is everybody?" Lancer said to Rook and
Rand as the three Cyclones entered the empty plaza.

"What'd you expect—the welcome wagon?" Rook
asked sarcastically. "After all, we didn't tell them Yellow
Dancer was coming to town. It's probably just siesta
time."

Rand took a look around the circle, certain he saw
people ducking away from the open windows and pulling
shutters closed on others. Even the central fountain was
deserted, but the damp earth around it suggested that
people had been there a short time ago. "You don't find
this a bit *strange*?" he asked Rook.

"You're both imagining things," she said. "It's not like
this hasn't happened before. Besides, there are two kids
right over there," she added, pointing to two young boys
munching on apples nearby.

Rand relaxed somewhat at that and swung his mecha
into a second lap around the well. He began to take
stock of the buildings now and realized that his expecta-
tions had been way off base: Instead of the stucco and
terra-cotta village he had envisioned, Roca Negra was
like something lifted from what used to be called Eng-
land. The architecture was of a style he had heard re-
ferred to as Tudor, with mullioned windows, tall gables,
nogging and timber facades, and steeply pitched tiled
roofs. "How about giving me a bite?" he heard Annie
shout to the kids as the van drove past them. Then he

spotted the restaurant: José's Café, according to the sign above the curved entryway.

Rook, Lancer, and Lunk followed Rand's lead, but only Lunk moved in to investigate. There were tables and chairs set up out front but no one on the scene to serve them.

"Bring me some peppermint candies!" Annie shouted to Lunk.

Lunk turned briefly to acknowledge her, and when he swung around, there was a mustachioed man standing in the restaurant's barroom swinging doors.

"The restaurant is closed during the emergency," the man began. He spoke with a Spanish accent and wore an apron and work shirt more suited to the trades than to the food biz, but he was gesturing Lunk to halt in a way that suggested he owned the place. "Our communications have been cut, and we're short on supplies of all kinds. The indications right now are that we'll be closed for about a month."

"But we've traveled such a long way!" Annie shouted out the open top of the van, disappointment in her voice. "We haven't had a decent meal in weeks."

"I told you what the situation is," the man fired back, raising his fist. Lunk was taken aback by the gesture. The man was slight, but his dark eyes were flashing with an anger that seemed to add to his aspect. "There's nothing I can do about it. We have no food to feed you. I suggest that you try the next town."

The man had moved past Lunk and was now overturning the café chairs and placing them legs up on the table. Lunk followed him, deciding to steer clear of the food issue for a moment and inquire as to the whereabouts of Alfred Nader, his dead friend's father. But the simple question seemed to unhinge the restaurant owner, who dropped one of the chairs at the mention of the man's name.

"What're you getting so upset about?" Lunk asked, concerned but not yet suspicious. "I only want to know how I can find Alfred Nader's house. Is that too much to ask, or are you as short on information as you are on food?"

The owner averted Lunk's penetrating gaze and busied himself righting the chair. "You must have the wrong town," he said distractedly. "I know everyone in town, and there's nobody named Nader living here."

"But you must have heard of him," Lunk pressed. "Alfred Nader? . . ."

"I tell you I never heard of him," the man said, raising his voice and moving back toward the swinging doors. "Now go away and leave me alone!"

"This is weird," Lunk said, turning around to face Rand and the others. "This guy tells me Alfred Nader doesn't live here. But he's lying, I'm sure of it." Lunk took a look back at the doorway and walked to the van. "Why the heck would he lie like that?"

"Something stinks," said Lancer. "Nader's here. We're just going to have to find him on our own."

"We'll split up," Rook suggested.

"All right, I'll go with Lunk," said Rand, already climbing into the van's shotgun seat. "We'll meet in an hour by the bridge outside town."

Lunk thanked his friends for their support and got behind the wheel. He swung the van around and headed it out of the plaza, followed closely by Rook and Lancer, who both ignored Annie's attempts to team up with them.

"Well, screw you guys!" she yelled as they roared off; then she spied Rand's untended Cyclone and smiled broadly.

* * *

Lunk and Rand headed up one of the streets leading from the plaza. There were a few people about, but without exception they disappeared as the van approached. Shutters slammed overhead, women carried their children indoors, and men shouted threats from the darkness of interior spaces. Much to Rand's surprise, Lunk seemed to know his way.

"My friend used to tell me all about this place," Lunk explained, a bit nostalgic. "He'd tell me all about his father, about how his old man was a big shot in town—a politician or something."

"And the restaurant owner never heard of him, huh?" Rand said knowingly. "What are they trying to cover up?"

"There's supposed to be a bakery somewhere along this street," Lunk said, leaving Rand's question unanswered and looking around. "There it is," he said a moment later. "A few more landmarks and I might be able to find my way to Nader's house without anybody's help."

Rand was silent while Lunk took one turn after another, the pattern of disappearances and threats unbroken. "You know, something just occurred to me," he said to Lunk when they had reached the outskirts of town. "Maybe they're trying to protect Nader."

"How do you mean?" Lunk asked, pulling the van over.

Rand turned to him. "These people don't know us. For all they know we could be sympathizers. If Nader was a politico, he could be in trouble."

"With who?"

Rand shrugged. "The Invid, for starters."

The rest of the team, having met with the same reception, had abandoned their search and were killing time at the edge of town, waiting for Lunk and Rand to show up.

Rook was on her feet, leaning almost casually against the stone wall of the bridge. Lancer and Annie were sitting on the grassy embankment above the stream.

"Lunk and Rand have got to pass by here eventually," Lancer was telling the others.

Rook agreed. "We're better off just waiting for them. But one of us is going to have to find Scott. Where do you think he put the Alpha down?... Hey! A truck!" she said suddenly. "Maybe the driver can shed some light on this thing."

Annie turned to glance at the truck. "Looks like they're stopping."

No one moved as the truck came to a halt on the bridge. They had seen two men in the cab and were looking there, when without warning a third man jumped from the canvased rear. It took them a moment to realize that he was wearing a gas mask and what looked like a twin-tanked oxyacetylene rig on his back. And by the time they had made sense of this it was too late: The man had brought the rig's torch out front and released a foul-smelling, eye-smarting gas into their midst.

Almost immediately Rook and Lancer began to cough uncontrollably. Beneath the cloud and consequently somewhat less affected by it, Annie tried to slide down the embankment and reach the stream. But the gas's effects caught up with her; she felt a searing pain work its way toward her lungs and doubled up into a fit of coughing. The cloud was as dense as smoke, but she could discern that several other men had followed the lead man from the back of the truck. They, too, had gas masks on, but they also carried bats and clubs. Just before Annie went under, she saw Rook and Lancer fall as roundhouse blows were directed against them.

* * *

There was an olive tree and a small circular well where there should have been a house. Otherwise the lot was empty, the buildings that surrounded it on three sides burned and abandoned. Puzzled, Lunk stood staring at the scene.

"Are you sure this is the place?" Rand asked him from the van. He had pulled out one of the former police vehicle's air-cooled autopistols and was resting it up against his collarbone now.

"Yep. He told me his dad had a well and an olive tree in his backyard. And there they are. Now all we have to do is find the house."

Rand frowned and stepped away from the van to join his friend. "There's got to be twenty houses in this town with an olive tree and a well in the backyard, Lunk. And even if this was Nader's place, he's obviously not here now. I don't know," Rand added skeptically. "Maybe he's dead, and that's why everybody's acting so strange."

Lunk was starting to reply when Rand heard the sound of footsteps behind him. He looked over his shoulder and found himself facing half a dozen angry-looking men, one of whom was carrying a kind of back-packed welding torch.

Rand swung back around, putting all he had into knocking Lunk to one side while he threw himself in the opposite direction. Lunk took the full force of the gas cloud in the back, but before the men could move in, Rand was through his roll and taking aim at the torch. He pulled off one quick shot that effectively decapitated the twin-spouted rod and gave the men pause. They began to scatter as Rand squeezed off three more shots, one toward the feet of each of the men who were standing guard by the van. The three leapt through a kind of impromptu dance and fled along with their comrades.

Rand called to Lunk and made a beeline for the van, throwing himself into the shotgun seat through the passenger-side door, Lunk just steps behind him.

Off to one side, the men were rallying for another attack.

"Make tracks!" Rand yelled, pounding a fist against the dash.

"You make good sense, buddy!" Lunk yelled back, putting the pedal to the metal.

CHAPTER
THIRTEEN

It has yet to be demonstrated that the Invid Regis was capable of direct dealings with each of her remote drones— Scouts, Troopers and Pincer Ships—prior to Scott Bernard's forcing her hand, so to speak. Commentators have pointed to the incident at Roca Negra as an example of changes in the previous hierarchical organization, in which each hive queen (sic) was made responsible for her own soldiers.

Bloom Nesterfig, *Social Organization of the Invid*

I N JOSÉ'S CAFÉ THE CHURLISH MAYOR OF ROCA Negra, a large, mustachioed man named Pedro, received word of the brutal attack on Rook, Annie, and Lancer.

"They beat them up!" he bellowed now, bringing his big fist down on one of the tables and rising to his full height of six foot four. His English, like José's, had a Spanish accent.

"Yes," José's wife, Maria, continued. She was a small, pretty woman who usually wore her auburn hair in a loose braid over one shoulder. "They put the three of them in the back of the truck, and then they sped off somewhere. But I think the two others got away."

José watched his wife from across the room but said nothing. It worried him to have her interfere in these matters, but she had been adamant about reporting the attack to the mayor, and when she was decided about something, there was nothing José could do to stop her. He only hoped that the rogues who captured the three strangers would not learn of her statements.

"Those no-good bums have done it this time," said Pedro, starting for the door.

Maria's thin hands were clutched at her breast. "You won't let them hurt the others, then?"

"When I get my hands on them, I'll *show* them who runs this town!" the mayor said without looking back.

José watched the doors swing to and fro. *Who* would he show? he asked himself. The rogues or the strangers who had come in search of Alfred Nader? Roca Negra could so easily fall victim to violence from either side. . . .

Meanwhile, Rand and Lunk were speeding toward the bridge to rendezvous with Lancer and the others, unaware that the bad part of town had already come calling.

"But why would they attack us?" Rand asked. "Just to drive us out of town, or what? And where the heck is Scott, anyway?"

"It has something to do with the disappearance of old man Nader," Lunk said firmly. He had the book out again and was regarding it while he drove.

"If that's true, we oughta rethink your idea of trying to get that book to him," Rand suggested.

Lunk shook his big head. "Uh uh, buddy, no way. I said I'd deliver this thing no matter what the odds. And if Nader's alive, I'll find 'im."

"Bravo," Rand replied, crossing his arms. "I just hope you don't get us both killed in the process." The van was closing in on the bridge now, and Lancer was nowhere to be seen. "They're supposed to be here. Where are they?"

"No sign of the Cyclones either," Lunk added, bringing the van to a halt and climbing out. He looked over toward the embankment, then down at tire marks in the dirt road—marks that didn't belong to the van. "Check this out," he told Rand. "Something's been by here earlier on—a truck by the looks of it."

Rand and Lunk bent down to inspect the tracks and in so doing took no notice of the men who climbed up from under the bridge. But Rand had thought to bring the autopistol with him and raised it threateningly as the men advanced. However, a second group joined the first after a moment, and although underarmed with clubs, axes, and farm tools, they stood fourteen strong.

"Some of you are gonna go down with me," Rand warned.

He was standing back to back with Lunk at the center of the wide circle that was forming around them.

"Get a load of this big bruiser with the knife," Rand heard Lunk say. He had no intention of turning around for a look but had to wonder about the size of the man if Lunk was calling him big. "If ever there was an *hombre* with no sense of humor, he's it."

"Well, this character with the ax isn't exactly my idea of a comedian either," Rand answered to let Lunk know how things were on his side of the circle.

"Ugly bunch of gorillas..." Lunk growled, lowering himself into a crouch and beckoning one of the men to come in on him.

"What are they waiting for?" Rand started to say, when one of the circle said, "We have your friends."

Rand felt Lunk straighten up behind him. "Throw the weapon down," Lunk told him.

"We're just going to let them take us?"

Lunk already had his massive arms raised. "Take it easy," he said to Rand under his breath. "My guess is they'll take us to Lancer and the girls. Then we'll make our getaway, all right with you?"

"Well, if you say so..." Rand gulped and tossed the autopistol to the dirt, much to the amazement of the circle. "It's your party," he shrugged as the men moved in to bind his wrists.

A short while later, in the back of the same truck that had surprised Lancer, Rook, and Annie at the bridge, Lunk had a change of heart. The truck had entered the plaza and was moving slowly past José's Café. Lunk spotted the owner standing in the doorway and said: "There's that bird José! I bet he knows where our friends are!"

And the next thing Rand knew, Lunk was standing up and shouldering his way toward the street. Rand jumped out of the truck and was right behind him. As the two of them rolled, got to their feet, and made a mad dash for the café entrance, propelled by blasts from the very weapon Rand had surrendered only moments before.

Lunk crashed through the swinging doors at full speed, knocking frail-looking José halfway across the room.

"I sometimes have my doubts about you, partner!" Rand said, out of breath and dodging blasts that were entering the bar from the street. The truck was backing up, disgorging men who were already closing in on the café. "Hope you have another plan ready," he added, noticing for the first time that there was a woman in the room.

Lunk was behind the bar, cutting the cords that bound his hands with a knife he had gripped between his teeth. José was cross-legged on the floor, shaking his head as if to restore himself to consciousness. The woman was kneeling beside him. Lunk freed himself and tossed the knife to Rand, who had to catch it in both hands and duplicate his friend's Houdini act.

"Okay, what's next?" Rand managed with his mouth full.

Lunk grinned and pulled a hand blaster from beneath his shirt. "Surprise," he said, shoving the weapon into José's ribs. "Now, my closed-mouthed friend, you're going to do a little talking."

Rand took a cautious look out the swinging doors and turned to Lunk. "I hate to bring up an unpleasant subject, but there's quite a crowd gathering out there, and since we've only got one blast—"

"In a minute," Lunk cut him off. "Start talking," he said to José, ignoring the pleas of the man's wife.

José swallowed hard. "What about? It isn't my problem."

"You can begin with where our friends are—and no stalling!"

"Maria," he said, looking imploringly at his wife. "What should I do?"

"Please believe us," she told Lunk from her husband's side. "We don't know what became of your friends. Only Pedro knows what happened to them."

"Fine. So produce Pedro."

"He is the mayor," Maria continued. "He's giving all the orders."

"Maria!" José yelled, trying to stop her.

"Then take us to him—*now*!"

"But how?" said José. "We can't get past that mob." He gestured toward the door.

"I've got an idea," Rand said from the door. "José, you've put on a pretty good act so far, and now you're going to do some acting on our behalf...."

José pulled Rand and Lunk through the café's swinging doors a few minutes later, leading them along on a leather leash. Their hands were now bound in front of them with white cloth napkins Maria had helped to knot, one of which dutifully concealed Lunk's blaster. The townsmen were suitably impressed (if somewhat bewildered) and moved in to retake custody of their prisoners, but José waved them off.

"Pedro has asked me to take them to him. He wants you men to stay here and capture their companion when he shows up."

"You're doing fine," Lunk complimented him under his breath. "Now just keep walking. Get us out of here and you'll save your skin. Tell the driver to take us to Pedro."

José motioned to the idling van one of the villagers had driven in from the bridge. "Is this their vehicle?"

The man behind the wheel nodded. José shoved his prisoners into the rear seats and joined them there. Maria rode shotgun.

"Be alert for their comrade," José reminded the men as he ordered the van off.

Away from the café, Lunk loosed the cloth knot and brought the blaster out for the driver to see. He ordered José and the driver out of the van when they reached the mayor's offices.

"Now don't get any funny ideas when we get inside," Lunk advised them, making his point with the weapon. "I don't want to hurt anybody, but I'll do what's necessary."

"You want me, too?" said the driver, Gómez.

"You, too," said Rand, giving him a light shove.

The building was a wooden two-story structure with tall, curved-top entry doors. Lunk and Rand stayed behind the two men as they climbed the staircase to the upper floor, but once at the office, José and Gomez burst through the doors shouting warnings to their friends inside. Lunk was only a step behind them, though, and fired a shot at the ceiling to quiet the room.

There were a dozen or so townspeople in the office,

not counting Lancer, Rook, and Annie, who were bound hand and foot on the floor in the center of the spacious room.

"Hands up!" Lunk bellowed.

"Well, hello, boys," said Rook as plaster rained down on her from Lunk's ceiling shot.

"Where's Scott?" Lancer asked.

Rand moved in to free his friends while Lunk threatened to air-condition the room unless someone directed him to the mayor.

"That's me," said a large man seated at a table.

"Be careful, Pedro," José warned him.

Lunk leveled the blaster at him. "We've got a few questions for you."

"Like where you hid the Cyclones," Rand said, moving to Lunk's side. Lancer and Rook had some nasty bruises, and a new anger was evident in Rand's voice.

But the mayor wasn't impressed. "We have them, and we mean to keep them," he told Rand. "You people are free to go, but we keep the machines."

Rand showed his teeth. "Hear me, mister, and hear me good: We're giving the orders now, not you."

"Give all the orders you want, but we'll do what we have to do."

Rand made an impatient sound and grabbed the blaster from Lunk's hands. "Talk to him, Lunk, before I do something I might regret."

The big man nodded and stepped forward. "All right, Mr. Mayor, forget the Cyclones for a moment. What I want now is the truth about Alfred Nader."

"I don't know anyone named Nader," Pedro said, meeting Lunk's glare. But the stifled gasps from others in the room told a different story.

Lunk slammed his fists down on the table. "I'm sick of listening to lies, pal!"

Rand put a hand on his friend's arm. "Hold on a minute," he started to say. But suddenly the building was shaking. Annie pointed at the window: Rand saw flashes of brilliant orange light in the skies above the mesa.

"Annihilation discs!" said Rand. "Invid patrol ships!"

"Now at least we know where Scott's been," Lancer chimed in.

Rand turned to the mayor, furious now.

"Your time is up, Pedro! We need those Cyclones!"

The mayor remained tight-lipped. "We don't want any more fighting in our village."

"If we don't get out there and help our friend, there won't *be* any more village," Lancer pointed out.

Pedro scoffed at him. "Do you imagine you heroes are going to repel an Invid attack by yourselves?"

"You better let us try," Rand said as the sounds of distant explosions infiltrated the room.

"I mustn't endanger the town!"

"We're trying to *help* your town," Rook told him.

Lunk took the blaster back from Rand and raised it. "That tears it! I'm not standing by while my friend dies for this stinking excuse for a town. Pedro, you've got ten seconds!"

"Wait!" José said, stepping into the projected line of fire. He turned to Gomez. "Tell them where the Cyclones are hidden."

"You're responsible for this, José," the mayor shouted. "If anything should happen to our village—"

"I'll take the responsibility then," José answered, whirling on him.

"They're in the warehouse," Gomez said softly.

The warehouse was a barn situated close to the bridge, an odds-and-ends storage facility for grain, farming tools, and rusting examples of early Robotechnology. The Cyclones had been rolled into a corner and covered over with a couple of mildewed canvas tarps.

Lancer, Rook, and Rand headed straight for their machines, activated them, and rode off to the sound of the guns. Annie and Lunk wished them luck and watched as the Cyclones reconfigured to Battle Armor mode. Lunk was heading back to the van when he heard his name called. It was Pedro, looking somewhat sheepish and conciliatory.

"Lunk, you're determined to go through with this?"

Lunk gestured to the by-now-distant Cyclones and said harshly, "That oughta answer your question."

Pedro nodded sullenly. "Then there's something I want you to see," he said, leading Lunk back into the barn. Inside, he motioned to an object concealed under a nylon cloth and pulled the cover away.

"I want you to have this."

Lunk knew it by its slang term—a "Stinger"—a lightweight autocannon no larger than a turn-of-the-century M-70 machine gun that ran on Protoculture and delivered piercing bursts of Reflex firepower. Stingers were the weapon of choice for the resistance early on, but with the Invid's control of Protoculture, the weapon had passed quickly into disuse. This one looked as though it had never been fired, but it hadn't been well cared for either.

"This was given to our town by a group of freedom fighters," Pedro began to explain while Lunk inspected the gun. "Before I was mayor, when...Nader was alive." Lunk straightened up at the mention of the name.

Pedro's voice took on a harder edge. "But Nader didn't want it used. He actually believed we could make a separate peace with the Invid and hid the gun, afraid that fighting back would end in death for all of us. But many of the townspeople misinterpreted his concern; they accused him of cowardice and worse. When he still wouldn't reveal where he had hidden the thing...they beat him to death. They burned his home, they..."

Lunk saw that Pedro was sobbing. "So that's your dirty little secret . . . the reason why those men attacked us. You're all ashamed of what happened here."

Pedro nodded. "May God have mercy on us. By the time we found the gun, it was too late to do anything. The Invid had overrun everything."

"And now you're the one who feels responsible for this place. You've inherited Nader's legacy."

"You could say that."

Lunk's hard look softened. "Pedro, maybe I've misjudged you."

"And I, you," returned the mayor. "A common enough mistake these days."

Out on the flats things were looking grim for Scott and the team. The arrival of the Cyclones had taken the pressure off him to some extent, but the Invid still outnumbered them three to one.

Shock Troopers again. Scott wasn't sure why they had showed up. It was possible that one of the Scouts they had tangled with earlier had gotten away. He had seen the first of the Troopers just as the team had been entering Roca Negra and had doubled back to deal with it. But on the tail of the first came a second, then a third and a fourth, and before Scott knew it, he was in the midst of a full contingent of Pincer units.

He dropped the Alpha in for a release run now, going after three grounded Invid who had pinned down Rook and Rand with cannon fire. The already cratered and fused terrain was being torn up by annihilation discs, the air above superheated and crosshatched by missile tracks launched from the Cyclones' forearm tubes. Scott loosed a flock of heat-seekers at the bottom of his dive and climbed sharply, looking back over his right shoulder to catch a glimpse of the results of his run. Two

Invid ships were flaming wrecks, collapsed and bleeding green nutrient. Another was badly damaged but still on its feet, one of its pincers blown away.

Scott swung his head as he thought the Alpha through a roll and saw Lunk's van streaking across the sands, seemingly on a collision course with three more Invid ships. Alert to the van's approach, the Troopers lifted off, forming up in a triangular pattern to deal with it.

But in a moment it was obvious that they had misjudged Lunk.

Scott caught sight of a brilliant flash at the front of the van an instant before one of the ships exploded in midair. A second flash and another Invid was blown to pieces. Scott realized that Lunk had mounted some sort of cannon to the van. Apparently the Invid also recognized the weapon, because they were suddenly giving the van a wide berth. Rook, Rand, and Lancer took advantage of the opportunity to deal out death blows of their own, managing to fell two additional Troopers with precision shots to the ships' optic scanners.

Scott smiled broadly and uttered a short, triumphant cry to the skies outside the Alpha's canopy. Not only had they cut the odds, they had won the battle.

The remaining Invid were actually turning tail and fleeing the area!

It was the first time Scott had ever seen them retreat.

Lunk returned to Roca Negra alone. He had a longer talk with Pedro and José about Alfred Nader. Both men had known Nader's son, Lunk's friend, and were sorry to hear that he had been killed.

The battle on the flats hadn't affected the rest of the town's attitude toward Lunk, but he understood this and pitied them the cross they had to bear. He had his own, and the emotional weight of it hadn't been lessened any by this brief stop at Roca Negra. In fact, he felt even more confused than before. Would Nader have turned out to be a sympathizer in the end? Would his town have been just another place where the people were too busy maintaining their separate peace to rally to the cause of a greater one?

Lunk spent some private time at what had once been Nader's ranch, picking up ripened olives from the tree and drinking cool water from the well. Lunk kept the book. More than the object of a promise now, it had become a symbol of confusion, of mistrust and treachery . . . markings engraved upon Earth's tortured and embattled landscape and upon the very fabric of Human life.

FOURTEEN

*Psychohistorian Adler Ripple traces Jonathan Wolff's
treachery to his illicit affair with Lynn-Minmei. He had met
her on Little Luna (the Robotech factory satellite), during
the Hunters' wedding and fallen in love with her while the
two of them were, for all intents and purposes, stranded on
Tirol. It's likely they would have married had the Sentinels
not come between them. (Minmei had vowed to steer clear
of soldiers after her brief and disastrous fling with Rick
Hunter. Ironically, she caught the bridal bouquet at
Hunter's wedding and in a sense felt destined to marry
Wolff. The subsequent degradation she fell into can be attributed in part to her learning about the wife and child Wolff
had left behind on Earth.) Ripple asserts that Wolff's decision to return to Earth was motivated by the broken engagement with Lynn-Minmei. Wolff was suddenly convinced that
he could take up where he had left off with the family he had
abandoned. When that didn't occur, he turned to drink and
drugs and embarked on a campaign of self-destruction. (Information that has only recently come to light suggests that
Wolff also had a brief affair with Dana Sterling—the daughter of Max and Miriya, who took Wolff's ship back into
space with the hyperdrive perfected by her former Southern
Cross comrade, Dr. Louie Nichols—and that Wolff had
learned the Invid were holding hostage both his wife Catherine and his son Johnny.)*

Selig Kahler, *The Tirolian Campaign*

A WEEK OF HARD RIDING BROUGHT DRAMATIC
changes in both the terrain and the social climate of the
settlements the team passed through. The land was
thickly forested except where it had been cleared for
farm cooperatives and villages. The road system was
well maintained, and food and supplies were readily
available. Lunk knew the reason for this: They were ap-

proaching one of the Invid's so-called Protoculture farms, where Human laborers were forced to toil endlessly in vast gardens, maintaining and harvesting the aliens' nutrient plant, the Flower of Life. But where the team had expected to encounter armies of Scouts and Troopers, they found none; and in place of a downtrodden populace, they found people in a celebratory mood. The Invid were said to have stopped their patrols a little over a month ago, and there were rumors to the effect that this had something to do with the arrival of a platoon of Robotech soldiers who were currently engaged in an assault on the Protoculture farm itself.

Scott was certain this unit was composed of men and women from the Mars Division attack wing. One of the predesignated rendezvous points set up by the mission commander was located some five hundred miles north of the team's present coordinates, and it was likely that a splinter group from the main force had moved south to engage the Invid at the farm. Scott was tempted to take the Alpha north to see for himself, but his sense of loyalty wouldn't permit leaving his friends on their own. At least not until each of them had found a peace of sorts or, better still, a home. It was no secret to any of them that the team was more like a family than the invincible military machine each member sometimes imagined it to be. And it was something none of them took for granted, least of all Scott, the most recent victim of the war's dispassionate savagery.

So they stayed together and eventually found their way to the city where the Robotech soldiers were supposedly garrisoned. It was an immense place, far larger than any of the places they had passed through thus far, a former military base (whose buildings had been adapted for civilian use) that had grown up within the confines of an enormous depression in the Earth's denuded crust, enclosed by the severe walls of an unnatural escarpment. The city now had hotels, restaurants, and a thriving population of five thousand or more.

Scott left the Alpha concealed outside the city and rode down into the bowl with Lancer and the others. As newcomers, they were questioned and searched at the main gate—an immense security fence watched over by armed guards stationed in nearby ultratech towers—but ultimately permitted to enter.

Scott, already searching for familiar faces, was perhaps a bit more hopeful than the others if no less puzzled. There were indeed soldiers all over the place, but they were hardly the strac troops Scott had convinced himself he would find. Nor were they Mars Division. Their high-collared, belted jumpsuits were the same ice-blue color as Scott's own, but the unit patches were unlike any he had seen. Scott glanced around some more, certain he would find what he was after. Here were three soldiers stumbling out of a bar; there, three more drinking on a street corner. Other troops in jeeps and personnel carriers were joyriding through the narrow streets, trash and empty liquor bottles in their wake. Even Annie was stunned.

"What's with this place?" she asked from the van. She was standing on the seat in the open back, her arms draped over the vehicle's roll bar.

"There's no shortage of 'Culture, that's for sure," Rand observed, motioning to the cruising jeeps.

Scott tuned in to a nearby conversation—soldiers, new arrivals by the sound of them: "This town's a gas!" one of them said. "Unbelievable," said another. "I didn't think I could ever feel this way again."

Scott heard tires squeal behind him and turned around. A jeep was accelerating drunkenly from the main gate, slaloming its way up the street, four soldiers laughing it up inside. It pulled up shortly next to Scott, one of the soldiers offering a bottle out of the top.

When Scott refused, the man said: "What's your problem, pal?" His glazed eyes took in the rest of the group. "You guys look like a war's going on."

"What about the Invid, soldier?" Scott snarled. "A couple hits of that stuff and you forget, huh?"

The soldiers looked at one another, speechless for a moment, then laughed. "Where you been, Colonel?" asked the driver. "They're history. We've been kickin' ass and takin' names all over this sector."

"It's no lie," said another. "Long as ya stick 'round here, ya got nothin' to worry 'bout. So, enjoy. The man's got it covered."

"You can get anything you want here, get me?"

"What man? What are you talking about?" Scott yelled as the jeep screeched off.

"At ease, Colonel!" one of them yelled, eliciting laughter from the others.

It was the same scene wherever they went: everyone talking up the town like it was paradise. Drunken soldiers, hookers, scammers, Foragers, rogues, and hustlers, all thrown together in the same pot, reveling and lifting their glasses in toasts to the mystery man who secured all this for them. The search for food and drink led the team into one of the many bars along the strip. Annie's attempt to flirt with the sideburned bartender ended with his walking off just as Lunk was about to order. Lunk was looking around for something to throw at the guy, when a soldier burst in through the bar's swinging doors.

"Wolff's back!" he yelled to the crowd at the top of his lungs.

Almost everyone got the message—out of sheer volume or at mention of the name itself—and many started for the door. Others, too drunk to move, got as far as lifting their heads from various tabletops. Scott took hold of a soldier within reach and spun him around.

"Who's Wolff?" he demanded of the man.

"The Wolff, bro," the man slurred. "*The* Wolff."

"Jonathan Wolff?" said Scott.

The man snapped his fingers, pointed, and winked at Scott, then shuffled off toward the door.

Rand saw the look of disbelief surface on Scott's face, but before he could ask about it, Scott was shoving his way through the exiting crowd and making for the street.

Rand and the others followed Scott out and found him amid a mob that had gathered around a jeep. Scott was standing rigidly by the curb, mouth half-open in amazement, staring at the man who was climbing out from the driver's side of the vehicle. A celebrity, Rand thought. Either that or a Robo officer who fancied himself one. The man was of medium build but square-shouldered and muscular. He had brown hair, thick and combed straight back, well-defined eyebrows, and a mustache, clipped clear in the center. He was wearing dark glasses and a gray uniform offset by a wide black belt and a red ascot. There was, however, something stern and humorless about him that made Rand wonder at the reception he was getting.

People in the crowd were firing questions left and right, some of which Wolff took the time to answer and others he ignored. At the same time, a wounded soldier in the rear of the jeep was singing Wolff's praises. "He saved my life," the man bit out. "Picked me up and carried me on his back through the Invid lines...then went back for the Protoculture canisters he knew we needed...."

"Celebration time!" yelled a black man behind Rand. "Drinks on the house!"

But Rand heard someone else mutter: "Wolff's a damn hero every time he comes back. How d' ya figure it?"

Scott swung around at the comment, his face dark and

angry, but said nothing. Until he turned back to Jonathan Wolff. Then Rand heard him say: "I can't believe he's alive—*alive*!"

Colonel Jonathan Wolff . . . Graduated first in his class from the Robotech Academy on Macross Island but missed the SDF-1's inadvertent jump to Pluto and the two-year odyssey that followed. Nevertheless, he had distinguished himself during that period by openly criticizing the Council's decision to turn its back on the fortress's crew and unwitting civilian population and was resolute in his opposition to Russo, Hayes, and Edwards and their plan to use the Grand Cannon against the Zentraedi. He rose to the fore again during the planet's two-year period of reconstruction and was finally handpicked by Admiral Hunter to head up the ground-base division of the Robotech Expeditionary Force.

But it was on Tirol that Wolff's name became legend and his special forces—known by then as the Wolff Pack—rode to glory. Throughout the Tirolian campaign against the Invid, it was Wolff's forces who turned the tide of battle time and time again. And it was Wolff who came to play a crucial part in the schism that all but destroyed the Pioneer Mission.

Even that wasn't enough for the man. Leaving Dr. Lang and his Saturn group in charge of things on Tirol, Wolff had gone off with Hunter and that group of galactic freedom fighters who called themselves the Sentinels. To Spheris, Gáruda, Haydon IV, to every world that had fallen to the Invid, to every world reduced to slave colonies by the Regent and his limitless army of Inorganics.

Then, for reasons few understood, he had volunteered for a more hazardous assignment: to follow in the tracks of Major John Carpenter in attempting to return a warship to the Earth all of them had left behind. An Earth that had been ravaged by the very Tirolian Masters the Pioneer Mission had aimed to disempower and now faced an even greater threat from the race those same Masters had turned savage and indomitable.

Wolff left Tirol, but not before he had saved the life of a young man who idolized him from afar . . . an assistant to the celebrated Dr. Lang named Scott Bernard. . . .

Silently, Scott ran over the facts and memories while waiting for a chance to speak with Wolff. It was incredible enough that the man had made it back from Tirol, given the then primitive state of the hyperdrive units, but for Scott to find him now, after all these years, was nothing less than miraculous.

From what he had managed to piece together since first seeing Wolff earlier in the day, Scott learned that Wolff had arrived on Earth shortly after the destruction of the Robotech Masters' fleet, approximately two years before the arrival of the Invid. His Wolff Pack had led the counteroffensive but had been decimated along with most of the Army of the Southern Cross. But Wolff himself had survived. Driven underground, he had spearheaded the resistance and ever since had been on the go continually, moving from place to place to recruit and reconnoiter, waiting for the moment when the rest of the Expeditionary Force returned to wage the final battle.

Still, the boisterous atmosphere of the town disturbed Scott. Where was the discipline that had made the Pack such a respected outfit? And why weren't the troops being organized for a coordinated assault against Reflex Point? Why, in fact, was Wolff here, so far south of the central hive, and where were the survivors of Mars Division?

Scott had all these things on his mind when he stepped into Wolff's personal quarters that night and offered salute.

"Lieutenant Commander Scott Bernard, Robotech Expeditionary Force, Mars Division."

Wolff was on the bed, his shirt-sleeves rolled up. "Mars Division?" he said, reaching for his dark glasses; then he laughed shortly: "Well, one of you made it through after all."

Scott lowered his hand from his forehead, somewhat stunned. "Then you haven't rendezvoused with any of the survivors, sir?"

Wolff got off the bed and walked over to the bureau. "Lieutenant—Bernard, you said?—you're the first I've seen." When he saw Scott agape, he laughed again. "Welcome to Earth, Lieutenant. Care for a drink?"

Scott declined and watched Wolff pour a tall one for himself. The small room reeked of stale sweat and liquor and was littered with the remains of half-eaten meals and empty bottles. Scott noticed that Wolff's hand shook as he downed the drink.

"Well, let's not stand on ceremony, Bernard," Wolff said exuberantly. "Have a seat. You can tell me about your ill-fated offensive and I'll tell you about mine."

"Sir, I'm not really here to socialize..."

"Oh, I see," Wolff said from the couch, with mock seriousness. "What's this about, then?"

Scott stared at the man before replying, fighting an impulse to turn around and leave the room before matters got worse. "You don't remember me, do you, sir? I knew you on Tirol. I was part of the Saturn group, an assistant to Dr. Lang."

Wolff's grin straightened; he turned his face away from Scott. "That was a long time ago, Bernard. And a lot of miles from here." He put the drink glass aside. "I'm sorry about this, Bernard. We lost quite a few good men today. And there's damn few left."

"Sir, about this town... The Wolff Pack—"

"This isn't the Wolff Pack, Lieutenant!" Wolff barked.

"The Wolff Pack is dead, every last one of them." He got up and returned to the bottle. "I know what you're thinking, Bernard. That the noble Jonathan Wolff is but a ghost of his former self and that he can't even control his troops. But you don't know the full story, Bernard. Not the half of it!"

Wolff scowled and set the drink aside without tasting it. "These men aren't soldiers—they're rogues and thieves and Foragers and every other kind of riffraff this planet has spawned during the past fifteen years. I do what I can with the few real soldiers I cross paths with. But this is Earth, not Tirol. And our enemy behaves differently here . . . As we all do."

Scott wasn't sure what to say, so he simply came to the point. "I'd like to be part of your team, sir."

Now it was Wolff's turn to stare. "You obviously know what you're in for, Bernard."

"I've fought my way through a thousand miles, if that's what you mean."

Wolff's eyebrows went up behind the dark glasses. "Impressive."

"In fact," Scott said excitedly, "if it's good troops you're looking for—"

"No," Wolff cut him off firmly. "I don't care how good they are. If they're not Robotech-trained, I don't want them." He turned his back to Scott to stare out the window.

"But, sir—"

"That will be all for now, Bernard."

Scott buttoned his lip and saluted. "Your orders?"

"Oh-five-hundred sharp at the main gate," Wolff said without turning around.

Four Cyclone riders suited up in battle armor left the basin base at sunrise, ascended the escarpment, and headed into the lush forests an hour's ride east. Wolff,

Todd, Wilson, and Bernard. Scott had made no mention of his meeting with Wolff to Rand or the others. He had gone as far as bunking with them in a room they had managed to secure in one of the base's barracks turned hotels and had crept out under the cover of darkness after leaving a scrawled note of explanation on his bedroll. He had to admit that it felt strange and discomforting to be without them, his surrogate family and personal "wolf pack." But he told himself it was time to begin distancing himself from them; his new loyalties would have to lie with Wolff and whatever missions lay ahead of them.

The four men left their Cyclones in the woods and followed Wolff's lead along a faint trail that coursed over low hills to an enormous clearing. Through the foliage, Scott caught glimpses of a massive red hemisphere of some sort. It troubled him that they had left the Cyclones behind and were closing on the Invid Protoculture farm armed only with hand weapons. Wolff's explanation made sense—that they wouldn't be able to get near the place on Protoculture-fueled mecha—but even so, it was hard to imagine that simple H–90's could effect much damage.

It was only when they reached the edge of the clearing that Wolff made the rest of the plan clear: It was imperative that they make off with enough Protoculture to fuel the massive rescue operation Wolff was planning. Each previous mission had brought him closer to this goal, and today's could complete the rescue team's requirements. Beyond that, the four of them simply had to keep themselves from being fried by annihilation discs. Scott had a clear view of the farm now and understood why Wolff hadn't attempted to describe the place earlier —it had to be seen to be believed. It was a hemisphere, all right, but one that stood more than three hundred feet high and was nearly a mile in circumference. It was a kind of blood-red, organic-looking geodesic dome, lit from within by a pulsing light. And from its techno-system base extended ten tentaclelike projections, each a good fifty feet around. Scott imagined that it must have resembled a jellyfish creature from above.

Wolff whispered a warning to his men. "Don't be fooled just because you don't see any Invid. They're around, you can be sure of it." Wolff had the faceshield of his Cyclone helmet raised; he had his dark glasses on.

Scott had to admit that the man was cool and alert, not the boozing, self-pitying Wolff he had seen the night before but the Wolff who had led the Pack up the glory road.

"There are two entry points above the foundation. The Protoculture is stored just inside these," Wolff said, gesturing to two arched portals in the membranous portion of the hemisphere wall. He told Todd and Wilson to take the south one. "Bernard and I will take the other one."

The three men nodded.

"Don't overburden yourselves," Wolff added. "Just take what you can carry without weighing yourselves down. Remember, you might need a free hand for those blasters." Wolff grinned. "But I hope it won't come to that."

Wilson and Todd moved off, using one of the tentacles for cover. Wolff waved Scott forward a moment later.

Halfway along one of the segmented tentacles, Wolff and Scott stopped, huddling down with their backs against the thing, waiting for Wilson and Todd to reach the south portal.

But something unexpected occurred just as Wilson was stepping through.

"Wolff!" Scott heard Todd shout over the suit's tac net. "There's a force field of some kind!" He and Wolff turned at the same moment: Wilson seemed to be suspended in the entrance, arms up over his head, his body shaking as energy coursed through his suit. The ground was rumbling all of a sudden, and before they could take a step toward their two comrades, an Invid Trooper erupted from the ground not twenty feet in front of them.

The shock of seeing the thing must have been enough to break the charge that held Wilson, Scott guessed, because now both he and Todd were heading back toward the woods at a run, dodging a pincer swipe along the way. Scott and Wolff adopted a similar tactic, only to find their route back to safety blocked by a second Invid. The Trooper emerged with enough force to throw Scott off his feet.

A third Trooper had cut off Wilson and Todd's retreat as well, and the two men were depleting their blaster charges against it.

Wolff was shouting for Scott to get up, all the while pouring energy from his handgun into the face of the alien. Peripherally, Scott saw a flash of white light and experienced a wave of searing heat; he turned in time to see Wilson and Todd disintegrate beneath a storm of annihilation discs, their death screams a piercing sound track through the net.

Wolff, meanwhile, had managed to chase off the Invid that had been looming over them only a minute before. Scott couldn't figure out how he had pulled it off but didn't stop to question it. He was on his feet now, Wolff's commands to run for it in his ears. The tree line was only fifty feet away, and he made a mad dash for it. . . .

CHAPTER

FIFTEEN

The incident with Jonathan Wolff dealt a severe blow to the team. Not only because the episode touched them more deeply than they thought possible—they were not as inured as they liked to think—but primarily because it seemed to shift the burden of responsibility entirely onto their shoulders: There was no resistance, except for their own meager efforts. But they would get over Wolff's treachery. How could they not, once confronted with the disillusionments that lay ahead?

Zeus Bellow, *The Road to Reflex Point*

THE NOTE SCOTT LEFT FOR THE TEAM ONLY MADE matters worse. It read: "Don't anyone worry. I can't tell you where I'm going or what I'll be doing, but I'll be back around sunset. Scott."

It was the secrecy that troubled Rand most. If Scott had simply disappeared for the day, Rand might not have given his absence a second thought, but when Scott failed to return with Colonel Wolff that afternoon, he and Rook decided to take matters into their own hands. They didn't bother with the formalities of the chain of command that kept Jonathan Wolff insulated from the city's rabble; they simply made their own way to his room and burst in on the man uninvited.

"Where's Scott, Colonel?" Rand said, out of breath from his run down the hall.

Wolff turned puffy eyes to them. He was seated at a table in the fetid room, a half-empty bottle of vodka in front of him. He had barely moved when Rand and Rook had thrown open the door and was now regarding them tiredly, with little concern.

"Scott who?" he said, refilling his glass.

"Bernard," said Rook. "We know he was with you this morning, and he hasn't returned since."

Wolff made a dejected sound and put down his glass. He reached for his dark glasses and slid them on. "Bernard . . ."

"Well?"

Tight-lipped, Wolff turned his gaze from them and shook his head.

Rand gasped. "You mean . . ."

"I can't say for sure. The Invid surprised us, and in the confusion I didn't see if he made it out or not. They were waiting for us, and we were overmatched. What more can I tell you?"

Struggling with the possible truth of it, Rand said nothing. But a suspicious look had begun to surface on Rook's face. "A whole lot more," she told Wolff. "How did you escape, Colonel?"

Wolff shrugged. "I was luckier than the others. That's the way it is."

Rook snorted. "From what I hear, that's the way it always is with you."

"What are you insinuating?" Wolff seethed, flashing her a cold look.

Rand gestured Rook to back off. He took two steps toward the table and slammed his hand down. "Just tell us where you were attacked."

Wolff's hand went out to steady the bottle. "If you're thinking about trying to go out there and find him, forget it. You won't make it."

Rand showed his teeth, then relaxed. "Look, we've

got an Alpha fighter hidden nearby. If there's even a chance that Scott's alive, you better believe I'm going out there to find him."

Mention of the VT seemed to bring Wolff around somewhat. He lifted the bottle but set it down without pouring. "Even a fighter might not be enough." Wolff gave Rand an appraising look. "Yes, Scott told me that you'd seen action together. But we're up against a hive, not a Scout patrol."

"It's still worth a try."

Wolff thought a moment, then said: "All right, I'll lead you out there."

"Great!"

Wolff stood up and went for his jacket. "We'll leave immediately."

Rand swung around to Rook. "Let the others know what I'm up to. We'll get Scott back!"

With that he rushed from the room, Wolff a few paces behind him. Rook stood dumbfounded for a moment, then followed him to the doorway. "What am I—your personal messenger or something?" she yelled to his back. But he didn't turn around. "Rand!" she shouted again, fuming.

Rand showed Wolff where the Alpha was hidden, but the colonel insisted they recon the area on Cyclones before bringing the Veritech into play. The fighter, Wolff insisted, would stir up the entire hive; it was simply too precious a commodity to risk, even for the life of a valued friend.

Rand saw the logic of it, disturbing as it was, especially after Wolff had led him to the hive.

"The place is a fortress!" Rand exclaimed, keeping his voice low. "I've never seen anything like it."

Wolff regarded him from behind the dark glasses, obviously pleased by Rand's shocked reaction. They were at the edge of the clearing now, suited up in Cyclone armor and armed with hand blasters. "It's just one of many," Wolff said. "There's a chain of these things that runs clear to Reflex Point."

Rand swallowed hard, discouraged. "It was around here that you last saw Scott?"

Wolff nodded and lowered the helmet's faceshield. "We'll search the perimeter first." He motioned Rand off to the right. "Stick to the woods, and I'll meet you on the other side. I only hope there's something left of Bernard to find."

Rand refused to allow the thought to register. He turned and was about to move off when the ground began to tremble. Wolff drew his blaster and pivoted through a 360, searching for some sign of the Invid's egress point. Rand managed to get his blaster unholstered and aimed in the same general direction as Wolff's.

In a moment the Invid Trooper showed itself, rising up through the earth and underbrush just outside the clearing. Wolff and Rand hit it full power, but neither of them was successful at directing a charge to any of the creature's vulnerable points. The Trooper seemed to sense their helplessness and opted to kill them with its claw rather than cannon fire. It had one of its pincers raised for a downward strike, when someone behind the two men stunned it with a Scorpion delivered to the head.

Rand turned in time to see Rook's red Cyclone's rear-wheel landing in the clearing. She slid the tail end of the mecha around and shouted through the externals for Rand to jump on.

"I told you you weren't leaving me behind," Rand heard as he raced to the Cyc. "And it's a lucky thing for you two that I decided to follow."

As Rand straddled the Cyclone's rear seat, he realized

that Wolff wasn't behind him. Over his shoulder he glimpsed Wolff waving Rook off. "Get going!" Wolff told them. "I'll make it back to my mecha!"

Rook wasn't about to sit around and argue. She toed the Cyclone into gear and sped off almost before Rand had secured an adequate handhold behind her. Meanwhile, the stunned Invid had come to life and was spewing a horizontal hail of annihilation discs into the trees. The Trooper pursued them, its shoulder cannons blazing. Rook pushed the Cyclone through a series of twists and turns, dodging explosions, plumes of fire and dirt.

Rand was thinking they were in the clear when the carapaced head of a second Invid appeared in front of them, pushing itself up from the soft forest ground, an unearthly land crab. Rook tried to launch the Cyclone over the thing before it completed its rise, but the Invid got one of its pincers free just as the mecha was directly overhead. Rand felt the jolt as the alien's claw impacted the mecha, and the next thing he knew he was on his butt in the grass, dazed, Rook similarly postured nearby. The Cyclone was nowhere in sight.

Rand shook his head clear and raised the helmet faceshield. "We've gotta find the Cyc," he shouted to Rook. "Split up."

Rook got to her feet; Rand waved her the okay sign and disappeared into the brush.

Splitting up was a bad idea, Rand told himself fifteen minutes later. The woods were thick, impenetrable in places; he had started working circles to fix his location, but he soon lost track of his own center—along with Rook and the missing Cyclone.

He was close to the hive clearing again, removing his helmet, when he heard sounds of movement close by. Rand turned, glimpsed Colonel Wolff, and almost called out to him. But something made him pull himself into concealment at the last moment. Wolff had holstered his blaster and looked as though he were waiting for a delivery of some kind. A Human-size figure was walking toward Wolff, but it was still too far off for Rand to get a good look at it. And even when it finally approached Wolff, he didn't know what to make of it.

Rand had his H–90 aimed at the thing now: It was taller than it had first appeared, perhaps eight feet tall, bipedal and suited up in bulky dark-colored battle armor. The creature's head—if that was indeed its head and not some kind of helmet—reminded Rand of a snail's foot. He told himself that it had to be an Invid. It certainly matched Scott's description of them, but Rand had for so long come to think of the aliens' ships as the creatures themselves that his mind refused to accept the idea.

Then Rand saw the Invid soldier hand Wolff a carry pack of Protoculture canisters.

He was tempted to kill them both—alien and traitor —but knew as the rage spread through him that he wanted Wolff to *know* who was taking him out when the moment came.

Rand lowered the weapon and silently began to work his way toward the conspirators. There was an outcropping of rock behind Wolff; Rand made his way to the top of this while the Invid walked back to the hive. Wolff had the Protoculture and was about to return to his Cyclone when Rand surprised him.

"So the hero's a traitor," Rand said from the outcropping, his blaster aimed down at Wolff. Wolff had been quick to raise his own weapon, but Rand went on, undaunted. "No wonder the city's full of laughing soldiers —it's so safe and secure now that you've arrived."

Rand risked a leap and in a moment was standing face to face with Wolff, who had yet to say a word. "The Robotech hero's made a deal with the Invid! For a few measly canisters of Protoculture, the great Jonathan Wolff leads his own soldiers to the Invid's doorstep. Isn't that it?"

Wolff fired.

The low-charge blast caught Rand in the right forearm guard, knocking the weapon from his grip and sending a jolt of searing heat to the flesh beneath the battle armor. He went down on one knee, as much from surprise as pain, and stared up at Wolff in disbelief.

"Go ahead and finish me," Rand spat. "I was meant to be Invid bait anyway...Just like Scott and all the others....It's how you always manage to return in one piece and well stocked with 'Culture...."

Wolff put the short muzzle of the blaster to Rand's head. "Easy, boy," he warned him.

Rand was shaking uncontrollably in spite of his best efforts to contain his fear. "How could you do it?" he asked Wolff. "Scott idolized you....He told me you'd saved his life once."

"Now you know about the dark side of heroism," Wolff said flatly.

Rand could feel the blaster's priming charge grounding on his skull. He wished he could see the man's eyes, know just what he was thinking. "I've seen it before—everyone out to save their own necks, trading lives... But why you, Wolff? Why?"

Wolff retracted the blaster. "Because they can't be beaten." He sneered. "Because it's better to have a few safe towns than an entire planet of slaves...And because...because of things you wouldn't understand, kid."

Rand scowled. "You better kill me, Wolff, because I'm gonna see to it that you're stopped."

Wolff stepped back and holstered his sidearm. "Go ahead and tell the town. See if they believe you."

Wolff turned and hurried off.

* * *

Rand unfastened the scorched battle armor from his forearm while he watched Wolff leave. Relieved that his burns weren't as serious as he had feared, he began to search the tall grass and brush for his blaster, wondering if he might be able to catch up with Wolff before he reached the Cyclones.

Go ahead and tell the town, Rand recalled Wolff telling him. *See if they believe you.*

Suddenly he heard Rook's voice and looked up. Scott was with her, one arm draped over Rook's shoulders for support. His battle armor was blackened in places, but he looked otherwise intact.

"I can't believe my eyes," Rand said, extending his hand to Scott. "Is it really you?"

"Barely," Scott returned.

"I found him in a hole in the ground." Rook laughed.

"And I miss it already." Scott disengaged himself from Rook and started to say something about a prehistoric-looking creature he had seen while in hiding, when he spied Wolff several hundred yards off. He tried a shaky step in that direction and said to Rand, "Is that Colonel Wolff? He came back to look for me?"

Rand put a hand out to restrain him. "Let him go, Scott." Scott looked over his shoulder, puzzled. "I've got something to tell you, and you're not going to like it . . . Wolff . . . Wolff's a traitor. He's got an arrangement with the Invid—he's been trading soldiers' lives for Protoculture."

"What are you talking about?" Scott's eyes were flashing.

"He's a traitor! I saw him with my own eyes. And an Invid, Scott, not a ship but—"

Rand didn't see the punch coming. Now, lying face-down in the grass, he couldn't even remember feeling it. "You're lying, you little coward!" Scott was yelling.

Rand rolled over and sat up, feeling a slight numbness beginning to spread across his jaw. "When I confronted him, he didn't deny it. I'm telling you, we were both led out here to be killed."

Scott roared something and launched himself, but Rook stepped in his way. In his weakened state he was no match for Rook and was easily held back. But she could do nothing about the curses he was hurling Rand's way.

All at once a fiery explosion effectively erased all traces of the struggle, the concussive force of it flattening Rook and Scott to the grass on either side of Rand. Through the smoke the three could see Trooper after Trooper issuing from the ground around them, blinding globes of incipient fire at the tips of shoulder cannons.

In a moment, annihilation discs were zipping into the area, pulverizing rocks and roots and whatever else lay in their path. Rand helped Scott make it to the safety of the stone outcropping, while Rook laid down cover fire with her hand blaster.

"The Cyclones—where are they?!" said Scott.

Rook indicated a direction. "I'll see if I can slow these things down some. Swing back around and pick me up."

Scott and Rand signaled their assent and rushed off, crouching as they ran.

Jonathan Wolff watched them from another part of the forest. He was surprised to see that Bernard had lived and was strangely relieved. Nevertheless, his escape had been but a minor stay of execution, for there were at least six Troopers going up against the three freedom fighters. Wolff could see that the woman was remaining behind to buy time for her comrades. But even if the other two were fortunate enough to make it to their Cyclones, it would just be a matter of time.

Unless someone came to their aid with the appropriate firepower.

An Alpha fighter, for instance, Wolff said to himself.

Rand got to the Cyclone first and doubled back to pick up Rook and convey her to the waiting red. Afterward he launched and went to Battle Armor mode, neatly disposing of one of the Troopers with a single shot to the thing's sensor.

Rook and Scott were similarly reconfigured now and going after a second alien. Scott dazzled the Trooper with in-close fancy flying, then boostered up and away from its pincer swipes to loose a Scorpion, which the creature blocked with its claw armor. In return the Invid pilot loosed a volley of annihilation discs against Scott, but in so doing had overlooked Rook and the missile she launched straight to its vulnerable scanner. The Trooper was blown to pieces, and the three teammates regrouped on the ground. The woods around them were crawling with Invid.

"We're surrounded," Rand thought to point out, his back to Rook and Scott. "Now what do we do?"

"What we always do," said Scott, almost laughing. "Fight our way out. Now, look alive."

Rand launched first, but critically misjudged his trajectory and ended up snagged by a Trooper's claw. Scott heard his desperate cry through the net, but even before he could think about how to free his friend, a bolt out of the blue took the Invid's pincer off at the elbow. An instant later, Scott saw the Alpha streak overhead. He was confused until he heard Rand yell, "Wolff! It's gotta be him!"

Wolff had the VT in Guardian mode. Missiles tore from undercarriage launch tubes, detonating like geysers of fire around one of the Troopers. But the creature survived the storm and struck back. Wolff rolled and tumbled the fighter through a steady stream of discs and dropped in to knock the troublemaker off its feet. He then switched to Battloid mode and came back down at the rest of them, the rifle/cannon discharging white death from its high-port position.

There were two Pincer ships in the skies now, and Wolff propelled the Alpha up to deal with them. One of the Invid had barely arrived in the arena when it was disintegrated by a flock of heat-seekers Wolff launched from the Battloid's shoulder racks.

On the ground, Scott was saying, "A traitor wouldn't handle an Alpha like that." He and the others had followed the fight and were now in the arid heights west of the base escarpment.

Wolff came on the net a moment later. "Just thought I'd give you a few pointers, flyboy."

"Be my guest!" Scott enthused.

Wolff kept the VT in Battloid configuration to take out the second Pincer ship before moving against the remaining Troopers. He literally stomped one of these senseless by bringing the mecha down full force on the alien's head. But the acrobatic act ended up costing him a precious few seconds: Wolff pivoted the Battloid in time to deal with the final Invid, but not before the Trooper succeeded in holing the techno-knight with an energy bolt that passed clear through it like a flaming spear.

Scott watched the crippled Battloid go down on one knee, then reconfigure to Guardian mode, seemingly of its own accord.

"Colonel Wolff!" he yelled, running over to the fighter. "Are you all right?"

The canopy went up, and Wolff managed to clamber out of the cockpit, one hand pressed to his side wound. He lowered himself to the ground, collapsing into Scott's arms. Gently, Scott laid Wolff on the ground, his own hands now awash in the colonel's blood. "You're bleeding, sir," he told Wolff hurriedly. "We've got to get you back to the base."

Wolff reached up and removed his dark glasses. "Too late, Bernard," he answered weakly, eyes closed. "Get yourselves out of here on the double."

"I won't let you die like this," Scott objected. "You're coming back with us!"

Wolff forced his eyes open and looked hard into Scott's own. "I'm a traitor, Commander—"

"Colonel—"

"And a traitor should be left to die out in the open . . ." Wolff shivered from a cold that began deep down in his guts. "When I think of the lives I traded to save my own skin . . ." Wolff screamed as something seemed to come loose inside him. Scott watched him blanch and felt the dying man's grip tighten on his arm.

"Colonel, hang on—"

"Catherine . . . Johnny . . . *Minmei*!" Wolff gasped, and died.

Scott shut the dead man's eyes, stood up, and saluted. In the distance he could see Lunk and Annie bounding toward the Alpha in the van. Alongside them rode Lancer on a Cyclone he had probably picked up at the base.

Scott looked over his shoulder at Rook and Rand; they looked back at him blankly, drained of emotion. Scott wondered whether they felt the same confusion he did. Gazing down at Wolff's body, gazing out at the smoldering remains of half a dozen Invid ships, he asked himself how this war could ever be won.

Or if indeed a war like this could ever have winners.

He thought about the long road ahead of them—his team, his family. Would it be as bloodstained a journey as these past few months? *Marlene*, he said to himself, reflexively reaching for the holo-locket around his neck.

To go through all this and yet never be able to win back your life!

METAMORPHOSIS

To Tim and Sara Robson
and Gary Stiffler—
staunch Robotech defenders

CHAPTER
ONE

> *How could so many of the principals in this vast struggle be so blind to the reason that one planet was at the center of it all? That is a secret we shall never know.*
>
> *On blighted Earth, arguably the most warlike planet in the Universe, the Flower of Life had taken root like nowhere else before—except for Optera (which may or may not have been its world of origin.) And in so doing, it set the stage for Act III of the Robotech Wars.*
>
> *And yet, inventively oblivious, Invid and Human alike attributed that to the vagaries of a plant.*
>
> Zeus Bellow, *The Road to Reflex Point*

NEVER HAS THE *FLOWER OF LIFE* WROUGHT MORE *strangely!* it occurred yet again to the Regis, Empress/ Mother of the Invid species. *Earth, your fate is wedded to ours now!*

How strange it was that Zor had chosen Earth, she thought, as she poised there in the center of the stupendous mega-hive known as Reflex Point. Or, more aptly, how *well* he had chosen by sending his dimensional fortress to the planet so long ago. Of all the worlds that circled stars, what had made him pick this one? The thought of Zor made her seethe with a passion that had long since turned to austere hatred.

Did he know that Earth would prove so fantastically fertile for the Flowers of Life, a garden second only to the Invid race's native Optera in its receptivity to the Flowers? It was true that Protoculture could bestow powers of mind, but even so, what had drawn Zor's attention across the endless light-years to the insignificant blue-white globe?

But Zor's decision didn't matter now. All that was important was that the Invid had finally found a world where the all-important Flower thrived. At long last, they had conquered their New Optera.

Of course, there was an indigenous species—the Human race—but they did not present any problem. The first onslaught of the Invid had left Human civilization in ruins; the aliens used many of the survivors to farm the Flower of Life.

A few Humans cowered in and around the shattered remains of their cities or prowled the wastelands, preying on one another and dreading the moment when the Invid would finish the job. The only use in letting the *Homo sapiens* survive a little while longer was to use them to further the Invid master plan.

Then the Humans would be sent into oblivion forever. There was no room for them on Earth anymore. And from what the Regis knew of the Human race's history, their absence would improve the universe as a whole.

And it *would* be done. After all, the last of the Regis's real enemies were dead. There was no one to oppose the might of the undefeated and remorseless Invid.

The Alpha Fighter bucked but cut a clean line through the air, its drives flaring blue. Wickedly fast, heavily armed, and hugging the ground, it arrowed toward the snowcapped mountains.

Lieutenant Scott Bernard eased back on his HOTAS—the Hands-on-Throttle-and-Stick controls. With so much power at his disposal, it was tempting to go for speed, to exercise the command of the sky that seemed like the Robotech fighter's birthright, and his own.

One reason *not* to speed on ahead was that there were others below, following along in surface vehicles—his team members. It would take them days, perhaps weeks, to cover mountain terrain he could cross in a few minutes. And he didn't dare leave them too far behind; his Alpha was the team's main edge against Invid hunter/killer patrols. The Alpha slowed until it was at near-stalling speed, its thrusters holding it aloft.

Another reason not to give in to the impulse to roar triumphantly across heaven was the fact that Humans *didn't* own the sky anymore.

He opened his helmet mike. "This is Alpha One to Scout Reconnaissance."

A young male voice came back over the tac net, wry and a bit impatient. "I hear you, Scott. What's on your mind?"

Scott controlled his temper. No point in another argument with Rand about proper commo procedure, at least not now.

"I'm about ten miles ahead of you," Scott answered. "We'll never be able to make those mountains before nightfall. I'm turning back; we'll rendezvous and set up camp."

He looked wistfully toward the mountains. There was so far to go, such a long, perilous journey, between here and Reflex Point. And what would be waiting there? The battle for Earth itself, the showdown of the Robotech Wars. The destruction of the greatest stronghold of the Invid realm.

But this group of oddly met guerrillas and a stranded Mars Division fighter pilot were not the Earth's sole saviors. Scott hadn't let his new companions in on it, but Humanity had a much more formidable ace-in-the-hole than them. And soon, soon . . . the demonic Invid would be swept away before a purging storm of Robotechnology.

He increased speed and took the Alpha through a bank, watchful for any sign of Invid war mecha that might have detected the fighter's Protoculture emissions. The fighter complained a bit; he would have to give its systems a thorough going-over with Lunk, the band's tech straw boss.

Scott was less proficient at flying in atmosphere than he would have liked. He had grown up on the SDF-3 expedition, and most of his piloting had been done in vacuum. There was an ineffable beauty, a *rightness*, to flying in Earth's atmosphere, but there were also hidden dangers, especially for a combat flier.

Still, he didn't complain. Things were going better than he had expected. At least the supplies of ordnance and Protoculture Scott's team had lifted from the supply depot of the turncoat Colonel Wolff would last them for a while.

Now all they needed was some luck. Somewhere, Scott's Mars Division comrades were getting ready for the assault. Telemetry had told him that a good part of the Mars Division had survived the orbital combat action and planetary approach in which his squadron had been shot to pieces, leaving him the only survivor. Scott still lived with the sights and sounds of those few horrible minutes, as he lived with memories even more difficult to endure.

Reflex Point waited. There the Invid would be repaid a millionfold—an eye for an eye.

From high overhead, Reflex Point resembled a monstrous spiderweb pattern. The joining lines, glowing yellow-red as though they were canals of lava, were formed by Protoculture conduits and systemry. The accessways were traveled by mecha and by the Regis's other servants.

At the center was the enormous Hive Nucleus that was Reflex Point proper. It was a glowing hemisphere with a biological look to it, and a strange foam of bubblelike objects around its base like a concentric wave coming in from all sides. The Nucleus was more than twelve miles in diameter. To Human eyes it might have resembled a super-high-speed photograph of the first instant of an exploding hydrogen bomb.

At the various junctures were the lesser domes and instrumentality nodes, though some of those were two miles across.

Deep within Reflex Point, at its center, was a globe of pure Protoculture instrumentality. This veined bronze sphere, with darker shadows moving and Shaping within it, responded to the will of the Regis. A bolt of blazing light broke from the dark vastness overhead, to create an enormous Protoculture bonfire.

The Regis spoke and her "children", half the Invid

race, listened; there was so much to tell them. With the incredible profusion of Flowers of Life that the Earth had provided, the Regis's children had increased in number, and the newly quickened drone zygotes must be instructed in their destiny. From within the huge globe, her will reached forth to manipulate the leaping Protoculture flames. "The living creatures of this world have evolved into a truly amazing variety of types and subtypes."

Images formed in the flames: spider, platypus, swan, rat, Human female. "Many of these are highly specialized, but extremely successful. Others are generalized and adaptable and many of those, too, are successful.

"Earth is the place the Flower of Life has chosen, and that is a fact that brooks no argument. And so it is the place where the Invid, too, shall live forevermore. For this, we must find the ultimate life-form suitable to our existence here and assume that form."

All across her planetary domain, the Invid stopped to listen. A few could remember the days long ago on Optera, before Zor, when the Invid lived contented and joyous lives. Other, younger Invid had access to those days, too, through the racial memory that was a part of the Regis's power.

On Optera, by ingesting the Flowers of Life, the Invid had experimented with self-transformation, and with explorations in auto-evolution that were part experiment, part religious rite. And, with the power of the Protoculture and its Shapings, they strove to peer beyond the present and the visible, into the secrets of the universe— into transcendent planes of existence.

Those days were gone, though they would come again when the Flowers covered the New Optera—Earth. For the moment though, evolution would be determined and enacted by the Regis.

"In order to select the ultimate form, the form we will assume for our life here, we are utilizing Genesis Pits for our experiments in bioengineering, as we did on Praxis."

More shadows formed in the otherworldly bonfire.

"We have cloned creatures from all significant eras of this planet's history and are studying them for useful traits at locations all across the globe. We will also study their interaction with the once-dominant species, *Homo sapiens.*"

Her disembodied voice rose, ringing like an anthem, stirring Invid on every rung of her species' developmental ladder, from the crudest amoeboid drone gamete to her most evolved Enforcer.

"Long ago, the Invid made the great mistake of believing alien lies; of believing in trust, of taking part in—" Her voice faltered a little; this final sin had been the Regis's alone.

"In love."

And the love Zor had drawn from her had been mirrored by her male mate, the Regent, as psychotic hatred and loathing. This had caused the Regent to fling himself —purposely and perversely—down and down a de-evolutionary path to monstrousness and mindlessness, to utter amorphous primeval wrath. But the other half of the Invid species, *his* children, worshipped him nonetheless.

The Regis steeled herself. Her mind-voice rang out again.

"But we have paid for those failures for an age! For an age of wandering, warfare, death, and privation! And once we have discovered the Ultimate Form appropriate to this planet, we shall assume that form, and we will secure our endless new supply of the Flower of Life. Our race will become the supreme power it was meant to be!"

But she shielded from her universe of children the misgiving that was never far from her thoughts. Here on Earth—the planet the Flower *itself* had chosen—the once-dominant life form was cast in the image of Zor.

And again the Regis felt herself fractured in a thousand ways, yet drawn in one direction. *What affliction is more accursed than love?*

Rand bent over the handlebars of his Cylone combat cycle as Annie yelled, her face pressed close so he could hear her over the mecha's roar, the passage of the wind, and the dampening effect of his Robotech armor.

"Look, there's Scott, at ten o'clock!"

Rand had already seen the hovering blue-and-white Alpha settling for a VTOL setdown. There weren't many useful-size clearings in the thick forest in this region. Certainly, there was nothing like a suitable airstrip for a conventional fighter craft within a hundred miles or more.

The designers who had given the fighter Vertical Takeoff and Landing capability of course knew how important that would be in a tactical situation in a conventional war. But Rand sometimes wondered if they had forseen how helpful the VTOL would be to a pack of exhausted guerrillas who were Earth's last committed fighting unit.

"I see 'im," Rand yelled back to Annie, rather than pointing out that he had been tracking Scott both by eye and on the Cyc's display screen. Rand didn't like to admit it, but he had developed a soft spot in his heart for the winsome, infuriating bundle of adolescent energy who had insisted on being a part of the team.

Annie had insisted on coming along with him on point, too. She was *determined* to do her share, take her risks, be considered an adult part of the team. Rand saw that a lot of her self-esteem was riding on the outcome and grumblingly admitted that he wouldn't mind some company. Scott and the rest had given in, perhaps for the same reason that they never questioned the pint-size redhead's outrageous claim that she was all of sixteen.

You could either accept Annie for her feisty self or risk shattering the brave persona she had forged, with little help or support, to make her way in a dangerous, despair-making world.

Now she banged Rand's armor. "Turn there, turn there!"

"Pillion-seat driver," Rand growled, but he turned down the game path, the cycle rolling slowly, homing in on Scott's signal. "We're about ten minutes ahead of the others, Scott."

Scott's voice came back over the tactical net. "Good. Still no sign of the Invid, but we can run a sweep of the area before the others get here."

None of them saw it or registered it on their instruments, but in the dim forest darkness, massive ultratech shapes moved—two-legged, insectlike walking battle-ships.

Just like armored monsters from a madman's nightmare.

Oh, great! We been shanghaied aboard Charon's Ark!

Remark attributed to Annie LaBelle by Scott Bernard

FOLLOWING THE PATH THEIR SCOUT TEAM HAD
taken, Lancer, Rook, and Lunk rode down the long, dangerous road toward Reflex Point. Lancer was riding his
Cyclone in the lead, wearing full techno-armor, the masculine, warlike side of his divided personality clearly
present. He was sure and confident, Rook Bartley
thought to herself, a practiced mecha rider and a deadly
warrior.

Rook, also in full Robotech panoply, had just caught
up on her red-and-white Cyc, having made sure that the
team wasn't being followed and it was safe to leave the
rear guard. She let Lancer hold the lead, glancing over to
make sure all was well with Lunk.

Things always seemed to be well with the big, burly
ex-soldier when he was on the road, riding in his beloved
all-terrain truck. Taking one look at Lunk, it was easy to
jump to the conclusion that there wasn't much going on
upstairs. His low forehead and the thick sideburns that

curled around and up under his eyes made him look like a comic-strip caveman.

But anyone who had talked to him, or looked closely into those soulful eyes, or seen him do the things Rook had seen him do, understood why conventional wisdom counsels against drawing quick conclusions.

As for Rook, she still found it strange to be riding with a gang again, even though Scott insisted on calling it a team, and everybody else kept insisting that they had their *own* agenda and that the alliance was temporary. She still wasn't sure how she had teamed up with them. It was too easy to say that she had shared danger, hardship, triumph, and defeat with them; she had done that with others before. She kept looking toward the time when she could ride as a loner once again.

Of course, there was Rand. . . .

Screw Rand! she snarled to herself.

From their places in the shadows of the great trees, the Invid Shock Trooper mecha kept watch, making sure the Humans were moving the right way. So far, the Troopers noted, these life-forms hadn't needed any herding.

The location of the nearest Genesis Pit was logical, situated along the easiest passageway through the mountains. The Entrapments were well deployed; the routine specimen collection was going well. The mecha floated along quietly and slowly, their thrusters muted as they awaited their moment.

"Heads up, Annie!" Rand's voice sounded a bit tinny through his helmet's external speaker. "Scott's right on schedule, of course."

Of course; what else? Would Scott Bernard, the rules-and-regs sole survivor of the massacre of his squadron be even a few seconds off?

Annie leaned out from the Cyclone and saw Scott's Alpha settling in the clearing. She pulled the bill of her trademark baseball cap, with its huge emblem that read E.T., lower "Um-hmm."

She tried not to let her relief sound in her voice. Although she had insisted on taking a turn at riding point, she was much more at ease riding next to Lunk in the truck (or APC, as Lunk insisted on calling it, since it was Armored and was indisputably a Carrier of Personnel). Annie wasn't even armed. Weapons made her a little queasy.

But now she didn't have to worry, because everything was going well. The Alpha had switched to Guardian mode for the VTOL landing.

The cockpit canopy slid back. Scott, armored in Robo-technology, stepped out, walked out to the forward edge of the swing-wing's fixed glove, and hopped down.

Annie looked around at the trees and the darkness they shed in the waning light, as Rand pulled up next to Scott in a spray of sand and gravel, some of it rattling and hissing off Scott's armor. "I guess this means we're staying here, huh?" She was tough despite her age, but she had done most of her surviving in settlements and cities. The wilds unnerved her.

Scott had gone around to the rear of the Guardian's portside leg to open a hidden compartment. "I'll get my Cyclone and we'll run a security sweep of the area before the others get here."

He pulled forth and activated the compact package that turned into his Cyclone, unfolding and reconfiguring. He thought about ordering Annie to wait in the cockpit of the fighter, but she had a special gift for getting into trouble, and so he discarded the notion. "Let's go."

Scott and Rand sped away, following the dry streambed, looking for an opportunity to leave it and move cross-country. Scouts seldom learn anything worth knowing on the main road, except when it's too late.

Acting as a scout for its unit just as Scott had done for his, an Invid Shock Trooper closed in on its target.

Normally the Invid were slow to detect Humans unless the prey had been specifically targeted, or there had been a sizable expenditure of Protoculture. This time, however, the Regis's fearsome war machines had been sent to guard a specific area and herd specimens into the Genesis

Pit. The Humans had come into their territory. By some oversight, there were no specific orders of any kind concerning Humans, and so the Troopers simply evaluated the interlopers as they would any other life-form, and decided they too would be worthwhile subjects of experimentation.

The Trooper kept its distance from the Humans, but some trick of the last filtering light of sunset piercing the dense trees betrayed it. Or perhaps Scott Bernard just had a *feeling* that they were being followed.

Scott slid to a side-on stop, ready to trigger and image the change that would meld his Cyclone and his armor into a Robotech killing machine. Rand stopped, too, Annie clinging close, white-faced. "What's wrong, Scott?" Rand's voice came over the tac net.

Scott shook his head slowly. "I'm sure I saw something moving. Back there."

But how could it be an Invid? Scout or Shock Trooper, their instant reaction was to attack.

"Don't tell me we're being watched!" Annie snapped at Scott, her lower lip trembling. "The Invid can't be *everywhere*!" She tried to get her arms all the way around Rand's armored midsection.

Contrary to its genetic programming, the Shock Trooper drew back—in accordance with the special instructions given to the sentinels of the Genesis Pits. Here were more samples from present-day life-forms to interact with the Regis's replicated marvels.

And an Entrapment intake waited near.

"Calm down, Mint," Scott was saying in that strangely relaxed tone he took on when other people's neck hair was standing on end. He had used Annie's team nickname—"Mint," from her ongoing affair with peppermint candy—to calm her.

"We've got to make sure the area's safe before the others get here. Or d'you want to see them ride into an ambush? No? Good. Rand, stay close. And cover me on the left."

The Cycs moved out, Protoculture engines gunning.

The Trooper floated back, almost delicately, close to the ground but leaving no print. As it circled it left its prey a clear path. All through this area, the Entrapments, a living part of the Genesis Pits, were growing in profusion, waiting to gulp down specimens.

Scott suddenly wondered if they should pull back; if he should send Annie and Rand hurrying for safety and cover their retreat with a barrage of Cyclone firepower.

But he realized that he and his companions had been led off to one side. Time had passed and Rook, Lancer, and Lunk were already near. It would be better to warn them first and then carefully withdraw.

He couldn't raise the other three over the tactical communication net, though, and couldn't tell if it was his position among the terrain features or whether the Invid were jamming the system. He spied a spot of high ground ahead and headed towards it, hoping for a clear commo link.

Then a shadow seemed to move across the hilltop—a shadow much larger than a bear or anything else that walked Earth's surface. It was going the other way, apparently oblivious to the scouts—heading for a point that would intersect Lancer and the others.

Ambush! Scott had no doubt. He revved his superbike, giving Rand a hand signal so that the Invid could not intercept a transmission. The sand felt a little treacherous, but that didn't matter under the circumstances. the two Cycs were fully armed, and for once, it seemed, the team had caught the Invid mecha with their iron trousers at half-mast.

He was about to order Rand to drop Annie off where she could take cover, then follow him on a stealthy approach-for-attack. But just then the ground opened up.

All Scott could see was that a flap of thick, brown-mauve stuff—like a flap of canvas twenty yards wide and seven yards thick—had been drawn back. It was thickly edged with long purple hairs, or perhaps they were feelers because in that horrible instant Scott could see that they were moving in different directions.

It seemed as though a monster's mouth had opened up in the Earth, ready to swallow them. But although Rand was extremely frightened and disgusted, he *knew* what this was. *A pit! Oldest trap of 'em all!*

The Entrapment's mouth was gruesome, bending inward at all four midspans rather than from the corners.

All thoughts of proper commo procedure faded like dew in the sunshine, and all Scott and Rand could hear over the tac net were one another's terrified howls; all they could hear over their external pickups was Annie's scream.

We're not fated to win after all, it occurred to Scott, as the Cyclones spun down into a deep, dark shaft that gleamed wetly like a gullet. The Cyc riders kept their seats by sheer instinct; Annie clutched Rand's waist. They fell into blackness, and what little light they had was cut off as the quadripartite Entrapment flaps above them closed serenely.

"Switch to Battle Armor!" Scott hollered, too loudly, over the tac net. He operated the gross hand controls on the Cyc, but more importantly, *imaged* the transition through the receptors in his helmet. He knew Rand would be doing the same. But just then Rand felt Annie lose her grip and drift free in the powerful air currents of the pit.

Mechamorphosis. That was the name Dr. Emil Lang had given these transitions so long ago, even before the start of the First War—that techno-origami shifting of shape.

One moment, there were two young men in armor tumbling through the moaning air currents of the Entrapment, and the next, there was *something going on*.

An onlooker might have thought that the Cycs were leukocytes destroying their riders, sliding up around them, Cyclone components meshing with armor components. The machines broke down into subunits to slide into their appointed places around the armor, as certain microorganisms might whip some critical hurt on certain other microorganisms.

The Cycs' tires were up high and out of the way on the Cycloners' backs, allowing them free play and unlimited fields of fire with their Robotech weapons. But even the thrusters in their suits didn't help them against the enormous vacuum that drew them down. There was no way back up.

Their armor flared anyway, to cushion the fall, and then somehow Rand heard a small, plaintive cry and realized that not everybody was protected.

"Hold still, Annie!"

It was a precision catch, possible only through Robotechnology. They were falling very fast, and simply rocketing armored arms under her would have only served to break the sweet, loudmouthed, red-haired soul of the team into three or—more likely—more pieces.

But as it was, Rand matched velocities and made the save.

He opened his helmet, careless of what might happen to *him*, holding Annie close—her pale face against his so that she could breathe the air his suit was pumping up in an effort to keep positive pressure.

Her small fingers moved, clasping the lip of his helmet's chinguard . . . then she was still, though she kept breathing. Rand hugged her to him, shielding her as much as he could. Neither Rand's armor's thrusters nor Scott's could stop their fall; whatever was pulling them down, it was more than just gravity and air currents. Scott wasn't even sure they *were* being drawn straight downward.

Rand, who was falling head first, was first to see it. "Scott! Look down there at that red glow coming right at us! Maybe there's a bottom floor after all!"

A lighted area on the shaft's floor? A lava pool? The light down there seemed to shift and waver, but it had the glow of extreme heat.

"A lot of good that'll do us if we go splat! Hit your burners!"

Rand and Scott simultaneously hit their burners, while Annie moaned and cried. But the retrothrusters did no good, and in another moment they plunged into the hellish fire.

CHAPTER
THREE

> Kraneberg, an oldtime historian of [North] American tech-
> nology, once said—in the form of a First Law—"Technology is
> neither positive, negative, nor neutral."
> Indeed. It is all three.
> And omnipresent.

Scott Bernard's notes

UH?"

Scott was amazed that he wasn't being boiled alive.
Instead, orange-yellow light played all around him,
Annie, and Rand, reflecting off their armor and helmet
facebowls.

The light seemed alive, moving like writhing eels. It
seemed to knot together in places with its ends exposed,
like twists in snarled barbed wire. Elsewhere it had settled into layers, like the colors in a sunset. The radiance
brightened, enveloping them.

Their facebowls polarized to shield them, while poor
little Annie squeezed her eyes shut and buried her head
against Rand's armored chest. Scott checked his instruments, but the sensors were not working. "I, I *think* we're
in some kind of energy field."

"Unbe*liev*able," Rand breathed. Then all at once the
light was above them, and they were plummeting through
utter blackness—or so it seemed, their facebowls still

17

darkened. "We went straight through it! Are we near the bottom?"

"Y'got me," Scott said, straining to see as his facebowl slowly depolarized. The place looked pitch black. The idea of a jagged rock floor racing up at them filled him with a cold despair.

"Emergency power to retros—" he was saying, just as the Cyclone warriors hit the water with a tremendous splash.

The first thing that Scott knew when he came to was that he had a monstrous headache. The next thing was that his eyes wouldn't focus properly, even taking into account the fact that he was trying to see through a helmet facebowl. He realized that he was sprawled out on his stomach. Before him, he saw his Cyclone armor's gauntlet-hand.

He groaned, trying to flex his fingers. They barely moved. He saw that he was lying on . . . on soil. Dirt.

He tried to see beyond the hand, his head trembling as he tried to lift it. His eyes were responding a little better, but what he saw made no sense.

Those giant fern things we saw on Praxis? No; wait a second . . . 'S not it . . . This's a diffr'nt planet . . . Earth . . .

It didn't look like any place he had ever seen or heard about on Earth. It looked . . . primeval. *Where are we, a swamp? What happened?*

Scott saw Rand sprawled out a few feet away, along the little stretch of sandy bank where they had landed.

Scott crawled over to him, groaning and hoping the pain he felt in his side wasn't a cracked rib. "Rand! Rand, are you okay?" He shook the Forager's shoulder pauldron. "Come on, fella, speak to me!"

Rand began to stir a bit. Through the external pickups, Scott heard a tiny moan. He looked beyond Rand and saw Annie lying a few yards away along the bank. She was making feeble attempts to sit up. "Annie, are you all right?"

She sat up suddenly, wide-eyed but apparently unafraid, blinking at the dawnworld landscape. "What happened to me?"

"We must've hit the bottom of the pit," he told her. Just then, Rand started coming around. "Take it easy, pal."

But Rand rose to his feet. "What, d'we miss a turn somewhere?"

He shook his head to clear it a bit. What he was staring at appeared to be seedferns. Cycads; club mosses and horsetails. Big and huge; small and almost microscopic. Off in the distance he could see what appeared to be conifers, ginkgoes, and more.

What is this, a damn coal forest?

Annie heard something that sounded a bit like a heavy-duty dentist's drill and ducked instinctively as something flashed by her ear. In a moment there was a cloud of them going past, though they seemed uninterested in the Humans. Their double wingsets were making silver blurs in the strange light of the place.

"Dragonflies!" Rand burst out. But these were dragonflies the length of his forearm, with enormous wings— slower than their modern counterparts.

Annie, seeing that they wouldn't hurt her, laughed with delight and skipped after them a few steps, the water splashing around her ankles.

Scott and Ran had instinctively reconfigured their armor, the Cyclone combat bikes under them once again. "And this water's nice and warm!" Annie was saying. She was wrinkling her nose, though; the air of the place was thick and steamy—the heaviness of rotting vegetation, of primitive life.

Annie's mood had turned to wonder, and she kicked up bright plumes of water. "Why don't you guys come in and give it a try?"

She was still trying to get them to join her when the surface of the water broke behind her, and something huge began to rise. "Annie! Behind you!" Scott shouted, his voice sounding a bit strange and processed over his suit's external speaker.

Both men were off their cycles, groping for their

sidearms. Annie stood rooted as a plated head the size of a small fishing coracle reared, shedding water in all directions. It opened its mouth and revealed rows of teeth like thick pegs. Rand's mind threw up a strange word, *Eogyrinus*?

Pieces of torn flesh still clung to the teeth, and it reeked of death and the marshes it hunted. Annie knew that through their helmets Scott and Rand couldn't even smell it.

Scott and Rand were jockeying for a clear line of fire. It was seemingly hopeless with Annie standing frozen right in front of the thing, hypnotized like a mouse before a rattlesnake. They were both armed with MARS-Gallant Type-H90s—the latest word in hip-howitzers, but that firepower was of little use with Annie in the crosshairs.

The thing had gotten very close. Rand saw that it was wide and flat, like a big croc with a bobbed, broad snout —no doubt an experienced shore hunter, just like the books said.

Scott hollered at Annie to get out of the way. She backpedaled and fell on her rump in the wet sandy shore. She stared into hungry, merciless eyes that, she could see, saw her as nothing more than another morsel of food. She threw herself flat on the ground just as the creature reared up to lunge for her. Then the neon-blue blaster-bolts flew, making a mewing sound.

As the H90s spat, the torrid air got even hotter. Rand fired with the modified two-hand stance that Scott had taught him. The thing heaved up as the dazzling hyphens of energy hit it. Pieces exploded from it as the furious heat of the shots turned the moisture in its cells into superheated steam, blowing it apart. There was no blood from those wounds; instead, the gaping holes in the thing had the look of broiled meat. The stench of it made the atmosphere that much more repugnant.

The monster thrashed and twisted. Roaring and bellowing, it swiped at the air with thick claws, snapping its jaws at the radiant bolts. Unable to understand what was happening, it nevertheless knew that it was dying. Its rage shook the air, the primeval plant-forest, and the sluggish lake waters. It fell back with a mighty splash, still quivering and contorting.

Annie kept screaming as Scott and Rand dragged her back to shore by her jacket. "Mint, he didn't bite you, did he?" Scott asked anxiously.

That seemed to bring her around a little. "N-no, but *almost*. And don't call me Mint, okay Scott?"

He held out his hand to her. "Sure thing. Come on; up you go." But even as she was scrambling to her feet, Rand yelled and pointed, sounding thoroughly rattled.

"Here comes more company!"

Three more of the things had surfaced and began ripping away at the first, while it spasmed. They tore out huge gobbets of flesh, snarling and whistling. Scott remembered hearing somewhere that real Earthly gators usually left their prey to rot, if it was too small to swallow in one gulp. That wasn't the case with this lunch crowd. In seconds, flesh, bones, blood, and viscera surged and rolled in the oily waters.

Rand gulped. "They passed on the salad course, I guess."

"Just look at them," Annie breathed.

Just then one of the three paused in its gorging to hiss a piercing whistle at them, giving them that same hungry, pitiless stare.

"They're looking *at us*!" she cried.

If we shoot these three, do nine more show up? he wondered. Even Robotech weapons had their limits. He grabbed Annie's arm. "Let's get out of here! Move, move!"

In another moment the armor had mechamorphosed, and the two Cyclones leapt away, Annie clinging to Rand once more, the tires automatically adjusting to travel over the soft soil. The *Eogyrinus*es came swarming up at them moments too late.

"Guess we lost 'em," Annie reported, glancing back over her shoulder to be sure. "I don't think they're built for long-distance events."

"But where did they *come* from?" Scott murmured.

Rand gazed upward. The sky held no sign of the energy field; instead there was a low gray haze. They sped up another dry watercourse, past tall, odd-looking conifers and cycads and some bennettitaleans.

"The Lost World," he said softly.

Lancer looked at Rook hopefully as he hopped down from the cockpit of Scott's abandoned Alpha fighter. *Let it be good news! Let her have found something!*

But as Rook slid her cycle to a stop, Lancer was already listening to negative results over the armored suits' tac net. "I followed the path north and cut a circle for a mile around. There wasn't a trace of them."

As she finished her report, Lunk showed up in his olive-drab APC truck. "If they circled back, they weren't leaving tracks," he reported.

That left another question. Scott's Cyclone was gone, and there were no tire marks anywhere. But why would they have gone straight to full armor and flown away, without leaving a message or trying to make commo contact with their teammates?

Maybe the tire tracks had been obliterated by someone? That would be easy enough to do in this kind of soil.

Lancer yelled out, *"They know better than to do this to us."* Rand might be a bit impetuous, and Annie was flighty to say the least, but Scott, a trained officer and team leader, would never simply ignore his responsibilities.

There was only one explanation that might make some sense of the situation, and that was the appearance of Invid.

"Shouldn't one of us scout ahead?" Rand asked as the two Cyclones sped through the eerie landscape of the subterranean world. "I've had enough surprises for one day."

"We'll stick together for now," Scott ordered.

"Well, do you have any idea where we're headed?" The instruments were all useless.

"No, Rand. But anywhere away from those reptiles will be fine with me—hey, power down! There's something up ahead—the end of the trail, maybe."

They stopped in an open part of the water course. What they saw ahead of them was a rampart of stone some hundreds of yards high, running away to the left and right with no breaks.

"A dead end!" Annie wailed. "And the cliffs and ceiling come together."

It was true. The overhead haze was broken by the downward sweep of the gigantic cavern's stone ceiling, which met the walls of the place in a tight seal. "No exit here," Scott observed.

"Maybe; maybe not," Rand corrected. "See up there?"

It was an opening of some kind, the mouth of a tunnel or cave, set high above the floor of the cavern. "That could be our rabbit-hole," Rand declared. "It's worth a look."

Scott couldn't argue with that. Their engines howled.

Elsewhere, the Regis noticed that something was amiss in one of her Genesis Pits. From Reflex Point, her consciousness reached out to join with the evolved mind of a Shock Trooper who was following the movements of the three Humans.

The Trooper's single, cyclopean optic sensor flashed red as she mindspoke. *Contaminants in the pit*! her angry thought reverberated through that trooper and the others assigned to the place. *Unless these intruders are contained and neutralized, the experiment will be ruined!*

But she paused, seeing the reasoning of her guards. Certainly these were Earthly biota, and under the Regis's broad guidelines they were valid candidates for inclusion in the pits. But these were Human, and they were armed with weapons and mounted on vehicles. A counterproductive anachronism here in the cavern of monsters!

Still, the introduction of machines and weapons might provide some instructive insights about the capabilities of the creatures she had bred here beneath the Earth. Their worth as contributors to the Invid's final, Evolved Form would be tested.

Yes; let it continue for now, at least until more observations had been made. The creatures of the cavern would probably cleanse the place of outsiders by themselves, and that would be most informative, too. Or if not . . .

There were other ways.

CHAPTER
FOUR

Fay Wray can have it!

Remark attributed to Annie LaBelle

THERE ARE IMPORTANT INSIGHTS TO THE STORY IN Rand's recounting of it in his voluminous *Notes on the Run*:

"I got even more worried when I saw that that tunnel through the bedrock was artificial. It had a low arc of roof, but the flat, level floor made it easy for us to go to cycle mode and race along.

"The obvious fact that someone had drilled the tunnel made me nervous, but let's face it: *everything* about that underground Lizard Lounge had me nervous by then. Scott had noticed it, too, I assumed, but we didn't mention it because we didn't want Annie hysterical.

"So we barreled down the tunnel. The Cycs' headlights cut the darkness, but only showed us the rock walls, the rock ceiling, and the rock floor. I would even have welcomed some motel art by that time. I had long since outgrown my graffiti stage, but I was tempted.

"I fibbed to Annie. 'Hang on tight! I've got a real strong feeling about this tunnel; in fact I'm sure it's gonna be our way out of this place!' If she knew I was bulling her, she was kind enough not to say so.

"But she did point to a bright light that was coming up before us. 'Hey, look at that!'

"Scott's voice sounded real relieved over the tac net, 'We made it!' That sort of surprised me; I figured a guy raised in starships most of his life wouldn't feel the claustrophobia as badly as I was feeling it, but I guess the weight of all those strata above us had been working at him.

"So I said, tempting fate a little, 'I knew it! Our troubles are over now!'

"All of a sudden the floor of the tunnel seemed to slope down. The next thing we knew, the Cycs were out in the open air and falling toward the lush vegetation down below.

"But we were pretty used to our mecha by then, although it had taken me some time to learn the ropes on a Cyc and Scott hadn't had much practice operating in an environment like Earth until he had crash-landed, a coupla weeks before. *Mox nix;* we hit our burners. I did my best to see that I didn't lose Mint, and somehow I made that landing on sky-blue, umbrella-shaped thruster flames.

"The terrain we landed on seemed okay at first, with boulders and some kind of fanlike growths coming from the ground. It was a little precarious but nothing those amazing Robotech scoots couldn't handle. If I had had my helmet open, maybe I would have noticed the smell; Annie was, I suppose, too strung out to.

"We were congratulating ourselves on making it when the ground beneath us began to move. We had landed in the middle of a bunch of big sail-backed things! Just before we thruster-jumped the hell *out* of there, I got a look down the maw of one of the things and saw it had two quite large front choppers. I guess it was a *Dimetrodon*, but I wasn't doing much note-taking and really couldn't tell you for sure if you asked me.

"Scott was howling something about 'more dinosaurs' but we were safe. The herd had re-settled for the night.

"We were all watching them to make sure that they weren't thinking about a bedtime snack, but I just happened to be looking off to one side when I caught the flash of movement. 'Hey, Invid!' I blurted out. But whatever it was had already ducked.

"Scott thought I was crazy, and we got a little sore at each other. Being that far underground and in a situation so insane had him kind of frayed. But then he backed off a bit, looking around thoughtfully. 'Maybe they *are* involved in all this. I suppose —'

"Scott interrupted his thought when he noticed that Annie was off an another caper, waving to us from a few yards away. She was balancing, with a lot of windmilling of her hat and shuffling of shoes, on a big, mottled, off-white ovoid thing that rolled under her. She was giggling and yelling, 'Watch me!'

"It was a typical Mint reaction to what we had just been through, driving it from her mind by clowning around. When I saw what she was doing, I could only think, *Oh, my god*! and I started to reach for my '90. Scott was yelling at her to get down off of there.

"Annie laughed right up until the second she realized that something big was coming up behind her—fast! I got my gun out. Maybe that *Daspletosaurus* actually wasn't the size of two Battloids one on top of the other, but that was how it looked to me at that moment.

"Certainly it was a little surprised to see Annie playing around with its eggs. I can only surmise that it had just laid them and hadn't had time to cover over its nest. It was fast and agile and brilliantly colored. It was just like the oldtime revisionist paleontologists said: a tower of bone and muscle in metallic blues and reds and pinks. Its teeth looked like sharpened baseball bats.

"I opened fire at it, and then Scott did, too. I have to give the lieutenant credit: he stood his ground and just kept shooting H90 rounds at it, even though it didn't look like he was doing *any* damage to the thing.

"If you're sitting someplace safe and reading this, I'll tell you something: It feels a lot different when *you're there*, and an animal bigger than any mecha is bearing down on you and you can smell it, and the best shots you can lay out don't seem to be making any difference. It takes a lot not to bolt, but I didn't have to make the choice because Scott Bernard was slightly in front of me, straddle-legged, whamming away. So I stood my ground, too.

"Then you live from microsecond to microsecond, and events all fuse together, because when you're about to die your life is suddenly an infinitely precious thing, no matter how lousy it's been to you.

"It was our good luck that the thing had a lot of ground to cover. I was aiming for the skull, hoping I might put its eyes out of commission or even get its brain somehow. It roared and staggered at us. But H90s were developed for use against Invid mecha, and no living organism, even one the size of that tyrannosaurid, could survive the kind of punishment we were giving it.

"We chopped away at its feet, legs, chest cavity, head —all while it was shrieking and snapping. Then Annie had the presence of mind to leap clear, as the *Daspletosaurus* fell across its own eggs, crushing some, dying and charred, never understanding what had killed it.

"I was yelling at Annie, who was white faced and contrite and promising not to go running off ever again, when I spotted familiar shapes: 'Hey, Scott! I *told* you I saw Invid!'

"But they had drawn back out of sight before Scott turned from Annie or she could spin around. And right away Scott and I were arguing again. How could he have seen them up above and yet not believe I had done the same down below? Either you trust your teammates or you don't.

"Of course, Mint put in her two-cents' worth, as the ancients say. She was scared enough as it was and wished I wouldn't see Invids behind every tree.

"For maybe the fourth time that day I bit back what I had been about to say. I knew Scott's military training revolved around reports and evaluations and source-dependability ratings and all that garbage, but either I was a teammate or I wasn't. I dropped the subject, though.

"'I can't help it if you're scared, kid,' I told Annie, turning away from Scott to kind of defuse things. 'I'm scared, too. But they *were* there, they're *still* there, and they're waiting for us.'

"I just couldn't get a handle on any of it. Prehistoric biota, and Invid who didn't attack. It just didn't make sense.

"But I could see that at least I had given Scott something to ponder.

"The fire we built on the beach of a tepid lake made Annie feel a lot safer. But I was still looking in every direction, waiting for Godzilla and the gang to show up expecting hot hors d'oeuvres. Scott coughed at the smoke but agreed with Annie that the fire was cheery.

"I stripped off my armor and put together a survival-type circle trident, to try to catch some supper. Up on the surface we could have just thrown some explosives in the water and waited for the catch of the day to come floating to us belly-up. But around here those tactics might just make something mad.

"So I crouched nervously on a rock on the beach, waiting, checking the deeper water every half second or so, I guess. Still, I'm a country kid, a Forager, and I had done that kind of thing a hundred times before. Pretty soon I had a hit.

"What I pulled up was all needle snout and kinked tail, some sort of freshwater, pygmy *Ichthyosaurus* whose grandmother had too many X-rays, I guess. I threw it down on the sand. Scott and Annie came over to find out what was wrong.

"Everything just got to me, because I started waving my arms around and babbling. The whole time scale had me going nuts.

"'This fish should've been dead, I dunno, sixty-five million years ago. Those pterosaurs and all the rest of these critters, same thing!'

"Annie was looking at me with eyes as round as full moons. 'S-so how can they still be alive?'

"Scott was shaking his head slowly. 'This is—it's beyond me.'

"I told them, 'Well *I'm* just wondering what *else* might be floating around out there.' Somewhere far off, we heard something very heavy break the water in a dive. It reminded me of the sound whales made in those prewar nature shows. Only, we knew it wasn't a whale, because it honked like a horny tractor-trailer.

"'At least *Annie* can sleep,' Scott said tiredly awhile later, as we sat in the firelight. We planned to take turns standing guard all night, and it was time for him to turn in.

"We had managed to talk Annie out of taking a watch with some excuse about needing her to help with the scouting the next day. Actually we didn't want her up alone and didn't really trust her with a gun. Even Scott saw the sense in letting her sleep. She snored softly, cap bill pulled down, hands clasped across her middle as she lay on her back. I shrugged. 'Kids: nothing bothers 'em.'

"We were finishing up the last of my impossible fish, and Scott grinned, 'Your *appetite* hasn't been bothered much, either.' I kept on chewing, looking into the fire, trying to think. 'Hey, Rand! Anybody home?'

"'I hear ya perfectly well, Scott. I'm just trying to piece a few things together, all right?'

"He took an unspoken offense and went to curl up by the other side of the fire. He probably thought that I was still upset that he didn't believe me about the Invid.

"I thought back to what had happened since we fell into that pit or whatever it was. The fire made it easier to visualize the energy screen we had fallen through.

"Scott had grown up out there in space somewhere, and lacked a lot of knowledge about Earth. And Annie—she was simply Annie. But one of the main things that originally drew me into the Forager life was that it was a way to find books. Books, films—the history of Earth, the Human race; the history that led to my being what I am, if that doesn't sound uppity.

"No, Scott knew next to nothing about Earth's prehistory, but I had read a small library's worth. What kid doesn't become interested in dinosaurs? And I had seen enough to know that what we had been thrown into was a huge potpourri: Paleozoic plants, Mesozoic reptiles. Everything was thrown in and mixed around, as if somebody was waiting to see what floated to the top.

"While there were a few swamp areas like the one in which we had found ourselves at the outset, most of the hundreds or thousands of square miles of the Lizard Lounge appeared to be flood plain, with seasonal bodies of water. We had no idea how the builders managed that. But it was no wonder the place was so enormous; the land creatures' lives revolved around the herbivores' need for a slow, constant feeding migration, and the carnivores' constant need to follow and hunt.

"We had seen dinos no bigger than chipmunks, and the real heavyweights as well; most or all of the biological niches were filled, including the ones for small, furtive mammals.

We had seen things that verified the work of Ostrom, Horner, Bakker, and the rest of the last great paleontologists. *Stegosaurus* actually *did* have a single row of bony plates on its back. Do they know, I hope?

"What we had stumbled into were warm-blooded dinosaurs—endotherms! The *Brontosaurus*es protected their young while on the move, like a herd of elephants. I watched huge duckbill females exhibiting maternal behavior, feeding and protecting their hatchlings. Of course, we didn't have any time to witness live births among the brontos: we were sorta busy keeping away from hungry meat-eaters.

"The predators were warm-blooded, and therefore had to eat a *lot*. They were fast-moving, very aggressive, and always ready for a meal. I watched a pack of swift *Deinonychuses*, running on bird-hipped hind legs, drag down a much bigger *Tenontosaurus*. The *Deinoychuses* tore the helpless giant to pieces and devoured it.

"Annie hid her eyes against my back, and while I was fascinated even though I was sickened, I made up my mind to try to spare her any similar sight, if possible.

"We had already had a few close encounters, though. Scott may go down in history as the only human being to ever kill a *T. Rex*; he did it with a rocket barrage of Scorpions from his Cyc's forward racks. We were safe for the time being, but how long could we last once we ran out of power and ordnance?

"I'm probably the last member of the legendary King Kong Klub, having passed the rigorous written and oral exams and proven my love for that movie. But in spite of my avowed devotion to stop-motion critters, I wished in those next hours that the Cycs were teleportation machines. I suspect we all did. You would have, too.

"I had forgotten that smell of blood. If you have ever had a serious laceration or been around major trauma, you know what I'm talking about. Fresh blood, spilled, lost. That smell was so thick down there that I swear it would have snuffed a candle.

"Still, that wasn't what I was trying to sort out while I sat watching the fire that night, to the sound of *Pachycephalosauruses* batting heads like bighorn sheep and oinking and spitting at each other. I was considering the awesome size of the artificial world around me.

"The Human race, even at its prewar height, didn't have the power or the knowledge to create this Lost World. It was pretty obvious who was behind it.

"But the Invid certainly had little motivation to build an Earth museum. Then I stopped thinking of the Invid I had been catching glimpses of in terms of soldiers and started trying to think of them as some other kind of force—say, park rangers? Guarding a sanctuary, perhaps?

"'Clear enough!' I was mumbling, and Scott sat up, rubbing his eyes, to look at me. 'This place is one big lab!' I cried. 'Now I'm beginning to understand! It's incredible!'

"'Well, *I'm* not beginning to understand,' he was grousing. 'Back up and try again.'

"He was right. I forced myself to slow down. 'I'm sure this is an Invid test facility. They're playing around with the history of life on Earth—evolution, from the start right down to today!'

"Were there other arenas where Tertiary organisms fought and strove, or basic Earth life-forms had been mutated with coldly clinical intent, against some possible future? There wasn't any time to think about that now; I was about to trip over my own tongue as it was. I tried again. 'They're doing evolution experiments—cloning, genetic engineering! Darwinism in the passing lane!'

"'Are you drunk?'

"'I wish! Listen, Scott: the Invid intend to make Earth their home, because that's where the Flower of Life grows best, right? Well, before they choose the final physical form—or forms—they'll take on, they're testing, studying!'

"Scott was standing up with a lot of well-now-hold-on-a-second-there talk and flat-handed calming gestures.

"'And now *we're* part of the experiment,' I yelled over him, sorry that Annie was going to have to wake up to bad news, because I was shouting it. 'They're using us as guinea pigs somehow; that's why the Invid keep hidden instead of showing themselves and attacking—'

"Scott was trying to shush me, but I backed away; I couldn't let him think I had had a hysterical episode, or he would *never* believe me. 'Scott, we've got to get out of here. Or at least get word to the others! This is more important than your damned Reflex Point! Once the Invid find a form that they figure will let them dominate the Earth, there'll be no more need for—uh!'

"At least, I *think* that was the sound I made. We had both stopped in midsyllable, mouths open, because the voice we heard then seemed to come from everywhere. It was female, and there was something slightly familiar about it. It was mostly alien and cold, yet with an arrogant undertone to it.

"I also got the feeling, somehow, that its words were being transmitted to and echoed by some multitude that spoke with a single voice, subordinate to the main one.

And I know this is strange, but—it sounded like a stage voice to me, like somebody doing Lady Macbeth through a lot of voice-processing equipment.

"It said, 'Humans, your time on this planet is almost spent!'

"We were both looking around for the source of the voice. And then I felt cold night air on my neck, because the hair there was standing up, because—*Annie came to a sitting position, arms folded across her chest.*

"She was still facing away from us, the firelight playing over the hair that looked so straggly after a day of roughing it in that sweaty theme park.

"Scott began, 'Um, Annie, are you feeling all—'

"That voice came again. 'The age of Humans is coming to an end!' What sat on the ground turned toward us, but the features we saw weren't Annie's anymore. It was something old and malign, using her face and form.

"'Now,' it gloated, 'a new era begins on Earth!'

"'What's she babbling about?' I said, but I didn't mean Annie.

"'Rand, she—sounds possessed,' Scott swallowed. And I had been hoping he would have some idea what we should do.

"The thing using Annie's body rose to its feet, standing across the camp fire from us. 'Humans, you do not know the extent of our power!'

"With that, the fire expanded, the flames leapt high above our heads. Scott and I backed off a step or two, shielding our faces.

"We saw Annie across the flames from us as she let them die down a bit, her hair floating as if windblown, her hands making passes as if she were a sorceress.

"'Humans are merely a dead end in the great scheme of evolution!' Annie gestured, and all of a sudden, so help me, we were seeing a moving form silhouetted in the blaze, a female form that didn't look quite Human. It threw its arms high in triumph, while that chilling voice went on exultantly.

"'The Earth is entering an era of domination by a different form of life, which has traveled a *different* evolutionary path.' The thing laughed evilly. 'Be warned . . .'

"But then the voice trailed away, until it was Annie's, moaning, and the expression on the face was one we recognized. Annie slumped, and we rushed to her."

CHAPTER
FIVE

Those which we call monsters are not so with God

Montaigne, *Essays*, Vol. II, XXX

THE TEAM'S SEARCH PATTERNS TURNED UP NOTH-
ing. Exhausted, they stopped for a few hours' rest before
they would continue with a night-sweep.

Lunk couldn't seem to stop himself from repeating the
same thing over and over: "What coulda *happened* to
'em?"

"I don't know where else to look," Lancer admitted
tiredly. "Our best hope is that they just—show up." He
ran his fingers through his long purple hair.

Lunk sat down next to him, leaning against the same
boulder in the firelight. He gnawed noisily on a drumstick
that they had scavenged from Wolff's supply depot. "I
suppose that's all we can do."

He looked to where Rook was curled up, a lithe form
in a blanket. There was only a single stray curl of strawberry-blond hair showing, brilliant in the firelight. "Isn't
she even worried about them? How can she sleep at a
time like this?"

Without turning over, she said, "I *can't* sleep, if you sit there blabbing and gorging yourself all night. How can you *eat* at a time like this?"

Lunk wore a hurt look. Lancer told him in a whisper, "The *real* reason she's awake is because she's worried, too, Lunk."

Rook lay watching the moon, listening to Lunk complain about how spooky it all was. After riding as a loner for so long, she was feeling again that special torment that she had promised herself she would always avoid—fear that harm had come to a loved one; an all-consuming concern for people who had become, though she had never meant to let it happen, family.

Annie came around again in a second or two, but when Rand and Scott told her what had happened, she claimed that they were both imagining things. As far as she was concerned, she had been having some crazy dream in which she married an Invid who looked like her old boyfriend.

That was Annie, mind never too far from the marriage that would, she was sure, let her live happily ever after. What the two men were telling her was upsetting her, and she gave them a wounded look, asking if they couldn't just drop the whole issue. Scott and Rand backed off.

But they would have had to stop talking about it anyway; just about then, a battle of the bipeds started up. In the dim nightlight glow from the haze overhead, they could just make out some big meat-eaters tangling with each other, probably over a kill or some carrion. Rand thought it was between two *Ceratosaurus*es and a larger *Allosaurus*, but couldn't see for sure and wasn't interested enough to stick around and find out.

Dangerous as it was traveling at night, the men snapped on their armor, started the Cyclones, and the moved out. They found the dry water course they had been traveling on, but they had no sooner increased their speed than the air was full of pterosaurs of all sizes and shapes, swooping and diving, beaks napping. Scott couldn't figure out if they had been stirred up by the blood and noiseof the fight, or if the Invid were somehow sending them at the Humans.

Luckily the flying things were getting in each other's way, so that evasive maneuvers saved the Cyclone riders for the moment. And lucky *was* the word; Rand saw one that had a fifty-foot wingspan. Scott's voice came over Rand's helmet phones, "You and Mint find cover! I'll fight them off and catch up!"

Rand couldn't argue; the armor gave the men a lot of protection, but Annie was completely vulnerable. Rand rogered and increased his speed, peeling away and heading for some tree cover. The soaring hunters concentrated on Scott.

Scott switched to full Battle Armor mode, rising on thrusters, Cyclone components becoming part of his powered suit. One blast from the H90 sent a small *Pteranodon* tumbling to the ground. With the flock hesitating, surprised at the blast, Scott landed in a blaring of backpack thrusters, to fight from the ground.

He blasted the wing off another as it stooped, but then had to duck and roll aside as a third came at him from the left. Its beak and wicked teeth would have taken off an unprotected arm, but the Robotech alloy saved him. He rolled onto his back, holding his H90 in both hands, firing at any pterosaur that came near.

The things shrieked as the blue bolts quartered the air, seeking them out.

"Scott's doing okay," Rand said, from the shelter of the trees, dividing his time between watching Annie and keeping an eye out for strays. "I don't think he needs our help."

"I . . . I kind of feel sorry for those creatures," Annie confessed.

"Aw, Mint, gimme a break!"

Scott was back on his feet again, shooting this way and that with a high degree of accuracy. Dead and dying soarers, whole or in pieces, lay all around him. As Rand and Annie watched, he nailed one that was coming straight down at him with folded wings; he got it dead center and its head exploded.

Then Rand noticed, from the corner of his eye, a glow coming from the foot of the nearby cliff-wall. It pulsed brightly, waned a bit, and brightened again.

"Hang on, Annie; we have to check something out."

High on a cliff ledge overlooking the savage battle, an Invid Shock Trooper mindspoke to itself and its companion. It was the Regis's voice, the same voice that was heard through Annie.

"The Human life-forms are most determined! Their will to survive is strong!"

Like the Zentraedi and the Robotech Masters, the dinosaurs were discovering that Humans weren't as easy prey as they looked. Yes, it seemed all this experimentation with life-forms from Earth's past and mutations of various ones from its present was pointless.

There would have to be further study of the Humans, to find out if their form would suit the Invid despite its aberrant behavioral patterns. But as for the ones below, they had done enough damage in the Genesis Pit. It was time to rid the place of contaminants.

Rand stopped some distance from the tunnel, which was at ground level. From the mouth of the tunnel, the light and heat pulsed so strongly that Annie hid in the lee of his armor except for an occasional peek.

"I *knew* something like this had to be here!" Rand cried. Heat, light, the energy field—perhaps even the force that kept the stupendous stone ceiling up—they had to be powered by some source. Some *Invid* source. Rand armed his forward Scorpions.

"Rand, what are you doing?" Annie asked sharply.

"It's time for 'Last Call at the Lizard Lounge,'" he said.

Eventually the pterosaurs broke off their attack, the slaughter having been too much even for them. Scott stood on the battlefield, the smoking remains all around him, fitting a fresh charge into his H90.

He rolled a body over with his foot, inspecting his work. "Must've been something he tried to eat."

Rand appeared, Annie still clinging to his waist, the Cyc skidding to a stop. "Are you all right?"

"All right so far."

"Listen, Scott, I've gotta tell you—"

But before Rand could get out his story about the Invid power source, or control center, or whatever it was, a new chorus of sounds came to them. They looked up to see that the sky was filled with every possible flying creature: dragonflies and other insects as well as pterosaurs.

"Something's stirring them up," Scott said.

"Something's got 'em *all* on the run!" Annie shouted.

They peered into the haze-light and, sure enough, the whole population of the strange sanctuary seemed to be headed their way.

"Looks like we're going to be right in the middle of rush hour," Scott was saying. Suddenly the ground began to tremble and dance beneath them. There was nothing they could do except lurch and teeter, trying to keep their balance.

"Earthquake!" Rand yelled. This wasn't the time to tell Scott about the two rockets he put into the Invid cave installation, or of the terrific secondary blast they had set off—or of the dark silence in the cave afterward. They could hear the grinding and cracking of uncountable tons of bedrock all around them.

A tree swayed like a giant flyswatter, and came down smack atop a *Triceratops* that just ignored it and kept bulldozing along. A big conifer broke the back of a smallish *Stegosaurus*; passing meat-eaters ignored it, continuing their flight. A boulder the size of a bus, falling from the ceiling, squashed an *Iguanodon*.

As the herd passed by, Rand and Scott changed modes and soared overhead on thrusters. Then they fell in behind the beasts, letting them lead the way.

"Scott, doesn't it occur to you that being in the middle of a dinosaur stampede could be bad for our health?"

"We don't know where we're going, Rand; maybe *they* do. Any better ideas?"

Rand muttered, "Oh, brother..."

Clouds of dust rose from the ground and fell from the ceiling. The haze began to grow dim. Rand figured that the energy field was losing the last of its power. It took every ounce of their skill to keep the Cycs going, but Scott insisted that they stay on the ground. The air was a storm of flying things that would have blinded them and perhaps even knocked them out of the sky.

Two big *Tyrannosaurus*es some distance in front of them simply disappeared, tails flailing, and Scott barely had time to give a warning. There was no time to brake, and the two Cyclones went off the edge, into the abyss that had opened in the ground before them. All three howled, Annie loudest of all.

As the armored men mechamorphosed, rising on their backpack thrusters again—the Cyc wheels repositioning up on their backs, out of the way—and Rand held Annie in his arms, something rose out of the chasm with them, flashing past.

"Invid Shock Troopers!" Scott shouted. Rand couldn't quite find the time to say, *Toldja*. In the distance, a thin, incandescent pillar of light suddenly stretched from the floor of the Genesis Pit up to its ceiling and beyond.

The Invid mecha swept out and around for an attack. "We'll have to take 'em on," Scott said grimly. Rand zoomed off to one side, to drop Annie off to safety on some rocks.

As Scott landed, one of the big, purple alien mecha came his way, firing annihilation discs from the bulky cannon mounted on either shoulder. Scott leapt clear with an assist from his thrusters, rolled, and came up with his H90 in his hand, firing. The Invid dodged his shots and came in at him.

Rand was standing shoulder to shoulder with Scott by then, the two trying to aim their shots while the ground heaved and jostled under them. Scott jumped off to the right and Rand launched himself high, barely eluding a swipe by a colossal metal pincer on a forearm the shape of a ladybug. Rand put more rounds into it, but the trooper crouched in a defensive posture beneath him, shielding itself with the thickest parts of its panoply.

Annie was screaming, pointing to the pillar of light. "Look, look! There's the exit, but it's disappearing!"

The energy field that had blocked the way out was gone. But the opening was shrinking, and the piller of light was getting narrower.

"It's our only chance!" Scott called to Rand.

Rand was so distracted that he was nearly mashed into the ground by a blow from an Invid. As it was, the mighty forearm got a piece of him, sending him sprawling. Rand managed to drive it back with wild shots from his side-arm, but the second Shock Trooper was angling for a shot of its own.

Rand back-flipped as Scott rushed in, the trooper getting off near misses, sending both men reeling back. Scott's targeting module deployed from its external shoulder mount and swung into place before his eye; he was staring at the Invid through a sighting reticle. He released a pair of Scorpions that missed, but drove the Invid back.

Suddenly, the invaders broke off the fight, turning and zooming off into the air, ignoring the Humans. "They're heading for the opening!" Rand saw. "We've gotta stop them, before they close it behind them!"

"Take care of Mint," Scott called back, already aloft. "I'll go after them." As he rocketed after them, he saw that the exit was closing quickly.

The Shock Troopers apparently realized they couldn't outrun their pursuer and turned to fight. Scott dodged another pincer swipe, just as Rand caught up, having dropped Annie off again. Scott evaded the swipe and vaulted to land atop the second Invid's crablike head. The first Trooper was so caught up in the battle that it swung again, missing Scott, who hurtled clear, but struck its comrade instead.

Scott dispatched another missile just as the first Trooper prepared to unleash its annihilation discs. He blasted it right through the opticle sensor that was its cyclops-eye. The warhead was a dud, but the missile penetrated the glassy circle, shattering it.

Green, thick nutrient fluid poured from the Shock Trooper, and it went flailing back like a falling scarecrow and hit the ground. The second Trooper charged at Scott, but Rand, in a close pass on raving thrusters, lashed out with his feet and smashed that one's eye, too.

"Hurry up!" Annie shrilled. "The exit's almost closed!" The entire place was shaking, raining boulders and dust, cracking apart, as monsters roared and bleated.

Rand lifted her up, and the three blasted through the air toward the shrinking ray of light. As they entered it, they were seized by the force that had drawn them into the Genesis Pit earlier, only this time it pulled them upward.

Within the Genesis Pit, the roof began to give way. The shallow waters churned, throwing up waves and living things that would soon be dead. The great beasts of land and sea threw their heads back and bellowed their agony to the world that had obliterated them once and was now doing it again.

The cliffs and ceiling gave way; the floor of the Genesis Pit fissured open, letting forth the magma the Invid had diverted to heat the place. A surge of molten fury gushed up the exit shaft behind the three Humans, threatening to overtake them.

Then the two armored figures and the little girl in her oversized battle jacket were flying upward under the moonlight. The magma stopped its upward motion and spread, igniting fires, and then it began draining down into the Pit once more.

All three Humans were laughing and cheering. Scott and Rand flew far away from the site to a distant hillside. The moon was full, but it looked to Rand as if rainclouds were moving in. Good; those fires wouldn't last long. "Isn't that a beautiful moon?" Rand said wonderingly.

But Annie's attention was elsewhere. "Look at the mountains!"

"The whole mountain range is sinking into that Pit," Scott said quietly.

The ground rumbled and moved again, clouds of dust obscuring the mountains, as a huge area went into subsidence, filling in the Genesis Pit. "That one was close" was all Scott could find to say.

Annie said mournfully, "But what about the poor dinosaurs?" She looked at Rand.

"The Invid created them," he told her. "And I think it's just as well that they left the dinosaurs down there to be destroyed. Conditions up here aren't right for them; there's just no place for them to survive anymore. Time simply passed them by."

Annie intertwined her fingers behind her back and scuffed the ground with one toe. "Y'mean, it's the same as when the Invid talk about the Human race being all finished?"

Rand was starting to nod when Scott interrupted. "No! Earth belongs to us; it's the *Invid* who are going to be extinct!"

He sounded ferocious. Rand knew all about Scott's fierce hatred of the species that had killed his fianceé and wiped out his unit, but this was no time for propaganda speeches. "All right, Scott; all right—"

"Hey!" Annie blurted. "Y'hear that?"

It was the sound of large engines. In a few moments mecha came into sight, seeking the source of the vast disturbances their instruments had detected. In another moment, the survivors spotted an aircraft.

"It's the Alpha Fighter!" Scott said. "And there's the rest of the team! It's about time."

Annie was dancing from foot to foot. "Wait'll I tell Rook what happened to me! Oboyoboy!'

"Y'better make sure she's sitting down," Rand said dryly. He wondered if Rook would care to hear *his* story. There was just no telling how the young lady would react sometimes. Still, maybe it would be worth the risk.

CHAPTER
SIX

> *The grand themes of the Robotech Wars are so dominant that the lesser ones are sometimes ignored. But those lesser themes, I insist, are more instructive.*
> *The matter of Marlene Foley's ultimate destiny is a primary case in point. Surely, Protoculture is a force to be reckoned with in our every thought.*

> Jan Morris, *Solar Seeds, Galactic Guardians*

THE FIVE INVID MECHA CRUISED SLOWLY ACROSS THE night sky, navigating with care, surveying the terrain below. They brought with them a sixth Robotech construct. Within it was a cargo of critical importance.

Two Shock Troopers brought up the rear, and a partially evolved Invid in personal battle armor—the so-called "Pincer Ship"—led the way. In the center of the flying convoy were two more Pincer Ships. Between them they carried a hexagonal canister. The canister was like a Robotech setting for a cosmic gemstone; inside its crystal cocoon there throbbed and shone a fantastic, translucent egg. The thing was luminous in deep corals, gentle reds, and flesh tones.

"We must know more about these new enemies," the Regis had decreed, in the wake of the Genesis Pit catastrophe. Her servants had been quick to act. Soon, a Simulagent, a triumph of Invid biogenetic engineering, would be in the enemy's midst. And before obliterating them, the Regis would know whether the Humans posed any possible danger to her grand scheme for her race.

The Simulagent was code-named "Ariel." Ariel had been replicated, with certain alterations, from a Human tissue sample that had been recovered while the Invid were examining the debris of the Human strikeforce they had destroyed weeks before. It was inconceivable that anyone on Earth would recognize Ariel as a clone, since the source of most of her genetic design was a dead woman from the long-gone SDF-3 expedition. . . .

The Invid flight leader's optical sensor scanned the area for any sign of Human presence, but there was none. The timing of the drop was important. The Simulagent's placement must be unseen, so that its origin would remain secret, and yet Ariel must not be left unprotected for long.

But the Invid had a recent fix on the Humans' route, which made things easier.

As the Invid formation neared its dropoff point, the crystal cocoon began to crack like an eggshell being pushed open from within. The strobing light from its center shone brighter.

Just as the formation flew low over a deserted, devastated village, the crystal shattered. The egg fell, lighting the night and the landscape below. It bounced from a tree branch to a half-demolished roof to the ground. Light and resilient and yet astonishingly strong, it suffered no injury. The flight of alien mecha turned around and started back toward Reflex Point.

The egg rested under a tree, casting its flesh-tone light all around. Soon it sensed the approach of its targets. Its glare grew, and it pulsed with the rhythm and sound of a quickened heartbeat. Darker colors swirled among the lighter ones now, and the egg stretched against the confines of its own skin with each beat.

This time Scott was flying directly over the rest of his team, keeping close in case of trouble, easing along in Guardian mode. The Veritech fighter looked like a cross between an armored knight and a robotic eagle.

The subsidence of the mountains into the Genesis Pit and the aftershocks had made the terrain dangerous and their maps useless. It had taken days to blaze a new trail through. They traveled at night, both to make up for lost time and because, at last, they had found a major highway.

Rand, Rook, and Lancer were all riding close to Lunk's APC. Like Scott, the Cyc riders had shed their armor; they all needed a chance to get out of its confinement after days of travel, and the scans and scouts indicated no Invid presence anywhere nearby. Scott flew his Alpha without his control helmet—the "thinking cap," in Robotech jargon—controlling it with the manuals alone.

Furthermore, it took Protoculture to power the armor, and they had used up a lot of their reserves in traveling the difficult mountain terrain. Several times, Scott had been forced to ferry the APC across unavoidable gaps, which was something he hated to do. By acting as a transport, the fighter was left highly vulnerable to sudden Invid attack. Also, since this task demanded very slow, deliberate, painstaking maneuvering, it ate up a lot of Protoculture. It was a workhorse role the fighter wasn't built for, and one that strained its autosystems.

At times like those Scott cursed the truck; but when he had to land and replenish his Protoculture and ordnance and service the Alpha, he blessed Lunk and the battered old APC.

Rand keyed his headset by chinning a button on the mike mouthpiece, both hands being occupied steering his Cyc. "Hey, Scott! Don'tcha think it's time for a rest? It's almost dawn, y'know."

Scott was well aware of it. The first rays of the sun were already lighting the surrounding mountain peaks, gleaming off granite and snow. They would shine through his cockpit well before they warmed his teammates below. "Quit griping! Point K is just a few more miles ahead."

"Say again?" Rook broke in sharply.

"Point K-as-in-king, Rook," Scott came back. "That's where all units from the invasion force I was in are supposed to rendezvous. They've probably already prepared an offensive aimed at wiping out Reflex Point."

Rook's voice sounded unsure. "You mean this Admiral Hunter of yours *knew the Invid were here*?"

"Negative. He didn't know *who* the enemy was, exactly, but he was aware that something was wrong back on Earth. Don't ask me how; it was all hush-hush stuff."

Even Annie, standing up in the truck's shotgun seat and resting her chin on her forearms, on the windshield frame, didn't have to ask Scott why he hadn't told them all that before. With the risk of capture or even desertion —"going my own way," as Rand or Rook would have called it—ever present, Scott simply couldn't take the chance.

Still, she kicked the glove compartment a little and pulled her E.T. hat down lower on her head, sticking out her lower lip. Lunk gave her a quick look, then went back to his driving.

Scott continued, "The way I figure it, there ought to be hundreds of Veritechs there, maybe a thousand or more. And ground units, assault mecha, supplies, and ammo—the works!"

Annie whooped into the dawn air. "Aw*right*! Now that's the way to show 'em how it's done!"

"Wait, Scott." Rand sounded edgy. "How can you hide an army that size?"

Scott was all confidence and can-do. "No more hiding. There's a secure base of operations there by now. From there we go island-hopping, cutting the links between Invid bases, until Reflex Point's isolated, and we can smash it."

Just then, Scott's displays began flashing and beeping for his attention. Computers sorted through the sensor information and flashed order-of-battle information, indicating that there was a large, friendly force just over the next ridge.

He caught a flash of bright metal off fighter tailerons, and in the valley below he saw ranked mecha in the predawn mist. "All right, boys and girls! There it is, just ahead!"

He increased power to the Guardian's foot-thrusters. "I'm going to go on ahead and report in." The Guardian flashed away, over the rise.

"Can't wait to see his playmates, huh?" Rand grumbled. This business about reporting in had reminded him that he wasn't on any army roster. Like Rook and Annie, he was just an irregular who had joined up with Scott to try to do his bit for the Human race. But he obviously had no place in a regulation strikeforce.

So, what happens to the rest of us now? "Thanks, and don't let the door hit you in the butt as you leave?"

The mists still swirled around the many hectares of grounded mecha. Scott figured the base was operating under blackout conditions, because he could see no lights or movement. He didn't receive any warn-offs or challenges, and he didn't get any indications that radar or sensors were checking him out, but he decided to land on the hillside and go in on foot anyway. The base might be using new commo procedures, and he had no desire to be shot down as a bogie.

The Guardian bowed its radome, and Scott hopped down. He stood breathing Earth's air for a few deep breaths, feeling the moment. *From this beachhead, we take our homeworld back!*

Rand and Rook had raced ahead of the others; their Cycs came leaping over the hill with a winding of Robotech engines. The sun was about to top a ridge to the east; Scott decided he might as well wait and ride down with his companions. He was painfully aware that, except for Lancer and Lunk, they had no place in this regular-army campaign.

Rand and Rook came to side-on stops, pushing up their goggles, and Lancer showed up moments later, with Lunk not far behind. Scott checked himself to make sure the mauve-and-purple flightsuit with its unit patches of his division, the Mars Division, and his knee-length, rust-red boots were all in order. Insignia, buttons, sidearm— he wasn't quite strac, but he wasn't looking too bad for somebody who had been stranded for so long.

Scott and his teammates were exchanging a few mild,

almost self-conscious congratulations—when Annie gave a dismayed yelp.

"The base! Look!"

They turned to look at the base just as the sun crested the ridge and its light shone off the snowy hills, brightening the little valley that was the home of Earth's liberation army.

But what they saw wasn't a home but rather a graveyard. Attack-transport spacecraft lay gutted like crushed eggs. Broken and burned-out mecha were everywhere. Ranks of parked Veritech Alphas had been holed and eliminated before ground crews and pilots could even reach them. Battloids and Hovertanks and MACs and logistical vehicles lay on the ground like shattered toys. And the stench of death wafted on the warming breeze.

The valley was filled with jutting, broken, blackened fuselages and skeletal, burned-off airframes and hulls. Barely keeping his balance, Scott stumbled to the edge of the rise, looking down, both hands buried in his dark hair.

The clearing of the mist only made it worse by the second. "I don't believe it; this, this can't be—" He howled across the valley, hoping the survivors would answer. He fired his H90 aimlessly into the air. The others sat in their vehicles and looked at one another in despair. At last Scott Bernard dropped the pistol, sank to his knees, and wept.

Earth's liberating army! The mist for its shroud; the vultures to caw taps over it.

One by one his friends dismounted and gathered around him.

They went down among the monolithic wrecks; there was no place else to go. Lunk opened up the last of their rations and Annie built a fire. Scott had wandered off.

He was sitting in the shade of a three-tube pumped-laser turret, looking off at nothing, eyes unfocused. Eventually, Rand came over with a plate of food and a cup of ersatz ration coffee, nudging them up against Scott. "Enough is enough. Time to eat, before you keel over."

He turned to go, then turned back for a moment. "You've got the team to think about, y'know." Rand walked away, the soles of his desert boots gritting in the sand. Scott stared blankly at the field of carnage.

Back at the campfire, Rook tried to sound positive, although cheerleading wasn't usually in her line of work; but everybody else seemed to be falling apart. "Look, here's a good idea: Why don't we get outta this dump right now?"

Lancer studied his ration can's contents, stirring them. "Not until we collect everything of use. Ordnance, supplies, weapons, perhaps Protoculture."

They all shivered a little, realizing how grisly that search would be. Lunk blew out smoke from a ration-pak cigarette, unsteadily. Rand returned.

"How is he?" Lancer asked, looking at the distant figure sitting with arms around knees.

Rand pulled up the hood of his sweatshirtlike windbreaker. "Catatonic. I dunno."

Lancer set down his ration can. "Come on, Scott! We're wasting time!"

Rand caught Lancer's arm. "Uh, I think I'm gonna go forage over *that* way. Maybe Scott can establish a commo base."

Like the others, Lancer caught what was in Rand's eyes. In another moment they were on the move, eager to replenish their supplies, eager to get away. As Rand sped off in a plume of soil, Rook raced after him.

The Robotech graveyard was a strange place for a two-ride, but Rand welcomed it. It came, really, just as he had decided it was pointless to try to get close to the onetime biker queen. By her city lights, he was just a hick, a wilderness Forager. She had made it clear to him that he wasn't one of the Bad Boys. Rand tried not to show his astonishment as she fell in with him, their tires stenciling parallel tread patterns among the looming derelicts.

They were moving slowly, searching; he had his hood down and his goggles up on his forehead. He glanced over at Rook, admiring the lissome grace her red-and-blue racer's bodysuit showed off. "Why'd you come along?" He had to yell, not wanting to key his headset. "Not that it bothers me or anything."

Her fair brows knit; the strawberry-blond hair blew around her freckled face. "Too depressing back there."

They came in a tight turn around a smashed tanker. Rand was saying, "I know what you—heyyyyy!"

They dug to a stop at the lip of a drop-off, looking down into a kind of arroyo ledge protected by drainage ditches. There stood a village—or at least, the remains of a village; its caved-in tile roofs and beaten-down walls and the general lifelessness of it somehow let them know it had suffered the same fate as the strikeforce.

"Two transgressors approach," the voice of the Regis said to her mecha warriors. "Remain in concealment!"

The war machines hunkered down, Scouts and Shock Troopers in personal battle armor, watching through optic sensors. Rand and Rook wound their way down the narrow lane.

Rand rode through the streets calling for any survivors, even though it might attract dangerous attention. But there was little time to search, and he hated the idea of leaving anyone, especially a child or someone who had been injured, behind. Rook was impressed with Rand's nerve, but she kept that to herself. She joined in the yelling.

They dismounted near the only building that was still in one piece, a large hacienda. Obviously the place had been too close to the strikeforce's rendezvous point, and it had been included in the slaughter. More carnage. But the two had grown callous to such scenes.

They were looking around the hacienda, not talking or meeting each other's gaze, when Rook smelled something strange and went to a spot where most of an adobe wall had been blown away. She stepped through into a garden, and knelt next to something jellylike and translucent, like a dying man-o'-war, draped across the swordleafed plants there. It was three or four inches thick, and had perhaps the surface area of a table cloth.

Rook knelt by it. "Careful," Rand grated, holding his gun uncertainly. But she touched it, then snatched her hand back with a hiss of pain.

"Damn thing burned my hand! And it's nothing to smirk about!"

"Well I *said* watch out."

She was suddenly as alert as a doe. Her voice came more softly, so intimate that it made him a little light-headed. She practically mouthed it, "Do you think the Invid are still around?"

He shrugged. She was up and moving; he had been staring, fascinated, at the blob of protoplasmic stuff, but now he couldn't take his eyes off the fit of her bodysuit, the shape of those slender legs, the swirl of the seemingly weightless cascade of hair. . . .

"I'll look outside; you check in back of the house." She pulled out her gun, and that brought him back to reality. His own gun was in his hand, fitted with its attachable stock and barrel extension, in submachine gun configuration now. He stepped back through the rift in the wall and thought about the blob of clear jelly.

A brief sensation of expanded awareness, as if his mind had been touched by another, swept through him. *Why do I feel like I've been through all this before?* The thought came unbidden and bemused him.

He heard a sound from back somewhere in the vaulted darkness of the hacienda. It might have been some debris falling as easily as it might have been some living thing blundering into a pile of rubble.

Rand warily followed the noise, his weapon raised. In a courtyard at the center of the place, he saw another sheet of the glistening, decomposing man-o'-war stuff, shrinking in the sun as he watched it. Its highlights twinkled like stars. He strained to remember what it reminded him of, as he moved on, footsteps echoing in the darkened hallways.

It looked almost...almost... But the image eluded him.

He heard a sound. He whipped around a corner with his weapon ready, braced to do battle. "*FREEZE*! Just fr—just, that is ..."

CHAPTER
SEVEN

> *Not even Zand, for all his PSI Sinsemilla, his Flower ingestion, had foreseen anything like it. And on and on, the Protoculture Shaped events.*
>
> Xandu Reem, *A Stranger at Home: A Biography of Scott Bernard*

SHE SAT IN A SHAFT OF SUNLIGHT THAT POURED down on her like a benediction from above. Her arms were crossed on her bare bosom, long, slim fingers clutching opposite shoulders. She stared aimlessly at the light.

Her hair was a deep red, like his own but waist-length, and luxuriant as some rare pelt. Her skin was so pale, her body so frail-looking—and yet it was a woman's. Highlights glistened from her—

Like the twinkling of stars.

Rand realized how close he had come to shooting by blind instinct. He also realized that she was naked, and he saw how beautiful she was there under the soft, almost loving sunlight.

"Ooo! That is . . . excuse me!" He brought the gun up and stared at it for a moment. He whirled, with a country Forager's sense of propriety. "That is, I'm sorry!"

She looked up at the strange figure, her long distraction broken. "Uhmm-ahh?"

The distraught Rand was trying to collect his wits. In the outlands where he came from, being found with a naked woman could have all sorts of horrible repercussions, especially if one were found with her by her male kin.

He jittered, staring at the pockmarked stucco wall. "Didn't mean to surprise you! But—won't you catch cold just sitting there like that? You know—Heh, umm, don't you have any—" He tried not to look at her. "—any *clothes* you could put on?"

She didn't know who or what she was. She looked up at the creature or object that had moved and made noises toward her. Following an ingrained program, she emulated: "Clothes...put...on?"

"Yeah, you know: anything to w-woo—" He was having trouble spitting it out, and he was having even more trouble keeping himself from ogling her.

"Have any thing w-wwoo—" she mimicked, completely baffled.

Just then, Rook dashed in. "Rand! I thought I heard voices!"

As she skidded to a stop, he was already waving his hands, trying to keep her from seeing the situation. "Um, don't come any closer! I don't think you want to see, er—maybe we should get back to the Cycl—"

But she had already seen the naked woman, and her open-mouthed surprise changed to anger. "Stop being an idiot!" She elbowed him aside and looked down at the young woman, who was trembling and looking up at them both, apparently in a state of shock.

Rook spun around and grabbed the front of Rand's pullover. "You *animal*! How could you *do* something like this?"

"Hey, honest! I found her like that! She wasn't wearing a single piece of *anything*!" He was astounded by the anger in her eyes, astounded that she could think he would assault someone. He was even more astonished by something else he thought he saw there. It was partially a look of despair, as if Rand had betrayed her, betrayed some emotional investment she had made in him.

She released him and began taking off her faded yellow hunting jacket, moving toward the young woman. "I'll just *bet* she wasn't, you scuzzwad!" She knelt to drape her jacket gently around the woman's shoulders.

"Tell me," Rook said kindly, "why are you here all by yourself?"

"Here all by yourself," Ariel repeated.

Rand told Rook, "That's all she does, repeat what you say!"

Rook rose and went back to him. "Now slow down and tell me what you're babbling about."

He shrugged. "Maybe she lost her memory."

Rook considered that. "You mean like through some sort of trauma?"

The young woman was staring down blankly at the straw on which she sat. The scintillating lights playing off her were fewer now.

Rand rode point, while Rook followed along with the frightened young woman huddled in her jacket.

They were observed by the optical sensors of a half dozen Shock Troopers and Pincer Ships.

"The Simulagent has been accepted," the Regis's voice rang among them. "Follow and observe! Make no attempt to contact—as yet!"

Annie, worried about Scott, stayed behind when the others went out foraging. Her few attempts to get him to talk met with utter failure. As the sun climbed higher, she idly inspected the nearby hulk, and kept one eye on Scott. He didn't move but sat beneath the gun turret, staring off into space.

Something bright in the sand caught her eye. "Hey, Scott, look what I found!" She swung it from its chain. "A pendant! Isn't it *beautiful*?"

But he never even turned her way. Annie's feelings were so hurt that she threw the glittering thing back toward where she had found it, then squatted miserably in the dust, eyes brimming with tears.

But a moment later she was distracted by the approach

of Scott's Alpha, still in Guardian mode. Annie jumped to her feet, waving and smiling up at the Veritech. "Hey, Lancer!"

A few seconds later, Lancer leapt down from the cockpit. Annie trotted over to greet him. "Did everything go all right? Didja find any Protoculture?"

He beamed, throwing back the long purple tresses. "I found something even better! Come on, while I tell Scott."

She dashed after, thrilled without even knowing what the news was. "Scott! Wait'll you hear this!"

Lancer stopped in front of the young lieutenant. "Scott, listen—" He stopped because Scott hadn't even bothered to look up at him.

Scott sighed listlessly. At last, still looking down, he said, "Yeah, what is is?"

But before Lancer could speak, they heard Lunk returning, laughing and beeping the horn of his truck. "Hey, everybody! Wait'll you see *this*! It's terrific!"

He was still carrying on as he stopped in a shower of gravel and sand and hopped out of the cab. Scott wasn't any more curious about Lunk's find than about Lancer's, but Lancer and Annie were eager to hear.

"You won't believe it!" Lunk chortled. "It's a new type of Veritech fighter I've never seen before!" He was waving a manual. "See? It attaches to the back of the Alpha, and it'll double or triple the range and firepower! It's called, uhh—"

He paused to thumb through the manual. Scott surprised everyone by saying quietly, "It's a Beta Fighter."

The other three went *"Huh?"* in concert, then Lunk continued. There was barely a mark on the Beta, and he had already repaired the slight damage there was. He unfolded one of the manual's diagrams and showed it to Lancer and Annie.

The Beta was bigger and more burly looking than the Alpha. It was a mecha of raw power that could also assume Battloid form and a kind of modified Guardian.

Then it was Lancer's turn. He had located two more Alphas that looked like they could be made combat-ready, especially given the surplus of spare parts lying around.

Lunk was still giddy. "With four fighters and four Cyclones, we'll just plain knock the Invid clear off this old world!"

Annie was picturing herself in a victory parade. "Scott, this is so exciting! We're going to have enough firepower to make us a miniature *army*!"

He looked at her angrily. "Four lousy fighters? What difference will that make against the Invid? The people who died here *were* an army, don't you understand that, any of you? This was part of Admiral Hunter's hand-picked force! And all we can do is end up *just like them*!" He slammed his fist against the torn hull furiously.

He hated himself for saying it. He had spent the morning hating himself for a variety of reasons: for the death of his fiancée Marlene in the initial attack, when Scott was the only survivor from his entire squadron. For leading the others along on this quixotic quest across a ruined Earth, with a lunatic vision of defeating the beings who had conquered an entire world. For the despair that had enveloped and disabled him completely, now that all his hopes were shattered. For the sad necessity of telling them, now, that it had all been a mistake, and they had to make their own way from here on, as best they could . . .

Annie was in tears and Lunk's big fists were balled. He looked a little like an angry gorilla. "That does it. Bernard! All right, you feel bad about your buddies; we understand, and we do, too. But is that any reason to take it out on Annie?"

Lunk took a step closer. "Get up." His ham-size, scarred fists were raised.

But Lancer intervened, almost frail and insubstantial next to Lunk, though they had all seen Lancer fight and knew differently. "Lunk, stop. Take care of Annie, will you? I'll talk to Scott."

Lunk hesitated, then obeyed. Lancer went to squat next to Scott, who seemed to be asleep.

"Don't say anything, please, just listen. We're all with you, and we're still ready to follow you in the fight against the Invid, because you—and we—are the last chance the Human race has. But if you give up now, the team falls apart, because you're the only one with the know-how to tackle Reflex Point.

"Now I want you to remember what *you* told *us*: we're all soldiers, and we have to do our duty, whatever the cost, whatever happens."

Scott's eyes had slowly opened, but he still stared out at the aftermath of the slaughter. Lunk, disgusted, led Annie off to begin work on the Alphas Lancer had found. After a moment Lancer followed them, leaving Scott alone and silent once more.

There's no way to defeat the Invid. You're insane, and now you've passed the insanity on to others.

He lost track of time until a sudden glint of light caught his eye. It was the sun shining off the pendant Annie had tossed aside. It was a cheap piece of jewelry; a lot of people in Mars Division and the other units had carried it or something like it. That made him remember something suddenly, and he dug out the locket Marlene had given him when they had parted—unknowingly—for the final time. It was a flat, heart-shaped metallic green locket with a blood-red holo-bead in the center, not very expensive but unutterably dear to him.

He activated it and it opened like a triptych. The air above the holo-bead was shot through with distortions, then the image of Marlene hung there, a Marlene perhaps six inches tall. Her uniform with its short skirt and boots showed off coltish legs. She was gamine and graceful; pale, wide-eyed, with long brown hair. Not beautiful, but very attractive.

The brief loop began playing in mid-message. "My love, I accept your marriage proposal with all my heart. I can't tell you what this means to me, or how long I've dreamt you would ask. Yes, Scott: I'd be *proud* to spend the rest of my life with you."

He had looked at it once, in the cockpit, just after she had given it to him, with nova-bright joy. But in the countless other times he had opened it, Marlene was superimposed on a scene of a flaming, plunging warcraft.

He clamped the locket shut once more, cutting off the loop. *Marlene!* Suddenly he heard the sound of powerful engines and looked up. The APC was returning with Rook at the wheel and Annie crouched nervously in the back seat. Rand was playing outrider on his Cyclone. The Alpha was playing mother hen to the bulky Beta Fighter. Scott figured Lunk was babying the Beta along; the big ex-soldier had some flight time, although he preferred the ground. But who was that in the APC's shotgun seat?

He got a better look and leapt to his feet without realizing it. *Marlene!*

The hair was a different color, but the face, the skin, the eyes—the very posture of her—these things *were* those of his dead fiancée.

It's finally happened. I've driven myself mad.

"It's like she's just learning to talk," Rook finished her story, "but she learns very quickly."

"How terrible the thing that happened to her must have been," Lancer said somberly.

Annie was sniffling. She wiped her eyes on the floppy sleeve of her battle jacket. "Well, I think it's awful!"

Rand looked grim. "The Invid did this to her, you can bet on that."

Lancer had assured himself that there was nothing obviously wrong with the young woman. There were no signs of bruises, wounds, or sexual assault. "We'd better get her to a town, somewhere where she can be helped."

The Simulagent had been staring at Scott, unnerving him, so that he stole only intermittent glances at her. Now though, still watching him, she shivered and groaned, then went down on one knee. Scott couldn't escape the feeling that it had something to do with him. *Or maybe I just want to believe that?*

It seemed impossible that anyone could be such a close match of another Human being. He had no faith in miracles, but he was beginning to think he would have to change his mind, because there was no other logical explanation.

But there was no time for insights; seconds later a

deep thrumming vibrated the air, and the freedom fighters whirled to see a flight of Invid mecha heave into sight from behind a crashed battlecruiser.

The war machines spread out into a skirmishing line and began their slow approach, gliding some thirty feet above the ground. Rand and Rook sprinted off toward their Cyclones. After a moment's confusion, Lunk and Annie knelt to gather up the young woman, as Lancer prepared to get to his Robotech bike as well.

Rand halted to look back at Scott, who still stood rooted. "Come *on*, Scott! Hurry!"

Lancer seized Rand's arm. "Forget about him and get to your Cyclone!"

Rand gave Scott a brief, bitter look. "Big talker." Then he rushed to battle.

Lunk and Annie got Ariel to take cover behind an exploded cruiser's hull. The three Cyclones raced out to meet the enemy. *We're lucky they didn't simply open fire*, Lancer thought. *With all of us caught in the open like that, it could have been a turkey shoot.*

The Pincer Ships and Shock Troopers laid down an advancing barrage of fire, patterning toward the oncoming riders. The annihilation discs from their shoulder cannons streamed down, fountaining sand and fire and debris wherever they hit.

Scott watched numbly. Part of him wanted to fight and part of him simply wanted to end it all. He wanted to give in to the seemingly endless weariness and bloodshed and pain, and accept his fate then and there. Then he realized that the woman was on her feet.

She seemed to be about to break down into tears. She stepped out of the cover into which Lunk had carried her and strode like a sleepwalker out onto the hot sand. She stared up at the oncoming Invid sortie, and whimpered. Lunk started to go after her and drag her back, but the nearby impact of two discs sent him falling backward.

Scott screamed, *"Hey, what are you trying to do, get killed?"* It occurred to him that someone else might as well ask the same question of *him*, standing out there in the open.

Lunk and Annie braved the alien volleys to reach her and try to carry her back to safety. But she was frozen there, and the Invid closed in, their fire sending up columns of flame to all sides. She put both hands to her ears and screamed, screamed.

As Scott watched her face, it was as though Marlene were screaming. The sound of it struck through every cell of him. It was the sound he had imagined a thousand times—her last scream as she died in the enemy onslaught.

Marlene!

Before he knew what was going on, he was vaulting for the Alpha's cockpit. He howled away into the air, pulled on his thinking cap, and buckled his harness. Scott changed to Alpha to Veritech mode, wings swept back for high-speed atmospheric dogfighting.

He had remembered what he was fighting for.

CHAPTER
EIGHT

People are mostly stupid and hateful and cruel to one another but—hell; let's save the world's ass anyway. It's better than being bored.

Rook

THE THREE PINCER SHIPS CAME AT SCOTT IN A TIGHT
V formation. He tagged the starboard wingmate with an
air-to-air missile and banked past the falling, burning bits
of it as the surviving two broke to either side to avoid
him.

He read the displays; the target acquisition computers
were working overtime. He launched another flight of
missiles; a Pincer dodged one only to be skeeted head-on
by another.

"All right; who's next?"

The third personal-armor Pincer was the next one to
come in at him, Frisbeeing the white-hot discs. Its claws
were bent close to it to decrease wind resistance and increase airspeed. Scott missed with a burst from his wing
cannon.

How the blazes do they manage to maneuver so fast?
But he knew he had been lucky; his whole team had. It
was miraculous that the Invid, catching them unprepared
and out in the open like that, hadn't incinerated them.

He looped, trying to get into the Invid's six o'clock position for the kill.

Rand brought his Cyc through a skidding 180°-turn, throwing up a shower of grit, as annihilation discs registered hits to all sides. The Shock Trooper stumped toward him, raising its immense claws, its two shoulder cannons pointing in his direction. Rand got off one round from the front-hub-mounted gun, cursing the fact that he hadn't had time to don his armor. Then he was flung back as a near miss from the Trooper's heavy guns blew him and his Cyclone backward through the air.

He landed in a shallow pit, stunned, waiting for an alloy claw to close around him and snip him in two or for a disc to burn him to ash. Instead he regained full consciousness in moments, spitting out sand and swearing. A thunder in the sky made him look up; the Shock Trooper roared by overhead, with Scott rocking it with cannon salvos.

Scott lost track of the Trooper, though, as the last Pincer Ship got on his tail and raked him with near-miss fire.

Rand, standing up in the pit, wiped the dirt off his face and invoked an all-embracing line from one of his favorite prewar motion pictures, shaking his fist at the sky. "I'm mad as hell and I'm not gonna take it anymore!"

Then he spotted the grounded Beta.

Lunk and Annie had the young amnesiac back under cover. "Don't worry," Annie told her. "The Invid won't hurt you, I promise! We won't let them!"

The Simulagent's face was warm and slick with tears.

Rand was studying the manual while he pulled on his thinking cap and warmed up the ship. He was trying to forget the fact that, except for a few hours in the Alpha under Scott's tutelage, he had never flown at all.

But the engines came up, deeper and more powerful than any Alpha's engine. Although the Beta was light on sensor gear and countermeasures equipment and certainly less maneuverable than an Alpha, it was fearsomely armed.

He was debating the best way to lift off when the heavy fighter rocked and nearly overturned. He saw through a stern monitor that a Shock Trooper had landed to take a swipe at it. Only the Beta's reinforced Robotech alloy armor had saved it—and him.

Rand grabbed the control grips, wrenched the stem back, and imaged the move to the receptors in the flight helmet. The Beta's engines erupted; the Shock Trooper was knocked backward tumbling, cracking open, becoming a pinwheel of flame. The Beta arrowed away from the standing start, riding a column of smoke, fire, and ground-shaking thunder.

Rand laughed to himself nervously. "Now! That's what *I* call—huh?"

The last Pincer Ship dove in at him, skimming annihilation discs from both shoulder mounts. He juked his ship inexpertly, trying to evade the Pincer, wondering if this was to be the briefest solo on record.

Then he heard Scott's voice, "Hold on, Rand!" These were the most welcome words he had ever heard in his life. Above and behind the Invid and closing in fast, Rand saw the Alpha launching a spread of missiles.

The Pincer Ship dodged and juked like a demon, but one air-to-air got a piece of it. The knee juncture of one of the monstrous, crablike legs exploded. The Pincer cut in all thrusters and went off, tumbling and blasting across the sky like some erratic comet.

Scott let it go, and fell in with Rand to try to talk him down. But there wasn't time. The Beta was flying upside down. Rand held his breath, fought off the impulse to close his eyes, and went in for a landing.

He managed to get rightside up at the last moment, but that was about all. The massive armor of the Beta got him through a landing that would have demolished on Alpha, or almost any other mecha. The ship skidded, punched completely through an empty troop carrier, skidded some more (while Rand recalled prayers he hadn't thought about in years) and ended up penetrating the hull of a tanker. She finally came to rest in the shadowy main hold, lit by the few rays of sunlight that found their way in through hull punctures. She was nose-down but intact.

Rand lay with his chin on the instrument panel, the rest of his body piled up behind, the operating manual on his head like an A-frame roof.

A perfect landing. In the sense that I'm gonna be able to walk away from it. Or at least be carried.

Extraction of the Beta and reactivation of the other Alphas took most of the rest of that long day. The team wanted to stay longer to get everything they could from the battlefield, but they didn't dare; there was no telling when the Invid would be back. They gathered what supplies, ordnance, Protoculture, and equipment they could and prepared to move out.

"Good fight," Scott told them, meeting everyone's gaze. But something showed in his eyes that hadn't been there before: an awareness that people had their limits, and that those limits were not so confining as he had thought.

Around them the Alphas were poised, noses almost touching the ground. The lower half of the Beta's nose was swung open like a trapdoor, its pilot's seat lowered for boarding. Lunk's truck was loaded. The team watched Scott.

"But as a result, we're short on Protoculture," he continued, "and we can't risk another tangle with the Invid, at least not now, if we can possibly help it. Remember that. Rand, do you think you can fly that thing without killing yourself?"

Scott pointed toward the white-and-olive-drab Alpha. Rand scratched his cheek near one of his numerous bandages. "As long as we don't have to turn right or left," he allowed.

"Improvise. Lancer, the Beta Fighter's yours. Rook, the other Alpha, okay?"

It was a VT with red-and-white markings. Rook wore a hungry, feline smile. "Just leave it to me."

They split up to get going. Annie and Lunk put Ariel into the truck.

As the Veritechs took off and Lunk gunned his engine, a lone figure stood watching them from a distant ridge. The Pincer Ship, its right leg blown away at the knee, relayed what it was seeing to Reflex Point, and to the Regis.

The wind whipped the Simulagent's scarlet hair, as she rode next to Annie. "Reception is perfect," the Regis's voice came to the mutilated Pincer Ship. "Maintain surveillance."

The subsidence of the mountains around the Genesis Pit and the danger of increased Invid patrol activity in the wake of events at rendezvous point K made Scott wary; progress was slow in the next few days. Roads and bridges had been shattered, and mountain passes were filled by quake and avalanch.

Time and again the Veritechs were forced to airlift the truck and its stores, until the Protoculture supply became critically low. Long-range aerial scouting missions were impossible; Invid patrol activity was too intense. At last the freedom fighters reached a mountain tunnel that a shifting of the Earth had permanently sealed.

With the Veritechs' remaining operating time drastically restricted, there was nothing to do but try to find a detour. A small town lay nearby, and the team members agreed to check it out as a first step.

But first they had to be sure the aircraft were safe. They parked the fighters in a part of the tunnel that was undamaged, near the entrance, then donned Cyclone armor. The team used the power-assisted metal suits to move boulders and wall in the VTs for safekeeping.

It was a strange sight—seven-plus-feet-tall gleaming giants lifting huge stones, in teams when the weight was extreme, but often alone, tossing them like medicine balls. After the task was completed, the team shed their armor so they wouldn't attract any attention from possible Invid patrols or from informers. They set off toward the town.

The one thing the team *hadn't* brought was extreme-cold-climate clothing; they hadn't counted on being forced to go so high into the mountains. As the Cyclones sped along, with Lunk's APC bringing up the rear, Rand shivered, "I can't s-stand it. I'm *so* cold!"

"All the more reason for us to get out of here before the *real* winter weather hits," Scott shot back.

The town lay in a valley at the confluence of a number of different mountain tracks and streams that might promise a path through. Two other roads from the lowlands ended there, reinforcing Lancer's contention that it was probably a jumping-off point.

Once they were down out of the heights they were more comfortable. The town itself, named *Deguello* according to a hand-lettered sign on weather-silvered wood at its outskirts, was more prosperous than Rand would have expected. Apparently there was some hidden resource. A hidden prewar supply depot, perhaps? His Forager instincts came to the fore.

The town was like a lot of others Rand and the rest had seen, a type Scott was getting to know. Stucco, tiled roofs, wrought-iron window bars, whitewash that had long since faded. Cracked plaster, drainage ditches that were mostly clogged. Still, somehow, there were some crops and meat and wares under the tattered awnings of the market stalls. Deguello was better off than many other places the team had seen.

It was evident that medical attention was available, but none too sophisticated. Most clothing was patched and frayed. This was a typical post-Invid settlement where virtually nothing was discarded; it was repaired, reused, recycled, cannibalized, or traded for something else. The day of the use-and-discard consumer society was nothing but a galling memory.

There were normal, struggling people trying to keep their lives together and trying to function in a normal way, side by side with seedy types. The townspeople eyed the newcomers and their Cycs with cold interest. Rook automatically noted the weapons she saw: knives and chains and conventional firearms; prewar military and hunting arms; some police and homemade-type stuff. She didn't notice any energy guns, which meant the team would have a tremendous edge if they ran into trouble.

Let's hope there's no trouble, though, she thought. *They look like they've been through enough.*

Just like everybody else on Earth.

As the group pulled into the town's main plaza, a man stirred and lowered his smeared plastic cocktail glass, looking them over, adjusting his much-worn wraparound shades. The grungy kerchief tied around his head and his thick black beard made him look like a pirate. He was wearing ratty brown shoes with no socks, threadbare khaki pants, and a grimy camouflage shirt, of the same fabric as his headband.

Scott dismounted first. Everyone knew that the plan was to look the town over and get some kind of handle on the local situation. They parked their cyclones and the APC without concern; in this postwar world, anyone with a vehicle had the sense to boobytrap it, and their nonchalance would be the most eloquent kind of proof that it would be wise not to meddle with the gleaming mecha.

Annie was pressing the idea that they all go shopping at the market. Scott was about to approve her expedition —it was as good a way to misdirect any watchers' attention as anything else he could come up with—when the man who had seen their arrival approached.

"Well, howdy there, folks." He kept his distance, as it was wise to do in greeting new people. Still, Scott could smell the odor from his body and from his mouth of broken yellow-and-black teeth.

The days of cosmetic dentistry and TV-hyped, brand-name personal hygiene were all over, and the beaten-down Human race was showing it. But people could be divided between those who still made the effort, with homemade soaps and pig-bristle toothbrushes, and those who had simply reverted to a medieval way of life and thought.

"Thinkin' about takin' a trip?" the man said. Lunk,

looking on, wondered if Scott intended to try to convince people that the team just happened to be up here on a pleasure jaunt. Or perhaps gathering daisies.

"Them mountains is crawlin' with Invid, y'know." Scott and Rand looked at him and said nothing. "Yeah, there's an Invid fortress smack-dab in the middle of that range; not even a rat could get through. But there *is* a map that'll show you a secret route. And it'll only cost you—"

He pulled an ancient pocket calculator. It was a solar-powered model that had been more of a novelty than a work tool before the wars, but was very dear in these days when batteries were scarce.

He squinted at their Cyclones, keying buttons. The calculator beeped with a final sum which he showed them. "—this much!"

Scott recoiled from the figure, payable in gold. "But—we haven't got that kind of money!"

The man looked the Cycs over. "Well, there're those in this town who've been known to do some barterin' and tradin'. Them fancy machines might do—"

"Forget it," Rand said flatly.

The man was about to argue, but stopped when he saw the look in the Forager's eye. "Have it your way, m'friend. But all the high-tone highway hardware in the world ain't gonna do you no good if you're stuck here. And I'll tell you one thing: Paradise is waitin' fer you, right on the other side of them mountains."

He turned to go. "Look around; see if I'm not telling you the straight gospel. If'n you change your minds, you can find me right over there, most any time."

"Without that map, we'll never get through the mountains! We're stranded here!" Annie said, close to tears.

"Within arm's reach of the Invid," Scott added. "Rand, you shouldn't have been so quick to refuse to bargain."

Rand made a sour face. "It's lucky for you you've got a Forager along, Lieutenant Bernard. You think somebody with a map that valuable would be lounging around in the street, looking like that?"

"Rand's right," Rook added. "Maybe there's a map, but it's not very likely that *that* pig has it. Why d'you think he was so anxious to cut a deal right away, before some other con artist could get to us?"

"It's a pretty good bet that this friendly little community is crawling with every kind of sharpie there is," Rand said. "The way I see it, our best bet is to split up, take a look around, and try to get the feel of the place."

Scott nodded in agreement. "All of you be careful. Is everyone armed? Lunk will stay here and guard the vehicles. Annie, you stick close to him, got that?"

Lancer said, "I've heard one or two things about this place." He was removing a pack from his Cyclone. "I want to check them out, but it's something I'll have to do alone."

Soon the team was setting off in various directions, hoping Deguello held some hope for their survival.

CHAPTER
NINE

> *Mom wasn't surprised at the way things were. I think she found grim irony in the fact that the one-percenters were in the majority at last.*
>
> Maria Bartley-Rand, *Flower of Life: Journey Beyond Protoculture*

LUNK WAS DEEPLY ENGROSSED IN HIS GEARHEAD window shopping. It was a great chance to examine some leftover war machinery. Annie put up with it for as long as she could and then, while he was on a mechanic's creeper under an APC like his own, she slipped away to check out Deguello for herself.

She was surprised at how much lowland food and other goods were available in this mountain outpost. Maybe somebody had discovered an emerald mine or something?

The fact that most of the people living in Deguello were from somewhere else wasn't so unusual; the first two Robotech wars and the Invid conquest had set most of the world adrift. And the fact that the team was in what had once been South America didn't really mean that much anymore, either. All nations were long since extinct; all cultures had been thrown together. Everyone was engaged in the struggle for survival.

But what struck Annie was strange was that so many folks seemed to be *waiting* for something. She saw people holding furtive negotiations in taverns and alleys, and others marking time in the square, looking this way and that as if expecting someone. Annie also noticed that people were selling or trading their personal possessions in return for gold or gems—apparently the only currency that counted here.

In some ways, it reminded her of a romantic oldtime motion picture that was one of her favorites, but there was no Rick's Café in Deguello, although she prided herself on looking just a little like a young Ingrid Bergman, when the light hit her just right, though Lunk and the others scoffed.

Still, it was nice to dream; her dreams were the only things she really owned. . . .

She scuffed her sneaker at a bit of garbage that lay on the pitted cobblestone sidestreet, aware that many eyes were following her. *Brother! I've been in some creepy places in my time, but this one takes the booby prize. What a slimebucket zoo!*

She was thinking that while watching a coughing, apparently tubercular man shuffling along and gagging in to a disgusting-looking rag. She was so distracted that she bumped right into somebody.

"Hey, ya little geek, why'n'cha watch where yer goin'?"

He was definitely one of the Bad Boys, a snake-lean, rat-faced guy in a dark, greasy jumpsuit open to his shrunken waist. There was a scorpion tattoo on his cheek. He wore a chain belt of massive links, and a blue Chicom Army–style cap, with a red bandanna tied around his thin left bicep. He had werewolf sideburns, a sawed-off 12-gauge side-by-side (a popular weapon in Deguello) in a shoulder rig, and there were fishhooks stitched to the knuckles of his fingerless black leather gloves.

Her street instincts resurfaced, and she realized that she had been traveling in the charmed company of Robotech heroes for so long that she had forgotten how vulnerable she herself was.

Uh-oh, Annie thought. It was her considerable luck that he merely clapped a hand down on her cap and shoved, to send her stumbling, arms thrashing. But quick hands caught her, saving her from landing on her derriere in the gutter.

"You should be more careful, little boy." She found herself looking up at a clean-cut, handsome face—a young man who couldn't be more than eighteen or so. He had big blue eyes, wavy black hair, and a blinding smile.

She squirmed to break free of his grip. *"I am not a little boy! What're you, blind? I'm a woman!"*

He let her go, surprised, plainly upset that he had hurt her feelings. "I'm terribly sorry! Forgive me. Um, my name is Eddie."

She took a closer look at him and noticed that he resembled—*let's see . . .*—James Dean! Only nicer! He was a dreamboat in a white T-shirt and a leather jacket!

She swayed toward him, almost melting. "Oboy! I, I mean, I'm Annie! Eddie's my *favorite name*! You can call me Mint!"

She vaguely recalled that she was supposed to be on a mission of espionage and derring-do. "Um, d'you live up in those mountains, by any chance?"

He chuckled; she sighed. "No, Annie. Only the Invid live up there. But beyond them is Paradise."

Her eyes were the size of poker chips. "You mean all that stuff is true?"

He nodded, pointing at the distant mountains. She thought he was as beautiful as a hood ornament. "Paradise is a city that was set up by the old United Earth Government and the Southern Cross Army, so that if there was an invasion or a catastrophe, the Human race would be able to go on. A kind of New Macross, I guess you could say.

"Paradise is like Earth used to be before the Invid, or the Robotech Masters, or the Zentraedi! People are free there, and safe."

Annie felt faint. A place where people were safe and free and happy! But what was Eddie saying?

"—the place for me. It's taken us a long time, but that's where my family's going. I—I wish the whole world could be like Paradise."

Annie launched herself straight up, throwing her arms around his neck, clinging there, swinging her feet. "Oh, Eddie! That's so beautiful! I love you! Please take me with you? *Pleasepleaseplease*?"

The mayor of Deguello's mansion was as grand as a small palace. The place had fallen into extreme disrepair in the latter twentieth century, especially with the privations of the Global Civil War, and the First and Second Robotech Wars. But now there were signs of a revivification. The reflecting pool and formal gardens had regained much of their glory; the mansion shone with light and elegance.

The mayor, son of the previous mayor and descendent of many, sat in the ballroom, holding the hand of a beautiful woman who in turn owned his heart. Donald Maxwell, so used to commanding the obedience of others, of navigating his way through the treacherous political waters of Deguello and the post-invasion world, thought there was a cosmic symmetry to it: everyone had their Achilles' heel, and his was love.

Under the ballroom's chandeliers, brilliant even in daytime, and the paintings as big as barn doors, portraits of a score of ancestors, he sat in his Louis XIV chair and she in hers. In its time the ballroom had been the most splendid and celebrated in a hundred mile radius. Now, though, its decor was stranger than anything its original builders could ever have envisioned.

"But we *must* talk about our wedding, Carla," he was saying. "It's long past time.

"Have you tired of my lovetalk? Then think about what you have to gain if you marry me! I've always given you everything, anything you wanted. But *this* I need from *you*! And when you're my wife, my only thought will be to make you happy!"

Maxwell's Northern European and North American bloodlines were evident in his blond hair, pale skin, and Anglo features. His meticulously tailored three-piece pinstripe suit—a traditional costume, as he regarded it—only served to set them off.

Carla, too, was fair-skinned. She was slim and willowy, a brown-haired, angel-faced young woman with a permanent air of sadness and a far-away look in her green eyes. She seemed about to speak, but then hesitant.

A servant entered and spoke softly. "Your pardon, sir, but your visitor has arrived."

Maxwell's hold on Carla's hand loosened a bit. Without turning he commanded, "Show her in." The servant bowed and left. To Carla he whispered, "Please! I need you so!"

She steeled herself. "Why? Donald, why do you insist on *possessing* me? Why can't you just accept what I'm willing to give?"

He rose, hearing the door open again, releasing her hand. "Because you can be much more than that," he whispered again, more harshly.

Then he turned away, and his fine, handmade shoes clicked on the polished dance floor. "Ah! The famous Miss Yellow Dancer! You honor us! Please do come in; I'm Donald Maxwell, Mayor of Deguello, very pleased to make your acquaintance!"

"You are so very kind," said Yellow Dancer with a shy lowering of her chin, her voice melodious and soft. She looked out at the ballroom in some wonder, through thick lashes.

Parked there were three fighter planes of Global Civil War vintage: a red Vampire jumpjet; a needle-nose Vandal all-weather fighter-bomber; and a Peregrine interceptor wearing the famous skull-and-crossbones insignia of the American VF-84 Squadron—the Jolly Rogers.

Maxwell had caught the look, was expecting it. "You find my old relics interesting? Maintaining them is something of an extravagance, of course, but—it's something of a matter of family pride, you see."

No visitor had failed to be astounded at the sight. Maxwell drew a certain sensual pleasure from seeing the sculpted brows of the renowned Yellow Dancer raised high. "Mr. Mayor—these planes still fly, then?"

He basked in the impact his collection had made.

"They haven't in many, many years, but—of course, or what would be the point of having them?"

He indicated the way with a slight bow; Yellow fell in, walking between the gleaming, sleek-lined sky hunters while he went on. "I'm no aviator, you see; they were refitted to fly by auto-pilot, the very last word in Human guidance systemry, before Robotechnology changed all that forever."

They had walked beneath the open landing gear bays, the poised wings. Yellow could see that the external hard-points and pylons were loaded with what seemed to be real, functioning ordnance, and that the jets looked fully operational.

"The planes basically flew themselves," Maxwell was saying. "These were my father's prized possessions; they're dear to me as he was dear to me. They're all I really have left of him, really."

They had come to two easy chairs over by the high windows, some distance from where Carla sat. Maxwell pointedly made no introductions. "Please sit down. Your note said that you're seeking employment?"

Yellow Dancer nodded, a purple wisp of hair falling across her cheek. "Yes, and I hear you are the owner of a fabulous nightspot here in town, correct?"

Maxwell nodded, his eyes searching Yellow's, drinking her in. Lancer had heard through resistance sources that Maxwell was a collector of Yellow Dancer's performance tapes and sound recordings. In fact, the mayor had made tentative inquiries with an eye to getting the legendary Yellow Dancer to perform in his mountain domain.

"I am indeed. And if the magnificent Yellow Dancer were to perform there, it would help my people by boosting the town's economy—and my own, of course."

Yellow Dancer chuckled slyly. Unnoticed, Carla suddenly broke her sad reverie, her head snapping up, eyes going toward where the two sat. "I'd be thrilled to, Mayor Maxwell," beamed Yellow Dancer. Carla's breath caught in her throat, and she put one hand on the arm of her chair, feeling faint.

It can't be! But—I've got to be sure! She forced herself to her feet.

The mayor was saying, "A bravura performance by Yellow Dancer will lift people's spirits. Certainly it will help in my reelection campaign." It didn't look or sound like Maxwell was very worried about being unseated, though.

Yellow Dancer looked up amiably, ready to greet the mayor's fiancée. A sudden astonishment came across the fine-boned, androgynous face.

Carla could only stare down at Yellow. *It* is *Lancer*!

Maxwell hadn't noticed Yellow's expression, because he was reaching up to take Carla's hand. He made the introductions and added, "I have a splendid idea! We'll have ourselves a deal, Yellow, if you promise to sing a ballad for our wedding! And I'll move the date up to tomorrow afternoon. Now how's that?"

Yellow barely heard what the mayor was saying. Like Carla, Yellow had the feeling that the gold of the sunset had engulfed the whole room, whisking them to some other time and place.

Maxwell's Club Inca was the finest spot in the region, but it was still a sad place, more of an echo of a bygone era than an evocation of it.

Carla sat watching Yellow Dancer move across the stage, dedicating the first number to the bride and groom. The groom was off somewhere attending to more of his seemingly endless business, and the bride was trying to hold back her tears.

The noontime wedding, at Maxwell's mansion, had been a joyless affair attended mostly by his attendants and a few local notables. Carla had refused an elaborate wedding gown, insisting on wearing a simple blue frock. She had gone through the motions like a zombie, barely aware of what she was doing, knowing only that Lancer hadn't come to her.

She had thought he would seek her out, and save her from the wedding. And then in time she realized that, for some reason, that wasn't going to happen.

But now, alone at her table at the Club Inca, she watched Yellow Dancer's every move. She couldn't be wrong! Lancer *must* have come back for her at last!

Yellow wore one of her most stylish outfits, a feminized version of the *Cabaret* MC's costume, complete with vest, bowtie, derby hat, and spats. Very Marlene Dietrich.

As promised, the song was an old Minmei number, sung for the mayor and the new Mrs. Maxwell. The alluring chanteuse broke into song, accompanied by recorded music because the house band just wasn't up to her level of performance.

How could it all have turned out this way? Carla wondered, staring into her champagne glass as though the answer were there.

Her memory strayed again, back to a time just after the Invid destroyed the planet Earth.

The brunt of the conquest was over in hours. Striking with beam weapons and energy effects that humanity still could not comprehend, the Invid exterminated over eighty per cent of the Human race. Many more died as the Invid mecha descended to ravage and slay.

The remnants of the Army of the Southern Cross rose to fight, were thrown back in defeat, regrouped, tried again against any sane hope, and were shattered beyond repair.

Still there were those who refused to surrender, as the aliens established themselves and began their pacification of the planet. One of these was a young aviator reservist named Lancer who had just begun to explore his love with a woman named Carla when the hordes from the stars struck.

Even as the Invid established their network of quislings, informers, and assassination squads, Lancer and a few others were plotting for a final attempt to strike at the heart of the Invid beachhead.

But the raid was a final disaster. Wounded, attempting to get back to her, Lancer had crash-landed his Veritech less than a mile from her door. Somehow, Carla had gotten him to what was left of her home.

By then, most of the people still alive were those willing to submit to the Invid. Some even served them—hunted down their enemies and offered them up to the triumphant invaders.

Lancer had barely come to in Carla's bed when the sounds of the hue and cry drifted up from the streets. Rifle butts were bashing at doors; hounds bayed.

In time, the manhunt came to Carla's house.

If you hold it against me that I was a little theatrical in what I did, and you don't care to consider The Scarlet Pimpernel *or* Zorro, *be kind enough to keep in mind what I accomplished, and let the record speak for itself.*

Of if not, either walk on by or step out back.

Remark attributed to Lancer

THAT TIME SEEMED SO REMOTE, CARLA THOUGHT, and yet it remained so crystal-clear in her mind.

Lancer had a fine record as a military officer, but he had left the Southern Cross sometime before the Invid attack because he had been unable to fight the urge he felt to be a performer. His soft, intimate way with some songs, his brassy, crowd-pleasing style with others, made him a natural; but there was another side to his art.

An interest in theater had led him to investigate the Japanese traditions of *No, Bunraku, Bugaku*, and especially *Kabuki*. He found that he loved to perform clownish *Saruwaka* antics more than he liked any *Aragoto* swaggering heroic lead, and in somewhat the same way, the martial juggling/acrobatics of the *Hoka* possessed him.

And he came, in time, almost against his will, to a fascination with the revered craft of the *Onna-gata*—the tradition of female roles portrayed by specializing male actors—and the gentle *Wagoto* style of acting.

Lancer found a strange understanding of himself through the *Musume*, the ingenue role, and dramatic masters encouraged him to study the art. In the West there was still, in many quarters, a horror at the blurring of gender lines. But in the *Kabuki* his talent was applauded, by men and women both, for its triumph of art over stereotype, and for its submersion of self in role.

Lancer returned to the Americas with new thoughts in his head. He began to revive the type of gender-blending pop music figure that had disappeared with the outbreak of the Global Civil War.

When he met Carla, she seemed immediately to understand everything. Carla became his co-conspirator, his lover, his confidant, his fiancée. She became a mainstay of his life, showing her affection for his *Musume* persona, joining him in a world where conventions and Western narrowness had no hold.

Everything was fine until the Invid came. While Earth passed into the flames, a young reserve aviator named Lancer lay listening to the tread of Shock Trooper mecha and the sound of rifle butts and hobnailed boots breaking down doors in the alley outside.

Carla was already nearly as adept at some parts of his craft as he. "There's only one way you can survive, and that's as Yellow Dancer," she said, even as she was setting out makeup.

When the Invid manhunters came in they found only two frightened women. Their insistent search turned up nothing—Lancer's VT armor having been left behind—and they went away grumbling, the Shock Trooper's optical sensor indicating nothing as the hulking war machine turned to go.

Carla leaned to kiss her lover longingly. 'You're Yellow Dancer now. You must be, *every moment*, or we're dead."

In retrospect, it seemed a happy time but sitting at the table in the Club Inca, Carla knew that it had been filled with fear and travail. By foot and ox cart and stolen bike and a half-dozen other means that they took as the occasion arose, she and Yellow Dancer moved toward some hoped-for safety. Yellow even began singing for their supper, when the opportunity came up. Not only did Yellow Dancer's persona submerge Lancer's; Yellow and Carla came to meld, in a way.

Then there came a day in a huge rail terminal, both of them clutching forged documents from the Resistance that would get them to a possible place of safety. The region they were in was somewhat neutral, and Carla's lover was Lancer once more. Dark thoughts seemed to have overtaken him once his male persona reasserted itself; the halcyon days of the escape were over, and aliens strode the Earth, exterminating Human beings at will.

And as the bullet train began moving, Lancer leapt from it. The doors shut and secured automatically behind him. He crouched, staring at the surface of the train platform so that he wouldn't have to meet her gaze. Lancer had to let the train take Carla to safety so that he could join the Resistance in the fight against the Invid.

Carla was gone from the sad little bridal party table by the time Yellow Dancer finished her encore set. Yellow went downstairs to her makeshift dressing room. What point would there have been in seeing Carla alone? The Invid kept the two apart, no less today than on that day in the rail station.

When Yellow Dancer opened the door, Carla sat waiting.

Yellow Dancer and Lancer surged and vied in a single mind. Carla seemed small and frail, sitting with her hands in her lap, facing the door, waiting only for Yellow's return. "After three years," she whispered. "You've come back for me at last!"

Tears ran down her cheeks as she watched Yellow sit down. "Time stopped having any meaning for me, do you know what that feels like? What happened to you? I've felt—my life has been so empty!"

What Yellow might have said will never be known; at that moment the door slammed open and Annie rushed in. "Lancer! Oops, didn't mean to interrupt, but—I'm in *love*!"

"That's all right, Annie," Lancer replied, but his eyes were on Carla.

In love, Carla thought. *Lancer* was looking at her now, not Yellow Dancer. "I-I was in love with someone once," Carla told Annie haltingly, wondering if she sounded deranged.

Annie appeared not to notice Carla's despair. "Fall in love again, okay? Then you'll be just as happy as *I* am!"

Annie gripped Lancer's hand. "Eddie and his folks are getting a map, an honest one, that'll tell them how to get through the mountains to Paradise. And they're taking me along! They're gonna be my family!"

It dawned on her that neither Yellow Dancer nor Carla seemed very happy for her. She jumped off the couch and resettled her E.T. cap. "I just couldn't leave without saying good-bye. Um, well, my dreamboat's waiting— g'bye!" She skipped out the door, tra-la-la-ing.

"Good-bye, Annie," Yellow Dancer said softly.

"Love," Carla mused, realizing what it was that she had seen in Lancer's eyes. "And ours is gone forever, isn't that what you were going to say?"

Annie caught up with Eddie where he was waiting for his father at the Central Deguello Bank. Mr. Truman came down the steps of the bank with a briefcase under one arm, looking up as he heard his son call out to him.

Eddie's father had been away for a few days, so Eddie said, "I'd like you to meet a very special friend of mine."

"Hi, Mr. Truman! My name's Annie LaBelle!"

Truman, a lean, stoop-shouldered man with salt-and-pepper hair and mustache, had a careworn face and wore much-repaired wire-rim glasses. He looked weary but friendly. "Well, Annie LaBelle, I'm very pleased to make your acquaintance."

He thought he knew why Eddie had taken a liking to Annie; she was so much like Eddie's little sister, Aly— Aly, dead these eighteen months since the White Virus cut its swath through the region.

To his son, Truman said, "Eddie, we'll be leaving soon —just as soon as I wrap up a few things. I found a buyer who wants the shop, and Mrs. Perio upped her offer for the house. Make sure everything's packed, and as soon as I get home, we'll be on our way."

Eddie shifted from foot to foot, hands in the pockets of his leather jacket. "Um, Dad, I told Annie she could come with us."

Truman let show a faint smile. "Why, of course you did, Son. Don't leave anything behind, Annie; we're getting out of here for good."

As Mr. Truman walked off, Eddie whooped and did a little war dance; Annie pirouetted, giggling deliriously. "Paradise, we're on our way!"

The ten-ounce gold bars, flat and wide as candy bars but much smaller, looked so insignificant there on the desk, Mr. Truman thought. And yet they had taken so much time and sacrifice and work to accumulate. The sunlight streaming through the tall windows made them so bright that they made him squint.

Across the wide desk, Mayor Maxwell said, "You should be proud, Mr. Truman. I know what you had to go through to get this, but not one man in a hundred succeeds like this."

Truman nodded tiredly. It had been explained to him, long since, why Maxwell's map cost so much. Certain parts of the route had to be changed constantly, to reflect new Invid activities and patrolling patterns. And there was the need for Maxwell's Lurp teams to set up safe resting places and resupply caches along the route. The cost of maintaining the teams was high, not to mention the fact that a cut of all proceeds went to the Resistance effort against the Invid.

Or so Maxwell insisted. There were rumors to the contrary, but there were rumors about everything in Deguello. Reliable people swore they had heard from friends and relatives who had made it to Paradise, and that Maxwell was a trustworthy man. Truman was too tired to hesitate anymore, too ground down by the loss of a daughter and the dead-end of life in Deguello. He just wanted to be on his way, to get his family to the safety of Paradise.

Maxwell handed over a folded, waterproofed bundle. "And here's a current map showing the safe route through the mountains. It was updated by my Lurps just this week; you'll be safe with this."

Truman accepted it with a trembling hand. "Thank you, sir."

"In Paradise, you'll live a better life," Maxwell said. "I'm glad you're the one getting this, Truman. I know what some people think of me, asking all the market will bear for these maps, but—the traffic along the secret route has to be kept to a minimum, and there's still the Resistance to finance. Still, I sleep better when the people I help deserve it."

Carla, on the other side of the ballroom, stared through the big tropical fishtank there, watching the scene played out as she had watched it played out dozens of times before. She looked at the map Truman held, wishing—struggling with herself.

Truman was quickly on his way, eager to get a start in what was left of the day. Carla sat in a wing chair near a window, looking up at the nearby mountains.

The team, minus Annie, was making a poor afternoon snack of a few canned party tidbits—salted nuts and the like—of prewar vintage, at an outdoor table. Buying local food, even at high prices, seemed wiser than eating current-dated Mars Division rations out where people might take notice.

All their inquiries had gotten them nowhere. There were other people with mysterious maps—in fact, it seemed to be one of the town's major industries. But what little reliable advice they had been able to get said that none were to be trusted—except, *perhaps*, the mayor's. And the price of the mayor's help, payable in gold, was beyond the team's reach.

Lancer had told the team about his contact with Maxwell. But he told them nothing of his old ties with Carla, and so there seemed to be no avenue of map-acquisition there; Maxwell was all businesss.

Scott was seriously considering letting Maxwell know who and what the team members were, but held off. More than one purported Resistance sympathizer had turned out to be an Invid stoolie.

Meanwhile, the team was concerned about Annie and her new adopted family. They couldn't blame her for wanting to restore some kind of stability to her life, even though her trip to Paradise did sound like a pipe dream. But Scott worried that she would inadvertently tell more than she should. However much she was sworn to silence, there was always the chance that she would betray the team's secrets.

Rand, chasing one of the few surviving pistachios around the dish, said, "They'll be serving free buffets in Deguello before we can ever scrape together the money for Maxwell's map! So what're we gonna do now?"

Scott stared down at his coffee. He had a plan to fall back on, and as much as he regretted using it, it seemed like the team's only hope now. Scott's plan was to pay a call on Maxwell, in full armor, with VTs in Battloid mode, and *force* the man to hand over the map. Then they would make a break for the mountains, leaving the mayor incommunicado. Hopefully they would get through before anybody could alert the Invid.

Scott was about to bring it up, but Rook spoke first. "Hell, it seems like *this one* never worries about *anything*." By that, she meant Ariel, who still wore Rook's jacket, and who still looked at the world with the lost expression of a total stranger.

And yet, Scott thought, it wasn't really irritation Rook was showing. Instead it was concern. Most traumatic-amnesia cases recovered in a few days, but this woman had been a blank for a week now.

Scott sighed. "I'm glad you brought that up. Isn't it about time we gave her a name of some kind?"

The Simulagent made a little questioning sound, aware

that they were talking about her. Rand smirked, "Hey Lunk! How 'bout *you* giving us a few suggestions?"

Lunk looked upset, as he always did when anyone asked him to take a lead. "I, ah, I bet Scott could come up with a nice name."

Scott had intended to say something else, but found himself asking, "Why don't we call her Marlene?"

Rook's brows knit; she knew the story of Scott's fiancée's death. Lancer broke in, "Why don't we just let her tell us when she's good and ready?"

Rook shrugged. "Until then, Marlene's as good a name as any."

But none of that solved the map problem. They discussed the situation again, until Lancer rose from the table. "I want to look into a few more things. I'll catch up with you later."

They watched him go. Rook thought, *Why do I get the impression he just made a decision*? She heard a murmuring and saw that the young woman was repeating the name *Marlene* to herself.

Maxwell was away on more of his unnamed business; and Carla invited Lancer in, bringing him to the balcony overlooking the ballroom. She poured some of the green tea she knew he loved, a true rarity in that part of the world nowadays, and made him sit by the grand piano Maxwell had bought her.

Carla played a soft Minmei melody, her touch much more deft than it had been two years before.

Lancer went to the open French doors, to stare at the snowcapped mountains. "Carla, tell me: how does Donald Maxwell make his money?"

Her smile slipped, then was back in place. "You know the lyrics to this one; would you like to—"

"What is Donald doing that you can't talk about?"

"I, I can't tell you."

He went and held her hands down so that the music stopped on a discordant note. "Now listen to me: there's something terribly wrong about this map business. Won't you tell me what it is, before somebody gets hurt? And then we can leave this place together, Carla. Carla, tell me!"

She hesitated, but swayed toward him for a moment, her eyes on his, as if some greater gravity had hold of her.

"I'll find us a place that will be much better for both of us," he promised.

She stood to look across at the balcony's opposite windows, to look west. "Lancer, let's go that way! To the warm sea breezes and the sunlight! I'll make you happy there, I swear it!"

"I've been down there, Carla. I'm being hunted, and so are the people with me. And we have a job to do. The only way out for us is over the mountains."

Her eyes dropped. In a very small voice, she confessed, "There's no way across those mountains, Lancer. The Invid control everything. Everyone who tries it dies, I'm sure of that now."

"Here's a copy of the map," Annie said in secret-agent tones, looking around, slapping it into Scott's gloved palm. "The *real* map, the *mayor's*!"

She was hitching up the pink brushed-suede rucksack she had been wearing when Scott first met her, the one that contained everything she had in the world. Scott gaped at her.

"I, um, borrowed it from Eddie's father and photocopied it!" she gushed. "I'm off now to Paradise with my new family. Eddie's mother and father are so-ooo nice! You guys make sure you follow quick, okay? The route'll probably change again in a coupla days, because the Invid are always changing their surveillance. Bye, Scott! Bye, Marlene! Bye, everyone!"

She frolicked away, laughing giddily.

Scott, watching her go, unfolded the map slowly. Rand and Rook and Lunk were ecstatic. The other team members went off to see to their vehicles.

Reflex Point was suddenly much nearer.

Scott looked at the map, matching it up with a hand

held display that showed aerial survey records from the memory banks of his Alpha. It didn't take long for his face to go from elation to scowling anger.

A fake . . .

CHAPTER
ELEVEN

Who will ride?
Who will fall?
Cyclone Psychos!

Deguello ballad

"THAT'S HIS BUSINESS, SELLING FAKE MAPS,"
Carla was telling Lancer.

"And nobody knows because nobody comes back. Did
he start the rumors about Paradise, too?"

She gulped and nodded. Lancer looked around him.
"And that's what pays for all of this. Sheer dumb, stub-
born Human hope and longing. Maxwell's going to
pay—"

He stopped as he heard an engine roar at the edge of
town. From his vantage point high up, Lancer could see
over the mansion wall to the street where Annie and
Eddie sat in the back of the Truman family's all-terrain
truck.

Most of the cargo bed was taken up by the Trumans'
good and baggage, lashed under tarps. As the ATT pulled
away, Maxwell and a half-dozen of his Lurp scouts waved.
Near them were two all-terrain jeeps.

"Annie!"

Lancer dashed for the door.

* * *

Armored and mounted, the team made final checks, ready to begin the pursuit. Cycs were tested for battle-readiness; Lunk made sure that the ammo well for the Stinger autocannon mounted in his APC's prow was filled to the brim with linked ammunition. Marlene sat next to Lunk, looking more bewildered than ever.

Scott was ripping up the map, though he already entered its directions in the displays, in order to trail the Trumans. "When I get my hands on Maxwell—"

Lancer snapped, "There's no time to think about Maxwell now! We've got to catch Annie before it's too late!"

All four Cycs went into wheelies, a way of releasing energy and yet not getting too far ahead while the APC accelerated. They streaked away toward the mountains.

Carla had watched from her vantage point in the mansion. Now she raced down the stairs and past the three silent fighter planes, flinging herself at the door, determined to steal a car or do whatever it took to catch Lancer and go on with him or die with him. She was determined not to be left behind ever again.

But Maxwell came through the door. "Hey! What're you doing, Carla? What've you been up to?"

"I told them, Donald! I told them everything!"

The team roared up the mountain roads, the Cyclones taking curves as only Robotech mecha could, Lunk doing his best to keep from falling behind. "We're comin', Mint!"

Marlene suddenly cried out, holding her head as if she had been hit by a migraine. "I, I heard them. Something . . . there's trouble!"

Truman slowed down his all-terrain truck, adjusting his glasses, squinting at the map. "I can't understand it. I can't orient this map; it doesn't make any sense."

His wife, a kindly woman with an open, fleshy face and hair pulled back in a black bun, looked on disheartenedly, doing her best not to distract him.

Suddenly she looked up in terror, as shadows crossed the windshield.

At the back of the cargo bed, Eddie was joking with Annie. She understood that he regarded her as a kid sister and had decided to wait until she got to Paradise to make her move. If a little makeup could work wonders for Yellow Dancer, she could imagine what it could do for Annie LaBelle!

Then she heard a roaring of thrusters, and bulky mecha heliographed the sun in a close pass.

"Invid!" She could see four Pincer Ships, claws folded close to them while they made their attack dives. Mr. Truman had seen them, too, and began swerving as the first annihilation discs hit. The all-terrain truck wove back and forth on the road, the Invid seeming to drive it almost playfully, until at last Mr. Truman swerved sidelong into a boulder, and Annie and Eddie were thrown from the cargo bed.

A strafing Pincer chopped a line of explosions along the road, and Eddie rolled into the ditch with Annie in his arms. Mr. Truman and his wife fell along after, clutching one another. The Pincer's wingmates held back while the leader came in for the kill.

Then there was an additional explosion and they saw that the leader was wobbling and tumbling through the air, like an unstrung, burning puppet. It erupted into a balloon of energy, smoke, and shrapnel just before it struck a nearby cliff.

Annie looked up, dazed. Suddenly there were Cyclone knights everywhere in the sky. All at once, the Invid were getting a costly lesson in dogfight tactics and learning that the sky was still a hotly contested killing ground.

Lancer pulled up nearby, still on his Cyc, and Lunk in his truck. "Get them out of here while we cover!" Scott's voice came over the tac net.

Rook's red-and-silver armor was sleeker, more maneuverable than the others', and had that wide-bore long-gun that was unique to it. Scott's blue-and-silver was more heavily armed than before, with an assault-rifle module acquired in the wreckage of his strikeforce's graveyard;

he stood straddle-legged, letting the Invid come at him, and held the trigger down.

Rand's armor, light-blue-and-silver, seemed more specialized for handgun-firing, and that suited him just fine, the armor wielding a bigger, more powerful version of the H90.

Then Lancer scooped up Marlene, who had dismounted in a numbed astonishment, set her behind him on his Cyclone, and started off. Annie and Eddie helped his parents into Lunk's truck, and it accelerated to catch up. The Cycs fell back in good order, firing, as the Invid came down at them, but then split up as the firing became too intense.

Scott jetted backward on thrusters that set the brush among the trees afire, awaiting his chance. He could see Rand and Rook doing the same. Trees and mounds of soil and rock exploded, the Invid lashing out at everything in their frustration.

At last the defenders were driven down to a lowermost verge. From that spot they could either go to the open sky, where they would be shot like clay pigeons, or to the forest that lay a few hundred yards below. Invid fire turned nearby trees into Roman candles.

Scott said, "We have to make them think they've won." *I hope Lunk and Annie and the rest have gotten far enough away!* He dismounted two missiles from a forearm pod, twisted their warheads to adjust, and waited, as the Invid rushed down. "On three! One . . ."

The armored Cycriders set up a network of fire, crisscrossing the sky with brilliant bursts, jostling the Invid as the Pincer Ships came within range.

Scott gave the warheads a final twist, then tossed the missiles down, and took up firing again. "Two . . ."

He and Rand and Rook were throwing up a furious barrage, heels hanging over the edge of the cliff, the dirt and gravel they had scuffed loose falling. The Invid's attack-pass cut the air.

"Three!"

The Cycs jumped back, dropped. Invid annihilation

discs hit the ledge where they had been standing, raising huge gouts of flame and debris and smoke.

Although the Regis's awareness was not in the Invid there, they spoke to one another with her voice. They did not know that Marlene was among the prey, and that she was part of a greater plan.

Instead they heard the Regis's standing orders in their minds, *Eliminate all resistance! Neutralize rebel forces. They must not be allowed to escape! Kill them all!*

Clinging to Lancer's armored middle, Marlene suddenly cringed. "The, the voices again!" She seemed about to faint. "Rand and the others—they ran!"

Lancer had his hands full with the pitched descent of the mountain road. But he wondered, *Does she mean Scott and the rest? And how does she know?*

Then Lancer, followed by Lunk, rounded a corner and had to stop. The way was blocked by Maxwell and a score of armed men.

They were equipped to tackle even Cyc armor, with old LAW rockets, RPGs, a few Manville X-18s, and a truck mounted with a heavy machine gun. Lancer fought off the urge to break away and come back later. But Maxwell might not let the others live long enough to be rescued, and above all, Carla was with the mayor, standing in the back of his staff car, her hand caught up in his.

Truman was standing up in the bed of Lunk's truck, gripping the cab frame. "Maxwell, you lied."

"I'm a good businessman and you're not; don't come crying to me. There *is* no way through the mountains. Congratulations on being the first to ever come back. However—"

Maxwell showed a thin smile. "Now that you know my secret, you can't be allowed to return. You understand, I'm sure. Will you please step down and line up over there?"

Maxwell's men had the angle on them from all sides with high-powered rifles, pump shotguns, and some Galil heavy assault pieces loaded, no doubt, with armor-piercing rounds. The Trumans, Annie, Lunk, Lancer, and Marlene dismounted and did as they were told. Lancer read his displays and braced himself.

Carla caught Maxwell's hand. "What are you doing?"

"They must be eliminated."

"No!" she wrestled against him for a moment. He threw her back against the bed of the converted truck, knocking the wind from her, ignoring her when she husked, "No, Donald . . ."

The blue-and-silver Cyclone rider had gathered the captives back some distance from the trucks, Maxwell noticed, most of them sheltering behind him. But Maxwell smiled. "This is the end of the road, folks." He raised his arm for the signal.

"If you move it, I'll burn it off," an amplified voice promised. Maxwell spun around just as Robotech weapons opened fire. Many of his men dropped their guns and all of them cringed, as the dazzling rays opened the ground around them and sent novaflame curling into the air.

Annie threw her arms wide and sang, "Good work, Rand!"

Maxwell ordered the rest of his men to throw down their guns, and he dismounted from the car, gaping at Lancer's H90, as Lancer advanced on him. "I-if you fire that thing, the Invid will be down on us immediately!"

"They're a little busy right now. We killed all the ones that came after us. Now, you've been feeding innocent people to the Invid for years, isn't that right?"

Lancer raised his gun. "Time for you to get a taste of your own medicine."

Maxwell drew a breath and said, "If you pull that trigger, you'll never find out how to get through these mountains alive. And the Invid are swarming after you."

The mayor met Lancer's gaze. "My precise map isn't just some children's story. It shows the way through underground warrens dating back to the Global Civil War. It leads into a camouflaged road through the mountains. You see—" He gave a slight smile. "I serve the Resistance, too; they pay me well. You can ask any underground contacts you want if you don't believe me."

Scott and Rand and the others were frisking Maxwell's henchmen. They rearmed their friends and armed the others with captured weapons: Eddie with a Manville, Mr. Truman with an ancient shotgun, Carla with an Ingram MAC 9. They tossed the other weapons into Lunk's truck.

"You spare my life and we all leave here alive," Maxwell was saying.

Lancer raised his H-90 and fired. The adjusted thread-fine beam burned away a piece of Maxwell's left ear, cauterizing what was left. His hair was singed but it did not catch fire. Maxwell fell to the ground, holding his wound and swearing in a monotone.

Lancer looked down at Donald Maxwell, "All right; we'll take you up on your offer. And if anything goes wrong, *you'll* be the first to die."

Carla ran after Lancer as he turned to go. "Wait! Lancer, wait for me!"

Maxwell lurched to his feet. "Carla, where are you going?"

She looked at him and her lip curled. "I've had enough of you!"

His protests—that he had done it all for her, that his wealth meant nothing without her—couldn't bring her back.

With Veritechs looming around him, Eddie shook his head to Annie's cries. "Why won't you come on with us, huh? Why?" she whined.

Eddie heaved a long breath. "Because you're going where there's more fighting, and that's not what I want, Mint. Paradise was just a lie. My dad's brother has a ranch down south; that's where we'll go. You can come with us if you want, but I'm not getting involved in any war! Besides, I have to look after my family."

Then he had dropped her hand and run to jump into the passenger seat next to his mother and father. "So long, Annie. Good luck."

"Eddie! Good-bye!" Annie called, but didn't move. The truck pulled away into the dusk. *"I love you!"*

She whirled and threw herself into Lunk's arms and wept. Lunk held her and wept for her, too.

Rand was sitting on and patting the crates of ordnance and the few precious Protoculture cells Maxwell had been forced to give up. "At least we got supplies and ammunition."

Rook still had her chin on her fist. "The chance to kill him against a few supplies? I still don't like the trade." Rand knew better than to try to reason with her in a mood like this.

Scott turned and saw the APC throwing up a trail of dust, speeding up out of Deguello. "We move out as soon as Lancer comes back."

Lunk's borrowed APC bounced up the road from the town, Carla's suitcase loaded in the back. Lancer somehow felt stiff and absurd sitting next to Carla. He tried again. "I simply don't want you mixed up in all this; same reason as before."

She looked across at him for an instant, then ahead through the windshield. "I'm not afraid to fight."

"I know that."

But Lancer wasn't so sure Maxwell would let her go, despite all the mayor's assurances. Then the subject changed from the abstract to the immediate; dashboard displays bleeped, showing three flights of Pincer Ships cresting a ridge nearby.

Lancer stepped hard on the accelerator, ignoring the danger of the curves. He felt a coldness right down at his center.

Good try, but—they've got us this time.

CHAPTER
TWELVE

How did the Regis lose contact with Ariel, such an important agent? The technically minded hindsighters will point out several reasons. The rest of us have learned better by now.

Nichols, *Zeitgeist Reconsidered: Alien Psychology and the Third Robotech War*

THE PINCER SHIPS SWEPT IN, BUT THERE WERE abruptly three new blips on the dashboard's scanners.

Maxwell's trio of prized autofighters swooped in hard at the Invid armor-piercing cannon rounds, loosing missiles and, breaking left, right, and upward, following the aero-maneuvering programs in their memories—maneuvers the Invid hadn't had the time or necessity to learn . . . until now.

Lancer stopped for only a moment, looking back to see the warplanes fighting their last battle. He saw the bright fireglobes of exploding Pincer mecha in the sky, and the whirling, flaring wreckage of enemy war machines.

Go get 'em! Lancer tromped his foot down hard on the accelerator.

Maxwell, in a secret tech-pit, watched his fighters roll up a score and then, one by one, be overwhelmed and sent down in flames. He liked to think that his father would have been happy at this last stand, even though it came late in the game.

At least Carla will be safe. So much for the jets. What does it matter? Not much, without Carla.

He leaned back in the control center chair and closed his eyes, wishing that he would never have to open them.

Snow had begun drifting down.

Lancer had his arm around Carla's waist. "Donald sacrificed all three of his father's fighters to save us—no, to save *you*."

He could see that she knew that; she was looking back at Deguello rather than at the smoking remains of the warplanes and mecha. Lancer wanted to wrap her in her coat and take her along with him.

"Why?" She was trembling.

A core of honesty made him answer. "You're everything to him. He wanted to save your life."

He was beginning to shiver, the flakes melting on his skin and the thin bodysuit. "What now, Carla?" He gripped her shoulders in strong hands. "I won't let him use you again!"

"Oh, Lancer! I have to—I'm going back." She reached for the satchel she had left in the APC. "This time I guess I'm the one who's jumping the train."

She reached up, held him close, kissed him with hopeless passion. "Good-bye Lancer; good-bye, Yellow."

Then she was going back down the road, walking to the lights of the mayor's mansion. Lancer walked slowly to the truck.

He automatically checked for the weapons the team had taken from Maxwell's goons and saw the pile was one gun light. The little palm-size shooter was gone.

Love or death; what will it be?

Lancer took a last look down the road at Deguello. As Yellow Dancer, he blew a last kiss to Carla. Then, as Lancer once more, he pulled on the parka Lunk had left on the seat, hardened his heart to all that had gone on before, and floored the accelerator, to go meet the Invid, to take them on on their own ground.

* * *

Maxwell had told the truth in at least one matter: the Invid fortress blocked the only usable pass.

The team had hoped to avoid it; the hidden road was perilous but had served for much of the way. A recent quake had brought the entire side of a mountain down, though, making further progress impossible. There was no choice but to tackle the fortress.

Watching the morning patrol of Pincer Ships and Shock Troopers return, Scott did his best not the hear Annie's teeth chattering and not to think about the silent shivering of Marlene and the others.

"It's a pattern," Lancer said, still grave after days journeying from Deguello. His skin was paler than ever from the high-country snow and chill. "The bulk of their mecha goes out at sunrise. That's the best time to make our move, Scott, whatever our move is going to be."

They were still bickering about the best way to deal with the alien stronghold when they heard a cracking and splintering of wood, and Rand's cry, "Tim-ber-rrrr!"

By nightfall, they were sitting around Rand's fire, wearing every stitch of clothing they had, and huddling under cargo pads from Lunk's truck as well. Under the draperied shelter of a rock overhang, Rand used the molecule-thin edge of a Southern Cross survival knife to carve skis, bringing them up every so often to sight down their lengths critically, while he explained.

"Okay; we can't get our mecha anywhere near that fortress without being detected, right? So one of us has to get cross-country to the fortress and knock out their Protoculture detection gear."

"And so you'll just ski on in there?" Lancer asked with a tug of a grin.

But Scott admitted, "It might work. What other chance do we have? When Rand signals us that he's knocked out their sensors, we'll run the gauntlet and hope nobody notices."

"There's only one hangup, isn't there, Rand?" Rook asked, giving him a look he couldn't quite read. "You don't have any idea what an Invid sensor looks like."

"I'll know it when I see it," he grumbled.

Annie grabbed one of the skis and began sighting along it as if she knew what she was doing. "Hey, Rand! You're gonna let me come along, aren't'cha?"

He shaved another paper-fine layer off the ski he was working on. "Actually, Mint, I'm afraid I cut these for somebody a little older and taller than you. With blue eyes and long, strawberry-blond hair and a shape that—"

A snowball hit him in the back of the head.

"I mean, a *team spirit* that we all admire," Rand amended.

"Well, you can count me out," Rook told him. "*This* dame isn't wandering around in the wilderness with *you*, country boy—"

It was just then that Marlene went into another seizure. Nobody but Rook saw how hurt Rand looked; nobody but Rand saw how confused Rook seemed by what she herself had said.

Lunk, Scott, and the others kneeling near Marlene didn't seem to be of much help and she appeared to come out of the fit by herself. Rook, standing and looking down at her, said, "It's almost as if she's got some horrible memory locked up deep inside, that's trying to push her over the edge."

Rand looked at Rook's profile in the firelight, and wondered how much of that was something Rook was projecting.

The Invid fortress was cut into a mountain face that resembled a miniature Matterhorn pockmarked with hemispherical openings.

"Look: I cut those skis down for you, Mint," Rand told Annie, "but don't get cocky. Practice runs are a lot different from what we're gonna have to do today."

"Don't call me 'Mint'!" was all she had to say, as she adjusted her improvised bindings.

The others looked on from the treeline. Watches had been synchronized, explosives packed, weapons charged —all of it checked a dozen times over and then checked again. Rand had managed to snatch a little sleep, but he doubted that Scott had slept at all.

The fact that Annie should accompany Rand was less and less of a surprise to them. Aside from the Forager, she was the only one with cross-country experience (she insisted that some undyingly devoted boyfriend had taught her). And aside from Rand, she was the only one who could hope to cross the open country to the fortress in a reasonable amount of time. The snow was so chancy that even snowshoeing was out of the question.

At five A.M., when the sun was beginning to light the sky, Rand and Annie moved out.

As Rand turned to go, snatching his makeshift ski poles out of the ground, Rook seemed to be about to say something or even grab his arm. But when she saw he was looking at her, she abruptly turned away.

Annie turned out to be a better skier than Rand himself, though neither of them was very good. Then Annie got fancy, Rand tried to chastise her—a bad move while skiing—and they both ended up in a snowbank.

It proved to be a heaven-sent spill; shadows crossed the snow and Invid Pincer Ships landed to examine things that had fallen from Annie's pink rucksack. Somehow, the skiers' tracks had been obliterated by the drift of snow on the slope.

"That's my bikini!" Annie yelped, struggling to get to her feet and take on the entire Invid horde by herself. Rand pushed her face down further in the snow, stifling her.

The Invid hooked the bikini bottom in question (*Why was she carrying it on a ski run*? Rand wondered) in its claw, and raised it close to its optic sensor for examination. The mini-pantie had in turn hooked one of the metallic submarine-sandwich-like charges the team had prepared for the fortress job.

Seeing it tottering there in the seat of the bikini, Rand pushed the struggling Annie even further into the snow. The sapper charge tottered and fell. Rand exhaled in relief when the charge proved inert. The Invid personal-armor mecha dropped the bikini bottom and rocketed away on a wash of thruster-fire.

Skiing to the base of the fortress mountain held no other terrors; they kicked off their improvised bindings. A modified grenade launcher got a grapnel up to an opening. There was terror in the climb, as they watched a patrol of Shock Troopers cruise by below them. But the Invid didn't notice the climbing rope, and the Humans pulled themselves up near the topmost access tunnel.

Annie nearly fainted back into Rand's arms; a Shock Trooper mecha was standing there.

Rand shoved the edge of his hand in Annie's mouth and she bit down so hard that she drew blood. But the Trooper appeared to be looking at the surrounding peaks with no more interest than an Alpine sightseer. It turned to go, each step sounding like a boiler being thrown down on a concrete floor, back down the dark, arched tunnel from which it had come. Rand rubbed his hand and wondered if Annie had had her shots lately.

The two pushed their goggles back and went in after the Trooper. The tunnel was a place of heat gradients, the chamber at the end being almost womblike in its warmth and moisture. It was a bizarre landscape of structures that looked like neurons and axons (or were they stalactites and stalagmites?). Dendrites bent and arched, and the undulating ceiling resembled Liver Surprise. Cable-thick creepers ran from the squishy-looking support members. A knee-high mist obscured everything. "All this place needs is bats," Rand whispered.

Bela Lugosi, where are you?

They sprinted through the echoing, gutlike halls of the Invid, trying not to breath. Annie had banished all rational thought from her brain, and so she was surprised when Rand hauled her behind one of the sticky-looking dendrite pillars.

There was a strange echo as the three smaller mecha stumped by, these ones only eight or nine feet tall, their optical sensors set in long snouts. They had the faces of metallic archer-fish. Even the two Humans heard the resonating message in the Regis's voice, the very armor of the enemy reverberating with it, "All my outlying units, report to transmutation chamber at once!"

Rand watched them lumber off. "This *could* be a lot harder than we figured."

He had pushed Annie into the shadows of a doorway of some kind, and she began experimenting with the wet-looking, illuminated membranes that looked like buttons.

A door-size sphincter opened next to her; she gasped, seeing what lay beyond, then giggled. *"Open Sesame!"* Words she had always dreamed of using, so appropriate now. There were certainly more than forty bad guys in *this* cave.

The two stepped into the next chamber, awestruck, gazing around them. Their stage whispers were lost in the size of the place.

"Wouldja look at—"

"Holy—"

It was the size of the biggest indoor arena Rand had ever seen, the one in the radiation-glazed deathtown they used to call Houston. He and Annie walked out on a gantrylike thing, which looked like a suspended arm with dangling Robotech fingers. They looked down.

Ringing the center of the huge dome were concentric ranks of egg-shaped objects: motionless protoplasmic things, with untenanted mecha sleeping inside like hunkered fetuses. And at the center of that vast place was a brilliant, shining dome. To Rand, it resembled those twentieth-century pictures of the first nannoseconds of a thermonuclear explosion. Around it grew a low, irregular palisade of things like budding mushrooms, but they stood ten yards high.

Annie looked down at the embryonic mecha. "Y'think they're all asleep, or something?"

Rand shrugged. "Y'got me, but if they *are*, maybe we can wake 'em up." His patented grin showed itself. "A riot in the Invid Incubator Room! That's gotta be *some* diversion."

Still, the ranks of huge eggs reminded him uncomfortably of an oldtime space flick he had seen as a kid, and he had no intention of having something leap up and give him some interspecies mouth-to-mouth. He held Annie back and kept his gun level as he pulled a coin out of a slit pocket over his midsection and tossed it.

The coin glittered in the red-orange-yellow light and bounced off the top of one egg. Rand was expecting a gelatinous quiver, but instead the coin bounced with a metallic *bonk*! and skipped, to land on the floor with a faint chiming. Nothing moved, nothing happened.

"My last quarter," Rand said ruefully. A 1/4-Cid piece from the city-state of España Nueva back down south. True, it wouldn't be much good on the road to Reflex Point, but still . . .

"Maybe they're in suspended animation," he considered, rubbing his jaw. "And maybe they won't wake up until they're supposed to."

He disregarded the idea of using his gun to experiment further; most likely, it would set off alarms and draw the enemy straight to him. Then Annie was crooning, "Uh-ohh-hh."

A saucer-shaped air-vehicle whose underside was all glowing honeycomb-hexagons had come floating silently from among distant dendrites. Its curved, mirrorlike upper surface showed four equidistant projections like knobbed horns. It came directly at Rand and Annie.

So? I thought you country boys could rub your psoriasis together and start a fire? Where's that pioneer spirit?

Rook, to Rand

THE FLYING SAUCER WAS FIFTY FEET WIDE. WHEN IT had covered most of the distance separating it from the intruders, it halted. It remained motionless, lying dead still without sound or motion.

Suddenly the honeycomb-cells began shedding harsh light, the saucer's underside a solid convex of brilliance. One of the embryo-mecha began to glow. Its egg expanded and rose into the air toward the saucer. Rand and Annie stopped their withdrawal and watched what was happening.

Again there was the regal female voice, reverberating from the saucer, the cross-echoes making it difficult to understand. But Rand thought he heard, "Nine-X-Nine-teen has been selected for transmutation. The quickening will begin. Retrieve a Scout pod and transfer it to Hive Center."

The egg had disappeared and the unborn Scout was enclosed in a larger globe of light, some sort of lifting field. It looked similar to the ones Rand and the team had fought. It was slowly unlimbering, its contours still curved to its confinement, the way a baby bird's are to its shell for the first few moments after it breaks free.

Rand and Annie watched the mecha borne away by the saucer. *He's being promoted?* Rand tried to puzzle out. He didn't know much about how Invid society really functioned; nobody did, or at least nobody who was talking.

Annie shook him and he realized that time was wasting away.

In the Hive Center lay one of the bio-constructs that was the Regis's direct contact with each installation and every individual of her far-flung realm. It was the center of the hive's reverence, obedience . . . adoration. It spoke to the hive members, and with them, and for them.

It was situated in a shallow nutrient pool about five or six yards wide, filling two-thirds of it. A half-dozen mature light-stalks blossomed around it, beaming down nourishing rays—radiating flowers like the Flower of Life and yet unlike it.

The darker chocolate-orange of the Hive Center's floor was broken across its entire span by large and small dark pink circles. It looked as if a hundred spotlights of various sizes shone there. But the only visible path of light was the incandescent beam that shone down on the Sensor, the coordinating intellect-clearinghouse of the hive.

Mecha stood by as the Regis spoke. Listening to her were a single looming Scout unit and a half dozen and more of the smaller, more highly evolved, trumpet-snouted Controllers.

"The proliferation of the Flower of Life on Earth has reached a critical phase, a triggerpoint," it said. "Soon the mass thriving of the Flower will be assured, and we will need the Human race no more, and Earth will be the homeworld that will replace our beloved Optera. But we *must* pass that triggerpoint, we *must* have more Human slaves to spread the Flower of Life to every corner of the Earth.

"And to increase our supply of slaves, we must have more mecha, as rapidly as the Evolving makes that possible. Prepare now for the arrival of the retrieval droid, and the quickening of a new Scout ship!"

One of the Controllers began making stiff-armed gestures to the others, like some ancient Roman military salute sequence. The other Controllers moved to their places, and in moments the hulking Scout ship, standing immobile on one of the lighted circles, began descending into the floor. In a moment it was gone and the aperture closed.

"I guess that thing there is the brains of the outfit," Rand whispered, where he and Annie poised in concealment behind two fibrous columns.

"Yeah, well, it may have it in the brains department, but—" She made a face. "Ugh! It gives a whole new meaning to 'ugly'!"

The thing that Rand thought was a Sensor was a huge mass of wetly glistening, sickly pink coils. It looked like someone had knotted a length of enormous small intestine beyond any unsnarling. Its stench clogged the warm, humid air of the hive center.

A retrieval pod entered, bearing aloft the hatchling it had fetched. "Scout Trooper ready for quickening," the Regis announced. The saucer set its burden down exactly where the previous one had stood, the hatchling booming as it landed. The lifting field disappeared as the saucer's underside dimmed. The retrieval pod whisked away.

The hatchling's optical sensor opened, exposing the vertical row of three lenses. "Activate canopy," the Regis commanded. Long segmented metal tentacles extended from somewhere above, their articulated fingers working quickly. The Scout's cranial area was opened and a broad plate or hatch swung up.

Rand could see a softly lighted area within the cranial compartment, but he couldn't tell much more about what was going on. "Insert drone Nine-X-Nineteen," the Regis's eldritch voice said.

From a conduit high in the wall, there came another egg, this one far smaller than the mecha's. Clusters of gracefully-waving tendrils, like undersea plants, floated at the top and bottom of the embryo.

Within the embryo was something curled up that looked shrunken and wizened even though its skin had the moist, hairless look of the unborn. It appeared to be mostly head, its arms and legs degenerated and vestigial. Its dark eyes were bottomless, liquid black slits; Annie couldn't decide whether they were as unseeing as a seconds-old kitten's, or windows to some all-observing intellect. Drone Nine-X-Nineteen's nose was a bony button.

A crest of hard plate made a ridge from its massive, convoluted brow back across its skull. Its skin seemed to be a lusterless gray-green, its brow and skull mapped by a craniological nightmare of bulges and eminences. It was all but chinless, its mouth seemingly a tiny bud.

Rand and Annie looked at the face of the enemy.

Drone Nine-X-Nineteen, still in its egg, was wafted by unseen forces, to nestle in the dimly lit womb of the Scout's head.

"Drone in place," the Sensor reported to itself.

"*Bad* place," Annie muttered. Rand nodded.

The tentacles closed the canopy of the quickened Scout; the optical scanner came alight, glowing red. "Transmutation completed," the Regis declared. "Prepare next Scout Trooper for quickening." The Scout that carried—or had *become*—Nine-X-Nineteen sank out of sight like its predecessor.

"Rand," Annie said plaintively, "I'm scared."

"So'm I, Mint. Let's get this thing over with and get out of here." A retrieval pod was bringing in another Scout. "Dammit! We must've gotten here right in the middle of Motherhood Week!"

Annie swallowed. "Then let's blow that Sensor thing and get out of here!"

"Fine with me, but we have to find it first, remember? And it could be *anywhere* in this maggot factory."

She looked at her watch. "That means it's time for Contingency Plan B, huh?"

Rand nodded, checking his own watch. "I hope Scott

and the others aren't napping." He looked around him. "I'd hate to be stuck in this neighborhood at night."

Scott was wide awake and swearing, looking at his military chronometer. He and the others were gathered under snow-covered firs behind a line of drifts, watching the pass from the shadows.

"They're late with their signal!" And he had no idea whether Annie and Rand were in trouble or had simply, in their sloppy civilian way, forgotten the timetable.

If they're goofing around up there . . .

But Lancer grabbed his armored shoulder. "There they are." He pointed.

Three quarters of the way up one of the peaks that flanked the fortress, light was flashing from one of the many niches or tunnel openings or launch bays or whatever they were.

Scott and Lancer trained their computer-coupled binocular on the spot. The binocular showed Annie, sitting on the edge of one of the niches, angling a mirror from her pack, using it as a crude heliograph. It would be impossible to answer by the same code, since the Invid might have picked up the flashes. He turned to Rook, who stood with Marlene and Lunk.

"Just as I figured: they need a decoy. Okay, Rook, get moving."

She nodded, snowflakes glistening in her long, strawberry-blond waves. "Wish me luck."

Annie continued her signaling, hoping the team had noticed it. It only made sense not to use a radio inside the fortress, but she would have felt better hearing Scott say, "Affirmative."

She heard the heavy tread of mecha round a corner, coming her way unexpectedly. Annie fumbled with the mirror and lost it as she dove for cover. She had no choice but to hang from the brink by her fingers, as two towering Controllers marched by.

"Unidentified intrusions registered along Perimeter Sixteen," the Regis's voice warned. "Investigate!"

After they had passed, Annie hauled herself back up again. But she felt a sinking unease. Suppose her signal hadn't been seen? She looked around for some other reflective surface that would serve, but could find none.

Maybe Rand and I are on our own? Maybe we'd better start improvising?

Rook activated a control, and her Cyc's tires extruded heavy snow studs. She left her thinking cap off, letting her hair blow in the wind on the chance that the aliens might think her less of a military threat if they didn't see that she was a Cyclone warrior.

She jumped from ridges and traveled under the tree canopy as much as she could, hoping that the enemy couldn't follow her back-trail through the snow and find signs of her teammates' presence. Then she howled out into the open, making the treacherous approach uphill toward the fortress. It wasn't long before a flight of Pincer Ships dove at her, their shadows flickering across the snow.

Rook gave a wild, scornful laugh, elated by the thrill and risk of it all. "Come on!" she called up. "I'll race you to the mountain top!"

The Pincers swooped close but held fire for the moment, trying to determine just what kind of threat they faced. Their scanners studied the racing cyclist.

In the Hive Center, sheets of light and electrical discharges raced across the heaving, visceral mass of the Sensor. "Patrol reports bio-energetic activity in the approaching vehicle. Protoculture emanations registered! All available units converge and intercept!"

Rand, watching from concealment, held Annie well back. "Keep your head down!"

"But—what's happening?"

Rand checked his watch again. "It all hit the fan just at

the time Rook was supposed to start her diversionary run!"

As the Invid closed the distance, Rook hit a switch on her right handlebar and tensed herself like a coiled spring.

A change in the din and the Saint Elmo's fire along the Sensor made Annie point and tug Rand's arm. "Look, it's stopping! Is that bad?"

Rook! he thought. He felt a stab of despair and loss so powerful that it nearly staggered him.

"Intercept and neutralize!" the Regis commanded, as the Pincers raced to obey.

Rook concentrated everything on her timing. Calculations meant less now than instincts and years of experience in evading the Invid. At a certain moment she slewed around a stand of pine and laid down the bike in a spume of snow, throwing herself clear of the on-purpose grounding, diving into a snow bank.

The Cyc lay dead, its Protoculture engine off. Rook lay doggo as the Pincers rounded the trees and went on past, following their Protoculture detectors, suddenly confused. They raced on, splitting up, casting about like bloodhounds for a scent.

Rook pulled herself up a little and smiled at the receding Invid personal-armor mecha. *"Ciao!"*

An instant later the smile disappeared. *Rand, get busy! Get out of there!* She was frowning at the fact that she was worrying so much over him—and Annie, of course . . .

She hadn't let anybody mean anything to her since she had quit her old biker gang. This caring for someone— especially a dumb country boy—was making her angry with herself and with him, too.

"It can't be a coincidence," Rand said tightly. "That heap o' guts out there—that *thing* is the Sensor we're looking for!"

Annie gripped his shirt. "D-d'you think it knows we're here?"

"If it does, we're in a lot bigger trouble than I thought."

The obscene loops of the Sensor were dark and quiet. Still, the quickening of Scouts went on. Rand watched as more Controllers went to take up positions near the stinking mass of the Regis's local embodiment.

Something occurred to him, and he gazed at Annie apprehensively. She had been possessed by an alien intelligence once before, in the Genesis Pit. What if it should happen again? But no, she seemed to be behaving normally—quaking with fear.

Rand tried to calm himself and take in the situation. "The place is crawling with guards."

"M-my skin's crawling, too!"

He picked a route and led the way from cover to cover. The Controllers were all concentrating on the quickening, gathered to one side of the Sensor. Then the two reached the opposite side of the monstrous mound of alien bowels. Annie skittered after Rand, quiet as a mouse, but she lost her footing and was about to go sprawling.

But Rand had turned, and he caught her. The descent of yet another Scout ship into the floor had covered the noise. "Watch what you're doing!" he wispered fiercely, turning her around and rooting through the pink rucksack.

She was puffing, wiping the sweat from her brow, fanning herself with the E.T. cap. Rand mumbled, "Where is it—ah!"

He drew out an instrumented cylinder the size of a pint beercan. A shaped-charge cobalt limpet mine, something the team had been saving ever since the raid on Colonel Wolff's goodies warehouse. "This should do the trick." *And we'd better not be hanging around when it does!*

Annie whispered, "Hey! I carried it; I think I ought to be the one to plant it—"

She dropped her cap and stifled a squeal as she reached frantically to catch the bomb, Rand having casually tossed it to her while the Controllers inserted another drone.

It was *supposed* to be totally inert until it was armed, but—"Talk about *dumb*," she said, giving him a venemous look. Then she turned to attach the limpet to the side of the Sensor's pool. She set the timer's blinking numerals. "One minute enough?"

He was setting a second sapper charge for sixty seconds. "Let's hope so." They couldn't take a chance on a longer setting; one of those enemy mecha might decide to take a stroll at any second.

They nodded to each other. *No going back now!* They stole off the way they had come. They were halfway across the floor when Annie realized her head felt cold. Even though she knew it was crazy, she looked back instinctively for her treasured cap. It still lay where she had dropped it.

Then, somehow, her feet had tangled up and she was falling, almost cracking her chin on the floor. From her loosened pack jounced an adjustable ordnance tool, ringing like an alarm bell.

"Disturbance in Hive Center!" thundered the Sensor, in the voice of the Regis.

CHAPTER
FOURTEEN

*Plutarch said courage stands halfway between cowardice
and rashness. Shakespeare said it mounteth with occasion.
What we've got here is living proof.*

Scott Bernard's mission notes

RAND SKIDDED TO A HALT, SPUN, AND SAW WHAT
had happened. "Typical!"

But he went dashing back, as Controllers turned to
converge on the spot where Annie lay. Their bulging arms
were raised and pointed, and their built-in weapons were
ready to fire. "Intruders. Two in number. Neutralize
them," the Regis exhorted her troops.

Annie levered herself up miserably. "No, please don't!
We didn't mean anything!"

Rand calculated time and angles. "Just hang tough,
Mint. These jerks won't know what hit them in a coupla'
seconds."

"Surrender, Humans, or be destroyed," the Regis demanded. Rand watched the Controllers close in, his hand
on his H90. Then he holstered it and put both hands over
his ears and opened his mouth wide, to lessen the impact
of the blast. Annie, terrified, did the same. "Humans,
this is your final warn—"

Most of the blast from the limpets' shaped charges was

directed inward, into the grotesque coils of the Sensor, but the backwash was more than enough to knock the leading three Controllers sideways.

The Sensor bore the brunt of a stupendous blast.

Marlene gasped.

Scott, too busy to notice, was watching through his binocular as smoke roiled from one of the snowpeak's upper openings. "They *did* it! Isn't that a beautiful—"

He lowered the binocular and turned, hearing Marlene cry out and then collapse into racking sobs. Rook and the others rushed to her side. "Is it the same thing as last time?" Lancer asked, gently trying to quiet her.

"She's screaming at me!" Marlene managed, through convulsing shudders.

Lunk's low brows met. "Who is?"

Rook tore her gaze away from the smoking fortress and tried not to fear that Rand had been hurt or killed. "Is there any way we can help, Marlene? Tell us what to do!"

Marlene was on her knees, holding her head in her hands. But she shook it no, her hair swinging.

"Let's get moving," Scott barked, to snap his team out of it. "Rand and Annie might need help even more."

"I . . . don't . . . believe it," Annie stammered, gazing upward.

Rand stood tranfixed near where she lay, looking up as well. "That—that *thing* . . ."

The Controllers were all down, smoking, either from the initial blast or from secondary explosions. And the Sensor had vanished from its nutrient bath, all right. But now sickly pinkish blobs of it, in various sizes, bobbed and drifted around the Hive Center. They tumbled like slow-moving meteors, drifting, caroming off each other, spreading like floating amoebas to fill the place.

My god! We hit it with enough wallop to knock off a half-dozen Shock Troopers, and yet— "It's dissolved into some kind of, of protoplasmic flesh!" He wasn't even sure what the phrase meant himself. *Perhaps*, he babbled to himself, *"Protoculture ectoplasm" would be more the term?*

Annie was struggling to get to her feet. "It's coming straight for us!" The deploying blobs had somehow located them, and were homing in from all over the chamber like evil clouds of murderous jelly.

Annie threw her arms around Rand's waist. "It's g-gonna eat me!"

Rand had his H90 out, gripping it in both hands. "Eat *this*," he told the remains of the Sensor, and began firing. But the bolts just split the flying lumps into smaller ones, and the firing somehow made them charge at high speed.

The Regis's voice came from every doughy lump, down to the least globule, as if from a vast chorus, *"Attack!"*

Rand fired hopelessly as Annie screamed.

One pilot short, the team still got all VTs into the air. The Beta was linked to Scott's Alpha, which increased its firepower and speed. The fighters moved forward on thrusters that shook the earth and started minor avalanches in the valley behind them. Down below, Lunk's APC, rigged for cold-weather work, moved cross-country almost as nimbly as a snow-mobile, bound straight for the fortress's main portal.

As they jumped off a snowbank and roared on again, Lunk said out of the side of his mouth, "I hope your stomach's stronger than your head, Marlene." But she sat hugging herself, eyes unfocused, shivering in spite of the outpouring of the heaters.

Rand tried not to retch, as wad after wad of the stuff that had been the Sensor splattered into him, coating him. The stuff had the consistency of runny putty but was warm to the touch. The most horrible thing about it, though, was that it moved by itself, snaillike, spreading wherever it hit. And it wouldn't come off.

The Sensor knew, even in its dispersed state, that it was dying. But it knew, too, who its enemies—its slayers —were, and it would have its revenge.

Annie's mind was about to snap. She closed her eyes as she rubbed and brushed at the stuff, uselessly tore it with her nails, batted it and shrilled, *"No, no, no, no, no!"*

She flung herself back at Rand, who was trying to clear the plugged muzzle of the H90. He was already wearing a pink mantle that was surging to cover his head. There was a waist-high pile all around them, making it impossible to run.

Rand beat, trying to shield Annie. "Annie, listen to me!"

"Aufff! It's getting in my mouth!"

The amorphous clots of residue streamed down at them from every quarter. He heaved at her. "Hang onto me and try to keep your head above it!"

Her voice was muffled by a mask of the stuff. "I can't breathe!"

His arms were all but paralyzed. "Annie, listen! Check the emergency tracking beam! *Is it still flashing?"* The crud was surging up around his face.

She gathered all her courage and forced down her panic. With a supreme effort, she got her head around and managed to get a glance down at the thing like a silvery fountain pen with a flashing tip that was clipped to one of her pockets.

She forced herself to get out the words, "I think so—yes!"

The Pincer Ships still casting about for Rook's trail weren't prepared for the sudden appearance of a vengeful trio of Veritechs. The dogfight had barely begun when four of the Invid personal-armor mecha were falling in whirling, flaming fragments. The team spent its missiles prodigally; their kill score climbed.

Lunk's truck, bounding and slewing across the open snowfield, attracted other attention. He saw cannons in a half-dozen niches in the cliff face open fire, and he began dodging and juking. Invid annihilation discs began Frisbeeing all around him. Snow was melted and earth blown high in fountains of flame and smoke. As was his habit, Lunk froze from his thoughts the image of what even one hit would do to him, Marlene, and the truck, in view of the ordnance and Protoculture they were hauling.

But Scott had seen what was happening, and dove in, loosing more missiles. The gun emplacements were knocked out in cascades of snow and broken rock, leaving only smoking holes like horizontal chimneys.

Rook and Lancer had vanquished the last of the opposition; the VTs made an attack run and blew open the main gate of the Invid fortress. The fighters slowed, moving on hoverthrusters, sailing into the colossal main corridor. Lunk's APC brought up the rear, his finger on the autocannon's steering wheel trigger.

They had little time to observe the fortress, with its bizarre and unnerving combination of alien technology and XT organics. Following Annie's tracer beam, they came to the Hive Center at last. The aircraft had been forced to slow down in the maze, so that Lunk pulled to a stop just as they grounded VTOL style.

The VTs knelt in a Hive Center of twisting, still-burning Controller mecha. The place was filled with thick smoke, the stench of incinerated organic material, and the reek of the disintegrating matter that had been the Sensor. The pilots jumped down, as Lunk and Marlene both coughed from the foulness around them.

At last they spotted the mound of pinkish stuff that had been the Sensor. Then they saw the dim flashing coming from its summit. Scott dashed toward it. "Gimme a hand here!"

The Sensor-stuff was beginning to melt; in another moment, Scott and Lunk had pulled two bodies free. Rand was barely breathing when they got him out, but he had shielded Annie in a little air pocket he had formed with his own body.

Rook stood to one side, staring down, not moving. She seemed about to speak, then was silent. But she never took her eyes off of Rand.

At last Rand's eyes opened. "W-what took you so long, pal?"

Rook let out a breath and pulled her features back into

their normal unconcerned, uncaring expression. And so when Rand eagerly looked at her, she gave him a casual look. He still managed a smile, grateful that she was alive, though he would have crawled back in under the Sensor offal before admitting it.

Lunk called over, "Annie sez she'll be all right once she brushes her teeth!"

Rand was already pushing Scott away from him, coming to his feet, clearing the last of the goo out of the H90, weaving a little. "I've *had* it! I'm gonna *slaughter* those walking tin latrines!" He steadied himself and lurched away. By the time Scott caught up with him, Rand was standing at a lower entrance to the huge dome where empty mecha waited in fetal repose.

Scott whistled low. "What is it, an incubator?"

Rand brought up his pistol. "Whatever it is, it's history!"

Something inside him knew he should be off somewhere ferreting out the place where the drones themselves were created—that he should be wiring *that* place up with all the explosives in Lunk's truck.

But he just wasn't made that way. The drones, for all their grotesqueness, were living things. And without their mecha, they were nothing.

Rand fired into the hemisphere in the middle of the dome—the thing that looked so much like the first instant of a nuclear explosion. He didn't know quite what would happen, but it turned out that the thing was fragile as stained glass. Sections of it geysered, then caved in, and black smoke roiled forth.

Rand was watching it in stonefaced satisfaction when, suddenly, Marlene's screech echoed to them down the alien halls.

They raced back to find the others trying to help, without any effect, as Marlene knelt, clutching her head. She wept that she couldn't *stand* it—though she didn't say what *it* was.

When Lunk wondered aloud what could be the cause of Marlene's seizures, no one answered until Scott said softly, "I wish I knew."

"Bad news, guys," Rook cut through their unease. She was standing by Lunk's truck, examining its beeping displays. "That Invid patrol that left the hive this morning is on its way home!"

Scott didn't take the time to wonder if it was because the raid had taken too long or because the destruction of the Sensor had alerted the mecha. "Okay, people: let's get out of here on the double. Rand, take the Beta Fighter."

Rand was already off and running. When the VTs hovered in the Hive Center and Lunk was racing his engine, Scott said over the tac net, "Listen up: you either break out of this rat's nest *now*, or you spend the rest of your lives as sharecroppers on an Invid Protoculture farm."

"What d'you mean 'you'?" Rand challenged. "What's *Bernard* gonna be doing while we're busting out?"

Scott tried to sound matter-of-fact. "I'm the one who got us into this."

"Nobody's arguing," Rand shot back.

"As you were! So, it's my place to take some of the heat off you. I'm going to block the front door for a while; don't lollygag getting out the back." His thrusters lit like blue novas, and his Alpha sprang away into one of the huge elevated conduit-passageways.

"Lancer, we should back him up," Rand said slowly, pulling on his thinking cap.

"Let him go, country boy; he'll be fine!" Rook snapped. "We've got enough problems of our own!"

Scott mechamorphosed to Battloid mode as he zoomed toward the shattered main gate. He met the first of the returning Pincer Ships with blasts from the mecha's massive rifle/cannon, a weapon with a muzzle as wide as a storm drain. The enemy flight was coming head-on, and Scott had little chance to dodge them. He blasted the first ship out of the air and scattered the ones near it.

But they came at him anyway, Frisbeeing their annihilation discs. He ducked into a side passageway, an upright Battloid, back and foot thrusters gushing blue. The Invid dove after him.

Then it was a game of evade and hide, ambush and run. The Invid were unrelenting, attacking him even though he had the advantage of standing or fleeing as he chose.

At last he darted like a huge wasp into a corridor that led to an intense light. At its mouth stood two Scout guards, so surprised at his appearance that they were slow to react. Scott knocked them off their feet, and they plunged backward, unable to attain a useful flying attitude. They tumbled and thrashed to their doom.

Scott found himself in a place that was miles wide. In its center was a tremendous globe that reminded him of the ancient ones in dance halls, the ones that reflected light. Only, this one was wired up with Invid Robotech hardware and organic wetware.

This must be the central power core for the fortress!

Pincer Ships entered the spherical vastness from three different conduits, and he felt the sweat run down his face. He eyeballed the power core quickly, spotting a glowing circular opening or access port a hundred yards across. Through it, he could see the scintillating mysteries of Invid Protoculture technology. His computers told him it was the alien equivalent of a main control matrix.

Scott made his decision, and the Battloid roared toward it. Invid noted his presence, drove toward him at full acceleration, claws outstretched to grip and rend, since they didn't dare fire there. Scott fooled them by hitting the core's outer hull, absorbing the impact with the Battloid's mighty legs, and springing away again.

The personal-armor mecha couldn't fire, but Scott felt no such compunctions. He whirled in midair and dispatched six air-to-ground Bludgeon missiles from his right and left shoulder pods. The Pincers dodged, thinking the missiles were meant for them.

One of the Bludgeons detonated on the rim of the access opening, but the rest lanced through into the power core's innards. Scott had already turned his Battloid on its heel to run like all hell.

CHAPTER
FIFTEEN

> *Homer posited two kinds of dreams, the "honest" one of*
> *Horn, and the "glimmering illusion" of Ivory.*
> *So Dad shot for Ivory, what else?*

> Maria Bartley-Rand, *Flower of Life: Journey Beyond*
> *Protoculture*

THE CORE'S VITALS SUDDENLY TURNED WHITE-HOT,
and the whole miles-wide spherical chamber lit up like the
interior of an arc furnace.

Although her Sensor was gone, the Regis spoke to her
remaining children. "Control Matrix breeched! Reflex
furnace overload!" All she could do was tell them that
they were all going to die, but at least they would hear
her voice in their final moments. Gargantuan sheets of
electrical discharge played all through the place.

The core came apart at its seams, like a soccer ball full
of Tango-9 explosive. The Pincers were vaporized; the
explosion raced outward.

Scott had turned and turned again, hurtling along at
max thrust, praying the walls and turns would muffle
some of the blast.

Then it caught up with him.

The Beta and the other two Alphas, shepherding
Lunk's truck, arrowed toward the titanic triangle of the

alien stronghold's rear gate. Beyond it, a snowy Earth shone.

"Nice of 'em to leave the back door open," Rook smiled. Then she felt her flesh goosebump as she saw that the light was dwindling; the two halves of the giant triangle's door were sliding in from either side.

"But not for long!" cried Lancer. "Lunk, *hurry!*"

Lunk gritted his teeth, floored the accelerator, and hit a few buttons. "Can't make it," he muttered, but the APC leapt ahead in a way that disputed that.

The VTs had to come through standing on one wingtip; the APC almost got its tailpipe caught. But they all made it, as the massive door halves ground shut.

"I think that one took some paint off my baby, here," Rook said cheerily, patting her instrument panel.

Lunk just tried to control his trembling; Annie was either meditating, praying, or passed out. Marlene looked comatose.

Rand glanced back over his shoulder at the fortress. *C'mon, Scott!*

Somehow, being slammed against walls and dribbled along the deck for a bit hadn't destroyed the superstrong Battloid. Even though the blast from the reflex furnace had shaken the whole mountain and had fissured walls, floors, and ceilings, it had somehow been relatively contained. But he was registering secondary explosions, and there was every chance that the core was going to explode again with an even more spectacular Big Bang.

Then it was on his tail, a fireball even bigger than the first. His sensors picked it up even while he was jetting for a secondary reargate, unable to find the main. Fast as it was, the Battloid had no chance of outrunning the flashflood of utter destruction for long.

And the bad news was that the gate he was headed for was closed.

He let the gate have everything he had left, his only hope being to break through. No room for explosives; he fired pumped-lasers.

Well, Scott: make-it-or-break-it time! he thought, all in

an instant, as the valve before him disappeared in a wash of demonfire.

Then he was through, the Battloid thrown into the clear like a marionette fired out of a mortar. But somehow the Robotech colossus held together, straightened itself, and regained flying posture, as the core explosion reached the open air on the mountain behind it. It was as if somebody had opened a floodgate into the heart of a star.

Scott dazedly shook his head, trying to image his mecha along, looking around him wonderingly, and tasting the special sweetness of being alive. *Well, what . . . do . . . you . . . know!* He went down to join the others.

Down below, Annie, Lunk, and Rook cheered as the mountain shook to its roots. Lancer was silent, but even he nodded approval.

But Marlene only watched dully, hearing the distant wailing of the Regis, and Rand was thinking to himself that somewhere thousands upon thousands of drones had been consumed. When he thought about the horrible things their quickening would have meant for Humans, he couldn't feel pity.

The stronghold itself began to sink, subsiding into the ground the way the mountains above the Genesis Pit had subsided. Passes everywhere were blocked with the snow shaken down by the fortress's passing, but at least now the way was open for any who might want to come after; for anyone who had had enough of the south and wanted to try a new life.

Who knows? Annie thought. *Maybe there* is *a Paradise!*

Far below the snow line they found a lake that, though cold, was a welcome place of respite. In no time, Annie was in the water, her much-touted bikini covered by a T-shirt. Rook was in, too, in bra and panties, eager to wash off the trail and the deaths and the killing. In no time, Annie had her engaged in a splash-fight. Both of them loved it, even though their lips were turning purple.

Marlene sat on the grassy shore, watching in bewilderment. Maybe if she could figure out this incomprehensible behavior it would help her figure out all the other enigmas that were her life. Thus far, she had simply gone along with the people who had found her, like a spore borne on the wind. But was that what she should be doing, even if it *did* feel appropriate? Nothing made any sense.

A few yards away, the men sat at ease after setting up camp. Annie had pointedly informed them that it was ladies first in the bath, and they would have to wait their turn.

Rand was shaking his head, saying, "Poor Marlene. All those attacks or whatever they are. And she *still* hasn't pulled out of that amnesia. I wish there was something we could do for her." He was looking in her direction, but it was also easy to shift focus just a little, and watch Rook splashing around in that skimpy outfit, which, drenched in water, was just about transparent. His breathing became a little ragged.

"Don't push it," Scott said. "She's been through some pretty rough times. She's got problems she's got to work through; who doesn't? She'll open up when she's ready."

Lancer was eyeing Scott, thinking about the matter of Marlene's naming, wondering what things the team leader was working through.

Annie was hollering for Marlene to come in and join the fun. Rook added, "Yeah, c'mon girl. It'll do you good."

Cold water immersion therapy? Rand wondered. *I could use some right about now.*

Then his predicament got even worse. Marlene said, "All right," to Annie's invitation, in a hesitant, unsure voice—as if complying came more easily than deciding.

She rose and began shedding clothes as innocently as a child. All four men stared, bug-eyed, but it was Rand who choked out, "Marlene, stop that! Are you trying to give me a cardiac?"

But she was already naked and seemed not to hear, feeling the sun and the wind on her skin, her fine, waist-length red hair stirred by the breeze. It was the slim-but-full, flawless female body Rand remembered so well trying not to stare at.

Framed there against the mountains with the sun gleaming from her, Scott thought Marlene was somehow a higher being. She seemed finer than other Humans—a creature possessed by an unconscious beauty and a natural grace so overwhelming that it caused an ache in your heart just to see it, and left you changed.

Lancer had calmly, almost gently, grabbed Rand by the earlobe to stop his raving. "Don't you know it's not polite to stare at a lady? You might make her feel self-conscious."

And who'd know better than you? Lunk thought, but not unkindly.

"Ow! Okay!" Rand was yelping, trying to squirm out of Lancer's hold. "I didn't mean to! I won't do it again! Uh, but maybe what I need's a swim—"

Lancer shoved him over in mock disgust. Rook, having watched from the lake, was suddenly scowling.

Gawdamn hick!

They were all to remember the interlude by the lake wistfully, though. Their route soon descended to a sand-blown desert region that didn't appear on twentieth-century maps. It was a desert more resembling those of North America than anything that had existed in the South before the devastations of the Zentraedi, Robotech Master, and Invid.

The terrain and climate hampered their rate of travel, but the enemy activity was much more of a problem. In the wake of the fortress raid, the Regis had saturation patrols scouring the countryside for them—consisting mainly of immense Shock Troopers now, with Pincers and Scouts in support roles.

They knew the aliens were concentrating a great deal of their resources on the freedom fighters, and Scott began to fear the team had attracted a fatal amount of attention to itself. What none of them could know was that the Regis was also enraged and frustrated that she had lost contact with her Simulagent—Marlene.

There came a time when the team was held up in a cave as a sandstorm raged outside and Shock Troopers paced the desert outside, searching for their trail. Though it should have been broad daylight, the world was a sand-red dusk, and even in the cave that tinted the air and layered everything, making their world monochrome.

Marlene, who had become ill once they had come down onto the desert, was nearly in a coma, shivering in her sleeping bag. In reality, she was suffering a delayed reaction to the impact of the Sensor's destruction and the PSI emanations' impact on her.

And their water supply was virtually gone; their main supply, in jerry cans rigged to Lunk's truck, had been shot up in a brief skirmish when they made their dash from the high country. Morale was so bad that Scott blamed Lunk for it, and Rand in turn jumped all over Scott; the argument almost had them at each other's throat. It didn't blow over so much as spread to the others. They were sick of seeing and hearing each other and being crowded into the cave with their mecha, the sand in everything, and the endless howl of the wind.

At last Marlene cried out in her fever-dream and startled everyone. There were some shamefaced apologies, as Rand knelt to squeeze some moisture into her mouth from a rag-twisted bit of cactus flesh. She opened her eyes at the taste of the juice and, despite its sour flavor, smiled up at him gratefully, almost adoringly. Outside, the rumble of Shock Trooper thrusters came over the wind, as the aliens went to search elsewhere.

Rand couldn't help smiling back, losing himself in those mysterious eyes, even chuckling to himself. But the others weren't laughing; they accused him—absurdly—of keeping the information about cactus moisture to himself.

He jumped to his feet, fists cocked. "A guy just can't win around you people, can he? Any Forager knows that trick; I guess I just assumed you weren't so dumb you'd just die of dehydration when there're cactus all around out there!"

He started for the cave entrance. "Did you see me

holding out? No! I gave what I had to Marlene, or are you all blind?"

"Rand, wait!" Rook spoke to him sharply, and yet there was a note of alarm in it.

"You want cactus? You'll get it!" She would have gone with him, but his hate-mask expression made it plain that he was in no mood for company. Rook watched him go, then turned to study Marlene, who had fallen back into a fitful sleep.

Even with his goggles on, Rand found himself all but blinded by the storm. He counted his steps and tried to remember the layout of the area. He had barely gotten thirty yards before he fell off the lip of a deep sandpit. He rolled and tumbled down its side, scraping skin and having the wind knocked from him.

Back in the cave, Marlene's eyes suddenly opened wide, though the others were busy making plans and didn't notice. The howl of the wind blotted out her one soft cry, "Rand!"

Rand was doing fine until an outcropping of sandstone grazed his head. Then he was seeing stars, and there was no desert, no earth, no *nothing* around him.

There were in fact cactus and other plants near where his body lay. The Invid Flower of Life took root where it willed, with no predictable pattern or limitation. Rand lay, out cold, in a miniature garden of them, with several of the tripartite Flowers crushed under him.

The sandstorm had stopped, and the beat of great, leathery wings, and the sound of a very special voice crying his name, roused him. He opened his eyes to a night sky, and saw that a dragon was passing overhead. And in its right forepaw, amid gleaming claws like sabers, it held—

"Marlene!" He was on his feet in an instant.

What the flamin', flyin'—"Stop!"

Then his Cyc materialized next to him and he was off to the rescue. The mechabike took to the air, and suddenly he was in armor, riding across a rectilinear land-scape. He went to Cyclone Guardian mode, only to dis-cover that the dragon had turned to fight.

Rand couldn't shoot without risking hitting Marlene. The dragon faked him out with a snap of its jaws, making him dart back. He managed to recover as Marlene yelled for him to save her.

His back burners ignited as he climbed back at the dragon for Round Two. "I don't know what's going on, but I'm coming, Marlene!" He bulldogged the dragon, assisted by the powered suit. The monster's saliva ate at his armor like acid. "Let 'er go, ya oversized iguana!"

Then it did, and she was falling, wailing. Rand went after her like a meteor and caught her, but the dragon was hot on their trail.

But all of a sudden, somehow, it was Rand and Mar-lene on the Cyc again, no armor, dodging and evading, while the beast blew flamethrower shots at them. Mar-lene, arms around his waist, cheek pressed to his back, called out, "Rand, listen: maybe this isn't happening."

"Huh?"

"Maybe you're dreaming all this."

"I like that idea better than being crazy as a restroom rodent!" Still, it was nice to feel her arms around his mid-dle.

The firedrake stayed in their six o'clock position over a Frazetta-scape of crags, peaks, and dire moors. It bird-dogged them through a long cave with a bright light at the other end. Rand wondered if he was supposed to be re-living his birth trauma or something, even though all he felt was scared. It chased them under an impossibly big, bright moon, and Rand wondered if the Cyc's silhouette resembled a certain oldtime movie production company logo.

Then it was daytime, the desert, and the pursuit was still on. Rand realized that Marlene was giving him the adoring look that said it all, and revised his opinion of the dream.

Next thing, somehow, they were back in the Hive Center, and Marlene had another one of her strange attacks, and Rand, staring at the Sensor, made the connection. "It's like a telepathic link with all the other Invid," Rand said slowly, eyeing the Sensor, "but why would *you* be so strongly affected by it, Marlene?"

No time to wonder; the dragon was back. Rand was on the Cyc and turned around to tell Marlene to get on, and then realized she was naked and unspeakably beautiful, as he had seen her by the lake.

CHAPTER
SIXTEEN

A trillion light-years high,
Expanding primordial fireball,
Your Universe is still
Your body

　　　　　　Mingtao, *Protoculture: Journey Beyond Mecha*

THIS ISN'T GONNA BE ONE OF THOSE NUMBERS WHERE *I*
find myself in school with no pants on, is it? Rand wondered.

Suddenly Marlene, clothed, was behind him on the
Cyc. But he saw that he was back in the Lizard Lounge.
Appropriately enough, the dragon showed up. At least
the Cyc wasn't mired in mud; he accelerated away past
dueling dinosaurs.

Then he had to dodge some Shock Troopers. *I told
Scott there were Invid here!* "I get the feeling this is some
kind of laboratory," he told Marlene, whose hands
pressed him tighter to her. "That the Invid are experimenting with the evolutionary processes of Earth. But
why?"

A ridge of rock rose up to send Rand and Marlene
head over heels. When he had crawled to her, to cradle
her head, she groaned, "You mustn't fight with Scott."

Scott? What's she telling me, here? "The two of us just

don't see eye to eye. I honestly don't think our lives—
any of us—mean a thing to him."

"Rand . . . water, please . . ."

But when he fetched it from a pool, she couldn't sip.
He brought some in his mouth, pressed it to her lips.
Then he was kissing her, and her eyes opened.

He laughed and tried to joke. "Um, in some places,
that would mean we were engaged."

But the roar of the dragon filled the cave as it came at
them like a bomber, and they were off again on the Cyc.
Off to one side was Annie, leering over the flames once
more in the Genesis Pit, speaking in the voice of the
Regis.

"Look, Human, into the flames of truth and tremble,
for it is your doom that you will see there. Even now the
final chapter of your people is being written in the great
Book of Time."

Annie wasn't finished. "Once the Invid were a simple
race, content with our own existence. But with our world
destroyed, our Flowers stolen, we were changed forever.
And once we have conquered the Universe we shall rise,
rise—we shall ascend beyond the physical. We shall rule
the higher planes of existence, as a race of pure intellect,
pure spirit!"

Rand saw again those mindshapes in the flames called
up by the possessed Annie. Somehow he saw Reflex
Point, and the very dwelling place of the Regis herself,
though he could not see her.

She said, "So we have come here, to regenerate, to
take Earth from the dying hands of Humanity. From the
ashes of your people we shall arise, reborn, like the Phoenix!"

There was a lot more to the dream, and it got even
weirder. The dragon snatched Marlene again, and Rand
found himself riding to the rescue with his teammates, all
of them dressed in combination Wagnerian–R.E. Howard
getups, but using mecha. And even Lunk's truck could
fly. Rand noticed that Rook seemed very displeased with
him.

Couldn't I just click my Ruby Slippers three times and call it a night?

Still, it was great to have a team to back him up, great to have friends. He realized that it was still a new thing to him, but he also realized that he had felt a little lonely back there, facing the Leaping Lizard all alone.

Somewhere along the line even the VTs got swords, gleaming silvery ones as big as telephone poles. When that dragon came at bay, the team *pureed* him.

But when demigoddess Marlene had thanked the warriors for saving her, and they were following the Eagles of Light homeward, after having been assured that a new day was dawning for the Human race, Rand could still hear the voice of the Regis. From the ashes of the Humans, the Invid would rise like a Phoenix.

What happened subsequently seemed dreamlike, but it hurt so much that he decided it wasn't. The sandstorm had passed and he was being helped back to the cave by Rook, who had come looking for him, and his scalp was matted with blood.

But when he saw the look of concern on her face, Rand reconsidered the possibility that he was still unconscious.

When the team—except for Lancer and Marlene—ran out from the cave demanding answers, Rand found himself slurring, "Listen, a new day is dawning, for the Dragon is slain at last. Shut up and listen! The, the day of oblivion's come f'r us all. Who th' hell were we, t'believe we could rule the Earth forever?"

There was a lot of crosstalk and some friction, some of them mad at Rand, others—especially Rook—telling them to lay off. But Rand plowed on, "The Invid have come here from across the Cosmos to regenerate themselves into a new form. They want to rule the physical Universe, and the higher planes of existence, too!"

"Wow! His brain's been fried!" Annie whispered.

"Naw, Annie," Rook countered. "The boy just hasn't woken up." She gave him a therapeutic slap on the cheek that she tried not to enjoy too much. Rand found himself back in the real world.

He took a few deep breaths and started again. "I know now why the Invid are here. They're trying to survive by plugging themselves into the Earth's evolutionary system. Don't look at me like that; you can't hardly blame 'em! We'd do it, too, if we faced racial extinction!"

Which we do, he realized.

Scott was close to taking a swing at Rand. "I couldn't care less whether the Invid survive or go the way of the Zentraedi and the Robotech Masters, just as long as they leave Earth. This is *our* planet!"

"Well, I wasn't saying that we—"

"I don't know what happened to you out there, Rand," Scott seethed, "but it seems to have knocked your loyalties out of whack."

"He was lying on a bunch of Flowers of Life," Rook blurted. "A whole little field of them. And the sandstorm hadn't bothered them, not even a bit."

While the others were thinking about that, Rand said, "What about Marlene? Is she all right?"

Rook looked at him for long seconds before she said, "She's still pretty weak, I'm afraid."

Rand went down on one knee next to her. Under his gaze, she stirred, wakened, smiled up at him as she had hours and an eternity ago. It had taken a look and a thought, not a kiss, to wake the sleeping damsel.

Well, Fair Milady, I don't know if you'll ever realize it, but you and I have just been on quite a spin. And I wouldn't have missed it for the world.

Rook, leaning against the cave wall with her arms crossed, glowered at the two. Maybe Marlene was brain-damaged, but that was no excuse to gaze up at a bumpkin like Rand with liquid, lambent eyes. He was nothing but a wasteland Forager!

"Hi," Rand smiled down gently. And now Scott, too, was scowling. In true military style, he didn't bother to consider his reasons for being irked at Rand. It was easier than examining his feelings for Marlene.

Rand touched Marlene's cheek. Her gaze gave him the

eerie feeling that she had truly been along on the all-time championship motocross run. Marlene smiled up at him.

A thought crossed Rand's mind. What was it Rook said he had been lying on?

Eventually, as Scott had fatalistcally expected, a patrol of Shock Troopers spotted them. The freedom fighters jumped the Invid right away.

They knew little about the Regis, but they were beginning to suspect something. The simple fact was that the Regis's attention was often diverted to matters elsewhere in her world-embracing scheme, and offworld as well. Although the whereabouts of her Simulagent and this persistently bothersome group of enemies were high on her priorities list, the Regis had a staggering number of projects and operations to control and guide.

All the freedom fighters knew was that there was still a chance to avoid disaster if the team could act quickly enough. Once more the VTs dodged and fired, barrel-rolled and spat missiles.

This battle took place over a strange landscape. The place *looked* like a jungle, except it appeared to have been *roofed over*. A translucent, shell-like pink covering stretched over hundreds of square miles of river valley. The roof, or whatever it was, had numerous irregular openings in it, openings so big that the VTs could fly in and out virtually at will. But so could the Invid.

The Humans were hampered by low Protoculture levels and ordnance supplies; Scott wondered if they would even have enough to get them through this latest mass dogfight. But Lancer was a tough, precise fighter jock, frugal with fuel and ammo when it was necessary, and he and Scott had taught Rand and Rook well. Trooper after Trooper went tumbling, burning, from the air under the weird shell-roof.

Down below, Lunk, Annie, and Marlene were having it a little tougher, as a Trooper noticed them and came swooping down at them. "Hey, you fancy fly-boys up there!" Annie squawked over the tac net, "you forgetting your friends here on *terra firma*?"

Rand broke away from the "ratrace" and, nearly at deck level, went after the Shock Trooper that was on the APC. But suddenly a bunch of trees came at him out of nowhere. *I think I zigged when I shoulda zagged*, he thought, as retros proved insufficient and the Beta hung up in a treetop.

A disc's explosion overturned the truck and the Trooper closed in for the kill, as the shocked Lunk, Annie, and Marlene watched. All in an instant, a bolt from a heavy VT cannon holed the enemy through and through, and it toppled.

The three looked up to where Rand's Beta hung like a fly in web. "Some shot, huh?" he beamed, although he was draped over his instrument panel at an undignified angle.

"Jeepers, what a dopey landing," marveled Annie.

Above, Scott and the others switched from Protoculture to reserve impulse power, and used their jamming gear and spread clouds of aerosol smokescreen behind them. Then they dived through one of the holes in the river valley's "roof," breaking contact. As they had hoped, the Invid went off in all directions, apparently mystified as to where the prey had gone.

The group made its camp and held council. With power and ammo levels so low, Scott unveiled what he considered to be the only workable plan for continuing the trip to Reflex Point.

"A raft?" Rand exclaimed.

Scott sipped from his mug. "There are two things to recommend the idea: We'll save what little Protoculture we have left, and we won't attract the Invid by activating our mecha."

Lancer blew on his coffee. "I think it's a brilliant idea. We'll just let the river do all the work."

Rand looked at the mecha. "You're talking about one

helluva raft, there. D'you *know* anything about rafts, spaceman?"

Annie started demanding that she be allowed to supervise and that the raft be named in her honor. Rook scolded her and said that this wasn't some dumb jungle movie where all you need is a couple of vines and a coconut.

Things began to turn into one of the team's signature free-for-alls. Lancer rose, stretched, and paced away toward the river. "Since I don't know the first thing about marine engineering, I volunteer for lookout duty."

"Probably afraid he'll break a fingernail," Lunk grunted.

Rand was agreeing, "The guy's just a lazy bum," when something heavy tapped his shoulder.

Scott was handing him the ax. "Country boy, it's time you showed us your stuff. I know this thing's a little primitive, but at least it works without Protoculture. Just think of a raft as a very large ski."

Lancer drank in the quiet beauty of the place. He found himself in a very quiet, serene world.

Coming to the shore of a fast-moving stream, he decided the current was too swift for predators and elected to bathe. In a moment, he had stripped, taken soap and personal articles from his belt pouch, and plunged in.

Several miles downstream from the team's landing spot, another Invid stronghold straddled the river on five asymmetrical legs. It looked like a bulbous insect with a glowing, low-hanging belly.

Inside was a Hive Center like and yet unlike that of the fortress. The Sensor there was identical to the other in its physical shape, but its color was a putrid, lit-from-within green. But in one particular way, this was a *very* different scene: The Regis had manifested herself.

An oval energy flux surrounded by a blue nimbus, its long axis vertical, hung over the Sensor. The mauve flux gave off solar prominences of light. Within it were swirling lights and within the swirl, barely discernible in the brilliance, was the female form of the Regis.

"Our Matrix is now approaching the bio-energy level needed for transmutation."

Regis and Sensor were attended by several Shock Troopers. One of these the Regis instructed, "Trooper, step forward!"

The Shock Trooper obeyed, somehow seeming subdued despite its immense size and armaments. The incandescence played across its armor as it stared at its ruler-deity, the Regis.

"You have proved yourself time and again," she told it, "as both a soldier and a shape-changer. In both these capacities you have helped ensure the survival of our race. Your outstanding achievements won you the honor of engaging the enemy in the Shock Trooper armor that now enfolds your being."

Her face was little more than a blank mask with shadowed eye sockets and the ridge of a nose. "Now the time has come for you to continue your evolution, to take the next step upward in the spiral of Protogenetic progress! Are you ready?"

The Trooper, watching her with its single optical sensor, made a biotechnic gurgling and a kind of hunching bow of obeisance.

"Very well! As I have spoken, so it shall be done! Prepare yourself for disembodiment and transmutation!" The Regis flung her arms wide, and the green Sensor was aglow. Energy crackled and sizzled through the Hive Center.

Vines of living Protoculture power snaked out from the Sensor to envelope the Trooper. In another moment it seemed to be in a rictus of agony, its superhard armor crumbling from it like plaster, as it stood in the center of a globe of transplendence.

Abruptly the armor was gone, and a pulsating egg hung in the center of the solar fury. "The disembodiment is complete," the Regis decreed. "You are yourself, unadorned, without identity, awaiting transmutation into the shell that will make you invincible!"

The egg beat like a heart. What it held was like the drone Rand and Annie had seen, and yet unlike it, the product of a long evolutionary progression.

The Regis gathered her indistinct hands to her blank breasts, palm to palm. "Behold the final stage in your evolution! Behold the Enforcer!"

SEVENTEEN

They had moved so fast they they had forgotten something. They were racing to save a world, and particularly the Human species, but nobody had ever said anybody was going to be grateful. It was just as well that they started getting used to that fact then.

Xandu Reem, *A Stranger at Home:*
A Biography of Scott Bernard

THE INVID ANOME HUNG BEFORE THE REGIS, A MINOR sun throwing off streamers of starflare. She threw her hands out wide, and the sunlet was swallowed up in a roaring pillar of ravening power. It burned upward like a huge searchlight beam, as something took shape within.

The light died and it was revealed. Twice the size of the Shock Troopers, it mounted a shoulder cannon like theirs but had a suggestion of the Controller's long muzzle. Its claws were proportionately smaller, adapted for finer work, but much more powerful than those of the mecha standing around it paying homage. It held all the power of the Matrix outpouring that had created it.

Its optical sensor fixed on the Regis, the Enforcer awaited her command.

The cool, clean water felt so good that Lancer could almost believe he was back at the *o-furo*, the bath. When he had lathered and rinsed himself, he began a little *Musume* exercise, like the ones his masters used to give him.

Using a theatrical depilatory, he removed the hair from his chest, legs, armpits, and so on. Then Yellow Dancer performed a maiden's bathing ritual, abandoning self for role. Each stylized gesture and movement would make an audience believe in the demure young girl; each pose and motion, handed down for centuries, contained a hundred subtleties.

But Yellow had become so clumsy, so out-of-practice! Surely Master Yoshida would have broken three sticks upon Lancer by now! Still, the exercise brought a feeling of calm serenity, a reminder of gentility and the frailty of beauty—a renewed faith in the high value and evasive exquisiteness of life itself.

Yellow emerged from the bath, still moving with the grace of the art. She held a towel close for modesty, even in that solitary place. She combed her long purple hair out carefully with her free hand. Then Yellow Dancer stretched out, stomach down, towel wound around middle, to nap in the warm sunlight that found its way down through gaps in the jungle roof and the forest canopy.

Gradually, Lancer reemerged, working on the problem of how to carry on the mission to Reflex Point. Had Scott's singlemindedness blinded him to the drawbacks in his rafting scheme?

A sudden sound made him look up, all freedom fighter now. He couldn't believe someone had managed to steal up on him; it had never happened to Lancer before. But it was too late; a knobby branch, padded by windings of creeper, thumped across the back of his skull.

"Tim-ber-rrr!"

Rand stepped back as the tree went down, dragging vines and creepers, branches from other trees with it. It sent up leaves and dust and all sorts of sounds as the creatures living in the tree fled in panic or anger.

"I'm gettin' pretty good at this Paul Bunyan stuff, huh?" he asked his teammates proudly.

But nobody seemed very impressed. Annie, looking up from where she and Rook and Marlene were making cross-members for the raft, snarled, "Whaddaya want, a standing ovation?"

Marlene giggled, and everyone stared at her. "Looks like our patient's finally starting to loosen up a bit," Scott smiled.

But inside, he was trying to sort out his feelings. If Marlene was improving—if she began regaining her memory—that might mean she would go her own way soon. He had tried not to think of that other life that she had obviously left behind. He tried not to think about the lover or even the husband who might be waiting for her, but now that was less and less possible.

In the midst of Scott's thoughts about Marlene, a long spear with a gleaming, machined-metal head suddenly arced out of the treeline and buried itself in a forest giant right next to him. The long shaft of stripped, dried wood bobbed slowly.

More spears followed, as Scott roared, "Follow me!" and led the way back toward the mecha. The rest of the group pounded after him. Miraculously, no one had been hit. They had to veer from a direct course, as a virtual hedgehog of spearpoints was thrust through a wall of undergrowth.

Scott detoured, hoping he wouldn't lose his bearings, gun in hand. He yelled for Lancer, but got no answer, and feared the worst. Scott had no idea who was attacking, but it clearly wasn't the Invid, and he had no wish to hurt any Human if he could help it. As the team members sprinted across a clearing, leaves and dirt flew as ropes of braided grass creaked, and all six travelers were hoisted aloft in an enormous net.

They were squashed in together against each other every which way, Scott losing his pistol, the others too tightly pinned to get to theirs. The world spun and swayed below them, but after a moment Scott saw people come out of concealment and into the open.

The spears had Rand expecting some lost tribe, a bunch of *Yanamamo*, perhaps, who had somehow survived the Wars and left their traditional territory. But instead, the team was looking down at men in factory-produced shoes and boots, albeit tattered and decaying ones, and trousers made from machine-woven fabric.

But the men were a bearded and mustached and headbanded bunch, carrying homemade bows, arrows, and spears, although the weapon heads were of metal. They wore beads and feathers and shell jewelry. Nothing made sense.

"W-whoever they are, they look like they're honked off about *something*," Annie observed.

An older fellow with snow-white hair and beard gestured up at them with a warclub whose head had been set with flakes of sharpened steel. "Bring them to the temple!"

The way he said "temple" had Rook expecting something from one of the venerated oldtime movies, but she was wrong. The natives marched them at spearpoint downriver to an aging, massive, hydroelectric power dam that looked to be in disrepair.

They were soon disarmed and standing out on a platform of lashed timbers on one of the dam crest piers. The green river valley seemed to stretch out forever, and the waters of the spillway basin fought and swirled far below them. All gates appeared to be open, and water fell in huge, white cascades, filling the area with mist.

Their hands had been tied, and each captive had been fitting with an ankle shackle rivetted to a heavy weight. Scott was looking around for some sign of Lancer, hoping that he had gotten clear and could come to their rescue.

"Now you will pay for your sacrilege!" the white-haired leader said. "You are outlanders and your presence in this place has offended the river god."

He gestured to where the open taintor gates and low-level outlets were letting the level of the reservoir fall. "It is because of you that the river god has turned his back on us and is leaving the valley!"

"Oh, come on!" Rand shouted, and some of the spearheads wavered close to his chest. "You're not telling me you're going to kill us just because this friggin' dam's had a malfunction?"

Scott already saw that that was *exactly* what the locals had in mind, but could make little sense of the matter. How could such a tribal society, such a primitive belief system, spring up in a single generation?

The only answer he could think of was the fact that the team was now in the region that had become a Zentraedi control zone, back when Khyron took refuge after the apocalyptic battle in which Dolza's force was wiped out. The Zentraedi would certainly have found good use for the hydroelectric power, but their giant size would've made it difficult for them to operate and maintain the dam. The answer would have been to spare a picked group of Micronian techs.

Most of the men in the group were in their mid-twenties or so, Scott judged. If a lot of the techs had been killed, inadvertently or otherwise, upon Khyron's departure, that would have left kids and a few oldsters—like the white-haired man with the slightly unhinged look in his eye—to put together a new society of their own. Perhaps they had borrowed elements of their crude culture from local Indians.

As to why the whole area had been roofed over, apparently by the Invid—Scott could only conclude that this was another of their experimental labs, a kind of grandiose ant farm.

"Silence!" the old man was howling. "The only way to bring back the river god's den is to sacrifice you!" He gestured to the shrinking reservoir.

He *must* be old enough to recall the days before the Wars, Scott saw—and certainly the days before the Invid and the Robotech Masters. But something had wrenched his mind away from the days of sanity and rational thought, and locked him into supersition.

"My lord, I think I have an idea," Scott interjected. "If we've sinned against your god, we plead ignorance. But we will set things right by bringing the river god's den back to your valley."

The old man looked at Scott; perhaps he recalled the techs in their worksuits—not so different from Scott's

uniform—who had once made the dam do their bidding.
"You can do this?"

"If, in return, you let us go."

The old man stroked his beard with gnarled, black
nailed fingers. "Very well, outlander. But if you fail, your
companions die!"

Scott angled a thumb at Lunk. "I'll need his help."
And I hope it's enough.

Scott surprised himself by recalling as much about dam
construction as he did from a years-ago Officer Candidate
engineering class.

Lunk followed him at a dead run, and they soon
reached the outlet control structure, further along the
dam. But when they got to the control room, they found
a musty room of half-corroded machinery and a bewildering collection of long-outmoded technology. Switches
were frozen in place; CRTs were dark and silent.

Scott had concluded that some malfunctioning auto-
system had opened the gates to release the reservoir
waters. "We'll shut off everything until we find the right
one," he told Lunk. Reopening them at a later time
would be the locals' problem.

"The outlanders have been gone a long time, Silverhair," a warrior said to the white-haired chief.

"Yes." Silverhair considered that. "Perhaps they abandoned their companions to save themselves."

"Hold on a second!" Rand protested. "If Scott says
he'll do something, then he'll do it! Just give him time!"

The old chief nodded slowly. "It is hard for you to face
the fact that they have deserted you. Ulu!"

The warrior addressed as Ulu brought up his spear
blade and leveled it at them.

After some time, Lunk stopped pulling levers and
spinning manual valve wheels at random and began reading designation plates on the various consoles. By miraculous good fortune, he found a mildewed manual. The
covers were rotted to soggy filth, but the schematics
themselves had been laminated.

Lunk might have his problems with social interaction, but he had never been outwitted by an inanimate object yet. He puzzled over the highpoints of the operating procedures for long minutes, then moved decisively. "Hey, Scott! I found it!"

It was a massive, two-bladed lever, an emergency manual control that would in cases of power failure close the gates by means of a fluidic backup system. But it, too, had suffered from the decades of neglect.

Lunk strained at it, the muscles of his shoulders and arms bunching and swelling. Scott threw his strength into the fight, too, their hands clamped around the switch.

Ulu's spear blade was close. "Trust us, will you?" Rook said, not able to take her eyes off it. "They'll do it and be back." The spearpoint edged closer, and a half dozen other warriors came after Ulu, to see that the job was done thoroughly.

The lever moved, an unbelievable quarter-inch, down its grooves. Scott and Lunk braced their feet against the console, teeth gritted, heaving for all they were worth. The lever moved another half inch.

"I warned your companions that all of you would pay the price of their failure," the chief said. The spear blades hemmed in the team members.

Suddenly there was a change in the sound of the water gushing through the gates and outlet. The flow was lessening.

"They did it," Rand exulted. "They shut off the valve!" Annie managed a cheer. As the team and the tribe watched, the flow was shut off, at both the top of the dam and the bottom.

"The valley is saved," the old chief said. "The river god is appeased at last!" His men were a little frightened by what they had seen, but joyous anyhow.

Scott and Lunk got back to the dam crest as fast as they could, only to find that their teammates had been unshackled and were receiving the tribesmen's clamorous thanks.

"We invite you to become members of our tribe," the old man said when Scott and Lunk got there.

"Thank you, but first there's a missing brother of *our* tribe we have to find," Scott deflected the invitation.

"Hey! Silverhair!" came a shout. "I did it! I got myself a wife!"

There was a barefoot kid in ragged cutoffs and T-shirt, maybe an undersized thirteen years old or so, coming their way. "I'm a man now!" he puffed, dragging a big, heavy old duffel bag after him.

"It's Magruder," said Silverhair the chieftain.

"Did he say 'wife'?" Rand murmured.

Magruder staggered to a stop before Silverhair and dropped the rope, as the warriors gathered round. "I captured myself a wife," he panted again, "so according to tribal law, you *have* to make me a warrior!" He pushed his narrow chest out proudly.

Rook got the distinct impression that Magruder was more excited about the prospect of being a warrior than about having a wife. Typical for his age, she decided.

Just then the duffel bag heaved and fell open. Everyone there gasped.

Protoculture Garden: Eden or Gethsemane?

Samizdat Reader's Digest article, November 2020

RAND FOUND HIMSELF LOOKING DOWN AT A FAMIL-iar mass of purple hair. "Lancer!"

Lancer, gagged, glared up at Rand and at the rest of the world. Scott turned to Magruder with a rare smile. "I'm afraid I've got some bad news for you, kid. Y'see, your fiancée is a man. And not one that I'd like to have mad at me, if you catch my drift."

Magruder looked stricken. "It can't be! That's my wife!"

The tribesman were beginning to guffaw, and Annie was giggling a bit hysterically. "Is this the missing brother you were talking about?" Silverhair asked.

Rand nodded, "Yeah; his name's Lancer."

Magruder had knelt to undo the gag. "Uh-oh."

Lancer looked at him mildly. "It was an honest mistake, little man. Now—" He drew a deep breath. *"Get me out of this thing!"*

Scott and some of the others stooped to help, Ma-gruder being too paralyzed. Everyone was united in laughter now, at the expense of woebegone Magruder. Rand was having trouble catching his breath. "I—I guess you haven't had much experience, huh, little guy?"

Annie was among the loudest, until she saw how hurt and mortified Magruder was. She stopped in mid-laugh, realizing that here was a mind of kindred spirit, another runt of the litter trying to make a place for himself and be accepted on equal terms.

The chief was ruffling the kid's hair; plainly, he was a sort of pest/mascot. "I hope you will forgive him, my friends. Magruder, these are our guests."

But Magruder broke free, grabbed up a spear, and ran fleetly for the jungle.

Annie made a stop at the truck, then followed Magruder's trail. She caught up with him in a little clearing at the edge of the stream where he had ambushed Lancer. She could hear him crying, so she backed up some distance, then made a lot more noise. "Yoo-hoo!"

He brought his spear around, swiping quickly at his eyes with the back of his hand. "Who is it?"

She struggled through the undergrowth into the clearing, trailing the long skirt she had scavanged back in New Denver. She was wearing a diaphanous top, and in her hair was a flower garland she had made that afternoon.

Annie struck a glamour pose, one hand behind her head, and batted her eyelashes at him. She sang, "*Hi*-ya. Ma*gru*der!" He gasped and dropped his spear; she sauntered over and sort of nudged her shoulder up against him.

He struggled to say, "Wh . . . what are *you* supposed to be?"

She smiled coyly. "You poor thing! You've got such a lot to learn about the opposite sex! Y'need a *real* woman to show you what makes the world go round, hmmm?"

He pulled away so fast that she almost toppled over, letting out a squawk. "And I suppose you're a real woman?"

Annie's lower lip thrust out and she made fists. "Hey,

listen, buster: don't forget your *last* girlfriend! I'm a damn sight closer than *he* was!"

He crossed his arms on his chest. "That's none of your business! Why don't you go away and leave me alone?"

"You'll never get a wife, you lamebrain!" she bawled at him. "A woman'd have to be nuts to hook up with a dippy squirt like you!"

"Oh, yeah?"

"Yeah! You're hopeless!"

They were snarling at each other, when Annie reminded herself why she had come out there. *Hold your horses, Annie! If you play your cards right, this guy could make you a jungle princess. Or a queen. Who knows? They might even make you a goddess!*

She turned from him, hands clasped to where her bosom was due to appear any day now. "I'm really sorry for shouting at you, Magruder," she sniffed. "It's just that—it's so difficult when a woman becomes emotionally involved."

Magruder looked like he'd been sandbagged. "Uhh! You're not crying, are you? Hey, don't do that!"

Everything was going just swell, Annie figured. In a week or two she would be running the valley. But then her schedule was thrown out the window: with a low rumbling, a trio of Shock Troopers flew by overhead. "Yikes! Invid!"

Magruder looked up at them stonily, as the flight of Troopers disappeared in the distance. "The Overlords have come back to their nest here in the valley."

Annie turned to him. "'Overlords'?"

He nodded. "My people hate them. Ever since they first came here, and made the great roof over this valley, hunting has been bad; they frighten the game."

He pointed downriver. "The strange three-in-one flowers grow thick down there, and so the Overlords built the great roof over the valley, to make this place their garden. The legends say that someday the river god will rise up to smite them, but"—a shrug—"so far that day hasn't come."

He turned and reached for his spear. Annie frowned,

"Um, Macky, you're not gonna try something stupid, are you?"

He hefted the weapon. "It's time I became a man!" he said. "I'll prove myself in battle!"

Hollering at him to use his head didn't help. He sprang away into the trees, nimble as a squirrel. Annie stumbled after him, tugging to free the hem of her skirt from some thorns. When she saw Magruder next, he was poised on a branch near a wide trail—a trail that had been beaten down by something a lot bigger than any wild game in the valley.

She hit the dirt as she heard the tread of mecha. When she lifted her head again, Magruder was swinging at the lead Shock Trooper on a vine, clutching his spear, yowling a fierce battle cry.

He landed with remarkable skill, on top of the lead alien's head canopy. "Now they'll stop laughing at me! I'll show all of them that Magruder is a man!"

Annie was prepared to see the spearpoint bounce off and Magruder either fall to his death or be plucked to bloody shreds. But instead, just as he struck, the Invid, apparently oblivious to him, fired its thrusters. Magruder lost his balance, caught his spear with both hands and fell. The spear lodged sideways in the grooves at the back of the cranial canopy; Magruder clung to it.

The next thing Annie knew, her new flame was being dragged away through the air, feet kicking, atop a Shock Trooper.

It took her a while to get the tribesmen and her own teammates to believe it. The LaBelle lower lip was thrust out again. "That's right! This place is some kind of Invid hothouse! Magruder took them on all by himself! He's convinced the only way he'll get you to stop laughing at him is become a macho sexist Tarzan!"

Silverhair shook his head. "That boy will be the death of me."

"The Invid are probably looking for *us*," Scott said.

"The tribesmen are going after Magruder!" Rand

shouted. "Scott, we've got to help these guys; the Invid'll wipe out every last one of 'em."

"We've barely enough Protoculture left to light a match," Lancer pointed out, "let alone fight a battle."

Scott was lost in thought, staring off at the dam. "Then, we'll have to improvise and maybe get a little hand from the good old river god."

Rand and Lancer began to get the idea, looking at their leader skeptically. It was funny how Scott wasn't very flexible until it came to fighting off the Invid.

"The trick will be in getting the Invid close enough to the dam. We may have to risk the last of our Protoculture reserves to lure them there."

Rand added, "Leave it to me. Those big boys just *love* to follow my Cyclone."

"Good. The rest of you, I want enough explosives planted on that dam to blow the whole business through those holes in the roof. Cobalt grenades, Tango-9—the works. And we're going to need Protoculture flares."

Lunk and Rook were smiling, though Marlene looked apprehensive and uncomprehending. Annie was off to one side, thinking. *I don't like this! Macky and me're being left out in the cold! My jungle darlin's just got to prove himself, or—ahh! Eureka!*

The Shock Troopers had been flying a slow spiral pattern, like searching wasps. They weren't flying very fast, but they were more than high enough for the young would-be warrior to make an unfavorable impression on the ground when he hit.

He held on, hoping they would pass over the reservoir or some other body of deep water soon. That was his only hope, and his hands were going numb. His fingers were slipping.

Then the alien mecha flew into the middle of a hail of boulders. The rocks bounced or broke harmlessly on the mecha. The Shock Troopers shielded themselves with the ladybug-shaped *targones* mounted on their forearms. They landed, looking around more in curiosity than in anger or alarm.

The Invid themselves didn't understand all the secrets of the Flower of Life. For some reason, the Flowers had chosen to thrive in this valley, and it was critically important to the Invid to understand *why*. Therefore, they had roofed the place, in order to control study conditions. They left the population of atavistic Humans unbothered.

At least, so far. The Troopers were hit by a rain of spears and arrows that shattered on or rebounded from them. Their optical sensors swept the jungle for enemies. Magruder managed to drag himself up. "Hey! Hold your fire!"

Silverhair shouted from the shelter of a leafy screen. "Quick, get down!"

But Magruder sprang to his feet, standing on the Trooper as if it were a mountain he had just scaled. "Look at me, Silverhair! I'm a man, and I'll prove it to you!"

Magruder felt that this was his moment. He grasped his spear and got ready to thrust it into the monster's brain.

But a figure swung out of nowhere, scooping him off the Shock Trooper's head just as the thing reached up to find out what was irritating it. Alloy claws clashed together on empty air.

Lancer, swinging across to safety with Magruder under one arm, laughed. "Keep trying to kill yourself and you won't live to be a very *old* man."

Annie saw where they would land and ran to meet Magruder. There wasn't much time left to get her plan in gear.

The Shock Troopers turned on the tribesmen, who were pelting them with arrows and spears again. The Invid advanced slowly, hoping to learn what had caused the change in these docile primitives.

"They've taken the bait!" bellowed Silverhair. "Hurry; back to the temple!"

Rand, leaning on a log next to his Cyclone, tossed pebbles at a leaf aimlessly and yawned. *I hate waiting! Let's get this turkey in the oven!*

He never heard the bare feet sneaking up behind him, and he only began to turn when he heard the swish of the creeper-wrapped wooden club. Then he was stretched out cold.

The Shock Troopers lumbered under the immense trunks of the deserted tree-city with the Regis's voice ringing within them. "The Robotech Rebels are somewhere in the vicinity! Scan for traces of Protoculture activity!"

It didn't take them long to find it and hear it. A Cyclone revved nearby and the optical sensors swung to fix on it at once.

Straddling Rand's Cyc with Magruder behind her holding the handlebars, Annie settled her goggles and shrilled her war cry. "Hit it!"

Magruder, it turned out, wasn't as primitive as he looked. He had some experience with the two-wheeled, battery-powered putt-putts that the dam engineers had once used to get around on. He gave the accelerator a twist, and the Cyc shot off along the wooden overhead walkway.

The Invid looked up, following the noise. Rand, lying trussed up back where he had fallen, shrieked through his gag, *Those brats stole my Cyclone!*

Magruder did a daring jump from one level to the next, right above the Invids' heads, and Annie didn't seem to realize just what danger she was in. "Yeah, there they are! Yoo-hoo! Come and get us!"

The Shock Troopers rocketed after them, slowed a bit by the need to watch out for the giant trees. Magruder zoomed down to the jungle floor and away; the aliens began making up the distance quickly. "Okay, remember to hold on tight now!" Annie yelled.

"I will!" Annihilation discs began crashing nearby.

Annie seemed undisturbed as the Cyc hurtled along, finding paths through the dense foliage that only the tribes-people knew. "Magruder, my little Ape-Guy, we're gonna make a man of you yet!"

* * *

Rook set her last cobalt grenade in place. There was only one limpet mine, and Lancer was placing that to the best advantage. The grenades and Tango-9 would have to do the rest of the job. She didn't want to think about what would happen if it wasn't enough.

Ironically, Silverhair and his people raised no objection to the whole plan. Deliverance in the form of the river god was what they had always looked for. It was the reason they had defended their god's den. It was obvious to the tribe that the freedom fighters were just messengers of the god, sent to assist him. Rook was beginning to think the religion wasn't as crazy as it seemed.

She listened, for the two-dozenth time, for the approach of Rand's Cyc. *Don't you dare screw up this one!* she thought to him silently. Then she wondered why she should even *care* about him.

Then she thought again, *C'mon, Rand. C'mon!*

Lancer set the last of his charges and delicately threaded a lilylike flower in one of its adhesion legs, for an artistic touch. He patted it, then turned and dashed for high ground.

The trooper caught up faster than Annie had calculated, jostling the Cyc with near misses in the long feeder tunnel that led to the dam. Magruder lost control just as they shot out of the tunnel and mecha and riders all ended up plunging through a screen of fronds and leaves and spilling in separate directions over lush grass.

The Invid appeared a moment later to land and stalk closer, spreading to either side. This Protoculture motorcycle was similar to the freedom fighters', but its riders seemed to have no armor, no weapons. There would have to be a little more examination before irrevocable disposition of the Humans was made.

That was the moment when Lunk blew the flares; all Invid heads turned automatically. A dozen Protoculture mini-suns burned on the dam's concrete face.

CHAPTER
NINETEEN

> *They were such disparate personalities—it's amazing that anyone could have believed they would come together as a result of random forces.*

> Crowell, *Remember Our Names!*
> *(The Road to Reflex Point)*

"PROTOCULTURE ACTIVITY ON THE DAM!" THE Regis's voice came to her children. "Investigate!"

The gleaming purple Shock Troopers boosted away, forgetting Annie and Magruder for the moment. Lunk came dashing off the dam crest roadway, getting clear of Ground Zero.

Scott watched with satisfaction as the Troopers, joined by the others who had been combing the valley, plummeted down to the blinding-bright Protoculture flares set along the dam face. He pushed the button.

Concrete blew out in a storm of conventional and Protoculture shaped charges, as the dam fractured and broke. The Invid mecha were stunned by what was happening and then they were thrown backward and down by the falling concrete cliff and the freshwater sea behind it. In a moment, a squadron of Invid were wiped away, smashed and flattened by forces that not even Robotech armor could withstand.

"And so the river god legend comes true," Scott

mused, looking down on the devastation from the heights. Just *lying* on top of some Flowers of Life had given Rand weird visions; perhaps *living* in the midst of a preserve of them had given the tribe some kind of altered perception, or prescience

The water quickly pushed up dirt and trees, hunks of mecha and vegetation. It was less a tidal wave than a moving wall of mud and solid debris that would plow down anything before it. A lot of Flowers were doomed. Maybe the Invid would even lose interest in the valley.

Lunk, Rook, and Lancer had come up behind him. Lancer spoke softly. "Did the tribe's *Visions* serve *us*, or..."

Annie pushed herself up, realizing that she had been lying on top of Magruder. Nearby, the Cyc rested on its side, smoking, but still intact. "Macky! My little Greystoke! Are you hurt?"

Magruder moved, then sat up, rubbing a bump on his head and knowing that by all rights he and Annie should have been torn limb from bough. Then he heard the din of the flood. They had barely made it high enough; a few yards away and several down, the broached reservoir had left its high-water mark.

Annie was offering him a handful of white silk, her gage for her jungle knight. "Need a hankie?"

His hands closed around hers. "Hey, we *did* it, Annie! Thank you, oh, thank you!" His face was alight; not even Silverhair could say no to him now!

Annie sat listening to the world-shaking noise of the flood recede. Sunlight came directly down on them through one of the holes in the Invid-built roof. It seemed a perfect moment, the kind she had always wanted to live, the kind she had always wanted to trap in amber.

"Believe me, Macky, it was my pleasure."

Rand was beginning to get a grip on the knots that held him. "If they've damaged my Cyclone I'll twist the skin off their heads and strangle 'em with it!"

He was blinded by salt sweat, but he was working

mostly by feel. He had an enormous headache from the shot he had taken. "What *is* it with kids these days, anyway?"

It was a holy night in the treetop town, both because the Invid had been driven out by the river god's righteous wrath, and because Magruder had at last proved himself a man of the tribe. (The team noticed that a number of people were breathing a sigh of relief about that, since they wouldn't have put up with any more of Magruder's pecadillos.)

Magruder and Annie, in the best raiment of the village, got to sit side by side in the high-backed chairs of honor in the tribe's council hall. Annie looked a little punchy but very happy. In addition to greeting Magruder as a man and a brother, Silverhair offered him his choice of any woman as his wife.

"All hail, Magruder!"

The river receded quickly, and for some reason the tribe didn't seem bothered by the loss of the dam, or the likelihood that the Invid would come again. Prophesies had been served, had been borne out, and thus other prophesies and Visions—which the tribemembers wouldn't discuss—would be, too. Therefore, all was well.

With the tribe's help, the building of a string of rafts went with surprising ease and speed. There were hidden warehouses, with empty oil drums, cordage, and tools. Several nights later, the team floated off downstream, on a string of rafts that supported them and their mecha.

Lunk had gotten a few powerful heat-turbine outboard engines going, and these were used for steering and minimal propulsion—enough to give the rafts headway. Even Marlene had to man a sweep, since the team was now one member short.

The shoreline still reeked of the stuff that had been washed up onto it during the flood. Watching the luminous fairy-grove of the tribe, each team member thought about what Annie had meant to him or her. All, that is, except for Rand, who stood by his outboard and looked downstream only, refusing to acknowledge that anything had happened.

The others silently manned steering engines or sweeps. At last he whirled on them. "Why the long faces? You all look like your gerbil just died. Try pulling yourselves together, okay? We're better off! You didn't have to look after her as much as I did, so trust me on this one. Now us big kids are free to get on with some down 'n' dirty freedom fighting!"

Rook, sitting with her back to a crate, hiked herself up a little, studying him. "Y'know, you're as transparent as glass."

Rand made a blustering objection, then turned away, his cheeks hot. Then he said in a low voice, "Hey, I think we've arrived."

It was just coming into view around a bend. The Invid Hive looked a little like a spider straddling the river. Its nodules were all alight now, like blister windows. Its curved underside glowed like a belly-furnace. As they watched, a flight of mecha left it, ungainly bats making their way out into the night.

"There *are* no Hives like that," Scott breathed. "That's the weirdest looking—" He drew breath. "All right, everybody; you know what to do."

They had tarped the mecha and Lunk's truck with camouflage covers, but that didn't hold much promise for the time when the string of rafts came in under the bright undergut of the Hive. It was like being a bug under a lamp beam, Rand reflected, as he huddled under a tarp, staring up at the fiery glare of the thing.

But somehow they weren't noticed. They couldn't decide whether it was because the Invid were in a turmoil after suffering losses, or simply that the aliens were looking for Protoculture spoor and ignoring everything else.

The stilted Hive made a bizarre sight, set against the delicate pink-lighted inner surface of the tremendous roof shell. At some point, the team realized that the light had grown less harsh, that they had passed out of the fortress's immediate area. They emerged from cover as the rafts drifted into darkness.

Something crossed the night sky. It was the patrol they had seen leave the fortress, exiting the valley through one of the giant holes. There were five Shock Troopers flying as the rear two echelons of a triangle, two followed by three. But what was at the apex made the team gasp.

"Hey, look at—" Rand began.

"I don't think I've ever heard of a Trooper like that before," Lancer said, the last of the Hive's light catching his pale skin.

Scott was shaking his head slowly. He had memorized every mecha-identification profile there was, and he had never seen this one. It was twice the size of the others. "What could it be?"

But there were no answers.

Once again, Rand's *Notes on the Run* offers an enlightening commentary on the subtler forces affecting the team:

"Another two days' rafting brought us to a deserted city where, wonder of wonders, we found a pinch of Protoculture in an old Southern Cross underground shelter— just enough to keep us going. It should have made us rubber-kneed with relief, really; it was a lucky find. But we were all still a little depressed about Annie. I kept expecting her to start yapping and pestering me.

"Unloading the mecha from the rafts was a lot easier once they were under power, and the Beta lifted Lunk's APC off like it was a toy. We decided to hole up in the downtown hub of that empty burg for a few days, to see what else there might be that we could use. The Forager in me didn't trust the place—those windy streets, echoing concrete canyons—but I knew there would be few other places to resupply between there and the coast.

"Figuring a few rest stops, Scott told us he estimated another eleven days' travel to the Pacific coast of Panama, where we would get ready for that hop to what all the old maps call Baja California. Most of Central America was an Invid bailiwick, and the Gulf of Mexico was their bathtub; we didn't have much choice but to go around. Scott said we might manage to be in the region of Reflex Point in as little as a month or so.

"Yippee. . . .

"While Scott and Lancer went over the maps, and Marlene sort of huddled in Rook's old jacket, watching Scott, Rook and Lunk and I rode off to see what else we could forage. Our headlights only made the city seem spookier and more ominous. Rook was grousing, something about the foolishness of scavenging in the dark.

"I told her, 'We'd be sitting ducks during the day—not that I feel a whole lot safer now. I'm beginning to think the Invid see equally well, day or night.'

"It wasn't much of a comment, I suppose. To tell the truth, I was still thinking about Marlene, and the looks she was giving Scott. If we had been living some oldtime musical, I would have said the two of them were about to burst into a somber duet. As for me, that intimate connectedness I had felt with Marlene seemed to be fading. And my feelings toward Rook changed from second to second.

"Anyway, there we were riding among leaning and teetering buildings, toppled wreckage, cracked streets with weeds growing up through them—and the Invid jumped us. A flight of Pincer Ships were following either that giant one we had seen back in the valley or its twin.

"They took a novel approach, blasting the top floors of buildings to pieces, raining cinderblocks and cement and pieces of girder and glass down on us. We did some stunt driving you won't find in any books, with dust coating our goggles and sticking in our teeth. A granite splinter opened a groove in Lunk's cheek.

"It seemed like we fled forever. Then we zazzed around this turn and Scott and Lancer were there, running neck and neck, Marlene riding pillion behind Lancer. We had gotten lax, maybe, because Scott was the only one in armor. Wearing that tin can never seemed to bother him; I had seen him sleep in it often.

"At any rate, he told us to find cover while he ran interference. It made sense; without our armor, the rest of us were just bikers in a bull's-eye. Then we heard his fireworks, and we poured on everything we had because as good as Scott was—and he was the best among us—he couldn't hold 'em for long.

"I was in the lead, and I spotted a major subway entrance. We went down, giving our kidneys a nice little massage on the steps. Scott was right behind Lunk's truck, and the Invid rounds were already melting the entrance canopy. We ran to the end of the platform and then hit the rails.

"Ladies and gentlemen, it was *dark* down there! Our headlights scared up rats as big as small dogs, and other things that didn't fit in any Audubon book *I* ever saw—mutations, of course.

"I figured we could put up a pretty good fight down there, because the Invid would have to bunch up and move slowly. But I made a note to slip on my helmet the second there was a chance; weapons make *noise*, and in the confinement of the tunnel a few shots would be plenty for a little short-term hearing loss.

"What I hadn't foreseen, though, was that the Invid would just shoot at us from the street above. They had tracked us by Protoculture emissions, I concluded. I bet that big bozo we had seen was the one doing the shooting; Pincer Ships simply didn't have that kind of raw power. Even Shock Troopers didn't pack such a wallop.

"Sure enough, the first one made me partially deaf and gave me the beginnings of a week-long headache. At every junction we looked for a way to go deeper.

"The Invid shots blew straight down through ceiling and floor behind us. The ceiling suddenly collapsed and Lunk's APC was nearly stuck, but somehow he churned free. I do believe that glorious old wreck *listened* when he talked to it.

"We shut down our Cycs so the Invid couldn't sense our Protoculture, but they must have gotten a final fix on Lunk's truck, because the last volley damn near nailed him. As it was, the whole tunnel began to break up.

"We all wriggled to shelter under some subway cars, except for Marlene, who had taken a spill, and Scott, who crouched over her, protecting her with his armor. I looked at the two of them and the way they looked at each other and I knew, in that bizarre instant flash you sometimes get, that they were what Vonnegut called a "Duprass"—a bonded pair. Something to do with fate, no doubt.

"It sounded like they were knocking whole buildings over up above; the tunnel was blocked by fallen debris and concrete back the way we had come. Lunk's beloved old jalopy was crumpled, too.

"Then it got quiet. We guessed that they had decided they had destroyed us. But there was no going back; our only chance, the way I saw it, was to look for another route out of the place—find a junction further down. And we had to do it fast, Lancer pointed out, because there might be Invid looking for a way in.

"Scott was mechamorphosing back to cycle mode while he was reminding us how persistent the Invid were —as if we hadn't seen that for ourselves. If Scott had one weakness as a leader, it was stating the obvious. But as he stripped out of his armor and went to look for an exit, his light showed that the tunnel had been sort of squooshed together like a toothpaste tube in that direction.

"We were sealed in."

CHAPTER
TWENTY

> *What is to become of men and women—males and fe-*
> *males—and the way they cope with one another and the differ-*
> *ences between them?*
>
> *Doesn't this go to the heart of the reason the Robotech*
> *Wars started in the first place? The Regis and Zor? The soul-*
> *lessness of the Masters? The Shaping of the Protoculture itself?*
>
> *Isn't it the question that must be answered before there's a*
> *love that's worthy of the name?*
>
> Altaira Heimel, *Butterflies in Winter: Human Relations*
> *and the Robotech Wars*

RAND CONTINUES:

"Scott hardly batted an eyelash. He just fell back to Plan W, or whatever letter he was up to by then. Can-do, that's the attitude they had drummed into him.

"But without any warning at all, Lunk suddenly lost it. The next thing we knew he was kneeling on Scott's chest, choking him, screaming about how Scott had gotten us into this, how it was his fault we were going to die. I think the first would be undeniable, but we had all had the chance to opt out, just like Annie, and so the second part just didn't stick. Maybe Lunk was regretting that he hadn't stayed behind to give Annie away at the wedding and settle down in a hammock someplace.

"When Lancer and I tried to peel him off, Lunk just flung us away with one sweep of his arm, growling and roaring like some berserk Neanderthal. Rook had no intention of letting it go on, but she was smarter than we were; I saw her edging her H90 out.

"Lancer saw, too, and so we made one more effort.

Lunk was foaming at the mouth, but I guess by then he had said everything he was thinking—basically, that he was afraid he was going to die. Lancer and I got armlocks on both sides, and this time we dragged him loose. Marlene cradled Scott's head to her and tried to stop the bleeding of his split lip.

"Lancer and I had our hands full, and Lunk was howling for us to leave him alone. Lancer stepped back and wound up for a punch. He got a lot of power into the uppercut—I made a mental note not to poke fun at Yellow Dancer ever again—but it barely rocked Lunk. Still, the big guy sort of came out of his fit.

"Lancer was apologizing, although I noticed he was poised to give Lunk a second dosage if the diagnosis called for it. But Lunk's madness seemed to have left him as quickly as it had come. Lancer reminded him that Scott hadn't led us down there; *I* had.

"And there I was, nodding, kind of smug, in a sneaky way, about how honest and forthcoming I was being. It served me right for letting my ego take over; when I wasn't looking, Lunk hooked *me*. It was a little like being struck by lightning. Next thing I knew, I was lying on the ground with loosened teeth.

"All I could think of to do was lie on the ground. I settled for giving Lunk my best mean look. "Feel better?" I drooled.

"And it worked. Next thing I know, Lunk's down on his hands and knees begging my forgiveness and blubbering that he didn't know what got into him—he was scared, he didn't belong on the team, didn't have what it took and so on.

"I opted for the high road. Rubbing my jaw, I told him that it seemed to me that he had had what it took just a second before. I sorta sneaked a look at Rook, hoping she had noticed now mature and big-hearted I was being, but she just sniffed at me and turned her nose in the air, and said, 'I guess he proved *that*, didn't he?'

"Sometimes I wish there was a third gender that would do nothing but referee.

"Marlene was looking around at us like we were crazy.

And I suppose we were; Christ, we were *all* crazy, the Robotech Irregulars off on a lark to blow up Reflex Point! No wonder it had brought us to a dead end.

"We gradually pulled ourselves back together. Scott said his head felt like somebody had been using it to crack walnuts.

"Lunk was worried about that same old thing, what else? Back in the war he had had to make tracks from a bad situation, and he saw himself as a coward. He was afraid he had cracked and let *us* down, too.

"Lunk had never asked me about this, but from what he admitted about that firefight, I don't think he could be blamed for what he did.

"I'm sure that it's a special kind of hell hearing your closest buddy scream for a pickup and having to stand pat. But when the transmission's coming from the middle of a walking-barrage of Invid cannonfire, and the rest of your unit's wiped out, and the man or woman shrieking at you is mortally wounded and beyond any possible rescue, I don't call it cowardice. It's part of the evil of war.

"Lancer had established himself as a sort of authority figure with that punch, I suppose you could say. But he tried to point out that Lunk was just Human. Lunk still didn't seem to know what to do and looked like he was about to burst into tears again. I gave Rook a little eye signal and said somebody should start hunting for a back door—that maybe there was something we had missed.

"She gave me a funny look, but didn't object. She and I got flashlights and started off. There was the very beginning of another platform at the far cave-in, and we got down to a lower level, but there was no exit. We walked amid handbills that had faded and gone to tatters, newsstands where the candy had been taken by the rats and the stacks of newspapers turned into cockroach settlements.

"The steady drip of water was everywhere and you could smell the stagnant pools of it, and the things rotting in them. There were constant skitters in the dark, distant squeaks and squeals. It wasn't terribly cold, but it was dank enough to make me shiver.

"I looked at the face of the woman on the last edition of *Mademoiselle* ever to be published and couldn't help wondering what I always wonder when I come across things like that.

"Did she survive the Invid holocaust? Had she lived through the turf-wars and the plagues and famines and slave-roundups? Had she been disfigured, or lived long enough to discover that her beauty could be a terrible curse in this post-apocalyptic world, and simply ended it all one day?

"Rook was strangely quiet, and I didn't feel like talking much because my jaw ached. Finally we were sitting on a platform, swinging our legs, gazing down at the third rail that would never know its surge of current again. Out of nowhere, I was admitting that I wasn't so sure there was any way out this time.

"I expected the worst, but for once she wasn't busting my chops. 'Don't give up hope. I'm sure we'll come up with a way out of here eventually.' Her voice sounded so different all of a sudden; the world seemed to change.

"I was flummoxed, as the ancients would say. To cover up, I said that even if we did get out, the team would never be the same. Rook just lay back with her head pillowed on her hands, looking up at the ceiling. I wanted to stretch out next to her the same way—nothing funny, you understand, just lie there together like we were out on a hill someplace looking at clouds. But I thought she might take it the wrong way, so I didn't.

"'I should tell you something,' she said. 'I've been thinking of quitting the team.'

"It was the last thing I expected her to say. But she insisted, 'It's been on my mind a long time, Rand.'

"'But we're counting on you more than ever now that—'

"'I'm tired of people counting on me! Or maybe I'm just tired of running for my life all the time.'

"I didn't know how to respond to that, so my mouth said, 'C'mon, you're just like me. You thrive on danger!'

"She was looking at me out of the corner of one eye, in

a very strange way. 'Up to a point.' From her, it was a major concession, agreeing with anything I said like that.

"So I gave in a little, too. 'You're right. I'm not being straight with you when I say fighting is fun. Maybe I just keep repeating it to keep from facing the fact that I'm scared sick a lot of the time.'

"Now she was watching me with both eyes. 'What d'you know? I never thought I'd hear you admit a thing like that.'

"I shrugged. 'It's all been working at me, Lunk and the Invid and all. Matter of fact, I wonder if this whole mission isn't just a hopeless effort. A half-dozen people just can't do it.'

"Now she was up on one elbow, and I couldn't help noticing how she moved in that shiny, skintight biker's racing suit. 'Rand, I just had a bright idea. Let's quit the team together. Hear me out! We'd be saving everybody's life. Scott would *have* to postpone the mission while we all go looking for more recruits. There are Resistance units. We might be able to assemble a real strikeforce.'

"I thought about that for a few seconds. An *hour* would not have been enough, but I didn't want her to think I was slow or indecisive now that she was just starting to be civil to me. 'I've got an even better idea: Why don't you and me just pull out and not come back?'

"Those fair, fine brows of hers came together. 'What are you saying?'

"'We could hop on our bikes and hit the highway again! You and I could get married, have us a coupla spare wheels—'

"It will, by now, be obvious to the knowledgeable reader that in spite of all the boasting I had done, I really didn't know much about women. Rook was giving me a glare that made me wonder if I should go get myself fumigated.

"But all at once she turned and started twirling a wisp of her forelock around one finger looking at it kind of cross-eyed. 'You've completely missed my point, Rand. The point was to pull out together so we could find more people and bring them back. Get me?'

"'I thought the point was to hit the road together because you feel the same way about me that I feel about you,' I opened up. 'We'd be perfect together. I'd follow you anywhere in the world. You *know* that.'

"'Have you completely lost your mind?'

"'*Huh*-uh. I've completely lost my heart.' God, what else did she want me to say? And so, of course, because (I'm pretty sure) I had made my point, she just—jumped to her feet! She just broke off the conversation! With that one move, she was calling the tune again.

"So I got up, too, and put my arm around her shoulders, not at all certain that she wouldn't flip me down over the third rail. But she stamped one foot and pushed my arm away and scolded me instead. 'The point of this deal is to save our friends' lives, not to establish a relationship. If, if you're willing to accept that, then I'm still game.'

"'Since you put it that way, I can hardly refuse, can I?'

"She chuckled softly, that throaty laugh that made me wish *so much* that we could be together. 'Boy, will Scott be mad,' she added.

"She laughed some more and it made me laugh, but really I was thinking the whole time what it would be like to hold her in my arms and have her embrace me instead of pushing me away. It made my head swim and I kind of forgot what we were supposed to be laughing about.

"Scott didn't think our dropping out was so funny, of course. We kept citing burnout and the need for more troops, without touching on the Lunk matter, and poor Lunk just stood there looking hangdog and miserable. Scott was hampered by the fact that, after all, none of us had ever signed an enlistment paper or sworn an oath of loyalty.

"Marlene was just puzzled, but I think Lancer wasn't fooled for a moment. Still, he kept his peace, for the most part, especially when I told them I had thought of a way that we might get out of that sepulcher. They heard me out, disliked my brainstorm, but gave in to it anyway.

"It didn't take long and it wasn't too sophisticated. We fastened our last spare Protoculture cells behind a kind of wedge we put on a length of rail that we cut loose with H90's. Scott mounted the wedge on a derelict subway car using his Cyc armor's strength. The rest was pretty obvious.

"Scott had yanked Lunk's truck loose and even straightened out most of the damage, with his powered armor. Everybody understood that there was a chance that we would bring the whole place down on our heads, but the air was starting to get thin, or so it felt, and we had all had enough of being buried alive; there were no objections.

"Lunk was calm again. He got the cells, primed them, and lashed them in place, steady, proficient—almost cheerful. The rest of us got into our armor, while Marlene and Lunk got to cover. Scott and Lancer stood ready to fire in case Invid came swarming through the hole we were hoping we would make.

"The car's motor was long dead, of course. But Rook and I started heaving and pushing against the back. The powered armor got that crate moving in no time, rusted parts freeing up with banshee shrieks. Then we hit our jets and the car was rocketing forward, faster than it ever traveled on the Urban Transmit System, I bet.

"We couldn't see, of course, because we had our shoulders to the wheel, but Scott told me later that the rail and the canisters of Protoculture just seemed to go into the rubble like an icepick. Lunk had mounted the cells just right, so that when they were several yards in, they went off like shaped charges.

"I never found out how Lunk rigged those cells, but suddenly there was a gap in the cave-in and the car was in it.

"The explosion rocked the car back and knocked Rook and me right on our butts, powered armor or no. We pushed the car off again with our feet, to keep the way clear.

"It turned out that Lunk had had the presence of mind to rig earplugs for himself and Marlene; none of us armored types had thought of it.

"Even before we could get up, Scott was scrambling

into the car, running to the forward end with armor-heavy steps that shook it. Lancer was about a half a high hurdle behind him. I thought they were being alarmist. But as I was getting a hand up from Rook I heard Scott yell over the tac net, 'Invid!'

"Apparently, a few personal-armor mecha had been hovering out there, trying to figure out what to do. Maybe they had been afraid to start digging because it might bring down the roof on themselves; maybe they had some sort of time frame, so that if we didn't dig ourselves out by its elapse we would be written off as dead. We'll never know.

"Scott and Lancer got in the first eight or ten shots and some missile hits, and that set the stage for a rub-out. Rook and I followed as fast as we could, but there really wasn't much to do but mop up.

"The next part's a little anticlimactic; we had to wait a bit for the tunnel to cool off from the heat of the firefight and the Pincer Ships' thrusters, but clearing a way with the powered armor was a cinch. In less than an hour, we were back on the surface, with no sign of any patrols and no hint of that big-bruiser enemy mecha.

"We took off our armor. I kept starting to put my arm around Rook's shoulders when she was looking the other way, and then deciding that she would take offense, then starting to edge my arm up again—then pulling it back, hoping nobody had noticed. I probably looked fairly spastic.

"Here's where it gets surprising again: When we finally trudged back to where we had left the VTs, Annie was standing there.

"She was wearing her olive-drab army surplus, that pink rucksack, and an E.T. cap just like the one she had lost in the fortress—a spare, it wouldn't surprise me. She was sort of moping around, but when she saw us her face lit up like a Christmas tree.

"After some reunion time, we got the story out of her —or at least, her version. 'Can you picture *me* as a jungle princess? They expected me to gather fruit and nuts and stand in the background while the men held council! So I said so-long! Dumb, hmm?'

"I suspected that there was probably also the problem that the tribe wouldn't rename itself in her honor. And that Magruder expected certain matrimonial accomodations. Annie was a lot like me: talked a better fight, in certain arenas, than she could deliver.

"It was pouring down rain by then and we were all standing under the Beta, which had been hidden in a parking garage. I had to interrupt Annie. I told her—and everyone else—that Rook and I were pulling out because we couldn't hack it anymore. Rook watched me and didn't say a word. Annie was shattered, poor kid, but then Rook spoke to back me up.

"Marlene said she would stay with Scott, and that seemed only as it should be. Lunk was in for the whole nine yards, as the ancients put it, to Reflex Point. To prove himself, he said. (Though I thought that was the wrong reason to go on a mission like that, I kept my mouth shut. I guess all motives and ideals were at least a little tainted, by then.)

"The way it turned out was just Rook and me riding away into a curtain of icy rain, while the others prepared to go on without us. Annie was crying her heart out on Lunk's shoulder. The farewells had hurt a lot more than they had helped.

"Some brilliant plan, Rand!

"Rook was tearing along way too fast for weather and road conditions, and almost slammed me with her Cyc when I mentioned it. So we rode on, with all of it eating at us and no possibility of talking it out.

"And we were thinking the same thing: The team was going to carry on the mission. Dropouts, losses, setbacks —none of that mattered. Something greater than themselves had taken hold of them.

"The last straw was when Scott and Lancer cruised slowly overhead in VTOL mode, a slow flyby and solemn salute. Suddenly my adored Rook wasn't there anymore; she had made a bandit turn on the slick street, risking her neck, and was charging back the way she had come. Back to greet Lunk and Annie; back to board the Alpha she had left behind.

"I turned more slowly; I just didn't feel like talking to anybody for a while. I was going to have to get Scott to land, because he had my Beta mated to his Alpha.

"I watched Rook speed through the rain like a Valkyrie on two wheels, a War Stormqueen. I didn't want to talk over the tac net or hear the brave words. I was staying because Rook had stayed; I would have left if she had left.

"Something greater than myself had taken hold of me."

CHAPTER
TWENTY-ONE

I suppose it's not a secret by now, though it was a long time till Pop knew it. When the team members complained about what bothered them the most, Rand agonized over how the books and films and tapes were dying—how Human history was passing away. And I guess sometimes he admitted he was trying to be a one-man databank/preservation society.

A lot of things happened after that, but if you want my opinion, that's when Mom fell in love for the first and the last time.

Naturally she didn't tell him right away.

Maria Bartley-Rand, *Flower of Life: Journey Beyond Protoculture*

THE EVOLUTION WASN'T FINISHED. IT WAS JUST BEginning.

The time had come for a form *beyond* that of the Enforcer. It was time for a new category of mecha—a new evolutionary step.

In the Hive Center at Reflex Point, the Regis looked down on two Enforcers. One was the one that had failed to eliminate the freedom fighters; the other had been quickened less than a week earlier. These two were the most intelligent, capable and adaptable of the Regis's children.

"You have been summoned here to assume your rightful place in the new order of our society," she told them. "First you must undergo transformation to the life form most suitable to this planet. Prepare for bio-reconstruction!"

Jagged nets of energy whirled out from the huge globe in the center of the dome, to ensnare the two Enforcers and etch them in light. They writhed as if in torment, then froze like statues. In moments, the mecha had been stripped away, dissolved to particles. In the midst of the Protoculture fires two figures, in fetal tuck, floated—the forms of two fully developed Humans—a male and a female.

"My children, you now share a part of my own genetic code. You are a prince and princess of our race, and shall be known hereafter as Corg and Sera."

The Regis appeared again in her almost-physical manifestation, the swirling barber-pole stripes of energy spiraling up and down around her. The Regis poured forth a purity of Protoculture power on a scale that only an Invid monarch was capable of ordaining or controlling. In moments, new mecha formed around the floating twins, Corg and Sera.

"We must soon begin the mass transformation of our people to the Human life form," the Regis went on, "the form in which I have conceived you. The most advanced and flexible configuration for survival on this planet—this world to which the Flower of Life has led us."

Two mecha stood side by side now, bigger than Enforcers. They were more humanlike in form than any of the other alien war machines. They looked like the powered armor the Zentraedi had used long ago, but they were larger. The upper torsos were heavy with weapon pods and power nacelles, so that the things gave a strange appearance of buxomness. The head area was quite small, sunk between massively armed and powered shoulders and immensely strong arms.

The mecha of Corg, who had so recently harried the freedom fighters in their underground escape, was drab gray-green, with highlights in an orange-tan color. Sera's mecha was purple, with trim of dark pink. The great Robotech digits worked and tested themselves; the Prince and Princess of the Invid had risen above the claw, the pincer.

"However," the Regis told them, "there may be hidden dangers in this physical form. An earlier experiment with Human reconstruction appears to be malfunctioning. Our spy, Ariel, whom the Humans call Marlene, has failed to establish communications with me. You must seek out Ariel and determine the cause of her disfunction, before we commit our race to a complete metamorphosis. You must prepare the way for the final phase of our domination of this planet! Go now, and prove yourselves worthy of your heritage!"

As the morning sun rose, the team stood on a cliff looking out at the Pacific. Scott was calculating the variables and the absolutes involved in a run for Baja California, but the others were just enjoying themselves. They were watching the crashing waves and the plaintive gulls, and enjoying the sight of the blue water and the broad beach.

From here on, according to fragmentary reports, the Invid watchposts and strongholds grew thicker and thicker. In order to avoid them, a sea-cruise seemed the only hope. The mecha were low on Protoculture again, and the ordnance was practically gone. But they had made it to the sea.

From here, anything was possible. Scott was thinking along the lines of a low, slow swing out over the ocean by night, leaving Lunk's truck and most of their other baggage behind—perhaps even abandoning one of the VTs.

That was when Annie pointed to her discovery. The team just stood there staring, while Annie asked them what in the world it was. Lancer answered.

"Abandoned Southern Cross base, Annie. Combination Navy Division/Jungle Forces installation, I'd say."

The place was a cluster of piers, radio towers, hangars, domes and quonset huts, barracks and operations center structures. Everything was decayed and overgrown with jungle plant life, and several of the roofs had collapsed. It was nothing new to the team; a gleaming town in good repair would have surprised them, but this was just one more pocket of earthly decline.

they were instantly thinking about food, weapons, maps, and charts, perhaps even equipment or a boat. in another second they were racing back to their mecha, eager to explore.

* * *

What pieces of mecha there were in the base were useless, but all other news was good. There was a fair amount of Protoculture, ordnance that was compatible with their VTs, sealed ration containers that had withstood the test of time, and a desalination plant that was still up to supplying a trickle of fresh water. But best of all, there were three boats.

Two of the boats were missile PTs, heavily armed for their size and extremely quick and maneuverable. The third was a cutter mounting missiles and a large pumped-laser battery. Finding the boats confirmed Scott's decision: The best way to make the run to Baja was by sea. It would save Protoculture and they would be able to stay below the Invid sky sensors. The VTs could take turns hitching a ride on the cutter, and the boats could carry a wealth of supplies and materiel.

Whatever had made the Southern Cross troops abandon their base, it had left them time to put their boats and other equipment in mothballs before they went. In no time, the team was getting everything in working order again. Aerosol cans' spray peeled off the sealant layers over the boats' engines and a lot of the other gear; special treatments had kept the hulls free of barnacles and such growth. They were immune to rot, and as ready to go as when they had been laid down.

Lancer, standing his turn at watch in the tower, a binocular raised to his eyes, couldn't help but feel that chill he got whenever things were going a little too well. It wasn't very many minutes later that he found himself staring through his binocular at a Shock Trooper whose optical sensor was looking right back at *him*.

"What I figure is," he was telling the others a minute later, "it's not sure yet that there's anything going on here. But I'd be shocked if the Invid don't come looking around very soon. If we want the element of surprise, we'd better get hopping."

Scott would have liked another two days to reconnoiter, double-check the boats from stem to stern, rest would only have brought on another spitting match over the tac net.

"But I owe you one," she grated, taking him completely by surprise.

In her cockpit, Rook looked down at the fizzling avionics, so badly shot up, and at the left thigh and bicep sections of her armor, which had been split open by flying shrapnel and Invid force ricochet. Blood seeped from her wounds.

Lancer scouted ahead, and in less than ten minutes the VTs had located a place to rest. They stopped in the midst of a tiny chain of islands not too far off shore. While Rand coached Rook in for a landing, Lancer went back to help Scott provide air cover and guidance, and convoy the boats in.

Their rest stop had been a resort only a generation before. A place where people came to worship the sun to the point of melanoma; pay for drinks with plastic beads; coo and woo under the coconut trees; surf; scuba.

To make love, Scott thought, looking around at the place. The bay was translucent blue and the sand powder-white. *Eat, drink, gamble.* The team was doing all those things now, he assumed, although he might be projecting a little on the trysting part. And the freedom fighters were gambling with and for things a lot more precious than plastic beads or casino plaques.

Annie had been reading manuals and instruction pamphlets, and decided to play nurse on Rook. The onetime biker queen gritted her teeth but sat still for it. Annie wound her upper arm and thigh in enough bandage to restrain a small moose. Rand watched interestedly without seeming to; Rook had certain soft spots, like the one for Annie, and he was determined to learn them. Then Rook scowled at him, and he turned his attention elsewhere.

Stripping to his shorts, Rand took the swim he had been thinking about since he had listened to the chorus of the gulls that morning. Lunk had promised Scott that he could patch up Rook's Alpha and the other damage the VTs had suffered, with minimum delay. But mean-

up, and perhaps even do a short sea-trial. But he 〈
even have two minutes.

Lunk had some experience with a Resistance quick
boat outfit, and he was the logical one to take command
of the missile cutter. He put out to sea with Annie and
Marlene joining him on the bridge. The two PTs were
towed by hawsers.

The VTs lifted off to rendezvous with the tiny flotilla,
but the minute they activated their Protoculture engines,
Shock Troopers came shooting up out of the trees. Annihilation discs hatched infernos all around them.

"This always happens, very time I go up!" Rand complained. "Don't those guys have anything better to do?"

The VTs went darting off on evasive maneuvers, the
pilots punching up weapons and targeting displays. The
Troopers folded their ladybug-shaped forearms close to
them and blasted after the VTs, firing from their
shoulder-mounted cannon. The fighters led the Invid on a
long swing out to sea, to keep them away from the boats.
The humans were breathing heavily from the g-forces,
legs locked, stomach muscles tightened to keep the blood
up in their heads where it was needed the most. The tac
net sounded like a wrestling tournament.

One Shock Trooper got a glancing hit at Rook's ship.
Rand heard her groan of pain over the tac net, and his
heart went cold. He turned around, thumbed the trigger
on his stick, and flamed a Shock Trooper that never even
knew what hit it. A second Trooper broke off its pursuit,
diving and sliding to avoid meeting a similar fate.

"Serves ya right for fooling around with the big kids!"
Rand cut in full military power and caught up with his
teammates.

Two more Troopers showed up but fell in with the
surviving one, and turned back toward the coast. Invid
patrol patterns were a little inflexible, Scott saw.

Rand slid in until his wingtip was under Rook's and
nearly touching her fuselage. "Hey, Rook? Are you
hurt?"

Her answer had a clenched-teeth sound to it. "Nothin'
I can't live with, farmer." He didn't press her about ʾ

while, all they could do was wait. Rook rested her chin on her fist and squinted balefully at Annie and Rand, who were frolicking in the surf.

Marlene, in a white mini kini made of knotted lengths of parachute silk, went running and yelling into the water. The wet silk made Rand gape, and then he looked away, swallowing with a loud noise.

Scott appeared, to say that everything would be ready when Lunk was done. Rand came out of the water sniffling and laughing and dripping—and happy. Rook's jaw muscles jumped a bit, but she held back her temper.

Then Rand was holding his hand out to her, more serious than she was used to seeing him. "I'm sorry you were injured, but—c'mon down to the water and enjoy yourself. Otherwise I can't be happy."

It shocked her so much that she didn't quite know what to say, but she saw that Rand suddenly wasn't smiling; he was just watching her.

She practically stuck the back of her hand in his eye. "I guess it can't hurt. Well? Aren't you gonna help me up?"

Marlene and Annie stopped splashing each other and shouted happily for Rook's recovery as Rand gallantly helped her up and led her down to where the waves were foaming. Rand called triumphantly, "Hey, look who finally gave in and decided to have some fun!"

Scott saw Rook's fingers, the ones on her free hand, curl into a fist and then open again, away from Rand's sight. It was like some quick debate.

Scott watched Marlene's lithe grace in the spray and surf. *Maybe they're right about this place. We should enjoy it while we can.*

Corg and Sera and the mecha they led split up to search the chain of islands for the rebels and for the Simulagent, Ariel. Sensor triangulations indicated that there was a strong possibility she was near.

They understood their orders. If possible, they were to contact Ariel. If not, they were to observe her interaction with the Humans in order to determine the cause of her

malfunction. Failing any of the above, they were to destroy her utterly, and the outcasts who had swayed her.

Lancer grew despondent looking at the pointless destruction the Invid had inflicted on the island. He followed a stream he had spotted from the air and found a
small waterfall in a grotto a few hundred yards up an
overgrown trail into the jungle. He tried not to reflect
upon all the people who had come that way before him,
and what their eventual fate had been.

This time he put aside the *Musume* persona. He waded
in and began washing the sweat of fear and battle and the
rankness of too many hours in the cockpit from him. He
sang loudly in Lancer's voice. He sang as if he were trying
to drown out some other tune, perhaps a funeral
dirge. . . .

It might have been memory of the Magruder ambush
that kept him alert. Even though the little waterfall was
splattering, he heard foliage parting and swinging back,
and caught the movement of a shadow out of the corner
of one eye.

Sera had picked up those strange auditory impulses
through the superattuned senses of her mecha. The Regis
had given her crowned offspring the means to know what
it was to be a demigod, to soar over oceans and continents—to see each movement of the blades of grass, hear
each bend of a leaf.

But the Regis never guessed what a trap that could be.
The strange sonic input kept Sera from firing on its
source. It kept her from contacting her brother Corg, or
the Pincer Ships. The only thing she could do was stalk
closer. She had heard the music of the spheres, but she
had never heard Human singing before.

Before she realized what she was doing, she was out of
the all-embracing armored safety of her mecha, padding
through the strange smells and sights and sounds of the
island, the terrifying *intimacy* of it. She was drawn by the
siren song.

She couldn't put a name to what she felt. She knew

that not *all* of her genetic coding came from the Regis, of course. Some of it was Human. Was that what was forcing her to this aberrant activity? She repressed any doubt; she must see what was making these compelling, beautiful sounds. Information wetware input told her that it was what the Humans called "singing" but that word was a mere cipher. . . .

The Human had long purple hair and was a male. He was standing under a precipitation runoff as some sort of an ablutionary function or perhaps a superstitious rite. The Human sang, and Sera hunkered down to listen. But her hand pressed frond to frond, which made slight noise and changed the silhouette of vegetation against the westering sun.

She saw him tense and look around, and she drew back. When she edged one eye up for another look, he was pressing into the heavier part of the waterfall, off to the right, where the view was screened from her by the thickness of the foliage and the weight of the water.

This was madness. She should kill him, summon her brother Corg, and eradicate all the rest of them. But there was something about the sounds he made. His "song" was so haunting, so soft and *knowing*, as if he had been given instruction in the things most intimate to her.

The feelings that stirred in her had no name. Sera pushed forward a little in the undergrowth to hear more before she would be obliged to still that voice forever.

She could hear nothing. She waited, standing on the rim of the waterfall's pool, looking this way and that. With the song ended, a measure of sanity returned. Better to kill the Human now and forget the aberration of his singing.

Two hands closed on her ankles, pulled, and Sera screamed. Then she was swallowing water.

CHAPTER
TWENTY-TWO

> *There were all these escapist books (as Rand called them)
> at the resort—I couldn't make out the name of the joint too
> well from the sign, but I think that for some reason or other it
> was called "Club Mud."*
>
> *These books were all about what fun everybody was gonna
> have living action-packed lives after some global disaster. They
> didn't mention radiation sickness and self-aborting children
> and plagues and famine and pillagers and—oh, you jaded old-
> timers! I'm sick of you!*
>
> *Escapist? From hot showers and hot meals and dentists and
> intercontinental airline flights and innoculations and a planet
> that belonged to the Human race? Escape me there!*
>
> Annie LaBelle, *Talking History*

SERA OPENED HER EYES AND SAW A PALE FACE
and purple hair riding the water lazily, before her.

Lancer saw an indistinct figure in some sort of body
suit. This certainly wasn't an Invid. That didn't mean it
couldn't be another turncoat. The person squirmed,
blowing breath in silver bubbles of alarm, thrashing to the
surface.

Lancer held his captive by one wrist, shaking the water
out of his own hair. "All right, pal! You're not going anywhere until . . . until . . . Um. You're a woman."

She seemed transfixed, a slim Human female, me-
dium-tall, with short-trimmed blonde hair and the *stran-
gest* red eyes—the kind of thing you see in a bad
flashphoto. Her hairstyle was, even wet, some short,
green-blonde upswept thing: *Peter Pan Meets the Razor
and Car Vacuum People.* She was dressed in a bodysuit of
colored panels of black, purple, and pink.

Lancer's nerveless fingers had gone limp on her wrist.
"Ah wo—mahn?" she repeated back at him, breathing

quickly, as nervous as—as someone he remembered. They were knee-deep in the pool now, and she just stared at him.

She lurched to get away from him, but Lancer cuffed his hand around her wrist again, more astounded than alarmed. "Sorry, but we'll have to know where you're from."

He looked over her dermasuit, a second skin. "At least you're not armed. Or is beauty your weapon?" His lips were close to hers.

She pursed her own, parted them, then suddenly struck at him, and struggled frantically to break free, sobbing.

Rand shook the water out of his thick red hair. Marlene, listening to a shell, flinched a bit as the water hit her but never lost her smile. She laughed at the water that was being sprayed at her; there was light everywhere she looked.

Rand was panting, leaning on the boogyboard he had found in the ruins of the resort. "Scott, you're missing a once-in-a-lifetime chance. Quit pretending to be a sand crab."

"Rand, I am not pretending to be a sand crab. Uh, what *is* a sand crab?"

"What're you talking about? At least take off that dumb flight suit!"

Scott had no way of refusing Rand's demands short of physical violence. Flight suit and all, Rand dragged him into the water. Rook watched them, easing her aching leg and arm. Rand seemed so young and limber and in the water, especially, he seemed slick and carefree as a pink sea otter. What hope could she have for a life with someone like that? He hadn't accumulated the chronicle of sins that she had. Rook sighed.

Scott confessed that he didn't know how to swim; virtually *none* of the spaceborne generation did. Rand only took that as a challenge to teach him. About thirty seconds of Rand's instruction had Scott spitting water, and heaving, and vowing to stick to solid ground from then on.

Out where the mecha were parked, Lunk was running repairs and listening to Annie's apparently endless heartbreak stories. "I'm beginning to think I'll die an old maid! I might even wind up as a librarian!"

That comment brought Lunk's head up out of the cockpit of Rook's Alpha, where he had been working. The only meaningful relationship he had had was a romance with a librarian. She was a fiery young woman who knew how to handle a gun and was determined that the books would live and that they would be there when *Homo Sapiens* eventually started picking up the pieces.

Lunk had had to run, but he had often thought back to the dark-haired, dark-eyed librarian—so impassioned. . . .

He drew a great breath and told Annie, "You're such a heartbreaker, you'll probably get married five or six times. Do me a favor and invite me to every wed ding."

She shrieked with laughter, grabbed the thick hair of his sideburns and showered his face with kisses.

Lancer thought he had spied his prey. He dodged into a clearing, but he saw that he had been fooled by a trick of the light. He stopped, froze, then called out, "Wait! I only want to talk to you! There may be Invid nearby! You may be in great danger!"

He heard a thrashing behind him, turned to see the pink along one flank as she ran, and yelled after her even as he sprinted to pursue. "Please stop—"

Sera could have gotten away if she had really wanted to. Why had she lingered? Why had she watched him?

"I just want to know who you are and where you're from! It's very important to me! *Hey!*"

Lancer could hear her ahead, sobbing and stumbling. He ran with an even breath, hopping some obstacles and ducking others. At last he bounded into a clearing where hot, blinding light shone down on him. He shielded his eyes with the flat of his hand and gazed up.

It was an alien mecha like nothing there had ever been before, anywhere. The late morning sun glinted all around it, and reflected off enormously strong purple components and pink trim, making the machine-mountain difficult to see.

Lancer blocked the light with his hand, moving a little. *It must have landed while I was swimming, but—it didn't attack me! It seems abandoned. But how could that be? According to all reports the drones are helpless eggs outside their mecha.*

He heard a sound and sensed some movement. The young woman stepped out from behind one of the machine's colossal legs. He saw now that the color pattern of her bodysuit reiterated the colors of the alien Trooper.

He stared at her as she watched him silently. "Y-you can't be the pilot! You're Human, not an Invid drone; where's the pilot, the alien?"

Something galvanized her; she leapt, incredibly high, as the mecha bent toward her, the turret in its muzzle blossoming open to receive her. Rather than the egg-nest described by Rand and Annie, the new Trooper's control nacelle was a padded cockpit completely encased in armor.

Lancer was still yelling to her as the cockpit closed and the Trooper's back and foot thrusters fired up. He was nearly blown from his feet and singed by the backwash; the invader lifted off, leaving the grass burned and smoldering where it had stood.

He blinked, coughing from the smoke and the sand she had kicked up. By the time he opened his eyes again, the Trooper was a diminishing meteor racing to the east.

This is unbelievable! She was the pilot of that mecha! Does this mean Humans are fighting for the Invid?

Shaken by her encounter with Lancer, and unable to unravel the complex series of feelings and impulses that had assailed her, Sera rejoined Corg and the contingent

of Shock Troopers. But she made no mention of what had
happened and that, too, confused her.

But Corg and the Troopers' sensors had detected
Lunk's test activations, as he checked his repair job. Sera
had barely rejoined them when they assumed attack formation and rocketed toward the island where Humans
had been sensed.

Rand eased himself into a frayed chaise longue next to
Rook. Scott threw himself down on all fours in the sand,
resolving never to go swimming in a flight suit again. As
he hunched around to sit down, his hand happened to
touch Marlene's shoulder.

She gasped as if she had been touched with a live wire,
and seemed to go into shock. "Must've pinched some
kinda nerve," Rand diagnosed.

"I tell you, I barely touched the woman!" Scott shot
back angrily, face reddening at the thought of how he
longed to caress her.

"Su-uure, Scott," Rook teased. "Probably just your
sexual magnetism." She looked to Marlene, who was gazing into empty air. "This might be a good sign, though, if
she's having flashbacks or something; maybe it means her
memory's returning."

"I hope so," Scott said, but he wondered if he *really*
did, or if he would be sorry on the day that happened.

Marlene abruptly clutched at her hair. "I feel them
coming closer! They're here!"

But the thunder of the attack had already made the
Humans look up. Down through the clouds plunged Corg
and Sera, leading their Pincer Ships and Shock Troopers.
"Invid squadron heading this way!" Rand hollered,
bounding out of his beach chair.

"Invid," Marlene was moaning. "Reflex Point...
Regis..."

"We're out of time, but I think we can still make a
break for it," Scott said, tight-lipped. "I'll run the boats.
Rand, Rook: suit up and make sure you're ready for my
signal."

They snapped to it, fast as any Mars Division elite troops, sprinting away, feet throwing up sand. Scott grabbed for Marlene's arm, but this time she showed no reaction to his touch.

The Invid completed several sweeps of the island, preparing to go in closer. Then they noticed the pair of PT boats moving out to sea at maximum speed.

Corg felt delighted at the chance to slay Humans. With voice and arm signals, he ordered the attack. Pincer Ships followed him for the first pass. Scott, on shore, watched and did his best to evade the enemy's strafing runs, but the jury-rigged remote controls were slow in responding.

Rand and Rook rushed to get into their armor, dragging the camouflage nets off their VTs even while Lunk was working, with infuriating deliberateness, to finish the last of his repairs on Rook's Alpha.

Two passes had both PTs leaking smoke and had blown open the weather bridge on one. Receiving no counterfire, the Invid dropped lower to recon. They saw the boat's wheel moving with no living hand upon it, and noted the remote transmissions it was receiving.

The Regis's voice spoke from their computer/commo net. "Scanners reveal no Human units in target vessels. Warning! Possible strategic entrapment maneuver!"

Scott figured he had played the possum hand for just about all it was worth. *Here we go; firing all missiles.*

The team had loaded the PT boats' racks with surface-to-air missiles, since surface-to-surface combat was unlikely. Now the launchers rose and traversed and targetted. Guided by their radars, the racks emptied, and sixteen Tarpon heat-seekers came boiling and corkscrewing up at the Invid. Caught by surprise, three of the Pincer Ships were blown to bits. The rest went into evasive maneuvers.

Corg studied the situation. The computer delivered its analysis in the Regis's voice. "Tracking sensors place origin of remote control transmissions at coordinates delta

6-5. Presence of Human life-form at that location is also confirmed."

Corg's optical sensor showed him another ocean craft, a bigger one, docked at a quay under a sheltering boat-yard roof. Corg dove toward it, with the Pincer Ships and, eventually, Sera falling in behind.

Scott watched as they neared the island.

Lancer charged into the clearing where the VTs were being readied for flight. "I just found out—something horrible," he panted.

Rand was armored, helmet in hands. "What is it? We just sprang the trap!"

"The repairs are all finished and it's time to scramble," Rook added. "What's the problem now?"

Lancer gave them a devastated look. "I just found out that the Invid are using Human pilots!"

Scott sat behind the controls of the cutter's main gun battery, in the forward turret. The pumped-laser cannon was outmoded by Mars Division standards, but it still delivered a terrific shot.

Corg and Sera, dodging the cannon blasts, homed in on the cutter like angry dragonflies. Scott had already shot down one Pincer Ship, but these new mecha were frustratingly fast and maneuverable. Their annihilation disc shots chopped up the water and the quay around the cutter, and Scott clenched his teeth. *C'mon Rand! Rook, Lancer! Don't let me down!*

Then the VTs were on the scene, closing in on the oncoming Invid, both sides pitching with all the firepower they had. The new-style mecha dodged, but two more Pincer Ships went down. The aliens broke and evaded, scattering to re-form and change their tactics.

Scott knew they would be back shortly though. He pulled himself from the turret as Annie, Marlene, and Lunk hurried over. Lunk tossed his tool cases in the direction of the little stern chopper pad, where his trusty truck was hidden—covered with a tarp in preparation for the voyage.

Scott assured Annie that he was all right and Lunk apologized for the repairs' having taken longer than he expected. Scott gave the big ex-soldier's shoulder a squeeze. "Save your breath; you worked miracles for us, Lunk."

As per plan, Lunk assumed command of the cutter while Scott ran off to get his VT into the air. Just as Annie and Marlene were preparing to help free up the berthing lines, a growling in the air made Lunk look out to sea.

The Pincer Ship Scott had winged, its portside claw missing, trailing smoke and fire, had come around for a suicide run. It was aimed straight for the cutter.

Lunk sent Marlene and Annie to seek shelter, then dove into the forward gun turret and began pounding away at the alien with the pumped-laser cannon. Because the Pincer Ship's aerodynamics had been changed by the damage it had suffered, it bucked and was buffeted by the air, evading Lunk's fire more effectively than it could have if it had been whole.

The alien filled his targetting scope. A moment later the world went dark.

CHAPTER
TWENTY-
THREE

By this time, the Mars and Venus Divisions should be well engaged in their battle with the Invid, and building toward the final blow at Reflex Point.

Air and ground forces of the Human race, we salute you and send you our best wishes! We know that, in your over-whelming numbers, and with the undeniable power of Human Robotechnology behind you, you will triumph!

Morale twix from Colonel Ackerman (G1 staff —SDF-3) to Earth relief strikeforce (never received)

SO FAR THE THREE VTS WERE WINNING THE AIR battle. Pincer Ships were no match for VTs in one-on-one dogfights. But the new enemy mecha had been hanging back, studying their opponents; Rand wasn't sure what would happen if they decided to jump in with both feet and a roundhouse swing.

Lancer had taken the Beta up. The purple-and-pink monster machine he had seen on the island came up fast and its back pods gushed forth a torrent of missiles. Lancer went into a ballistic climb, cutting in all his jamming gear, side-slipping, and weaving. Warheads detonated behind him and missiles fizzled past in near misses.

Then Annie's voice came up over the tac net. "Lancer! Come in!"

"I'm right here, Annie. What's up?"

"I can't raise Scott. We're on the ship and we're in trouble. Lunk's been hit!"

"Annie, this is Scott. I just got to my Alpha; I heard your last transmission."

"Scott, this is Lancer. Hook up our fighters and take the Beta. I'm taking over for Lunk."

It only made sense; aside from Lunk, Lancer was the only one with any real experience at the helm of a large vessel. "I copy, Lancer. Meet you at the cutter."

Seconds later, the Beta settled in on its blasts and lowered the bottom half of its cockpit like a dinosaur opening its mouth. As the pilot's seat was lowered, Lancer yelled over the tac net to Scott, "It's all yours, pal! Go get 'em!" Then he jumped to the ground and got clear.

The Beta shifted components slightly, preparing for interlock. Scott's Alpha backed in at its nose, tailerons folding, and a complex joining took place in seconds, with a clanging of superhard alloy. The latched fighters formed a single ship that sprang away into the sky at incredible boost.

Lancer ran for the cutter.

Scott scattered the remaining Pincer Ships and the new enemy mecha, intimidating them with the combined fighters' speed and the volume of fire they could spew. Corg and Sera broke in different directions, cautious, deciding to feel out their enemy's strengths and weaknesses —if any.

"Follow me, you guys," Scott radioed to his wingmates. "We'll try to lead them in front of the gunboat—in range for a knockout." He cut in full thrust, rushing to catch up with Rand and Rook. Corg and the two surviving Pincer Ships climbed after, but Sera's mecha poised in midair, as she listened to her computer and the Regis's voice.

"Scanner confirms Human life-forms now aboard third flotation target mecha." Far below, the cutter was under weigh, racing for the open sea.

Lunk eased his arm in its sling and grated his teeth against the agony of the burns and what he figured was probably a hairline fracture. There were painkiller ampules in the med supplies, but he wanted a clear head for battle.

"Sorry about getting you into this, Lancer." He was crowded into the bridge with Marlene and Annie, all of them doing their best to give Lancer room to man the wheel.

Lancer, helmet cast aside, spared one gauntleted hand from the wheel for a moment, to give a blithe wave. "You did great, Lunk. The cutter's still in one piece, isn't she? *I* got no complaints."

Indeed. The kamikaze Invid had taken a hit at the last instant and broken up in the water just in front of the cutter's bow, showering it with flaming wreckage. A chunk of it had hit the optical pickup for the pumped-laser's scope, blowing it up in Lunk's face. A major piece had hit the turret, throwing the unbelted Lunk out of the gunner's saddle and giving him some considerable lumps and burns—and damaging the main battery beyond repair.

Scott's voice came over the net. "Lancer, Lunk! Heads up! We're going to try to draw the enemy down to you!"

Lancer had barely gotten finished acknowledging and begun preparing for a make-or-break shootout, when something enormous blocked out the sky. Everyone on the bridge cringed, seeing the immense tower of Robotechnology that was Sera's mecha. Lancer tried to reverse-all, hoping he wouldn't blow every bearing in the power train or tear apart a propellor shaft.

It did no good; the alien advanced at what was for it a slow approach-speed, with something like a deliberate vindictiveness. Rather than fire, it drew back one titanic fist, bracing to put it right through the bridge. The freedom fighters could only steel themselves, and dread the impact.

In her cockpit, Sera made an animal snarling, her teeth locked, eyes like red coals of anger fixed on the cutter. So many Pincer drones had died! So many conflicting emotions had interfered with her devotion to her Queen-Mother, the Regis! Now it was time to thrust aside confusion and prosecute the war these Humans seemed determined to fight.

And breaking this toylike water-vessel to bits with her mecha's hands, sending it and its crew to the bottom, was the ideal place to start.

She drew back her mecha's hand, wrapped in a fist the size of an oldtime tank. She could see, through her mecha's eyes, the terrified looks on the faces of the Humans. Three of them dropped to the deck, the fourth clung to the wheel despite the swells set up by her machine's back thrusters.

Sera drew a quick, almost whistling breath. The one at the wheel was *him*, the one with the purple hair who had made those strange, seductive, achingly beautiful sounds.

Her mecha answered her thought-images; it drew back, hanging there on thrusterfire. Although her mecha was nearly as big as the cutter itself and well able to break it to matchwood, it held back.

Lancer thought about the woman he had confronted in the quiet jungle clearing. *Why doesn't she shoot? Who is she, and what's going through her mind?* He was frozen at the wheel, waiting for the missile, the annihilation disc, the single blow of a mecha fist that would make four Human Beings into scraps of fishfood.

He wanted more than anything to run from the bridge and scream, *Wait! I don't want to be your enemy! I don't want you to be mine!*

Sera shrank back from the visual displays before her, eyes still fixed on the male with the purple hair, pressing the back of her hand harshly against her lips, whimpering, sobbing.

Rook's voice came over the tac net. "Lancer, hang on! I'm almost in range!" Lunk's eyes flickered to the target-acquisition displays and saw that there was no alternative; the cutter was helpless before this Invid.

Sera's indecision gave way to conviction. She couldn't harm the man.

All the rest was murky: whys and wherefores and what

might happen next. She had failed her Regis, and yet something had been born in her that was *herself*, that was *Sera*, and not something that had been put there. It was frightening, and it was at the same time wonderful.

Her mecha was jolted by an Alpha energy volley. She looked and saw Rook diving at her like an angry hawk, going to Battloid. Sera whirled her mecha away, leaking fire and smoke, dodging further damage.

Rook hovered close, confronting her, whamming away with the Battloid's fearsome rifle/cannon. Sera gathered herself and sprang away into the air faster than any rocket, unable to tell if she had won some personal victory or suffered a disastrous defeat—or both.

Lancer watched her go, his heart beating hard, pulse throbbing against the collar ring of his Robotech armor.

Scott's voice crackled. "Lancer, we're almost to you! Coming into range now! Get set!" Lancer glanced aside; target-acquisition displays had them.

"Ready Scott." He could see the VTs and their Invid pursuers.

"Breaking on three! One, two—" Lancer clutched the remote firing grip, his finger curled just off the trigger. "Three!" Scott finished. "Fire!"

But Lancer had seen his three friends break away, and was already triggering. The cutter's fore and aft launchers belched; racks of Tarpons emptied, and thick flights of Copperheads went up as well. "Firing!"

Two Copperheads broke in burning wrack across Corg's mecha but were otherwise insignificant. But other missiles savaged the Pincers that had made it that far, and not a single personal-armor machine survived. Corg's mecha closed its bulky, armored forearms around its cranium, protecting its pilot, while an inferno washed past it. Sera, soaring in to join her brother—unsure of what she would do—pulled clear, as the missiles drew instant lines of contrail across the sky.

Rand, Rook, and Scott stayed out of the demon's brew of detonating warheads until there was quiet again. There was no sign of the enemy anywhere. They banked and headed for the cutter, which sailed along on an impossibly placid ocean, a Pacific unaware of the carnage that had ended seconds before.

Sera landed on a beach from which she could watch the cutter and its accompanying VTs dwindle from sight toward the horizon. Soon Corg landed, and the two sky-scraper mecha stood shoulder to shoulder.

"Patrol escorts destroyed," their computers told them in the Queen-Mother's voice. "Abandon further pursuit. Do not risk loss of royal mecha at this time."

Corg emerged from his upholstered nacelle. He was a sharp-featured, handsome young man with lean good looks and mysterious, oblique blue eyes. His shoulder-length hair was blue as well, lying flat and fine against his skull and lending itself to his cruel, ascetic look. He snarled at the escaping enemy, then looked to his twin's mecha.

Sister, what possessed you?
Brother, I—I do not know. . . .

Lancer stood looking out over the fantail, as he had for so much of the voyage. Annie showed up in her usual ebullient mood, rejoicing that land had come into view. He said he would be along to the bridge in a moment. Annie gave him a dubious look, but then frolicked off, ecstatic with the idea of getting away from shipboard confinement.

He brushed the long lavender stands from his face, but the wind only fluttered them back there again.

Who is she? How did I lose a piece of myself so quickly?

"Hard to believe we've come such a long way in such a short time," Rand said, breaking the long silence of the net. He looked over to where Rook cruised close, but she didn't even glance aside at him or otherwise show that she had caught the implication.

Rand trimmed his Alpha. Where Rook was concerned, silence was a kind of a start.

* * *

Baja California gleamed ahead. The imperatives of history and the Vision that had moved Zor across the years and light-years were pulling together; their warp and woof were almost complete. What was to be, would be.

But that wasn't how it felt to anyone on the team. If Corg and Sera were confused by Human emotions, the freedom fighters were at least dazed by them, each in his or her own way—arguably, they were disabled in some measure. But if emotions had been taken from them they would have fallen like scythed wheat, and the Third Robotech War would have ended right there and then.

As it had been ordained from the beginning, the deciding force in the Robotech Wars was something neither side would ever see or understand, but everyone involved had felt it.

And just over the horizon, a Phoenix waited to spread its wings.

SYMPHONY
OF LIGHT

For the West Coast contingent:
Julia, Jesse, and Daniel

CHAPTER
ONE

I am intrigued by these beings and their strange rituals, which center around this plant their language calls "the Flower of Life." This world, Optera, is a veritable garden for the plant in its myriad forms, and the Invid seem to utilize all these for physical as well as spiritual nutrition—they ingest the flower's petals and the fruits of the mature crop, in addition to drinking the plant's psychoactive sap. The Regis, the Queen-Mother of this race, is the key to unlocking Optera's mysteries; and I have set myself the goal of possessing the key—if I have to seduce this queen to make that happen!

Zor's log: *The Optera Chronicles* (translated by Dr. Emil Lang)

IT WAS NEVER SCOTT'S INTENTION TO MAKE CAMP AT the high pass; he had simply given his okay for a quick food stop—if only to put an end to all the grousing that was going on. Lunk's stomach needed tending to, Annie was restless from too many hours in the APC, and even Lancer was complaining about the wind chill.

Oh, to be back in the tropics, Scott thought wistfully.

He had always been one for wastes and deserts—weathered landscapes, rugged, ravaged by time and the stuff of stars—but only because he knew of little else. Here he had been to the other side of the galaxy and remained the most parochial member of the team in spite of it. But since their brief stopover in the tropics, he had begun to understand why Earth was so revered by the crew of the Pioneer Mission, those same men and women who had raised him aboard the SDF-3 and watched him grow to manhood on Tirol. In the tropics he had had a glimpse of the Earth they must have been remembering: the life-affirming warmth of its yellow sun, the splendor of its verdant forests, the sweetness of its air, and the miracle that was its wondrous ocean.

Even if Rand *had* insisted that they try that *swimming!*

Scott would have almost been willing to trade victory itself for another view of sunset from that Pacific isle . . .

Instead, he was surrounded by water in the forms more familiar to him: ice and snow. The thrill the team had experienced on reaching the Northlands and realizing that Reflex Point was actually within reach had been somewhat dampened by the formidable range of mountains they soon faced. But Scott was determined to make this as rapid a crossing as was humanly possible. Unfortunately, the humanly possible part of it called for unscheduled stops. It was Lunk's APC that was slowing them down, but there was that old one about a chain being only as strong as its weakest link.

The land vehicles were approaching the summit of the mountain highway now. Rook and Lancer, riding Cyclones, were escorting the truck along the mostly ruined switchback road that led to the pass. The ridgeline above was buried under several feet of fresh snow, but the vehicles were making good progress on the long grade nonetheless.

Scott was overhead in the Beta, with Rand just off the fighter's wingtip. Short on fuel canisters, they had been forced to leave Rook's red Alpha behind, concealed in the remains of a school gymnasium building in the valley. Scott planned to retrieve it just as soon as they located a Protoculture supply rife for pilfering. Down below, Annie and Marlene were waving up at the VTs from the back seat of the APC; Scott went on the mecha's tac net to inform Lunk that a rest stop was probably in order.

The two Robotech fighters banked away from the mountain face to search out a suitable spot, and within minutes they were reconfiguring to Guardian mode and using their foot thrusters to warm a reasonably flat area of cirque above the road and just shy of the saddle. By the time they put down, the sun had already dropped below one of the peaks, but the temperature was still almost preternaturally warm. The weather was balmy enough for the two pilots to romp around in their duo-therm suits, especially with the added luxury of residual heat from the snow-cleared moraine. There was a strong breeze rippling over the top of the col, but it carried with it the scent of the desert beyond.

The rest of the team joined them in a short time. Lunk, Rook, and Lancer began to unload the firewood they had hauled up from the tree line, while Rand went to work on the deer he had shot and butchered. Moonrise fringed the eastern peaks in a kind of silvery glow and found the seven freedom fighters grouped around a sizzling fire. The northern sky's constellations were on display. Scott had developed a special fondness for the brilliant stars of the southern hemisphere, but Gemini and Orion were reassuring for a different reason: They reinforced the fact that Reflex Point was close at hand. He had to admit, however, that it was foolish to be thinking of the Invid central hive as some sort of end in itself, when really their arrival there would represent more in the way of a beginning. He wondered whether the rest of the team understood this—that the mission, as loose as it was, was focused on destroying the hive, or at the very least accumulating as much recon data as possible to be turned over to Admiral Hunter when the Expeditionary Force returned to Earth for what would surely be the final showdown.

Glancing at his teammates, Scott shook his head in wonder that they had made it as far as they had, a group of strangers all but thrown together on a journey that had so far covered thousands of miles.

Scott regarded Lunk while the big, brutish man was laughing heartily, a shank of meat gripped in his big hand. He had done so much for the team, yet he still seemed to carry the weight of past defeats on his huge shoulders. Then there was Annie, their daughter, mascot, mother, in the green jumpsuit that had seen so much abuse and the ever-present E.T. cap that crowned her long red hair. She had almost left them a while back, convinced she had found the man of her dreams in the person of a young primitive named Magruder. It wasn't the first time she had wandered away, but she always managed to return to the fold, and her bond with Lunk was perhaps stronger than either of them knew.

Rand and Rook, who could almost have passed for siblings, had had their moments of doubt about the mission as well. They had formed a fiery partnership, one that seemed to rely on strikes and counterstrikes; but it was just that unspoken pact that kept them loyal to the team, if only to prove something to each other.

More than anyone, Lancer had remained true to the cause. Scott had grown so accustomed to the man's lean good looks, his lavender-tinted shoulder-length hair and trademark headband, that he had almost forgotten about Yellow Dancer, Lancer's alter ego. That feminine part of the Robotech rebel was all but submerged now, especially so since the tropics, when something had occurred that had left Lancer changed and Scott wondering.

But the most enigmatic among them was the woman they had named Marlene. She was not really a member of the team at all but the still shell-shocked victim of an Invid assault, the nature of which Scott could only guess. It had robbed her of her past but left her with an uncanny ability to *sense* the enemy's presence. Her fragile beauty reminded Scott of the Marlene in his own past, killed when the Mars Division strike force had first entered Earth's atmosphere almost a year ago. . . .

"You know, just once I'd like to sit down and eat steak until I pass out," Lunk was saying, tearing into the venison like some ravenous beast.

"Just keep eating like you're eating and you might get your wish," Rand told him, to everyone's amusement.

"I've never met anyone who had such a thing for food," Rook added, theatrically amazed, strawberry-blond locks caught in the firelight.

Scott poured himself a cup of coffee and waited for the

laughter to subside. "You know, Lunk, we've still got a full day left in these mountains, so I'd save some of that for tomorrow if I were you." *Always the team leader*, he told himself. But it never seemed to matter all that much.

"Well, you're not me, Scott," Lunk said, licking his fingertips clean. "Sorry to report that I've eaten it all."

"You can always catch a rabbit, right, Lunk?" Lancer told him playfully.

Annie frowned, thinking about just how many rabbits they had dined on these past months. "I'm starting to feel sorry for rabbits."

Rand made a face. "They like it when one of them gets caught, Annie. It gives them a chance to go back to the hutch and—"

Rook elbowed him before he could get the word out, but the team had already discerned his meaning and was laughing again.

Even Marlene laughed, eyes all wrinkled up, luxuriant hair tossed back. Scott was watching her and complimenting Rand at the same time, when he saw the woman's joyous look begin to collapse. Marlene went wide-eyed for a moment, then folded her arms across her chest as though chilled, hands clutching her trembling shoulders.

"Marlene," Annie said, full of concern.

"Are you feeling sick or something?" Lunk asked.

But Lancer and Scott had a different interpretation. They exchanged wary looks and were already reaching for their holstered hip howitzers when Scott asked: "Are the Invid coming back, Marlene? Do you feel them returning?"

"Form up!" Rand said all at once, pulling back from the circle.

"Weapons ready!"

Annie went to Marlene's side, while the others drew their weapons and got to their feet, eyes sweeping the snow and darkness at the borders of the firelight.

"Anyone hear anything?" Rand whispered.

No one did; there was just the crackling of the fire and

the howl of the wind. Rand had the H90 stiff-armed in front of him and only then, a few feet away from the fire, began to sense how cold it was getting. There was moisture in the wind now and light snow in the air. Behind him, he heard Rook breathe a sigh of relief and reholster her wide-bore. When he turned back to the fire, she was down on one knee alongside Marlene, stroking the frightened woman's long hair soothingly.

"It's all right, Marlene. Believe me, you don't have a thing to worry about. We're safe now, really."

Marlene whimpered, shaking uncontrollably. "What's wrong with me, Rook? Why do I feel like this?"

"There's nothing wrong with you. You just have to understand that you had a terrible shock, and it's going to take a while to get over it."

Lancer put away his weapon and joined Rook. "Maybe I can help," he told her. Then, gently: "Marlene, it's Lancer. Listen, I know what you're going through. It's painful and it frightens you, but you have to be strong. You have to survive, despite the pain and fear."

"I know," she answered him weakly, her head resting on her arms.

"Just have faith that it'll get better. Soon it'll get better for all of us."

Still vigilant, Rand and Scott watched the scene from across the fire. The young Forager made a cynical sound. "That sounds a little too rich for my blood."

"Optimistic or not, Rand, he's right," Scott returned.

Rand's eyes flashed as he turned. "I only wish I felt that confident."

Not far from the warmth and light of the fire, something monstrous was pushing itself up from beneath the snow-covered surface. It was an unearthly ship of gleaming metals and alloys, constructed to resemble a life-form long abandoned by the race that had fashioned it. To Human eyes it suggested a kind of bipedal crab with massive triple-clawed pincer arms and armored legs ending in cloven feet. There was no specific head, but there were aspects of the ship's design that suggested one, central to which was a single scanner that glowed red like some devilish mouth when the craft was inhabited. And flanking that head were two organic-looking cannons, each capable of delivering packets of plasma fire in the form of annihilation discs.

Originally a race of shapeless, protoplasmic creatures, the creators of the ship, the Invid, had since evolved to forms more compatible with the beings they were battling for possession of Earth. This creative transformation of the race had its beginnings on a world as distant from Earth as this new form was distant from the peaceful existence the Invid had once known. But all this went back to the time before Zor arrived on Optera; before the Invid Queen-Mother, the Regis, had been seduced by him; and before Protoculture had been conjured from the Flower of Life. . . .

The Regis had failed in countless attempts at fashioning herself in Zor's image but had at last succeeded in doing so with one of her children—the Simulagent Ariel, whom the Humans called Marlene. Then, upon losing her through a trick of fate, the Queen-Mother had created Corg and Sera, the warrior prince and princess who were destined to rule while the Regis carried on with the experiment that would one day free her race from all material constraints.

It was Sera's ship that surfaced next, the heat of its sleek hull turning the glacial ice around its feet to slush. Purple and trimmed in pink, the craft was more heavily armed than its companion ship, with a smaller head area sunk between massive shoulders and immensely strong arms. Momentarily, four additional ships of the more conventional design surfaced around the Humans and their windblown fire.

Sera heard the Queen-Mother's command emanate through the bio-construct ship that had led the squad to the high pass.

"All Scouts and Shock Troopers: you may move into your attack positions at this time! Sera, you will now take command. You are personally responsible for the elimination of these troublesome insurgents."

Sera signaled her understanding with a nod of her head toward the cockpit's commo screen. She had dim memories of a time not long ago when she had fought against these Humans in a different climate, and accompanying this was a dim recollection of failure: of Shock Trooper ships in her charge blown to pieces, of an inability on her part to perform as she had been instructed by the Regis ... But all this was unclear and mixed with a hundred new thoughts and reactions that were vying for attention in her virgin mind.

"As you command, Regis," she responded as confidently as she was able, her scanners focused on the seven Humans huddled around the fire. "We now have them completely surrounded. And with our superior abilities, we will succeed in carrying out your ... your orders." Somewhat more mechanically, she added, "Nothing will stop us."

Had the Regis heard her falter? Sera asked herself. She waited for some suggestion of displeasure, but none was forthcoming. It was only then that she allowed herself to increase the magnification of her scanner and zero in on the Human whose face had caused her lapse of purpose.

It's him! she thought, once again taking in the fine features of the one whose strange, seductive, and achingly beautiful sounds had drawn her to that jungle pool; the one who had surprised her there, stood naked before her, holding her in the grip of his strong hands and assaulting her with questions she could not answer. And it was this same Human she had glimpsed later during the heat of battle when her own hand had betrayed her. . . .

"Sera! You're waiting too long!" the Regis shouted through the bio-construct's comlink.

Sera felt the strength of the Queen-Mother begin to creep into her own will and force her hand toward the weapon's trigger stud, but one part of her struggled against it, and at the last moment, even as the weapon was firing, she managed to swing the ship's cannon aside, so that the shot went astray. . . .

Lancer was just commenting on the beauty of the snowfall when the first enemy blast struck, flaring overhead and erupting like a midnight sun in the snowfields near the grounded VTs—a single short burst of annihilation discs that had somehow missed their mark. Scott was the first to react, propelling himself out of the circle into a tuck-and-roll, which landed him on his knees in the perimeter snow, his MARS-Gallant handgun raised. But before he could squeeze off a quantum of return fire, a second Invid volley skimmed into the team's midst, sending him head over heels and flat on his face. He inhaled a faceful of snow and rolled over in time to see a series of explosions rip through the camp, brilliant white geysers leaping from plasma pools of hellfire. On the ridgeline he caught a brief glimpse of an Invid Trooper before it was eclipsed by clouds of swirling snow.

The rest of the team had already scattered for cover. Scott spied Lancer hunkering down behind an arc of moraine slide and yelled for him to stay put as Invid fusillades swooshed down into a gully below the ridge, throwing up a storm of ice and shale. Rand, meanwhile, was closing on the Alpha Fighter, discs nipping at his boot heels from two Invid Troopers who had positioned themselves just short of the saddle. Running a broken course through the snow, he clambered up onto the nose of the Veritech and managed to fling open its canopy. But the next instant he was flat on his back beneath the radome of the fighter, a Shock Trooper towering above him. Frantically, Rand brought his hands to his face, certain the Trooper's backhand pincer swipe had opened him up. But the thing had missed.

Now, he thought, *all I've gotta do is keep from being roasted alive!*

Radiant priming globes had formed at the tip of the cannon muzzles; as these winked out, platters of blinding orange light flew toward him like some demon's idea of

Frisbee. Rand cursed and rolled, thinking vaguely back to that deer he had killed down below. . . .

Two hundred yards away Scott was on his feet, blasting away at the Invid command ship positioned on the ridge. Unless his eyes betrayed him, it was the same ship that had been sent against them during their ocean crossing to the Northlands. And that was a bad sign indeed, because it meant that the Regis had finally gotten around to singling the team out as a quarry worthy of pursuit. He squinted into the storm and fired, uncertain if the ship was still there. The wind had picked up now, and icy flakes of biting snow were adding to the chaos. From somewhere nearby he heard Lancer shout: "Behind you, Scott!" and swung around to face off with a Trooper that was using the Veritechs for cover. Scott traded half a dozen shots with it before a deafening explosion threw him violently out of the fray; he felt an intense flashburn against his back and was eating snow a moment later. Coming to, he had a clear view of the ridge, of the pastel-hued command ship standing side by side with a somewhat smaller Trooper. The Trooper had lifted off by the time Scott scrambled to his feet; it put down in front of him, sinking up to its articulated knee joints in the snow. Scott stumbled backward, searching for cover, while the Invid calmly raised its clawed pincer for a downward strike.

A short distance away, Rook sucked in her breath as she witnessed Scott narrowly escape decapitation. Fortunately, the snow beneath his feet had given way and he had fallen backward into a shallow ravine at the same moment the Trooper's claw had descended. But now the thing was poised on the edge of the hollow, preparing to bring its cannons into play. Rook turned her profile to the ship, the H90 long gun gripped in her extended right hand, and fired two blasts. Given the near-blizzard conditions, it was too much to ask that her shots find any vulnerable spots—although her second burst almost made a hole through the ship's eyelike scanner. The Trooper swung toward her, almost the impatient turn one would direct toward a mischievous child, and loosed two discs in response, one of which tore into the earth twenty yards in front of her with enough charge to blow her off her feet.

By now, five Invid Troopers had put down in the cirque; their colorful commander was still on the ridge monitoring the scene. The team, meanwhile, had been herded toward the steep glacial slope at the basin's edge. Scott leapt up out of his hollow after Rook took the heat off him and waved everyone toward his position. "Everyone over the side!" he yelled into the wind. "Slide down the slope back to the tree line!"

"But the mecha!" Rand returned, gesturing back to the basin.

"Forget it! We've gotta make for the woods!"

Scott saw Annie go over the side and ride down the chute on her butt, trailing a scream that was half fear, half thrill. Lancer and Marlene took to the slope next, then Lunk and Rand. Scott waved them on, yelling all the while and triggering the handgun for all it was worth against the Invid who had nearly taken his head off a few moments before. He managed a lucky shot that blew the thing's leg off, and it settled down into the basin snow and exploded.

Only Scott and Rook remained in the cirque now, along with the four undamaged Troopers that were moving toward them with evil intent.

"Rook! Are you all right?!" Scott yelled.

She gave him the okay sign and started to make her way toward his position, pivoting once or twice to get a shot off at her pursuers. The Invid were pouring a storm of discs at them, so they had to flatten themselves every so often as they attempted to close on the chute. Scott continued to send out what his blaster could deliver and wasn't surprised to see the enemy split ranks and head off for a flanking maneuver. Rook was a few yards in front of him when the two of them went over the side. Scott tried to dig his heels in, then realized why the rest of the team had disappeared so quickly. Under a thin layer of snow the chute was a solid sheet of glacial ice.

* * *

Sera saw the apparent leader of the group whipping down the slope and lifted off to pursue him. She paused briefly on the edge of the slide to issue instructions to her troops, then engaged the thrusters that would send her down toward the tree line along the Humans' course.

Although Lancer might have given Sera pause, she had no bonds with the rest of the team. She came alongside Scott, realizing that he could see her through the command ship's transparent bubble, and trained her cannons on him. But at the last minute, Scott's heels found a bit of purchase and he suddenly ended up somersaulting out of harm's way, each of Sera's shots missing him as he rolled down the slope.

The Invid princess came to a halt at the bottom of the chute where the others had taken up positions behind groupings of terminal moraine boulders. Lunk was loosing bursts against the cockpit canopy that made it impossible for Sera to tell in which direction the leader had headed.

Sera allowed the brutish Human to have his way for an instant, then turned on him, aware of the blood lust she felt in her heart. But all at once one of the Human's teammates ran from cover and pushed the big one off his feet and out of the path of her shots. Angered, Sera traversed the command ship's cannons to find him, realizing only then that it was the lavender-haired Human.

Her hand remained poised above the weapon's oval-shaped trigger, paralyzed.

Elsewhere, the rebels and Shock Troopers continued to trade fire.

Marlene cowered behind a boulder as lethal packets of energy crisscrossed overhead, her hands pressed to her head, as if she were fearful of some internal explosion.

"Fight or die!" she screamed, her words lost to the storm. "There must be another way . . . another life!"

Then, a moment later, the fighting itself surrendered.

Scott heard an intense rumbling above him and looked up in time to see enormous chunks of ice fall from the buttresses surrounding the cirque, avalanching down into the basin, scattering the Invid Troopers and burying the Cyclones and Veritechs under tons of crystalline snow.

CHAPTER
TWO

Scott had assumed that the "waning" [sic] of Yellow Dancer had something to do with Lancer's infatuation with Marlene; but while Scott was certainly on the right track, he had the wrong cause—a fact that contributed to the rivalries that arose later on. Had the two men sat down and talked things out, perhaps they would have realized that Marlene was not the amnesiac Scott wanted to believe she was, nor Sera the Human pilot Lancer assumed her to be. Time and time again this failure to communicate would undermine the team's movement toward unity, right to the end.

Zeus Bellow, *The Road to Reflex Point*

IT WAS SCOTT'S IDEA THAT THEY SEPARATE INTO three groups. The avalanche had indeed buried the VTs and Cyclones, but at the same time it had forced the Invid out of the basin area and bought some breathing space for the team. Reunited, they had picked their way farther down the mountainside, splitting up when they reached the tree line. There they left obvious evidence of their separate paths in the snow, hoping the Invid commander would similarly redeploy her Troopers. This way, Scott hoped, his irregulars would stand a better chance of circling back to the chute and retrieving the mecha.

Somehow.

The squall had moved through, but the temperature had actually risen a couple of degrees. Nevertheless, the freedom fighters were soaked to the skin and feeling the chill. Annie felt it more than the others—her jumpsuit had little of the thermal protection afforded Rook by the

Cyclone bodysuit, and she simply wasn't as inured to the cold as Rand. As a result, she had ridden piggyback into the woods, her shaking arms draped around Rand's neck.

"It'll get better when we get into the trees," Rand had assured her. "I can't promise you a fire right away, but at least you'll be out of this wind."

At this point Rand had no real plan beyond finding temporary shelter where they could regain some of their strength. All of them had taken a beating, and Rook had some severe facial burns. Rand didn't imagine that Scott and Lunk were in much better shape, and even though Lancer had been spared real harm, he had Marlene to look out for, which was in some ways worse than being out there alone. Rand had berated himself for having left his survival pack in the Alpha. For the past few weeks he had been complaining to Scott that everyone was becoming too reliant on the mecha systems for survival, and now here he was out in the woods with nothing more than a handgun and his fenceman's tool. But a few steps down the forest's wide trail his attitude began to improve considerably, especially after he spied the snare.

Evidently at one time the place had been occupied by others who were less than sympathetic to the Invid. There were three small, almost igloolike shelters containing foodstuffs, tools, and lengths of cord and cable, but more important, the trees along the trail had been rigged to repel intruders.

Rand left Annie in Rook's care in one of the shelters and went off into the moonlight to investigate. That the designers of the traps had been after big game was immediately obvious, but each of the tree and cable mechanisms was in need of attention, and Rand realized that he was going to have to work fast if the snares were to serve their purpose. So while Rook and Annie warmed themselves, he went to work replacing worn cables, resecuring counterbalances, and sharpening stakes. He had to fell several medium-size trees, but he had been careful to select only those that would topple with the least amount of noise. And thus far there had been no sign of the Invid.

He was busy on a final piece of handiwork now, down on his knees in the snow using cutters on the cable that guyed the central snare.

"Aren't you finished yet?" he heard Rook ask behind him.

He turned from his task to give her a wry look. She was ten feet away, arms folded and a smirk on her face. "Hope you and Mint have been comfortable," he answered with elaborate concern.

Rook made an affected gesture. "Oh, we'll manage until the servants arrive. Have you been having fun with your cat's cradle?"

Rand twisted a final piece of cable around itself and stood up, regarding the contraption in a self-satisfied way.

"Sometimes I amaze myself."

Rook walked over and gave the wire a perplexed tug. "*This* is the better mousetrap you promised us?"

"You two just stay put in the shelter and leave the metal nightmares to me, okay?"

She scowled. "Your confidence is underwhelming."

"*Pretend* to believe in me," he quipped.

Just then Annie ran into the clearing, breathless and pointing back toward the foot of the chute.

"They're coming!"

Rand told Rook to see if she could do something about the tracks they had left in the snow, so she and Annie went to work with conifer switches while he smoothed the snow around the snare. He briefed his teammates on its workings and ran rapidly through the contingency plan he hoped they wouldn't have to resort to. Fifteen minutes later, he was climbing up into one of the trees and Annie and Rook were back in the shelter.

Rand squirreled around a bit until he found a good place for himself in the upper branches, then cupped his hands to his mouth and shouted, "Help! Help me, I'm hurt!" directing his false alarm along the trail that led to the base of the snowslide. Rook and Annie heard his call and hunkered down in the shelter, peering out at the clearing through a narrow slot in the wall. Soon they heard the sound of heavy footfalls, and a Trooper lumbered into the clearing, its blood-red scanner searching the trees.

Rand drew his H90 and reminded himself to remain calm. He could see that the Trooper was following the footprints they had purposely left intact on the trail.

"A little farther..." Rand encouraged, whispering to himself through gritted teeth.

The Invid took two more perfectly placed steps, which brought each of its cloven feet down into the trap's ring mechanisms. Cables cinched and tightened, while others grew taut, straining at turnbuckles and activating pulleys that had been concealed high in the surrounding branches. Elsewhere, poles and trees began to spring loose, groaning as they straightened up, released at last from their bowed bondage. The Trooper's feet were pulled out from under it, and suddenly it was being hauled into the air, captive and inverted.

Grinning in delight, Rand moved out onto the branch to view the hapless thing's ascent. But a moment later his smile was collapsing: the snare had been well engineered but underbuilt. Either that or the lashed trees had seen too many seasons. One after another they were beginning to splinter under the Trooper's weight; cables stretched and snapped, and pulleys were ripped from their moorings. As the ship plummeted headfirst toward the snow, Rand armed his weapon and squeezed off four quick shots, only one of which connected. But all that served to do was alert the Invid to his presence. Before he could react, the Trooper's cannons came to life and discharged a blast that connected squarely with the trunk a few feet below his shaky perch. The tree came apart, and Rand and the upper section were blown backward by the explosion.

He and the Trooper hit the ground at almost the same instant, both of them knocked senseless by their falls. But the Invid was the first to stir. As the Trooper rose slowly to its feet, Rook and Annie saw the ship's scanner wink into awareness. Rand was still unconscious, facedown in the snow, one outstretched arm hooked around the base of the tree he had slammed into on his way down. Annie began to scream.

Horrified, Rook watched the Invid take three forward steps and position itself over her fallen teammate. She barreled out of the shelter, yelling for Rand to wake up, raising her blaster even as the Trooper was raising its claw. She had to put five shots into the alien's back before it swung around, and when it did, it was clever enough to use its pincer as a shield. Undaunted, Rook continued to fire until she saw those telltale globes of priming light form at the ship's cannons; then she spun around and hastily tried to retreat. The Invid dropped her with a disc that threw her into a headlong crash. She rolled over, struggling to regain her breath as the Trooper approached, uncertain if she should be thankful that the thing had let her live. Suddenly she heard Annie's taunting voice close by and watched amazed as her diminutive friend began to pelt the towering ship with snowballs.

Rook raised herself and resumed fire, hoping to draw the Invid's attention before Annie succeeded in enraging it. Rand had meanwhile come around and was contributing his own bursts, and together they somehow managed to send the Trooper to its knees.

"Go, go!" Rand yelled, motioning Rook and Annie past him.

They both knew what he was up to and broke for the trail where Rand had rigged the second trap. Rook turned around to see if he was following.

"I'm right behind you!" she heard him yell.

And so was the Trooper, looming up over them and the trees, monstrous-looking in the moonlight, like the nightmare it was.

But it performed just as Rand had expected, stepping boldly along the path, unaware that one area held a special surprise. And in a moment the Trooper was sinking to its waist through the snow, down into a pit that had been dug underneath the trail.

"Cut your lines!" Rand shouted to the women.

Rook ran to the area he had indicated and drew her knife. She severed the cables as he called out the numbers. Instantly, sharpened logs swung down toward the trapped Trooper from the surrounding treetops. Thrusters blazing against the pit's hold, the Invid dodged the first two and parried the third with its pincer targone, but the fourth punched through the ship's scanner and immobilized it. The Trooper was lifted up out of the pit and sent flat on its back in the trail. The sharpened log protruded out of its blood-red eye like a stake thrust into a vampire's heart.

"God . . . we did it," Annie said in disbelief.

Rook wiped sweat from her brow. "Too close this time, just too close."

"Not bad." Rand smiled, striding over to the bleeding ship. "A bit primitive perhaps, but I had confidence in it."

Rook scoffed at him. "Sure thing, Rand. And I suppose almost getting yourself killed was part of the plan?"

"That's always part of my plan," he told her. "Just to impress you a bit."

"You're never scared?" Annie said, taken in.

Rook looked over at Rand, then down at Annie. "Only when no one's looking at him," she told her.

Somewhat closer to the chute, Scott and Lunk were attempting to bring their own primitive plan into play. They had skirted the edge of the woods, keeping themselves just above the tree line, then worked back toward the western buttress of the cirque. As hoped, the Invid commander had split its forces—*her* forces, Scott was now telling himself—but two of the four Troopers had picked up their trail and were narrowing the gap.

The avalanche had touched off secondary slides in several of the tributary crevasses below the basin, and in one of these, an exposed grouping of moraine boulders perched precariously above the gully's narrow floor. Scott thought that if they could lure the Troopers into the ravine, then somehow manage to loosen those boulders . . .

Lunk was skeptical, but he didn't see that there were any alternatives. The VTs and Cyclones hadn't been completely buried by the snow, but they couldn't even think about reaching them until they had cut the enemy down to size. So he volunteered to go up top and see if he could pry some of the rocks free, while Scott set out to bait the two enemy ships.

Lunk had found what he considered to be a persuasive boulder that would force the entire group into a slide, and he had his shoulder to it when Scott entered the ravine at a run, the Troopers right behind him. The lieutenant reached the end of the ravine and turned to fire a few shots at his pursuers, meant more to antagonize than to inflict any damage. But more than that, Scott's short burst was aimed at keeping the Troopers at bay for just the few seconds Lunk needed to send the boulder crashing down toward them.

"Hurry!" Lunk heard between H90 reports. "They're in position!"

Lunk shoved his bare shoulder to the stone, boots trying to find purchase in the snow. Down below, one of the Troopers opened fire on Scott. The anni discs threw up a fountain of snow that momentarily buried him, but Lunk saw Scott shake himself out of it. And perhaps it was the sight of his friend's peril that gave him the extra push he needed, because all at once the boulder was toppling over and commencing its slide and tumble toward the pack.

Scott heard the rock impact the mass and decided to help things along by training his weapon on the ledge itself. The charges from his MARS-Gallant did what sheer momentum alone couldn't, and in a moment the whole mass was avalanching toward the bottom of the ravine with a ground-shaking, deafening roar. Scott threw himself up the opposing slope, figuring the Invid would blast free of the ravine, giving him and Lunk a chance to reach the VTs. He never hoped they would actually catch the Troopers unaware, but that was exactly what happened. They had both tried to lift off, but the bounding rocks had shattered the ships' sensors, and in the confusion the things got caught up in the slide and were overturned and buried.

When the snow settled, Lunk appeared at the top of the ravine, a triumphant look on his face.

"Not bad, eh, Commander?!" he yelled down.

Scott surveyed the damage they had wrought and could only regard it in wonder. "Yeah, great, pal," he called back. "Just like we planned."

Lancer and Marlene had run clear through a finger of woods. They were not far from Rand and the others, but their trail had led them to the edge of a deep gully, with a river of snow several hundred feet below them. They had no way of knowing that the one Trooper on their tail was the last of the four.

Marlene seemed unaware of where she was or what it was they were running from. Lancer had simply pulled her along like a helpless child, often shielding her with his body from debris flung up by the Trooper's discs. But now all he could do was gaze hopelessly across the ten feet of empty space that separated them from the gully's opposite face.

"Maybe if we hurry we can double back around," Lancer told her, trying to make it sound feasible.

But as he took hold of her thin wrist again and prepared to set off, he saw the Trooper emerging from the woods, closing in on them fast. Marlene understood that they would have to jump across the abyss. She nodded to Lancer, her forehead wrinkled up in apprehension.

They gave themselves several yards of runway and made a mad dash toward the ledge, hand in hand as they soared across the chasm. And they almost made it. But they fell short by a foot, catching hold of the edge—which was really little more than snow—and falling backward to what they thought would be the chasm bottom.

Instead, however, they landed on a narrow ledge approximately ten feet below the lip.

Lancer was thinking that things couldn't get much worse, but of course they could. Above them, the Invid command ship came into view. But to his surprise, he watched as the control nacelle sprang open and a Human pilot jumped down from the padded cockpit. It was the same brainwashed captive he had seen on the island: a slim female of medium height with punked out green-blond hair and eyes as red as a Trooper's scanner. She wore a bodysuit of colored panels that emphasized the body's major muscle groups in swaths of black, purple, and pink—like the colors of the command ship itself.

"I know you," Lancer called to her as she peered down at them. "Why are you fighting for the Invid?"

The woman's only response was to mock him with a short laugh.

Lancer pointed at her accusingly. "You're a traitor! Answer me: Why are you fighting for them?"

Sera continued to stare at the Human, angered and confused at the same time. *I should destroy this thing called man*, she thought. *But for some reason I cannot.*

The Trooper who had pursued Lancer and Marlene through the woods appeared on the opposite ledge now, but it, too, held its fire.

Lancer regarded the ship warily, then swung back around to confront the woman, who was obviously in command of the situation. "Can't you understand me?!" he demanded. When he failed to get a response, he altered his tone to one of cynical surrender. "Then get it over with. But spare this woman. She's done no wrong."

Marlene and Sera met each other's gaze. And during the exchange, which Lancer thought brief, a wealth of racial memories was transmitted.

That face . . . thought Marlene. *It's as though time has stopped and I can look into my past and my future simultaneously . . .*

Sera's face had dissolved, but Marlene seemed to follow those flashphoto eyes on a journey through space and time. Cosmic vistas opened up before her, stains and weblike filigrees of brilliantly hued clouds, swirls and spirals of galactic stuff strewn like diamonds on velvet. She beheld a vision of Optera through Sera's eyes, of the Invid as they were before the coming of Zor, of the Flowers before the Fall. Then Sera's unconscious unlocked for her the horrors of days since. Marlene saw the quest for their stolen grail; the transmutation of the race to an army of relentless warriors, burdened with a need for mecha and Protoculture that rivaled the Masters' own; the trip across the galaxy to this planet they now called their own; and the dispossession of its indigenous beings, just as they themselves had once been dispossessed. . . .

And there was a voice in Marlene's mind—one that she could not identify but that at the same time seemed to be her own:

"Reach into the cosmic consciousness of your race, Ariel," the voice told her. *"And although you feel you are dreaming, watch and observe the beauty of your home. For we are a race of powerful beings destined to control the universe with our intellect and power, and you, Ariel, are a part of that power. Come back to us, my child; come back, Ariel, and rejoin the hive . . ."*

Marlene stared at Sera as her face took form once again, the journey through space-time concluded, and thought: *I know her: we're like sisters somehow . . .*

Then without warning, explosions were rocking the ledge and erupting around the base of Sera's command ship. Scott and the rest of the team had positioned themselves on the ridgeline above the gully and were firing bursts against the command ship and its sole minion.

Momentarily confused by the renewed fighting, Sera broke off her contact with Marlene and returned to the cockpit of her ship, lifting off at once and joining her charge on the opposite side of the chasm. But no sooner did she touch down than the ledge gave way and the two dropped together, impacting rocks and outcroppings as they fell.

Lunk and Rand pulled Lancer and Marlene to safety. It seemed unbelievable that they had all survived and that all their crazed plans had worked. But even more unsettling was the Human pilot who had once again demonstrated a bewildering ambivalence. Scott refused to believe that the woman had purposely stayed her hand; he pointed out how she had fired on him earlier without compunction. Lancer, however, knew better than to accept Scott's explanation that the woman had been *distracted* by their sudden fire. And he also saw that something inexplicable had transpired between the woman and Marlene. Both Rand and Annie had been touched by the Invid consciousness in the past, but their psychic encounters had been brief and transient. Marlene, on the other hand, had been profoundly affected.

"I don't belong with you," Marlene told Lancer later, when the others had moved off in the direction of the buried mecha. "Please, Lancer, I'll just bring trouble for all of you. . . ."

He tried to comfort her as best he could by offering himself as her protector. And that did seem to calm her a bit. But it brought him little succor.

Who would be next to feel the enemy's mind probe? he wondered, shivering as he led Marlene away from the abyss.

CHAPTER
THREE

> *In quieter moments I find myself wondering about the men and women I have served with during these long campaigns. I think about the ones left behind, like Max and Miriya, and the ones sent away, like John Carpenter, Frank Tandler, Owen, and the rest. The list goes on and on. Would I have joined that crew had it not been for the Sentinels; abandoned these dark domains for even a chance at seeing Earth's blue skies once again? I think: Absolutely. But what can my homeworld offer me now? Certainly not peace, that endangered species. Retirement, perhaps. How Lisa would laugh!*
>
> Admiral Hunter, as quoted in Selig Kahler, *The Tirolian Campaign*

FREEING THE VERITECHS AND CYCLONES FROM THE snowslide proved to be a greater challenge than anyone had expected. The team brought the collective heat of their MARS-Gallant H90 hand blasters to bear against the massive chunks of ice that had been loosed during the avalanche, by sunrise they had succeeded in defrosting the Alpha Fighter. Tango-9 explosive and the VT's thrusters did the rest of the work in a tenth the time, but Annie and Marlene sustained mild cases of frostbite nonetheless. And despite Scott's optimistic projection, it took the team several false starts and another two days to cross the Sierra range. But waiting for them was the desert with those warm highland winds, and with it came a renewed sense of purpose and determination.

This was the same arid expanse crossed by pioneers and adventurers during North America's push toward its western horizon, but few would have recognized it as such. Over the course of the last two decades the region had seen periods of devastation to rival those of its geoformative years. Dolza's fleet of four million had not overlooked the cities that had grown up here, and neither had Khyron after New Macross had risen to the fore. Vast stretches of the territory were cratered from the thousands of annihilation bolts rained upon it, host still to equal numbers of rusting Zentraedi dreadnoughts, thrust like war lances into the ravaged land. Just north of the team's present route were the remains of Monument City, which had played such a pivotal role in the Second Robotech War.

Population centers had grown up in some of the craters, but most of these were abandoned now, their onetime residents returned to life-styles more befitting the territory's original nomadic tribespeople than the Robotechnologists who had once tried to breathe new life into the wastes.

Scott had listened intently to Lancer and Lunk's information; he of course had read and heard accounts of Macross and Monument, and the team's propinquity to those legendary cities filled him with an awe usually reserved for sacred places and archeological power spots. It made him think about the long road that had taken him back to this land of his parents' birth and the treacherous one that lay ahead. The team was close to Reflex Point now—the presence of an Invid tower assured him of this much—but he had to wonder how many more twists and turns they would have to negotiate before they stood at the portal of the Regis's central hive, how many Invid stood in their way, and how many more deaths their journey would entail.

There were many such communication towers placed around the hive complex, and Scott knew from past experience that the team's further progress toward Reflex Point would depend on how many of these they could circumvent, or better still, destroy. Options were discussed while the team made temporary camp near a meandering river where cottonwoods and conifers pro-

vided a narrow green ribbon of safety and shade. In the
end it was decided that Scott and Rand would recon the
outlying area; nearby were the ruins of a deserted city
and what appeared to be an inhabited town. Annie insisted on tagging along, hoping they would run across a
cowboy or two.

The three freedom fighters set out on Cyclones, Annie
in her customary place on the pillion seat behind Rand.
Only Scott was suited up in battle armor. Rand had tried
to talk him out of it but soon recognized that Scott fancied himself the only law and order between here and
Reflex Point.

A short ride brought them into the town they had
glimpsed from the Veritechs, a curious combination of
high-tech modular buildings and wooden structures fashioned after centuries-old designs, complete with elaborate
facades, shaded boardwalks, and hitching posts for horses
and pack animals. The dirt streets were empty, but this no
longer came as any surprise. Scott was certain the townsfolk were well aware of their arrival and were merely
concealing themselves until the proper moment. As they
powered the Cyclones down the town's main street, he
could almost feel the weapons being trained on them
from upper-story windows.

The one thing he hadn't figured on was getting ar-
rested.

But that's just what the residents of Bushwhack had in
mind when they finally did show themselves, twenty or so
strong, dressed in Twentieth-century garb and armed with
antique rifles, shotguns, and revolvers. They formed a
broad circle around the rebels and ordered Scott and
Rand away from their mecha. Scott was willing to
comply—even to go as far as removing his battle armor
—until he saw the ropes come out. But by then it was too
late to do much about it. He and Rand were stripped of
their weapons, tied up, and led by the jeering mob to the
sheriff's office.

He was a short, stocky man with curly black hair and a
handlebar mustache. He was wearing a beat-up felt fe-

dora and a sheepskin coat. Scott didn't see any badge displayed, but when the sheriff pointed a six-gun at him, he stopped looking.

"Anybody who goes around dressed like that is just *lookin'* for trouble," the sheriff told him, gesturing to the heap of Cyclone armor Scott had piled in the street. "I reckon you're under arrest, strangers."

"But we haven't done anything!" Rand protested, struggling against the rope coiled around his arms. Silently he cursed himself for having listened to Scott's harebrained logic about uniforms and earning respect.

"Well, you look like you *might* do something," the sheriff answered him, putting the muzzle of the revolver close to Scott's head.

"It's illegal!" Scott argued, trying to step away.

"Yeah, you can't arrest us without charges," Annie added.

The sheriff's dark eyes narrowed. "Z'at so? Well, I reckon I'll be the one to decide that, young 'un. You renegade soldiers and your catch try to take over everything. But we're not lettin' you take over this town."

"Who'd want to, anyway?" said Annie.

"But we're not renegades," Scott argued. "I'm from Mars—"

"From Mars?!" The sheriff laughed and turned to the crowd. "Here that, folks? He's from Mars!" The crowd started whooping it up. "Reckon you better tell it to the judge, robby."

"Fine," Scott said through gritted teeth. "Lead us to him."

The sheriff flashed a smile and pushed his hat back on his head. "You're lookin' at 'im."

Again the crowd got into the spirit, laughing and jeering. One dangled a noose in front of Rand's face, while a second began to inspect Rand's boots with an evil glint in his eye. There was what amounted to a festive atmosphere brewing, so much so that no one took notice of the two strange figures who were watching the scene from nearby. One was perhaps two feet shorter than his companion, but both were clothed alike, in bottletop goggles, helmets, cowls, and full-length cloaks.

"Looks as though these strangers are going to be occupied for a spell," said the taller of the two.

"Then I guess they won't be needin' their Cyclones, huh, Roy?"

"I feel it only right that we see to it that no harm comes to them."

"The Cyclones, you mean."

"Now what else would I mean?"

"Well, you coulda meant the strangers."

Roy made a face. "Now, have you ever heard me express any concern for strangers before?"

"No . . . but—"

"And is it *likely* that I would be concerned about the strangers?"

"Well, no. But—"

"Then I think it would be prudent for you to adhere to our original plan."

"Adhere, Roy?"

"As in 'stick to.'"

"I should get the truck?"

Roy let out an exasperated sound. "Yes, Shorty, you should get the truck."

Back at the camp on the outskirts of town, Lancer, Lunk, Rook, and Marlene were doing what they could to camouflage the VTs with strategically placed branches and bunches of sagebrush and tumbleweed. They had moved the fighters to a kind of natural shelter Lancer discovered, a rock outcropping with plenty of surrounding scrub. It seemed a senseless task, but at least it was keeping everyone busy.

Lancer hadn't been in favor of Scott's heading off into town; whenever Scott disappeared, it usually spelled trouble for the rest of them. It was some comfort to know that Rand and Annie were with him, but not enough to keep Lancer from worrying. The major source of his concern, however, was Marlene. She had said little these past two days, and it was obvious to Lancer that her confrontation with the Human pilot of the Invid command ship had had a devastating effect. Was it possible, he asked himself, that Marlene herself had once been used in a similar fashion? Perhaps she had escaped after her own command ship had been destroyed. There was a certain logic to it, since, like the blond pilot, Marlene seemed to have no recall of her past life.

I don't belong with you, Lancer could hear her say. *I'll just bring trouble.*

Marlene was aware of Lancer's concerns and smiled weakly at him as she continued to tug handfuls of tall grass from the sandy earth. Then suddenly she was down on her knees, moaning and clutching her pale hands at her temples. Lancer jumped down from the radome of the Alpha, but Rook beat him to Marlene's side and was already stroking the tortured woman's long hair and speaking soothing words into her ear by the time Lancer got to her.

"She must be sensing the Invid again," Rook told Lancer and Lunk. "I *told* Scott this would happen if we camped too close to that communications tower."

Lunk shook his head. "We're not that close to the thing. But maybe there's a Protoculture farm around here."

Lancer knelt down to take Marlene's hand. "Marlene, can you tell us what you're feeling? Can you tell from the pain whether it's a patrol or a hive?"

Marlene pressed the heel of her hand to her forehead and made an agonized sound.

"You're asking a lot of her, Lancer," said Lunk.

"Look," Lancer said, turning around. "I know what I'm asking. But it could be that Scott and Rand are in danger, and Marlene might be able to lead us to the source of it."

Rook looked at him as though he had just sentenced Marlene to the rack. "The closer she gets, the more unbearable the pain becomes. I don't have to tell you that."

"No, you don't. But *all* of us are at risk here—not

just Marlene." He touched Marlene's cheek with his fingertips, and she opened her eyes. "The decision's yours. Do you think you can lead us to the source of your pain?"

"I can . . . try," she responded weakly.

Lancer tightened his mouth and nodded. "Then we're going out together," he said, getting up.

Rook and Lunk were dead set against it, but Lancer convinced them that there was really no other choice. Marlene was part of the team, with strengths and weaknesses just like the rest of them. And it only made sense to exploit her strengths, especially when that early warning system of hers was kicking in. So an hour later Lancer and Marlene were cruising out over the wastes, side by side in the APC that Lunk had reluctantly given up.

"Are you all right?" Lancer asked her after they had been driving for some time.

She nodded without saying anything.

"Is the pain still there?"

"Not now. It's like someone just switched it off inside me."

"It would help if you could remember something about your past."

"I feel like I was born on the day you people found me, Lancer. There's nothing beyond that—I'm empty."

He looked over at her. "Still, you *had* a life. We just need to find out who you were."

Marlene shrugged. "How much do you remember about the day you were born?"

"Not very much," he started to say. Then all at once there were two men on horseback positioned in front of the vehicle. Lancer brought the APC up short, instinctively extending his right arm across Marlene; the horses reared, their riders leveling rifles.

"One false move and I'll make a lead mine outta yer innards!" warned one of the men. "How's that fer threats?" he asked his partner.

The second rider repeated the warning to himself and shook his head. "I don't like it. Too...*cryptic*." He brought his rifle to bear on Lancer. "Supposin' you tell us what yer doin' in these here parts, Lavender Locks."

Lancer suppressed a grin. The man had on a bandanna and a tiny pair of tinted goggles. His voice sounded like sandpaper on cement. "We were just out driving around, and we got lost," he told them sheepishly.

"Yeah?" said the first rider. "'Pears to me you had sumthin' on yer mind 'sides yer drivin'." He began to laugh knowingly, leering at Marlene.

Lancer smiled and put his arm around Marlene, pulling her close. "Well, shucks," he mimicked the rider. "Iffen you have to know, we're newlywed honeymooners."

"Well, no wonder yer all distracted," the rider exclaimed, lowering his weapon. "I would be, too!"

"Stop cackling and tend to business, Jesse," his cohort told him. "You folks might not know it, but there's an outlaw gang operatin' out here, an' yer lucky ya didn't go and git yer car 'n' everythin' stole out from under ya." He disarmed his weapon.

"Worse'n that, yer headed right smack dab straight into Invid territory."

"Garldarn," said Lancer, playing it up. "Me and my little bride 'preciate yer bein' so neighborly as to warn us like that."

The gruff-voiced man seemed to offer a grin beneath the bandanna. "Seems we speak the same language, stranger, so I tell ya what we're gonna do: We're gonna show ya where you can buy some mighty fine weapons to defend yerselves." He tugged at the reins to bring his mount about. "Ya jus' follow us."

The two riders began to gallop off. Lancer kept the APC close behind. Their trail angled east along the remains of a once-broad highway.

"Why are you trusting them?" Marlene asked.

"I'm not. But I'm curious about these weapons. Maybe there's a resistance group operating around here."

The highwaymen led them down into one of the devastated crater cities Scott and Rand had flown over earlier that day. Its once-tall towers were nothing but empty shells now, burned and collapsed like fallen layer cakes. Some time ago a river had altered course and turned most of the crater into a polluted lake. But adjacent to the resultant waterfall, practically beneath its thunderous flow, was a massive tunnel that led to an arena of some sort, and it was into this that the riders disappeared. "Hole in the wall," they called it. Inside, however, was an even greater surprise: the rusting remains of a Robotech battle fortress. It had put down on its belly and somehow seemed to be fused to its ruined surroundings.

Lancer couldn't help but register his astonishment. The ship was nothing like the cruisers developed during the Second Robotech War; it had more in common with the organically fashioned Zentraedi battlewagons of the First. And yet it was not quite Zentraedi, either. The sleek sharklike bow and massive triple-thrustered stern were closer to the hybrids he had heard about—ships constructed on Tirol and sent home under the command of a certain Major John Carpenter. Lancer said as much to the two riders. They had dismounted and doffed their helmets and cowls; in place of the techno-outlaws who had stopped the APC stood two silver-haired old-timers with thick mustaches and faces aged from a myriad of suns.

"Yep, and she's old and rusty, just like her crew," said the one called Jesse, who affected a headband and had a crazed way of laughing.

"Then you were part of Admiral Hunter's command," said Lancer.

"That's something we don't talk about around here, sonny," returned Frank, who may have had a few years on his saddlemate. His hair was shorter than Jesse's, and his mustache lacked the same outlaw droop.

Just then a third member of the gang stepped through an open hatchway in the grounded ship. He had a cooking pot in one hand and a ladle in the other. With his clean-shaven face and trimmed black hair he appeared to be much younger than either of his companions; more-over, he wore a sky-blue uniform that bore some resemblance to Scott's. Lancer saw, however, that there was no sign of life in the soldier's dark eyes. He tried to question the man as he passed by the driver's seat of the APC but got no response.

"Don't pay no attention to him," Jesse told Lancer. "Gabby hasn't spoken a work to anybody since he came here."

Frank motioned them toward the ramp that led to the hold of the battlecruiser. "Come on in here, stranger, so's we can show you what we got."

Lancer and Marlene followed them in. Piled high inside were high-tech crates Lancer knew to contain laser-array ordnance of all description.

Jesse made a broad sweep with his arm. "Welcome to the best-stocked tradin' post in the whole West!"

Back in town, the sheriff was trying to follow the rapid, angry flow of Scott's words. He and his men had tossed the three renegade soldiers into a cell, but it hadn't put an end to the leader's ranting and raving.

"Just in case you're interested, *Sheriff*," Scott was saying now, his hands gripped on the bars of the cell, "I happen to be an officer with Mars Division. We were sent here from Tirol by Admiral Hunter to liberate Earth from the Invid's hold. As far as I know I'm the only survivor of the assault group, but regardless, my orders are to locate and destroy the Invid Regis and the central hive at Reflex Point. Short of that I—"

"Enough!" the sheriff shouted, holding up his hands. The man had been going on like this for more than an hour, and he couldn't take much more of it—all this talk about assault groups and an attack fleet on its way to Earth from the other side of the galaxy. . . . Every so often one would hear this sort of thing from people who had come wandering in off the wastes looking like they had just received communiqués from the Lord Almighty, but that didn't mean that he had to sit still and listen to every last one of them. "You're just wastin' your breath if you expect me to believe such a cock-and-bull story. Besides, I heard tell of a better one than that by the last group of waste wackos who showed up here."

Scott was about to take up the argument from a different front when he heard a shot ring out from outside the sheriff's office. A moment later one of the sheriff's men burst through the front door.

"Rustlers, Sheriff! They got the motorsickles!"

Scott shook the bars and cursed.

Rand shouted: "Don't let them get away, Sheriff!"

The sheriff made it to the door in time to see two of his men emptying their revolvers at a truck that was tearing down the main street. He could just discern a figure in the open back, a cloaked and helmeted figure yelling above the noise of gunfire: "Much obliged, Sheriff! We never woulda gotten away with 'em iffen you hadn't locked away the strangers!"

The sheriff glanced in at the jail cell through the open office door, then once more at the truck.

"You're responsible for this, Sheriff!" Scott called out, furious.

"You've endangered our entire mission," said Rand.

"You dumb hick!" Annie added.

The sheriff contemplated his position: the rustlers were well known to him, and he certainly didn't fancy tangling with them. At the same time, he was responsible for the strangers' property. So it only made sense to let the strangers go after their own machines. He turned to one of his deputies and said: "Saddle up a coupla fast horses."

"This model must date clear back to the war against the Robotech Masters," said Lancer, hefting one of the samples from the opened crate. It was really not much different from the laser rifles the team was used to, except that the muzzle was somewhat thicker and the trigger mechanism more complex.

"Gen-yoo-wine army issue," Jesse said proudly.

Lancer brought the rifle up to high port position. "Guess it wouldn't be considered good taste to ask where you got them, huh?"

"Why should you care?" Jesse wanted to know.

"Good customers don't ask too many questions," cautioned Frank, swigging from a bottle of whiskey.

Jesse laughed. "Frank's right, Lavender. But I reckon there's no harm in tellin' ya."

He came across the hold to explain himself, close enough for Lancer to see the space madness in his eyes.

"Way back when, we was soldiers. The army issued these weapons to us."

"So you're part of this ship's rusty old crew." Lancer grinned. "Then why aren't you out fighting the Invid with all this firepower instead of playing rustler?"

Jesse scowled and looked away for a moment. "We had our fill of fightin'. We were with Admiral Gloval on the SDF-1; after, we signed up fer duty with the Expeditionary mission. Traveled clear across the galaxy, sonny, a godfersakin' place called Tirol. Then we made one heck of a mistake and tied in with Major Carpenter. 'Course, we finally made it back all right, but by then General Leonard and his boys had their hands full with the Robotech Masters. So we jus' kinda *retired*, if you know what I mean. Now we sell supplies to resistance fighters, so I reckon we're doin' our part."

Marlene saw Lancer's face begin to flush and did what she could to calm him down by sliding under his arm and laying her head against his shoulder. But Lancer's anger was not so easily assuaged.

"Making a nice profit for yourselves, aren't you?"

Jesse laughed. "Reckon we are at that."

"You're nothing but a pack of deserters," he started to say. But suddenly there were new sounds wafting in from outside the hold. A truck had pulled up in the arena. Lancer heard someone shout: "Look what we got!" followed by a wild "*yaahoo!*"

Jesse and Frank were standing by the hatch. "Wonder

where they stole those?" Jesse said before the two men stepped outside.

Lancer heard the Cyclone engines.

"Why don't you see if you can make a little more noise?" yelled Frank. "I don't think them thangs can be heard more'n twenty miles away!"

"Aw, the sheriff didn't even bother to send a posse after us," the new arrival yelled back, laughing as wildly as Jesse had a moment before.

"Keep that talk down, Shorty," Frank ordered. "We got company."

As Lancer and Marlene were stepping down the hold ramp, Jesse swung around to ask them if they were interested in buying a couple of Cyclones. Lancer saw two men in cloaks and helmets astride mecha they had ridden out of the back of the truck. It took him a moment to recognize the Cycs, and he had to quiet Marlene before she said anything.

"Young folks, meet Roy and Shorty," said Frank, gesturing to the men. Roy was tall, with a blockish, bald head. Shorty had crossed eyes and a pinched-up face. He bristled at Frank's introduction.

"I told you not to call me Shorty, Frank!"

"Well, we gotta call you *something*," Frank answered him.

Jesse leaned across the Cyclone's handlebars to thrust his chin at Shorty. "We'd call ya by your real name if ya could remember what it was, *Shorty*!"

Shorty raised himself on the footrests. "That ain't funny!"

It looked as though he might have taken a swing at Jesse just then, but Gabby appeared out of nowhere with his pot and put a quick end to it by ladling some hot stew onto Shorty's bare hand.

Shorty screamed and clutched himself, while the rest of the band had a good laugh.

"Gabby ain't too fonda Shorty," Jesse told Lancer and Marlene. "Ain't that right, Gabby?"

Gabby stood still, almost catatonic, oblivious to it all.

"Fact is, Gabby ain't too fond of nobody," Frank chimed in. "He's a little funny in the head."

Lancer looked over at the uniformed man and experienced a rush of compassion. Gabby seemed to pick up on it and walked toward the hatchway, proffering the pot of stew to Marlene.

"Look out, folks!" Shorty warned them. "He might throw it at ya!"

But instead, he simply held the pot out until Marlene took it from his hand.

Frank felt his chin. "Well, I'll be hornswaggled. He's offerin' it to you."

Marlene thanked him.

"Well, isn't *this* a day for surprises?" said Roy.

Shorty nursed his burned hand. "First time I ever seen him do anything nice for anyone."

"He tried to rejoin Hunter's outfit when those kids from the 15th ATACs got hold of Jonathan Wolff's ship," Frank explained. "But his Veritech got shot down before he could make it."

Jesse snorted. "Durn fool wuz tryin' to git back into the war agin. He's gotta be crazier'n a bedbug."

The four old veterans collapsed in laughter.

CHAPTER
FOUR

Dr. Lang considered him an army brat and tried on more than one occasion to instill him with some sense of objectivity, but Scott was a lost cause. If he couldn't persuade, his inclination was to force. And this kind of behavior was simply not tolerated in the lab. Lang would tell him: "You can't force experiments or people to conform to your world view! The universe just doesn't work that way!" Scott heard him but was not so easily convinced. He had little patience in those days and was often accused of being arrogant and judgmental. Type A, all the way.

Xandu Reem, *A Stranger at Home: A Biography of Scott Bernard*

LANCER ASKED HIMSELF HOW SHORTY AND ROY could have come across Scott and Rand's Cyclones. There was some talk about a local sheriff and how he had been foolish enough to leave the Cycs unattended. It was beginning to sound like Scott had gotten himself into another fix, but Lancer had yet to find out why or where his teammates were being held. He had barely enough scrip to purchase one of the laser rifles, let alone buy back the Cyclones, but he wondered if he couldn't persuade the Robotech veterans to rescue Scott for old time's sake. After all, they had all been on the SDF-3 together, and chances were that Frank or one of them had at least *heard* of Scott Bernard, the Pioneer Mission's youngest member.

They had all moved back into the hold of the cruiser, which functioned as the group's living quarters as well as their high-tech trading post. Marlene and Lancer had gorged themselves on Gabby's delicious stew. The shell-shocked soldier had taken to them and, in his eerily silent fashion, was treating them more like honored guests than potential customers. Frank, Jesse, Roy, and Shorty were engaged in a wild game of cards that required two full decks and seemed to be a hybrid of gin rummy and draw poker.

"Come on, Lady Luck," Shorty was saying now, "give me the card I want." He took one from the facedown stack just as Jesse was throwing one faceup beside it.

"You can have this one, Shorty."

But Shorty was too busy kissing the card he had picked to respond to Jesse's offer. "Jus' the one I wanted," he crowed. "How 'bout that!"

Frank looked at his hand and made a disappointed sound. The cards were an inverted fan in his left hand; his right gripped a whiskey flask.

"Don't need this 'un either," said Jesse, discarding another.

"Gentlemen, I fold," Roy announced stiffly, although he kept the cards in his hand.

Shorty started bouncing up and down in his seat. "Frank, y' ole coot, ya gonna play or not?"

"Hang on, I'm jus' tryin' to decide how much to raise you."

"Yer bluffin'!"

Gabby served a cup of steaming tea to Marlene, who smiled and thanked him. Lancer watched the man shuffle off into an adjoining compartment separated from the hold by cinched curtains. Gabby sat down at a communications console and began to throw switches.

"Is that transceiver in working condition?" Lancer asked loudly enough to cut through the card-table conversations.

Frank answered him. "Like everything else around here, it's wore out." Dismissively, he threw his cards to the table. "We still receive transmissions from the Expeditionary Force, but we can't respond to 'em."

Jesse grunted and laughed. "Gabby keeps turnin' it on like maybe he's expectin' a message from somebody."

Gabby seemed to hear the men ridiculing him; forlornly, he got up from the console and left the hold.

"What do the transmissions say?" Lancer asked after Gabby had gone.

"Who knows?" Shorty cackled. "We don't pay no attention to 'em."

Lancer leaned back in his chair. *What a sad bunch*, he thought. *Soldiers who have lost the will to fight . . .* He was about to launch into the speech he hoped would rekindle their spirits, when Marlene suddenly shot to her feet and let out a low groan of pain. Lancer stood up and took hold of her quaking shoulders; she had her eyes closed, her fingertips pressed to her temples.

"What is it, Marlene? Are you hearing the Invid broadcasting towers again?"

The four veterans voiced a shocked "*Whaaatt*?!"

"The tower must be broadcasting again," Lancer explained without thinking.

Alarmed all at once, Frank stood up. "You mean she can hear 'em?" He gestured to the others. "Git 'em, boys! I reckon these two to be Invid spies!"

"You're wrong," Lancer told them, shielding Marlene.

"Well, I think Frank's right," Jesse said menacingly.

"I knew there was sumthin' funny 'bout 'em," snarled Shorty.

Frank leveled a hand blaster that resembled an antique short-barreled staple gun. "Don't make a move," he warned Lancer. "If she *ain't* an Invid, how come she hears their signals?"

Lancer took Marlene into his arms while she sobbed. "She's been traumatized by them. It affected her hearing somehow—it's more sensitive than ours."

Jesse scoffed. "That's 'cause we're Human and she's an Invid!"

"That's not true," Lancer shouted, leading Marlene slowly away from the couch and closer to the external hatch. "She's suffered more from the Invid attacks than any of you! You can see for yourselves the agonizing pain their broadcast signals put her through."

Shorty took a step forward. "You're whistlin' in the wind, pretty boy. We ain't buyin' it!"

Roy uttered a kind of growl and began to move in bearlike, his huge mitts raised. Lancer backed Marlene against the bulkhead and turned her in his arms. "Think she's an Invid, huh?" He pulled her to him and kissed her full on the mouth. Startled at first, Marlene began to relax and return his tenderness. The veterans went wide-eyed.

"Whoa!" said Jesse. "Don't reckon he'd kiss an Invid like that, do you, Frank?"

"They might be aliens, but they sure ain't *strangers*," laughed Shorty.

"Hol' up, kids, 'fore ya short out our pacemakers."

Lancer broke off his embrace. "That was the most pleasant way to prove a point I could ever imagine," he whispered, looking into Marlene's eyes.

Frank tucked away his blaster and sat down on the edge of the table. "No hard feelings, kids. Consider yourselves among friends."

Lancer saw his chance to enlist their aid. "Does that mean you'd be willing to help us?"

Frank looked at him questioningly. "What possible help could we be? We're just a bunch of old—*huh?!*"

An explosion rocked the ship.

"The telltale sound of trouble," said Roy, reaching for a weapon.

From the hatchway they saw two Troopers complete a pass over the arena. Gabby, some sort of tote bag clutched in his right hand, was running a jagged course toward the ship. A single charge from one of the Invid ships tore into the already ruined street, throwing him off his feet. Roy had a rocket launcher on his shoulder; he fired and caught the Invid with a glancing shot to its underbelly.

"Lay down some more cover fire!" Frank yelled. "I'll go try to fetch 'im!"

"No, wait," Lancer said, pulling the launcher from Roy's grip. "I can move faster. I'll get him."

Lancer raised the weapon and darted out into the arena. The second Trooper was swinging around and preparing for another pass. "Make a run for it!" he told Gabby, helping him to his feet. "I'll keep you covered."

Wordlessly, Gabby struggled to his knees, but instead of heading for the escort, he doubled back to retrieve the tote bag he had dropped. The Trooper, meanwhile, was coming in low overhead. Lancer seated the launcher on his right shoulder, centered the ship in the weapon's laser sight, and triggered the missile. His shot was sure, straight to the Invid's optic core; a brief fireball and the enemy disintegrated.

Gabby was still on his hands and knees but now had the bag tight in his arms.

"Leave it!" Lancer barked, hearing the sound of the first Trooper's thrusters. "Whatever it is, it isn't worth risking your life!" But he had begun to wonder. Gabby looked up at him, words of explanation in his eyes, and fumbled with the bag's latch. Puzzled, Lancer went down on one knee to gaze at the contents: it was Gabby's battle armor.

All at once the ground rumbled. Lancer reshouldered the launcher and twisted. The first Trooper had put down behind them, its right pincer raised for a crushing blow. Lancer squeezed off a second projectile, which tore into the Invid's scanner, dropping it instantly. He was on his feet watching the thing bleed green when he heard Rand's voice in the distance.

"We've been looking all over for you!"

Rand was waving at him from atop a heap of slacked steel that had once been part of the arena's superstructure. Scott and Annie were with him, along with the horses they had ridden in on.

Not exactly the cavalry arriving in the nick of time, Lancer said to himself while returning the wave, but it was good to see them just the same.

* * *

Lancer led his teammates to the Robotech ship; Scott filled him in on their brief incarceration and the theft of the Cyclones, and Lancer primed Scott for the surprises in store. Everyone remembered the incident with Jonathan Wolff, and Rand especially was concerned about Scott's reaction to all this. It was certainly good news that the Cycs were safe, but Rand knew that Scott wouldn't let it go at that—not when the rustlers were soldiers who had once served with the illustrious Expeditionary Force.

The veterans claimed never to have heard of Scott Bernard. This didn't surprise Rand, given the fact that some of them apparently couldn't even recall their own names. Besides, from what Scott had told him, the Pioneer Mission had had an enormous crew, and Major Carpenter's contingent had separated from the main body of the force early on in the mission. They had been lost in space for approximately ten years, but Scott wasn't about to cut them any slack.

Frank was the first to catch Scott's wrath—square on the side of his jaw.

"You cowardly scum!" Scott raved, sending the old man backward into the arms of his companions. "I hate to even dirty my fists on you."

Rand kept his mouth shut, but he wished for once that Scott could control his temper.

"We ain't soldiers any longer," Jesse was telling Scott, wagging a bony finger in the lieutenant's face. "And we don't take orders from the likes of you or anyone else! So if ya wanna attack the Invids, you'll jus' have to do it on yer own!"

"You're all traitors!" Scott bellowed back, grabbing Jesse by the shirtfront and glaring at him.

Lancer put his hand on Scott's shoulder. "Back off, Scott, you're wasting your time. They fought bravely against the Zentraedi, but the fight's gone out of them. Obviously they're no match for the Invid now."

Scott growled and propelled Jesse backward into Roy's arms. It looked for a moment like he was ashamed of himself, but just then he caught the telltale sounds of the transceiver. He rushed into the adjoining cabin, where Gabby was seated at the console.

"A working transceiver?" Rand heard Scott say before roughly snatching the headphones from Gabby's grip and shoving him aside. "Calling Admiral Hunter," Scott began. "Come in, Admiral Hunter..."

Frank, Jesse, and the others burst out laughing until Scott turned on them.

"What's so damned funny?"

"The transmitter doesn't work," Lancer explained while the old men tried to stifle their chuckling. "Just the receiver."

Scott looked at the console in disbelief. "It what—"

Suddenly the monitor screen flashed, and the external speakers crackled to life. "This is the Expeditionary Force calling all Earth stations. Do you read us? Come in Earth stations...."

"We receive you, com base," Scott spoke into the headset, desperation evident in his voice. "This is Earth station receiving Expeditionary Force command...."

The face of a young man began to resolve on the screen. It was a clean-shaven face with blue eyes, fine-featured and framed by shaggy brown hair.

"If anyone is reading this message, your orders are to rendezvous with the Expeditionary Force at Reflex Point. Ships of the main fleet will be entering Earthspace within two weeks Earthtime this transmission...."

"Admiral Hunter jus' won't give up," Jesse commented.

"He's sure a spunky one, ya gotta give 'im that," said Shorty.

The image had de-rezzed by now. Through it all Gabby had been staring at the screen as though he had seen a ghost. While Scott continued to fiddle with the console controls, Gabby shuffled mindlessly toward the hatch.

"We've got to take out the broadcast towers," Scott was saying to no one in particular. "If we can cripple even some of them... Hey! Where's he going?"

Rand stepped back to permit Gabby access to the
hatch; he noticed that the man was clutching something in
the palm of his hand, but he couldn't make it out. "Let
him go," he told Scott. "He can't help, anyway."

Lancer volunteered to take the APC out to the camp
and bring in Rook and Lunk. It was dark by the time he
returned, and in addition to Rook and Lunk, the APC
carried what remained of Gabby's body. Lancer explained
that they had seen flashes of annihilation disc fire in the
vicinity of the broadcast tower; they had gone in when the
fighting stopped and discovered the flaming wreck that
was Gabby's jeep. Close by, they had found Gabby, clad
in the battle armor he had retrieved only a short while
before.

They had the man laid out in the escort hold now;
Gabby's fractured helmet sat on the floor next to him,
and the holo-locket taken from his burned hand lay atop
the sheet Lunk had thrown over the body.

"He was a brave and loyal soldier, all the way and then
some," Frank said soberly.

Shorty tugged in a sob. "We're gonna miss ya, Gabby."

Marlene stooped to place a flower on the sheet; she
gathered up the holo-locket, accidentally activating it as
she stood up. A handsome, uniformed youth appeared in
an egg-shaped aura of purple and gold light. "Hi, Dad,"
the holo-image saluted. "Like father, like son; so here I
am in the army now, and I just hope you'll be as proud of
me as I am of you." Marlene thought she recognized the
youth but said nothing.

"Poor Gabby," Jesse said, kneeling down to lift a
corner of the sheet.

All at once Frank grabbed Jesse by his lapels and
pulled him to his feet.

"Are we gonna jus' sit around and let the Invid kill us
off one by one, or are we gonna do somethin' about it?!"
He shoved his friend aside and drew his blaster. "I'm
gonna finish the job Gabby started!"

Lancer came up behind Frank and caught him up in a

full nelson, trying to reason with him. "You can't do it alone, Frank."

The old man told Lancer to butt out but ceased his struggling as a second transmission began to flash from the communications console. On the screen was the face they had seen earlier, and the young man's message was much the same: The Expeditionary Force was preparing for an offensive, and all resistance groups were urged to move against the central Invid hive, designated Reflex Point.

Marlene reactivated the holo-locket and compared the two images.

"It's him!" exclaimed Jesse. "That's Gabby's boy on that screen!"

Lancer let go of Frank. "No wonder he spent so much time trying to make that transceiver work," he said, turning to the body. "With it he could stay in touch with the one person he loved the most."

Frank hung his head. "It's a goldurn pity. Gabby could see his son, but the boy couldn't see him. An' he never told us nuthin' 'bout it."

"Listen to me, everybody," Scott said in his best take-charge voice. "I'm going to get that broadcast tower if it's the last thing I do. How about it—are you with me or not?"

The team, of course, rallied, but the veterans remained unmoved.

"What's your plan?" Rand thought to ask Scott as the freedom fighters raced toward the hatch.

"We'll decide on the way!"

Terrific, Rand said to himself.

"But what about the old cowboys?" Annie wanted to know, gesturing to Frank and his men.

"You heard them, Annie," Scott told her. "Their fighting days are over!"

Frank knew what he had to do; he just couldn't seem to bring his body to understand. It was as if the young lieutenant's words were true after all: The fight had gone out of him. He had, however, gotten as far as suiting himself up in his rusting armor and struggling his way to the bridge of the ship. He was sitting in one of the command chairs now, trying to bolster his courage with long pulls from his flask, but even the whiskey was failing him.

"This ain't no help," he muttered, giving the flask a toss toward the rear of the bridge.

"Thank ya, Frank, but we don't need it either."

Frank swiveled in the chair to find Jesse grinning at him, the flask gripped in his right hand. Roy and Shorty were with him, all three of them squeezed into armor that barely fit them anymore.

Jesse laughed, shutting his eyes. "You ain't goin' nowhere without us, Cap'n."

"Reportin' fer duty," saluted cross-eyed Shorty, hand to the helmet he was rarely without.

"He's correct," said Roy, a smile playing across that sagging face of his, his bald pate gleaming in the console lights.

Frank rose out of the chair, suppressing the smile he wanted to return. "Well, what're ya waitin' for, then? Git to yer battle stations."

Jesse tossed the flask back to him and straightened his headband. "Aye, aye, sir!" he said smartly.

A moment later the aged cruiser's lift-off thrusters came to flaming life. Like some predatory fish, the ship began to rise, disentangling itself from the techno-debris that had ensnared it for so long. And in response the devastated city rumbled its applause, buildings and ruined roadways vibrating in sympathy. At an altitude of five hundred feet, the ship's Reflex engines kicked in, triple-thrusters blazing like newborn suns, to direct it along its final course, straight into the heart of the Invid domain.

The blunt top of the broadcast tower resembled the glowing hemispherical hives Scott and the others had already gone up against, except for the fact that it was set atop an organic-looking stalk some eight hundred feet

high. As the three Veritechs closed on it—Scott's Alpha
and the uncoupled Betas—scores of rust-brown Pincer
Ships poured out to engage them. And the odds had
never been worse.

"God, there are too many of them!" Scott yelled into
his helmet mike, suddenly questioning the impulsive nature of their attack. Two of his three heat-seekers found
their targets, but the skies were literally dotted with alien
ships. "We'll never get through them!" As a storm of annihilation discs was directed against him, he loosed a
cluster of four more missiles. Three more Invid ships exploded, sending teeth-jarring shock waves and flashes of
blinding light clear into the VT's cockpit. Scott zigzagged
through a second salvo of enemy fire and was triggering
off another missile flock when he heard Rand's voice cut
through the tac net.

"Scott, look! Those crazy old men have actually gotten
that junk heap off the ground!"

Scott edged himself up in the seat; he saw the cruiser
off to the right below him, barely above treetop level.

"Watch your mouth, sonny," Frank was telling Rand.
"This ain't no junk heap, and we're gonna prove it by
showin' you whippersnappers what a real combat crew
looks like!"

Scott wanted to take back all the things he had said to
them. He had heard those words of newfound courage
before, and the ending was always the same.

"Get that ship out of here!" he roared.

"Jus' like the good ole days!" Jesse yelled over his
shoulder to Roy. He had the base of the broadcast tower
centered in the console's targeting screen, but it was not
the tower he was after—not yet. First there were all
those ships to take out. So he flipped the weapon selector
switch to maximum burst and depressed the trigger button.

A fan of laser-array energy spewed into the field, annihilating countless ships. But the combat troops were
quick to even up the score. Ignoring the Veritechs for the

moment, they massed against the cruiser and refocused the might of their collective firepower. Without shields, the Robotech ship had little immunity to the discs. Fiery explosions erupted across the cruiser's bow as blast after blast flayed armor and superstructure and blew away gun turrets.

On the bridge Shorty was thrown screaming from his station as an angry white flash holed the ship.

"Dadburn it!" Jesse cursed, seeing his friend go down. "I'll show 'em!"

He slammed his hands against the trigger button again and again, but for every Invid ship that flamed out there were two more returning fire. They were buzzing around the cruiser now, slashing at its damaged areas with their pincers and opening irreparable wounds in its hull. Discs found their way into these, and soon the warship was a flaming, smoking wreck locked in a new struggle with gravity itself.

Scott watched helplessly as the cruiser began to fall. "Use your escape pods!" he pleaded with them. "Abandon ship while you've got time!" But Frank spoke the words Scott knew he would hear:

"No way, sonny. This crew don't give up."

"Don't be foolish, old man! There's nothing more you can do!"

"There's still a job to be done," Frank told him weakly.

Scott was alongside the ship now, trying to get a look in through the bridge viewports. "You're not going to prove anything by this!"

"We can prove we ain't cowards, Lieutenant."

Scott realized that they were trying to pilot the cruiser into the very base of the broadcast tower. He would have given anything to have been able to prevent them, and yet the tower had to be taken out, and it was doubtful that the Veritechs could do it alone. So Scott pulled up and away from the ship's suicidal plunge, ordering Rand and Rook back at the same time.

The cruiser pierced the stalk like a lance, some two hundred feet below the hemispherical cap.

On the bridge, Roy turned a knowing look to Frank at the adjacent station. "I've removed the safety locks from all the missiles, Commander."

Frank nodded. "Are we all in agreement about what must be done?" he asked his crew. "Shorty, what d' ya say?"

Mortally wounded, Shorty had managed to struggle back into his seat. His head was resting on the console. "Commander, how many times do I have to tell you? Don't call me Shorty."

Scott's voice boomed through the speakers. "There's still time. Set the charges and get yourselves to the pods. We'll come in and pick you up."

"Sorry, sir," said Frank. "Our radio's been damaged, an' we can't hear a word you're saying." Rand tried to make them understand, but Frank just shook his head. "No, it's better this way. . . . Shorty, you ready?"

Shorty coughed once. "It's a funny thing, Commander, but I just remembered what it really is—my name, that is. It's—"

Frank brought the heel of his fist down on the self-destruct button.

The tower exploded, a stalk in a firestorm.

The three Veritechs swooped in for a flyby.

"We mustn't let the world forget them . . . loyal, courageous . . . *soldiers*."

"They'll be awarded medals of honor," Scott said softly.

Down below, Lunk, Annie, Lancer, and Marlene watched the fireball climb and mushroom overhead.

"Who were they, anyway?" Annie asked.

Perplexed by the conflicting emotions she felt, Marlene thought back to Gabby's kindness, Jesse's laugh, Frank's gruffness, the brief holo-locket image of Gabby's son. . . .

"They were heroes," she sobbed.

CHAPTER
FIVE

*They thought they had stumbled into Denver, but in fact
they had lucked into Delta-Six, a top-secret subterranean installation attached to the Cheyenne Mountain complex, constructed to ensure that America's heads of state would survive
any form of attack leveled against the continent. But they
weren't thinking of the Zentraedi then, and certainly not of
Dolza's four million.*

"Northlands" *History of The Third Robotech War,* Vol.
LXXXVI

THE TEAM SWUNG NORTH, THEN EAST, LEAVING THE
desert behind and entering the foothills of the Northlands
central range. The Rockies, they were told. They chose to
avoid southern routes across the continental divide in
favor of the less traveled northern passes, even though
this made for more difficult ascents. But there were numerous satellite hives in the warmer valleys to the south,
and since the team's reserves of Protoculture were low,
they couldn't afford to risk all-out engagement. They had
managed to procure a few canisters of fuel, but Scott had
insisted they be used for the red Alpha, which Rand and
Rook had retrieved.

The weather was against the team, however, and although a week went by without an enemy encounter,
their progress was slow. When at last they crossed the
spine, they began to sense the nearness of the prairielands
beyond. But tectonic upheavals brought about by the

Zentraedi Rain of Death had so altered the terrain here that they often felt off the map; and given their precataclysm charts, indeed they were.

It was snowing now in this final pass that had no right being there. Fearful of calling attention to themselves and careful to conserve what little fuel remained, they had decided to keep the Veritechs grounded. Lunk had secured chains for the APC and fashioned skids and tow bars for the fighters using plate and barstock he had scavenged from what had been a recreational ski area. They had the APC rigged as a kind of tow vehicle, but most of the real propulsion was derived from battery-driven thrusters in the VTs' raptorlike legs. Annie and Marlene were riding up front with Lunk; the rest of the team was currently on foot.

"It's so cold," Annie whimpered to Marlene, shivering and clutching the hooded poncho to her neck. "It feels like my nose is going to fall off or something."

Marlene pressed herself closer to Annie and brought some of her own poncho around Annie's shoulders.

Scott, Lancer, and Rook, similarly attired in cold-weather ponchos, were alongside the red Alpha at the middle of the caravan. "Soup," said Rook, daydreaming. "Nice, hot soup. A cup of thick soup, a *bathtubful* of piping hot, steaming soup . . ." She felt Lancer's hand on her shoulder.

"Don't. It only makes it worse."

Then she heard Rand: "Hold up a minute, guys!"

He was behind them at the Beta's wingtip, preoccupied with his latest acquisition—the thermograph Jesse had given him shortly before the assault on the broadcast tower. It was about the size of a small chain saw, with a muzzlelike sensor and top-mounted carrying handle. Rook saw that he was kneeling down, sweeping the instrument across the snow.

"Lunk! Stop the sleds!" Scott called out over the wind.

"It's amazing. . . . There's something underneath us!" Rand was saying as Scott, Lancer, and Rook approached.

"Yeah, we know. It's called ice," Rook told him.

Scott motioned her to lighten up. "What are you picking up?"

Rand double-checked the indicator readings. "A large heat source. Massive, way off the meter."

"Volcanic?"

Rand shook his head, loosing wet snow from the poncho. "Definitely not."

"Then the thermograph is on the fritz," Rook said through chattering teeth. "Either that or it's your brain."

Rand ignored the comment and began pushing snow aside, as if to get a glimpse of something beneath the ice. "It's gotta be a generator of some kind . . . just below this layer of snow . . ."

Rook made an impatient sound. "Come on, man, you're wasting our time."

He looked up knowingly and got to his feet. "Wasting our time, huh?" All at once he was beside her, pushing her toward the window he had excavated.

"Quit your shoving!" she protested.

"Well, Miss Know-it-all, why don't you take a look for yourself?"

She glared at him for a moment, then went down on her knees, wiping away flakes of new snow and peering in. The ice was virtually transparent, as clear as Caribbean water. But her mind refused to accept what her eyes were telling her: she seemed to be looking down on a turn-of-the-century building bathed in artificial light— one of those twenty-story milk cartons she had seen pictures of. There was steam or something issuing from exhaust elbows on the roof, and below that she could discern other buildings and lit streets.

Overwhelmed by a sudden sense of vertigo, she had to turn away.

"It's a city!"

"Told you," said Rand.

Scott looked at both of them and frowned. "Sorry, guys, but it's no time to play archaeologist."

"We just need a pickax and some ropes!" Rand said excitedly. He was already up and running toward the

APC. "Think of the food and supplies that are down there!" He threw off his poncho and made a mad leap for the vehicle's shotgun seat, mindless of Lunk's bewildered cries. He was rummaging around in the storage compartment beneath the seat when the ground started to give way.

It was too late for the warnings Scott and the others were shouting out; the APC fell through, almost dragging the VT caravan with it. Instinctively, Scott grabbed hold of the Beta's skids, but momentarily the fighter train came to a halt of its own accord, with the blue Alpha perched precariously at the edge of the hole, its radome dropped, like the beak of a bird searching for worms in a hole.

Down below, Annie felt herself for broken bones. She looked around and saw that Rand, Marlene, and Lunk were performing similar self-examinations. She had no idea what they had fallen into or onto, but it seemed to be some sort of roof. The APC was upright nearby, the chains that had connected it to the lead Veritech snapped. Overhead, Scott and the others were leaning in to inquire if everyone was all right. Annie got to her feet and felt a strong uprush of heated air.

"Hey, I think we can get down to street level!" Rand was shouting. He had thrown open the door to a boxlike structure that housed the building's stairway. Atop it were the jetting exhausts Rook had seen from above.

Rand disappeared through the door, and Annie followed him without a thought.

The rest of the team had lowered themselves to the roof by now and had discarded their ponchos. Above the jagged rend in the ice the snowstorm was still howling. Scott moved to the edge of the roof and looked around in amazement: It was indeed an underground city, intact and apparently deserted. He turned to gaze up at the hole and realized that the city was not only subterranean but fully enclosed by a protective dome of what appeared to be fabriplex. Somehow the place had been spared destruction by both the Zentraedi fleet and subsequent geological shifts. Over the years it had become buried by earth and snow. He wanted to run this by Lunk and Lancer, but Lunk had other concerns on his mind.

"The landing gear's been damaged," he told Scott, indicating the undercarriage of the still suspended blue Alpha.

"I guess that means we're stuck here for a while," said Rook, not exactly unhappy about it.

Scott scowled. "Another delay," he muttered under his breath.

Rand and Annie, meanwhile, had hit the streets. They had taken the forty flights warily, and Rand had his blaster out even now, but there was no sign of activity. The ground-floor levels of many of the buildings were illuminated, as were numerous signs and street lights. Still, there were indications that the place had been abandoned in haste, and it was an eerie feeling to walk through it all. There were no vehicles, and the only sound was that of the city's self-contained atmosphere being sucked toward the breach they had opened in its protective umbrella.

Annie wasn't quite as put off by the emptiness as Rand. "It's magical," she enthused. "I've never seen a city this big in my whole life."

Rand holstered his weapon.

"I wonder what keeps it running. It looks like it dates back to the prewars period." He caught a glimpse of Annie's look of enchantment and laughed. "And to think, it's been buried here just waiting for you and me to come along."

"Like out of a fairy tale!"

Rand took hold of her hand, and they ran off to explore.

Scott sent Marlene and Rook off to locate Rand while he, Lunk, and Lancer carefully disengaged the caravan and piloted each of the Veritechs to the roof of the building. A search for tools brought them down into the low-ermost of the building's subbasements, where Lunk discovered the source of the city's power: a generator that tapped thermal power deep within the Earth itself. Lancer also came up with something that explained where they were: it was a teletype evacuation notice addressed to the residents of "Denver," issued on the eve of Dolza's devastating barrage of death.

"They were in such a big hurry, they forgot to turn out the lights," Lunk smirked. "They're gonna get stuck with *some* utility bill."

Rook had managed to find Rand. It wasn't difficult: she simply started with the toy stores, then worked her way through the supermarkets and delis.

She was off gathering supplies now, while Rand, Annie, and Marlene were sampling foodstuffs from the plastic wrapped, bottled, and canned goods smorgasbord they had spread out on the floor around them. They had found bags of marshmallows and jars of peanut butter, cookies, dried fruits and frozen pies, cans of soda and bars of chocolate, cereals, beans, soups, and assorted sweets.

"Mmmm, mint chocolate," Annie said with her mouth full. She tore open a second package and broke off a piece for Marlene. "Try it, you'll love it. I could live off this stuff."

Marlene nibbled at it and raised her eyebrows. "It is good."

"Peppermint!" Annie exclaimed, picking another item from the floor. "This is my most favorite thing in the whole world!" She pillowed her head against the bag and closed her eyes lovingly.

Nearby, Rand popped open a Coke. "You got mints on the brain, kid." He gulped some down and took a bite from the hero he had defrosted.

"I don't care what the Invid do as long as they don't take away our peppermint."

"Nice attitude, Annie. But I gotta agree with you: this is the life. Somebody pinch me so I know I haven't died and gone to heaven."

Rook, pushing a cartful of supplies, came by just then to remind him. "How about a kick in the teeth instead?" She gave the three of them her best disapproving look. "What a mess. We're supposed to be foraging supplies, not packing them away in our stomachs. Ever think that Scott and Lancer might be hungry, too?" She shook her head at Rand. "Sometimes you make me wonder."

He showed a roguish grin in response and tossed a can over to her. "Ever seen these before?"

Rook read the label. "Vienna sausages? What's a 'vienna'?"

Rand saw Annie and Marlene's puzzled looks. "You mean none of you have tried these?"

"Are they peppermints?" Annie said, getting to her feet.

Rook made a face and tossed the can over her shoulder to Rand. "What a disgusting thought."

Rand shared a wink with Annie and said, "Let's find out."

She kneeled down and pulled on the can's ring-seal. "Oh, they're cute!" she laughed, fishing out sausages for Rand and Marlene. She popped one into her mouth. "Ter-ri-fic . . . Not peppermints, but pretty good anyway."

Rook was watching them all munching away, her forefinger to her lower lip. "Lemme try one," she said, kneeling down, hands between her knees.

Rand dangled a sausage between his fingers. "I don't know. . . . You think you should?"

"Just gimme it," she barked, snatching it from his grip. She chewed the thing up and swallowed: salty and too soft, but it tasted better than anything she had had in weeks.

Annie saw the look of delight on her face, laughed, and pointed her finger accusingly. "Now our food supply's *really* gonna be in trouble!"

Scott had left the VT repairs to Lancer and Lunk and had gone off to look for Rand and Rook. He couldn't blame them for wanting to explore the city; it was like some museum of prewar life, the life some of the oldest members of the Pioneer Mission had spoken of.

He was standing in front of a bridal shop now, staring at a lovely white dress in the display window. The dress reminded him of a picture he had once seen that was taken on his mother's wedding day. There was even something about the mannequin that reminded him of her, the short upswept brown hair adorned with a red flower.... He was so caught up in the memory that he wasn't aware of his teammates' presence until Annie spoke.

"Jeepers, look at that dress! What I'd give to be married in that!"

Embarrassed, Scott swung around, certain they had read his thoughts somehow. Marlene and Rook were nodding in agreement. They had three shopping carts loaded with supplies.

"Hey, Scott, who's the lucky girl gonna be?" Rand joked.

But Scott saw his friend's smile quickly collapse after Rook nudged him on the arm. Now it was Rand who was embarrassed for having forgotten about Marlene—*Scott's* Marlene, who had died during the Mars Division assault.

The foursome began to move off. Scott returned to his musings for a moment more, then called out for them to stop.

"Where do you think you're going? I want to get these supplies to the ships. Maybe you've forgotten, but we have an appointment to keep at Reflex Point."

Rand made a dismissive gesture. "Ah, give it a rest, Scott. What's an hour or two gonna matter?" Then he softened his tone somewhat. "Look, I know this place might not be very important to you...."

"But we were born right here on Earth," Annie filled in. "And leaving this place now would be like turning our backs on our heritage."

Even Rook chimed in. "We deserve a little R&R, don't we?"

The three of them didn't wait for his answer and

started off down the street. But he didn't try to stop them; there was no denying the truth of their arguments.

"You're such an old stick-in-the-mud sometimes," Annie said over her shoulder.

Scott regarded the mannequin once again, only now it was Marlene, his fiancée's face, that he saw there. *Oh, come on, Scott,* he fantasized her saying. *Loosen up a little. It's a beautiful dress. And who knows, maybe they'll give us a break on the price. . . . It is our wedding, after all. . . .*

"Marlene," he said softly.

"I'm right here, Scott," the other Marlene said behind him. "What are you thinking about?"

He turned to her and stammered: "Uh . . . about another dress a long time ago that was similar to this one."

She had a sympathetic look on her face. "Do you think they're right about me being a stick-in-the-mud?"

She was about to reply that she had no idea what that meant, when Scott's face brightened suddenly and he put his hand on her shoulder.

"Marlene, how about an unguided tour of the city— just you and me?"

She smiled and let him take her hand but an instant later was down in the street on her butt.

"Whoa, are you all right?" Scott was asking her. He was kneeling beside her on the pavement, regarding her ankle boots and frowning. "We're going to have to find you some better shoes and some warmer clothes."

She took Scott's hand between hers and pressed it to her cheek. "Mmmm . . . You're not cold?"

Scott nuzzled her hair. "No. All of a sudden, I feel very warm."

They walked the deserted streets arm in arm, content to say little and enjoying their closeness. Marlene spied a display of lingerie in a shop window and ran to it, fingertips to the plate glass. Here was a pair of yellow bikini briefs with a matching spaghetti-strapped bra, a lavender camisole, a rose-colored teddy.

"Aren't they beautiful, Scott?"

"Uh, that's not quite what I had in mind," he said from a safe distance, blushing all the while. He put his arm around her shoulders to move her away. "Believe me, you'd freeze in those things," he told her.

In a shoe store, he feigned a foreign accent and tried to interest her in a pair of low-impact approach boots, but she playfully demanded to be shown something more feminine.

"But these things will keep you from churning in the snow."

"Feminine, I said."

He round a pair of white pumps in her size and squatted down to place them on her feet. "They're not very practical," he started to say, but she was already up and twirling around on one foot, laughing.

"There," she told him. "Much better for dancing."

Scott smiled up at her. *Dancing*, he thought. But the more he watched her, the more her face began to blend with memories of his lost love, and ultimately he had to look away. She saw the sadness in his eyes and asked him to talk about it.

"I was just dreaming of a better time, Marlene. Of dancing . . ."

Then all at once he was on his feet, the excitement back in his eyes, putting his hands atop her shoulders.

"And now to complete the picture . . ."

He led her off at a run to a dress shop and rummaged through the racks until he had found what he was after: a strapless gown cut like a mermaid's tail, pale lavender above a kind of pleated base of white skirt.

"It was made for you."

She held it up to herself, flattered by his choice.

"Go ahead, try it on," he urged her.

And she was about to, but there was something vague in her memory that prevented her. Scott picked up on it immediately, even though she hadn't a clue as to why she had stopped.

"Stupid of me," he said, smacking the heel of his hand

against his head. He scanned the shop for a dressing room and when he had located it, rushed over to station himself like a guard by its curtained entrance.

"If you'll just step this way, mademoiselle . . ." he suggested with a theatrical bow.

She disappeared inside and cautioned him about peeking, recalling the way Rand had looked at her when she had innocently stripped off her clothes to swim. . . .

Scott jumped back as though scalded. *She's reading my thoughts*, he told himself. He swallowed hard as he watched her discarded clothes pile up on the floor below the curtains. And when the curtains parted, she was the most beautiful thing he had ever seen.

She stood still, her hands crossed at her neck, allowing him to take her in; then she gathered her hair in one hand and turned her back to him.

"Would you zip me up, Scott?"

He regarded the open zipper and took halting steps toward the dressing room, his eyes fixed on the graceful curve of her back, the pale perfection of her skin.

*Why the sudden shift from Lancer to Scott? many have
asked. But the answer is immediately evident once we are reminded of Ariel/Marlene's original programming as Simulagent. Then it seems entirely natural for her to seek out the
leader, and, as it were, the team's weakest line of defense.*

Bloom Nesterfig, *Social Organization of the Invid*

RAND SANG TO HIMSELF WHILE HIS INDEX FINGERS
worked the machine's flippers: *Sure plays a mean pinball*
...The left paddle caught the ball just right and sent it
careening around the cushioned arena, up the forward
ramp, and smack into the belly dancer's navel for a bonus
score of one thousand points. But propelled free, the
steel sphere fell like one of Galileo's own and shot directly through the Flipper Straits, lost to the game's mechanical bowels.

"You Khyron!" Rand cursed, whacking the machine
with his hands.

Beside him, Rook made a bored sound at her own
machine and moved off to one of the arcade's plastiform
seats.

"Don't tell me you're giving up already?" he asked
over his shoulder.

"Too boring." She yawned.

"Well, how do you ever expect to improve at anything if you just keep giving up?"

He was still angry with her for the elbow she had given him earlier while they were washing their clothes in the Laundromat. Annie had wandered off, and Rand had spotted Scott and Marlene strolling by arm in arm. He was leaping up to give Fearless Leader a round of applause when the gut shot had been delivered without forewarning.

Of course, it wasn't really the case—that Rook had a habit of giving up—but that was beside the point. In any event, she ignored his comment, so he turned back to the machine, angering it just short of tilt after another ball plunged home.

"No good piece of—"

"This place just makes me feel . . . lonely," Rook interrupted him.

Nice, Rand said to himself. *We finally get to spend a few peaceful moments together and she feels* lonely. "So what does that make me—part of the furniture?" he said without turning around.

He heard her laugh. "C'mon, you don't want me to answer that, do you?"

Rand compressed his lips to a thin line. He was going to place the next shot right between her eyes. . . .

Up on the roof, Lancer and Lunk were making final repairs to the damaged Alpha. Lancer was down on one knee operating the torque wrench. It was a rare occasion when the two men worked side by side; Lunk was continually worried that Yellow Dancer would make some unannounced appearance, and the last thing he wanted to do was to be caught alone with her, er, *him*! But today had been different; they had talked shop, and they had talked about the Invid.

"We've really got our work cut out for us now," Lunk was saying. "These new ships they keep throwing at us are a lot more maneuverable than the Troopers."

"You're right about that," Lancer said absently.

"I mean, we were just plain lucky the last time they surprised us in the mountains. If that ledge hadn't given way..."

Lancer recalled the fall of the pink and purple ship. And its female pilot. He found himself wondering if he would see her again—wondering with a mixture of fear and anticipation. But Annie's voice brought him from his musings before he had to grapple with the emotions behind them. She came running onto the roof from the stairway cubicle dressed like a June bride.

"Look what I found!"

The dress was a soft pink, with a white ruffled collar and matching bonnet. But it was at least four sizes too large for her, so she had most of the train gathered up in her arms.

"Just what are you supposed to be?" Lunk asked her.

Lancer laughed and stood up, wiping his hands on his trousers. "She's a bride—and a pretty one at that." He formed his hands into an imaginary camera and brought them to his eye. "What I'd give to have my old Pentax."

Annie put up her hands to stop him. "Wait! I want my bridegroom in this photo!" And with that she jumped up, threw her arms around Lunk's neck, and hung there, the hem of the gown touching the floor now.

Lunk went rigid for a moment, then scooped her up and cradled her in his arms, his dismayed expression unchanged.

Lancer threw his head back and laughed.

"Perfect!" he enthused.

Scott couldn't get that zipper out of his mind, except now he was wondering what it would be like to *undo* it. Since Marlene's death he had been convincing himself that celibacy had been written into his destiny, but suddenly this nameless goddess, this new Marlene, was bringing all the old allegiances into question. Was it wrong for him to be having these thoughts? he asked himself. Would his Marlene have wanted him to remain faithful to her no matter what? He sensed that the phrasing was wrong, perhaps even the questions themselves, because he knew that his love for Marlene could never be extinguished. But these new feelings had more to do with happiness and companionship.

The two of them were exploring a department store. Scott had located the sound system and an original Lynn-Minmei disc—probably the first one she had ever recorded. He knew her well from Tirol, but how different that Minmei seemed from the innocent girl whose bright eyes shone from the CD jacket. It seemed ages ago, Scott realized, before all the troubles with Edwards, before Minmei's devastating encounter with Wolff. . . .

"Stagefright," one of the singer's most popular numbers, was blasting through the PA speakers. Marlene, still in that strapless gown that fit her like a glove, was trying on jewelry. Scott watched her in wonderment. They picked out a silver and brass collar and a bracelet of gold. He found her a leather shoulder bag and a floppy blue hat.

They exchanged meaningful looks. And Scott asked her about love.

"Was there anyone, Marlene? Were you ever in love?"

"Love?" she asked him.

He could see that she had no understanding of the emotion. How traumatized she must have been to have had even that erased from her past!

He began to envy her.

In the next store they separated, as two people might drift apart in a museum, lost in private thoughts and personal moments. It was the toys that fascinated Marlene: wind-up clowns and talking bears, music boxes and transformable gadgets, drummer boys and lively ballerinas. She switched all of them on, filling her world with a symphony of transistorized sounds and songs. She was handling a fragile glass giraffe when the gorilla showed up.

Marlene uttered a frightened scream and fell back, dropping the small figurine to the floor. Of course it was only Scott in a mask, but how was she to know that?

She ran to him after he had taken it off, seeking shelter in his arms. "Hold me, Scott," she whispered. But he held back and gently pushed her to arm's length, his hands on her shoulders.

"Marlene, I . . . I want to know all about you."

She gave him a helpless look. "I wish I could tell you," she apologized. "I wish I knew the words. . . ."

But what he saw in her eyes was enough. "We don't need words," he told her, drawing her in. They kissed lightly, tentatively, exploring each other.

Then suddenly *she* pulled back, overcome first by dread, then pain. "They're coming!" she managed. "It's hopeless, hopeless!" Her mane of red hair was shaking back and forth. "There's no escape from them!"

Scott did what he could to comfort her and began to look left and right in desperation. "We're trapped down here!" he berated himself. "Trapped!"

There was no escape!

Far above them in those displaced mountains that towered over the buried city, Corg, the crown prince of the Invid horde, had zeroed in on the rend the freedom fighters had inadvertently opened in the dome. He was a sharp-featured young man with lean good looks and mysterious oblique blue eyes. His hair, which was also blue, lay flat and fine against his skull, lending itself to his somewhat cruel and ascetic look. Corg had been created from the lifestuff of his race by the Regis herself, to rule at Sera's side in the new order.

His command ship was like hers: somewhat acephalic, top-heavy, and buxom-looking with its heavily weaponed torso pods and power nacelles.

Accompanying him were two Enforcer ships that represented the most recent examples of technological innovation from the Regis's weapons factories. They were not unlike their crablike prototypes but somehow appeared almost naked beside them. They were bipedal and seemingly four-armed, their optic scanners were more Cyclopean in placement, and there was a phallic, muscular flexibility to the top-mounted cannons that was absent in the more cumbersome-looking Shock Troopers and Pincer Ships.

Corg chose to make his own opening in the city's dome and did so with a massive charge from his ship's shoulder cannon. Then he began his hellish descent, his two underlings following him down into the breach.

The freedom fighters were waiting for them, though. Scott had alerted the rest of the team to Marlene's premonition, and they had elected to draw the Invid down into the city and utilize the more maneuverable Cyclones to battle them in the streets.

In Battle Armor mode, Scott, Lancer, Rand, and Rook were assembled at street level when the first two Invid blasts shook the city, impacting against the upper storys of one of the tall towers and showering them with chunks of concrete and shards of plate glass.

"We won't stand a chance head to head against these guys," Scott said over the tac net. "We've got to take advantage of their clumsiness!"

"Gotcha!" Rook returned as everyone took to the air.

Rand lingered behind and was almost slagged because of it. "We'll make mincemeat out of them," he was saying when an energy bolt exploded in the street. He caught up with Rook a moment later in an alleyway, but the newfangled Enforcer had pursued him and loosed a shot that nearly fried both of them where they stood. They launched and took up ground-level positions on either side of the alley's exit and poured return fire into the Invid ship as it rounded the corner.

The Enforcer found Rand first and swung toward him, the triple nodes of its cannon primed for fire. Rand leapt away just in time, amazed to see two steady streams of crimson fire where he had expected annihilation discs.

Elsewhere, Scott and Lancer were facing off with the second Enforcer. They had their backs to the wall as the Invid came at them, its rear thrusters keeping it airborne, a flying insect nightmare in the city's twilight.

"I'll draw its fire," Scott told Lancer. "Get above and do some damage!"

The Enforcer's cannon muzzles came to life, spewing two deadly beams, which converged and struck the base of the building, sending shock waves through the streets. Glass was now raining down from everywhere, along with snow that was avalanching through the dome's ruptured skin. Both freedom fighters jumped aside, but Lancer stayed in the air while Scott attempted to lure the enemy onto a wider boulevard. He dug in at the end of the street and waited for the Enforcer's approach; then, with the thing scarcely two hundred yards away, he launched two time-charged Bludgeons from the right forearms tubes of his battle armor. The missiles detonated in the air over the Invid's back, with a collective force great enough to throw the thing face-first to the street. Lancer was in position now, and on Scott's command he activated nearly all his suit's launch tubes; missiles arced from the open compartments and racks and fell like a fiery hail on the immobilized alien ship, destroying it even while its own cannons were blazing away. To add insult to injury, Scott launched another missile into the dome overhead, loosing a fall of massive ice chunks, which sealed the Enforcer's fate.

Rand and Rook were still being pursued by the first ship, whose pilot was obviously the more experienced of the two.

"Boy, this high altitude's beginning to affect me," Rand told his teammate, fighting for breath.

They had stopped to go face-to-face with the ship after realizing that Scott and Lancer were coming in to out-flank it. Now all four of them opened up at once, throwing everything they had against the Enforcer and what was left of the devastated dome, burning and burying it much as they had its companion ship.

But suddenly there was another ship in the arena: a drab gray-green command ship with orange-tan highlights. They had seen this one before and had hoped they wouldn't see it again.

"Scott, behind you!" Rook warned.

The team scattered, but the command ship stuck with Scott, pursuing him through several blocks—literally *through* the buildings, although Scott was using the doorways and the alien was simply making his own. Ultimately they squared off, the giant insectlike ship and the diminutive Cyclone, and Scott flicked on his externals to say: "I had a sick feeling you would show up again."

The Invid raised its cannon arm and would have slagged him then and there had it not been for Lancer and the others, who distracted it with rooftop fire. Scott seized the moment to leap away, but the command ship continued to stalk him—probably angered by the earlier comment, Scott had the temerity to say to himself. Even Lunk, Annie, and Marlene had joined the fray by this time; they were packed into the APC, riding circles around the Invid's feet while spraying it ineffectually with machine-gun fire. Down on his butt with the alien looming over him, Scott wondered how they had gotten the vehicle down to street level, but he didn't dwell on it for long, because the Invid was ignoring the trio and raising that handgun again....

Just then Annie somehow succeeded in angering the thing with some silly comment; the Invid switched targets, reangled its handgun, and fired off a rapid burst that nipped at the carrier's tail. The APC was unscathed, but something had been thrown from the rear seat—something pink and soft-looking...

Scott realized it was a dress of some sort but couldn't believe his scanners when he saw that Marlene was running back to retrieve it! Lunk had brought the APC to a halt and was yelling at her to forget about it.

The Invid ship swung around and took one giant step, aiming menacingly at its defenseless prey. In the cockpit, Corg stared down at the sister his race had lost to the Humans and could not bring himself to fire.

Scott, meanwhile, had launched himself straight up, crying out Marlene's name and launching half a dozen Scorpions straight into the Invid's back. Leaking fire from its seams, the alien whirled on him and raised its cannon, but Scott was again quicker to the draw with two more missiles that managed to sever the ship's right arm.

The cannon hit the floor with a thunderous crash, but Corg wasn't about to retreat just yet. He turned and stomped after Scott, shouldering the ship through the walls of the building and out into the street.

There, the reunited rebel team ganged up on the command ship, paralyzing it with missile fire and opening up the rest of the dome. It was as though a dam had collapsed: hundreds of tons of snow and ice were pouring into the city. The Invid struggled against the slides but eventually succumbed to the sheer weight of the fall. It went down on one knee, systems sputtering and shorting out, then tipped to its side.

"To the Alphas, everybody!" Scott commanded.

"Well, there goes the world's shortest vacation," Rand said in response.

Lunk, Annie, and Marlene were waiting for them on the roof. Once more, Scott couldn't figure out how the APC had managed it, but he didn't stop to ask. He reconfigured his mecha to its two-wheeled mode and told Lunk to stow the four Cycs in their Veritech compartments. Marlene was frightened but unhurt. Scott wanted nothing more than to hug her, his battle armor notwithstanding, but he contented himself with simply touching her shoulder.

Shortly they had the Veritechs in the air, the APC slung from the undercarriage of the Beta.

"Sorry about the accommodations," Scott apologized to Lunk, Annie, and Marlene, "but the fresh air will do you good."

Lunk swung himself around in the driver's seat of the APC to look back at the massive holes in the ice dome that had kept the city a secret from its surroundings for the past twenty years. In his hand he held an electronic detonator he had rigged to the computer control system of the city's thermal furnaces.

"Now or never," he said out loud, and thumbed the trigger button.

Five minutes later the city exploded with near-volcanic force; a swirling pillar of fire shot up into the winter skies, vaporizing snow and ice and capturing the resultant thaw and clouds of steam. The sound of follow-up explosions echoed in the mountains, catching the Veritechs in their roar. They fought to stabilize themselves in the shock waves and newborn thermals, the jeep rocking to and fro like a pendulum beneath Scott's fighter.

"What the hell happened?!" Rand's panicked voice boomed over the net.

Lunk flipped on the APC mike. "I rigged the main generator to feed back on itself," he explained.

"Bu-but *why*?!"

"Because that city had no place in this world." There was a kind of anger in Lunk's voice.

"Well, it sure doesn't anymore," Rand said.

"Some fireworks, though," Rook commented.

"Well, golly gee, Miss Rook, sure glad we were able to bring some excitement to your day. Least you won't have to be *bored* anymore."

"Who asked *you*?!" Rook returned.

Scott listened to them go at it, then reached out to lower the volume in his cockpit. He craned his neck to see if he could get a glimpse of Marlene, below him in the personnel carrier. *She knew they were coming*, he told himself. But what was the strange link they shared? What channel had the Invid opened in her shocked mind that allowed her to sense their coming? And could the team somehow tap that frightening frequency?

He thought back to the command ship's momentary paralysis when Marlene had appeared to pick up Annie's lost dress. *Why didn't the alien pilot fire?* he wondered, thinking back to the blond pilot's similar reluctance. The Invid had her right in its sights, and yet it was almost as if the thing had *recognized* her.

Almost as if Marlene was . . . *one of them*.

CHAPTER
SEVEN

> *Opinions vary: there are those who give Annie LaBelle's age as thirteen and others who give it as seventeen; and there's enough contradictory background data to give strength to either argument. Subsequent research has yet to reveal enough to persuade or dissuade either camp. Rand, in his voluminous* Notes on the Run, *states that "Annie was thirteen going on seventeen," while elsewhere he opines that "she may be seventeen, but she acts like she's thirteen." It is a minor controversy, to be sure, but one that is still argued over. Ms. LaBelle has not been helpful in laying this matter to rest.*
>
> Footnote in Bellow, *The Road to Reflex Point*

THE PRESENCE OF INVID SCOUTS PATROLLING THE outer perimeters of the central hive forced the team to keep to the mountains and turn south once again. There was still no sign of Hunter's invasion force, and the Protoculture reserves in the VTs were simply too low to permit any worthwhile reconnaissance behind the enemy lines. No one was really put off by the delay; even Scott breathed easier knowing that Reflex Point was temporarily out of the question. Besides, the snow was behind them, even though the land itself was no less rugged. Travel since "Denver" had been almost due south—into what Scott's maps indicated had once been called western Texas.

Scott, Rook, and Lancer had done most of the flying; Lunk's APC was back on the ground where it belonged, with Rand's Cyclone to keep him company. Annie was in the mecha's buddy seat, urging Rand through the old highway's twists and turns. It was a warm, blue-sky day, and she felt gloriously alive and uncommonly optimistic. Indeed, she had good reason to feel this way.

"It's my birthday!" she shouted into Rand's ear when they had exited one of the road's many tunnels.

"If you don't stop screaming in my ear, it'll be the last birthday you celebrate," Rand warned over his shoulder.

They had lost sight of the VTs on the other side of the tunnel, so he took the turn fast, hoping to spot them before entering the figure-eight switchbacks that led down into the valley. All at once, Rook's red Alpha came whipping around the shoulder, scarcely ten feet above the roadbed. Rand told Annie to hold on and locked the Cyclone's brakes, stabilizing the mecha through a long slide as Rook was setting the fighter down. Lunk had a clearer view of things and managed to bring the APC to a more controlled stop behind the Cyc.

"Why don't you look where you're going?!" Rand shouted even before Rook had opened the canopy.

"Are you trying to kill us?!" Annie threw in.

"Just the opposite," Rook said peevishly over the Alpha's externals. "There's an Invid hive on the other side of the ridge, and at the rate you two were going, you'd have been on it in no time."

Rand's eyes went wide, but instead of thanking her or apologizing, he simply said: "Way down here? Choicest spot around."

Rook was correct about the hive; what she didn't realize was that the Invid were already aware of the team's presence and were heading toward them. About the same time she was warning Rand away, the Invid Regis was issuing new instructions to her troops through one of the hive's bio-constructs.

"Shock Trooper squadron, prepare to relieve incoming patrol drones," she announced. "Projected course of Robotech rebels from last point of encounter should bring them into our control zone during the next eight hours. Evidence of Protoculture activity on the outlying limits of

scanning perimeter indicates possible presence of Robotech mecha within control zone even now. All scanning
systems on full alert."

On foot, Rook, Rand, and the others joined Scott and
Lancer at the top of the ridge, where the two had concealed themselves among some rocks. The VTs had been
shut down and left on the roadbed.

"I don't like the looks of all this activity," Lancer was
telling Scott when the rest of the team approached. He
had a pair of high-powered scanning binoculars trained
on the hive dome. Shock Troopers and Scouts were buzzing in and out of the hemisphere, and several Pincer units
were in assembly on the ground, as though receiving
orders from some unseen commander. "I think they're
expecting us."

"But they weren't expecting us to spot them first,"
Scott said gruffly.

"How does it look?" Rand called out behind them.

Lancer lowered the binoculars and stepped away from
the outcropping. "In a word—bad."

"We've got to double back," Scott told them. "There's
a high road that keeps to the ridgeline above this valley.
We might be able to get through before their sensors pick
us up. It's going to be slow going, but I don't see that we
have any choice."

The refrain, Rand said to himself as he trudged back to
his mecha.

Scott, Rook, and Lancer led the slow, silent uphill pro-
cession, relying once more on the battery-operated thrusters that had seen the Guardian-configured Veritechs over
many a northern pass. But once over the ridge, they
risked increasing the pace somewhat and brought the
Protoculture systems back into play. They kept to the
road nevertheless but were now hovering fifteen or so
feet above its rough surface. But this still wasn't fast
enough for Annie.

"Some birthday," she griped to Rand. "No party, no presents, and no fun."

He had been hearing this for the better part of three hours now and was beginning to tire of it. "Count your blessings," he told her. "We're lucky to be alive. Isn't that right, Marlene?" he added, hoping to gain some support.

But Marlene didn't have much to say beyond a soft "Uh-huh" from the front seat of the APC. Her head felt as though it was splitting open, but she was determined not to let the others see how much pain she was in.

The three pilots became more brazen on the downhill stretches and were soon winging the fighters along at a good clip. Encouraged (and seeing an opportunity to raise the noise level of the mecha above that of Annie's nonstop complaining), Rand began to feed the Cyclone more throttle.

"Mint, what d' ya say we goose this thing a little. That sound good to you?"

Annie hammered her fist against his shoulder. "Don't call me Mint—*Whoa*!"

With a turn of his wrist, Rand saw to it that her words were left behind. The three Veritechs had disappeared around the bend, but with a bit of fancy weaving under the foot thrusters, Rand thought he could not only catch up but pull out into the lead. As soon as he made his first move, however, the first Invid ship appeared on the scene. It elevated into view from the trees at the base of the slope and skimmed two streams of annihilation discs straight into Rand's path. Consequently, he had to bring that fancy maneuvering into play sooner than planned, but he did succeed in dodging the energy Frisbees of the enemy's first volley.

Of course, it meant leaving the road entirely to do so.

But at least we're alive! he screamed to himself as the Cyclone was bounding down the steep slope toward the trees, Annie hanging on for dear life, in and out of the pillion seat half a dozen times before they hit the flat ground at the base of the cliff. Rand risked a look over his shoulder and saw that the APC had also left the ledge roadbed.

What he didn't see, however, was that Lunk's landing was far from smooth. A second discharge of disc fire had forced Lunk to swerve at the last moment; the nose of the vehicle connected with some large rocks and overturned, sending Marlene sprawling while Lunk rode out the roll. The same Invid ship swooped down for a close pass over the fleeing Cycloners, loosing a barrage as it fell, but Lancer's Alpha was on the thing now and holed it before it could manage a follow-up burst. Rand, meanwhile, was closing on the trees at top speed, heartened when he heard the Pincer unit explode behind him, but panicked when he saw two more rise unexpectedly out of the forest.

"They're everywhere!" he shouted.

"Rand! Get into your battle armor!" he heard Scott say over the mecha's tac net. "I'll keep you covered."

Rand halted the Cyclone and began to snatch sections of armor from one of the storage compartments. Off to his right he saw Lunk leading a dazed Marlene to shelter among the rocks at the base of the slope and told Annie to join them there. She ran off, holding her cap on her head with one hand.

Rand struggled into the "thinking cap" and launched for reconfiguration. A moment later he was back on the ground in Battle Armor mode, squaring off with one of the ships. The thing tried an overhand pincer swipe that missed, then a quick spray of disc fire after Rand had aggravated it with two Scorpions from the Cyclone's forearm launchers. The discs tore into the earth at Rand's feet and threw him flat on his back, but he countered with three missiles that found their way into seams in the ship's alloy. The Invid had enough life left in it to attempt a second pincer crush, but Rand rolled out from under it and watched as the ship collapsed onto its face and exploded.

Elsewhere, Rook was in pursuit of the second new arrival; Scott was several lengths behind her as she chased the ship across wooded valleys and dry fingers of foot-hills. The lieutenant's face came up on the red VT's cock-pit commo screen.

"That's enough, Rook—let it go."

"But we can't let this one report that it found us," she pointed out. "We've gotta finish it."

"Forget it," Scott told her more strongly. "They're on to us already, or we wouldn't have had that little skirmish back there. Swing around."

Rook glared at Scott's screen image, then began to ease the VT off its pursuit heading. She couldn't help but notice how beautiful the land was below her—green hills and meadows, in startling contrast to the barrenness of the high ground. She saw a town and alerted Scott to her find.

"It doesn't look like anybody's home," she commented as the two fighters completed a quick flyby.

Scott was silent for a moment, then said: "That'll be perfect."

"Perfect for what?" she asked him. But he had nothing further to say.

They all agreed that the village must have been a de-lightful place when it was alive. Now it was just a motley collection of buildings and houses (spanning several hundred years of architectural styles), but nothing could diminish the tranquillity of the valley itself or the beauty of the surrounding mountains.

Scott ordered the Veritechs in and instructed Rand to assist Lunk with whatever repairs the APC required; af-terward the two men were to join the others in town, but Marlene and Annie were to wait until they received an all clear before coming down from the hills.

A building-to-building search of the place revealed lit-tle in the way of supplies, but Lancer stumbled across one item that prompted a scheme to turn the tables on the Invid Troopers in the nearby hive—as well as carry out the more prosaic surprise Scott had in mind for Annie. What he had found—hidden in a barn on the outskirts of town—was a device known as a bio-emulator, a Protoculture-powered instrument that was capable of mimicking the energy emanations of a supply-sized cache of the pure stuff. It had been developed not by the resistance but by the black market racketeers at the close of the Second Robotech War, for luring Southern Cross personnel to their deaths.

Given top billing in Scott's reworked plan was an unusual building that dominated the town, a circular structure with a columned cupola adorning its domed roof that had once served as an armory. Installation of the bio-emulator setup required a certain amount of group effort to conceal wiring and such, but the original plan, the prosaic one, called for little more than setting up several strategically placed rocket launchers and breaking out some of the supplies the team had brought with it from the Rocky Mountains underground complex. The freedom fighters split up into two teams, with Rook and Rand handling the indoor chores while Lunk and Lancer worked together rigging the armory building with charges. Scott did what he did best: he supervised.

Then Rand was sent to fetch the two women.

The sun was setting, huge and golden, and Annie and Marlene were still waiting in the mountains, sitting side by side on the rock with a western view.

"I guess birthdays are very special days," Marlene was saying consolingly. "I wish I could remember if I ever had one."

"Oh, you've had one," said Annie. "I don't think there's any way around that."

"Do they always make you unhappy?"

Annie brought her knees to her chest and put her head in her hands. "Let's just say that it's hard to be happy when every single one of your birthdays is a disaster."

"But Annie, were they all bad?"

The young girl was sniffling now, her eyes closed.

There was a time, she recalled, when things could have been pleasant but weren't. A time before the Invid inva-

sion, when her parents and Mr. Widget were still alive,
when the Northlands were embroiled in war with the Robotech Masters, and the Southlands prospered. Before
the bombs . . . when she still had a home.

She could see herself in that simple shingled house,
dressed in her yellow pants and blouse, reading the card
they had given her and gazing at the cake her mom had
bought at the market, left alone to puzzle out why they
couldn't stay to enjoy it with her, why they always seemed
to have more important things to do. She could hear her
mother's voice still: *Your father and I won't be back till
late, Annie, so when you've finished your little party, be
sure to clean up all the dishes and put yourself to bed at a
decent hour, all right? Well, good-bye, honey, and, oh yes,
happy birthday. . . .*

"I don't know how many times I prayed that just once
I could have a real birthday party with friends and family
like everybody else in the world."

"I don't think there's anything worse than being alone
on your birthday. Well, I guess I wasn't completely alone
. . . at least my friend Mr. Widget was there to help me eat
my birthday cake."

"Who?"

"He was my cat. . . . He's gone now. . . ."

"Oh," Marlene said softly, trying to understand.

Annie looked up into a pale yellow sky, wisps of lavender clouds. "Jeez, when did it get so dark? I wonder
where the others are." The sun was already down now.
"Thank goodness it won't be my birthday for much
longer," she sighed.

All at once the two women heard growling noises
coming from the trees behind them. They wrapped their
arms around each other and waited for the worst. The
growling grew louder, and Annie began to scream,
clutching at her friend; then Rand appeared out of the
darkness with a big hi and a smile on his face.

"Rand, you *jerk*!" Annie yelled.

He snorted and walked over to them. "All right, all
right, calm down. I should've known you'd be a nervous

wreck by now. But let's get going; we have to go meet the others."

"But where's the Cyclone?" Marlene wanted to know, her arm still around Annie's shoulders.

Rand shook his head. "I'm afraid I can't offer you a ride. It's too risky to use any of our mecha. This whole area is crawling with Invid."

Marlene gasped. Strange that she didn't *feel* their presence.

"Scott and the others are holed up in the village," Rand added after a moment. "There's no way we can get through."

"That tears it. . . ." said Annie.

Marlene gave her a reassuring hug. "I'm afraid it's going to be another birthday without a party, Annie. We're sorry."

Rand made a scoffing sound. "I hate to tell you this, but we've got a lot more important things to worry about than Annie's birthday. Now, come on."

He led them off through the woods to the edge of the hill overlooking town, trying to maintain that same hard look that wouldn't give away the surprise. But he knew that the act must be killing her and began to wonder about the more sinister side of surprises.

"That big house down there on the left," he gestured. "We've gotta try and make a run for it."

"It's so spooky-looking," Annie said, burying her face in Marlene's breast. "I'm scared."

"Are you sure Scott's down there?"

"Everybody's down there," Rand told her. "At least, they were when I left. . . . I hope nothing's happened." He started off down the hill. "Follow me."

It was a simple brick affair with a large chimney, curved-top windows and doors, and two small dormers. They hid together behind a tree at the edge of the walk. Rand ran to the door and motioned for them to join him quietly but quickly. Annie was making frightened sounds.

"It's dark in here, so watch out," he cautioned them as

he opened the door. "Scott, I'm back," he whispered into the darkness. "Where are you?"

Annie was the last through the door, and by that time Marlene and Rand were gone. She called out to them, quietly at first but with increasing panic in her voice. "What happened to everybody?" she asked pleadingly as she moved across the floor, unable to see her hand in front of her face.

"Why does everybody always abandon me?"

"Annie, over here," someone called out from somewhere.

"Rook, is that you?" she answered, her voice a tremolo.

Suddenly there were flashes of light in the blackness, then a brightness she had to hide her eyes from. But again someone called out to her: "Open your eyes, Annie."

And when she looked, she saw all her friends, gathered around a round table that had been set for seven, with plates and wine goblets and platters of food and a large birthday cake decorated with seventeen candles. And everyone was wishing her happy birthday.

Lunk was standing over her with the cake in his hands.

"Are you putting me on?" she asked them.

"It's your favorite," he told her. "Mint chocolate."

"And look what I made for you," Rook said, showing her a knitted scarf.

"Happy birthday, Annie," said Marlene. "At last."

Annie stared at everyone for a moment, found that she couldn't take it, and ran outdoors to weep; there she said thank you to the stars.

CHAPTER
EIGHT

Dad didn't plan a career as a voyeur—at least, not consciously. He just kept finding himself looking here when he should have been looking there, stumbling onto this when he should have been busying himself with that... Until the incident at the baths. But I sometimes wonder how much Mom encouraged Dad's behavior. I asked her about it once, and the only thing she would tell me was that Dad got what he had coming. Then she grinned.

Maria Bartley-Rand, *Flower of Life:*
Journey Beyond Protoculture

THE CAKE, THE SWEETS, AND THE GIFTS WERE ONLY
the start of the surprises Scott and the team had in store
for Annie, but after a few sips of wine it turned out that
Annie had some surprises of her own.

She was playing the celebrity host to their toasts and
compliments now, using her wineglass as a prop microphone and modeling the pink chiffon dress Rook had
given her. Her hair was brushed and parted in the center,
for once free of the funky E.T. cap she was seldom seen
without.

"To the cutest little freedom fighter around," Scott
said from the table, lifting his glass.

"Thank you, thank you, ladies and gentlemen," Annie
directed to her audience. "I would also like to thank my
designer, Miss Rook Bartley, for this elegant gown."

Rook took in the cheers with a noticeable blush. She
hadn't done more than tailor the dress down to Annie's

size. And unfortunately, she had gone a little high on the hem; the dress made Annie look about six years old, but no one was pointing this out. The yellow knee socks and brown pumps didn't help any, but they had taken what they could from the sub city, with little thought given to coordinating an outfit.

"Rook, I didn't know you were so...so *domestic*," Scott said from across the room.

Rook saw the bemused look on his face but ignored it. "It looks great on you," she told Annie, throwing the lieutenant a look out of the corner of her eye.

"Thanks! I feel like a beauty queen!" Annie tried a pirouette, giggling all the while, and almost lost her balance.

Cross-legged on the floor, Rand stifled a laugh. "One thing's for sure—you're no ballerina!"

Annie looked at him and shook her head as though to clear it. "And now the moment you've all been waiting for," she said like an emcee. "Approaching the judges' runway is our next contestant for the title of Miss Birthday Girl!"

Lunk and the others caught on to the act and applauded.

Annie switched to a squeaky parody of her own voice. "Thank you," she said into the wineglass. "My name's Annie. I'm four-foot-seven with blue eyes, and I'm often complimented on my personality." As she sauntered by Rand, she flashed some thigh and slipped him a wink. "And my legs aren't bad, either, big boy."

"I'll say," Rand enthused, knocking back another goblet of wine.

Annie cozied up to Lunk next. "Oh, I can't tell you how happy I am to be here! It's just too thrilling for words!" She gave him a light peck on the cheek and moved away from the table, snatching up his glass of wine.

"Hey, wait a second, that's not fair!" Rand protested while everyone else laughed. "If a contestant kisses one of the judges, she's gotta kiss all of them."

Annie had backed away tipsily to clink glasses with Lancer.

"Gee, do I have to?"

"Yep. Them's the rules."

"Well, pucker up then," she said on her way over to Rand. But as he stood up and offered his lips, she stuck one of the wineglasses in his mouth. Annie dismissed the laughter and sidled up to Scott, who was leaning against the wall. "Now, don't anybody move, because my very favorite part is coming up next—the *swimsuit competition*!" As Scott's eyebrows went up, she reached up and shut his eyes with her fingertips. "But *you* don't get to watch, you dirty old man!"

"That's telling him, Annie!" Rook encouraged her.

Rand said, "Well, she's got my vote."

"Yeah," from Lunk, getting to his feet.

Rook seconded the vote, and everyone else said, "Agreed!"

"It's unanimous, Annie," Rook announced. "You are the new Miss Birthday Girl!"

Annie skipped over to the curtained window while they toasted her easy victory. "Jeepers, I don't know what to say!" Then suddenly it was her natural voice once again, full of emotion and sincerity:

"Except that this is the happiest night of my life."

But far above the spirited celebration, some uninvited guests were converging on the deserted village: an Invid patrol from the nearby hive, now under the leadership of Corg himself. He had narrowly escaped being blown to bits by the explosions that had destroyed the underground city, and the Regis had granted him a new command ship of the same design as the original.

"Are we approaching the site of the disturbance?" Corg inquired into his cockpit communicator.

The source of active Protoculture readings recently received by the hive monitors had been traced to the village, and the Regis was certain that the Robotech rebels had made their way here. She was just as certain there would be no escape for them now.

"Estimated arrival time: five point two minutes," she told Corg through the command net that linked her with her troops.

Corg glanced out over the landscape from the cockpit of his ship and thought: *The thrill of approaching victory makes me feel almost . . . Human!*

The women were cleaning up—by choice, not design. Normally they wouldn't have even bothered to tidy up, but there was something about the house and the town itself that brought out sentiments most of them thought they had left behind. Marlene was a little puzzled by it all, but she volunteered to help Rook clear the table and clean the glasses and plates. The luxury of running water was more than enough for Rook, and she really had her mind on the hot bath she planned to take once the supplies were repacked.

"I've never seen Annie so excited," she was telling Marlene now. "This is one birthday she'll never forget." Annie was peacefully asleep in a chair nearby. "I never thought I'd live to see her wearing a dress like a regular little girl."

Scott was outside the window, eavesdropping, his handgun raised. Lancer found him there and wondered what it was all about.

"You're concerned about Marlene, aren't you?"

"Well, what about you, Lancer? Don't you get the feeling there's something mysterious about her? And I don't just mean the amnesia. It goes beyond that . . . like she's never had a past to remember. Like . . ."

"Like what, Scott? Go on, say it."

But Scott simply tightened his mouth and shook his head.

Lancer sighed knowingly but wasn't about to open up his own thoughts if Scott couldn't bring himself to do the same. "I don't think that she's going to murder us all in our sleep, Scott. But I agree that she's an unusual woman. Maybe we just have to give her some time to come out of it."

Scott gave him a dubious look and was about to press the point, but just then Rand broke into the conversation.

"Hey, guys, do you really think the Invid might show up tonight?"

There was something about Rand's tone that suggested more than his usual concern, almost as if he had other plans. But Lancer chose to reply to his remark, not to the unsaid things. "There's no sign of them yet," Lancer told him. "And believe me, that's just the way I want it. I think I've had more than enough entertainment for one day."

Rand tittered, delighted. "Well, maybe you've had enough. But as far as I'm concerned the party's just beginning."

Lancer beetled his brows. "Rand, what exactly do you have in mind?"

When Rook and Marlene finished the dishes, they woke Annie up and surprised her with a bag of peppermints they hadn't brought out at the party.

"Peppermints!"

Rook patted her on the shoulder. "I knew those bags you took wouldn't last."

Annie was handling the bag lovingly one moment, and the next she was crying. "When I think that I'm having a real birthday after wanting one so badly...with peppermints and everything..." She buried her face against Marlene.

"We're just glad you enjoyed it," Rook said, smiling. "The only problem is we only get to do it once a year." She yawned and stretched. "And now, something for the three of us to enjoy together...."

The bathroom was in the rear of the house; it was a completely tiled room with a shower stall and a sunken tub large enough for four. Rand had been there when Rook made the discovery, and he knew it was only a mat-

ter of time before she would go back to avail herself of
the pleasures of an honest-to-goodness hot bath. So he
had already stationed himself below the room's only window well before the time Rook, Marlene, and Annie entered. He couldn't believe his luck when he realized that
all three were about to take the plunge.

He had actually convinced himself that he had no idea
just what the room contained. As far as he or anyone else
was concerned, he was merely standing guard out here
while the rest of the guys dillydallied out front, cleaning
their weapons and waiting for the Invid to home in on
that device Lancer had rigged in the armory. Therefore, it
was entirely understandable that he poke his head up to
that window at the first sign of any unusual noises, because who knew what was lurking around in these supposedly deserted villages?

What he hadn't figured on was the damn window being
quite so high; he was forced to stand on the rather shaky
woodpile underneath it in order to peer in. And it was
only then that he realized the window glass itself was
frosted—not opaque but certainly a lot less clear than he
would have liked. And the steam from all that hot water
wasn't helping any, either.

Nevertheless, he was able to discern a good deal of
what was going on. He knew, for example, that that was
Marlene stepping out of her pants, and Annie discarding
her dress, and Rook slipping off her jumpsuit and bra and
panties. . . . It was just the *details* that were left to his
imagination. And the need to know those details soon
had him on tiptoe atop the woodpile, eyes and cupped
hands pressed to the glass.

Annie was already in the sunken tub when the first
logs began to slip under his feet.

"It sure is warm enough," she was saying. "I feel like a
lobster." Naked, Rook and Marlene were laughing playfully but not loud enough to cover up the sounds from
outside the window.

Rand gripped the windowsill, held his breath, and
tried to *will* the logs silent, but they just kept rolling off

the top of the pile and crashing against the side of the house. At first he wasn't sure if the women had heard anything, nor could he be sure they were looking his way. But the bathroom was awfully quiet all of a sudden. . . .

I'm just investigating these strange sounds, Rand said to himself over and over. *I'm just investigating these strange sounds—*

"Hey, is there somebody out there?!" Annie asked.

Rand heard her and started to back off, but the pile gave way again and sent him down on his butt to the ground. By the time he turned around, the window had been thrown open, and in addition to clouds of steam came a bucketful of ice-cold water that caught him squarely on the back and seemed to lift him right off the ground.

"That oughta cool you down, Rand," he heard Rook saying.

"That's what I get for trying to be helpful?!" he shouted in return, running off toward the front of the house.

Overhead, the Invid squadron closed in on the village, a constellation of evil moving across the heavens.

"Estimated three point seven three minutes to objective," Corg told his troops. "Focus scanning systems on Protoculture activity. And remember: These are Robotech rebels. They are not to be neutralized for the farms; they are to be destroyed."

Scott and the others had moved indoors by the time Rand entered, towel-drying his hair and trying to work some warmth into his scalp. Lunk was spreading out the sleeping bags, and Scott seemed to be spit-polishing the muzzle of one of the assault rifles.

"I'm starting to think maybe the Invid aren't as stupid as we thought they were," Lancer was saying from the window.

"Don't worry, they won't let us down," Scott told him. "Just keep your eyes peeled."

Shivering, Rand draped the towel around his neck. "Whew!" he said loudly enough to capture everyone's attention. "I've never been able to figure women out. They go on and on about how men don't appreciate them, and when we *do* go out of our way to appreciate them, they start screaming bloody murder like it was all news to them."

Lancer threw him a disapproving look. "There's a big difference between appreciating them and leering at them, Rand."

"Ah, what do *you* know about it?" Rand countered angrily.

Scott ignored the two of them and asked Lunk about the so-called Roman candles he had set up outside.

"It's just my part of the surprise for Annie's birthday," Lunk explained.

Meanwhile, the birthday girl was back in the tub having her hair washed by Rook. She asked Marlene if she had ever been in love.

"Scott asked me the same question," Marlene said, soaping herself up, "and I have to give you the same answer I gave him: I know it must sound strange, but I honestly don't remember."

"How can you not remember if you were in love?" Annie said in amazement.

Marlene shrugged. "I've forgotten everything. I'm a living, breathing, walking blank—I can't even remember what my *purpose* in life is."

"Your purpose in life is to find a man," Annie told her with certainty. "Everyone knows that. Rook has found herself a man."

Rook stopped massaging Annie's hair and gently twisted her head around. "If you're talking about Rand," she said into Annie's face, "let me enlighten you about a thing or two. First of all, about this business of *needing* a man—*huh*?!"

Marlene was staring at them in stark terror.

"They've come!" she screamed. "The Invid are here!"

Inside the armory the bio-emulator continued its false siren song.

The men were also aware that the Invid had arrived, and the ships were doing just what the plan called for: forming a circle around the building.

"Remind me to congratulate the wise guy who invented that bio-emulator," Lancer said, arming his blaster. "It's working like a charm."

Scott was the first through the open window. "Lunk, stay with the women. And Rand, grab those detonators on your way out. Time for this evening's next surprise."

While Scott, Lancer, and Rand were stealing away from the house, Corg was issuing orders to his troops. They had put down in formation fifty yards from the circular structure and were spreading out to take up positions. The voice of the Regis came across the communications net.

"You have reached the focus of the disturbance."

"Deploy for complete encirclement of the Robotech rebels," Corg ordered. "None of them must be allowed to slip through our grasp."

"Scanners indicate the Protoculture emanations are definitely Robotech in origin. . . ." the Regis updated as the combat units fanned out.

"We will not fail you this time, my queen," Corg started to say, but the Regis had something to add.

"However, the nature of your readings is disturbing. The Protoculture activity is unusually steady in its dispersal pattern. We detect no modulations or fluctuations of any kind—almost as if the matrix waverings were being synthetically produced."

"Nonsense! Humans are incapable of such deception!" He already had the cannon arm of his ship raised.

The cockpit displays in Corg's ship began to flash as new data was received and transmitted. "Our bio-detectors register no sign of Human movement within the structure," the Regis continued. "Probability cortex indicates likelihood of a trap, increasing by a factor of one hundred for every five seconds you remain in present situation. . . ."

Corg reached out and shut down the audio signals. "Open fire!" he commanded.

Streams of annihilation discs began to tear into the circular walls of the armory, and explosions erupted across the face of the dome, filling the cool air with the sound of thunder and throwing pyrotechnic light into the night sky. Corg continued to scream "Fire! Fire!" urging his troops on to greater heights of destructive catharsis, pouring out all the misunderstood feelings and frustrations that were part of the life the Regis had given him.

But outside the circle of pincer-clawed ships, the Humans had some feelings of their own to express. And suddenly there were explosions coming from the trees that surrounded the building, explosions Corg could not understand. He watched as his Troopers were hurled violently against one another and sent smashing into the building's stone walls. Others were lifted off the ground by the force of the blasts. Claws, scanners, and pieces of hardware became fiery-hot projectiles blown from his decimated squadron. The hull of his own ship was holed with shrapnel and pieces of airborne debris, and all at once he felt himself overturned, felled by a storm of enemy fire. Shock Troopers were taken out while they attempted to lift off, erupting like brilliant balls of flame, raining pieces of themselves throughout the field.

"Easy as shooting fish in a barrel," Rand said from the perimeter.

Lunk, too, was yahooing from the window of the house. The women had joined him in the front room, clad only in bath towels. Annie was so excited, she leapt clear out of her towel, breasts bobbing up and down, but Lunk was too preoccupied with the explosions to notice.

"*Ka-boom!* Yeah! I *love* this stuff!"

"Wow! This is the *best* birthday present of all!"

Meanwhile the few remaining Invid ships, including the command ship, were taking to the skies in retreat.

"Okay, we're free to use the Alphas," Scott told Lancer and Rand. "Let's move it!"

The three men ran past the house to the concealed fighters, waving back to Lunk and their towel-clad teammates. Lancer stopped to say: "Don't anyone go to bed yet, because we fly-boys have one more surprise in store!"

"Another surprise?" Annie asked him, adjusting her towel. "Just what are you guys up to now?"

"Just you wait and see," Lancer said, running off to catch up with Scott.

Lunk had jumped out of the window and was showing Annie an enigmatic grin. "I've got one of my own," he added, rushing away.

The women exchanged puzzled looks and then some as the sky began to fill with starburst explosions.

Rook laughed. "He wasn't kidding: they really are Roman candle launchers."

Annie looked at her. "You mean you knew all along?"

"Only some of it."

Scott was glad to see that the fireworks had only added to the enemy's confusion. The Invid ships were streaking away, trying desperately to evade the fireworks, fooled into thinking they were some sort of lethal missile.

In fact, Corg was reporting as much to the Regis while he led his ragtag troops back toward the hive.

But Scott didn't call for pursuit. Instead, the Alphas formed up on his lead and went through the unrehearsed moves they had discussed earlier that day.

"It's wonderful, isn't it, Annie?" Marlene said from the window of the house.

"I've never had a birthday like this," the teenager was saying.

"I don't think *any* of us have had a birthday like this," said Rook.

And it's really happening . . . it's not a dream!

The women could see the skywriting now, and Rook read the words: "Happy . . . Birthday. . ."

Up above, Rand said: "I'll bet Admiral Hunter never had you guys doing this with your Alpha Fighters, huh, Scott?"

Scott smiled, then realized that Rand was off course somehow. "What are you doing down there?" he asked.

Rand made no response and completed his part of the skywriting moves. From the window, the three women watched as his Alpha spelled out "Mint" under the birthday greeting.

Rook snorted. "So *that's* why Rand wanted to write your name."

"Oh, well," Annie sighed, turning away from the window for a moment. "I guess it's a lot better nickname than 'Peewee.'"

CHAPTER
NINE

The planet [Earth] secured, the Regis then had to decide what to do about the surviving Human population. She knew from past experience that Humans could be a dangerous lot, even these Terrans, who seemed somehow inferior to the Tirolian species. Eventually it would occur to her to use a percentage of the survivors as laborers in the Protoculture farms, but that was only after what can best be described as a trial-and-error period, during which an unlucky assortment were subjected to experiments too gruesome to dwell on. Fortunately, most of the laboratory cases died outright or soon thereafter, though a scant few remained to wander their ravaged homeworld less than Human.

Bloom Nesterfig, *Social Organization of the Invid*

AS RAND TOLD IT:

"The soldiers had been dead a week, but the town was just getting around to burying them when we rode in . . . I have to admit that I had put no stock in the rumors we had been hearing on the road, but sure enough, the town had its own contingent of Robotech soldiers, Mars Division, like Scott, survivors from that same ill-fated assault on Earth. It was remarkable enough to come across a populated village so near the Invid control zone, but to find fellow soldiers as well was almost more than Scott could bear. I still have an image of him parked in the middle of that town's dust bowl of a main street, straddling the Cyc with a big grin on his face and broadcasting our arrival to one and all over the mecha's externals. When only a handful of folks wandered out to greet us, I remember thinking: *Here we go again; just another ghost town run by a bunch of rubes and rogues*. But then we learned that everyone that counted was at the graveyard.

"That's where Scott ran into the robbies. Not straight away, though; there was a funeral service in progress, so we all just hung around on the outskirts of the action until the crowds thinned. There were church bells ringing in the distance. After that, Scott went in to introduce himself to the one soldier who seemed to be in charge—a tall officer, wearing shades and a high-collared gray uniform like Scott's. I never did catch the dude's name; come to think of it, I don't think the two of us exchanged more than a brief handshake the whole time we were in town.

"It turned out that they had been there for some months; they had put down as a unit somewhere south of Reflex Point and worked their way into the Northlands, hoping to come across other Mars Division survivors. They saw a lot of action early on, but now they were just hanging on, waiting for the big one to go down. They had all heard of Scott and were excited to learn that the Expeditionary Force was indeed on its way. They had a good deal of intelligence dope on Reflex Point, but there was something they needed to talk about before getting down to basics.

"There were three fresh graves in the cemetery, marked by simple wooden crosses, one of which was crowned with a 'thinking cap,' its faceguard shattered. I naturally assumed that the Invid had paid the town a visit and left their usual calling cards, but that wasn't the case. It seems that the three had been gunned down by some lone biker who went by the name of Dusty Ayres. These latest murders brought the total to eleven.

"Scott was flipped out to learn that someone other than the Invid were killing soldiers; he asked the officer about Ayres.

"'We don't know much about him,' the man replied. 'Except that he seems to have it in for soldiers.' The officer threw his men a dirty look. 'Some people claim he can't be killed.'

"I didn't like hearing this, but for Scott it explained

how three soldiers could be brought down by one loner. I didn't bother to point out that a man needn't be *invulnerable* to get the better of a group, because it was obvious that Scott was already thinking *Invid*. No *Human* could do such a thing. As if he had to be reminded about the sympathizers we had met along the way. Wolff, to name just one . . .

"'Sounds like a real mystery man,' Lancer offered. 'And nobody knows why he's here, huh?'

"Scott said more firmly, 'You must know more about this guy.'

"I was glad to see that I wasn't the only suspicious one among us. But the officer wasn't swayed to say any more about Ayres. 'I wish I had more.' The man shrugged. 'Everything's just rumors right now.'

"'Dusty Ayres, you say,' Scott repeated.

"'That's the only name I've ever heard him called.'

"Lancer brought up the sympathizer idea.

"Lunk punched his open hand. 'I just wish he'd try to start something with us. I'd break his face.'

"*Terrific*, I thought. I looked at the three graves and wondered how our helmets would look on those crosses.

"'He's got to be hunted down,' the officer told Scott. 'Will you join us, Lieutenant?'

"Scott was wary. 'I'm not going to involve any of my people until I know more about this matter.'

"'Sure thing, Lieutenant. You take your time. While the rest of us die . . .'

"I sucked in my breath; you just didn't go around saying things like this to Scott unless you were already holding an H90 to his head. Fortunately, Lancer stepped in to intervene. Only thing was, he actually took it upon himself to volunteer our services. Lunk, the big lug, seconded it, and I guess that was enough for Scott.

"'You won't regret it, Lieutenant,' the officer thanked us.

"I, of course, *already* regretted it; but everyone else was talking tough and anxious to get started."

* * *

"We left Annie and Marlene behind—much to our birthday girl's dismay. After all, she had been 'seventeen' for a full week now, and didn't that entitle her to share in the 'fun stuff'? Those were her words: *'It simply isn't fair!'*

"Rook got a big charge out of this but didn't bring it up until later, after we had split up into several groups.

"'Fair? Did she really say "fair"?'

"I repeated Annie's exact words into my helmet mike and laughed. We were both in battle armor now and cruising side by side across the barren stretch where Ayres had last been seen, close to where the bodies of the three soldiers had been found. The area had once been called 'the Panhandle,' for reasons unknown, but it was just plain desert to us, no different from the wastes we had been traveling through since leaving the mountains behind. Scott and Lancer were off somewhere south of us, and Lunk was riding with a few of the other soldiers.

"I confessed to Rook how pissed off I was by the whole deal. 'I mean, what happened to Reflex Point? Suddenly we're a posse for hire, or what?'

"For once, Rook actually agreed with me. Strange, because she had been ignoring me since the stunt I pulled at the bathroom window. I had been taking a kind of apologetic, conciliatory tone with her ever since and now suggested that we split up to cover more ground. But she didn't want to hear it.

"'If it's all the same to you, I'd feel better about this if we stayed together.'

"I certainly didn't need to be told twice, and I'm sure I was smiling inside my helmet when the Invid ships appeared over the hills.

"'Guess we're just not meant to be together!' Rook shouted over the net just before we separated.

"There were five ships bearing down on us: four rust-brown pincer-armed combat units led by one of the new blue and white monsters we had been up against in the underground city. It was bound to happen—our Cycs were probably putting off the only 'Culture vibes for miles around—and I had said as much before we split up, but nobody wanted to hear it.

"The leader dropped some fire at our tails, but we were flat out now and just out of range. The big guy stuck with me after we separated, but Rook had her hands full with the Pincer craft. I saw her slalom through a field of explosions, then launch and reconfigure to Battle Armor mode. She put down almost immediately and took out one of her pursuers with a single Scorpion loosed in the nick of time. I wanted to applaud her, but I was too busy dodging blasts from that leader ship. There was a low mesa directly in my path, and I used it to my advantage by snaking around its base and going over to Battle Armor before the Invid ship completed its own turn. I hovered near the eroded wall of the butte, trading shots with the ship, but I couldn't zero in on any vulnerable spots. The Invid was up on its armored legs, towering over me, loosing anni discs from two small weapons ports tucked under its chin—guns I didn't know existed until just then. But after a minute of this I took off to find Rook. As the two of us landed side by side, she said, 'We've gotta stop meeting like this.'

"I would have laughed if another blast from the leader hadn't forced us into a rapid launch. And when we put down again, there was panic in Rook's voice. 'It's bad, Rand! There's just too many of them!'

"'It's *always* bad!' I shouted back. 'Just range in on the big one and give it your best shot!'

"The four remaining ships had regrouped and were closing in on us. We both raised our forearm launch tubes, and it was then that Rook spied something atop one of the nearby hills. I turned in time to catch a metallic glint.

"'What is that?' Rook asked.

"I told her I had no idea. 'But if it's not friendly, we're in real trouble.'

"The Invid had also caught sight of the thing, and it was apparent an instant later that they found it to be a more appealing target. The ships zoomed past us without a shot, making straight for the hilltop. I thought it might be Scott or maybe Lunk in the APC, but I had to guess again, because instead of attacking, the ships simply moved off, as though recalled unexpectedly.

"'I guess it's friendly,' Rook was saying, stepping out for a better view of the thing. But that didn't make sense, I told her, following her lead. If it was friendly to us, it would have been fired upon. My guess was that it was an Invid command ship—perhaps that orange and green one we had been seeing lately.

"But as the thing came into view, we saw that it was some kind of sidecarred cycle, piloted by a man wearing a poncho and Western-style hat. We were trading looks with him when he suddenly fell off the bike, obviously *shot*!"

"The rogue was hurt, but well enough to ride. Rook insisted on seeing what she could do for the wound in his arm, and he led us to a patch of forest that bordered the river we had crossed on our way into town. He was tall and good-looking in a derelict sort of way. His hair was parted in the center and fell below his shoulders, and he was in need of a shave and a good scrubbing, but none of that seemed to bother Rook. She was playing nurse to his silent cowboy and enjoying herself. I pretended to interest myself in the guy's mecha, which *was* unusual—it had twin scrambler-type exhaust stacks and a multimissile launch rack (the thing I had taken for a sidecar)—but I didn't miss a word of their conversation. I had already convinced myself that the guy was an Invid plant. He claimed to be as surprised as we were that the Invid had flown off without frying all of us, but I wasn't buying any of it.

"Rook and I had taken off our battle armor. The stranger was sitting down with his back against a tree, the poncho draped over one shoulder, letting Rook probe around inside his wound with a pair of tweezers from one of the Cyc's first-aid kits. What she fished from his arm turned out to be an old-fashioned *bullet*! But even this didn't seem to faze Rook.

"'This should help some,' she said, dropping the small projectile on the ground and treating the wound with antiseptic solution.

"The man thanked her in the same flat, clipped tone I was already beginning to dislike. A breeze rustled through the woods just then, and I gazed up and saw something that reinforced my suspicions about the guy. The wind revealed what the poncho had intended to hide: that his arm and a good portion of his chest were covered with some sort of gleaming alloy. Rook must have seen it, too, because I heard her gasp while asking the rogue's name.

"'Excuse me, mister. I didn't mean to embarrass you,' she hastened to add. 'What happened to you?'

"'Well, I'm glad you didn't run away when you saw it,' the stranger drawled. 'That's how most react. . . . Let's just say it's a little present from our friends the Invid. You could say I'm just lucky that they left me alive at all.'

"Rook made a face. 'I guess it could've been worse. . . .' She asked the man to remove his poncho and dabbed at the wound with gauze before beginning to dress it. 'At least you got away from them.' Rook winked at him flirtatiously. 'Now, I'm no doctor, so you better not let this rest until you see one.'

"The rogue almost smiled—or maybe that tight-lipped grin *was* his idea of a smile. But in any case, he said: 'What'd you say your name was, missy—Rook? Well, Rook, I just can't thank you enough for helping a stranger out.'

"Rook had a blushing response all ready for him. I saw her gesture to the bullet. 'But this isn't from any Invid,' she started to say. 'They don't have anything this primitive in their arsenal.'

"The stranger was about to reply, but I stepped in with my Gallant drawn and aimed at his midsection. 'You're right, Rook. And those Invid ships didn't just forget about us, either. This rogue's a spy.'

"'What are you doing?!' Rook shouted at me. 'Put that thing away!'

"'Not till I find out what it is about his guy that makes the Invid run away, or how he ended up with a bullet in his arm.'

"The rogue just stared, like he was sorry for me or something. 'If you have to know, the bullet came from my own gun. It discharged by accident. Check near the seat of the cycle if you don't believe me, kid. You'll find an antique six-gun under—'

"'You're an Invid agent,' I snarled, ignoring the bit about the gun because it sounded too much like the truth.

"'If that was true, you'd be dead, kid.'

"This also sounded right, but I ignored it and motioned with the blaster for him to get up. Rook was already on her feet, cursing me.

"'He's not our enemy, Rand. Besides—he's *hurt*!'

"I told her to stand out of the way and ordered the guy to his feet. He got up slowly, almost tiredly, and said we had helped him and he was grateful. 'I don't want anybody to get hurt.'

"I had the weapon straight out in front of me, and I guess I really didn't expect him to go for his gun. I even fired a warning shot into the tree behind him as his hand inched toward the holster, but he went for it anyway, confident that I wasn't about to kill him in cold blood, and caught me in the right hand with a stun blast, knocking the Gallant from my two-handed grip.

"That made *twice* when I should have fired first and asked questions later—first with Wolff and now with Mr. Clint McGlint. But so help me, if I'm ever drawing a bead on someone again...

"Anyhow, Rook ran over to me to take a look at my hand, dismissing it roughly when she saw that I was only mildly burned.

"'I hope you're satisfied!' she seethed. "You could have been killed!'

"The stranger threw me a look. 'Like I said, kid, if I was one of them, you woulda never left the sands alive.'

"I looked over at Rook, trying to sort through my feelings, and decided that it was all her fault for being so . . . *friendly.*

"Back then I was still struggling with jealousy."

"I let Rook and the stranger have a few moments of privacy by the river while I nursed my hand and wounded pride. But I didn't let it go on for long. The sun was going down, and I was certain that Scott and the others would be worrying about us. I had all but forgotten about Dusty Ayres and the search that had brought us out here to begin with.

"Rook and her new hero were too far off for me to hear, but I could tell by her posturing that things were getting a little too chummy, so I finally banged the Cyc into gear and rode in to break it up.

"'Sorry to *interrupt*, but it's time we headed back to town,' I told her. 'Thank your friend for his *hospitality* and let's get moving.'

"The stranger regarded me, then turned back to Rook. 'I have to leave anyway.'

"'Sorry to hear it,' I said.

"He ignored the comment. I tried to hurry Rook along and roared off, wanting no part of whatever good-byes the two planned to exchange.

"Rook caught up with me a few minutes later, and we rode a long way before either of us spoke. She repeated that I had been wrong about the man from the start—the man with no name. As he told it, he had been used as a guinea pig in some gruesome experiments the Invid had carried out shortly after they had defeated the Earth forces; apparently, the whole right side of his body had been vivisected and replaced with prostheses and alloy plating. Worse than that, his friends had stood by and made no attempt to rescue him. He was an unusually sensitive man, Rook insisted. and I had acted like a complete moron.

"I don't know why I didn't put two and two together then and figure out who the stranger was; I guess I was just too wrapped up in Rook's attachment to him to see the obvious. 'I have some unfinished business to take care of,' he had told her in response to her invitation to join us.

"Well, by the time we got back to town, I was convinced that I had been wrong and full of forgive and forget toward Rook. The open invitation didn't exactly *thrill* me, but I somehow managed to swallow my protests and keep still about it.

"'Rand, level with me,' Rook said when we were getting off the Cycs. 'Was I wrong to befriend that stranger?'

"'No,' I told her. 'You've gotta follow your feelings sometimes, no matter what.' Naturally I thought she was trying to get to the heart of the possessive feelings I had displayed. It was only later that I realized what was really on her mind: she had known all along just who it was she was helping and befriending. The question had nothing to do with *us*; it had to do with loyalties of an entirely different sort. . . .

"We had tracked down Scott and the gang to a saloon-restaurant straight out of an old Western movie. But if the place took me by surprise, the sight of Yellow Dancer nearly floored me. I suppose I had started to think of her as gone—a missing person—someone who had traveled the road with us for a short while and vanished, a casualty of this bizarre war. So to see Lancer now, in his turquoise tunic and helmet/bonnet, his pink belt and skin-tight pants, filled me with contrasting feelings. Scott and Lunk were at the bar knocking back a few while Yellow sang a very subdued 'Lonely Soldier Boy.'

"A couple of the town's soldiers came in just then, announcing that they had finally dug up a photo of this Dusty Ayres character, and they wanted to pass it around to us. Rook and I stood at the bar with the rest of them as the photo circulated. It was of course the face of our mysterious stranger. The cigarette in his mouth made him look even more sinister than he had appeared in the flesh.

"I was waiting for Rook to say something or at least throw me a look, but she didn't do either. I turned to her, my face all twisted up, and said:

" 'You *see*?—I was right all along!' "

CHAPTER
TEN

> *If the Ayres incident proved one thing, it was that Humans and Protoculture were basically immiscible. Invid and Protoculture? That was something else, as we shall see.*
>
> Mingtao, *Protoculture: Journey Beyond Mecha*

ROOK EDGED AWAY FROM THE BAR AND LEFT THE saloon. The sight of Dusty's photo in the hands of all those soldiers who were eager to see him killed, all those soldiers who had allegedly lost friends at his hands, had brought into question her earlier efforts on his behalf. Her flirtations. She sat in the dark on the saloon steps, while inside the soldiers drank and swore vengeance, and wondered why she always seemed to fall for the bad boys, the loners and rogues. It went back to Cavern City, she supposed, to Romy and the Angels and the days when she had been something of an outlaw herself. She couldn't deny, however, that she had seen something noble in Dusty's character. She thought back to that brief glimpse she had had of his chest plates and prosthetic arm. "My friends did nothing to stop them," she recalled him telling her. "They made no attempt to rescue me, or

at least put me out of my misery. . . . " Not that that justified his going on a murder spree.

Rook heard Rand's voice and glanced over her
shoulder in the direction of the saloon. He was telling the
men that he knew where Dusty could be found. But he
made no mention of the time he and Rook had spent with
him. He was being his usual protective self, and yet Rook
found that she was angry instead of grateful; she didn't
want to thank him as much as throttle him. Because
Rand, underneath all the arrogance and sarcasm, was actually a pretty sensitive man—in a hick sort of way.

Rook shut her eyes and pressed her hands to her forehead, as though in an attitude of prayer. *I knew he was
the one they were searching for, but it just doesn't seem
possible that he could be so cold-blooded. And maybe
Rand is right—maybe he is an Invid agent.* When she
looked up, she found Marlene standing in front of her.

"Are you all right?" Marlene asked her. "I saw how
upset you got in the saloon."

"I'm touched," Rook said nastily as Marlene sat down
beside her.

Marlene made a puzzled expression. "I guess I must
deserve that for some reason. . . . You see, I don't mean to
pry, but you just looked like you could use a friend."

Rook sighed and took Marlene's hand. "I'm sorry,
Marlene. In fact I was just thinking about friendship."

"Do you want to talk about it?"

Rook made Marlene promise that what she was about
to say would remain between them; then she told her
about the brief skirmish with the Invid ships and the
wounded rider she had helped. "It was Dusty Ayres,"
Rook confessed. "I think I knew right from the beginning, but I just didn't want to believe it. And after he told
me what he had been through, I started to feel sorry for
him. I probably wouldn't have said anything if that photo
hadn't turned up. Now I'm going to have to lie about it."

"But Rand won't say anything. He doesn't know what
you were feeling."

Rook showed a thin smile. "Oh, he knows, Marlene, he knows. . . ."

A light rain had begun, but a moment passed before Rook took any notice of it. She could hear the soldiers in the saloon discussing their plans to hunt Dusty down. Suddenly, she shot to her feet, startling Marlene. "I won't be able to rest until I see him again. Maybe I can convince him to surrender before he gets himself killed!"

Rook raced off, leaving Marlene alone in the rain.

An hour later, Scott was leading a Robotech posse across the sands. Rand was overhead in one of the Alphas (the Beta was close to depleted), directing the five Cyclone riders to where he and Rook had last seen the outlaw Ayres. The APC was trying to keep up with the group; Lunk had two of the town's soldiers with him. No one knew where Rook had gone; Rand had an idea, but he wasn't saying.

A heavy rain was falling, and the barren land had all the charm of a landscape in hell. But Scott was inured to the idiosyncrasies of the Earth's weather. Besides, he was obsessed with Ayres's capture, even though he had wanted no part of it initially. Perhaps it was because he was convinced that there was more to the story than anyone was telling him. A supposedly invulnerable outlaw who was systematically killing off Robotech soldiers . . . And yet the man wasn't thought to be an Invid agent, and *no one* had the slightest idea what was motivating him to murder. It just didn't add up. Scott was even beginning to suspect *Rand* of holding something back. It was obvious from the things he had said back in the saloon that he and Rook had had more than a passing encounter with Ayres. But why would Rand lie about it? Scott wondered. With Reflex Point almost close enough to touch (and with the new information the town's soldiers had supplied him), it was imperative that the mystery be solved so everyone could get back on track.

As if to reinforce Scott's concerns, a squadron of some fifteen Invid ships appeared suddenly out of the clouds.

"Invid at twelve o'clock!" Lancer reported over the net. "A bunch of 'em, too!"

Scott made a motion for the Cycloners to fan out. "Here we go, Rand," he sent up to the Alpha. "Standard battle plan!"

In the Veritech cockpit, Rand had to laugh. *Standard battle plan*. That was their little joke, meaning: *Do your best and we'll all try to keep from killing one another in the process.*

Rand wished them luck and threw his fighter into the thick of things. The squadron was composed of Pincer units and one blue leader that he could see; he managed to destroy one of the ships straight away but spent the next few minutes juking and dodging discs and laser fire from the rest. The blue especially was riding his tail with a vengeance.

"Too many of them!" he shouted over the net, upside down now and enmeshed by angry red bolts and streams of annihilation discs. "Where the hell is Rook when we need her?"

Elsewhere on the sands, Rook was confronting the outlaw. Ayres had almost fired on the red Veritech when it appeared but had stayed his hand at the last minute when he recognized Rook inside the cockpit. She was standing by the fighter's kowtowed nose now, mindless of the rain. Dusty was dressed in the same poncho and hat he had worn earlier; his all-terrain war machine was idling softly behind him. "You took a chance coming out here, Rook," he was telling her.

"I know that. But it was a chance I had to take, Dusty."

He grinned at her knowingly. "So you know my name, huh? And you just had to find out more about the mysterious killer. Is that it?"

"I suppose so," she started to say, wondering if she could bring herself to admit more.

"Well, there's nothing more to find out," he answered

before she could go on. "So get back in your fighter and forget about trying to involve yourself in this."

"But I'm *already* involved," Rook shouted. "I knew who you were this afternoon. I didn't need to learn that in town. And all I'm asking you for is an explanation."

Dusty started back to his cycle. "I've got things to do, Rook. I don't have time for this."

Rook pushed wet hair back from her face. "I guess I was naive to think I could keep you from killing again, so you leave me no choice...." She drew her blaster and leveled it at him. "I'm a soldier, Dusty, just like the rest of them. I have friends to protect."

She could see that she had surprised him, but he made no move for his weapon. "I don't want to hurt you, Rook—"

"Don't move or I'll fire," she warned him.

"You're making a mistake," he said after a moment. "Just put the blaster away and listen to me. Don't make me do something I'm going to regret."

Rook's nostrils flared, but she couldn't keep Dusty's words from undermining her will. She recalled how he had shot Rand, and she recalled the stories of his invulnerability... At last she lowered her weapon, and Dusty thanked her.

"You remember what I told you at the river, Rook? About the Invid's experiments with me?" He tossed the poncho over one shoulder and opened his shirt to give her a good look at the alloy plates that covered half his chest. "My *friends* let this happen to me, Rook. They stood by and let those monsters use me like a laboratory animal. They replaced my entire right side piece by piece with Protoculture-generated organs and these metallic prostheses." Ayres glared at her. "Do you really blame me for hunting them down?"

Rook lifted her head to answer him. "It must have been unbearable," she began on a sympathetic note. "But think about it, Dusty: you were a soldier once. Maybe your friends couldn't get to you. Maybe they tried and failed. And look what you're doing now: you're killing the only people who can avenge you. Your enemies are the Invid. How can you be sure they didn't implant something in your brain when they were carrying out those experiments—something that would *compel* you to attack your own friends."

Rook waited for him to respond. The latter possibility made a lot more sense to her than the former, because if Dusty's friends really had made an attempt to rescue him, why were they now acting like the whole deal was one big mystery to them? It was a moot point, though: Dusty was shaking his head, rejecting what she had said.

He raised his prosthesis into the cycle's headlamp and indicated eleven crosshatched marks engraved into the forearm alloy. "Each mark is a name I'd just as soon forget," he told her. "But I won't forget until I've killed every one of them!"

More than the marks, Rook could see the madness in Dusty's eyes. "I understand," she said softly.

He uttered a short maniacal laugh. "I was hoping you would, Rook." He goosed the cycle's throttle and pulled the hat down on his forehead. "I've got no gripe with your friends, but don't try to stop me—any of you."

Rook allowed him to ride off. *We'll meet again*, she told herself. *And I'll do what I have to do....*

Rand took out another Pincer unit with heat-seekers from the undercarriage launch rakes and reconfigured to Battloid mode, bringing the rifle/cannon out in the mecha's metalshod right fist.

"It looks like we've gotten ourselves into a hole this time," Lunk said from the ground, where the soldiers were pouring fire into the sky.

Employing the foot thrusters to stabilize the ship, he raised the weapon to high port position and bracketed yet another Invid in his sights. He triggered off a burst, catching the ship midsection. "Just keep firing," Rand told Lunk, while the enemy fell like a meteor.

Scott screeched his mecha to a halt and stood up,

straddling the seat to bring his assault rifle into play. In the distance at ground level, he saw a bright light moving toward him. "Something's coming!" he alerted the others.

"Let's hope it's on our side," said Lancer.

Lunk lowered his weapon to have a look at it. "It's sure moving fast!"

Suddenly the Invid ships ceased their attack and began forming up on the blue leader, as though to observe the arrival of the newcomer. Then Rand's voice cut through the net: "That's Dusty Ayres's machine!"

With a dozen Invid ships still overhead, Rand expected Scott would have had sense enough to pull back and regroup, but instead, he heard Scott say, "Let's get him!" and launch himself in pursuit of the outlaw. Two of the other Robotech soldiers followed his lead.

Dusty Ayres saw the Cyclones speeding toward him and flashed a satisfied grin. *Well, well, Steve and Kent driving out with their greetings*, he thought. *How considerate of them.* The launcher's panel slid to, and Ayres let his thumb hover over the trigger button. "Now *die!*" he screamed, and fired.

Missiles streaked from the rack and found their targets; the two riders were blown to bits. Scott squinted as flames geysered up out of the sands, instantly superheating the air and filling it up with the stench of death. "Outflank him!" Scott commanded Lancer and the fifth Cycloner. "We'll try a cross fire!"

The three Cyclones and the APC converged on the lone rider, announcing themselves with a horizontal storm of lethal rounds. But Ayres appeared to be weathering it all; his clothes were torn to shreds and aflame, but the man himself was unscathed.

"They were right, Scott! The guy's indestructible!" Lancer exclaimed.

Ayres answered the challenge with shots of deadly accuracy, first taking out the Cycloner, then picking off the soldiers in the APC one by one before loosing missiles against the vehicle itself. Lunk was thrown a good twenty feet from the fiery wreck; when he looked up, he saw

Scott hovering over Ayres in Battle Armor mode, dumping everything the mecha had against him. Lancer pulled up a moment later, and Scott put down beside the two of them.

"Nice shooting," said Lancer as the three of them regarded the ruin that was Dusty's cycle.

But it wasn't over yet: Ayres—at least something that *resembled* Ayres—was stepping from the flames.

"I must be seeing things!" Lunk cried.

Scott's eyes went wide beneath the helmet faceshield. "I wish I could say you needed glasses, but I'm seeing it, too!"

In the meantime, everyone had forgotten about Rand —all except the Invid Enforcer, that is. The rest of the ships were still in formation overhead, but the commander had pursued Rand to the ground. Still in Battloid mode, he was trying to go one on one with the thing, but his reconfigured fighter was an infant to the enemy's giant.

Fortunately, Rook came roaring to his aid not a moment too soon, somehow managing to pilot her red VT right through the Pincer combat units without a fight. Together, the two Veritechs turned on the Enforcer and brought it down with enough explosive heat to turn the rain to clouds of steam. When the Pincer Ship pilots saw this, they broke formation and fell on the Humans; but by now Rand and Rook were back to back, with the VTs' weapons systems synchronized. On Rand's command they launched all their remaining cluster rockets, and in the fireworks display that followed, every Invid ship was destroyed.

At the same time, Lancer was seeing fireworks of his own. The first to attack Ayres, he was the first down, toppled by a blow from the outlaw's bionic arm. Lunk was already out—he had fainted from shock—but Scott stepped forward now, raising his weapon and cautioning Ayres not to move. Confident inside the reconfigured mecha, Scott reasoned that Lancer's battle armor hadn't been enough to withstand the Human monster's strength, but surely Ayres couldn't bring a Cycloner down....

Scott tried to reason through it again a moment later, when he found himself flat on his back with Ayres standing over him aiming a blaster at his heart. He couldn't even recall the punch Ayres had thrown.

"Stay there," said Ayres. "Don't get up."

Who is to say what he might have done had the two Veritechs not put down on either side of him just then? Rook and Rand had the fighters in Guardian mode now; Rand leveled the rifle/cannon on Ayres while Rook leaped from her cockpit to face off with the gleaming half-Human outlaw.

"You told me it was just revenge, Dusty. That you weren't after the rest of us, remember?"

"They tried to kill me," Ayres threw back, training his hand weapon on her. The implication was clear: if Rand fired, Rook was going to die as well. No one was even certain at this point that the VT could really take Ayres out.

"Well, what did you expect them to do?" Rook screamed. "You're a murderer." She took two steps toward the muzzle of the weapon. "So you might as well start with me, because these people mean more to me than life itself. And if I thought that my helping you had contributed to their deaths, I couldn't live with myself." She gestured to her breast. "Go ahead, Dusty: right here, right here ..."

Scott, Lancer, and Lunk were urging Rook to get back, but she stood her ground.

Ayres glowered at her and extended his weapon, but a moment later, much to Rand's amazement and everyone else's relief, he lowered it.

"I couldn't do that," he said, unable to meet her eyes. "I just couldn't.... Maybe if I'd had friends like you, none of this would have happened. I told you: I've got no argument with any of you people."

In the midst of all this, the Invid Enforcer had struggled to its feet and was now taking halting steps toward

the Humans. Scott and the rest of the team swung their
guns off Dusty to train them on the approaching ship. But
Ayres told them not to worry about it. "I can tell by the
way it's moving that it's no threat to us anymore."

Scott, who figured he knew the Invid just about as well
as anyone, disagreed and told his team as much. So it
seemed that only Dusty was surprised when the ship's
cannons flared to life. He pushed Rook aside, raised his
handgun, and fired, bull's-eyeing the ship's scanner.

Rook hid her face from the ensuing blinding flash and
follow-up explosion. She thought she heard a bloodcurdling scream pierce through it all, one of agony and
release, and when she looked up Ayres was gone, disintegrated along with a great portion of the Invid ship itself.

The team spent the rest of the night picking up the
pieces. Rook filled everyone in, grateful for Rand's efforts to support her but in the end overriding his objections. No one blamed her, really; they had all seen so
much in the way of revenge, betrayal, and deceit this past
year that Ayres's story was nothing new.

"I told him his real enemies were the Invid," Rook
explained. "I'm sure they put something in his head; they
had more control over him than he realized."

"More than he wanted to admit, that's for sure," said
Lancer. "Those ships pulled back to see what we'd do up
against their toy. He was probably an early experiment to
see if they could use us against one another."

"And it's obvious they can," Scott added. He exchanged a brief look with Lancer. They were both thinking about the blond pilot they had seen in the tropics and
then again in the snow-covered Sierra pass.

And they were thinking about Marlene.

"Well, at least he had a friend in his last moments,"
Lunk said to Rook.

She gave him a wan smile. "He died for us. . . ."

"Stop it, Rook," Scott said harshly before she could
continue. "Don't make him out to be some kind of hero."

Rand saw the hurt look surface on his friend's face and

moved quickly to Rook's side to take her hand. "Scott's right," he said softly. "Dusty wasn't a hero, Rook."

"Then what was he, Rand?" she wanted to know.

Rand's lips compressed to a thin line.

"He was a victim."

CHAPTER
ELEVEN

> *Oh, what a place this was! A city? The city. These nine-foot techno-horse-headed gestapos with their black armor and fancy blasters ... They wouldn'a drawn second looks in this town.*

Remark reported by Rand in his *Notes on the Run*

ANOTHER WEEK WENT BY AND THERE WAS STILL NO sign of advance units from the Expeditionary Force. Nevertheless, Scott and his team put the time to good use reconning the southern and eastern perimeters of the central hive complex. Thanks to information supplied to him by the Robotech officer (whose remains were now housed in the same graveyard Dusty Ayres helped to fill), Scott was beginning to form an overview of Reflex Point; it was not, as initially believed, a single hive but rather a group of hives, at the hub of which was the Regis's stronghold. The complex covered a vast territory that stretched from the Ohio River Valley to the Great Lakes and from what had once been Pennsylvania west to Illinois. The week's recon had established that the perimeter was most penetrable from the northeast; this constituted something of a lucky break for the team, as it placed Mannatan (formerly New York City) close enough to their route to justify a short detour. Burdette, the late Robotech officer, had furnished Scott with the location of a relatively unpoliced Invid storage facility within the island city, where there was more than enough canister Protoculture to restock the team's dwindling supplies.

Mannatan was the largest surviving city in the Americas, Northlands and Southlands. It had been shaken and scorched by Dolza's annihilation bolts, but many of its enormous structures had survived intact. So much death had been rained around it, however, that the city had had to be evacuated. Few of the millions of evacuees who had fled into the irradiated surroundings had survived, but by the end of the Second Robotech War, people and mutant birds with condorlike wingspans were finding their way back to the cracked and fissured towers, and the abandoned city slowly began to repopulate. Before the Invid arrived, hopes ran high that the city would rise once again to become the great center it had been in the previous century, but those plans were dashed with the aliens' first wave. Still, the Regis saw no reason to destroy the place; she merely constructed one of her hives atop the tallest structure—the 1,675-foot Trump Building, which the hive encased like a wasps' nest just short of its summit—and moved all potential troublemakers to nearby Protoculture farms. With Reflex Point at close proximity, the city's residents (who numbered less than one-tenth of one percent of the city's prewars population) posed no threat to the Regis's domain, and Mannatan was one of the few places where her Controllers and bio-constructs actually patrolled the streets on foot.

Everyone was naturally eager to visit the city, but Scott was wary about all of them entering at once. He wasn't sure just how closely the Regis had been monitoring their recent movements, but given the reappearance of the green-haired Human woman and the orange and green command ship, it seemed reasonable to assume that the team was still a high-priority concern at Reflex Point. And with access to the city limited to a single two-tiered bridge near the northern tip of the island, Scott was against taking any unnecessary risks. Lancer was the obvious choice for advance man because he had already seen the city—years ago, before the Invid invasion, when Mannatan was on the ascendant. Rand would serve as backup, and Annie would accompany them, if only to keep up appearances. The two men would carry hand blasters.

Scott's intuitions proved correct, inasmuch as the Regis had indeed made elimination of the team one of her top priorities, especially since she had lost Ariel to them, and was noticing a certain reluctance on Sera's part. But in some ways this was as intriguing to her as it was baffling—allowing her to recall her own attractions to Zor so long ago. So she elected to place Sera and Corg in temporary command of the city's central hive to observe the results. She did this mostly because she had pressing concerns of her own at this point. The long-awaited trigger point of the Flower of Life was drawing near, but at the same time there was evidence of the imminent arrival of the Human forces who had battled her husband, the Regent, on Tirol and other worlds. And if they arrived before the Flowers came to full fruition, the entire scheme of the Great Work would be jeopardized.

Nine Urban Enforcers marching in a diamond-shaped formation were patrolling a quadrant in the lower part of the island city just now, an area where the towers were especially tall, making the sunless streets feel all the more narrow. Security had been breached earlier that same day; sensors had detected the presence of an unauthorized entry into the city and the energy signatures of Robotech mecha. Shock Troopers and Pincer Ships were hovering overhead, while Scouts covered the miles of waterfront.

"Urban Enforcer squadron," boomed the Regis's voice over the foot soldiers' command net. "Proceed in formation to the East River, divide into units, and search all abandoned buildings for any sign of the rebels. They must not be allowed to slip through our grasp this time."

The nine were huge cloven-foot, bipedal creatures outfitted in black-and-white battle armor, with rifle/cannons affixed to both forearm sheaths. Their smooth eyeless heads were almost comically small, almost dolphinlike beneath the helmets, with a single round scanner for a mouth —a red jewel in the elongated jaws of the helmet. Over what could have been the bridge of the leaders' snout was an inverted triangular marking of rank.

Most of the residents had scattered from the streets and returned to their homes. Street stalls had shut down, and mongrel dogs were having a field day. There were two Humans, however, who made no move as the soldiers approached. They were hunkered down on the sidewalk, their backs to the wall of a ruined building, tattered clothing pulled tight around them, hats pulled low on their heads. Their temerity would have been suspicious had the pair not been representative of that class of Humans who had a penchant for street life and were often addicted to any number of intoxicating concoctions. Nevertheless, in light of the present emergency, one of the soldiers saw fit to stop and investigate the duo.

"Investigating Human life-forms . . ." the Invid told his superior, aiming a scanner. "Sensors indicate no active Protoculture, yet their lack of reaction warrants further observation."

The squad stopped to have a look, but after a moment the leader made a dismissive gesture with its right arm. "Do not waste time with these derelicts."

"But they do not fit the standard Human profile," the soldier began to object.

"Do as I command," the leader said more harshly. "These could hardly be the rebels we seek."

As the soldiers moved off, a whispered and muffled voice rose through the clothing of one of the men. "Can we get up now? I can't breathe—the kid's smothering me in here!"

"Not yet," said his companion, taking care to keep still. "Let them get a little farther down the street."

Shortly, Lancer straightened up, removed the brown cap, and flashed a self-satisfied grin at the now deserted street. "Okay," he said.

Beside him, Rand was in a panic. "Come on, Annie, open up the blanket! I've got about thirty seconds worth of air left!"

Lancer stood up in his tatterdemalion threads, while Annie tossed aside the blanket she had wrapped around her shoulders. She had been sitting on Rand's shoulders beneath the makeshift cape for the past ten minutes or so. Adroitly now, she leapt off him and removed her dark shades and gray fedora.

Behind her Rand was massaging circulation back into his score neck. "My head! Jeez, Annie, why couldn't you have—"

"Lancer, I thought you said they called this place Fun City," she complained, ignoring Rand. "Well, it's been a pretty big disappointment so far! All we've done is dress up like bums and hide from the Invid. When do we get to have some real fun, huh?!"

"When are you gonna learn?" Rand said angrily, waving a fist over her head. "What d' ya think, we're in an amusement park or something? Remember what we're here for."

She made a face and stuck her tongue out at Rand.

Lancer had stripped off his costume and was back to his usual black trousers, tank top, and leather knee boots. "Knock it off," he told Annie. "We have about fifty blocks to cover, so let's move it."

Burdette was right about the place being unguarded. There were a few Urban Enforcer troops stationed out front, but the trio had no problems getting around them and were soon in the basement of the building, closing on the duct system the Robotech officer's map indicated would lead them to the main storage room. It was at this point that they were supposed to head back downtown to rendezvous with Scott, but Lancer insisted that they make certain the information was correct and follow through with the break-in without waiting for the diversions Rook and Lunk had planned.

Rand went along with the idea (Annie didn't have to be convinced), and in a short while they were pushing out the grate of the duct that emptied into the Protoculture storage area itself. It was a dimly lit theater with an elaborate stage, but all it housed now were stacks and stacks of crated Protoculture canisters. Rand went over to one of the crates and pried open the lid.

"There's enough here to take a whole army to Reflex Point!" he whispered excitedly, hefting one of the soda-can-sized fuel canisters.

"Provided we can get it out without being spotted," Lancer said absently.

"Ha! Don't worry about a thing, sir," Rand began to joke. "Protoculture Express at your service! We deliver overnight or you get your money back."

"Guaranteed!" Annie joined in. "In fact, if we don't make good, *we* pay *you*!"

"Now all we've got to do is get back downtown and tell Scott about this," Rand said. "Right, Lancer? . . . Lancer, are you okay?"

Lancer was glancing around the theater, amazed. "Sorry," he said, turning to his teammates. "I was just thinking what a beautiful place this used to be."

"What do you mean?"

"This is Carnegie Hall," he explained with a sweep of his arm. "I guess it doesn't mean much to you, but before the Robotech Wars this was one of the finest concert halls in the world. I remember reading about it. The people who used to sing here . . ." He smiled at the thought. "I used to dream of playing here. Now there isn't much chance of that, I suppose."

"Culture of a different sort," Rand mused. "Maybe the Invid will start holding auditions, huh?"

Lancer ignored the ribbing and allowed himself a momentary fantasy that featured Yellow Dancer on stage, singing "Lonely Soldier Boy" to a packed house. . . .

I won't let the Invid destroy my dreams! he promised himself.

It was that promise that enabled Lancer to justify going along with Rand's spur of the moment plan to take what they could get their hands on straightaway rather than risk a second entry into the place. It also made sense from a practical point of view, because they would have enough fresh Protoculture to recharge the Beta and utilize it in a follow-up raid if it came down to that.

They were in the midst of packing away a few six-packs of the stuff when they heard loud footsteps echoing in the hall and headed in their direction. They had already secreted themselves among the maze of stacked crates when one of the Invid foot soldiers entered, seemingly on patrol.

"Keep under cover," Lancer warned as they made themselves small. "We don't want to fight it out if we don't have to." He and Rand had their handguns drawn. Annie was wide-eyed, trying to hold on to the armful of canisters she hadn't had time to set down.

Lancer cautiously peered over the top of one of the crates. He could see the soldier moving systematically through the aisles formed by the stacks. "It may just be on an inspection tour," he said softly. "It'll probably go away if it doesn't find anything wrong, but be ready, just in case." Silently, he stole across the aisle and repositioned himself for cross fire.

Rand looked over at Annie and her precariously balanced load. "Try not to move. Don't even breathe if you can help it!"

She shut her mouth tightly and rearranged the canisters as judiciously as she could, but there was one that insisted on sliding. She made a nervous sound.

The Enforcer stomped past their aisle and stopped, as though alerted to something. Rand drew a bead on the thing's back. *Here we go again*, he told himself. *Sitting ducks . . . !*

The Invid began to move off, but Annie was suddenly desperate. "Rand, help me! They're slipping—they're gonna *fall*!"

And a moment later they did, hitting the floor with a sound of toppling bowling pins. Rand managed to stifle Annie's scream with his hand, but the Enforcer had heard enough to warrant a second pass along the aisle.

"They slipped," Annie explained in a panic after Rand took his hand away. "I'm sorry, I couldn't help it—"

"Here comes trouble," he interrupted her, arming the Gallant. "Just keep quiet."

The Invid raised its rifle as it began to retrace its steps, but its pace remained unchanged. Lancer threw a quick nod to Rand and leveled his own weapon, wondering just where you had to hit these creatures to have it count. He chose the scanner as a likely target and bracketed it in his sights.

"Just a few steps closer," Rand was whispering to himself when he heard the cat.

At least it sounded like a cat—a rather large cat at that. It growled twice more and then launched itself from wherever it had been perched. Rand went up on tiptoe and just caught a glimpse of the animal's shadow as it leapt from stack to stack. *It was even bigger than its growl had indicated!* He could see that the Invid soldier had swung its snout to the sound and was also tracking the shadow now. The cat took a few more leaps, making one hell of a racket in the process.

Rand breathed a sigh of relief when he saw the Enforcer's rifle begin to lower. Obviously it was satisfied that the animal had been responsible for the noise. *It's going to fall for it!* he thought.

He let himself collapse in sheer nervous exhaustion when the Enforcer exited the room, and Annie came over to him thinking he had been hit or something. Then suddenly the cat was back, snarling a long meow and executing an incredible tumble from the box seats near the hall's stage. Only now Rand was sure the thing wasn't some ordinary cat.

And in fact it wasn't: it was a young, curly-haired Hispanic boy wearing elbow pads, sky-blue dancer's tights, pale yellow leg warmers, and a tank top emblazoned with a large *J*.

"Well that was easy!" the boy laughed, one leg crossed over the other and hands behind his head after his upright landing.

"Have you been here the whole time?" Lancer said once he had gotten over his amazement.

The youth nodded. "That was my Persian. Wanna hear my Siamese now?"

Annie still didn't get it. "You mean that was you? There wasn't any cat?"

"Okay, so you do a good feline impression," Lancer said warily, gesturing with his weapon. "What are you doing in here?"

The boy's eyebrows went up. "What are *you* doing here is more like it, *mano*. As for me, I hang out here sometimes—but I know a lot of easier ins and outs than using the air ducts."

"So you saw us," said Rand. "Hope you're not nursing any ideas about turning us in . . ."

The youth laughed again. "Wha'—for foraging a little 'Culture? Be real, Red. 'Sides, I'm no symp, if that's what you're thinking." He motioned to Lancer's blaster. "Look, I'm not complaining or anything, but how 'bout lowering the hard-tag?"

Lancer glanced down at the weapon and deactivated it.

"That cop's gonna be making another pass pronto," the youth warned. "We better make tracks, unless you're dying to use your juice."

Rand got up, his H90 casually aimed in the boy's direction. "Lead on, Lightfoot," he told him. "We're right behind you."

*   *   *

There were indeed quicker ways out of the place than the route they had taken in, and in a short time the youth was leading the trio down an east-west street a few blocks from the Carnegie Hall storage facility. The Protoculture canisters had been safely stashed away for the time being.

"I guess we owe you an apology and our thanks," Lancer was saying. "What are you called?"

"Jorge," the youth answered him. "I've got a nest in the balcony back there."

"You can enter that place at will?" Rand asked, impressed.

Jorge turned a gleaming smile up at him. "Shit, man, there's no place in this whole city we can't go if we want to."

"But the Invid—they're crawling all over this place."

"Yeah, but they don't bother us if we don't bother them."

"That was some display you put on," Lancer said, changing the subject. "You're quite an acrobat."

"A *performer*," Jorge emphasized proudly. "Fact is I was on my way to rehearsal before I had to stop and save your necks." He laughed at their chagrin. "Why don'cha come with me and check us out."

Lancer looked over to Rand, who returned a shrug of consent.

"Well, I'm all for it," said Annie, quick to take Jorge's arm. "I'm gonna have some fun in this place if it kills me!"

"It should be a great show," Jorge was telling them a few minutes later.

He and the rebel trio were on a staircase landing overlooking a small stage, where a dozen male and female dancers were executing syncopated martial kicks under colored lights. It was a kind of historical piece, harkening back to the frenzied, *kata* routines of the turn of the century, with some break dancing and pelvic thrusts thrown in for variety.

"They're good," Lancer commented. *I wonder if their dreams will survive this alien nightmare?*

But on stage some of the performers were wondering whether they would survive the director. He was nothing if not the consummate perfectionist. "Hold it! Stop! Stop!" he was shouting now, an effeminate curl to his voice. He was twice the age of the oldest on stage but well built nonetheless. He had a pencil-thin mustache and brown hair, save for a section of bleached forelock. "This is awful, just aw-ful. Harvey," he continued, pointing, "I swear you dance like a moose in heat. And Arabella: You look like you're waltzing, for heaven's sake. Remember, *everyone*, this is supposed to be 1990, not 1770! So could we please *try* not to embarrass ourselves?"

The dancers had all adopted hangdog expressions by now, and Jorge took advantage of the lapse in the music to call out: "Simon! Hey! Up here!" When the director looked up, Jorge gestured to Lancer and the others. "I brought some friends to watch the rehearsal, okay?"

Simon scowled at him. "Absolutely not! You know my rules about people—" He broke off his scolding and was staring at Lancer. "Am I seeing things? Is that the face that launched a thousand slips?! Lancer, is that you?! Or should I say Yellow Dancer?"

Lancer smiled and went downstairs to take Simon's hand. Jorge, Rand, and Annie tagged behind.

"Lancer, I still can't believe it," Simon exclaimed. "I've thought about you a lot. . . . What's it been, something like two years? In Rio, wasn't it? What are you doing here? I want to hear *everything*."

Lancer looked over his shoulder at Rand. "Well, we're just passing through."

"Passing through?" Simon said, surprised. "Since when does anyone enjoy the privilege of 'passing through' anymore? You can't be serious."

"We've got transportation," Lancer said, holding back.

Simon stepped back to regard the trio quizzically. "Perhaps it's not in good taste to ask too many questions," he said after noticing Rand and Lancer's sidearms.

"Probably not." Lancer smiled.

"Well, you've just *got* to come to the show tonight, that's all there is to it," Simon enthused.

"The Invid are permitting performances?" Lancer asked.

"They haven't tried to stop us yet. I guess they figure it keeps the slaves happy and out of their way."

Meanwhile, in the hive atop the Trump Building, Sera was engaged in an argument with her brother/prince, Corg. The Robotech rebels had not been located, and Corg was in favor of taking matters into his own hands by simply exterminating every Human in the city.

"I will not permit it," Sera told him. "Observation of these life-forms has not yet been completed. They require more study, even if that means the rebels live for a time more."

"Your lenience is a sign of weakness," Corg answered her. "I say destroy them now."

She glared down at him from the massive throne—a monolithic two-horned affair set atop what appeared to be a thick-stalked, flat-topped mushroom, adorned along its outer edge with a band of glossy red discs. Beneath the cap stood two Urban Enforcers, as silent and motionless as statues. The domed room itself resembled the inside of a living neural cell.

"You seem to forget our instructions, my brother. We are to study the Humans' behavior patterns and learn from them."

Corg made a disgruntled sound. "The experiment is as good as complete. It is time to exterminate these life-forms. I'll proceed with my program, regardless of instructions."

She knew that he had been defeated on every occasion and wondered whether this was influencing his behavior, but she didn't want to point this out to him. "I'm warning you, Corg, do not challenge my authority in this matter. The Regis has placed me in charge."

"For the moment," he snarled.

"What makes you so sure of that?"

"It's perfectly obvious. You have no stomach for destruction. But you've known all along that our plan calls for the eradication of these creatures. And I intend to begin that process immediately."

Corg disappeared through the floor of the hive even as Sera was ordering him to call off his attack. She reseated herself to digest his words.

Maybe he is right, she began to tell herself. *Perhaps I don't have the determination to carry out this task.* She had to admit to herself that she had no grasp of the emotions that were keeping her from destroying the rebels— especially that one who had touched her with his voice. Surely she should have killed him when they had faced each other at the chasm. But she had let him live, and now Corg was beginning to suspect her. All at once it seemed imperative that she speak with Ariel, because in that brief confrontation with her lost sister she had come close to understanding some of the changes that were going on inside her.

Sera shot to her feet.

I must try to find her . . . !

Corg wasted no time assembling his Shock Troopers and commencing his murderous assault on the city's Human population.

Across the Hudson River, where Scott and the rest of the team were awaiting word from Lancer, Marlene sensed the warlord's destructive swing and screamed as those hellish emotions assailed her consciousness once again.

Scott was by her side in an instant. "Where?" he asked as he tried to comfort her. "Where are they attacking?"

"The city," she managed to bite out, hands pressed to her head, body rocking back and forth in Scott's arms. "They're going to wipe out the entire city!"

"But you've got to be mistaken," Scott started to say

when the sound of the first explosions reached him. He grabbed a binocular scanner and ran to the edge of the roof that was their temporary camp. Training it on the city, he saw countless flashes of intense light, and within minutes it seemed that the entire northern portion of the island was ablaze.

CHAPTER
TWELVE

There is some truth to the claim that Corg contributed to the Invid's defeat, such as it was; but only in the sense that his premature blood lust succeeded in alienating Sera that much sooner. On the other hand, the so-called parallels with the Zentraedi Khyron are rather forced and remain unconvincing. To be honest, who can we point to that did not contribute to the defeat? One might as well blame Marlene, Sera, Zor, for that matter. Lay the blame on love, if you will, on Protoculture.

Dr. Emil Lang, *The New Testament*

CORG ASSEMBLED HIS URBAN ENFORCER SQUADrons at the northern tip of the island and commanded them to begin a southward march, sanitizing the city top to bottom. Shock Trooper ships would back them up, creating apocalyptical fires to flush the Humans from their dwellings.

The residents thought they were witnessing some sort of drill until the first streams of annihilation discs hit the streets; then there was sheer panic. People fled from burning buildings only to be caught up in volleys of fire from the Invid ground troops. Block after block burned, filling the evening sky with infernal light. The brick and concrete facades of buildings collapsed into the avenues, sending up storms of glowing embers and acrid ash. Hundreds were trapped in the rubble, and hundreds more perished in the alleyways and streets, in shafts and courtyards. No one could comprehend what was occurring.

Had they brought this on themselves somehow? Had they transgressed or violated some Invid regulation no one had been aware of? Or was this simply the way it would always end from now on? No more old age or disease, no more heart attacks or accidents; just random bursts of blinding light, spurts of systematic extermination...

Corg smiled down on the ensuing destruction from the cockpit of his command ship. *There, Princess*, he laughed to himself. *Observe your life-forms now!*

Downtown, in Simon's dance theater, Jorge held a note that had just been delivered by one of the underground's black eagle courier birds. The sounds of distant explosions had already reached into the building, and an atmosphere of dread prevailed. "Listen up, everybody!" he announced. "The Invid are on a rampage. They're offing everyone! Sweeping through the whole city, north to south!"

"Oh, my God!" muttered Simon. "They're through with us! I knew it would come to this someday!"

Lancer looked over at Rand, his face all twisted up. "It's because of us, Rand," he seethed, just loud enough for his friend to hear. "We brought this on. Just our being here..."

Rand accepted it with a kind of shrug and took another bite from the sandwich Jorge had fixed him before all hell broke loose.

"We've got to get out of here," one of the dancers was telling the rest of the troupe. "They're getting closer!"

The man was right, Lancer realized; the explosions were louder now, near enough to shake the theater itself. The first blast to strike the building threw everyone to the floor. The lights flickered once and went out; a few people screamed.

"We have to help these people get to shelter," Lancer told Rand when intermittent power returned. Dust and particles of debris filled the air. Lancer had his weapon drawn.

Rand, who had almost swallowed the sandwich whole,

pulled it from his mouth and gasped for his breath. "Get *them* to shelters? What about them getting *us* to shelters?"

Jorge was standing beside them, helping a petrified Annie to her feet. "We can reach the subway from the basement," he said rapidly. "We'll be safe there."

"Depends on how *serious* they are," Rand started to say. But Jorge was already herding his fellow performers toward the exits.

Two more crippling explosions erupted in their midst just then, and all of a sudden the interior of the theater was in flames. Most of Simon's troupe had already made it through the exit doors, but the director himself was standing stock still, as though in shock. Lancer ran over to him and spun him around, catching the look of devastation in his eyes.

"Simon, you've got to leave!"

"My theater . . ."

Lancer put his hands on Simon's shoulders, steering him away from the blaze that had already scorched both their faces. "Listen to me . . . The theater's gone. And it won't help anybody if you go up with the rest of it."

"It's over," Simon said flatly, overcome.

"Come on, man. There'll be other shows; we'll get through this."

Simon offered a wan smile. "Maybe . . ."

A column collapsed behind them, bringing down a portion of the balcony and fueling the fire.

"Of course there will!" Lancer yelled. "Unless we don't get you out of here right now!" Rand was by the door, one hand shielding his face from the heat, yelling for them to get a move on. Lancer grabbed hold of Simon's hand and led him off at a run.

"Unbelievable," Scott was saying on the rooftop across the river. "It looks like they're trying to destroy the whole city and everybody in it." He scanned the infrared binoculars north to south, then lowered them.

Rook and Lunk stood silently by the retaining wall,

mesmerized by the fiery spectacle. Marlene was off to one side, hugging her arms to herself. Scott swung around to Lunk.

"How much Protoculture will we have if we cannibalize the Cyclone power systems?"

"Maybe a dozen canisters."

"We have to act quick," Rook told Scott. "Annie and the boys are somewhere in the middle of that firestorm."

Scott tightened his mouth. *Why haven't they contacted me as planned?* he asked himself, already dressing them down. With a dozen canisters of fuel, they would have just enough to power the three Veritechs for a short time. But unless they were able to resupply afterward, that would effectively finish the mecha, fighters and Cyclones both. And even the instrumentality nodes of Reflex Point were a good three hundred miles west of the city.

"Come on, Scott," Rook was saying, her mind made up. "Let's switch the canisters and get out there."

Scott issued a silent nod of consent and went down on one knee by Marlene's side while Rook and Lunk moved off. "You better stay behind," he told her. "I don't want to risk bringing you any closer to that place. I can see what you're already going through."

"I-I'll be all right here," she stammered, as though chilled to the bone. "But promise me you'll be careful, Scott."

They touched briefly, and he was gone.

In the central hive, Sera had been alerted to the wave of death her brother was unleashing against the populace. She sat rigidly at the top of the mushroomlike dais now, hands clasped tight to the arms of the throne, as views of the destruction reached her via a circular projecbeam.

"This is intolerable!" she screamed to her Enforcer guards, who stood unflinching below the dais cap. "Corg is deliberately sabotaging the experiment! The defeats he has suffered at the hands of the Humans have affected his conditioning!"

Everywhere the projecbeam took her, the scene was

the same: buildings ablaze, Human life-forms in postures of agony, and more. But all at once Sera gasped as an image of Lancer filled the holo-field. He was out in the madness, his Gallant stiff-armed in front of him, returning insignificant blasts of vengeance against the overwhelming power of Corg's war machine.

The Earth rebel who has caused so much disturbance within me! she kept saying to herself. But Lancer's presence meant that Ariel must be nearby. Sera leapt from the dais and headed straight for her command ship.

If Sera had continued watching the projecbeam a moment longer, she would have realized that Lancer's shots were not to be so easily dismissed. True, an H90 seemed insignificant when compared to Corg's mobile arsenal, but Lancer and Rand had nevertheless managed to clear the streets of more than a dozen Urban Enforcers.

"That's that," Lancer was saying now as number fifteen fell, its chest plates laid open and oozing green nutrient fluids.

Annie, Jorge, and Simon stepped out from cover to join them in the street. Most of the ground troops had moved further south, but in their wake the city crumbled and burned, turning night to day.

"At least no one in the company got hurt," said Jorge. "Everyone made it into the subway tunnels in time."

"I wish the rest of the city was that lucky," Annie added, stifling a sob.

Lancer checked the blaster's remaining charge and frowned. "We better get underground ourselves."

Suddenly Annie raised her arm and let out a bloodcurdling scream. Two Trooper ships had dropped to the street out of a slice of orange sky, their cloven hooves ripping into the pavement.

Lancer and Rand raised their weapons at the same moment and fired, instinctively finding the same target. The Trooper caught both blasts just above its scanner and ruptured like a lanced cyst, spewing thick smoke and sickly fluids. The second turned to watch its companion go down, then swung back around, its cannon tips aglow with priming charge. But out of the blue something holed the thing with a perfectly placed shot to the midsection, and it too dropped, almost crushing Rand and Annie on the way down.

Simon, Jorge, and the freedom fighters looked up in time to see three Veritechs swoop through the canyon formed by the buildings and fade into the glow.

"It's Scott!" Rand shouted, amazed. "How the hell did they find us?!"

"I don't think they did," Lancer said, watching the VTs bank out of sight. "Just be glad that they chose to zero in on that particular Trooper." He felt a hand on his shoulder and turned.

"Lancer, I've got an idea," said Simon. "I want you to help us go ahead with the show." He paid no attention to Lancer's look of disbelief. "I know it's a lot to ask, but we're going to need help if this city is to survive."

Lancer thought it over; over Simon's shoulder he could see Annie and Rand nodding their heads in encouragement. "Sure," he said at last.

Jorge flicked his fingers together with an audible snap. *Ejole!* "This'll be the show of a lifetime!"

The three Veritechs flew north to the edge of the worst conflagrations and split up to double back. The thruster fires of Invid Trooper ships were just visible in the southern skies. "Let's make sure the streets are clear of any ground units," Scott told the others over the net. "Then we'll go after the ships."

"Nothing on my scanners," Rook reported a moment later.

"Mine either," added Lunk.

Scott looked out over the city and shook his head in despair. The Invid had cut a north-to-south swath of death four blocks wide along the west side of the island. Searching for any signs of Enforcer activity, he dropped down into the canyons again and was almost at street level when his radar displays suddenly came to life.

"Hold on, I've got something!"

By the time he realized what it was a blast had seared the upper sections of his fighter, nearly destabilizing it, but he managed to pull the Beta up and out of its plunge and soon had a visual on the enemy ship even as the displays were flashing its signature.

"Command ship," said Scott, staring down at the orange and green crablike thing that was hovering below him at rooftop level. "It's that damn command ship! Let's take it!"

Corg, as though reading Scott's designs, chose that moment to loose his first stream of annihilation discs. Scott banked sharply and fell; the Invid ship shot up at the same time, and Human and alien ended up exchanging places, discs, and laser-array fire in an aerial duel. Rook streaked in from behind and landed two heat-seekers, but Corg's ship shook them off and stung back, igniting a row of rooftops with its misplaced shots.

Scott and Rook went wingtip to wingtip to launch a salvo of missiles, but again the Invid outmaneuvered them, diving down into the city's hollows, where Lunk almost fell victim to the command ship's wrath.

"That thing is dangerous!" he shouted over the net as explosive light lit up the inside of his cockpit.

"All right, let him go for now," said Scott. He turned to make certain the Invid was willing to give it a rest and exhaled with relief when he saw the ship arrow off. "We've got to find Lancer."

"Yeah, but where do we start looking?" asked Rook, disheartened by the inferno below, to say nothing of the complexity of the city's intact landscape and terrain.

"Just keep your external receivers open," Scott told her.

Hopeless, she thought. *Just what kind of sign does he expect us to see from up here?*

Two hours later, the three Veritechs were still circling. They were all running dangerously low on fuel, and there had been no sign of Lancer, Annie, or Rand. Or the Invid, which was a lucky break. Then Rook picked up

something on the receiver and reported her coordinates
to Scott and Lunk. She supplied them with the frequen-
cies as they came into view on her display screen.

"Tune in and tell me who that sounds like."

Lunk fiddled with his controls, listened for a moment,
and heard the strains of "Look Up" coming across the
cockpit speakers.

"Hey, that sounds suspiciously like an old buddy of
mine."

Rook laughed shortly. "Scott, you wanted a sign, huh?
Well, how's that one down there at three o'clock?" She
tipped the VT's wings once or twice over the source of the
transmissions: a tall, squeezed pentagon of a building
whose rooftop was currently the scene of some kind of
concert or show.

Scott completed a flyby and signaled Rook in a similar
manner. He could discern the words PAN AM at the top of
the building, above a huge lightboard sign that was flashing the word HERE.

"That's Lancer all right," Scott started to say. Then he
noticed that his radar display was active once again: The
command ship had returned with reinforcements. "Follow
my lead to the street," he told his teammates. "And activate cluster bombs on my mark."

The Invid ships pursued them just as he had hoped
they would, and when the three VTs were properly positioned, he called for a multiple missile launch. Warheads
streaked from the fighters, arcing backward and detonating in advance of the Invid ships; several of the Troopers
were destroyed, and even the command ship was brought
up short by the force of the explosions.

"I'm going back for Marlene," Scott reported as the
Veritechs climbed. "I'll rendezvous with you at the
source."

Rook and Lunk kept their fighters airborne until the
concert ended; then they hovered down in Guardian mode,
just as Scott was returning from the Jersey side of the river.
Yellow Dancer, who had borrowed makeup and a

flashy pink outfit for his part of the show, was already out of character by the time everyone regrouped.

"I got a bone to pick with you three," Scott yelled as soon as the VT canopy went up.

"Save it, Scott," Rand answered him from the roof. He tossed a canister of Protoculture fuel up to Rook. "Figured you might be a quart low by now."

Scott lost most of his stored anger while he listened to a quick rundown of the events of the day. He couldn't really find fault with their actions, especially in light of what had followed. There was certainly no going back to the storage facility now, but what they had managed to carry out was more than enough to take the team the rest of the way to Reflex Point. Once they finished here, of course.

Scott pulled Marlene aside while Lunk set about refueling the mecha energy systems. "We're going to have to go back up," he explained, his hands on her shoulders.

"Yes, I know."

He wanted to say more, but Lancer was now standing alongside them, urging Scott to hurry it up. "I don't mean to break you kids up, but we've got lots of work to do."

Embarrassed, Scott withdrew his hands. "See you," he said, blushing, and ran for the Beta.

Lunk and Annie remained with Marlene as the two Alphas and the now separate components of the Beta lifted off. *Hurry back*, Marlene was saying to herself when Lunk stepped up behind her.

"You miss him alread—"

An explosion erased the rest of his words and threw both Lunk and Marlene ten feet or more in opposite directions.

Marlene was first to come around. Unsure how long she had been out, she stood up and coughed smoke from her lungs. One section of the roof was holed and in flames, and she could hear screams of panic in the darkness. Lunk was on his back nearby, apparently unconscious; Annie was nowhere in sight. Someone yelled,

"Ariel," and for some reason she found herself turning around.

It was the green-haired woman they hadn't seen since the mountain attack. She was stepping from the flames that were licking at the armored legs of her towering command ship.

"Ariel," the woman repeated, and again Marlene felt something stir within her. "I am Sera, princess of the Invid, and I have come for you."

Trembling, Marlene stared at her. "But my name is . . . Marlene. I don't understand why you've come for *me*. . . ."

"Because you have turned against your people and I must know why, before we begin transmutation of our race. *Why* have you disobeyed the Regis?"

Marlene gasped. *What is this woman talking about?* "I don't believe what I'm hearing," she said, as if Sera were some hallucination she could banish through an effort of will. "I'm not an Invid."

Sera was taking steps toward her now, her crimson eyes flashing a kind of anger that burned deep into Marlene's soul. "You were placed among the people of Earth to learn their ways, so that we might profit from your discoveries. The Regis has been awaiting your reports, and yet you choose to ignore our commands. Do you expect me to believe that you have forgotten who you are and why you are here?"

Marlene shook her head back and forth; she tried to deny the words her heart seemed eager to affirm. "No . . . it can't be."

The woman regarded her quizzically. "What can't be, Ariel? Search your thoughts, search them for the truth."

"You're lying! You must be!" Marlene screamed as an explosion tore up another section of the roof.

Sera leaned away to shield herself. "I must stop Corg, before the battle comes any closer," she said. Then her eyes found Marlene. "I will deal with you later."

Marlene watched Sera race off to her ship. Behind her,

Lunk was coming around, wondering aloud what had happened. But she hardly heard him.

It can't be true, she thought. *It can't be true!*

Down below, the battle was raging in the streets. Reconfigured to Battloid mode, Scott's section of the Beta was backed against a building, the rifle/cannon in both hands laying down a thunderous sweep of fire into the face of an advancing Trooper. Elsewhere, two Pincer Ships pursued Lunk through the city's right-angle canyons. Two more had ganged up on Rook's red Battloid, forced it into a corner, and were now attempting to open it with their claws.

She called for help over the net. "These cursed things are trying to rape my ship!"

Rand came to her aid a moment later, his Battloid hovering overhead and taking out each ship with a single shot. But the next moment he was facedown in the street, felled by a blast to the back by none other than Corg himself.

The Invid put down behind the crippled Battloid and moved in to finish it off, but Lancer blew it back into the air with a massive Bludgeon release from the reconfigured burly hindquarters of the Beta. At rooftop level, Corg countered with a wave of annihilation discs that pinned Lancer to the wall, but the Invid prince recognized that he was outnumbered and darted off to muster support.

Scott moved in to check on Rand's status, the rifle/cannon upraised and ready for action. Rook joined him shortly.

"Looks like they're pulling back," said Lancer, while his ship launched and reconfigured. "What do you say we call it a day, Scott?"

"We're not done yet; there's still the hive."

Rand whistled over the net. "The hive! Don't you think you're asking a lot out of four little fighters?"

"Yeah, Scott," Rook chimed in. "Have you got a secret army or something?"

"No, but I've got a plan," he told them. "Obviously the Regis never figured on a direct attack, or she wouldn't have had her workers build the hive in such an accessible spot. My bet is we can bring the whole thing down with a few well-placed cobalt grenades."

There wasn't much time to discuss the pros and cons because Corg had returned with three Pincer Ships to back him up. So the three Battloids launched to join their leader and boostered off toward the hive, the four Invid ships in close pursuit.

In the hive, the Regis's voice reached into the very thoughts of her unsuspecting children.

"Attention, perimeter guard: Four Earth fighters are preparing to launch an attack against the hive."

But Sera was nowhere to be found, and without her the Invid drones and Enforcers could do little more than scurry about in a kind of blind panic. And by the time Corg understood the Humans' intent, it was already too late to stop them.

The VTs had climbed to an altitude of several thousand feet and were now falling on the hive like metallic birds of prey. They directed their warheads into the conical summit of the tall structure that housed the hive, and the energy of the ensuing explosions funneled down through the building like a bomb dropped through the top of a chimney. The hive took the full force of the contained blast and blew apart, raining great clumps of organic mass to the streets.

Corg felt the collective deaths pierce him like a lance. In the face of the hive's collapse he broke off his pursuit and cursed the Humans for their barbaric act.

I will have my revenge for this day, he promised the stars.

Lancer insisted on saying good-bye to Simon.

"There's no way we can ever thank you for what you and your friends have done," Simon told him. "Why don't you stay here and leave the rest of it to them, Lancer? Surely you've done your part by now."

The city's survivors were leaving the subway shelters, taking stock of what had been leveled against them. Simon, Jorge, and the freedom fighters were near Carnegie Hall, having just finished loading the VTs with as much Protoculture as they could safely carry.

Lancer knew that Rand had heard Simon's remark and was waiting for his response. Lancer flashed him a brief look and said: "I've been with these people for a long time, Simon, and I plan to be with them right to the end."

Simon offered an understanding nod.

"This was just a skirmish in a much bigger war," said Rand.

"Well, I hope all of you will return someday. And when you do, we'll have the celebration you deserve." Simon embraced Lancer and wished him luck.

On their way out of the city (Lancer, Annie, and Marlene squeezed into the Beta's cramped storage space), the team flew over the remains of a metal statue that had once stood proudly in the harbor. It had once symbolized liberty, Lancer explained.

Scott regarded it and said: "I only hope we can return that to the world someday."

CHAPTER
THIRTEEN

Reflex Point consists of a central hemispherical hive (located close to what was once the city of Columbus, Ohio) and several attendant structures linked to it by numerous Protoculture conduits and instrumentality lines. There appear to be seven secondary nodes—one at twelve o'clock, a second at two, a third at four, a fourth and fifth at seven, and a sixth and seventh at eleven—along with an unattached and somewhat larger dome, south at six o'clock. And that's about the best we can offer you right now, fellows. We hope you'll be able to tell us more once you get down there.

An excerpt from the Mars Division premission briefing, as quoted by Xandu Reem in his biography of Scott Bernard

SHE WAS MOST DEFINITELY HUMANOID BUT OF IN-determinate, often variable height. The form was as close an approximation of Zor's as was possible for the Invid Queen-Mother; with her children she could work wonders, but to become like them she would need to divest herself completely, a thought beyond contemplation. Her cranium was well shaped but hairless, her large, exotic eyes a deep royal-blue, elongated to near slits, with sparse lashes and pencil-thin brows. She was attired in gloves and a full-length red robe whose curious collar encased her ears like a kind of neck brace. Two oval-shaped sensors were set into the robe's collar; they matched a third that was affixed to her breast.

She was deep inside the hemispherical hive that was the living heart of Reflex Point, positioned beneath an enormous globe of Protoculture instrumentality, her link with the outside world in which her children lived and died. The trigger point for the Flower of Life grew near, but the recent events had made her more fearful than encouraged by its timely approach. The experiment in racial transmutation had become hurried and desperate now, in the face of an imminent Human onslaught from the far reaches of space, from that very world that had once doomed her own Optera to death—the Tirol that haunted her memories and dreams.

How like those war-hungry creatures I have become in my drive to possess this world! she told herself. But wasn't this a condition of the body she inhabited?

It was strange that this very Human form should be deemed the one best suited to her designs for racial transmutation, that these very beings she and her children had labored to enslave should prove the form most suitable to the planet itself. And yet didn't she know somewhere in her heart that this would *have* to be the true form, the form that she had grown to love, the form that Zor had inhabited when he first seduced the secrets of the Flower from her innocent and trusting nature?

The Regis was well aware of the recent destruction of her outpost in the Human city of tall towers and artificial environments, and that the Robotech rebels who had so far eluded her were quickly closing in on the central hive complex. But she couldn't hold Corg or Sera accountable for their failures, or even Ariel, now that she understood. It was this physical form itself that was to blame; once instilled with consciousness, a subtle sabotage began to occur, an undermining of all spiritual vigor. It was like the Protoculture itself, that artificiality the Robotech Masters had conjured from her precious flowers. These bodies took over the stuff of soul and subverted its true purpose, enslaved it to emotions and whims and unfathomable interior currents.

But if these things were not far from her mind, they were at least somewhat removed from her priorities—the continuation of the Great Work. And the Human form, however gross, would have to serve them in this purpose;

it would merely represent a stage on the way to the final realization, the *transcendence* itself.

The sky above the western horizon was drained of color and angry with flashes of intense light, brighter than the midday sun. It was all the world's lightning in concert, a blinding stroboscopic show that could be seen and felt for a radius of one hundred miles.

Scott looked into the face of it, hands shielding his eyes from random bursts of unearthly whiteness. *The assault has begun*, he told himself with a mixture of excitement and terror. *Hunter's forces have arrived and are attacking the hive complex itself.*

The team was at the eastern perimeter of Reflex Point, Veritechs and Cyclones grounded after Scott's advance sightings and subsequent commands to regroup. They were in an area that had seen relatively recent tectonic upheavals, jagged outcroppings that looked as though they had been thrust up from the bowels of hell and had no place in this otherwise stable terrain of soft grasslands and rolling hills.

Annie stared at the sky in wonder. "Is it some kind of storm? A tornado, maybe?"

Rand and Rook exchanged grim glances. "I wish it were," Rand told his young friend. Bass sounds were rumbling across the sky, seconds late of the explosions that birthed them.

"It has to be Admiral Hunter," Scott said behind them. Squinting, he could discern dark shapes streaking through that celestial chaos. *Hundreds* of shapes—fighters, mecha, and surely the Invid ships launched to engage them. "Let's move in," he said firmly. "We can't just stand here and watch."

They kept to the high ground and began a slow forward advance. Oddly enough, the light show seemed to wane as they approached, and when at last they reached the arena itself—a wooded valley, host to a wide, meandering river—they understood why.

"We're too late," Scott informed everyone over the net.

They could see for themselves what he meant from their vantage on a cliff overlooking the battleground. The landscape was littered with the smoldering remains of Veritechs and Invid Pincer Ships and Trooper craft. Patches of forest across the valley were burning, and layers of smoke and gas hovered above the valley floor like some nefarious fog; it was as though the land itself had belched up fire and gas from its seething nether regions. In the distance, the uppermost portion of a hemispherical hive was visible, squadrons of Invid closing on it like wasps returning to their nest. A huge gunship crashed and burned while the team watched helplessly.

"It's too horrible," Annie sobbed, putting her face in her hands, and remembering Point-K and similar horrors. Marlene put her arm around Annie's shoulder and pulled her close. Lunk turned around in the front seat of the APC to stroke Annie's back.

"I've never seen ships like these," Lancer said from the seat of the Cyclone. Rand and Rook were nearby on their mecha. Of the three VTs, only the Beta had been moved in, and Scott was overhead now, hovering at the edge of the cliff.

"They must be the latest upgrades," said Lunk. "But I guess there's still some flaws in the design, huh?"

Scott heard the comment. "Can that talk, Lunk," he barked over the net. "This was only an advance group. The admiral is probably trying to ascertain the defensive strength of the hive complex. But he'll be back—you can count on that now."

Lunk grunted an apology.

"I'm going in to check things out down there," Scott continued, bringing up the Beta's rear thrusters. "Stay put until you receive my all clear."

"Somebody wake me up," Annie pleaded, rubbing her eyes. "This has to be just some terrible nightmare."

* * *

Scott's signal came an hour later, and the seven team members gathered by the river to honor the dead. Scott had looked everywhere but hadn't found a single survivor. The smoky aftermath of the battle was beginning to disperse, but the stench of death lingered in the cool air.

"What now, Scott?" asked Lancer.

Annie grabbed hold of Rook's elbow. "Can't we just leave? I hate this place."

Rook had turned to answer her, but the ground beneath their feet was suddenly quaking and rending open. Everyone fell back as an Invid Pincer Ship pushed itself up out of the earth. No blasters were drawn, however, because it was obvious that the thing was finished; it had been lethally shot and was leaking nutrient.

"Back!" Rand cautioned the others. The ship pitched forward on its face, spewing the viscous green fluid from its wounds. "You don't want to get any of that stuff on you!"

They all remembered when he had been slimed and couldn't get the smell off him for a week. Nevertheless, they were intent on watching the puddle spread and turned away only when they heard the sound of a muffled command ring out behind them.

"Hold it right where you are! Don't move!"

Scott swung around anyway, hand at his weapon, but stopped short of raising it. The source of command was a soldier who was aiming some sort of shoulder-mounted device at them, but underneath that shiny black helmet and gleaming body armor the soldier was Human, Scott was certain of that much.

"Who are you?" the soldier demanded in a curious voice, panning the device across the faces of the team. There was no hostility in the voice but a certain intensity Scott couldn't immediately identify.

"Are you with the Expeditionary Force?" he asked.

The soldier shushed him and fiddled with the controls of the device. Scott realized that it was a video camera.

"Let's try it again—and no questions this time. Now: who are you?" The soldier swung the camera on Scott.

"I'm Lieutenant Scott Bernard, Twenty-first Squadron, Mars Division, but—"

"Teeming Tirol!" The soldier exclaimed, pausing the shot. "Mars Division? And the rest of you?"

"These are my personnel," Scott began. "We've been together—"

"Freedom fighters! I got it, I got it!" the soldier said, recommencing to shoot the team. "Lieutenant—Bernard, did you say? . . . Lieutenant Bernard and his ragtag band of freedom fighters, weary after their long journey to Reflex Point and disheartened by the devastating defeat suffered by the first wave of Admiral Hunter's assault group, contemplate their next—"

"That's about enough of that, mister!" Scott interrupted, taking a threatening step forward. "Just who are you and what the hell do you think you're doing?!"

The soldier shut off the camera and doffed the helmet.

Scott's mouth fell open. Not because she was that beautiful—although her long black hair and piercing green eyes *had* been known to stop men in their tracks—but simply because he hadn't figured on confronting a woman.

"My name is Sue Graham," the photographer was saying. "I'm a photojournalist attached to the Thirty-sixth Squadron, Jupiter Division."

"Then you're with the Expeditionary Force," Scott said excitedly. "When is the rest of the fleet due?"

"Soon," Graham answered him absently, training her camera on the fallen Invid's leaking wounds. "Maybe I can get a shot of you and the admiral shaking hands. That's something that should be included in the archives: Hunter congratulates one of his officers on a job well done." Graham looked at Scott. "You *have* been doing a fine job, haven't you, Lieutenant? Where are the rest of the Twenty-first?"

"Dead," Scott said nastily.

Graham glanced at the nearby wrecks of Veritechs and

troop carriers. "Guess that gives us something in common."

Scott glowered at her. "I don't think so, Graham. I didn't just stand around shooting footage while my comrades died."

"Oh, really? Just what exactly were you doing while your comrades were dying, Bernard?"

Rand snarled, "Listen, you," and started to move in, but Scott gestured for him to stay put.

Graham regarded Scott and his team. "Look, don't you think we should get out of here before the Invid show up? Or would you rather stand around and argue?"

"You heartless bitch," Scott seethed, bringing up his fists.

Lancer stepped between Scott and Graham. "Take it easy, Scott. If she can watch her friends die without so much as flinching, there's nothing we can say to put a dent in her."

Graham snorted. "Bunch of soft sisters."

Lancer had to get Scott in a full nelson to restrain him. But he might have broken free anyway had it not been for another of Marlene's early-warning-system headaches.

"Scott," she said, pained. "They're coming!"

Rook armed her blaster and looked around for cover. "Let's go, boys, let's go . . ."

"Push over your Cyclones," Graham shouted, scooping up her helmet and gesturing to the mecha. "Deactivate the systems so the Invid will think the pilots have been killed."

Rand made a face at her. "Jeez, space cadet, you think we need to hear that from you? We've been fighting these—"

"Here they come!" Lunk warned. Everyone turned their eyes west: The sky was dotted with hundreds of alien ships, black spots on the face of the setting sun.

Scott tore himself away from the scene and glanced nervously right and left; ultimately he fixed his sights on the mecha. "We better do as she says. Then make for the trees, everybody!"

* * *

More than a dozen Invid ships put down where Scott and the team had stood no more than an hour before—Pincer craft mostly, seemingly under the command of a blue leader. Curiously enough, they didn't fan out to search the woods but wandered around the battle wreckage instead, as though searching for something. On several occasions they came close to crushing the overturned Cyclones, and a mindless pincer swipe almost sent the APC off the slope (where it was supposed to appear crashed) and down into the river below.

From the edge of the woods, Scott's team of irregulars watched the aliens' movements with growing alarm. The search party represented more collective firepower than any of them had yet witnessed, and Scott couldn't help but wonder about it. He was saying as much to Rand, when Sue Graham suddenly stood up and began filming the Invid.

"Graham, what are you doing?!" Scott whispered from behind the fallen tree that concealed them. "You're going to give away our position!" It was getting dark now, but that was no reason to take chances.

"Every piece of footage adds to our knowledge, Lieutenant," she answered him calmly. "Besides, I don't have any decent shots of these things on two feet. Most of it's aerial sequences, and I'm not about to lose the opportunity now."

Scott reached over and grabbed her ankle, twisting it and forcing her to sit down. "You do that on your own time, Graham," he grated. "Not when there are other lives at stake."

A short time later, the Invid patrol left the area and the team began to relax somewhat. Lunk, Rand, and Lancer stole their way to the APC and returned with the sleeping gear and provisions. They made camp in a small cabin fifty feet into the woods.

Meanwhile, Sue Graham filled Scott in on what she knew about the Earth forces' imminent invasion. She had spent the past year aboard the SDF-3 as Admiral

Hunter's personal photographer, and she couldn't say enough good things about the man. She didn't say what had made her join the ranks of Jupiter Division, but it was obvious to Scott that there was some intrigue connected to the move. They spoke of Tirol and Fantoma, of Rem and Cabell, and of other notable people they both knew. Scott felt himself growing strangely homesick for deep space if not for Tirol itself, and even his attitude toward the journalist was softening somewhat. The red bodysuit she was wearing in place of the armor helped.

"The third attack unit is in preliminary maneuvers at a base on the far side of the moon," Graham was saying now. She had set her camera up to project some of the holographic footage she had shot, and everyone was gathered around. "Here's a shot of the site," she narrated as views of deep space and the warships of the Expeditionary fleet lit up the darkness.

"The admiral's fleet is due to rendezvous with the advance units any day now. Squadrons of new-generation Veritechs will arrive with the fleet. They've been code-named Shadow Fighters."

Scott, Lunk, and Lancer leaned toward the holo-image for a better view. The craft looked something like the standard VTs but were colored a nonreflective gray-black and had a more pronounced delta-wing design.

"Why 'Shadow Fighter'?" Lunk wanted to know.

Graham changed discs; technical readouts now filled the holo-field, replacing the space footage. "The Protoculture generators of the new-generation VTs have been redesigned to include a fourth-dimensional configuration that renders the Shadow Fighter invisible. The Nichols drive, it's called."

Scott had a hundred more questions in mind, but once again it was Marlene who threw him off track. She uttered a low moan and began to sink into that posture of agony they had all witnessed so often. Sue Graham looked at the red-haired woman skeptically and asked: "What's with this one, anyway?"

Scott ignored her and crept to the edge of the woods to

search the skies. Sure enough, the Invid squadron was returning, their thrusters blazing in the night. Scott ordered everyone forward, and silently they made for the valley floor to investigate the enemy's reappearance. Marlene, even though breathless with pain, was the first to notice that the cockpit of the blue leader was opening.

And out of the innards of the ship stepped what looked like a Human being: a young man with long blond hair in a tight-fitting broadly striped uniform of black and green. He issued a command the team strained to hear, and two of the Pincer Ships appeared to acknowledge him with raised claw salutes.

"Human pilots!" Graham said in amazement.

"Another turncoat," said Rand. "Just like that woman we saw . . . The Invid must have a thing for blondes."

"Quiet!" Scott told him. "I'm certain they know we're here."

"Maybe not, Lieutenant," said Graham almost casually, the camera perched on her shoulder.

Rook turned around to look up at her. "Then what? Some piece of Robotech mecha?"

"Exactly. A syncro-cannon."

Scott was the only one who knew what she was talking about; the rest of them were scratching their heads while he cursed Graham for not telling him earlier that the assault group had been equipped with such a weapon.

"It's a particle-beam weapon," he explained. "The cannon was developed by Dr. Lang for use against the Invid."

"It must pack one helluva wallop if the Invid are bothering to look for it," Rand commented.

"It does," Sue told him, still filming the aliens' movements. "That's why I hid it from them."

Scott shot to his feet and yanked the camera out of Graham's grasp. "Where, Graham? And no games."

"In a cave." She gestured without looking. "About a click or so upriver."

Roughly, Scott shoved the camera back into her hands.

"We've got to get that weapon before they find it."

"Count me out, Lieutenant," said Graham.

"Ever hear of loyalty, or self-sacrifice?"

She smirked. "We've all got our jobs to do. For me, it's this." She patted the camera.

"Please, Scott," Marlene said, cutting them off, reaching up for his hand. "Don't try to go out there. You'll be killed."

Scott squeezed her hand and smiled thinly. "I'll see that weapon destroyed before I see it fall into their claws." He turned to glare at Sue Graham. "That's my job . . . but I can't expect you to understand."

Graham laughed shortly, patting the camera again. "Just give me some good footage, hero. I'll make you a star."

CHAPTER
FOURTEEN

God knows Rick and I have had our share of difficulties, Max, especially during the weeks following his decision to join the Sentinels, as you probably recall. But this is worse than that, and it's beginning to prey on me. Sue's with him day and night lately, and Rick doesn't seem to mind it one bit—the lecher. He claims Sue sees him as some kind of father figure, but just who does he think he's kidding? She's infatuated with him, and I'm worried that he is going to fall for it one night— the loneliness of command and all that rot. Max, can't we just see about getting her transferred? Who'd be the wiser?

Lisa Hayes-Hunter in a letter to Max Sterling

ODDLY ENOUGH, SOME OF THEM MANAGED TO GET a little sleep. Marlene had made Scott promise to wait at least until morning before making an attempt to go after the syncro-cannon. He had given his word, proverbial fingers crossed behind his back, if only to calm her down. She had appeared especially stressed out for the past week, and Scott was worried about her, so he wasn't surprised to hear her call out in the middle of the night. He slipped out of his sleeping bag and went to her side; she seemed to sense his presence and come around, smiling weakly up at him in the moonlight.

"I feel so strange, so alone, Scott. . . ."

He reached out to stroke her luxuriant hair. "It's because we're so close to Reflex Point, Marlene. I'm afraid this would happen; that's why I wanted you to stay with Simon. . . ." He was suddenly aware that she wasn't listening to him but staring instead at the holo-locket that had slipped from his shirt.

"You'll never forget her, the woman in your pendant. . . . She was very special, wasn't she?"

Scott held the heart-shaped memento in the palm of his hand and regarded it for a moment. "She *was* special, but so are you, Marlene." He placed his hand against her cheek. "I wear this to remind me. . . . Sometimes it's the only thing that gives me the strength to go on."

"I'm sorry I brought it up," she said sleepily, and rolled over in her bag.

Scott heard the roar of thrusters and went to the door and looked up. Through the trees he could see three Invid patrol ships streak across the night sky. Lancer was beside him now; he had the watch and had returned to the cabin at the sound of Marlene's cries. "Everything all right?" he asked.

Scott led him away from the doorway. "Nobody has enough strength left to hold on to, Lancer. If we don't finish this thing soon . . ." Scott let it go and uttered a soft curse aimed at the stars. "What's keeping Hunter? Doesn't he realize—"

"Don't, Scott," Lancer said, cutting him off. "We just have to keep taking things one step at a time."

"I suppose you're right." Scott turned to look back at his sleeping friends and teammates. "We've just got to— Lancer, where's Rand?!"

Lancer swung around and saw the empty bedroll— then another. "Annie's missing, too."

Scott stepped deeper into the woods to whisper their names in the dark. "They're with Graham, I'm sure of it," Scott told Lancer angrily. "Wake everyone up. We've got trouble."

Ten minutes later, what remained of the team was ready for action; Lunk and Marlene were helping Scott, Lancer, and Rook into their battle armor. "My guess is that Graham is leading them to the syncro-cannon," Scott was saying now. They were gathered at the edge of the woods and could see that the Invid were still patroling the area. "We have no choice—we have to get the Veritechs up."

"I can't believe Rand would be foolish enough to listen to that woman," said Lancer. "And to take Annie with him . . ."

Rook snorted. "Doesn't surprise me any. I think he's hot for that photographer." She disregarded the fact that Rand had tried to take Graham's head off earlier in the day.

"I know why he did it," Marlene offered, looking away from them. "Because I made such a scene about Scott going."

Lancer flashed her an understanding look. "Still, why would he take Annie?"

"That was probably Graham's idea," Scott answered him. "Can't you understand what she's up to?" he continued, seeing their puzzled looks. "The whole idea is to try to get some terrific action footage for herself. Think about it: Annie and Rand, two freedom fighters far from home."

Scott was correct on every count, including his hunch that Sue Graham had set the whole thing in motion. She and Rand and Annie were picking their way across a steep, rock-strewn incline now, nearing the place where Graham claimed to have hidden the Robotech weapon. Neither Rand nor Annie minded in the least that Graham was getting it all down on disc; after all, this was a heroic undertaking, and who along the long road they had traveled had taken such an interest in their actions? And while it was true that Rand had been affected by Marlene's concern for Scott's safety, his motivations were more selfish than considerate.

What Graham had termed a cave was actually a kind of pocket in the hillside, well concealed and protected by a broad earthen overhang. Several Invid patrol ships had overflown the area, but the cannon had thus far escaped detection. Rand wasn't all that impressed by his first sight of the thing. But the weapon was massive, he had to admit, with a boxcar-sized barrel that had a kind of mitered muzzle. There was an adjacent drive unit, its front cockpit portion enclosed by a bubble shield. The whole arrangement was mounted on a three-legged circular base that housed the weapon's thrusters and hoverports. It reminded Rand of some of the artillery used by the Army of the Southern Cross in the Second Robotech War.

Rand and Graham scrambled down the slope while Annie waved good luck from the overhead ledge. The photographer trained her camera on the young girl, then swung around to catch Rand as he was seating himself at the cannon's controls.

"On second thought, this thing looks awesome," he said, grinning for the lens. "But I'm sure I'll be able to handle it. Why, when I think back to some of the spots we've—"

"Get started!" Graham yelled from the ground. "I want to get a shot of you coming out of the cave."

Rand's face reflected his disappointment, but a moment later he was pushing buttons and flipping switches, the cannon's thruster fires roaring to life beneath him. He had had limited experience with Hovercraft of any sort, but what he knew was enough to send the weapon free of its rocky enclosure and place it to strategic advantage on a high ledge overlooking the valley floor, the river a dark, sinuous ribbon below him. Infrared scanners told him where the Invid patrol ships were thickest, and without much thought as to the consequences, Rand slipped on a pair of targeting goggles and began to arm the gun.

Back at Annie's side now, Sue Graham aimed her camera and readied herself for the shot.

The syncro-cannon erupted, spewing a flash of blue fire into the night. The first blast tore right through four Invid Enforcer ships, a streaking projectile through paper targets. *No more looking for vulnerable spots now*, Rand said to himself. He grinned and triggered three follow-up bursts, two directed into the midst of the patrol ships and one to take out the survivors that were making for the skies.

Suddenly patrol craft and Troopers were lifting off all across the valley. It was as though someone had tossed a smoke bomb into a bee's nest. And Rand kept firing, scorching earth and air alike with the cannon's devastating salvos. Then, out of the corner of his eye, he saw Graham, in her armor now and astride a black Cyclone.

"Hey, what are you up to?" he asked her over the tactical net. He saw Graham gesture to her camera.

"I've got work to do."

"But we're going to need you now that we've stirred everything up!" Rand yelled, but she was already gone.

Scott and the others took to the Veritechs at the cannon's first discharge. Rook hadn't witnessed such an incredible display of power since the early battles between the last of the Southern Cross and the first Invid wave. But even so, this was Reflex Point, not some low-echelon outpost hive staffed with Scouts and a couple of Trooper ships. For every ten Invid the cannon destroyed, there were ten more in the air, and Rook began to curse Rand for taking it on himself to confront them.

The three Veritechs had a bad time of it; that they survived at all was in no small way a result of the pandemonium Rand's shots were causing. Numerous though they were, the Pincer Ships and Troopers seemed to be buzzing around in a blind rage, desperate to counterattack but at a loss as to direction; in some cases they were even annihilating one other. Consequently, Scott, Rook, and Lancer were able to inflict a good deal of secondary damage as the syncro-cannon continued to send swaths of blue death into the field.

But the Invid ultimately located the cannon, and their forces proved to be more than Rand could handle. Recalling what Scott had said earlier—that he would rather see the cannon destroyed than fall to the enemy—Rand saw to it that that was the case, arming the syncro's self-destruct mechanism even as Pincer Ships were moving in to overwhelm him. He had rejoined Annie and was shielding her with his own body when the thing finally blew, taking twenty or more Invid ships with it.

"I didn't want to blow the damn thing up," Rand explained to Annie as dirt and rocks rained down on them. "But it was better than letting them get their steely paws on it!"

Shortly, the Beta was hovering over them, a rescue rope dangling blessedly from its undercarriage. Rand was shocked to find Marlene in the rear compartment, but Scott told him that they couldn't risk leaving anyone behind. Lunk was off somewhere in the APC. Rand sent Annie back to sit with Marlene and climbed into the Beta's rear cockpit seat.

"Prepare for mecha separation," Scott told him over the net. He said nothing about Graham and nothing about Rand's action, hoping to make Rand feel all the worse about it.

"I'm ready, Commander," Rand said by way of apology.

He then turned to the women and told them to brace themselves.

Sue Graham was overjoyed at the shots she had been getting: entire squadrons of Invid Pincer Ships reduced to slag heaps by blasts from the syncro-cannon; Veritechs and alien Troopers going at it tooth and claw in Earth's night skies; the ground-shaking self-destruction of the cannon itself—Invid craft clasped onto it like so many frenzied land crabs; the frightened look on the face of the young female freedom fighter as she climbed toward the safety of the hovering Beta Fighter. It was splendid stuff, fantastic—the kind of footage that would earn her awards.

She knew that Lieutenant Bernard had caught sight of her once or twice during the chaos and was well aware of what he thought of her. But she found it easy to dismiss him from her concerns. It might be a bit uncomfortable later on, Sue told herself, but with the main fleet already overdue, she wouldn't have to put up with the lieutenant's flak for very long. She had to admit, though, that he had certainly provided her with some of the day's best action sequences—especially now that his Beta had undergone mecha separation and his motley band had all reconfigured their fighters to Battloid mode. It had been a long time since she had seen techno-knights dishing it out. She kept her camera trained on the skies for a time, singling out the red Alpha and its attractive pilot.

But suddenly her lens found an even more interesting subject: the blond Human who had stepped from the Invid command ship the day before. She had seen his craft off and on during the battle, but now she had him fully in her sights. And so, apparently, did the pilot of the Beta's rear component—that daredevil Rand. The two ships, Battloid and Invid commander, exchanged hyphens of laser fire and flocks of heat-seeking missiles; they darted across the valley like two insects in a kind of death ritual. But in the end it was the Earthling who prevailed; his missiles tore into the hovering, perhaps depleted ship and holed it top to bottom, blowing away one of its cannon arms and sending it into a lethal dive.

Sue reconfigured her Cyclone to Battle Armor mode and zoomed in to meet it, a gleaming figure in black hopping across the battle-scarred terrain. Most of the drone ships had also taken note of their commander's demise and were fleeing the arena in the direction of the central hive.

Sue raised her camera and took a few steps toward the fallen ship, its pilot on the ground motionless beside it. He had scampered out of the ruined cockpit and collapsed, but Sue was certain he wasn't dead. As she stepped closer, the blond man got up, gasping. She centered him in the lens brackets and asked: "Who are you? How long have you been fighting for them? What's the Regis really like?"

The pilot dropped to his knees, hands tight against his abdomen and stared at her uncomprehendingly. Then he was on his feet again, taking shuffling steps.

Sue heard the angry rasp of thrusters behind her and turned to look up at the source of the sound. It was one of the few remaining Pincer Ships, evil on its mind. She broke into a wild run, but the first discs were already on their way. For a brief instant her eyes met those of the blond pilot, before white light erased the world. . . .

Scott got off a few rifle/cannon shots at the retreating Pincer Ship, but the thing got away. He ordered a sweep of the area, then put down where he had seen the command ship crash and Sue Graham shoot her last footage. Lunk, Lancer, and the rest joined him after a moment.

"Hey, is this guy really an Invid or what?" Lunk said, standing over the body of the blond man as though afraid to touch it.

Scott went over to the photographer and gently removed her helmet. Alive but mortally wounded, Sue let out a long, deep moan. Scott tried to cradle her head in his lap, but the bulky armor of the Cyclone prevented it. He pushed her hair away from her face.

"It seems I've got pictures of an Invid with the body of a Human," she managed to say, looking up at Scott through glazed eyes.

"Were they worth dying for, Graham?"

Behind him, Annie was making disgusted sounds. She and Lunk and Marlene watched as green blood pulsed from the pilot's wounds. "Anybody that bleeds green blood must be an Invid," she announced. "But how come they look like us all of a sudden? I mean, he looks almost Human, doesn't he, Marlene?"

"Like that other blond pilot," said Lancer. "That woman."

Annie turned around to find out why Marlene wasn't answering her; she saw that Marlene was staring wide-eyed at a wound she had received to her left shoulder. Alarmed, Annie reached out. Then she noticed the blood.

It was green.

Annie collapsed to her knees in disbelief. Was it possible that through all their months together she had never seen Marlene bleed? *It had to be some kind of mistake—a hallucination!*

Annie's actions had drawn everyone's attention, and all eyes were now fixed on Marlene. No one knew how to react: someone might as well have told them that Marlene was suffering from a fatal disease. The pale woman looked from face to face, then put her hands to her head in a gesture of complete shock. "No! No!" she screamed, tossing her head back and forth.

Scott left Sue's side to calm Marlene, uncertain himself and denying the evidence with each step. He put his hand out to touch the wound, to see for himself if this wasn't just some trick of the night. . . .

The two of them exchanged looks of dismay as they regarded the blood on his fingertips. "Marlene . . ." he stammered. "I . . ."

She stared at him, tears streaming down her face, turned, and ran off. Only Rand made a move to stop her, but Scott restrained him.

"But we can't just let her leave!"

Scott's lips were a thin line when he turned to his friend. "She'll be back," he promised. "I don't know what's going on here . . . this pilot, now Marlene . . . but I know she'll never be able to live among the Invid again. We're her family, Rand. *We're her family!*"

CHAPTER
FIFTEEN

> *Captain, there's something wrong with the engines! They're just not responding!*
>
> Remark attributed to someone in the SDF-3 engineering section

ON THE FAR SIDE OF THE MOON, THE WARSHIPS OF the main fleet dematerialized from hyperspace—sleek, swanlike destroyers with long tapering necks and swept-back wings. They were enormous battlecruisers shaped like stone-age war clubs with crimson underbellies; dorsal-finned tri-thrusters and Veritech transports that resembled clusters of old-fashioned boilers; and of course the squadrons of new-generation assault mecha, the so-called Shadow Fighters.

On the bridge of the flagship, General Reinhardt waited for word of Admiral Hunter's arrival, while the rest of the fleet formed up on his lead. Filling the front viewports was the Earth they had come so far to reclaim. Reinhardt regarded the world as one would a precious stone set on black velvet. *Almost sixteen years*, he thought to himself. *Is this a dream?*

He shook his head, as if to clear thoughts of the past

from his mind, and turned his attention to the monitors
above the command chair. Here were displayed views of
local space, Earth's silver satellite, and the gleam of a
thousand hulls touched by sunlight. But there was still no
sign of the admiral. Reinhardt slammed his thin hand
against the chair's communicator button. "Anything yet?"

"No sign," the astrogation officer responded.

"That damn ship's jinxed," Reinhardt muttered to
himself. "I told Hunter something like this would
happen. . . ."

The bridge controller flashed him a look across the
bridge. "Recommend we initiate attack sequence, sir. We
can't afford to wait much longer for the SDF-3. All approach vectors have been plotted and locked in, and conditions now read optimum status."

Reinhardt drew his hand across his face. "All right,"
he said after a moment. "Issue the codes."

The controller swung around to his console and tapped
in series of commands, speaking into the mikes while his
fingers flew across the keyboard.

"All units are to proceed to rendezvous coordinates
Thomas-Victor-Delta. Attack group three will remain
and await instructions from SDF-3 command. Attack
group two will continue to objective Reflex Point, activating cloaking device at T minus five minutes and
counting. . . . Good luck, everyone, and may God be with
us for a change. . . . "

Ground force units and their companion VT strike
groups had already landed. Scott and the team had been
on hand to greet them, and in the ensuing excitement
everyone forgot about Marlene for a few moments. She
hadn't been seen since dawn, when the painful realization
of her identity had led to her flight.

Sue Graham was dead.

The Invid hadn't shown themselves either, which in
itself was a positive sign. Scott still didn't know what to
make of the Human or humanoid pilots they were apparently using. He wanted desperately to believe that Mar-

lene was in fact the amnesiac captive he had come to love—that that green blood was something the Invid had done to her—and that they would reunite when all this was finished once and for all. But there were just too many reasons to think otherwise, and for the first time in over a year he found himself recalling Dr. Lang's theories concerning the Invid Regis and her ability to transmute the genetic stuff of her children into any form she chose. These were fleeting thoughts, however, glossed over while preparations got under way for a full-scale invasion of the central hive.

The irregulars had been attached to the ground forces under the command of Captain Harrington, a dark-haired, clean-shaven young man who thanked Scott for the recon information he had gathered and promptly dismissed it. They were all in a group now, atop a thickly wooded rise that overlooked Reflex Point's centermost and largest hive, a massive hemisphere of what looked like glowing lava surrounded by five towering sensor poles and a veritable forest of Optera trees—those curious thirty-foot-high stalk and globes that were the final stage of the Flower of Life. There was no Invid activity, ible activity, except for random flashes of angry lightning, which in their brief displays suggested a domelike barrier shield that encompassed the hive itself.

"At last . . . we finally made it," Scott was saying. He was in Cyclone battle armor, as were Lancer, Rook, Rand, Lunk, and most of Harrington's troops. Veritechs had taken up positions in the woods all around the hive, and the grassy slopes to the rear were covered with squads of Cyclone riders.

"I don't want to burst your bubble," said Harrington, "but we've still got a Protoplex energy barrier and a couple of thousand Invid Shock Troopers to get through."

Scott had a defensive reply in store for the captain but let it go. How could the man be made to understand what Reflex Point meant to Scott's team? True, the Expeditionary Force had come a long way for this showdown, but Scott reckoned that the distance of the overland journey to this moment as incalculable.

"I want to make certain that the main Alpha force stays out of this until we punch a hole in the barrier," Harrington was advising his subordinates. "We don't want to repeat yesterday's mistake and get them too stirred up. We'll let them think we're of no consequence." Harrington turned to Scott. "Lieutenant, I'm counting on you to be ready with your fly-boys as soon as you receive my word, understood?"

"Sir!" said Scott. Lancer and Lunk joined him in a salute.

"I'm so excited I could just scream!" Annie enthused from the sidelines.

"It's going to be awesome," Rand said beside her.

Scott threw Rand, Rook, and Annie a stern look. "Forget it, you're not coming. This is strictly a military operation."

"You're lucky to be out of it," Lancer added at once and almost cheerfully, hoping to mitigate Scott's pronouncement somewhat.

Rook went from sadness to anger in an instant. "Well, we sure don't want to interfere now that the big boys have arrived, do we? I mean, all that action we've seen together—that was just *play fighting*, right?"

Rand, too, was seething but was determined not to show it. "Personally, I'm in no hurry to get myself killed, *Lieutenant*, so it's fine with me."

Annie looked up at her two friends, then over at Scott, Lancer, and Lunk. "But it's not fair to break us up like this just 'cause you guys were soldiers. We're still a team —a *family*! You can't just tell us to split up!"

Rook tried to soothe Annie while she cried. "I suppose this is good-bye, then." She had packed away all her snide comments. "Good luck, Scott."

Harrington gave orders for the attack to begin before Scott could answer her. Veritechs configured in Guardian mode lifted out of the woods to direct preliminary fire against the hive, filling the air with thunder and felling scores of Optera trees. And as fiery explosions fountained around the hive, awakened Invid Shock Troopers emerged from the ground to engage the Earth forces one on one. Scott rushed to his fighter, but Lancer stopped to say a farewell to his friends, even as Veritechs roared by overhead.

"I can't say it's always been fun, but it's certainly been terrific," Lancer yelled over the tumult. "You three take care of yourselves, okay?"

"*You* take care," said Rand. "Remember, I expect to see Yellow Dancer perform again."

Lancer smiled coyly. "Don't worry, you will."

"You promise?" Rook asked.

Lancer leaned over to kiss her lightly on the cheek. "Till we meet again."

It was a little too sweet and fatherly for her liking, but Rook said nothing. Lancer behaved the same toward Annie.

"Now, don't go and get married behind my back."

"I won't," Annie said tearfully.

Lunk pulled up in the APC to wave good-bye as Lancer headed for his Alpha. "I'm a soldier again," he shouted, gesturing to his spotless battle armor. "I'll be seeing you guys!"

Rand watched his friend drive off. "A soldier again? What the heck does everyone think we've been doing this past year?" He frowned at Rook. "They're all riding off into *battle*, right? So how come I feel like we're the only ones without invitations to a party?"

A short distance away, Scott waved good luck to Lunk and threw a salute back to his former teammates.

"That tears it!" Rand cursed. "I should've figured he'd say good-bye like that. A robby, through and through."

"Would you want it any other way?" Rook asked him, returning Scott's salute and smiling.

Rand thought it over for a moment, then brought the edge of his hand to his forehead smartly.

Scott turned to his console and displays, lowering the canopy and activating the VT's rear thrusters.

Good-bye, my friends, he said to himself. *Whatever happens now, at least I'll know the three of you will get out of this alive.*

Veritechs and Invid Shock Troopers were clashing throughout the field now. Hundreds of Pincer Ships had joined the fray and were buzzing around the hive in clusters four and five strong. Only a few Cyclone riders had reconfigured their mecha to Battle Armor mode; most of them were riding against the hemisphere in a kind of cavalry charge, pouring all their fire against the hive's flashing barrier shield.

Bursts of blinding light strobed across a sky littered with ships and crosshatched by tracer rounds and hyphens of laser fire. Rand watched from the edge of the woods as Veritechs swooped in on release runs and booster-climbed into the sunlight. The sounds of battle rumbled through the surrounding hills and shook the ground beneath his feet. He could see that the battalion was meeting with heavy resistance, despite what Captain Harrington had said about underplaying their hand. The Invid knew exactly what was at stake, and they weren't about to be tricked.

I can't do it, he thought. *I can't just stand here and watch them go!*

Without a word to Rook or Annie, he donned his helmet and made for his Cyclone. They called out after him.

"I'm not going to sit it out after coming this far," he told them. "I figure the time has come for a little well-meaning insubordination."

Rook tried again to stop him, to talk some sense into him, but her words lacked conviction—even *she* didn't believe what she was saying. "That idiot's going to get himself killed without somebody to look after him!"

Annie saw what was coming but didn't bother to try to stop her other than to shout a halfhearted, "Wait!"—and that was only because she didn't want to be left behind. She began to chase after them, leaving the woods and risking a mad unprotected dash across the battlefield, but it was Lunk she ultimately caught up with.

He had been riding escort to various Cyclone squads, adding his own missiles to the riders' laser-array fire, when an Invid command ship he had finished off with heat-seekers almost toppled on him, sending the APC out of control. Suddenly he was flung into the shotgun seat, and the vehicle was skidding to a halt in the thick of the fighting. And the next thing he knew Annie was in the driver's seat, practically standing up to reach the pedals and shouting: "I'll show you how to handle this thing!"

"What the heck are you doing here?" he demanded, grateful and concerned at the same time.

Annie accelerated, pinning him to the seat.

"What's it look like I'm doing?!"

"Come on, Mint, gimme the wheel—"

"Forget it!" she yelled into his face as he made a reach for it. "I'm not gonna be left behind anymore, Lunk!"

Lunk backed off and regarded her. She was a trooper, he had to admit, a regular workout.

Deep within the hive, the instrumentality sphere glowed with images of the battle—a Cyclone charge, an aerial encounter, death and devastation. A living flame of white energy now, the Regis beheld the spectacle and understood.

"The Earth people have risen in great numbers against us," she addressed her troops, in position elsewhere in the hive. "And now they dare to attack our very center, to threaten all that we have labored to achieve. But this time we will put an end to it. Corg, I call upon you to defend the hive. Destroy them, as they would us, for the greater glory of our race!"

"It will be my pleasure and my privilege," Corg answered her from the cockpit of his command ship. Behind him, his elite squad of warriors readied themselves as the hive began to open, the subatomic stuff of the barrier shield pouring in to fill the drone chambers with white radiance.

But Corg was suddenly aware of a Human-sized figure silhouetted against that blinding light. "No, wait! You mustn't!" it shouted.

Ariel, in her Human guise and garb, was below him, searching for sight of him in the cockpit. "So, you've returned. . . . What do you want?"

"I want to speak to the Regis. Let me through—this madness must be stopped!"

"Madness?!" he shouted, stepping his ship forward menacingly. "What are you saying?"

Ariel gestured to the outside world. "They're only fighting to regain the land that is rightfully theirs . . . the land we've taken!"

"You've lived among them too long, Ariel," Corg told her. "Or should I call you *Marlene*? . . . Now stand aside!"

Corg leapt his ship over her head, nearly decapitating her, but she had ducked at the last instant and was on all fours now, weeping, Sera's pink and purple ship towering over her.

"Sera, you must listen to me," Marlene pleaded, getting to her feet. "Have we forgotten our past? You yourself opened my mind to these things. Have we forgotten that our own planet was stolen from us? What gives us the right to inflict the same evil on these people?"

Sardonic laughter issued through the ship's externals. "So suddenly our Ariel remembers," sneered Sera. "And you would have us surrender. . . . Well, we have traveled too far to concern ourselves with this barbaric life-form's needs. Soon this will be our world, and our world alone."

"We've traveled far, and yet we have learned nothing."

Sera engaged her ship's power systems and leapt into the light, the roar of the thrusters drowning out Marlene's anguished pleas.

Outside, the barrier had been breached by antimatter torpedoes delivered against it by two Veritechs and subsequent blasts from the battalion's destabilizer cannons. Cyclone riders and Battloids were now punching through

the rend and battling Pincer Ships on the ground nearest
the hive wall.

The outpouring of Protoculture energy released from
the shield was working a kind of seasonal magic across
the landscape, reconfiguring not only local weather patterns but the life processes of the flora itself. Rand and
Rook, riding at the head of a contingent of Cycloners,
moved from winter to spring in a matter of seconds.
Spores and pollen clusters the size of giant snowflakes
were wafting through the newly warmed air; young grass
was spreading like some green tide across the valley, and
trees and flowers were blossoming in vibrant colors.

"*This* sure wasn't in the forecast!" Rand commented
over the net.

"Look at all these wildflowers! Poppies, marigolds—"

"Yeah, but I don't like the look of that big cornflower
up ahead."

Rook saw a blue Enforcer ship surfacing in front of
them, its cannon tips already aglow with priming charges.
"Fan out," Rand ordered the rest of the Cyclone group as
energy bolts were thrown at them. The two freedom
fighters launched their Cycs and changed over to Battle
Armor mode.

"Draw its fire!" said Rook, boostering up and off to
the left.

Rand remained at ground level, taunting the blue devil
with trick shots, while Rook came in from behind to drop
the thing. But a second Invid suddenly appeared out of
nowhere and swatted her from the air with a cannon twist
that smashed one side of the armor's backpack rig, shear-
ing away one of the mecha's tires. She went into an uncontrolled fall with her back to the larger ship, but Rand
swooped in to position himself between the two of them.

"It's okay, I've got you covered."

"Leave it to me!" she told him, voice full of anger, as
Rand triggered off a series of futile shots.

"If I'd left it to you, you'd be a pile of smoking rubble
by now, and I'm just too fond of you to let that happen!"

"You're what?!"

Rand risked a look over his shoulder at her. "You heard me—I'm fond of you, dammit!"

It was a hell of a time to be confessing his feelings, she thought, but it was turning out to be one of those days. "I—I don't know what to say. . . . "

Rand swung back to his opponent and saw that the Invid ship's cannons were about to fire. "Don't say anything," he yelled in a rush, "just *moooove*!"

The cannons traversed and followed the Cycloners up, but the pilot's aim was off, and Rand managed to sweep in and bull's-eye the ship from behind.

"Nice shooting there, cowboy," Rook said, coming alongside him later. "I bet you try to impress all the girls that way."

There was a sweetness in her voice he had never heard before and a smile behind the faceshield of her helmet that lit up his heart. "No, only the ones who can outshoot me," he laughed.

They were both some fifty feet off the ground, almost leisurely in flight, as though the battle had ended. Then, without warning, there was something up there with them: a kind of towering diamond-shaped flame of white energy inside of which, naked and transcendent, was a Human female with long, flowing red hair. . . .

The vision, if that indeed was what it was, also appeared to Lunk and Annie, who were down below in another part of the arena.

"What the devil is that thing?!" Lunk said, back behind the wheel of the APC now.

At that the flame seemed to tinkerbell across the sky, as though calling to them. Annie swore to herself that she was seeing Marlene up there but dismissed the thought as wishful thinking. The flame, however, *did* seem to be beckoning to them.

"Do you get the feeling it wants us to follow it?"

"That seems to be the idea," said Lunk, putting the vehicle into gear. "And I've learned that you never say no to a hallucination."

* * *

At the same time, almost directly over the hive, where the fighting had been fast and furious, Scott and Lancer were reconfiguring their fighters to Battloid mode in the hope that some of the Expeditionary Force fly-boys would follow their lead. The air combat units had been sustaining heavy losses, and Scott reasoned that the boys had been flying far too long in zero-gee theaters. He recalled the fear he had felt when Lunk first surprised him with the Alpha—and back then he was only going up against two or three Troopers ships, nothing like the swarms of Invid craft that were in the skies today.

Reconfigured, the two teammates demonstrated what a year of guerrilla fighting had taught them; they dropped down close to the hive, rifle/cannons blazing, and took out one after another Invid ship—even the most recent entries to the aliens' supply: the Battloid-like Retaliator ships, upscale versions of the Invid Urban Enforcer street machines. Lancer went so far as to bat a couple of them with the rifle/cannon, showing just how to make gravity work to one's advantage.

Then suddenly there was a kind of flame whisking along beside them, tipped on its side and incandescent.

Lancer said: "It's some sort of vapor cloud, I think. But I can't get a decent fix on it. See if you can get close to it."

Scott banked his fighter toward the apparition and trained his scanners on it. But it was his eyes that gave him the answer: Inside the flame cloud a naked figure swam, larger than life and recognizable.

No, it can't be! Scott thought.

All at once Lancer's voice pierced the cacophony of sounds coming over the tac net.

"I'm hit, Scott! The gyro-stabilizers are shot! I can't get myself turned around! Can't get the canopy up, either. I'm down and out, buddy! . . . A memory!"

CHAPTER
SIXTEEN

> One of the intriguing (and unanswered) questions of [the
> Third Robotech War] is how Ariel/Marlene accomplished her
> minor miracle in the skies above Reflex Point. Nesterfig (in her
> controversial study of the social organization of the Invid) ad-
> vances the theory that Ariel somehow "borrowed" Protocul-
> ture energy leaking from the hive barrier shield—the same that
> so affected the surrounding countryside. But this does not
> really answer the question. Neither Corg nor Sera was en-
> dowed with similar abilities, and most experts agree that they
> were the most highly evolved of the Regis's creations. The
> Lady Ariel herself was never able to shed light on this curious
> incident.

> Zeus Bellow, *The Road to Reflex Point*

IN THE COCKPIT OF HER COMMAND SHIP, SERA FLASHED
a self-satisfied smile at her display screen. The Human
pilots had hoped to get the better of her troops by reconfiguring their craft, but, vastly outnumbered, they were
sustaining the same losses in Battloid mode as they had in
Guardian. But suddenly her scanners revealed that
Lancer's fighter had been one of those to feel the Invid
wrath, and although his ship had not been destroyed, it
was plummeting toward Earth, hopelessly out of control.
As she watched him fall, memories of his face played
across the screen, and when she could bear no more of it,
she engaged the thrusters of her ship and fell in to rescue
him.

Ariel's words came back to her now: *We have learned
nothing Sera, nothing*! And she answered back: "You're
wrong, Ariel. I have learned to love at least one of our
enemies, enough to betray my own people."

Lancer caught sight of the rapidly approaching Invid command ship and guessed that it was coming in to finish him off. He had been struggling with the canopy release switches but had since abandoned any idea of freeing up the jammed mechanisms. His teeth were gritted now, and he was resigned to death. But all at once the Invid was actually scooping up his wounded ship in its armored arms, and far from annihilating him, the enemy was pulling him out of his fall. He glanced up and saw through his canopy and the enemy ship's bubble cover that it was the blond woman pilot. Whether she was XT or Human had yet to be learned; but whoever, she was saving his life.

"Why?" he shouted. "Why?!"

And somehow her voice found its way through the VT's command net to answer him: "Don't ask me to explain," she told him. "But in saving your life I have forfeited my own!"

At the same time her ship let go of his, but the Alpha's systems were revived now, and the foot thrusters were able to maintain it at treetop level. Lancer had the Battloid's rifle/cannon raised, and it would have been a simple matter to destroy the command ship, but instead he let it escape unharmed, confused by this latest turn of events.

Closer to the hive, Scott was still staring at the flame cloud Marlene inhabited. Several other Battloids were similarly suspended, awed by the sight.

"Marlene . . . is it you?" Scott asked the thing hesitantly. "Is it really you?"

In response, the flame leapt toward the hive. Cocooned within its radiance, Marlene, like some living filament, stretched out her arms, and sinuous waves of lightning leaked into the sky.

Scott engaged the VT's boosters and shot after her. Lancer was right behind him.

Corg's ship was not far off; while he watched the two Earth mecha streak off in pursuit of Ariel's projected image, the voice of the Regis entered his ship, informing him of Sera's betrayal.

"She did what?" Corg said in disbelief.

"It is true, Corg," the Regis repeated. "She has saved the life of one of the Robotech rebels."

"Then she is as tainted as Ariel." How was it that this Human species could make his sisters abandon their duty? he asked himself.

He vented his rage against two Battloids and three Alphas, destroying all of them with blasts from the forearm cannons of his ship; then he soared after Ariel and her rebel friends.

But if the flame had begun to alter itself, so had the weather. The land had suddenly passed from spring to summer, and now autumn leaves were falling. Rand and Rook were still following Marlene's form, a flickering sun trailing tendrils of light.

"Marlene," Rand shouted over the net, hoping she could hear him. "What does all of this mean?! What's going on?"

If they had any doubts that what they were seeing was truly Marlene, the voice they heard put an end to all of them.

"Can't you understand?" the flame seemed to ask, oscillating as it moved, its naked filament regarding them over her shoulder, long red hair streaming out behind as though it were a part of the light itself. "We are only trying to find a place where we can live in peace and security."

"Yeah, but you forgot something," Rand reminded her angrily. "This planet is our home, not some Invid retirement community."

"You must believe me, it was never our plan to destroy Humanity."

Marlene's flame shot ahead of them, a free-floating electrical disturbance against the crimson and yellow surface of the hive.

"Then what was your plan?"

"I am neither Human nor completely Invid. I am a new form of life that is a blending of the two. I see that now, although my Regis does not. I can see that it was never our destiny to remain in this Human form. But I must somehow make her understand."

Even though they were scattered, the rest of the team —Scott and Lancer, Lunk and Annie—were monitoring the conversation.

"And this new form of life is planning to replace the old one, I suppose," said Lancer, still thinking about the humanoid pilot who had saved his life.

"My friends, follow me into the central core, the heart of the Invid civilization. There all your questions will be answered."

With that the flame dove into the hive, opening a radiant portal in the side of the dome.

"She went in," Annie said in an amazed voice from the shotgun seat of the APC. "You're not going to follow her, are you?" she added, tugging on Lunk's arm.

"You better believe I am," he told her firmly. "Listen, Mint, if you're scared, you can hop out. I'll be back for you."

"I'm not *scared*," she harumphed, turning her back to him. "I don't think. . . ."

They were approaching a blinding white hole in the side of the hive now, driving entirely out of their own world, destined perhaps never to return.

It was a little like being underwater or within a living bloodstream, replete with cells and corpuscles. In the distance they could discern a blinding white sphere, bisected by a horizontal ray that spanned the field from one side to the other.

And Marlene's form was still leading them in.

"I can't believe it," Rand said to Rook over the net. "We're *inside* Reflex Point. I thought we were supposed to be destroying this place, not taking the grand tour."

"I think I prefer the view from the outside. Where do you suppose she's taking us?"

"Over the rainbow," said Rand.

Almost everyone emerged at the same moment: Rook and Rand, still in Battle Armor mode, Lunk and Annie in the APC, and Lancer and Scott in their fighter mode Alphas. The place was a huge cavernous chamber, filled with light and supported by what seemed to be webwork strands of living neural tissue. Suspended overhead was an enormous globe of pure Protoculture instrumentality, a kind of veined bronze sphere with dark shadows moving and shaping within it, responding to a will that was fearful to contemplate.

They were all shocked to see each other, but where Annie was excited, Scott was angry; he threw off his "thinking cap," raised the canopy of the alpha, and hopped out, storming over to the two Cycloners.

"I thought I told you two to stay put," he began. "You're not soldiers!"

Rand marveled that the man could even be entertaining such thoughts given the circumstances.

"Well, since we're not soldiers, we don't have to follow your orders, do we?" Rook threw back at him, raising the faceshield of her helmet.

"Marlene led us to this place," Annie explained, climbing down from the APC.

Scott looked around uncomfortably. "She led all of us here, I guess."

Suddenly Rand was pointing up to the sphere; its interior was growing brighter by the second. The glow culminated in a flash of threatening light.

"Foolish Humans," an omnipresent deep but female voice began, "you have come here seeking to look upon the face of the Invid Regis. . . . So be it. You shall see her."

Over the rainbow, indeed! Rand said to himself.

The next thing anyone knew, someone had pulled the

plug, plunging the Regis's inner sanctum into darkness, except for the inner glow of that sphere, directed down on them now like stage light. Then a towering flame formed beneath the base of the sphere. It was similar to the one that had encompassed Marlene earlier, only this one was larger and more menacing. And within it they could discern a hairless humanoid figure, thirty feet high and dressed in a long red robe and strange gloves that dangled a kind of tail.

"Behold, I am the Invid. I am the soul and the spirit. I have guided my people across the measureless cosmos, from a world that was lost to a world that was found. I have led my people in flight from the dark tide of the shadow that engulfed our world, one that threatens to engulf us even now. I am the power and the light. I am the embodiment of the life force, the creator-protector. In the primitive terminology of your species, I am . . . the *Mother*!"

While she spoke they had views of nebulae and star systems, the journey the Invid had taken from Optera to Tirol and on to all the worlds that had led them eventually to Earth.

Light returned to the chamber, and they had a full view of the blue-eyed creature, the Invid mother.

"You are surprised. . . . So were we, when we discovered that the planet to which we were led by the Flower of Life was inhabited by the very species who had destroyed our homeworld."

"I'd say 'inhabited,'" Rand started to say.

"That is of little consequence. . . . Your species is nothing when weighed against the survival of my people. . . . The Invid life force will not be denied. . . ."

"No, that's not right!" a small voice rang out to argue with her. Everyone turned and saw Marlene enter the domed chamber from somewhere, just as they remembered her in her yellow jacket and blue denims.

Scott called to her.

"So, Ariel, it is true: you *are* a traitor. Was it you who led these children of the shadow into the hive?"

"They are not children of the shadow," Marlene contradicted her. "They have a life force almost as strong as our own."

"They are the enemies of our race."

"If they oppose us, it's because we are trying to do the same thing to them that was done to us so many years ago!" She turned to her friends now. "Scott, listen to me: Perhaps if we could begin again, we might be able to find a way for our two races to share this planet together, in peace."

Scott closed his eyes to her and shook his head. "I'm sorry," he told her. "But you must realize that's impossible."

"So you'd rather have the death and destruction continue?"

"That's right, Marlene," Lunk cut in. "To the bitter end if we have to!"

Marlene made a stunned sound; she had not expected this.

"Lemme tell you something," Lunk continued. "Maybe you've forgotten that your species invaded our world—*remember*?!"

"I do remember," she said softly.

At the edge of Earthspace the third attack group was moving into position above Reflex Point, the Shadow Fighters that rode its wake dematerializing as the command was received for activation of the Protoculture cloaking device.

"There are still no signs of the SDF-3," the controller updated. "All other ships are present and accounted for."

"*Jinxed!*" Reinhardt muttered.

"Ground forces report successful penetration of the hive barrier shield, with heaviest losses sustained by the Veritech squadrons. Invid command is either unaware of our presence or unconcerned. My guess is that the cloaking device has been successful."

"All right," the commander said, turning to the forward viewports. "Signal the fleet to form up for final attack formation and prepare to engage." Reinhardt exhaled slowly, exhausted by the weight of his responsibility. His confidence had been bolstered by the controller's report, but he couldn't help but dwell on the possible consequences of failure. Hunter had called for the use of neutron bombs, which while sure to annihilate the Invid would also spell doom for much of the Earth's population.

Over the battlefield Corg was taking out ship after ship in an effort to offset Sera's betrayal. And now his sensors were indicating the presence of Robotech mecha inside the hive itself. He dealt out death to two more Veritechs and headed through the remnants of the shield into the heart of the hive.

In the inner sanctum, the alien the Humans knew as Marlene was still trying to get over Lunk's remarks. "But you've traveled with me," she was telling him, the hurt evident in her voice. "I even thought that you liked me, or at least accepted me. I'm no different now than I was then, Lunk. So why have your feelings changed?"

"What d' ya mean, you haven't changed?" Lunk's face was red with rage beneath the lifted faceshield of his helmet. "You're an *alien*! You think we woulda taken you along if we knew that? You're a spy!"

"But the fact that I *could* travel among you as a friend should tell you something, Lunk. Isn't it possible that we're not so different, after all . . . your people and mine?"

The Regis had been following these exchanges with interest, and she learned more about the Humans in the past few minutes than she had in the past three years. But Ariel still had a lot to learn. "Look at these friends of yours," she said to Ariel and directly into the minds of the Humans. "Notice how they stare at you in fear and confusion—emotional states that in their species inevitably lead to hatred . . . and *violence*!"

"Yes, they're confused because they feel I betrayed them," she argued, "but they're not full of hatred."

"Your contact with them has blinded you to their true nature, my child. It is their genetic disposition to destroy whatever they cannot understand."

"Now just wait one damn minute, Dragon Lady!" Rand interrupted her, willing to risk a step forward. "I've had about enough of this! How do you know what we're thinking? I'm willing to take Marlene as she is—and I think Lunk feels the same underneath all that armor of his. I don't *hate* her. Especially now, knowing what she stands to lose by coming to our defense like this. But *you* are another matter. As far—"

No one saw the crimson paralyzing rays until it was too late; they seemed to bubble up out of her blue eyes like dye, and they knocked Rand off his feet—the proverbial look that could kill—but his battle armor saved him.

"It is natural to them," she explained to Marlene/Ariel, barely missing a beat. "As natural as breathing itself. Their entire history is a catalog of murder, conquest, and enslavement, all directed against others of their own species."

"That's not true!" Sera now threw back, suddenly materializing in the chamber. "Ariel's right, Regis. Forgive me, please, but I too have begun to doubt whether we are any better than they are." She looked briefly at Lancer before continuing. "You say this species is guilty of murder and enslavement, but how is that any different from what we're doing to this planet?"

"So, Sera, you *and* your sister have been turned against us."

Sera, Lancer thought to himself, watching her.

Ariel was now gesturing toward the Humans. "Look at them, Regis. They're not . . . animals or barbarians. They are a brave and noble people trying to protect what is rightfully theirs, just as we tried to do." She offered Scott an imploring look, hoping he would understand and forgive her. Something in his eye told her he would.

Corg had by now joined them also, not in the flesh like

Sera but via the instrumentality sphere, where his image appeared five times life size.

"Have all of you gone mad?" he shouted. "How did these Humans gain entrance to the hive?! Sera, remove them at once!"

Sera thrust out her chin. "I was not aware that I had to obey your orders, Corg."

He scowled at her. "Your contact with the rebels has made you weak and spineless."

"And it has made a monster out of you," she returned. "Consumed by vengeance and evil passions. *You* are a child of shadow, Corg, not the Humans."

"What are you saying?" he bellowed. "This pathetic species you've become so fond of cannot be allowed to stand in the way of our future. Have you forgotten what we have been called to do?"

"If you keep fighting, there won't be a future for any of us," Lancer said from the floor of the chamber.

Corg dismissed the threat without a word. "Enough. I am called to battle—where my duty lies!"

"I've got to stop that lunatic!" Scott yelled, ignoring Marlene's pleas for him to wait and racing for the cockpit of his fighter.

The Alpha gave chase to the alien ship through that same netherworld of moving cells Rand and Rook had navigated earlier. *I've got you now!* Scott thought, training his weapons on Corg even before the two of them had left the hive. But the XT swung his craft around and loosed a stream of discs before Scott could get off his shot, and an instant later they were outside, dogfighting in the skies over those recently altered autumnal forests. Red-tipped heat-seekers and anni discs cut through the air as the two aces put their ships through their paces, dodging and juking, climbing and dropping against each other.

Views of the battle were displayed inside the chamber, where the rest of the freedom fighters were still gathered, along with Ariel and Sera.

"I don't like just standing around and watching this," Rand told Rook. "What do you say, do we stay here or go out there and help him?"

"I don't know anymore, Rand. I'm all confused. . . . "

All at once the sphere's images de-rezzed, only to be replaced by space views of the approaching Expeditionary fleet.

The Regis's lapis eyes narrowed. "No! They have come! The dark tides of the shadow have come to engulf us again!"

"It's the rest of Hunter's fleet!"

"Wow! I didn't expect so many ships!"

"Well, that does it," Lancer said softly, filled up with a sudden despair. "Any hope of a peaceful settlement has just gone down the drain."

CHAPTER
SEVENTEEN

Throw water on her! Throw water on her!

Remark attributed to Rand (unconfirmed) on seeing
the Invid Regis for the first time

MOST OF EARTH'S POPULATION WAS UNAWARE OF
the Expeditionary fleet's arrival, let alone of the Olympian battle that was taking place in the skies above Reflex Point. But even as far off as the remote areas of the Southlands, people knew something was up. The Invid were suddenly taking their leave—from cities, towns, communications outposts, and Protoculture farms, a steady stream of Troopers and Pincer units, all headed north for some unknown purpose.

Meanwhile, in one small section of those embattled northern skies, a green and orange Invid command ship was going one on one with a Veritech, each oblivious to the ferocious fighting going on around them, as though these two had been chosen representative combatants. And in some ways they had. . . .

For Corg, the alien prince, there was no thought of defeat, only the glory of victory. Showing a malicious grin, he raised the right cannon arm of his ship and loosed a bolt of red death at the approaching fighter.

But Scott was well prepared for it and already thinking the Beta through an avoidance roll; he returned two bursts to Corg's one, reconfiguring to Battloid mode as the VT came full circle.

Corg darted left and right, almost playfully, then threw his ship into a frontal assault, even as the Battloid's rifle/cannon continued to pour energy his way. The two crafts collided and grappled in midair, thrusters keeping them aloft while they flailed at each other with armored fists. Scott tried to bring the cannon down on the ship's crown, but Corg parried the blow and punished the VT with body blows. Scott twisted and hurled his opponent way; once again he brought the cannon into play, and once again Corg seemed to laugh off the attempts.

The alien's voice seethed over the tac net: "Your pitiful attempts make your defeat at my hands all the more pleasurable!"

Scott snorted. "I'll be satisfied with boring you to death, then!"

The Battloid had the cannon in both hands now; the first volley missed, and the second impacted harmlessly against the command ship's crown. In response Corg loosed a flock of missiles from his ship's shoulder-mounted racks, and Scott met the stakes with an equal number of his own. The projectiles destroyed themselves in midair between the two ships, but Corg had followed his missiles in, emerging from the smoke and bringing the metalshod foot of his ship against the VT's control modules before Scott had an opportunity to take evasive action. Electrical discharges snapped around the inside of the Beta's cockpit like summer lightning as circuits fried and systems shorted out. Scott sat defenseless in the seat as shock poured through his armor and the displays cried out last warnings. Corg's ship was behind him now, cannon raised. Scott thought he would feel the final blow against the Battloid's back, but Corg played his hand for insult instead. He targeted and zapped the Beta's thrusters, incapacitating the ship.

The Battloid commenced a slow facedown descent, trailing thick smoke from its leg and neck. . . .

Corg watched it for a moment, laughing out loud in his cockpit, then turned to deal with the half dozen fighters that had suddenly appeared to avenge their commander.

"How quaint," he sniggered to himself.

He positioned himself central to their assault and let them take their best shots, which he avoided with ease. Then, as they came in at him, he showed his teeth and counterattacked, taking out the first as it swooped past him, then a second, third, and fourth as they strived to ensnare him.

At the same time, Corg's Troopers were taking the battle to the edge of space. The so-called Mollusk Carriers and squadrons of Pincer units a thousand strong had moved in to engage the main fleet. Laser fire crisscrossed and lined local space, spherical explosions blossoming like so many small novas.

Hundreds of Invid ships were annihilated by mecha they could not even see, let alone fight. Squadrons of Enforcers and Pincer ships were wiped out; Mollusk Carriers exploded before they could even release their brood. And yet they continued to come, more and more of them.

On the bridge of the fleet flagship, Reinhardt received the latest updates. "Estimate of Invid troop capability is coming in now, sir," Sparks reported.

"I want a full status report on the assault force entry into Reflex Point," he demanded.

"They're continuing to meet heavy resistance, sir."

Reinhardt studied the monitors and displays. "If push comes to shove we're going to be forced to use the neutron S missiles."

"But our troops . . ." said Sparks, alarmed.

"I'm aware of the consequences," Reinhardt answered him grimly. "But is there a choice? Either we eliminate them and reclaim the planet or give it all away. We can deal with the ethics later on."

"I understand," Sparks said softly.

"Shadow Fighter launch is complete," a female tech said over the comlink.

"This is it, then," said Reinhardt. "Wish them Godspeed for me, Lieutenant."

In the hive chamber, Lancer, Lunk, Annie, and Sera had their eyes fixed on the Protoculture globe as glimpses of the battle in space were relayed to the Regis's *sanctum sanctorum*. It was obvious to the Humans that the Regis was growing concerned now; she was no longer the omniscient being they had first met.

"All units regroup," she was telling her troops. "Repel the invaders at all costs!" As she swung around to face her small audience, her eyes found Sera. "Your defection has cost us much, my child."

No one really understood what she meant by it, least of all Sera. It was true that she had stayed her hand when it had come to killing Lancer, but it was beyond her how her presence in the current battle could have affected things or altered the outcome any. "It can't be," she answered her Queen-Mother, knowing guilt for the first time.

Lancer was about to add something, when he saw one of the cells of the communication sphere black out. It was the third time he had seen it happen now, and it suddenly occurred to him that the sphere was tied in not only to the Regis in some direct way but to her offspring as well. He turned his attention to the battle images again: A squadron of Enforcers was being decimated by laser-array fire erupting from what seemed to be empty space; and as the last of the ships were destroyed, another cell faded and was gone. Annie noticed it, too.

"Hey, look at that!" she said, pointing to the dark patch on the underside of the globe.

"It loses power with each Invid loss," Lancer explained. "Isn't that right, Regis?"

The alien looked down at him imperiously. "You are perceptive, Human.... And as you have observed, our entire race feels the loss when even one of our children ceases to exist."

The pain she must have known, Lancer found himself thinking. Even over the course of the past year, to mention nothing of what had happened before, with the Tirolian Masters, then Hunter and the so-called Sentinels....

"Those Shadow Fighters are chewing them up!" Lunk enthused as more and more Invid ships disappeared in fiery explosions and seemingly sourceless cross fires.

Lancer took a step toward the pillar of flame that was the Invid Queen-Mother. "Your forces can't detect those fighters," he told her. "Your children are defenseless, don't you understand? Now you're the only one who can end this destruction."

Unmoved, the queen regarded him. "Twice in our recorded history we were forced to relinquish our home and journey across the galaxy.... But this time we shall not leave!"

"Don't you know when to take no for an answer?!" Lunk shouted at her. "Your children are dying!"

Sera glanced at Lunk, then looked up to the Regis. "Mother, perhaps we should listen to him...."

"You have the power to transform any world you choose," Lancer argued. "Some planet you won't have to fight for!"

"You cannot understand," the Regis said, almost sadly. "The Flowers of Life exist on this world and this world only. They are our strength; they are our life. Without them, we would perish."

Scott opened his eyes to Marlene's face and a world of pain. He was in his battle armor and propped up against a tree not far from the smoldering remains of a crashed fighter. He had no recollection of the events that had landed him there.

"Scott," Marlene was saying, dabbing at his head with a moistened rag. "Is your head any better?"

Scott saw blood on the rag and raised his fingers to the wound. Even this slight movement brought a wave of pain along his left side; at the very least his ribs were cracked under the armor's chest plate. "Agh...what happened?" he groaned.

Marlene gestured to the VT, "You were shot down. I saw you fall and—"

"Where's the Beta's component?" He tried to raise himself and collapsed; Marlene laid her hand and cheek against his chest.

"You shouldn't be moving, Scott. Stay here with me!"

"I've got to get back...." He saw that she was staring at him in a peculiar way and couldn't understand it. The revelations of the previous day and the sequence inside the chamber of the hive were lost to him. "Marlene, what's wrong?" he asked her, almost warily.

"I...I don't know how to explain it," she stammered. "I feel so strange, so concerned about you....Do you think you could love me, Scott? Even if only for a little while?"

Some of it was coming back to him now, scenes of battle, memories of *Corg*! He looked at her like she was crazy to be saying these things. "Marlene, I'm capable of only one thing, and that's fighting the Invid!" Refusing her offered lips, he managed to struggle through the pain and get to his feet.

Marlene chased after him as he ran off. "But, Scott," she screamed, "I love you!"

Elsewhere, two Battloids were moving through the chaos like lovers taking a Sunday stroll in the park. Rand's had just suffered a near miss, and Rook was teasing him about it over the tac net.

"I think you need some lessons in how to maneuver, kiddo. My grandmother could do better than that."

"All right," he told her in the same teasing voice. "But the next time you're in trouble, don't come to me for help."

"*Who'll* come to *who* for help?"

Rand smiled for the screen. "Love you, too."

"Same goes for me," Rook started to say, but Corg's approach put a quick end to the flirtation.

He split them up with fire from his hand cannon. They had arrived on the scene too late to see what the alien had done to Scott, so it took Rand by surprise when Corg moved against him hand to hand—something seldom done in midair—effortlessly knocking the rifle/cannon from the Alpha's grip. Rook stared out of her cockpit amazed, watching the two ships begin to duke it out, moving in to exchange rapid flurries of blows, then separating only to thruster in against each other all over again, trying to punch each other's lights out. But Rand was nothing if not resourceful, and somehow he managed to get the Invid ship in a kind of full nelson, which left Corg vulnerable to all frontal shots.

"Okay, I've got him!" Rook heard Rand yell over the net. "Blast him!"

Rook tried to depress the HOTAS trigger button, but her fingers simply refused to obey the command. If she didn't catch the alien just right, Rand would be destroyed along with him. Her face was beading up with sweat and the HOTAS was shaking in her grip as though palsied, but she couldn't bring herself to fire with Rand's safety at stake. He was screaming at her, telling her not to concern herself. . . .

Corg was just as confused as Rand: the red Battloid had a clear shot at him, but instead of firing the pilot was throwing herself against him, trying to batter him with the mecha's cannon. It was a tactical blunder and one that gave him all the time he needed to reverse the Battloid's hold. Corg grinned to himself and fired off a charge into his opponent's right arm, taking it off at the elbow; then he threw open the command ship's arms to propel the Human mecha backward. Engaging his thrusters now, he fell against the red ship, striking it with enough force to stun the mecha's female pilot.

Rook came around as Corg's ship was surfacing in her

forward viewport, the hand cannon primed and aimed at her. But just then Rand rammed the thing from behind, and although he had managed to interrupt Corg's shot, he received the blast that had been meant for her.

Rook could hear his scream pierce the net as his crippled Battloid began a slow backward fall, bleeding smoke and fire and sustaining shot after shot from Corg's weapons. Rook came up from behind to try to slow his descent, but Rand protested loudly:

"Rook, it's useless. . . . He's coming in for another run. You've gotta save yourself!"

"You're out of your gourd, mister," she told him, "I'm not letting you go now!"

Corg had the two Battloids centered in his sights and was preparing to fire the one that would annihilate them both, when an energy bolt out of the blue impacted against the back of his ship.

Scott's voice came over the tac net as Rook saw the component section of the Beta come into view.

"Get Rand out of here. I'll take care of things up top."

"Roger," she exclaimed, wrapping the arms of her mecha more tightly around that of her crippled friend.

The Beta and the alien mecha went at it again, only this time both of them knew it would be for keeps. Enough of Scott's memory had returned to make him aware of what Corg had done to him.

The two ships spun through a series of fakes and twists, drops and booster climbs, slamming each other with missiles and volleys from their cannons. Again, flocks of projectiles tore into the skies and met in thunderous explosions, throwing angry light across the field. But then Scott saw a way to prey on the alien pilot's technique: He made a move as though to engage Corg hand to hand, then surreptitiously loosed a full rackful of heat-seekers as Corg hovered open-armed and defenseless.

Even Corg wasn't aware of how much damage the Bludgeons had done to his ship and sat for a moment, complimenting the Human pilot on what had been a clever if underhanded maneuver. But all at once his ship's autosystems were flashing the truth, even as the first explosions were enveloping him, searing flesh and bone from the humanoid form that had been created for his young soul. . . .

Scott shielded his eyes: Fire and green nutrient seemed to gush from the ship at the same instant as the explosion quartered it, arms and legs blown in different directions. But as important as it had been for him personally, Scott knew it for what it was: a minor battle in a war that was still raging all around them.

Scott put down a few minutes later to see about his friends. His mecha's missile supply was virtually depleted, and it was time to let the fleet VT squadrons take charge of things for a while. He asked Rand if he was all right, but instead of the thanks he thought he was due, Rand said: "What the heck did you say to Marlene?"

"Yeah," added Rook, "we can't get a word out of her."

"I'd rather not talk about her," Scott started to say. But without warning Rand was all over him, head bandage or no, his hands ripping at the armor at Scott's neck.

"You're gonna *tell* me whether you like it or not! You think you can just walk out on this thing? She's got some crazy idea that she loves you—as if she had some idea of what that means. But you're gonna see to it that she understands, pal! I think you would have loved her, too, if you hadn't found out she was an Invid."

Rook separated the two of them. Then she had a few things of her own to say to Scott. "Stop torturing yourself over your dead girlfriend and come back to life, will you?"

"How can I ever forget that she was killed by the Invid—by Marlene's race?"

"So you're going to hold that against Marlene?" Rand seethed. "It wasn't like she pulled the trigger, you know. Besides, what about all the Invid you and the rest of Hunter's troops killed? This war has made victims out of all of us. When are you going to realize that the Invid are just our latest excuse for warfare?"

"Rand, you've lost it—you've gone battle-happy. *They* started it; they attacked our planet—"

"Listen, there were wars before we even heard of the Invid or the Robotech Masters or the Zentraedi. You might've lost your Marlene fighting other Humans."

Scott shook his head in disbelief, but even so he sensed some *rightness* in Rand's words. Not the way he was phrasing it; more in the sentiments he was trying to express, the sensibilities. . . .

After a moment, he said: "If only we could have avoided this. . . . "

Scott Bernard might as well have asked to negate his own birth.

The so-called trigger point was that point at which Flower production would have provided the Regis with adequate supplies of liquid nutrient for the conversion of her hibernating hive drones to quasi-Human form. Once this had been accomplished, her soldiers (with their Protoculture-fueled ships—the Troopers, Pincers, and Enforcers, would have been turned loose to eradicate the remaining Human population, including those who had comprised the labor force in the Protoculture farms, which (with more than enough Protoculture on hand to maintain a standing army) would have been shut down. Presumably ... But would this then-reformed race have taken up where they had left off on Optera? Would they continue to employ the Flower that had been central to their society there? Would they have become somewhat Humanized by the Reshaping? ... We are open to suggestions.

Zeus Bellow, *The Road to Reflex Point*

WITH THE ARRIVAL OF THE INVID LEGIONS FROM the Southlands the tide began to turn on the Expeditionary Force. It was a matter of sheer numbers.

Even though the Shadow Fighters had been initially successful in decimating the enemy ranks, the odds had now changed. The alien hordes were now punching through Reinhardt's forward lines and launching strikes against the fleet warships themselves. Consequently, contingents of Shadow Fighters had fallen back to protect their mother craft, leaving vast regions of space unprotected and vulnerable to infiltration. And though the hive barrier shield had been breached, the Terran ground troops had yet to gain entry to Reflex Point itself. Reinhardt, of course, had no way of knowing that six Humans

not only had been inside the hive but had met the Invid
Regis face to face.

"Three cruisers wiped out!" Sparks reported from his
duty station as the flagship was rocked by another volley
of enemy fire. "They're all over us, Commander. Even
the Shadow Fighters can't stop them!"

Reinhardt swiveled in the command chair to study one
of the threat board displays. "Blast it! What in heaven's
name is preventing Harrington's men from getting into
that hive?!"

"Sir, the Second, Third, and Fifth Divisions are reporting extremely heavy casualties. I can't raise the Fourteenth at all."

Reinhardt cursed. If the fourteenth was wiped out, it
meant that responsibility for the entire assault had fallen
to the Cyclone squadrons. And they would have to accomplish that without air support.

"At this rate we won't be able to hold out for more
than a few hours," Reinhardt muttered. "Order one of
the Shadow squadrons to prepare for a direct assault
against the hive. I don't care how they accomplish it—
even if we have to pull everyone back for a diversionary
move. Tell the air wing commander that I'm instructing
cruisers in the fleet to concentrate their firepower in sector six. We'll guarantee a hole, but the rest is up to
them."

Sparks swung to his tasks.

Reinhardt sucked in his breath and waited.

In the hive chamber the Regis regarded the Protoculture globe with growing alarm. Though her children were
meeting with success, the battle was far from won. And
could it ever be? she began to ask herself.

"This planet retains the malignant spirit of the Robotech Masters," she said out loud to Sera and the three
Humans. "Whether one race or the other emerges victor-
ious is of little consequence now, because such lingering
hatred will only breed greater hatred into the race that

survives. This world is contaminated, and I am only just beginning to understand. . . .

"The conflict will rage from generation to generation unless every last Human is wiped out, and that still won't be enough. Because *we* have inherited that evil bent. Our gene pool is polluted by it."

Cocooned within her column of cold white fire, the Regis turned slowly to gaze down upon Sera. "My child, this is not what we seek. This is not what we have traveled so long to achieve. But I begin to see a way clear of the treachery that has ensnared us . . . the truth I refused to grasp on Haydon IV. It is almost as if *he* were speaking to me across the very reaches of space and time . . . as though he had some inkling of the injustices he unleashed even then, when his Masters first directed their greed against us. . . . "

She could see Zor's image in her mind's eye, and it came to her now that the Flower that had been the cause of it all was about to bring their long journey full circle. That the Protoculture he had conjured from its seeds was to provide her with the energy she needed to complete the Great Work and ascend with her children to a higher plane, the noncorporeal one at last, that timeless dimension. *No earthly chains to bind them* . . . no emotions, no lust, only the continuous joys and raptures to be found in that realm of pure thought.

But could he really have seen this all along, been so omniscient? she asked herself. Such a precise vision, such an incredible realtering and reshaping of events . . . Sending his ship away to this world, then drawing the Masters and their gargantuan armies here, only so that the Flower could take root and flourish, so that the Invid might follow.

And now these returning ships with their untapped reservoirs of Protoculture—destined from the start to be her *mate* in the new order.

She had been so misguided in assuming his form; in so doing she had been captured by the rage and fears and emotions that blinded her to Protoculture's true purpose.

It was not simply to supply mecha with the ability to transform and interact with its sentient pilots; it was meant to merge with the race that had passed eons cultivating its source. They had used the Flowers for nourishment and sustenance and spiritual succor, and for all these millennia the Flower had been trying to offer them something more.

And Zor had played the catalyst.

"My child," the Regis continued, "I see now the new world that calls to us. And we shall consume and bond with that blessed life that provides our passage."

"Do you understand what she's saying?" Lancer asked Sera as the Regis seemed to reincorporate with the chamber globe.

Sera nodded, her attention still fixed on the battle scenes displayed there. Lunk and Annie gasped as the latest view was flashed into the inner chamber: Shadow Fighters, visible now, piercing through the hive's protective envelope.

And Reflex Point was beginning to react to their entry. Colored lights began to strobe into the chamber from unseen sources, dissolving the weblike neural arrangements supporting it and eliciting a threatening tide of organic waste and refuse from those collapsing cells.

"Well, the takeoff may be decided, but she just ran outta time," said Lunk.

Sera started off in the direction of her command ship, but Lancer put his arm out to stop her. "Let me go," she pleaded with him. "I must protect the Regis and the hive until she has assured our departure."

"I want to help you," Lancer told her.

She stopped struggling and turned to him. "You will be fighting against your own people."

Tight-lipped, he nodded. "If they knew what I know now . . . they'd understand."

"*We* understand," Annie encouraged him. She grabbed hold of Lunk's arm and led him toward the APC. "Now let's get out of here before this whole place comes apart."

* * *

Word of the Shadow Fighters' successful penetration of the hive was relayed to the flagship, but Reinhardt was still not encouraged. Six cruisers had been taken out in the past hour, and it had required over fifty fighters to get a mere four through the hive's defenses. And if those few survivors didn't make it into the central chamber, Reinhardt asked himself, what then?

"Sir?" Sparks said from his station.

Reinhardt looked at him wearily. "I have no choice. . . . I want all neutron missiles armed and ready for an immediate launch against Reflex Point."

Sparks swung around to his console. Reinhardt listened while his orders were radioed to the rest of the fleet. He wondered what the other commanders must be thinking of him. But there was no alternative; they had to realize that. . . .

"T minus fifty and counting," he heard Sparks say.

At the edge of Earthspace, the thrusters of two dozen mushroom-shaped droneships flared briefly, propelling their armed warheads toward the target area.

The hive corridor was oval-shaped and surgeon's-gown green. Lancer had no idea as to its purpose or its direction. But Sera appeared to know where she was going, and that was all that mattered. She was at the controls of her pink and purple command ship; he was alongside her in a Cyclone he had taken from the VT, reconfigured in Battle Armor mode.

"I consider it an honor to be fighting side by side with you," Sera told him over the comlink.

Yes, we're both fighting on the same side now, he thought. And in a sense they were a nonallied counterforce, separated from the Human as well as the Invid cause.

"You know, I've been thinking about how we met. . . . " he said leadingly.

"Lancer, would it be possible for you to love one of my race?"

He thought back to Marlene. And Scott. "I think I could. And what about you?"

She sighed over the net. "I only hope we have time to find out."

Two Shadow Battloids were fast approaching them from the corridor terminus.

"T minus ten seconds and counting," the tech reported.

Reinhardt was standing at the control center now, Earth's beautiful oceans and clouds filling the bridge veiwports. Short-lived explosions flashed across the field, and off to port a holed cruiser floated derelict in space. He had already inserted the override key into the console lock; he gave it a quarter turn and commenced arming the main switches as the countdown continued.

"Seven, six, five, four..."

Reinhardt hit the secondaries and slammed home the final crossover; now the S missiles were beyond anyone's control, no matter what followed.

"Three, two, one, *zero!*"

Reinhardt could discern bursts of white light below him against the seemingly tranquil face of the planet.

"God forgive me," he said under his breath.

The Regis's voice boomed out, omnipresent. It was as if she had become the entire hive now, and each part of it her.

"The final attack has begun. And a terrible error has been made. But in seeking to reach our own goal we shall see to it that these creatures have a chance to reach theirs as well. The shadow of the Robotech Masters has been allowed to rule this world for too long.... Now it will be dispersed!"

Sera's ship took a hit to the shoulder from one of the Battloids in the corridor, but she rallied and returned fire, taking out not only the one who had shot her but two more. Lancer hovered clear off to one side, unable to assist. But he had already done his part by destroying the first two, and it pained him even now to think about those Human lives he had taken.

Suddenly two more Shadow Fighters streaked into view.

"We'll never be able to stop all of them!" he shouted to Sera.

She was about to reply when unexpected fire from behind them devastated the intruders. Lancer twisted around to find Scott's VT behind them in the corridor.

"Figured you could use some help," the lieutenant said flatly.

"You're a welcome sight, Human" Sera told him.

"Yeah, well I'd love to stay and chat about that," Scott said after a moment, "but I suggest we get ourselves out of here on the double."

Lunk and Annie made it out of the hive before the three pilots. Rook and Rand and Marlene were also in the clear, a few miles off when the hive began to undergo the first changes.

In the shotgun seat of the APC, Annie gulped and found her voice. "Lunk," she said, pointing, "tell me what's happening!"

As if he could explain it.

The hive had gone from a crimson, almost bloodred color to steely blue. It was also more transparent now, and some sort of huge spherical nodes had been made visible in the deep recesses of the dome—perhaps those same round commo devices Lunk and Annie had stood beneath only minutes before. With the barrier envelope disappeared, the Shadow Fighters had direct access to the Regis's lair, but they couldn't get near it because of the intense electrical discharges that were surging up throughout the area.

And somehow the voice of the Invid queen was reaching all of them where they fought, died, or waited.

"Hear me, my children," she intoned. "When we sensed the first faint indications of the Flower of Life resources on this world, we thought we had at last found the home for which we searched."

The hive was barely visible now. It was engulfed in a kind of swirling storm of blinding yellow light from which rays of raw energy poured into the sky, while a crazed network of lightning and electrical groundings danced overhead. It was more like a contained explosion than anything else, as though the hive had become an epicenter for all the world's random energy, as though the very processes of universal creation were gathering together and being run through at an extraordinary pace. The hive had become the vessel for the Great Work, the merging of opposites—the pleroma. Here was the meeting place of the red and white alchemical dragons: the point of transcendence. The air was crackling, local storms unleashed and billowing clouds tearing through darkened skies as though in a time-frame sequence. And the land was changing and reconfiguring. The trees surrendered their leaves as an intense chill swept in from all sides, minitornadoes swirling around the sunlike fires that glowed within the hive. Invid ships—Scouts, Troopers, and Pincers—were streaming into it like insects drawn to the flame that annihilates them.

"We had called together all of our children scattered throughout the galaxy to begin life anew on this planet. We began rebuilding a world that had nearly been destroyed by evil. And we constructed the Genesis Pits in order to pursue the path of enlightened evolution. But it was not enough."

Suddenly light and shadow seemed to reverse themselves, and the world drained of color. Where the hive had stood there was now only an impossible tower of radiant amber light, launching itself through hurricane clouds with blinding determination, a pillar of raw but directed energy.

It was a mile-wide circular shaft of horrific power that erupted from the hive, mushrooming up with a rounded, almost penile head into that feminine void above, a million blast furnaces in concert.

* * *

Overhead, at the edge of the envelope that was Earth's protective shield, the neutron missiles were falling toward their target, but now that target was now coming up to meet them, with a face as different as any could be, a face only the once-dead would recognize. . . .

Reinhardt and his bridge staff saw it coming and would not have been able to move away from it had they had the power to do so; they were transfixed, in awe, in some sort of splendiferous, almost holy, reverie. Before their eyes the light was changing shape even as it pierced through Earth's atmosphere and entered the vacuum out of which it had been born. It was anthropomorphic here, contorted into a dragon's face there, with its fanged mouth opened wide, its tongue a lick of solar fire, ready to engulf all that dared stand in its way. It struck like a serpent, twisting and flailing about as though charmed by its own existence, charmed by its own imminent swan song.

Reinhardt saw the creature—for that's what he termed it to be, a living light: energy and life combined on some new and unimaginable scale—encounter the warheads he had launched against it, and he saw those alloyed death machines slag and melt away in the creature's wake. And he realized that this was to be his own fate as well. . . .

There was nothing but brilliant yellow light in the viewports now; throughout the fleet men and women stood naked before it, unable to comprehend what was happening but aware that it was something that had never occurred before. They were unable to understand that they had come all this way to meet death face to face, like the Zentraedi and Robotech Masters before them. It was as though they had been chosen to reap the whirlwind that had blown in from the other side of the galaxy. And they were unable to understand that they had been chosen to unite with the Invid in some inexplicable way, in the same manner that the Invid were uniting with the wraiths of the Protoculture. They were the homunculi, the Micronians who had been used by the conjurer Zor in the carrying out of the Great Work.

Some people, in ships at the perimeter of the fleet, saw that tower shoot up from Earth's surface like a lance of pure light, only to be joined as it pierced the night by coils of unequaled brilliance delivered up from the planet itself, encircling it for a brief moment like the shells encompassing an atomic nucleus. For this really was a kind of cosmic orgasmic fusion.

"Come with me!" the Regis's voice rang out, like the music of the spheres. "Discard this world and follow the spirit of light as it beckons us onward. And let our leave-taking heal this crippled world and reshape its destiny."

Then that light contacted the warships of the main fleet and digested and assimilated their strengths and weaknesses as it had the bombs sent against it, incorporating into itself all the contradictions and ironies and, most of all, Humankind's ability to wage war.

The dragon seemed to yawn and bellow its triumph as the light streaked on into the void.

"Our evolutionary development is complete," the racial voice continued.

"To all of my children scattered throughout the cosmos...Follow me to a new world, a new plane. Abandon this tortured life and follow the spirit of light as it spreads its wings and carries us to a new dimension...."

And those few who survived told of the ray's complete and total transmutation. To a feline face with bright blue eyes, through one that was surely Human in form. And then it had collected itself into one mass...like a phoenix on the wing, a radiant bird with outstretched wings wider than the world it was leaving behind, soaring away quicker than thought to another plane of existence.

EPILOGUE

Which came first: the Flower or the Protoculture?

Louie Nichols, *BeeZee: The Galaxy Before Zor*

Life is only what we choose to make it;
Let's just take it,
Let us be free.

Lynn-Minmei, "We Can Win"

THERE WERE FEW SALVAGEABLE VERITECHS LEFT after the Transformation, but Scott Bernard had managed to secure one of them. Most of the crew and ships of the main fleet had perished with the Invid's departure—*gone with them*, as some were saying.

A month had passed, and Earth was indeed beginning to heal itself, as the Regis's voice had promised it would. Grass and nascent forest covered what had been wasteland before, and regions that had been hot since Dolza's rain of death were showing markedly lower levels of radioactivity. Even the devastated area around the central hive had been sanitized by the light's leave-taking.

But two of the Regis's children remained. . . .

Scott was saying good-bye to one of them now on a rise overlooking the scene of what was to be Yellow Dancer's last concert, an outdoor amphitheater not far from the city that had once been called New York. People had been drawn to the concert from all over the North-lands and Southlands, seeking some explanation for what had occurred, almost as though the Invid's departure had been something of a Second Coming. There was a sense that the Earth had come to play a pivotal role in events that were beyond anyone's ability to comprehend, that the world had been used somehow to further one species' progress toward an end that awaited all of them. And in the process Humankind had been saved from self-annihilation, so that Earth, too, might someday follow along the same path.

A feeling of peace prevailed, of lasting calm few had ever known. War had been placed out of reach. And if one were to be fought, it would have to rage without Protoculture, for almost all that precious substance, along with all the Invid Flowers, had vanished from the face of the Earth. It would have to be a war fought with sticks and stones by a species that had been returned to a kind of primitive innocence; to childhood, perhaps.

But these issues were far from Scott's teammates' thoughts that day; rather, they were dwelling on endings and beginnings of a different sort. For now that they had done their part in allaying everyone's initial fears and confusion, the time had come for them to think about their own individual paths and the inevitable farewells those steps toward the future would entail. And amid all that returning splendor, there was an awkwardness they had never experienced with one another.

As for Scott Bernard, his mind was made up. The SDF-3 had never appeared out of spacefold, and Scott was going out to look for it aboard the only fleet cruiser that had survived the Transformation.

"But why?" Marlene wanted to know, raising her voice above the music booming out from the concert shell below them, where Yellow Dancer held center stage.

"Really, Scott, what's the point?" Rand said, backing Marlene up even though he knew it was futile. "You can start a new life here."

"I've got to go back," Scott insisted, turning the "thinking cap" over and over in his hands.

"But how will you figure out where to begin looking?"

Annie asked him. "I mean, couldn't you be happy staying down here on Earth with your friends and everything? Gee," she added, tears welling up in her eyes, "I miss you already."

How could he explain it to them? That although their friendship had meant so much to him this past year, he had other friends as well. Dr. Lang, Cabell, and so many others. He *had* to find out what had become of the SDF-3. And more to the point, space was his home, more than the Earth ever was and perhaps more than the planet would ever be.

He looked down at Annie and forced a smile. "Admiral Hunter's lost out there, and someone's got to find him and his crew. We've got to try while there's still one ship left with enough reflex power to make the fold." He glanced over at Rand and Rook, Marlene and Lunk. "Fate brought us together for a journey none of us will ever forget. But we've reached the end of that road, and there're only individual ones left for us now." Scott shook his head. "I don't know, maybe to spread some of what we learned while we were together. Does that make any sense to you?"

Rand caught Scott's eye and smiled broadly. *So it's not meant to be a winding down, after all*, he told himself, *but a gearing up for new quests. . . .*

"Well, good luck," Lunk said dubiously, walking over to shake Scott's hand. "I think I'm through with the road for a while." He gazed appreciatively at the green hills above the festival grounds. "I'm going to do a bit of farming, try and pay back the debt I owe to good ole Earth for shooting it up the past coupla years. Especially now that I've got some real fine volunteer help," he added, looking over at Marlene and Annie and grinning.

"What about you, Rand? Any ideas?" Rook asked leadingly. The two of them were sitting side by side in the grass, their backs against a tree.

Rand leered at her fondly. "Well, yeah, I do have a

notion or two. I'm thinking of going back to the South-lands to write my memoirs."

Rook grimaced. "You've got to be kidding. Who the heck cares, anyway? Besides, you're just at the beginning of your life, not the end of it."

Rand thrust out his chin. "Hey, I think people would be interested to read about some of the adventures we've been through."

"*We*?" she said excitedly. "Well, that's different! But I think those books are going to need a feminine point of view, just to keep things balanced, of course."

"And you're applying for the position."

"I am uniquely qualified to edit you, rogue."

Rand was about to agree, when a tremendous cheer rose from the crowds down below.

But the cause of the commotion wasn't Yellow Dancer, who had just finished her rendition of "We Will Win"— the anthem of the First Robotech War—but Lancer himself. He had thrown off his wig and female attire and was now attempting to explain himself to the audience.

"Thank you, everyone, thank you. You've made Yellow Dancer's final concert the greatest ever. Thank you all, you're wonderful!"

Those in the front rows saw that he was directing a lot of his delivery to one person in particular: an unusual-looking woman with short spiky green-blond hair and eyes that glowed like embers . . . For who else but an out-of-this-world woman was so well suited for Lancer?

Only he wasn't getting the response he had expected; the audience seemed almost *indifferent* to his visual confession. In fact, they were prepared to follow him in any guise he chose; after all, it was just *the stage*, wasn't it?

Up above, Scott had kissed Marlene good-bye and was headed for the cockpit of the Alpha. What would become of her and Sera? he wondered, and found himself thinking about Max and Miriya Sterling's daughter, Dana.

He waved to his friends as the VT lifted off, tuning his receiver to the broadcast frequency of Lancer's concert.

He really did it, Scott chuckled to himself. *It was certainly a month for revelations.*

"I want to dedicate my last number to a very special group of friends," Lancer was saying from the stage. "And to one friend in particular. . . . He's leaving Earth behind, and with it the most precious of possessions: his friends—the people who love him most. But I want him to know that when he returns, we'll be here to welcome him home with open arms."

As Scott listened to Lancer's latest composition, he found himself recalling the names and faces of the people who had emerged as heroes during Earth's quarter of a century of devastating warfare. Rick and Lisa Hunter; Max, Miriya, and Dana Sterling; Lynn-Minmei and Bowie Grant and Louie Nichols . . . And all those who hadn't lived to see this day: Admiral Gloval, Roy Fokker, Claudia Grant, Rolf Emerson, and countless others. Scott felt a bittersweet wave pass through him as Lancer's words crept into his mind, Earth dwindling now in the Alpha's cockpit display screen.

> She finds him strong and brave
> And how she wants him so, so much
> So much she knows she needs that touch
> To lead the way to love.
>
> He spies a gentle soul
> Waiting for her to find someone so
> So very sweet and kind
> To lead the way, the way to love.

"The Way to Love," Scott repeated, meditating on the words. And it suddenly occurred to him that it was love after all that had tipped the scales in each of those terrible wars. Love had won out over the greed, the hatred, and the betrayals, redressing the evil the Robotech Masters had first unleashed, and perhaps even atoning for some unknown sin that was Zor's alone.

> And now they have their space
> They've run the final race
> Love's given them a place
> Where love can live
>
> Heaven is where they are
> With love, they have no need to roam
> Just look at them to see how she,
> She led them to love
>
> They are in love
> They are in love . . .

Marlene! he thought, leaning out as though to catch a glimpse of her. But there were only Earth's oceans and clouds now, and stars winking into view above him. And he made a promise on one of them: a promise to return after he had found that jinxed ship and its long-lost crew.

Scott listened a moment more, choking back his sadness, and hit the Alpha's thrusters, boosting up and away from the world he had helped to liberate, one he hoped he would see again. . . .

Far below, Lunk, Marlene, and Annie had climbed into the battered APC and were headed down to the festival grounds to pick up Lancer and Sera. There were wisps of sunset clouds in a warm-looking sky, clear all the way to tomorrow. The Moon was rising, brilliant and seemingly closer than it had ever been. Lunk glanced up at it and said:

"You know, sometimes I think that's the most beautiful sight in the whole world. And I don't know why anyone would want to leave it behind."

Annie saw the VT's contrails caught in the western sky's final moment of color and sighed.

"And it might be a long time before anyone leaves it again." She smiled.

Marlene put her arm around Annie and hugged her close.

"Good-bye, Scott," she said softly. "May you find what you're after. May all of us."

APPENDIX

Because the original printings of the Robotech novelizations pre-dated digital typesetting, it was not practical to re-typeset the entire book in a timely manner for this compilation. However, we have included the following errata list to note some discrepancies with the continuity of the animated series. Please visit Robotech.com for more information about the Robotech universe.

INVID INVASION

PAGE 3: When the Regess departed for Earth in 2030, Rick was approaching the age of 41.

PAGE 4: The spelling of Jonathan "Wolfe" has been adopted in more recent Robotech texts, as Carl Macek had used that spelling in *Robotech Art 3*.

PAGE 6: The Invid queen's name is correctly spelled "Regess" (feminine of "Regent").

PAGE 7: The mainstay airborne Veritech of the Southern Cross was actually the VF-8 Logan.

PAGE 9: At this time in 2042, Veritech Fighters had been in development for nearly 40 years.

PAGE 12: The Invid Sensor Nebulae had first been detected eleven years earlier with the Invid Invasion of the Earth in 2031.

PAGE 18: In the animated series, the Invid only used variants of the Scout mecha in space.

PAGE 39: The Invid Invasion began only a year after the end of the 2nd Robotech War.

PAGE 77: The text implies that Lunk and Lancer (*Metamorphosis* p.80) were part of the Southern Cross, though they are too young to have been veterans of previous Robotech wars. Flashbacks in the animated series show their origins to be from the Mars Division.

PAGE 147: Breetai was killed in McKinney's Sentinels novel *Rubicon*, before being able to return to Earth to meet Scott and his group.

PAGE 185: In *Robotech: Love & War* from DC Comics, Jonathan Wolfe is seen among the crew of the SDF-1 as a young flight instructor.

METAMORPHOSIS

PAGE 2: Though the text states that the last of the Regess' enemies were dead, they do not account for her revelations of the "Children of the Shadow" at the end of the animated series.

PAGE 45: Marlene's last name is actually "Rush", not Foley.

PAGE 46: While the novel describes that the Invid Ariel was genetically derived from the late Marlene, the animated series explicitly made no such connection.

PAGE 132: The Cyclone is a dual-mode mecha that can only transform between Cycle and Battloid configurations; it does not support a "Guardian" mode.

SYMPHONY OF LIGHT

PAGE 33: Major Carpenter returned to Earth in a Tokugawa-class vessel. In the television episode *Ghost Town*, the old veterans are visibly operating a smaller Garfish-class vessel.

PAGE 152: The animated series never addresses the Shadow Devices as "Nichols drives" and *Robotech: The Shadow Chronicles* shows that Dr. Louis Nichols himself is not the source of the underlying Shadow technology.

PAGE 182: These weapons were called "Neutron-S" missiles in the animated series.

— *list compiled by Jonathan L. Switzer*